New Masterpieces of Horror

New Masterpieces of Horror

Edited by John Betancourt

Associate Editor, Richard Gilliam

BARNES
&NOBLE
BOOKS
NEW YORK

Contents

Introduction

Welcome to *New Masterpieces of Horror*, a selection of some of the best and most compelling short fiction of the last few years. The stories here cover a wide territory, from monsters to psychological suspense to traditional ghost stories to variations on fairy tales. The one thing they have in common is quality of craftsmanship, storytelling power, and a clear insight into what keeps us on the edge of our seats . . . until it goes for the jugular!

What *is* a masterpiece of fiction, anyway? More than a well-told story, it's a story that lives beyond the paper it's printed on. A story that haunts the dreams, that flashes from the subconscious at odd moments, that lingers on in the imagination after weeks or months or years. Edgar Allan Poe had that quality—stories such as "The Tell-Tale Heart," "The Fall of the House of Usher," and "The Pit and the Pendulum" endure, and will continue to endure, because they carry images of such power that they have become almost pulp icons. People know these stories even if they've never read them. They have become, in effect, icons of pop culture, much as Elvis and Marilyn and so many others have.

People forget, though, that classics don't reach such fame overnight. Poe labored for years and only made a few dollars from his fiction in his lifetime, despite the quality of his work. H. P. Lovecraft—another mainstay of horror fiction—likewise labored in near-obscurity and near-poverty throughout his life.

As you read through the stories in this book, as you explore the fevered imaginations of some of the best contemporary writers in this or any other genre, ask yourself one question: Will this story last forever, taking its place alongside the work of such standard-bearers as Poe and Lovecraft and all the rest we now regard as classic?

Leading off is Robert Bloch's "The Chaney Legacy," a story about the makeup kit of Lon Chaney, Sr., the first of the great horror movie stars. Bloch (1917–94) himself must surely need little intro-duction these days: among his many claims to fame is the novel *Psycho*, which became a rather successful movie. His career began in the 1930s, and he was a member of the Lovecraft Circle. An active writer to the end, his work grew steadily more accomplished. "The Chaney Legacy" will stand alongside the best of his work.

Another writer who needs little introduction is Harlan Ellison, who over the last thirty years has written more classic fiction (and won more awards for it) than anyone else in the field. "Soft Mon-key" contains no fantastic element, but it's one of the most grip-ping—and horrifying—suspense stories you'll ever read.

Classic writer Ray Bradbury, who reached fame with his science fiction and fantasy, has always dabbled with the horror subjects. His story "The Troll" is a modern fairy tale with enough of a sly dark note to fit in here. Of late Bradbury has been concentrating on mysteries and poetry, so his excursions into the fantastic are more rare—and all the more welcome.

Peter Straub is yet another author who needs little introduction. His best-selling novels, particularly *Ghost Story*, have introduced mil-lions of readers to his work. "The Ghost Village," though, is one of those short works that should have reached a wider audience than it did in its first publication. Despite winning a World Fantasy Award, it remains unjustly obscure.

William F. Nolan's chief claim to fame may well be the *Logan's Run* trilogy, but his dozens of other novels and hundreds of short stories continue to thrill readers. "The Yard," one of his more recent works, is as good as they get.

Novelist, short story writer, poet, teacher—Joyce Carol Oates is a talent to be reckoned with in any genre and at any job she undertakes. Her fiction has always had a dark edge to it, and over the last decade she has published many stories in genre horror publications. "Blind" is a creepy exercise in claustrophobia.

The multi-talented F. Paul Wilson only recently cut back on his medical practice in favor of more writing, which no doubt pleased his many fans (and disappointed his many patients). Although he has been moving away from classic horror lately with a string of best-selling medical thrillers such as *The Select*, "Ménage à Trois" showcases his strong handling of characterization, plot, and medical knowledge.

S. P. Somtow, a multi-talented writer/composer/film director, began as a science fiction writer in the 1970s before finding his true calling in horror, producing such now-classic novels as *Vampire Junction* (widely cited as the first proto-"spatterpunk" horror novel for its beautifully and poetically written ultra-violence). Here he returns to the darker side of urban life, reinventing a famous fairy tale in contemporary terms in "Gingerbread."

Joe Haldeman will always be remembered for his science fiction novels, particularly the Hugo and Nebula Award-winning *The Forever War* (widely considered science fiction's answer to *Catch-22* and one of the great anti-war novels of all time). Like many science fiction writers, he's always dabbled in fantasy and horror as well. His creepy story "Graves," for instance, showcases his powerful writing and military background at once. It also won a World Fantasy Award for best story of the year.

One particularly chilling sentence, written by Dennis Etchison and published as the opening line of his story "The Dead Line" in a 1979 issue of a small press magazine called *Whispers*, has stayed with me ever since: "This morning I put ground glass in my wife's eyes." Now, sixteen years later, in preparation for writing this introduction to his story, I came across a quote by Ramsey Campbell in which he cites that same sentence as "the most horrifying first line ever written." It seems I wasn't the only one hooked by Etchison's razor-edged writing when he burst onto the horror scene. His first collection, *The Dark Country*, a hardcover that featured "The Dead Line" and many other early stories, set sales records for its publisher. Its title story, "The Dark Country," which is presented here, also won a World Fantasy Award, and justly so: It's a decadently rich collage of images, emotions, and horrifying events just south of the border.

British master Ramsey Campbell has always specialized in quiet, moody, atmospheric horror stories, and his "The Old School" is a prime example: very British, very subtle, and all the more effective for it. Nobody but Campbell could have written this story.

One of the highlights of anthology editing is turning up stories in the research stage that you missed in their original publication. Elizabeth Massie's remarkable "Brazo de Dios" is one such story: so emotionally wrenching that it lingers in your memory long after the last paragraph. Remember her name and watch for her work.

Thomas F. Monteleone, who won a Bram Stoker Award for his novel *The Blood of the Lambs* several years ago, has been writing cross-over thrillers of late. "Nobody's Perfect" is his short work at its best: deceptively straightforward, but packing a punch. His current novel is *The Resurrectionist*.

Connie Willis is one of science fiction's best talents, and her Hugo Award-winning story "Death on the Nile" (a play on words in more ways than one) showcases her every strength. To say more than that might give away some of the story's punch.

Nina Kiriki Hoffman's work is often compared to that of Ray Bradbury, only darker and more sensuous, with a modern sensibility. As her body of work has grown in recent years, so has critical recognition. Her first novel won a Bram Stoker Award. "The Third Dead Body," a zombie story, is among her very best.

John J. Ordover works mostly behind the scenes in publishing these days, editing many best-selling science fiction books for a major New York publishing company, but his all too infrequent short stories, of which "All Flesh Is Clay" is a prime example, have always attracted attention. Recently he has been seduced by the lure of Hollywood, and the careful viewer may have noticed his name among the author credits for a *Star Trek: Deep Space 9* episode entitled "Starship Down."

About a decade ago, Alan Rodgers edited one of the magazines that reshaped contemporary horror, *Night Cry*, the digest-sized all-fiction companion to *The Twilight Zone Magazine*. There he helped audiences discover the likes of David J. Schow, John Skipp, Craig Spector, and many more. "The Boy Who Came Back from the Dead" was Rodgers's first foray into fiction writing on his own, and, like many Rodgers stories that followed, it blends tabloid science and horror into a unique style. This story garnered Rodgers a World Fantasy Award with good reason, and it remains one of his very finest works.

Jane Yolen is much loved for her many children's books, such as the Commander Toad series, though she has always found time to write fabulous stories for adults. "The Snatchers" finds her, as usual, in top form.

After John Bellairs passed away (and after an exhaustive search), Brad Strickland was selected to complete several of Bellairs's books . . . which he has now done to strong reviews. "Her Wild Wild Eyes" finds him exploring more familiar territory.

Charles L. Grant recently celebrated the publication of his one hundredth book. His story "Peacemaker" is a perfect example of the "quiet horror" he is known for . . . moody, atmospheric, and all the more effective for it.

Some writers are born to work at a specific length; just as Stephen King seems most comfortable at novel length, Steve Rasnic Tem is a master of the short story. Tem's "In the Trees" is a perfect example of a compact horror story—one told at exactly the right length, in exactly the right way.

New writer Gregory Nicoll isn't really that new—we co-founded the Giants of Science Fiction (a group for tall writers, nobody under six feet three inches need apply) in the mid-1980s at a World Science Fiction Convention in Atlanta, Georgia—but he has begun to attract an increasing amount of interest with his horror fiction. "Dead Air" has all the marks of a mature talent: the smooth prose, the deft characterizations, the easy narrative voice. Look for his work in many current anthologies.

One of the first of Joe R. Lansdale's stories to attract major attention was "Night They Missed the Horror Show," which won a World Fantasy Award. It showcases all his strengths: believable characters, a clear Texas narrative voice, and a shocking ending that you won't see coming. He's another author to watch, both for his comics work and his dark suspense novels from The Mysterious Press.

"The Great Lover," by Dan Simmons, finishes up the book: a historical novella by a vastly talented writer who has won every award the science fiction, fantasy, and horror fields have to offer, and with good cause. "The Great Lover" seamlessly melds fact, fiction, and fantasy, set against a World War I backdrop.

—John Gregory Betancourt
1996

The Chaney Legacy

Robert Bloch

This story is dedicated, with gratitude, to Harlan Ellison.

Nobody thought Dale was crazy until the trouble started.
True, he'd been a film buff ever since he was a kid, the way other youngsters sometimes get hung-up on baseball, football, or even chess. If they follow their hobby into adult life such interests can become an obsession, yet no one thinks it's a sign of insanity.

In Dale's case his studies led him into teaching a course on film history at the university, which seemed sensible enough. Certainly he appeared to be normal; he wasn't one of those wimpy professors seen in comedy films aimed at the junk-food generation.

Actually Dale was rather attractive. Debbie Curzon thought so. She was a newscaster on local radio where she met and interviewed many of the stud celebrities in sports or films; Dale must have had some *charisma* for her to choose him as a lover.

The two of them might have ended up together on a permanent basis if Dale hadn't leased the Chaney house.

That's what the realtor called it—"the Chaney house"— although Dale couldn't verify the claim and the ancient escrow was clouded. The place was really just a small cottage halfway up Nichols Canyon in the Hollywood hills. Huddled amidst a tangle of trees and underbrush on a dirt side-road which turned to quicksand during the rainy season, the weatherbeaten frame dwelling offered no exterior charm or interior comfort. Debbie's reluctance to share it was understandable, but once he found it Dale couldn't wait to move in.

"All right, do as you please," Debbie told him. "If that dump is
more important to you than sharing a brand-new condo with
me—"

"It's not just a dump," Dale protested. "This is the *Chaney*
house. Can't you understand?"

"Frankly, no. What makes you want to hole up in a place like
this just because some dumb actor may or may not have hung out
here sixty years ago?"

"Lon Chaney wasn't dumb," Dale said. "He happens to be one
of the finest performers in silent films, perhaps the greatest of them
all."

"Who cares?" Debbie's voice honed to a cutting-edge. "I just
hope your wonderful Mr. Chaney knows how to cook and is good
in bed, because from now on you'll be living with him, not me."

It was open warfare, but Dale found no weapon to pierce the
armor of feminine logic. In the end Debbie told him to bug off,
and he had no choice but to obey the entomological injunction.

A week later Dale moved into the Chaney house and by then
everybody thought he'd flipped out. Turning down a renewal of his
teaching contract now at the end of the fall semester meant losing
his chance at tenure, and that certainly was a crazy decision, because he gave no reason for leaving.

But Dale knew exactly what he was going to do. He would
vindicate himself in the eyes of Debbie and the academic world by
writing a Hollywood history of his own—a definitive work which
would answer the questions which lurked behind the legends. Who
killed William Desmond Taylor, and why? Did Thomas Ince meet
his death because of illness or was it murder? What really kept
Garbo from returning to the screen? Had there been cover-ups in
the case of Thelma Todd or Marilyn Monroe? So much had been
surmised, so little verified. And for a starter, he meant to solve the
Chaney mystery.

Of all the stars of silent films, Lon Chaney was by far the most
mysterious. There were books on his films but no full-length biog-
raphies except for a reporter's inaccurate magazine series following
Chaney's untimely death from cancer in 1930. Chaney's first wife
died without breaking silence and his second left no memoir. His

son Creighton, who later changed his name to Lon Chaney, Jr., was estranged from his father for many years and avoided painful memories. To this day Chaney's private life remains an enigma. "Between pictures," he told reporters, "there is no Lon Chaney."

The coincidence of moving into one of the actor's former residences challenged Dale. Come what may, he meant to learn Lon Chaney's secret.

But first there were more practical questions to deal with. Once furniture arrived and utilities installed, he had to renovate his surroundings. The cottage had been unoccupied for many years—no wonder the realtor offered him such a bargain rental—and it was time for a thorough housecleaning.

So Dale called an agency and secured the services of a Hispanic lady named Juanita. She was short, plump, but surprisingly strong; perched on a rickety ladder she scrubbed away at the ceiling and side-walls, then descended to attack the floors with mop and brush. And on the second day she made her discovery.

Finishing up her work, she cleared out old boxes and empty cartons from the bedroom closet. The last carton, wedged in back under a jumble of debris, was not entirely empty.

"Look what I find," Juanita said, holding up her trophy for Dale's inspection.

He took the tin box from her, hefting it with both hands. Then he lifted the lid and his eyes widened.

"What is it?" Juanita asked.

The box was empty but its interior was divided into a number of small compartments lined with smudged cloth. And the underside of the lid was covered by a mirror.

"Some kind of a kit," Dale said.

It was hard to keep his voice from quavering, hard to conceal rising excitement as he paid and dismissed Juanita. When she left, Dale picked up the box again and now his hands were trembling. His hands, holding Lon Chaney's makeup kit.

Dale had seen publicity stills of Chaney displaying a different and much larger kit with side-trays, so this obviously wasn't the only one. What made it unique was that this box was here, in Chaney's secret hideaway.

Or was it?

Dale forced himself to face facts. In spite of the realtor's claim, he couldn't be certain that Lon Chaney ever lived here. For all he knew, the kit might have belonged to any one of a thousand actors residing in these hills when Hollywood was young.

What Dale needed was proof. And staring at the bottom of the box, he found it.

Wedged against the base was a coil of paper, a small square scrap which must have peeled off after being pasted below the mirror. Dale picked it up, smoothed it out, then read aloud the lettering typed across its surface.

"Property of Leonidas Chaney."

Leonidas!

This was proof and no mistake. While the general public knew the actor as Lon and most filmographies listed his first name as Alonzo, Dale was one of the few aware that the star's birth certificate identified him as Leonidas.

Chaney, born on April Fool's Day, had fooled his public. And considering his passion for privacy it seemed odd he'd put his real name here. But perhaps he'd fixed on his deception later in his career. Dale's inspection told him that this battered box was old, perhaps dating back to pre-Hollywood days when Chaney was a struggling actor in traveling shows. Could this actually be his very first makeup kit?

One thing seemed certain—Chaney *had* lived here. But when?

Dale pondered the question as he sat in gathering darkness alone, with the makeup kit on the table before him.

From what little he knew, Chaney's homes were modest by Hollywood standards, even after he attained stardom, but he would never have settled his family here. Which left only one other plausible answer.

Suppose this place was really a hideaway, a place his family didn't know about, a place he came to secretly and alone? According to publicity he did have a cabin up in the mountains where he went fishing between films. Could it be that he actually spent some of that time here, perhaps even without his wife's knowledge?

And if so, why? Dale quickly dismissed the notion of a secret love-life; Chaney was never a womanizer, and even had he been, this was hardly the setting for a romantic rendezvous. Nor was he a closet alcoholic or drug-addict. In any case there'd be no reason for him to keep a makeup kit hidden here.

Dale leaned forward, peering at the box through the twilight shadows which fell across its murky mirror.

But the mirror wasn't murky now. As he stared, something in the mirror stared back.

For a moment Dale thought it was his own face, distorted by a flash of fading sunlight amidst the coming of the dark. Even so, he realized that what he saw was not a reflection. There was another face, a face *in* the mirror, a ghastly white face with painted features that glowed and grinned.

With a shock he realized what it was—the face of a clown. And before Dale's widened eyes the face was melting, changing, so that now a second clown loomed leering out at him—cheeks spotted with paint and tufts of hair suddenly sprouting above a bony brow.

Dale turned, seeking a glimpse of someone else, some intruder who must have stolen silently into the bedroom to stare over his shoulder.

But save for himself the room was empty. And when his eyes sought the mirror again the face—or faces—had vanished. All he saw now was his own face reflected in the glass, its features fading in the dark.

Dale rose, stumbling across the room to switch on the overhead light. In its welcome glare he saw the makeup box and the perfectly ordinary mirror mounted within.

The clown-images were gone. They had existed only in his imagination—or was it his memory? For there had been two clowns in Chaney's life.

Hastily Dale sought his bookshelves, fumbling and finding the volume containing Lon Chaney's filmography. He riffled through it until a page fell open upon a photograph of the actor in the title role of *He Who Gets Slapped.* And now it was Dale who felt the slap of recognition. The picture showed the face of the first clown he'd seen in the mirror.

Turning pages, he located the still photo of another clown with daubed cheeks and patches of hair clumped on the bone-white skull. Chaney again, in *Laugh, Clown, Laugh.*

But there was no mirth in the painted face, and none in Dale's as he banged the book shut and left the room. Left the room, left the cottage, left the canyon to drive down to the shelter and sanity of lighted streets below.

He parked on Fairfax and entered a restaurant, taking comfort in its crowded quarters and the presence of a friendly waitress who urged him to try tonight's special. But when his order came he had no appetite for it.

Tonight had already been too special for him, and he couldn't forget his confrontation at the cottage. Had he really glimpsed those faces in the mirror, or had the images been evoked from memories of the films seen in retrospective showings long ago? A mirror is just a sheet of silvered glass, and what it reflected must have come from his mind's eye.

Dale forced himself to eat and gradually the tension ebbed. By the time he finished and drove back up the canyon his composure returned.

Inside the cottage the lights still blazed upon commonplace surroundings, safeguarding against shadows and dispelling doubts. If Chaney had lived here at all, that time was long-gone and the actor himself was long-dead. There were no ghosts, and the box on the bedroom table was merely an old makeup kit, not a miniature haunted house.

For a moment Dale had an impulse to lift the lid and examine the mirror for added reassurance, then dismissed it. There was no point in dignifying his apprehensions; what he needed was a good night's sleep and a clear head for tomorrow.

Truth to tell, he felt drained after the emotional stress of the day, and once he undressed and sought his bed Dale quickly fell into dreamless slumber.

Just when the change occurred he did not know, but there *was* a change, and the dream came.

In the dream he found himself awakened, sitting up in bed and staring through darkness at the black blur of the box on the table.

And now the impulse he'd rejected upon entering the bedroom returned with an urgency he could not deny.

Sometimes dreams seem oddly like films—movies of the mind in which one's own movements are silently commanded by an unseen director—a series of jump-cuts and sudden shifts in which one is both actor and audience.

Thus it was that Dale both felt and saw himself rise from the bed, captured in a full shot as he moved across the room. Now a cut to another angle, showing him poised above the makeup kit. Then came a close shot of his hand moving down to raise the lid.

Moonlight from the window sent a silvery shaft to strike the surface of the makeup mirror, flooding it with a blinding brightness that seethed and stirred.

Faces formed in the glass—contoured countenances which seemed frighteningly familiar, even in the depths of dream. Faces changed, and yet there was a lurking linkage between them, for all were oriental.

Some Dale had seen before only in photographs—the evil Chinaman from the lost film *Bits of Life*, the benevolent laundryman in *Shadows*. Then, in rapid shifts, the vengeful mandarin of *Mr. Wu*, the bespectacled elderly image of Wu's father, and a final, frightening glimpse of the chinless, sunken-cheeked, shrivelled face of the aged grandfather. They formed and faded, smiling their secret smiles.

Now others appeared—the two pirates, Pew and Merry, from *Treasure Island*, a bearded Fagin out of *Oliver Twist*, followed by figures looming full-length in the mirror's depths. Here were the fake cripples of *The Miracle Man*, *The Blackbird*, *Flesh and Blood*. Then the real cripple of *The Shock* and the legless Blizzard in *The Penalty*. Now came a derby-hatted gangster, a French-Canadian trapper, a tough sergeant of Marines, a scarred animal-trapper, an elderly railroad engineer, and Echo, the ventriloquist of *The Unholy Three*.

In his dream Dale stood frozen before the glass as faces flashed forth in faster flickerings—the faces of madmen. Here was a crazed wax-museum attendant, a bearded victim of senile delusions, a deranged Russian peasant, the insane scientists of *A Blind Bargain* and *The Monster*. They were laughing at him, grinning in glee as Dale closed his eyes, hands clawing out to close the lid of the makeup kit.

Then he staggered back to the bed. There were no images here, only the darkness, and Dale fell into it, fleeing the faces and seeking surcease in sleep.

It was morning when Dale's eyes blinked open, welcoming the sanity of sunlight. He stirred, conscious now that last night had been a dream, knowing he'd seen nothing in the mirror; indeed, he had never even left his bed.

As he rose he glanced over at the box resting on the table, remembering how he'd closed it in reality before retiring, then closed it again in his nightmare.

But now the lid was up.

For a moment Dale recoiled, fighting the irrational explanation until sunlight and common sense prevailed.

The makeup kit was old, its hinges worn or even sprung. Sometime during the night the catch must have loosened and the lid popped up.

It was a logical answer, but even so he had to force himself toward the table, steel himself to gaze down into the mirror set inside the lid and gaze on what was reflected there.

Sunshine formed a halo around the image in its glassy surface— the image of his own face.

And as his features formed a smile of rueful relief, Dale turned away. The mirror in the makeup kit held no terrors for him now, any more than the one he faced as he shaved. He dressed and sought the makeshift kitchen, taking comfort in the familiar ritual of preparing his breakfast, then eating eggs and toast with a copy of the morning *Times* propped up before his coffee-cup. Even the news offered an odd comfort of its own—the familiar headlines and stories of wars, terrorist bombings, political corruption, street crime, drug-busts, accidents, epidemics, natural and unnatural disasters that filled the newspaper pages. However grim, these were realities; realities which he and everyone else in the world faced with fortitude born of long familiarity. They had nothing to do with the unhealthy fantasies which took form when Lon Chaney stalked the screen—fantasies which existed now only in Dale's imagination.

Glancing at his watch, he folded the paper and rose quickly. There was a busy day ahead, and time was already running short.

Leaving the cottage, he drove down to Hollywood Boulevard, turned right, then made a left on Fairfax. He reached Wilshire and headed west, weaving through noonday traffic until he found a parking-space before the imposing structure of the Motion Picture Academy of Arts and Sciences.

Here, upstairs in the Margaret Herrick Library, he turned his attention to the files he requested. Lon Chaney wasn't the only movie monster he meant to deal with in his projected history; there was research to be done on other stars of the horror film. And unlike the case with Chaney, there was ample material on men like Karloff, Lorre, and Lugosi.

But even as he scribbled notes Dale found something lacking in the interviews and biographical data of these celebrated actors who seemingly made no mystery of their careers.

The one missing element common to all was that of explanation. Why had a gentle gentleman like Boris ended up playing monsters? What led Peter Lorre, the rabbi's grandson, to the portrayal of psychopaths? How did Bela Lugosi, who played parts ranging from Romeo to Jesus Christ in early European appearances, transform himself into the dreaded Count Dracula?

William Henry Pratt, Laszlo Loewenstein, Béla Blasko—all three men had changed their names, but what had changed their natures?

Dale found no answer in the files, but the last item he read before leaving the Academy offered a hint. It was an interview with an actress who toured with Lugosi in *Dracula.*

She told of how the genial cigar-smoking Hungarian prepared for his famous role, sitting before his dressing-room mirror and donning the costume and makeup of the vampire. But that was only a preliminary to performing. The next and most crucial step came as he rose, wrapped in the black cape, face contorted and eyes blazing. As he confronted himself in the mirror his deep voice invoked an incantation. "I am Dracula," he intoned. "*I* am Dracula. I *am* Dracula." Over and over again he repeated the words, and by

the time he strode out upon the stage the words became reality.
Lugosi *was* Dracula.

"He psyched himself up," the actress explained. And as the years
passed, a part of him became the part he played; when he died he
was buried in Dracula's cape, with Dracula's ring on his finger.

Dale jotted down his notes, then hurried out into the afternoon
sunshine. Now it was time to drive into Beverly Hills for a medical
appointment.

It had been made a month ago, just an annual checkup, as a
matter of routine. But now, as he arrived and took a seat in the
crowded waiting-room, Dale felt uptight. He felt no worry about
possible physical illness, but what about psychological stress? Last
night's dreams might be a symptom of mental disturbance. What if
Dr. Pendleton told him he was cracking up?

By the time the receptionist called his name and a nurse led him
to the examining-room he knew his pulse was pounding and his
blood-pressure had risen. So it came as a pleasant surprise when the
doctor made no comment on his readings other than remarking he
thought Dale was underweight and seemed overtired. Reports on
blood tests and urine-specimen would be available in a few days,
but nothing indicated cause for concern.

"Slow down a little," Dr. Pendleton said. "Pace yourself. And it
won't hurt if you put on a few pounds."

Armed with that advice Dale left. Relieved, he headed for a
seafood restaurant on Brighton Way and there he ordered and
actually enjoyed his meal. The doctor was probably right, Dale
decided; he *had* been working too hard, and the tension flaring up
after his break with Debbie took an added toll. He resolved to
follow orders, rest and relax. Then, perhaps, it might be possible to
come to terms with himself, and with Debbie too. He really missed
her, missed the hours they spent together, and the breach must be
mended. All in good time.

As Dale left the restaurant he sensed a change in the air; the chill
breeze hinted at rain and a muted murmur of distant thunder
confirmed its coming.

The first drops spattered the windshield as he turned onto the
canyon side-road, and by the time he parked in the driveway a

flicker of lightning heralded the downpour that followed. Dale hurried into the cottage beneath the wind-tossed trees. Once inside he flipped the light-switches as he moved from room to room. It was only upon reaching the bedroom that he halted when its overhead light came on.

Standing in the doorway, he stared at the open makeup box on the table, forehead furrowed in doubt.

Hadn't he closed the lid before he left? Dale shrugged in uncertainty. Perhaps the loose catch was the culprit once again; he'd better examine it and put his mind to rest.

Rain drummed the rooftop in a faster tempo and lightning flashed outside the window as he crossed to the table. Then, as he reached it, a clap of thunder shook the walls and the lights went off, overhead and throughout the cottage.

Power-outages were not uncommon hereabouts during a storm and Dale wasn't alarmed; perhaps the lights would come back on in a moment. He waited, but the darkness persisted and prevailed. Maybe he'd better look for his flashlight.

Then its illumination was unnecessary as the lightning-bolt struck somewhere close outside the window, filling the bedroom with a greenish glare. As it did so Dale peered down at the mirror inside the lid of the makeup kit and froze.

The reflection peering up at him was not his own.

It was the face of Singapore Joe—the role Chaney played in *The Road to Mandalay*—the half-blind man whose left eye was covered with a ghastly white cast.

But the image seemed strangely blurred; Dale blinked to clear his vision as lightning faded and the room plunged into darkness again.

Dale's shudder wasn't prompted by the roar of thunder. It was what he'd seen that traumatized him. *The Road to Mandalay* was one of the lost films; he knew of no print in existence. But Singapore Joe existed, in the mirror, existed in an indelible image leering up at him through the dark.

And the dark must be dispelled. Dale turned and blundered his way into the hall. Reaching the kitchen he stooped and opened the cabinet beneath the sink. Lightning outside the kitchen window came to his aid and in its moment of livid life he found and grasped the flashlight. It was not just an ordinary cylinder-type but one which terminated in a square base, projecting a strong beam of almost lantern-like intensity.

Dale switched it on, and the ray guided him back to the bedroom. As he walked his relief faded with the realization that his vision had faded too.

He was seeing only with his right eye now. The left was blind. Blind—like the eye of Singapore Joe.

You're having a nightmare, he told himself. But he wasn't asleep, and if there was a nightmare it had to be in the mirror of the makeup kit. Unless, of course, he was hallucinating.

There was only one way to find out, and Dale knew what he must do. Rain swept across the rooftop above, doors creaked and groaned against the onslaught of the wind, lightning glimmered, thunder growled. Only the light he gripped in his hand was reassurance; a magic lantern to protect him on his way. *Magic lantern*— that's what they called the movies in the old days. Was there such a thing as magic?

Forcing himself toward the bedroom table, he gazed down at the glass reflected in the lantern-light.

Half-blind he stared, but what he saw with his right eye was just a mirror after all. A shining surface reflecting his own familiar face.

And now his left eye cleared and he could see again. Dale took a deep breath, then expelled it hastily—for now the mirror blurred and a piercing pain shot through his lower limbs, causing him to crouch. Something pressed heavily against his spine, bowing his back.

He was changing, and the image in the mirror was changing too. He saw the tousled hair, the gargoyle grimace, the twisted limbs, the body bent beneath the hideous hump. No need to ask the identity of this image—he was gazing at Quasimodo, the Hunchback of Notre Dame.

It was Chaney he saw in the glass but he himself felt the weight of the hump, the constriction of the harness binding it to his body, the pain inflicted by the mass of makeup covering his face, the jagged teeth wired into his mouth, the mortician's wax masking his right eye.

Realization brought relief. It was makeup, and only makeup after all. Gradually the image diffused and Dale's feeling of physical restraint faded until once again he stood erect.

Thunder rolled as the image dispelled. Dale sighed with relief; now was the time to slam down the lid of the kit once and for all.

He started to reach for it, but his hands were gone.

His hands—and his arms.

Illusion, of course, like the illusion of Chaney's face and form coming into focus beneath the mirror's shiny surface. Dale's eyes met those of the visage peering out at him from under the broad brim of a Spanish sombrero. Chaney was armless, and now Dale felt the agony of numbed circulation, the constriction of his own arms bound against his body by a tight, concealing corset. That, he remembered, had been Chaney's device when portraying the armless knife-thrower in *The Unknown*.

With the recollection his panic ebbed, and once more features and form receded into the mirror's depths. The numbness was gone from his arms now; he could lift his hands and close the lid.

Then he fell.

His legs gave way and he slumped to the floor, sprawling helplessly, the box on the table beyond his reach. All he could do was elevate his gaze, see the shaven-headed creature crawling across the glass, dead legs dragging behind him. It was Phroso, the paralyzed cripple in *West of Zanzibar*.

No makeup had been involved in the simulation of the man who had lost the use of his lower limbs; it had been Chaney's artistry which made the role seem reality.

Knowing that, Dale strove to rise, but there was no feeling in his legs—he couldn't command them. The face in the mirror glowered at him in the lamplight, bursting into brightness as lightning flashed outside the window. The eyes were mocking him, mocking his plight, and now Dale realized that the mirror's monsters sensed his purpose and were summoned to prevent it. Their appearance in the mirror gave them life, his awareness gave them strength to survive, and that strength was growing. Closing the kit would condemn them to darkness and it was this they fought against. They know he couldn't close the lid, not if he were blind, armless, or paralyzed.

Frantically Dale balanced himself on the palm of his left hand, extending his right arm upward, inching to the table-top. Then his fingers gripped the lid of the makeup kit, wrenching it down. With a rasp of rusty hinges the box slammed shut.

The mirror disappeared from view, but Dale's paralysis persisted. Try as he would, he couldn't raise himself. All he could do was wriggle, wriggle across the floor like a snake with a broken back, and lever his arms against the side of the bed. Pulling his body upward, he lifted himself, gasping with effort, then collapsed upon the cool sheets which dampened with the sweat of fear pouring from his fevered forehead.

Fever. That was the answer; it had to be. The doctor was wrong in his diagnosis. Dale was coming down with something, something that twisted mind and body. Labeling it psychosomatic brought no relief.

Dale rolled over to face the telephone resting on the night-stand beside the bed. If he could reach it he could call the paramedics. But as his hand moved forward he felt a sudden tingling in his legs, then kicked out with both feet. The paralysis, real or imaginary, was gone.

No reason to summon paramedics now, but he still needed help. In the dim light cast by the flash-lantern standing on the table across the room he dialed Dr. Pendleton's number. The ringing on the line gave way to the mechanical message of an answering-service.

"Dr. Pendleton is not in. Please leave your name and number and he will get back to you—"

Dale cradled the receiver, frowning in frustration. Sure, the doctor would get back to him, perhaps in an hour, maybe two or three. And then what?

How could he explain all this? If he minimized his condition he'd get that take-two-aspirins-and-call-me-in-the-morning routine. And if he came on too strong the doctor would probably order up an ambulance on his own. Pendleton was a practitioner of modern medicine; he wouldn't come out in the storm to make a house-call merely to humor a hysterical patient with his presence.

But Dale had to have someone's presence here, someone to talk to, someone like—

"Debbie?"

He'd dialed her number automatically, and now the very sound of her voice brought relief.

"Dale! I was hoping you'd call."

Then she *did* care. Thank God for that! He listened intently as the warmth of her response gave way to concern.

"What's wrong? Are you sick or something?"

"Something," Dale said. "That is, I'm not sure. No, I can't explain it on the phone. If you could just come over—"

"Tonight? In all this rain?"

"Debbie, please. I know it's asking a lot, but I need you. I need you now—"

"And I need you." Debbie sighed. "All right. Give me half an hour."

The phone went dead, but as he replaced the receiver Dale came alive again. She was coming and he'd told the truth; he did need her, needed her desperately.

Listening, he realized the rain was slowing. It was a good sign. Perhaps by the time she arrived the storm would be over and they could talk without the punctuation of thunder. He'd tell her what had happened, make her understand.

But just what *had* happened—and why?

Dale rolled over on his back, staring at the shadows on the ceiling, facing up to the shadows surrounding the question in his own mind.

And the answer came.

He'd found it today at the Academy, found it when he read the actress's description of Bela Lugosi preparing for his portrayal.

"He psyched himself up." That was her explanation of how Lugosi became Dracula, and that was what Lon Chaney must have done.

No wonder he'd established a secret hideaway! Here, in this very room, he did more than experiment with physical disguise. Dale pictured him sitting alone on a night like this, creating contrivances to deform his body, refashioning his face, staring into the mirror at the creature reflected there. And then, the final transformation.

"Make up your mind." A figure of speech, but Chaney had given it a literal application, one beyond the mere application of makeup from his kit. Seated here in the shadowed silence, this man of mystery—this son of deaf-mute parents whom he communicated with through the power of pantomime—confronted the reflections of monsters in the mirror and whispered the words. "I am the Frog. I am Blizzard. I am Dr. Ziska, Sergei, Alonzo the Armless, the Blackbird, Mr. Wu." Each time a different incarnation, each time a new *persona*, each time a litany repeated hour after hour from midnight to dawn, willing himself into the role until the role became reality.

And psyching himself up, he'd psyched-up the mirror too. The intensity of total concentration had been captured in the glass forever, just as it was later captured on the blank surface of nitrate film used for silent pictures. The filmed images decayed in time but the makeup kit mirror preserved Chaney's psychic power forever—a long-latent power revived by Dale's own glimpses into the glass, a power that grew greater with each succeeding gaze.

Dale remembered the first apparitions—how fleetingly they appeared and how little effect they had beyond the initial shock of recognition. It was his repeated viewing which gave strength to the shifting shapes until they transformed his body into a semblance of what he saw.

But he wouldn't repeat the mistake. From now on the makeup kit would remain closed and he'd never look into that mirror again.

The rain had ended now and so had his fear. Thunder and lightning gave way to a calm matching his own. Knowing the truth was enough; he wouldn't repeat all this to Debbie or try to convince her. Instead he'd just tell how much he needed her, and that was true too.

But first he must dispose of the kit.

Dale shifted himself over to the side of the bed, sitting up and swinging his feet to the floor. The power-outage hadn't ended; he'd shut the kit away in the closet, then take the flash-lantern with him and guide Debbie up the path when she arrived.

All was quiet as he crossed the room to the table where the lantern-light shone on the closed box beside it. That's what the kit was, really; just a battered old box. Lon Chaney's box—Pandora's box, which opened for evils to emerge. But not to worry; the lid was down and it would stay down forever.

His hand went to the flash-lantern.

At least that was his intention, until he felt the chill of cold metal at his finger-tips and found them fixed upon the lid of the makeup kit.

He tried to pull away but his hand remained fixed, fixed by a force commanding his movement and his mind, a power he could not control.

It was the power that raised the lid of the box, a power that seethed and surged, and in the uptilted mirror he saw its source.

Two eyes blazed from a face surmounted by a beaver hat and framed by matted hair; a face that grinned to display the cruel, serrated teeth. But it was from the cruel eyes that the power poured—the burning eyes of the vampire in *London After Midnight*. Dale knew the film, though he'd never seen a print; knew its original title was *The Hypnotist*. And it was a hypnotist who glared up at him, a hypnotist's power which had compelled him to open the box and stand transfixed now by the vision in the glass.

Then suddenly the face was fading and for a moment Dale felt a glimmer of hope. But as the face disappeared into the mirror's distorted depths, another face took form.

It was a face Dale knew only too well, one which had lain buried in his brain since childhood when he'd first seen it fill the screen from behind a ripped-away mask. The face of madness, the face of Death incarnate, the face of Chaney's supreme horror; the face of Erik in *The Phantom of the Opera*.

No wonder he'd blotted out all memory of the terror which tormented his nightmares as a child, the terror he'd hidden away in adulthood but which still survived in his unconscious. It was suppressed fear that lay behind his inexplicable interest in Lon Chaney, a fright disguised as fascination which guided him to this ultimate, inevitable confrontation with the gaping fangs, the flaring nostrils, the bulging eyes of a living skull.

The Phantom stared and Dale felt the flooding force of the death's-head's overwhelming power, to which he responded with a power of his own, born of utter dread.

For an instant, for an eternity, his gaze locked with that of the monster and he realized a final fear. The face was looming larger, moving forward—attempting to emerge from the mirror!

And then, with savage strength, Dale gripped the box in both hands, raising it high; panting, he dashed it down upon the floor. The makeup kit landed with a crash as the Phantom's image shattered into shards of splintered glass glinting up in the lantern-light.

Chaney's power was broken at last, and with it the power of the Phantom. Dale gasped, shuddering in relief as he felt full control return.

As the knocking sounded its summons he picked up the flash-lantern and carried it with him down the hall to the front door. Debbie was here now, his hope, his angel of salvation. And he went to her proudly and unafraid because he was free of Chaney, free of the mirror's magic, free of the Phantom forever. This was the beginning of a new life, a life of love and beauty.

Dale opened the door and saw her standing there, smiling up at him. It was only when he lifted the lantern and Debbie saw his face that she began to scream.

Psychologists specializing in ethology know of the soft monkey experiment. A mother orangutan, whose baby has died, given a plush toy doll, will nurture it as if it were alive, as if it were her own. Nurture and protect and savage any creature that menaces the surrogate. Given a wire image, or a ceramic doll, the mother will ignore it. She must have the soft monkey. It sustains her.

Soft Monkey

Harlan Ellison

At twenty-five minutes past midnight on 51st Street, the wind-chill factor was so sharp it could carve you a new asshole.

Annie lay huddled in the tiny space formed by the wedge of locked revolving door that was open to the street when the document copying service had closed for the night. She had pulled the shopping cart from the Food Emporium at 1st Avenue near 57th into the mouth of the revolving door, had carefully tipped it onto its side, making certain her goods were jammed tightly in the cart, making certain nothing spilled into her sleeping space. She had pulled out half a dozen cardboard flats—broken-down sections of big Kotex cartons from the Food Emporium, the half dozen she had not sold to the junkman that afternoon—and she had fronted the shopping cart with two of them, making it appear the doorway was blocked by the management. She had wedged the others around the edges of the space, cutting the wind, and placed the two rotting sofa pillows behind and under her.

She had settled down, bundled in her three topcoats, the thick woolen merchant marine stocking cap rolled down to cover her ears, almost to the bridge of her broken nose. It wasn't bad in the doorway, quite cozy, really. The wind shrieked past and occasionally touched her, but mostly was deflected. She lay huddled in the tiny space, pulled out the filthy remnants of a stuffed baby doll, cradled it under her chin, and closed her eyes.

She slipped into a wary sleep, half in reverie and yet alert to the sounds of the street. She tried to dream of the child again. Alan. In the waking dream she held him as she held the baby doll, close under her chin, her eyes closed, feeling the warmth of his body. That was important: his body was warm, his little brown hand against her cheek, his warm, warm breath drifting up with the dear smell of baby.

Was that just today or some other day? Annie swayed in reverie, kissing the broken face of the baby doll. It was nice in the doorway; it was warm.

The normal street sounds lulled her for another moment, and then were shattered as two cars careened around the corner off Park Avenue, racing toward Madison. Even asleep, Annie sensed when the street wasn't right. It was a sixth sense she had learned to trust after the first time she had been mugged for her shoes and the small change in her snap-purse. Now she came fully awake as the sounds of trouble rushed toward her doorway. She hid the baby doll inside her coat.

The stretch limo sideswiped the Caddy as they came abreast of the closed repro center. The Brougham ran up over the curb and hit the light stanchion full in the grille. The door on the passenger side fell open and a man scrabbled across the front seat, dropped to all fours on the sidewalk, and tried to crawl away. The stretch limo, angled in toward the curb, slammed to a stop in front of the Brougham, and three doors opened before the tires stopped rolling.

They grabbed him as he tried to stand, and forced him back to his knees. One of the limo's occupants wore a fine navy blue cashmere overcoat; he pulled it open and reached to his hip. His hand came out holding a revolver. With a smooth stroke he laid it across the kneeling man's forehead, opening him to the bone.

Annie saw it all. With poisonous clarity, back in the V of the revolving door, cuddled in darkness, she saw it all. Saw a second man kick out and break the kneeling victim's nose. The sound of it cut against the night's sudden silence. Saw the third man look toward the stretch limo as a black glass window slid down and a hand emerged from the back seat. The electric hum of opening. Saw the third man go to the stretch and take from the extended hand a metal can. A siren screamed down Park Avenue, and kept going. Saw him return to the group and heard him say, "Hold the motherfucker. Pull his head back!" Saw the other two wrench the victim's head back, gleaming white and pumping red from the broken nose, clear in the sulfurous light from the stanchion overhead. The man's shoes scraped and scraped the sidewalk. Saw the third man reach into an outer coat pocket and pull out a pint of scotch. Saw him unscrew the cap and begin to pour booze into the face of the victim. "Hold his mouth open!" Saw the man in the cashmere topcoat spike his thumb and index fingers into the hinges of the victim's jaws, forcing his mouth open. The sound of gagging, the glow of spittle. Saw the scotch spilling down the man's front. Saw the third man toss the pint bottle into the gutter where it shattered; and saw him thumb press the center of the plastic cap of the metal can; and saw him make the cringing, crying, wailing victim drink the Drano. Annie saw and heard it all.

The cashmere topcoat forced the victim's mouth closed, massaged his throat, made him swallow the Drano. The dying took a lot longer than expected. And it was a lot noisier.

The victim's mouth was glowing a strange blue in the calcium light from overhead. He tried spitting, and a gobbet hit the navy blue cashmere sleeve. Had the natty dresser from the stretch limo been a dunky slob uncaring of what *GQ* commanded, what happened next would not have gone down.

Cashmere cursed, swiped at the slimed sleeve, let go of the victim; the man with the glowing blue mouth and the gut being boiled away wrenched free of the other two, and threw himself forward. Straight toward the locked revolving door blocked by Annie's shopping cart and cardboard flats.

He came at her in fumbling, hurtling steps, arms wide and eyes rolling, throwing spittle like a racehorse; Annie realized he'd fall across the cart and smash her flat in another two steps.

She stood up, backing to the side of the V. She stood up: into the tunnel of light from the Caddy's headlights.

"The nigger saw it all!" yelled the cashmere.

"Fuckin' bag lady!" yelled the one with the can of Drano.

"He's still moving!" yelled the third man, reaching inside his topcoat and coming out of his armpit with a blued steel thing that seemed to extrude to a length more aptly suited to Paul Bunyan's armpit.

Foaming at the mouth, hands clawing at his throat, the driver of the Brougham came at Annie as if he were spring-loaded.

He hit the shopping cart with his thighs just as the man with the long armpit squeezed off his first shot. The sound of the .45 magnum tore a chunk out of 51st Street, blew through the running man like a crowd roar, took off his face and spattered bone and blood across the panes of the revolving door. It sparkled in the tunnel of light from the Caddy's headlights.

And somehow he kept coming. He hit the cart, rose as if trying to get a first down against a solid defense line, and came apart as the shooter hit him with a second round.

There wasn't enough solid matter to stop the bullet and it exploded through the revolving door, shattering it open as the body crashed through and hit Annie.

She was thrown backward, through the broken glass, and onto the floor of the document copying center. And through it all, Annie heard a fourth voice, clearly a fourth voice, screaming from the stretch limo, "Get the old lady! Get her, she saw everything!"

Men in topcoats rushed through the tunnel of light.

Annie rolled over, and her hand touched something soft. It was the ruined baby doll. It had been knocked loose from her bundled clothing. *Are you cold, Alan?*

She scooped up the doll and crawled away, into the shadows of the reproduction center. Behind her, crashing through the frame of the revolving door, she heard men coming. And the sound of a burglar alarm. Soon police would be here.

All she could think about was that they would throw away her goods. They would waste her good cardboard, they would take back her shopping cart, they would toss her pillows and the hankies and the green cardigan into some trashcan; and she would be empty on the street again. As she had been when they made her move out of the room at 101st and First Avenue. After they took Alan from her . . .

A blast of sound, as the shot shattered a glass-framed citation on the wall near her. They had fanned out inside the office space, letting the headlight illumination shine through. Clutching the baby doll, she hustled down a hallway toward the rear of the copy center. Doors on both sides, all of them closed and locked. Annie could hear them coming.

A pair of metal doors stood open on the right. It was dark in there. She slipped inside, and in an instant her eyes had grown acclimated. There were computers here, big crackle-gray-finish machines that lined three walls. Nowhere to hide.

She rushed around the room, looking for a closet, a cubbyhole, anything. Then she stumbled over something and sprawled across the cold floor. Her face hung over into emptiness, and the very faintest of cool breezes struck her cheeks. The floor was composed of large removable squares. One of them had been lifted and replaced, but not flush. It had not been locked down; an edge had been left ajar; she had kicked it open.

She reached down. There was a crawlspace under the floor.

Pulling the metal-rimmed vinyl plate, she slid into the empty square. Lying face-up, she pulled the square over the aperture, and nudged it gently till it dropped onto its tracks. It sat flush. She could see nothing where, a moment before, there had been the faintest scintilla of filtered light from the hallway. Annie lay very quietly, emptying her mind as she did when she slept in the doorways; making herself invisible. A mound of rags. A pile of refuse. Gone. Only the warmth of the baby doll in that empty place with her.

She heard the men crashing down the corridor, trying doors. *I wrapped you in blankets, Alan. You must be warm.* They came into the computer room. The room was empty, they could see that.

"She *has* to be here, dammit!"

"There's gotta be a way out we didn't see."

"Maybe she locked herself in one of those rooms. Should we try? Break 'em open?"

"Don't be a bigger asshole than usual. Can't you hear that alarm? We gotta get out of here!"

"He'll break our balls."

"Like hell. Would he do anything else than we've done? He's sittin' on the street in front of what's left of Beaddie. You think he's happy about it?"

There was a new sound to match the alarm. The honking of a horn from the street. It went on and on, hysterically.

"We'll find her."

Then the sound of footsteps. Then running.

Annie lay empty and silent, holding the doll.

It was warm, as warm as she had been all November. She slept there through the night.

The next day, in the last Automat in New York with the wonderful little windows through which one could get food by insertion of a token, Annie learned of the two deaths.

Not the death of the man in the revolving door; the deaths of two black women. Beaddie, who had vomited up most of his internal organs, boiled like Chesapeake Bay lobsters, was all over the front of the *Post* that Annie now wore as insulation against the biting November wind. The two women had been found in midtown alleys, their faces blown off by heavy caliber ordnance. Annie had known one of them; her name had been Sooky and Annie got the word from a good Thunderbird worshipper who stopped by her table and gave her the skinny as she carefully ate her fish cakes and tea.

She knew who they had been seeking. And she knew why they had killed Sooky and the other street person: to white men who ride in stretch limos, all old nigger bag ladies look the same. She took a slow bite of fish cake and stared out at 42nd Street, watching the world swirl past; what was she going to do about this?

They would kill and kill till there was no safe place left to sleep in midtown. She knew it. This was mob business, the *Post* inside her coats said so. And it wouldn't make any difference trying to warn the women. Where would they go? Where would they *want* to go? Not even she, knowing what it was all about . . . not even she would leave the area: this was where she roamed, this was her territorial imperative. And they would find her soon enough.

She nodded to the croaker who had given her the word, and after he'd hobbled away to get a cup of coffee from the spigot on the wall, she hurriedly finished her fish cake and slipped out of the Automat as easily as she had the document copying center this morning.

Being careful to keep out of sight, she returned to 51st Street. The area had been roped off, with sawhorses and green tape that said *Police Investigation—Keep Off*. But there were crowds. The streets were jammed, not only with office workers coming and going, but with loiterers who were fascinated by the scene. It took very little to gather a crowd in New York. The falling of a cornice could produce a *minyan*.

Annie could not believe her luck. She realized the police were unaware of a witness: when the men had charged the doorway, they had thrown aside her cart and goods, had spilled them back onto the sidewalk to gain entrance; and the cops had thought it was all refuse, as one with the huge brown plastic bags of trash at the curb. Her cart and the good sofa pillows, the cardboard flats and her sweaters . . . all of it was in the area. Some in trash cans, some amid the piles of bagged rubbish, some just lying in the gutter.

That meant she didn't need to worry about being sought from two directions. One way was bad enough.

And all the aluminum cans she had salvaged to sell, they were still in the big Bloomingdale's bag right against the wall of the building. There would be money for dinner.

She was edging out of the doorway to collect her goods when she saw the one in navy blue cashmere who had held Beaddie while they fed him Drano. He was standing three stores away, on Annie's side, watching the police lines, watching the copy center, watching the crowd. Watching for her. Picking at an ingrown hair on his chin.

She stepped back into the doorway. Behind her a voice said, "C'mon, lady, get the hell outta here, this's a place uhbizness." Then she felt a sharp poke in her spine.

She looked behind her, terrified. The owner of the haberdashery, a man wearing a bizarrely-cut gray pinstripe worsted with lapels that matched his ears, and a passion flame silk hankie spilling out of his breast pocket like a crimson afflatus, was jabbing her in the back with a wooden coat hanger. "Move it on, get moving," he said, in a tone that would have gotten his face slapped had he used it on a customer.

Annie said nothing. She *never* spoke to anyone on the street. Silence on the street. *We'll go; Alan; we're okay by ourselves. Don't cry, my baby.*

She stepped out of the doorway, trying to edge away. She heard a sharp, piercing whistle. The man in the cashmere topcoat had seen her; he was whistling and signalling up 51st Street to someone. As Annie hurried away, looking over her shoulder, she saw a dark blue Oldsmobile that had been double-parked pull forward. The cashmere topcoat was shoving through the pedestrians, coming for her like the number 5 uptown Lexington express.

Annie moved quickly, without thinking about it. Being poked in the back, and someone speaking directly to her . . . that was frightening: it meant coming out to respond to another human being. But moving down her streets, moving quickly, and being part of the flow, that was comfortable. She knew how to do that. It was just the way she was.

Instinctively, Annie made herself larger, more expansive, her raggedy arms away from her body, the dirty overcoats billowing, her gait more erratic: opening the way for her flight. Fastidious shoppers and suited businessmen shied away, gave a start as the dirty old black bag lady bore down on them, turned sidewise praying she would not brush a recently Martinized shoulder. The Red Sea parted miraculously permitting flight, then closed over instantly to impede navy blue cashmere. But the Olds came on quickly.

Annie turned left onto Madison, heading downtown. There was construction around 48th. There were good alleys on 46th. She knew a basement entrance just three doors off Madison on 47th. But the Olds came on quickly.

Behind her, the light changed. The Olds tried to rush the intersection, but this was Madison. Crowds were already crossing. The

Olds stopped, the driver's window rolled down and a face peered out. Eyes tracked Annie's progress.

Then it began to rain.

Like black mushrooms sprouting instantly from concrete, Totes blossomed on the sidewalk. The speed of the flowing river of pedestrians increased; and in an instant Annie was gone. Cashmere rounded the corner, looked at the Olds, a frantic arm motioned to the left, and the man pulled up his collar and elbowed his way through the crowd, rushing down Madison.

Low places in the sidewalk had already filled with water. His wing-tip cordovans were quickly soaked.

He saw her turn into the alley behind the novelty sales shop *(Nothing over $1.10!!!)*; he *saw* her; turned right and ducked in fast; *saw* her, even through the rain and the crowd and half a block between them; *saw it!*

So where was she?

The alley was empty.

It was a short space, all brick, only deep enough for a big Dempsey Dumpster and a couple of dozen trash cans; the usual mounds of rubbish in the corners; no fire escape ladders low enough for an old bag lady to grab; no loading docks, no doorways that looked even remotely accessible, everything cemented over or faced with sheet steel; no basement entrances with concrete steps leading down; no manholes in the middle of the passage; no open windows or even broken windows at jumping height; no stacks of crates to hide behind.

The alley was empty.

Saw her come in here. *Knew* she had come in here, and couldn't get out. He'd been watching closely as he ran to the mouth of the alley. She was in here somewhere. Not too hard figuring out where. He took out the .38 Police Positive he liked to carry because he lived with the delusion that if he had to dump it, if it were used in the commission of a sort of kind of felony he couldn't get snowed on, and if it were traced, it would trace back to the cop in Teaneck, New Jersey, from whom it had been lifted as he lay drunk in the back room of a Polish social club three years earlier.

He swore he would take his time with her, this filthy old porch monkey. His navy blue cashmere already smelled like soaked dog. And the rain was not about to let up; it now came sheeting down, traveling in a curtain through the alley.

He moved deeper into the darkness, kicking the piles of trash, making sure the refuse bins were full. She was in here somewhere. Not too hard figuring out where.

Warm. Annie felt warm. With the ruined baby doll under her chin, and her eyes closed, it was almost like the apartment at 101st and First Avenue, when the Human Resources lady came and tried to tell her strange things about Alan. Annie had not understood what the woman meant when she kept repeating *soft monkey, soft monkey,* a thing some scientist knew. It had made no sense to Annie, and she had continued rocking the baby.

Annie remained very still where she had hidden. Basking in the warmth. *Is it nice, Alan? Are we toasty; yes, we are. Will we be very still and the lady from the City will go away? Yes, we will.* She heard the crash of a garbage can being kicked over. *No one will find us. Shh, my baby.*

There was a pile of wooden slats that had been leaned against a wall. As he approached, the gun leveled, he realized they obscured a doorway. She was back in there, he knew it. Had to be. Not too hard figuring that out. It was the only place she could have hidden.

He moved in quickly, slammed the boards aside, and threw down on the dark opening. It was empty. Steel-plate door, locked.

Rain ran down his face, plastering his hair to his forehead. He could smell his coat, and his shoes, oh god, don't ask. He turned and looked. All that remained was the huge dumpster.

He approached it carefully, and noticed: the lid was still dry near the back side closest to the wall. The lid had been open just a short time ago. Someone had just lowered it.

He pocketed the gun, dragged two crates from the heap thrown down beside the Dempsey, and crawled up onto them. Now he stood above the dumpster, balancing on the crates with his knees at the level of the lid. With both hands bracing him, he leaned over to get his fingertips under the heavy lid. He flung the lid open, yanked out the gun, and leaned over. The dumpster was nearly full. Rain had turned the muck and garbage into a swimming porridge. He leaned over precariously to see what floated there in the murk. He leaned in to see. *Fuckin' porch monk—*

As a pair of redolent, dripping arms came up out of the muck, grasped his navy blue cashmere lapels, and dragged him headfirst into the metal bin. He went down, into the slime, the gun going off, the shot spanging off the raised metal lid. The coat filled with garbage and water.

Annie felt him struggling beneath her. She held him down, her feet on his neck and back, pressing him face-first deeper into the goo that filled the bin. She could hear him breathing garbage and fetid water. He thrashed, a big man, struggling to get out from under. She slipped, and braced herself against the side of the dumpster, regained her footing, and drove him deeper. A hand clawed out of the refuse, dripping lettuce and black slime. The hand was empty. The gun lay at the bottom of the bin. The thrashing intensified, his feet hitting the metal side of the container. Annie rose up and dropped her feet heavily on the back of his neck. He went flat beneath her, trying to swim up, unable to find purchase.

He grabbed her foot as an explosion of breath from down below forced a bubble of air to break on the surface. Annie stomped as hard as she could. Something snapped beneath her shoe, but she heard nothing.

It went on for a long time, for a time longer than Annie could think about. The rain filled the bin to overflowing. Movement under her feet lessened, then there was hysterical movement for an instant, then it was calm. She stood there for an even longer time, trembling and trying to remember other, warmer times.

Finally, she closed herself off, buttoned up tightly, climbed out dripping and went away from there, thinking of Alan, thinking of a time after this was done. After that long time standing there, no movement, no movement at all in the bog beneath her waist. She did not close the lid.

When she emerged from the alley, after hiding in the shadows and watching, the Oldsmobile was nowhere in sight. The foot traffic parted for her. The smell, the dripping filth, the frightened face, the ruined thing she held close to her.

She stumbled out onto the sidewalk, lost for a moment, then turned the right way and shuffled off.

The rain continued its march across the city.

No one tried to stop her as she gathered her goods on 51st Street. The police thought she was a scavenger, the gawkers tried to avoid being brushed by her, the owner of the document copying center was relieved to see the filth cleaned up. Annie rescued everything she could, and hobbled away, hoping to be able to sell her aluminum for a place to dry out. It was not true that she was dirty; she had always been fastidious, even in the streets. A certain level of dishevelment was acceptable, but this was unclean.

And the blasted baby doll needed to be dried and brushed clean. There was a woman on East 60th, near Second Avenue; a vegetarian who spoke with an accent; a white lady who sometimes let Annie sleep in the basement. She would ask her for a favor.

It was not a very big favor, but the white woman was not home; and that night Annie slept in the construction of the new Zeckendorf Towers, where S. Klein-On-The-Square used to be, down on 14th and Broadway.

The men from the stretch limo didn't find her again for almost a week.

She was salvaging newspapers from a wire basket on Madison near 44th when he grabbed her from behind. It was the one who had poured the liquor into Beaddie, and then made him drink the Drano. He threw an arm around her, pulled her around to face him, and she reacted instantly, the way she did when the kids tried to take her snap-purse.

She butted him full in the face with the top of her head, and drove him backward with both filthy hands. He stumbled into the street, and a cab swerved at the last instant to avoid running him down. He stood in the street, shaking his head, as Annie careened down 44th, looking for a place to hide. She was sorry she had left her cart again. This time, she knew, her goods weren't going to be there.

It was the day before Thanksgiving.

Four more black women had been found dead in midtown door-ways.

Annie ran, the only way she knew how, into stores that had exits on other streets. Somewhere behind her, though she could not figure it out properly, there was trouble coming for her and the baby. It was so cold in the apartment. It was always so cold. The landlord cut off the heat, he always did it in early November, till the snow came. And she sat with the child, rocking him, trying to comfort him, trying to keep him warm. And when they came from Human Resources, from the City, to evict her, they found her still holding the child. When they took it away from her, so still and blue, Annie ran from them, into the streets; and she ran, she knew how to run, to keep running so she could live out here where they couldn't reach her and Alan. But she knew there was trouble behind her.

Now she came to an open place. She knew this. It was a new building they had put up, a new skyscraper, where there used to be shops that had good throwaway things in the cans and sometimes on the loading docks. It said Citicorp Mall and she ran inside. It was the day before Thanksgiving and there were many decorations. Annie rushed through into the central atrium, and looked around. There were escalators, and she dashed for one, climbing to a second storey, and then a third. She kept moving. They would arrest her or throw her out if she slowed down.

At the railing, looking over, she saw the man in the court below. He didn't see her. He was standing, looking around.

Stories of mothers who lift wrecked cars off their children are legion.

When the police arrived, eyewitnesses swore it had been a stout, old black woman who had lifted the heavy potted tree in its terra-cotta urn, who had manhandled it up onto the railing and slid it along till she was standing above the poor dead man, and who had dropped it three storeys to crush his skull. They swore it was true, but beyond a vague description of old, black, and dissolute looking, they could not be of assistance. Annie was gone.

On the front page of the *Post* she wore as lining in her right shoe, was a photo of four men who had been arraigned for the senseless murders of more than a dozen bag ladies over a period of several months. Annie did not read the article.

It was close to Christmas, and the weather had turned bitter, too bitter to believe. She lay propped in the doorway alcove of the Post Office on 43rd and Lexington. Her rug was drawn around her, the stocking cap pulled down to the bridge of her nose, the goods in the string bags around and under her. Snow was just beginning to come down.

A man in a Burberry and an elegant woman in a mink approached from 42nd Street, on their way to dinner. They were staying at the New York Helmsley. They were from Connecticut, in for three days to catch the shows and to celebrate their eleventh wedding anniversary.

As they came abreast of her, the man stopped and stared down into the doorway. "Oh, Christ, that's awful," he said to his wife. "On a night like this, Christ, that's just awful."

"Dennis, *please!*" the woman said.

"I can't just pass her by," he said. He pulled off a kid glove and reached into his pocket for his money clip.

"Dennis, they don't like to be bothered," the woman said, trying to pull him away. "They're very self-sufficient. Don't you remember that piece in the *Times?*"

"It's damned near Christmas, Lori," he said, taking a twenty dollar bill from the folded sheaf held by its clip. "It'll get her a bed for the night, at least. They can't make it out here by themselves. God knows, it's little enough to do." He pulled free of his wife's grasp and walked to the alcove.

He looked down at the woman swathed in the rug, and he could not see her face. Small puffs of breath were all that told him she was alive. "Ma'am," he said, leaning forward. "Ma'am, please take this." He held out the twenty.

Annie did not move. She never spoke on the street.

"Ma'am, please, let me do this. Go somewhere warm for the night, won't you . . . please?"

He stood for another minute, seeking to rouse her, at least for a *go away* that would free him, but the old woman did not move. Finally, he placed the twenty on what he presumed to be her lap, there in that shapeless mass, and allowed himself to be dragged away by his wife.

Three hours later, having completed a lovely dinner, and having decided it would be romantic to walk back to the Helmsley through the six inches of snow that had fallen, they passed the Post Office and saw the old woman had not moved. Nor had she taken the twenty dollars. He could not bring himself to look beneath the wrappings to see if she had frozen to death, and he had no intention of taking back the money. They walked on.

In her warm place, Annie held Alan close up under her chin, stroking him and feeling his tiny black fingers warm at her throat and cheeks. *It's all right, baby, it's all right. We're safe. Shhh, my baby. No one can hurt you.*

Death on the Nile

Connie Willis

Chapter One: Preparing for Your Trip—What to Take

To the ancient Egyptians,' " Zoe reads, " 'Death was a separate country to the west—' " The plane lurches. " '—the west to which the deceased person journeyed.' "

We are on the plane to Egypt. The flight is so rough the flight attendants have strapped themselves into the nearest empty seats, looking scared, and the rest of us have subsided into a nervous window-watching silence. Except Zoe, across the aisle, who is reading aloud from a travel guide.

This one is Somebody or Other's *Egypt Made Easy.* In the seat pocket in front of her are Fodor's *Cairo* and Cooke's *Touring Guide to Egypt's Antiquities,* and there are half a dozen others in her luggage. Not to mention Frommer's *Greece on $35 a Day* and the Savvy Traveler's *Guide to Austria* and the three or four hundred other guidebooks she's already read out loud to us on this trip. I toy briefly with the idea that it's their combined weight that's causing the plane to yaw and career and will shortly send us plummeting to our deaths.

" 'Food, furniture, and weapons were placed in the tomb,' " Zoe reads, " 'as provi—' " The plane pitches sideways. " '—sions for the journey.' "

The plane lurches again, so violently Zoe nearly drops the book, but she doesn't miss a beat. " 'When King Tutankhamun's tomb was opened,' " she reads, " 'it contained trunks full of clothing, jars of wine, a golden boat, and a pair of sandals for walking in the sands of the afterworld.' "

My husband Neil leans over me to look out the window, but there is nothing to see. The sky is clear and cloudless, and below us there aren't even any waves on the water.

" 'In the afterworld the deceased was judged by Anubis, a god with the head of a jackal,' " Zoe reads, " 'and his soul was weighed on a pair of golden scales.' "

I am the only one listening to her. Lissa, on the aisle, is whispering to Neil, her hand almost touching his on the armrest. Across the aisle, next to Zoe and *Egypt Made Easy*, Zoe's husband is asleep and Lissa's husband is staring out the other window and trying to keep his drink from spilling.

"Are you doing all right?" Neil asks Lissa solicitously.

"It'll be exciting going with two other couples," Neil said when he came up with the idea of our all going to Europe together. "Lissa and her husband are lots of fun, and Zoe knows everything. It'll be like having our own tour guide."

It is. Zoe herds us from country to country, reciting historical facts and exchange rates. In the Louvre, a French tourist asked her where the *Mona Lisa* was. She was thrilled. "He thought we were a tour group!" she said. "Imagine that!"

Imagine that.

" 'Before being judged, the deceased recited his confession,' " Zoe reads, " 'a list of sins he had not committed, such as, I have not snared the birds of the gods, I have not told lies, I have not committed adultery.' "

Neil pats Lissa's hand and leans over to me. "Can you trade places with Lissa?" Neil whispers to me.

I already have, I think. "We're not supposed to," I say, pointing at the lights above the seats. "The seat belt sign is on."

He looks at her anxiously. "She's feeling nauseated."

So am I, I want to say, but I am afraid that's what this trip is all about, to get me to say something. "Okay," I say, and unbuckle my seat belt and change places with her. While she is crawling over Neil, the plane pitches again, and she half-falls into his arms. He steadies her. Their eyes lock.

" 'I have not taken another's belongings,' " Zoe reads. " 'I have not murdered another.' "

I can't take any more of this. I reach for my bag, which is still under the window seat, and pull out my paperback of Agatha Christie's *Death on the Nile.* I bought it in Athens.

"About like death anywhere," Zoe's husband said when I got back to our hotel in Athens with it.

"What?" I said.

"Your book," he said, pointing at the paperback and smiling as if he'd made a joke. "The title. I'd imagine death on the Nile is the same as death anywhere."

"Which is what?" I asked.

"The Egyptians believed death was very similar to life," Zoe cut in. She had bought *Egypt Made Easy* at the same bookstore. "To the ancient Egyptians the afterworld was a place much like the world they inhabited. It was presided over by Anubis, who judged the deceased and determined their fates. Our concepts of heaven and hell and of the Day of Judgment are nothing more than modern refinements of Egyptian ideas," she said, and began reading out loud from *Egypt Made Easy,* which pretty much put an end to our conversation, and I still don't know what Zoe's husband thought death would be like, on the Nile or elsewhere.

I open *Death on the Nile* and try to read, thinking maybe Hercule Poirot knows, but the flight is too bumpy. I feel almost immediately queasy, and after half a page and three more lurches I put it in the seat pocket, close my eyes and toy with the idea of murdering another. It's a perfect Agatha Christie setting. She always has a few people in a country house or on an island. In *Death on the Nile* they were on a Nile steamer, but the plane is even better. The only other people on it are the flight attendants and a Japanese tour group who apparently do not speak English or they would be clustered around Zoe, asking directions to the Sphinx.

The turbulence lessens a little, and I open my eyes and reach for my book again. Lissa has it.

She's holding it open, but she isn't reading it. She is watching me, waiting for me to notice, waiting for me to say something. Neil looks nervous.

"You were done with this, weren't you?" she says, smiling. "You weren't reading it."

Everyone has a motive for murder in an Agatha Christie book. And Lissa's husband has been drinking steadily since Paris, and Zoe's husband never gets to finish a sentence. The police might think he had snapped suddenly. Or that it was Zoe he had tried to kill and shot Lissa by mistake. And there is no Hercule Poirot on board to tell them who really committed the murder, to solve the mystery and explain all the strange happenings.

The plane pitches suddenly, so hard Zoe drops her guidebook, and we plunge a good five thousand feet before it recovers. The guidebook has slid forward several rows, and Zoe tries to reach for it with her foot, fails, and looks up at the seat belt sign as if she expects it to go off so she can get out of her seat to retrieve it.

Not after that drop, I think, but the seat belt sign pings almost immediately and goes off.

Lissa's husband instantly calls for the flight attendant and demands another drink, but they have already gone scurrying back to the rear of the plane, still looking pale and scared, as if they expected the turbulence to start up again before they make it. Zoe's husband wakes up at the noise and then goes back to sleep. Zoe retrieves *Egypt Made Easy* from the floor, reads a few more riveting facts from it, then puts it face down on the seat and goes back to the rear of the plane.

I lean across Neil and look out the window, wondering what's happened, but I can't see anything. We are flying through a flat whiteness.

Lissa is rubbing her head. "I cracked my head on the window," she says to Neil. "Is it bleeding?"

He leans over her solicitously to see.

I unsnap my seat belt and start to the back of the plane, but both bathrooms are occupied, and Zoe is perched on the arm of an aisle seat, enlightening the Japanese tour group. "The currency is in Egyptian pounds," she says. "There are one hundred piasters in a pound." I sit back down.

Neil is gently massaging Lissa's temple. "Is that better?" he asks.

I reach across the aisle for Zoe's guidebook. "Must-See Attractions," the chapter is headed, and the first one on the list is the Pyramids.

"Giza, Pyramids of. West bank of Nile, 9 mi. (15 km.) SW of Cairo. Accessible by taxi, bus, rental car. Admission L.E.3. Comments: You can't skip the Pyramids, but be prepared to be disappointed. They don't look at all like you expect, the traffic's terrible, and the view's completely ruined by the hordes of tourists, refreshment stands, and souvenir vendors. Open daily."

I wonder how Zoe stands this stuff. I turn the page to Attraction Number Two. It's King Tut's tomb, and whoever wrote the guidebook wasn't thrilled with it either. "Tutankhamun, Tomb of. Valley of the Kings, Luxor, 400 mi. (668 km.) south of Cairo. Three unimpressive rooms. Inferior wall paintings."

There is a map, showing a long, straight corridor (labeled Corridor) and the three unimpressive rooms opening one onto the other in a row—Anteroom, Burial Chamber, Hall of Judgment.

I close the book and put it back on Zoe's seat. Zoe's husband is still asleep. Lissa's is peering back over his seat. "Where'd the flight attendants go?" he asks. "I want another drink."

"Are you sure it's not bleeding? I can feel a bump," Lissa says to Neil, rubbing her head. "Do you think I have a concussion?"

"No," Neil says, turning her face toward his. "Your pupils aren't dilated." He gazes deeply into her eyes.

"Stewardess!" Lissa's husband shouts. "What do you have to do to get a drink around here?"

Zoe comes back, elated. "They thought I was a professional guide," she says, sitting down and fastening her seatbelt. "They asked if they could join our tour." She opens the guidebook. " 'The afterworld was full of monsters and demigods in the form of crocodiles and baboons and snakes. These monsters could destroy the deceased before he reached the Hall of Judgment.' "

Neil touches my hand. "Do you have any aspirin?" he asks. "Lissa's head hurts."

I fish in my bag for it, and Neil gets up and goes back to get her a glass of water.

"Neil's so thoughtful," Lissa says, watching me, her eyes bright. " 'To protect against these monsters and demigods, the deceased was given *The Book of the Dead*,'" Zoe reads. "'More properly translated as *The Book of What is in the Afterworld*, *The Book of the Dead* was a collection of directions for the journey and magic spells to protect the deceased.'"

I think about how I am going to get through the rest of the trip without magic spells to protect me. Six days in Egypt and then three in Israel, and there is still the trip home on a plane like this and nothing to do for fifteen hours but watch Lissa and Neil and listen to Zoe.

I consider cheerier possibilities. "What if we're not going to Cairo?" I say. "What if we're dead?"

Zoe looks up from her guidebook, irritated.

"There've been a lot of terrorist bombings lately, and this is the Middle East," I go on. "What if that last air pocket was really a bomb? What if it blew us apart, and right now we're drifting down over the Aegean Sea in little pieces?"

"Mediterranean," Zoe says. "We've already flown over Crete."

"How do you know that?" I ask. "Look out the window." I point out Lissa's window at the white flatness beyond. "You can't see the water. We could be anywhere. Or nowhere."

Neil comes back with the water. He hands it and my aspirin to Lissa.

"They check the planes for bombs, don't they?" Lissa asks him. "Don't they use metal detectors and things?"

"I saw this movie once," I say, "where the people were all dead, only they didn't know it. They were on a ship, and they thought they were going to America. There was so much fog they couldn't see the water."

Lissa looks anxiously out the window.

"It looked just like a real ship, but little by little they began to notice little things that weren't quite right. There were hardly any people on board, and no crew at all."

"Stewardess!" Lissa's husband calls, leaning over Zoe into the aisle. "I need another ouzo."

His shouting wakes Zoe's husband up. He blinks at Zoe, confused that she is not reading from her guidebook. "What's going on?" he asks.

"We're all dead," I say. "We were killed by Arab terrorists. We think we're going to Cairo but we're really going to heaven. Or hell."

Lissa, looking out the window, says, "There's so much fog I can't see the wing." She looks frightenedly at Neil. "What if something's happened to the wing?"

"We're just going through a cloud," Neil says. "We're probably beginning our descent into Cairo."

"The sky was perfectly clear," I say, "and then all of a sudden we were in the fog. The people on the ship noticed the fog, too. They noticed there weren't any running lights. And they couldn't find the crew." I smile at Lissa. "Have you noticed how the turbulence stopped all of a sudden? Right after we hit that air pocket. And why—"

A flight attendant comes out of the cockpit and down the aisle to us, carrying a drink. Everyone looks relieved, and Zoe opens her guidebook and begins thumbing through it, looking for fascinating facts.

"Did someone here want an ouzo?" the flight attendant asks.

"Here," Lissa's husband says, reaching for it.

"How long before we get to Cairo?" I say.

She starts toward the back of the plane without answering. I unbuckle my seat belt and follow her. "When will we get to Cairo?" I ask her.

She turns, smiling, but she is still pale and scared-looking. "Did you want another drink, ma'am? Ouzo? Coffee?"

"Why did the turbulence stop?" I say. "How long till we get to Cairo?"

"You need to take your seat," she says, pointing to the seat belt sign. "We're beginning our descent. We'll be at our destination in another twenty minutes." She bends over the Japanese tour group and tells them to bring their seat backs to an upright position.

"What destination? Our descent to where? We aren't beginning any descent. The seat belt sign is still off," I say, and it bings on.

I go back to my seat. Zoe's husband is already asleep again. Zoe is reading out loud from *Egypt Made Easy*. " 'The visitor should take precautions before traveling in Egypt. A map is essential, and a flashlight is needed for many of the sites.' "

Lissa has gotten her bag out from under the seat. She puts my *Death on the Nile* in it and gets out her sunglasses. I look past her and out the window at the white flatness where the wing should be. We should be able to see the lights on the wing even in the fog. That's what they're there for, so you can see the plane in the fog. The people on the ship didn't realize they were dead at first. It was only when they started noticing little things that weren't quite right that they began to wonder.

" 'A guide is recommended,' " Zoe reads.

I have meant to frighten Lissa, but I have only managed to frighten myself. We are beginning our descent, that's all, I tell myself, and flying through a cloud. And that must be right.

Because here we are in Cairo.

Chapter Two: Arriving at the Airport

So this is Cairo?" Zoe's husband says, looking around. The plane has stopped at the end of the runway and deplaned us onto the asphalt by means of a metal stairway.

The terminal is off to the east, a low building with palm trees around it, and the Japanese tour group sets off toward it immediately, shouldering their carry-on bags and camera cases.

We do not have any carry-ons. Since we always have to wait at the baggage claim for Zoe's guidebooks anyway, we check our carry-ons, too. Every time we do it, I am convinced they will go to Tokyo or disappear altogether, but now I'm glad we don't have to lug them all the way to the terminal. It looks like it is miles away, and the Japanese are already slowing.

Zoe is reading the guidebook. The rest of us stand around her, looking impatient. Lissa has caught the heel of her sandal in one of the metal steps coming down and is leaning against Neil.

"Did you twist it?" Neil asks anxiously.

The flight attendants clatter down the steps with their navy-blue overnight cases. They still look nervous. At the bottom of the stairs they unfold wheeled metal carriers and strap the overnight cases to them and set off for the terminal. After a few steps they stop, and one of them takes off her jacket and drapes it over the wheeled carrier, and they start off again, walking rapidly in their high heels.

It is not as hot as I expected, even though the distant terminal shimmers in the heated air rising from the asphalt. There is no sign of the clouds we flew through, just a thin white haze which disperses the sun's light into an even glare. We are all squinting. Lissa lets go of Neil's arm for a second to get her sunglasses out of her bag.

"What do they drink around here?" Lissa's husband asks, squinting over Zoe's shoulder at the guidebook. "I want a drink."

"The local drink is zibib," Zoe says. "It's like ouzo." She looks up from the guidebook. "I think we should go see the Pyramids."

The professional tour guide strikes again. "Don't you think we'd better take care of first things first?" I say. "Like customs? And picking up our luggage?"

"And finding a drink of . . . what did you call it? Zibab?" Lissa's husband says.

"No," Zoe says. "I think we should do the Pyramids first. It'll take an hour to do the baggage claim and customs, and we can't take our luggage with us to the Pyramids. We'll have to go to the hotel, and by that time everyone will be out there. I think we should go right now." She gestures at the terminal. "We can run out and see them and be back before the Japanese tour group's even through customs."

She turns and starts walking in the opposite direction from the terminal, and the others straggle obediently after her.

I look back at the terminal. The flight attendants have passed the Japanese tour group and are nearly to the palm trees.

"You're going the wrong way," I say to Zoe. "We've got to go to the terminal to get a taxi."

Zoe stops. "A taxi?" she says. "What for? They aren't far. We can walk it in fifteen minutes."

"Fifteen minutes?" I say. "Giza's nine miles west of Cairo. You have to cross the Nile to get there."

"Don't be silly," she says, "they're right there," and points in the direction she was walking, and there, beyond the asphalt in an expanse of sand, so close they do not shimmer at all, are the Pyramids.

Chapter Three: Getting Around

It takes us longer than fifteen minutes. The Pyramids are farther away than they look, and the sand is deep and hard to walk in. We have to stop every few feet so Lissa can empty out her sandals, leaning against Neil.

"We should have taken a taxi," Zoe's husband says, but there are no roads, and no sign of the refreshment stands and souvenir vendors the guidebook complained about, only the unbroken expanse of deep sand and the white, even sky, and in the distance the three yellow pyramids, standing in a row.

" 'The tallest of the three is the Pyramid of Cheops, built in 2690 B.C.,' " Zoe says, reading as she walks. " 'It took thirty years to complete.' "

"You have to take a taxi to get to the Pyramids," I say. "There's a lot of traffic."

" 'It was built on the west bank of the Nile, which the ancient Egyptians believed was the land of the dead.' "

There is a flicker of movement ahead, between the pyramids, and I stop and shade my eyes against the glare to look at it, hoping it is a souvenir vendor, but I can't see anything.

We start walking again.

It flickers again, and this time I catch sight of it running, hunched over, its hands nearly touching the ground. It disappears behind the middle pyramid.

"I saw something," I say, catching up to Zoe. "Some kind of animal. It looked like a baboon."

Zoe leafs through the guidebook and then says, "Monkeys.

They're found frequently near Giza. They beg for food from the tourists."

"There aren't any tourists," I say.

"I know," Zoe says happily. "I told you we'd avoid the rush."

"You have to go through customs, even in Egypt," I say. "You can't just leave the airport."

" 'The pyramid on the left is Kheophren,' " Zoe says, " 'built in 2650 B.C.' "

"In the movie, they wouldn't believe they were dead even when somebody told them," I say. "Giza is *nine* miles from Cairo."

"What are you talking about?" Neil says. Lissa has stopped again and is leaning against him, standing on one foot and shaking her sandal out. "That mystery of Lissa's, *Death on the Nile?*"

"This was a *movie*," I say. "They were on this ship, and they were all dead."

"We saw that movie, didn't we, Zoe?" Zoe's husband says. "Mia Farrow was in it, and Bette Davis. And the detective guy, what was his name—"

"Hercule Poirot," Zoe says. "Played by Peter Ustinov. 'The Pyramids are open daily from 8 A.M. to 5 P.M. Evenings there is a *Son et Lumière* show with colored floodlights and a narration in English and Japanese.' "

"There were all sorts of clues," I say, "but they just ignored them."

"I don't like Agatha Christie," Lissa says. "Murder and trying to find out who killed who. I'm never able to figure out what's going on. All those people on the train together."

"You're thinking of *Murder on the Orient Express*," Neil says. "I saw that."

"Is that the one where they got killed off one by one?" Lissa's husband says.

"I saw that one," Zoe's husband says. "They got what they deserved, as far as I'm concerned, going off on their own like that when they knew they should keep together."

"Giza is nine miles west of Cairo," I say. "You have to take a taxi to get there. There is all this traffic."

"Peter Ustinov was in that one, too, wasn't he?" Neil says. "The one with the train?"

"No," Zoe's husband says. "It was the other one. What's his name—"

"Albert Finney," Zoe says.

Chapter Four: Places of Interest

The Pyramids are closed. Fifty yards (45.7 m.) from the base of Cheops there is a chain barring our way. A metal sign hangs from it that says "Closed" in English and Japanese.

"Prepare to be disappointed," I say.

"I thought you said they were open daily," Lissa says, knocking sand out of her sandals.

"It must be a holiday," Zoe says, leafing through her guidebook. "Here it is. 'Egyptian holidays.' " She begins reading. " 'Antiquities sites are closed during Ramadan, the Muslim month of fasting in March. On Fridays the sites are closed from eleven to one P.M.' "

It is not March, or Friday, and even if it were, it is after one P.M. The shadow of Cheops stretches well past where we stand. I look up, trying to see the sun where it must be behind the pyramid, and catch a flicker of movement, high up. It is too large to be a monkey.

"Well, what do we do now?" Zoe's husband says.

"We could go see the Sphinx," Zoe muses, looking through the guidebook. "Or we could wait for the Son et Lumière show."

"No," I say, thinking of being out here in the dark.

"How do you know that won't be closed, too?" Lissa asks.

Zoe consults the book. "There are two shows daily, seven-thirty and nine P.M."

"That's what you said about the Pyramids," Lissa says. "I think we should go back to the airport and get our luggage. I want to get my other shoes."

"I think we should go back to the hotel," Lissa's husband says, "and have a long, cool drink."

"We'll go to Tutankhamun's tomb," Zoe says. " 'It's open every day, including holidays.' " She looks up expectantly.

"King Tut's tomb?" I say. "In the Valley of the Kings?"

"Yes," she says, and starts to read. " 'It was found intact in 1922 by Howard Carter. It contained—' "

All the belongings necessary for the deceased's journey to the afterworld, I think. Sandals and clothes and *Egypt Made Easy*.

"I'd rather have a drink," Lissa's husband says.

"And a nap," Zoe's husband says. "You go on, and we'll meet you at the hotel."

"I don't think you should go off on your own," I say. "I think we should keep together."

"It will be crowded if we wait," Zoe says. "I'm going now. Are you coming, Lissa?"

Lissa looks appealingly up at Neil. "I don't think I'd better walk that far. My ankle's starting to hurt again."

Neil looks helplessly at Zoe. "I guess we'd better pass."

"What about you?" Zoe's husband says to me. "Are you going with Zoe or do you want to come with us?"

"In Athens, you said death was the same everywhere," I say to him, "and I said, 'Which is what?' and then Zoe interrupted us and you never did answer me. What were you going to say?"

"I've forgotten," he says, looking at Zoe as if he hopes she will interrupt us again, but she is intent on the guidebook.

"You said, 'Death is the same everywhere,' " I persist, "and I said, 'Which is what?' What did you think death would be like?"

"I don't know . . . unexpected, I guess. And probably pretty damn unpleasant." He laughs nervously. "If we're going to the hotel, we'd better get started. Who else is coming?"

I toy with the idea of going with them, of sitting safely in the hotel bar with ceiling fans and palms, drinking zibib while we wait. That's what the people on the ship did. And in spite of Lissa, I want to stay with Neil.

I look at the expanse of sand back toward the east. There is no sign of Cairo from here, or of the terminal, and far off there is a flicker of movement, like something running.

I shake my head. "I want to see King Tut's tomb." I go over to Neil. "I think we should go with Zoe," I say, and put my hand on his arm. "After all, she's our guide."

Neil looks helplessly at Lissa and then back at me. "I don't know. . . ."

"The three of you can go back to the hotel," I say to Lissa, gesturing to include the other men, "and Zoe and Neil and I can meet you there after we've been to the tomb."

Neil moves away from Lissa. "Why can't you and Zoe just go?" he whispers at me.

"I think we should keep together," I say. "It would be so easy to get separated."

"How come you're so stuck on going with Zoe anyway?" Neil says. "I thought you said you hated being led around by the nose all the time."

I want to say, Because she has the book, but Lissa has come over and is watching us, her eyes bright behind her sunglasses. "I've always wanted to see the inside of a tomb," I say.

"King Tut?" Lissa says. "Is that the one with the treasure, the necklaces and the gold coffin and stuff?" She puts her hand on Neil's arm. "I've always wanted to see that."

"Okay," Neil says, relieved. "I guess we'll go with you, Zoe."

Zoe looks expectantly at her husband.

"Not me," he says. "We'll meet you in the bar."

"We'll order drinks for you," Lissa's husband says. He waves goodbye, and they set off as if they know where they are going, even though Zoe hasn't told them the name of the hotel.

" 'The Valley of the Kings is located in the hills west of Luxor,' " Zoe says and starts off across the sand the way she did at the airport. We follow her.

I wait until Lissa gets a shoeful of sand and she and Neil fall behind while she empties it.

"Zoe," I say quietly. "There's something wrong."

"Umm," she says, looking up something in the guidebook's index.

"The Valley of the Kings is four hundred miles south of Cairo," I say. "You can't walk there from the Pyramids."

She finds the page. "Of course not. We have to take a boat."

She points, and I see we have reached a stand of reeds, and beyond it is the Nile.

Nosing out from the rushes is a boat, and I am afraid it will be made of gold, but it is only one of the Nile cruisers. And I am so relieved that the Valley of the Kings is not within walking distance that I do not recognize the boat until we have climbed on board and are standing on the canopied deck next to the wooden paddlewheel. It is the steamer from *Death on the Nile*.

Chapter Five: Cruises, Day Trips, and Guided Tours

Lissa is sick on the boat. Neil offers to take her below, and I expect her to say yes, but she shakes her head. "My ankle hurts," she says, and sinks down in one of the deck chairs. Neil kneels by her feet and examines a bruise no bigger than a piaster.

"Is it swollen?" she asks anxiously. There is no sign of swelling, but Neil eases her sandal off and takes her foot tenderly, caressingly, in both hands. Lissa closes her eyes and leans back against the deck chair, sighing.

I toy with the idea that Lissa's husband couldn't take any more of this either, and that he murdered us all and then killed himself.

"Here we are on a ship," I say, "like the dead people in that movie."

"It's not a ship, it's a steamboat," Zoe says. " 'The Nile steamer is the most pleasant way to travel in Egypt and one of the least expensive. Costs range from $180 to $360 per person for a four-day cruise.' "

Or maybe it was Zoe's husband, finally determined to shut Zoe up so he could finish a conversation, and then he had to murder the rest of us one after the other to keep from being caught.

"We're all alone on the ship," I say, "just like they were."

"How far is it to the Valley of the Kings?" Lissa asks.

" 'Three-and-a-half miles (5 km.) west of Luxor,' " Zoe says, reading. " 'Luxor is four hundred miles south of Cairo.' "

"If it's that far, I might as well read my book," Lissa says, pushing her sunglasses up on top of her head. "Neil, hand me my bag."

He fishes *Death on the Nile* out of her bag, and hands it to her, and she flips through it for a moment, like Zoe looking for exchange rates, and then begins to read.

"The wife did it," I say. "She found out her husband was being unfaithful."

Lissa glares at me. "I already knew that," she says carelessly. "I saw the movie," but after another half-page she lays the open book face-down on the empty deck chair next to her.

"I can't read," she says to Neil. "The sun's too bright." She squints up at the sky, which is still hidden by its gauzelike haze.

" 'The Valley of the Kings is the site of the tombs of sixty-four pharaohs,' " Zoe says. " 'Of these, the most famous is Tutankhamun's.' "

I go over to the railing and watch the Pyramids recede, slipping slowly out of sight behind the rushes that line the shore. They look flat, like yellow triangles stuck up in the sand, and I remember how in Paris Zoe's husband wouldn't believe the *Mona Lisa* was the real thing. "It's a fake," he insisted before Zoe interrupted. "The real one's much larger."

And the guidebook said, Prepare to be disappointed, and the Valley of the Kings is four hundred miles from the Pyramids like it's supposed to be, and Middle Eastern airports are notorious for their lack of security. That's how all those bombs get on planes in the first place, because they don't make people go through customs. I shouldn't watch so many movies.

" 'Among its treasures, Tutankhamun's tomb contained a golden boat, by which the soul would travel to the world of the dead,' " Zoe says.

I lean over the railing and look into the water. It is not muddy, like I thought it would be, but a clear waveless blue, and in its depths the sun is shining brightly.

" 'The boat was carved with passages from *The Book of the Dead,' " Zoe reads, " 'to protect the deceased from monsters and demigods who might try to destroy him before he reached the Hall of Judgment.' "

There is something in the water. Not a ripple, not even enough of a movement to shudder the image of the sun, but I know there is something there.

" 'Spells were also written on papyruses buried with the body,' " Zoe says.

It is long and dark, like a crocodile. I lean over farther, gripping the rail, trying to see into the transparent water, and catch a glint of scales. It is swimming straight toward the boat.

" 'These spells took the form of commands,' " Zoe reads. " 'Get back, you evil one! Stay away! I adjure you in the name of Anubis and Osiris.' "

The water glitters, hesitating.

" 'Do not come against me,' " Zoe says. " 'My spells protect me. I know the way.' "

The thing in the water turns and swims away. The boat follows it, nosing slowly in toward the shore.

"There it is," Zoe says, pointing past the reeds at a distant row of cliffs. "The Valley of the Kings."

"I suppose this'll be closed, too," Lissa says, letting Neil help her off the boat.

"Tombs are never closed," I say, and look north, across the sand, at the distant Pyramids.

Chapter Six: Accommodations

The Valley of the Kings is not closed. The tombs stretch along a sandstone cliff, black openings in the yellow rock, and there are no chains across the stone steps that lead down to them. At the south end of the valley a Japanese tour group is going into the last one.

"Why aren't the tombs marked?" Lissa asks. "Which one is King Tut's?" and Zoe leads us to the north end of the valley, where the cliff dwindles into a low wall. Beyond it, across the sand, I can see the Pyramids, sharp against the sky.

Zoe stops at the very edge of a slanting hole dug into the base of the rocks. There are steps leading down into it. "Tutankhamun's tomb was found when a workman accidentally uncovered the top step," she says.

Lissa looks down into the stairwell. All but the top two steps are in shadow, and it is too dark to see the bottom. "Are there snakes?" she asks.

"No," Zoe, who knows everything, says. "Tutankhamun's tomb is the smallest of the pharaohs' tombs in the Valley." She fumbles in her bag for her flashlight. "The tomb consists of three rooms—an antechamber, the burial chamber containing Tutankhamun's coffin, and the Hall of Judgment."

There is a slither of movement in the darkness below us, like a slow uncoiling, and Lissa steps back from the edge. "Which room is the stuff in?"

"Stuff?" Zoe says uncertainly, still fumbling for her flashlight. She opens her guidebook. "Stuff?" she says again, and flips to the back of it, as if she is going to look "stuff" up in the index.

"*Stuff*," Lissa says, and there is an edge of fear in her voice. "All the furniture and vases and stuff they take with them. You said the Egyptians buried their belongings with them."

"King Tut's treasure," Neil says helpfully.

"Oh, the *treasure*," Zoe says, relieved. "The belongings buried with Tutankhamun for his journey into the afterworld. They're not here. They're in Cairo in the museum."

"In Cairo?" Lissa says. "They're in Cairo? Then what are we doing here?"

"We're dead," I say. "Arab terrorists blew up our plane and killed us all."

"I *came* all the way out here because I wanted to see the treasure," Lissa says.

"The coffin is here," Zoe says placatingly, "and there are wall paintings in the antechamber," but Lissa has already led Neil away from the steps, talking earnestly to him.

"The wall paintings depict the stages in the judgment of the soul, the weighing of the soul, the recital of the deceased's confession," Zoe says.

The deceased's confession. I have not taken that which belongs to another. I have not caused any pain. I have not committed adultery.

Lissa and Neil come back, Lissa leaning heavily on Neil's arm. "I think we'll pass on this tomb thing," Neil says apologetically.

"We want to get to the museum before it closes. Lissa had her heart set on seeing the treasure."

" 'The Egyptian Museum is open from 9 A.M. to 4 P.M. daily, 9 to 11:15 A.M. and 1:30 to 4 P.M. Fridays,' " Zoe says, reading from the guidebook. " 'Admission is three Egyptian pounds.' "

"It's already four o'clock," I say, looking at my watch. "It will be closed before you get there." I look up.

Neil and Lissa have already started back, not toward the boat but across the sand in the direction of the Pyramids. The light behind the Pyramids is beginning to fade, the sky going from white to gray-blue.

"Wait," I say, and run across the sand to catch up with them. "Why don't you wait and we'll all go back together? It won't take us very long to see the tomb. You heard Zoe, there's nothing inside."

They both look at me.

"I think we should stay together," I finish lamely.

Lissa looks up alertly, and I realize she thinks I am talking about divorce, that I have finally said what she has been waiting for.

"I think we should all keep together," I say hastily. "This is Egypt. There are all sorts of dangers, crocodiles and snakes and . . . it won't take us very long to see the tomb. You heard Zoe, there's nothing inside."

"We'd better not," Neil says, looking at me. "Lissa's ankle is starting to swell. I'd better get some ice on it."

I look down at her ankle. Where the bruise was there are two little puncture marks, close together, like a snake bite, and around them the ankle is starting to swell.

"I don't think Lissa's up to the Hall of Judgment," he says, still looking at me.

"You could wait at the top of the steps," I say. "You wouldn't have to go in."

Lissa takes hold of his arm, as if anxious to go, but he hesitates. "Those people on the ship," he says to me. "What happened to them?"

"I was just trying to frighten you," I say. "I'm sure there's a logical explanation. It's too bad Hercule Poirot isn't here—he'd be able to explain everything. The Pyramids were probably closed for some Muslim holiday Zoe didn't know about, and that's why we didn't have to go through customs either, because it was a holiday."

"What happened to the people on the ship?" Neil says again.

"They got judged," I say, "but it wasn't nearly as bad as they'd thought. They were all afraid of what was going to happen, even the clergyman, who hadn't committed any sins, but the judge turned out to be somebody he knew. A bishop. He wore a white suit, and he was very kind, and most of them came out fine."

"Most of them," Neil says.

"Let's *go*," Lissa says, pulling on his arm.

"The people on the ship," Neil says, ignoring her. "Had any of them committed some horrible sin?"

"My ankle hurts," Lissa says. "Come *on*."

"I have to go," Neil says, almost reluctantly. "Why don't you come with us?"

I glance at Lissa, expecting her to be looking daggers at Neil, but she is watching me with bright, lidless eyes.

"Yes. Come with us," she says, and waits for my answer.

I lied to Lissa about the ending of *Death on the Nile*. It was the wife they killed. I toy with the idea that they have committed some horrible sin, that I am lying in my hotel room in Athens, my temple black with blood and powder burns. I would be the only one here then, and Lissa and Neil would be demigods disguised to look like them. Or monsters.

"I'd better not," I say, and back away from them.

"Let's go then," Lissa says to Neil, and they start off across the sand. Lissa is limping badly, and before they have gone very far, Neil stops and takes off his shoes.

The sky behind the Pyramids is purple-blue, and the Pyramids stand out flat and black against it.

"Come on," Zoe calls from the top of the steps. She is holding the flashlight and looking at the guidebook. "I want to see the Weighing of the Soul."

Chapter Seven: Off the Beaten Track

Zoe is already halfway down the steps when I get back, shining her flashlight on the door below her. "When the tomb was discovered, the door was plastered over and stamped with the seals bearing the cartouche of Tutankhamun," she says.

"It'll be dark soon," I call down to her. "Maybe we should go back to the hotel with Lissa and Neil." I look back across the desert, but they are already out of sight.

Zoe is gone, too. When I look back down the steps, there is nothing but darkness. "Zoe!" I shout and run down the sand-drifted steps after her. "Wait!"

The door to the tomb is open, and I can see the light from her flashlight bobbing on rock walls and ceiling far down a narrow corridor.

"Zoe!" I shout, and start after her. The floor is uneven, and I trip and put my hand on the wall to steady myself. "Come back! You have the book!"

The light flashes on a section of carved-out wall, far ahead, and then vanishes, as if she has turned a corner.

"Wait for me!" I shout and stop because I cannot see my hand in front of my face.

There is no answering light, no answering voice, no sound at all. I stand very still, one hand still on the wall, listening for footsteps, for quiet padding, for the sound of slithering, but I can't hear anything, not even my own heart beating.

"Zoe," I call out, "I'm going to wait for you outside," and turn around holding onto the wall so I don't get disoriented in the dark, and go back the way I came.

The corridor seems longer than it did coming in, and I toy with the idea that it will go on forever in the dark, or that the door will be locked, the opening plastered over and the ancient seals affixed, but there is a line of light under the door, and it opens easily when I push on it.

I am at the top of a stone staircase leading down into a long wide hall. On either side the hall is lined with stone pillars, and between the pillars I can see that the walls are painted with scenes in sienna and yellow and bright blue.

It must be the anteroom because Zoe said its walls were painted with scenes from the soul's journey into death, and there is Anubis weighing the soul, and, beyond it, a baboon devouring something, and, opposite, where I am standing on the stairs, a painting of a boat crossing the blue Nile. It is made of gold, and in it four souls squat in a line, their kohl-outlined eyes looking ahead at the shore. Beside them, in the transparent water, Sebek, the crocodile demigod, swims.

I start down the steps. There is a doorway at the far end of the hall and if this is the anteroom, then the door must lead to the burial chamber.

Zoe said the tomb consists of only three rooms, and I saw the map myself on the plane, the steps and straight corridor and then the unimpressive rooms leading one into another, anteroom and burial chamber and Hall of Judgment, one after another.

So this is the anteroom, even if it is larger than it was on the map, and Zoe has obviously gone ahead to the burial chamber and is standing by Tutankhamun's coffin, reading aloud from the travel guide. When I come in, she will look up and say, " 'The quartzite sarcophagus is carved with passages from *The Book of the Dead.*' "

I have come halfway down the stairs, and from here I can see the painting of the weighing of the soul. Anubis, with his jackal's head standing on one side of the yellow scales, and the deceased on the other, reading his confession from a papyrus.

I go down two more steps, till I am even with the scales, and sit down.

Surely Zoe won't be long—there's nothing in the burial chamber except the coffin—and even if she has gone on ahead to the Hall of Judgment, she'll have to come back this way. There's only one entrance to the tomb. And she can't get turned around because she has a flashlight. And the book. I clasp my hands around my knees and wait.

I think about the people on the ship, waiting for judgment. "It wasn't as bad as they thought," I'd told Neil, but now, sitting here on the steps, I remember that the bishop, smiling kindly in his white suit, gave them sentences appropriate to their sins. One of the women was sentenced to being alone forever.

The deceased in the painting looks frightened, standing by the scale, and I wonder what sentence Anubis will give him, what sins he has committed.

Maybe he has not committed any sins at all, like the clergyman, and is worried over nothing, or maybe he is merely frightened at finding himself in this strange place, alone. Was death what he expected?

"Death is the same everywhere," Zoe's husband said. "Unexpected." And nothing is the way you thought it would be. Look at the *Mona Lisa*. And Neil. The people on the ship had planned on something else altogether, pearly gates and angels and clouds, all the modern refinements. Prepare to be disappointed.

And what about the Egyptians, packing their clothes and wine and sandals for their trip. Was death, even on the Nile, what they expected? Or was it not the way it had been described in the travel guide at all? Did they keep thinking they were alive, in spite of all the clues?

The deceased clutches his papyrus and I wonder if he has committed some horrible sin. Adultery. Or murder. I wonder how he died.

The people on the ship were killed by a bomb, like we were. I try to remember the moment it went off—Zoe reading out loud and then the sudden shock of light and decompression, the travel guide blown out of Zoe's hands and Lissa falling through the blue air, but I can't. Maybe it didn't happen on the plane. Maybe the terrorists blew us up in the airport in Athens, while we were checking our luggage.

I toy with the idea that it wasn't a bomb at all, that I murdered Lissa, and then killed myself, like in *Death on the Nile*. Maybe I reached into my bag, not for my paperback but for the gun I bought in Athens, and shot Lissa while she was looking out the window. And Neil bent over her, solicitous, concerned, and I raised the gun again, and Zoe's husband tried to wrestle it out of my hand, and the shot went wide and hit the gas tank on the wing.

I am still frightening myself. If I'd murdered Lissa, I would remember it, and even Athens, notorious for its lack of security, wouldn't have let me on board a plane with a gun. And you could hardly commit some horrible crime without remembering it, could you?

The people on the ship didn't remember dying, even when someone told them, but that was because the ship was so much like a real one, the railings and the water and the deck. And because of the bomb. People never remember being blown up. It's the concussion or something, it knocks the memory out of you. But I would surely have remembered murdering someone. Or being murdered.

I sit on the steps a long time, watching for the splash of Zoe's flashlight in the doorway. Outside it will be dark, time for the *Son et Lumière* show at the Pyramids.

It seems darker in here, too. I have to squint to see Anubis and the yellow scales and the deceased, awaiting judgment. The papyrus he is holding is covered with long, bordered columns of hieroglyphics and I hope they are magic spells to protect him and not a list of all the sins he has committed.

I have not murdered another, I think. I have not committed adultery. But there are other sins.

It will be dark soon, and I do not have a flashlight. I stand up. "Zoe," I call, and go down the stairs and between the pillars. They are carved with animals—cobras and baboons and crocodiles.

"It's getting dark," I call, and my voice echoes hollowly among the pillars. "They'll be wondering what happened to us."

The last pair of pillars is carved with a bird, its sandstone wings outstretched. A bird of the gods. Or a plane.

"Zoe?" I say, and stoop to go through the low door. "Are you in here?"

Chapter Eight: Special Events

Zoe isn't in the burial chamber. It is much smaller than the anteroom, and there are no paintings on the rough walls or above the door that leads to the Hall of Judgment. The ceiling is scarcely higher than the door, and I have to hunch down to keep from scraping my head against it.

It is darker in here than in the anteroom, but even in the dimness I can see that Zoe isn't here. Neither is Tutankhamun's sarcophagus, carved with *The Book of the Dead*. There is nothing in the room at all except for a pile of suitcases in the corner by the door to the Hall of Judgment.

It is our luggage. I recognize my battered Samsonite and the carry-on bags of the Japanese tour group. The flight attendants' navy-blue overnight cases are in front of the pile, strapped like victims to their wheeled carriers.

On top of my suitcase is a book, and I think, "It's the travel guide," even though I know Zoe would never have left it behind, and I hurry over to pick it up.

It is not *Egypt Made Easy*. It is my *Death on the Nile*, lying open and face-down the way Lissa left it on the boat, but I pick it up anyway and open it to the last pages, searching for the place where Hercule Poirot explains all the strange things that have been happening, where he solves the mystery.

I cannot find it. I thumb back through the book, looking for a map. There is always a map in Agatha Christie, showing who had what stateroom on the ship, showing the stairways and the doors and the unimpressive rooms leading one into another, but I cannot find that either. The pages are covered with long unreadable columns of hieroglyphics.

I close the book. "There's no point in waiting for Zoe," I say, looking past the luggage at the door to the next room. It is lower than the one I came through, and dark beyond. "She's obviously gone on to the Hall of Judgment."

I walk over to the door, holding the book against my chest. There are stone steps leading down. I can see the top one in the dim light from the burial chamber. It is steep and very narrow.

I toy briefly with the idea that it will not be so bad after all, that I am dreading it like the clergyman, and it will turn out to be not judgment but someone I know, a smiling bishop in a white suit, and mercy is not a modern refinement after all.

"I have not murdered another," I say, and my voice does not echo. "I have not committed adultery."

I take hold of the doorjamb with one hand so I won't fall on the stairs. With the other I hold the book against me. "Get back, you evil ones," I say. "Stay away. I adjure you in the name of Osiris and Poirot. My spells protect me. I know the way."

I begin my descent.

Ménage à Trois

F. Paul Wilson

Burke noticed how Grimes, the youngest patrolman there, was turning a sickly shade of yellow-green. He motioned him closer. "You all right?"

Grimes nodded. "Sure. Fine." His pitiful attempt at a smile was hardly reassuring. "Awful hot in here, but I'm fine."

Burke could see that he was anything but. The kid's lips were as pale as the rest of his face and he was dripping with sweat. He was either going to puke or pass out or both in the next two minutes.

"Yeah. Hot," Burke said. It was no more than seventy in the hospital room. "Get some fresh air out in the hall."

"Okay. Sure." Now the smile was real—and grateful. Grimes gestured toward the three sheet-covered bodies. "I just never seen anything like this before, y'know?"

Burke nodded. He knew. This was a nasty one. Real nasty. He swallowed the sour-milk taste that puckered his cheeks. In his twenty-three years with homicide he had seen his share of crime scenes like this, but he never got used to them. The splattered blood and flesh, the smell from the ruptured intestines, the glazed eyes in the slack-jawed faces—who could get used to that? And three lives, over and gone for good.

"Look," he told Grimes, "why don't you check at the nurses' desk and find out where they lived. Get over there and dig up some background."

Grimes nodded enthusiastically. "Yes, sir."

Burke turned back to the room. Three lives had ended in there this morning. He was going to have to find out what those lives had been until now if he was ever going to understand this horror. And when he did get all the facts, could he ever really understand? Did he really want to?

*   *   *

Hot, sweaty, and gritty, Jerry Pritchard hauled himself up the cellar stairs and into the kitchen. Grabbing a beer from the fridge, he popped the top and drained half the can in one long, gullet-cooling swallow. Lord, that was *good!* He stepped over to the back door and pressed his face against the screen in search of a vagrant puff of air, anything to cool him off.

"Spring cleaning," he muttered, looking out at the greening rear acreage. "Right." It felt like August. Who ever heard of eighty degrees in April?

He could almost see the grass growing. The weeds, too. That meant he'd probably be out riding the mower around next week. Old lady Gati had kept him busy all fall getting the grounds perfectly manicured; the winter had been spent painting and patching the first and second floors; April had been designated basement clean-up time, and now the grounds needed to be whipped into shape again.

An endless cycle. Jerry smiled. But that cycle meant job security. And job security meant he could work and eat here during the day and sleep in the gatehouse at night, and never go home again.

He drained the can and gave it a behind-the-back flip into the brown paper bag sitting in the corner by the fridge.

Home . . . the thought pursued him. There had been times when he thought he'd never get out. Twenty-two years in that little house, the last six of them pure hell after Dad got killed in the cave-in of No. 8 mine. Mom went off the deep end then. She had always been super religious, herding everyone along to fire-and-brimstone Sunday prayer meetings and making them listen to Bible readings every night. Dad had kept her in check somewhat, but once he was gone, all the stops were out. She began hounding him about how her only son should join the ministry and spread the Word of God. She submerged him in a Bible-besotted life for those years, and he'd almost bought the package. She had him consulting the Book upon awakening, upon retiring, before eating, before going off to school, before buying a pair of socks, before taking a leak, until common sense got a hold of him and he realized he was going slowly mad. But he couldn't leave because he was the man of the house and there was his younger sister to think of.

But Suzie, bless her, ran off last summer at sixteen and got married. Jerry walked out a week later. Mom had the house, Dad's pension, her Bible, and an endless round of prayer meetings. Jerry stopped by once in a while and sent her a little money when he could. She seemed to be content.

Whatever makes you happy, he thought. He had taken his own personal Bible with him when he left. It was still in his suitcase in the gatehouse. Some things you just didn't throw away, even if you stopped using them.

The latest in a string of live-in maids swung through the kitchen door with old lady Gati's lunch dishes on a tray. None of the others had been bad looking, but this girl was a knockout.

"Hey, Steph," he said, deciding to put off his return to the cellar just a little bit longer. "How's the Dragon Lady treating you?"

She flashed him a bright smile. "I don't know why you call her that, Jerry. She's really very sweet."

That's what they all say, he thought, and then *wham!* they're out. Stephanie Watson had been here almost six weeks—a record in Jerry's experience. Old lady Gati went through maids like someone with hayfever went through Kleenex. Maybe Steph had whatever it was old lady Gati was looking for.

Jerry hoped so. He liked her. Liked her a *lot.* Liked her short tawny hair and the slightly crooked teeth that made her easy smile seem so genuine, liked her long legs and the way she moved through this big old house with such natural grace, like she belonged here. He especially liked the way her blue flowered print shift clung to her breasts and stretched across her buttocks as she loaded the dishes into the dishwasher.

"You know," she said, turning toward him and leaning back against the kitchen counter, "I still can't get over the size of this place. Seems every other day I find a new room."

Jerry nodded, remembering his first few weeks here last September. The sheer height of this old three-storey Gothic mansion had awed him as he had come through the gate to apply for the care-taker job. He had known it was big—everybody in the valley grew up within sight of the old Gati House on the hill—but had never been close enough to appreciate *how* big. The house didn't really fit with the rest of the valley. It wasn't all that difficult to imagine that a giant hand had plucked it from a far-away, more populated place and dropped it here by mistake. But the older folks in town still talked about all the trouble and expense mine-owner Karl Gati went through to have it built.

"Yeah," he said, looking at his calloused hands. "It's big all right."

He watched her for a moment as she turned and rinsed out the sink, watched the way her blond hair moved back and forth across the nape of her neck. He fought the urge to slip his arms around her and kiss that neck. That might be a mistake. They had been dating since she arrived here—just movies and something to eat afterwards—and she had been successful so far in holding him off. Not that that was so hard to do. Growing up under Mom's watchful Pentecostal eye had prevented him from developing a smooth approach to the opposite sex. So far, his limited repertoire of moves hadn't been successful with Steph.

He was sure she wasn't a dumb innocent—she was a farm girl and certainly knew what went where and why. No, he sensed that she was as attracted to him as he to her but didn't want to be a pushover. Well, okay. Jerry wasn't sure why that didn't bother him too much. Maybe it was because there was something open and vulnerable about Steph that appealed to a protective instinct in him. He'd give her time. Plenty of it. Something inside him told him she was worth the wait. And something else told him that she was weakening, that maybe it wouldn't be too long now before . . .

"Well, it's Friday," he said, moving closer. "Want to go down to town tonight and see what's playing at the Strand?" He hated to sound like a broken record—movie-movie-movie—but what else was there to do in this county on weekends if you didn't get drunk, play pool, race cars, or watch TV?

Her face brightened with another smile. "Love it!"

Now why, he asked himself, should a little smile and a simple *yes* make me feel so damn good?

No doubt about it. She did something to him.

"Great! I'll—"

A deep, gutteral woman's voice interrupted him. "Young Pritchard! I wish to see you a moment!"

Jerry shuddered. He hated what her accent did to the "*r*"s in his name. Setting his teeth, he followed the sound of her voice through the ornate, cluttered dining room with its huge needlepoint carpet and bronze chandeliers and heavy furniture. Whoever had decorated this house must have been awfully depressed. Everything was dark and gloomy. All the furniture and decorations seemed to end in points.

He came to the semi-circular solarium where she awaited him. Her wheelchair was in its usual position by the big bay windows where she could look out on the rolling expanse of the south lawn.

"Ah, there you are, young Pritchard," she said, looking up and smiling coyly. She closed the book in her hands and laid it on the blanket that covered what might have passed for legs in a nightmare. The blanket had slipped once and he had seen what was under there. He didn't want another look. Ever. He remembered what his mother had always said about deformed people: That they were marked by God and should be avoided.

Old lady Gati was in her mid-sixties maybe, flabby without being fat, with pinched features and graying hair stretched back into a severe little bun at the back of her head. Her eyes were a watery blue as she looked at him over the tops of her reading glasses.

Jerry halted about a dozen feet away but she motioned him closer. He pretended not to notice. She was going to want to touch him again. God, he couldn't stand this.

"You called, ma'am?"

"Don't stand so far away, young Pritchard." He advanced two steps in her direction and stopped again. "Closer," she said. "You don't expect me to shout, do you?"

She didn't let up until he was standing right next to her. Except for these daily chats with Miss Gati, Jerry loved his job.

"There," she said. "That's better. Now we can talk more easily."

She placed a gnarled, wrinkled hand on his arm and Jerry's flesh began to crawl. Why did she always have to touch him?

"The basement—it is coming along well?"

"Fine," he said, looking at the floor, out the window, anywhere but at her hungry, smiling face. "Just fine."

"Good." She began stroking his arm, gently, possessively. "I hope this heat wave isn't too much for you." As she spoke she used her free hand to adjust the blanket over what there was of her lower body. "I really should have Stephanie get me a lighter blanket."

Jerry fought the urge to jump away from her. He had become adept at masking the revulsion that rippled through his body everytime she touched him. And it seemed she *had* to touch him whenever he was in reach. When he first got the caretaker job, he took a lot of ribbing from the guys in town down at the Dewkum Inn. (Lord, what Mom would say if she ever saw him standing at a bar!) Everybody knew that a lot of older, more experienced men had been passed over for him. His buddies had said that the old lady really wanted him for stud service. The thought nauseated him. Who knew if she even had—

No, that would never happen. He needed this job, but there was nothing he needed *that* badly. And so far, all she had ever done was stroke his arm when she spoke to him. Even that was hard to take.

As casually as he could, he moved out of reach and gazed out the window as if something on the lawn had attracted his attention. "What did you want me to—"

Stephanie walked into the room and interrupted him.

"Yes, Miss Gati?"

"Get me a summer blanket, will you, dear?"

"Yes, ma'am." She flashed a little smile at Jerry as she turned, and he watched her until she was out of sight. Now if only it were Steph who couldn't keep her hands off him, he wouldn't—

"She appeals to you, young Pritchard?" Miss Gati said, her eyes dancing.

He didn't like her tone, so he kept his neutral. "She's a good kid."

"But does she *appeal* to you?"

He felt his anger rising, felt like telling her it was none of her damn business, but he hauled it back and said, "Why is that so important to you?"

"Now, now, young Pritchard, I'm only concerned that the two of you get along well. But not *too* well. I don't want you taking little Stephie away from me. I have special needs, and as you know, it took me a long time to find a live-in maid with Stephie's special qualities."

Jerry couldn't quite buy that explanation. There had been something in her eyes when she spoke of Steph "appealing" to him, a hint that her interest went beyond mere household harmony.

"But the reason I called you here," she said, shifting the subject, "is to tell you that I want you to tend to the roof in the next few days."

"The new shingles came in?"

"Yes. Delivered this morning while you were in the basement. I want you to replace the worn ones over my room tomorrow. I fear this heat wave might bring us a storm out of season. I don't want my good furniture ruined by leaking water."

He guessed he could handle that. "Okay. I'll finish up today and be up on the roof tomorrow. How's that?"

She wheeled over and cut him off as he tried to make his getaway. "Whatever you think best, young Pritchard."

Jerry pulled free and hurried off, shuddering.

Marta Gati watched young Pritchard's swift exit.

I repulse him.

There was no sorrow, no self-pity attached to the thought. When you were born with twig-like vestigial appendages for legs and only half a pelvis, you quickly became used to rejection—you learned to read it in the posture, to sense it behind the eyes. Your feelings soon became as calloused as a miner's hands.

He's sensitive about my little Stephie, she thought. Almost protective. He likes her. He's attracted to her. *Very* attracted.

That was good. She wanted young Pritchard to have genuine feelings for Stephie. That would make it so much better.

Yes, her little household was just the way she wanted it now. It had taken her almost a year to set it up this way. Month after month of trial and error until she found the right combination. And now she had it.

Such an arrangement would have been impossible while Karl was alive. Her brother would never have hired someone with as little experience as young Pritchard as caretaker, and he would have thought Stephie too young and too frail to be a good live-in maid. But Karl was dead now. The heart attack had taken him quickly and without warning last June. He had gone to bed early one night complaining of what he thought was indigestion, and never awoke. Marta Gati missed her brother and mourned his loss, yet she was revelling in the freedom his passing had left her.

Karl had been a good brother. Tyrannically good. He had looked after her as a devoted husband would an ailing wife. He had never married, for he knew that congenital defects ran high in their family. Out of their parents' four children, two—Marta and Gabor—had been horribly deformed. When they had come to America from Hungary, Karl invested the smuggled family fortune in the mines here and, against all odds, had done well. He saw to it that Lazlo, the younger brother, received the finest education. Lazlo now lived in New York where he tended to Gabor.

And Marta? Marta he had kept hidden away in this remote mansion in rural West Virginia where she had often thought she would go insane with boredom. At least she had been able to persuade him to decorate the place. If she had to stay here, she had a right to be caged in surroundings to her taste. And her taste was Gothic Revival.

Marta loved this house, loved the heavy wood of the tables, the carved deer legs of the chairs, the elaborate finials atop the cabinets, the ornate valances and radiator covers, the trefoil arches on her canopy bed.

But the decor could only carry one so far. And there were only so many books one could read, television shows and rented movies one could watch. Karl's conversational capacity had been limited in the extreme, and when he had spoken, it was on business and finance and little else. Marta had wanted to be out in the world, but Karl said the world would turn away from her, so he'd kept her here to protect her from hurt.

But Marta had found a way to sneak out from under his over-protective thumb. And now with Karl gone, she no longer had to sneak out to the world. She could bring some of the world into the house.

Yes, it was going to be so nice here.

"Tell me something," Steph said as she rested her head on Jerry's shoulder. She was warm against him in the front seat of his old Fairlane 500 convertible and his desire for her was a throbbing ache. After the movie—a Burt Reynolds-type car-chase flick, but without Burt Reynolds—he had driven them back here and parked outside the gatehouse. The top was down and they were snuggled together in the front seat watching the little stars that city people never see, even on the clearest of nights.

"Anything," he whispered into her hair.

"How did Miss Gati get along here before she had me?"

"A lady from town used to come in to clean and cook, but she never stayed over. You're the first live-in who's lasted more than a week since I've been working here. The old lady's been real choosy about finding someone after the last live-in . . . left."

Jerry decided that now was not the time to bring up the last maid's suicide. Steph was from the farmlands on the other side of the ridge and wouldn't know about her. Constance Granger had been her name, a quiet girl who went crazy wild. She had come from a decent, church-going family, but all of a sudden she became a regular at the roadside taverns, taking up with a different man every night. Then one night she became hysterical in a motel room—with two men, if the whispers could be believed—and began screaming at the top of her lungs. She ran out of the room jaybird naked and got hit by a truck.

Jerry didn't want to frighten Steph with that kind of story, not now while they were snug and close like this. He steered the talk elsewhere.

"Now you tell me something. What do you think of working for old lady Gati?"

"She's sweet. She's not a slave driver and the pay is good. This is my first job since leaving home and I guess I'm kinda lucky it's working out so well."

"You miss home?"

He felt her tense beside him. She never talked about her home. "No. I . . . didn't get along with my father. But I get along just fine with Miss Gati. The only bad thing about the job is the house. It gives me the creeps. I get nightmares every night."

"What about?"

She snuggled closer, as if chilled despite the warmth of the night. "I don't remember much by morning, all I know is that they're no fun. I don't know how Miss Gati lived here alone after the last maid left. Especially without any legs. I'd be frightened to death!"

"She's not. She tried out girl after girl. No one satisfied her till you came along. She's a tough one."

"But she's not. She's nice. A real lady. You know, I make her hot chocolate every night and she insists I sit down and have a cup with her while she tells me about her family and how they lived in 'the Old Country.' Isn't that nice?"

"Just super," Jerry said.

He lifted her chin and kissed her. He felt her respond, felt her catch some of the fervor running through him like fire. He let his hand slip off her shoulder and come to rest over her right breast. She made no move to push him away as his fingers began caressing her.

"Want to come inside?" he said, glancing toward the door at the gatehouse.

Steph sighed. "Yes." She kissed him again, then pulled away. "But no. I don't think that would be such a good idea, Jerry. Not just yet. I mean, I just met you six weeks ago."

"You know all there is to know. I'm not hiding anything. Come on."

"I want to . . . you know I do, but not tonight. It's time for Miss Gati's hot chocolate. And if I want to keep this job, I'd better get up to the house and fix it for her." Her eyes searched his face in the light of the rising moon. "You're not mad at me, are you?"

"Nah!" he said with what he hoped was a reassuring grin. How could he look into those eyes and be mad? But he sure as hell *ached.* "Crushed and heartbroken, maybe. But not mad."

She laughed. "Good!"

There's plenty of time, he told the ache deep down inside. And we'll be seeing a lot of each other.

"C'mon. I'll walk you up to the house."

On the front porch, he kissed her again and didn't want to let go. Finally, she pushed him away, gently. "She's calling me. Gotta go. See you tomorrow."

Reluctantly, Jerry released her. He hadn't heard anything but knew she had to go. He wondered if her insides were as churned up as his own.

"Hurry and drink your chocolate before it gets cold," Marta Gati said as Stephie returned from down the hall.

Stephie smiled and picked up her cup from the bedside table. *A lovely child,* Marta thought. *Simply lovely.*

Her own cup was cradled in her hands. It was a little too sweet for her taste, but she made no comment. She was propped up on her bed pillows. Stephie sat in a chair pulled up to the side of the bed.

"And what did you and young Pritchard do tonight?" Marta said. "Anything special?" She watched Stephie blush as she sipped her chocolate.

Marta took a sip of her own to hide the excitement that swept through her. *They're in love!* This was perfect. "How was the movie?" she managed to say in a calm voice.

Stephie shrugged. "It was okay, I guess. Jerry likes all those cars racing around and crashing."

"Don't you?"

She shrugged. "Not really."

"But you go because young Pritchard likes them. And you like him, don't you?"

She shrugged shyly. "Yes."

"Of course you do. And he likes you. I can tell. I just hope he hasn't taken any liberties with you."

Stephie's color deepened. Marta guessed she wanted to tell her it was none of her damn business but didn't have the nerve. "No," Stephie said. "No liberties."

"Good!" Marta said. "I don't want you two running off and getting married. I need the both of you here. Now, finish your chocolate and get yourself to bed. Never let it be said I kept you up too late."

Stephie smiled and drained her cup.

Yes, Marta thought. *A lovely girl.*

The gatehouse was one room and a bathroom, furnished with a small desk, a chair, a bureau, and a hide-a-bed that folded up into a couch during the day. A sort of unattached motel room. But since he took his meals up at the house, it was all that Jerry needed.

The lights had been off for nearly an hour but he was still awake, rerunning his favorite fantasy, starring the voracious Steph and the inexhaustible Jerry. Then the door opened without warning and Steph stood there with the moonlight faintly outlining her body through the light cotton nightgown she wore. She said nothing as she came forward and crawled under the single sheet that covered him.

After that, no words were necessary.

Dawnlight sneaking through the spaces between the venetian blinds on the gatehouse window woke Jerry. He was alone. After she had worn him out, Steph had left him. He sat on the edge of the hide-a-bed and cradled his head in his hands. In the thousand times he had mentally bedded Steph since her arrival, he had always been the initiator, the aggressor. Last night had been nothing at all like the fantasies. Steph had been in complete control—demanding, voracious, insatiable, a wild woman who had left him drained and exhausted. And hardly a word had passed between them. Throughout their lovemaking she had cooed, she had whimpered, she had moaned, but she had barely spoken to him. It left him feeling sort of . . . used.

Still trying to figure out this new, unexpected side to Steph, he walked up to the house for breakfast. The sun was barely up and already the air was starting to cook. It was going to be another hot one.

He saw Steph heading out of the kitchen toward the dining room with old lady Gati's tray as he came in the back door.

"Be with you in a minute," she called over her shoulder.

He waited by the swinging door and caught her as she came through. He slipped his arms around her waist and kissed her.

"Jerry, no!" she snapped. "Not here—not while I'm working!"

He released her. "Not your cheerful old self this morning, are you?"

"Just tired, I guess." She turned toward the stove.

"I guess you should be."

"And what's that supposed to mean?"

"Well, you had an unusually active night. At least I hope it was unusual."

Steph had been about to crack an egg on the edge of the frying pan. She stopped in mid-motion and turned to face him.

"Jerry . . . what on earth are you talking about?"

She looked genuinely puzzled, and that threw him. "Last night . . . at the gatehouse . . . it was after three when you left."

Her cranky scowl dissolved into an easy smile. "You must really be in a bad way!" She laughed. "Now you're believing your own dreams!"

Jerry was struck by the clear innocence of her laughter. For a moment, he actually doubted his memory—but only for a moment. Last night had been real. Hadn't it?

"Steph . . ." he began, but dropped it. What could he say to those guileless blue eyes? She was either playing some sort of game, and playing it very well, or she really didn't remember. Or it really never happened. Neither of those choices was the least bit reassuring.

He wolfed his food as Steph moved in and out of the kitchen, attending to old lady Gati's breakfast wants. She kept glancing at him out of the corner of her eye, as if checking up on him. Was this a game? Or had he really dreamed it all last night?

Jerry skipped his usual second cup of coffee and was almost relieved to find himself back in the confines of the cellar. He threw himself into the job, partly because he wanted to finish it, and partly because he didn't want too much time to think about last night. By lunchtime he was sweeping up the last of the debris when he heard the sound.

It came from above. The floorboards were squeaking. And something else as well—the light sound of feet moving back and forth, rhythmically. It continued as he filled a cardboard box with the last of the dirt, dust, and scraps of rotten wood from the cellar. He decided to walk around the south side of the house on his way to the trash bins. The sound seemed to be coming from there.

As he passed the solarium, he glanced in and almost dropped the box. Steph was waltzing around the room with an invisible partner in her arms. Swirling and dipping and curtsying, she was not the most graceful dancer he had ever seen, but the look of pure joy on her face made up for whatever she lacked in skill.

Her expression changed abruptly to a mixture of surprise and something like anger when she caught sight of him gaping through the window. She ran toward the stairs, leaving Miss Gati alone. The old lady neither turned to watch her go, nor looked out the window to see what had spooked her. She just sat slumped in her wheelchair, her head hanging forward. For a second, Jerry was jolted by the sight: She looked dead! He pressed his face against the solarium glass for a closer look, and was relieved to see the gentle rise and fall of her chest. Only asleep. But what had Steph been doing waltzing around like that while the old lady napped?

Shaking his head at the weirdness of it all, he dumped the box in the trash area and returned to the house through the back door. The kitchen was empty, so he made his way as quietly as possible to the solarium to see if Steph had returned. He found all quiet— the music off and old lady Gati bright and alert, reading a book. He immediately turned back toward the kitchen, hoping she wouldn't spot him. But it was too late.

"Yes, young Pritchard?" she said, rolling that "r" and looking up from her book. "You are looking for something?"

Jerry fumbled for words. "I was looking for Steph to see if she could fix me a sandwich. Thought I saw her in here when I passed by before."

"No, dear boy," she said with a smile. "I sent her up to her room for a nap almost an hour ago. Seems you tired her out last night."

"Last night?" He tensed. What did she know about last night?

Her smile broadened. "Come now! You two didn't think you could fool me, did you? I know she sneaked out to see you." Something about the way she looked at him sent a sick chill through Jerry. "Surely you can fix something yourself and let the poor girl rest."

Then it hadn't been a dream! But then why had Steph pretended—?

He couldn't figure it. "Yeah. Sure," he said dully, his thoughts jumbled. "I can make a sandwich." He turned to go.

"You should be about through with the basement by now," she said. "But even if you're not, get up to the roof this afternoon. The weatherman says there's a sixty percent chance of a thunderstorm tonight."

"Basement's done. Roof is next."

"Excellent! But don't work *too* hard, young Pritchard. Save something for Stephie."

She returned to her book.

Jerry felt numb as he walked back to the kitchen. The old lady hadn't touched him once! She seemed more relaxed and at ease with herself than he could ever remember—a-cat-that-had-swallowed-the-canary sort of self-satisfaction. And she hadn't tried to lay a single finger on him.

The day was getting weirder and weirder.

Replacing the shingles on the sloping dormer surface outside old lady Gati's bedroom had looked like an easy job from the ground. But the shingles were odd, scalloped affairs that she had ordered special from San Francisco to match the originals on the house, and Jerry had trouble keeping them aligned on the curved surface. He could have used a third hand, too. What would have been an hour's work for two men had already taken Jerry three in the broiling sun, and he wasn't quite finished yet.

While he was working, he noted that the wood trim on the upper levels was going to need painting soon. That was going to be a hellish job, what with the oculus windows, the ornate friezes, cornices, brackets, and keystones. Some crazed woodcarver had had a field day with this stuff—probably thought it was "art." But Jerry was going to be the one to paint it. He'd put that off as long as he could, and definitely wouldn't do it in summer.

He pulled an insulated wire free of the outside wall to fit in the final shingles by the old lady's window. It ran from somewhere on the roof down to the ground—directly *into* the ground. Jerry pulled himself up onto the parapet above the dormer to see where the wire originated. He followed it up until it linked into the lightning rod on the peak of the attic garret. *Everything* connected with this house was ornate—even the lightning rods had designs on them.

He climbed back down, pulled the ground wire free of the dormer, and tacked the final shingles into place. When he reached the ground, he slumped on the bottom rung of the ladder and rested a moment. The heat from the roof was getting to him. His tee-shirt was drenched with perspiration and he was reeling with fatigue.

Enough for today. He'd done the bulk of the work. A hurricane could hit the area and that dormer would not leak. He could put the finishing touches on tomorrow. He lowered the ladder to the ground, then checked the kitchen for Steph. She wasn't there. Just as well. He didn't have the energy to pry an explanation out of her. Something was cooking in the oven, but he was too bushed to eat. He grabbed half a six pack of beer from the fridge and stumbled down to the gatehouse. Hell with dinner. A shower, a few beers, a good night's sleep, and he'd be just fine in the morning.

It was a long ways into dark, but Jerry was still awake. Tired as he was, he couldn't get to sleep. As thunder rumbled in the distance, charging in from the west, and slivers of ever-brightening light flashed between the blinds, thoughts of last night tumbled through his mind, arousing him anew. Something strange going on up at that house. Old lady Gati was acting weird, and so was Steph.

Steph . . . he couldn't stop thinking about her. He didn't care what kind of game she was playing, she still meant something to him. He'd never felt this way before. He—

He heard a noise at the door. It opened and Steph stepped inside. She said nothing as she came forward, but in the glow of the lightning flashes from outside, Jerry could see her removing her nightgown as she crossed the room. He saw it flutter to the floor and then she was beside him, bringing the dreamlike memories of last night into the sharp focus of the real and now. He tried to talk to her but she would only answer in a soft, breathless "uh-huh" or "uh-uh" and then her wandering lips and tongue wiped all questions from his mind.

When it was finally over and the two of them lay in a gasping tangle of limbs and sheets, Jerry decided that now was the time to find out what was going on between her and old lady Gati, and what kind of game she was playing with him. He would ask her in a few seconds . . . or maybe in a minute . . . soon . . . thunder was louder than ever outside but that wasn't going to bother him . . . all he wanted to do right now was close his eyes and enjoy the delicious exhaustion of this afterglow a little longer . . . only a little . . . just close his eyes for a few seconds . . . no more . . .

"Sleep well, my love."

Jerry forced his eyes open. Steph's face hovered over him in the flashing dimness as he teetered on the brink of unconsciousness. She kissed him lightly on the forehead and whispered, "Goodnight, young Pritchard. And thank you."

It was as if someone had tossed a bucket of icy water on him. Suddenly Jerry was wide awake. *Young Pritchard?* Why had she said that? Why had she imitated old lady Gati's voice that way? The accent, with its roll of the "r," had been chillingly perfect.

Steph had slipped her nightgown over her head and was on her way out. Jerry jumped out of bed and caught her at the door.

"I don't think that was funny, Steph!" She ignored him and pushed the screen door open. He grabbed her arm. "Hey, look! What kind of game are you playing? What's it gonna be tomorrow morning? Same as today? Pretend that nothing happened tonight?" She tried to pull away but he held on. "Talk to me Steph! What's going on?"

A picture suddenly formed in his mind of Steph going back to the house and having hot chocolate with old lady Gati and telling her every intimate detail of their lovemaking, and the old lady getting excited, *feeding* off it.

"What's going *on!*" Involuntarily, his grip tightened on her arm.

"You're hurting me!" The words cut like an icy knife. The voice was Steph's, but the tone, the accent, the roll of the "r"s, the inflection—all were perfect mimicry of old lady Gati, down to the last nuance. But she had been in pain. It couldn't have been rehearsed!

Jerry flipped the light switch and spun her around. It was Steph, all right, as achingly beautiful as ever, but something was wrong. The Steph he knew should have been frightened. The Steph before him was changed. She held herself differently. Her stance was haughty, almost imperious. And there was something in her eyes— a strange light.

"Oh, sweet Jesus! What's happened to you?"

He could see indecision flickering through her eyes as she regarded him with a level stare. Outside, it began to rain. A few scattered forerunner drops escalated to a full-scale torrent in a matter of seconds as their eyes remained locked, their bodies frozen amid day-bright flashes of lightning and the roar of thunder and wind-driven rain. Then she smiled. It was like Steph's smile, but it wasn't.

"Nothing," she said in that crazy mixed voice.

And then he thought he knew. For a blazing instant, it was clear to him: "You're not Steph!" In the very instant he said it he disbelieved it, but then her smile broadened and her words turned his blood to ice:

"Yes, I am . . . for the moment." The voice was thick with old lady Gati's accent, and it carried a triumphant note. "What Stephie sees, *I* see! What Stephie feels, *I* feel!" She lifted the hem of her nightgown. "Look at my legs! Beautiful, aren't they?"

Jerry released her arm as if he had been burned. She moved closer but Jerry found himself backing away. Steph was crazy! Her mind had snapped. She thought she was old lady Gati! He had never been faced with such blatant madness before, and it terrified him. He felt exposed, vulnerable before it. With a trembling hand, he grabbed his jeans from the back of the chair.

Marta Gati looked out of Stephie's eyes at young Pritchard as he struggled into his trousers, and she wondered what to do next. She had thought him asleep when she had kissed him good night and made the slip of calling him "young Pritchard." She had known she couldn't keep her nightly possession of Stephie from him for too long, but she had not been prepared for a confrontation tonight. She would try for sympathy first.

"Do you have any idea, young Pritchard," she said, trying to make Stephie's voice sound as American as she could, "what it is like to be trapped all your life in a body as deformed as mine? To be repulsive to other children as a child, to grow up watching other girls find young men and go dancing and get married and know that at night they are holding their man in their arms and feeling all the things a woman should feel? You have no idea what my life has been like, young Pritchard. But through the years I found a way to remedy the situation. Tonight I am a complete woman—*your* woman!

"Stephanie!" young Pritchard shouted, fear and disbelief mingling in the strained pallor of his face. "Listen to yourself! You sound crazy! What you're saying is impossible!"

"No! Not impossible!" she said, although she could understand his reaction. A few years ago, she too would have called it impossible. Her brother Karl had devoted himself to her and his business. He never married, but he would bring women back to the house now and then when he thought she was asleep. It would have been wonderful if he could have brought a man home for her, but that was impossible. Yet it hadn't stopped her yearnings. And it was on those nights when he and a woman were in the next bedroom that Marta realized that she could sense things in Karl's women. At first she thought it was imagination, but this was more than mere fantasy. She could feel their passion, feel their skin tingling, feel them exploding within. And one night, after they both had spent themselves and fallen asleep, she found herself in the other woman's body—actually lying in Karl's bed and seeing the room through her eyes!

As time went on, she found she could enter their bodies while they slept and actually take them over. She could get up and walk! A sob built in her throat at the memory. To *walk!* That had been joy enough at first. Then she would dance by herself. She had wanted so much all her life to dance, to waltz, and now she could! She never dared more than that until Karl died and left her free. She had perfected her ability since then.

"It will be a good life for you, young Pritchard," she said. "You won't even have to work. Stephie will be my maid and housekeeper during the day and your lover at night." He shook his head, as if to stop her, but she pressed on. "And when you get tired of Stephie, I'll bring in another. And another. You'll have an endless stream of young, willing bodies in your bed. You'll have such a *good* life, young Pritchard!"

A new look was growing in his eyes: belief.

"It's really you!" he said in a hoarse whisper. "Oh, my dear sweet Lord, it's really you in Steph's body! I . . . I'm getting out of here!"

She moved to block his way and he stayed back. He could have easily overpowered her, but he seemed afraid to let her get too near. She couldn't let him go, not after all her work to set up a perfect household.

"No! You mustn't do that! You must stay here!"

"This is sick!" he cried, his voice rising in pitch as a wild light sprang into his eyes. "This is the Devil's work!"

"No-no," she said, soothingly. "Not the Devil. Just me. Just something—"

"Get away from me!" he said, backing toward his dresser. He spun and pulled open the top drawer, rummaged through it and came up with a thick book with a cross on its cover. "Get away, Satan!" he cried, thrusting the book toward her face.

Marta almost laughed. "Don't be silly, young Pritchard! I'm not evil! I'm just doing what I have to do. I'm not hurting Stephie. I'm just borrowing her body for a while!"

"Out, demon!" he said, shoving the Bible almost into her face. "*Out!*"

This was getting annoying now. She snatched the book from his grasp and hurled it across the room. "Stop acting like a fool!"

He looked from her to the book and back to her with an awed expression. At that moment there was a particularly loud crash of thunder and the lights went out. Young Pritchard cried out in horror and brushed past her. He slammed out the door and ran into the storm.

Marta ran as far as the doorway and stopped. She peered through the deluge. Even with the rapid succession of lightning strokes and sheets, she could see barely a dozen feet. He was nowhere in sight. She could see no use in running out into the storm and following him. She glanced at his keys on the bureau and smiled. How far could a half-naked man go in a storm like this?

Marta crossed the room and sat on the bed. She ran Stephie's hand over the rumpled sheets where less than half an hour ago the two of them had been locked in passion. Warmth rose within her. So *good*. So good to have a man's arms around you, wanting you, needing you, *demanding* you. She couldn't give this up. Not now, not when it was finally at her disposal after all these years.

But young Pritchard wasn't working out. She had thought any virile young man would leap at what she offered, but apparently she had misjudged him. Or was a stable relationship within her household just a fool's dream? She had so much to learn about the outside world. Karl had kept her so sheltered from it.

Perhaps her best course was the one she had taken with the last housekeeper. Take over her body when she was asleep and drive to the bars and roadhouses outside of town. Find a man—two men, if she were in the mood—and spend most of the night in a motel room. Then come back to the house, clean her up, and leave her asleep in her bed. It was anonymous, it was exciting, but it was somehow . . . empty.

She would be more careful with Stephie than with the last housekeeper. Marta had been ill one night but had moved into the other body anyway. She had lost control when a stomach spasm had gripped her own body. The pain had drawn her back to the house, leaving the woman to awaken between two strangers. She had panicked and run out into the road.

Yes, she had to be very careful with this one. Stephie was so sensitive to her power, whatever it was. She only had to become drowsy and Marta could slip in and take complete control, keeping Stephie's mind unconscious while she controlled her body. A few milligrams of a sedative in her cocoa before bedtime and Stephie's body was Marta's for the night.

But young Pritchard wasn't working out. At least not so far. There was perhaps a slim chance she could reason with him when he came back. She had to try. She found him terribly attractive. But where could he be?

Sparks of alarm flashed through her as she realized that her own body was upstairs in the house, lying in bed, helpless, defenseless. What if that crazy boy——?

Quickly, she slid onto the bed and closed her eyes. She shut out her senses one by one, blocking off the sound of the rain and thunder, the taste of the saliva in her mouth, the feel of the bedclothes against her back . . .

. . . and opened her eyes in her own bedroom in the house. She looked around, alert for any sign that her room had been entered. Her bedroom door was still closed, and there was no moisture anywhere on the floor.

Good! He hasn't been in here!

Marta pushed herself up in bed and transferred to the wheelchair. She wheeled herself out to the hall and down to the elevator, cursing its slow descent as it took her to the first floor. When it finally stopped, she propelled herself at top speed to the foyer where she immediately turned the dead bolt on the front door. She noted with satisfaction that the slate floor under her chair was as dry as when she had walked out earlier as Stephie. She was satisfied that she was alone in the house.

Safe!

She rolled herself into the solarium at a more leisurely pace. She knew the rest of the doors and windows were secure—Stephie always locked up before she made the bedtime chocolate. She stopped before the big bay windows and watched the storm for a minute. It was a fierce one. She gazed out at the blue-white, water-blurred lightning flashes and wondered what she was going to do about young Pritchard. If she couldn't convince him to stay, then surely he would be in town tomorrow, telling a wild tale. No one would believe him, of course, but it would start talk, fuel rumors, and that would make it almost impossible to get help in the future. It might even make Stephie quit, and Marta didn't know how far her power could reach. She'd be left totally alone out here.

Her fingers tightened on the arm rests of her wheelchair. She couldn't let that happen.

She closed her eyes and blocked out the storm, blocked out her senses . . .

. . . and awoke in Stephie's body again.

She leapt to the kitchenette and pulled out the drawers until she found the one she wanted. It held three forks, a couple of spoons, a spatula, and a knife—a six-inch carving knife.

It would have to do.

She hurried out into the rain and up the hill toward the house.

Jerry rammed his shoulder against the big oak front door again but only added to bruises the door had already put there. He screamed at it.

"In God's name—open!"

The door ignored him. What was he going to do? He had to get inside! Had to get to that old lady! Had to wring the Devil out of her! Had to find a way in! Make her give Steph back!

His mother had warned him about this sort of thing. He could almost hear her voice between the claps of thunder: *Satan walks the earth, Jerome, searching for those who forsake the Word. Beware—he's waiting for you!*

Jerry knew the Devil had found him—in the guise of old lady Gati! What was happening to Steph was all his fault!

He ran back into the downpour and headed around toward the rear. Maybe the kitchen door was unlocked. He glanced through the solarium windows as he passed. His bare feet slid to a halt on the wet grass as he stopped and took a better look.

There she was: old lady Gati, the Devil herself, zonked out in her wheelchair.

The sight of her sitting there as if asleep while her spirit was down the hill controlling Steph's body was more than Jerry could stand. He looked around for something to hurl through the window, and in the next lightning flash he spotted the ladder next to the house on the lawn. He picked it up and charged the solarium like a jousting knight. Putting all his weight behind the ladder, he rammed it through the center bay window. The sound of shattering glass broke the last vestige of Jerry's control. Howling like a madman, he drove the ladder against the window glass again and again until every pane and every muntin was smashed and battered out of the way.

Then he climbed in.

The shards of glass cut his bare hands and feet but Jerry barely noticed. His eyes were on old lady Gati. Throughout all the racket, she hadn't budged.

Merciful Lord, it's true! Her spirit's left her body!

He stumbled over to her inert form and stood behind her, hesitating. He didn't want to touch her—his skin crawled at the thought—but he had to put an end to this. Now. Swallowing the bile that sloshed up from his stomach, Jerry wrapped his fingers around old lady Gati's throat. He flinched at the feel of her wrinkles against his palms, but he clenched his teeth and began to squeeze. He put all his strength into it—

—and then let go.

He couldn't do it.

"God, give me strength!" he cried, but he couldn't bring himself to do it. Not while she was like this. It was like strangling a corpse! She was barely breathing as it was!

Something tapped against the intact bay window to the right. Jerry spun to look—a flash from outside outlined the grounding wire from the lightning rods as it swayed in the wind and slapped against the window. It reminded him of a snake—

A snake! And suddenly he knew: *It's a sign! A sign from God!*

He ran to the window and threw it open. He reached out, wrapped the wire around his hands, and pulled. It wouldn't budge from the ground. He braced a foot against the window sill, putting his back and all his weight into the effort. Suddenly the metal grounding stake pulled free and he staggered back, the insulated wire thrashing about in his hands . . . just like a snake.

He remembered that snake handlers' church back in the hills his mother had dragged him to one Sunday a few years ago. He had watched in awe as the men and women would grab water moccasins and cotton-mouths and hold them up, trusting in the Lord to protect them. Some were bitten, some were not. Ma had told him it was all God's will.

God's will!

He pulled the old lady's wheelchair closer to the window and wrapped the wire tightly around her, tying it snugly behind the backrest of the chair, and jamming the grounding post into the metal spokes of one of the wheels.

"This is your snake, Miss Gati," he told her unconscious form. "It's God's will if it bites you!"

He backed away from her until he was at the entrance to the solarium. Lightning flashed as violently as ever, but none came down the wire. He couldn't wait any longer. He had to find Steph. As he turned to head for the front door, he saw someone standing on the south lawn, staring into the solarium. It was old lady Gati, wearing Steph's body. When she looked through the broken bay window and saw him there, she screamed and slumped to the ground.

"*Steph!*" What was happening to her?

Jerry sprinted across the room and dove through the shattered window onto the south lawn.

Marta awoke in her own body, panicked.

What has he done to me?

She felt all right. There was no pain, no—

My arms! Her hands were free but she couldn't move her upper arms! She looked down and saw the black insulated wire coiled tightly around her upper body, binding her to the chair. She tried to twist, to slide down on the chair and slip free, but the wire

wouldn't give an inch. She tried to see where it was tied. If she
could get her hands on the knot . . .

She saw the wire trailing away from her chair, across the floor
and out the window and up into the darkness.

Up! To the roof! The lightning rods!

She screamed, *"Nooooo!"*

Jerry cradled Steph's head in his arm and slapped her wet face as
hard as he dared. He'd hoped the cold pounding rain and the noise
of the storm would have brought her around, but she was still out.
He didn't want to hurt her, but she had to wake up.

"Steph! C'mon, Steph! You've got to wake up! Got to fight her!"

As she stirred, he heard old lady Gati howl from the solarium.
Steph's eyes fluttered, then closed again. He shook her. "Steph!
Please!"

She opened her eyes and stared at him. His spirits leaped.

"That's it, Steph! Wake up! It's me—Jerry! You've got to stay
awake!"

She moaned and closed her eyes, so he shook her again.

"Steph! Don't let her take you over again!"

As she opened her eyes again, Jerry dragged her to her feet.

"Come on! Walk it off! Let's go! You've *got* to stay awake!"

Suddenly her face contorted and she swung on him. Something
gleamed in her right hand as she plunged it toward his throat. Jerry
got his forearm up just in time to block it. Pain seared through his
arm and he cried out.

"Oh, God! It's you!"

"Yes!" She slashed at him again and he backpedaled to avoid the
knife. His bare feet slipped on the grass and he went down on his
back. He rolled frantically, fearing she would be upon him, but
when he looked up, she was running toward the house, toward the
smashed bay window.

"No!"

He couldn't let her get inside and untie the old lady's body.
Steph's only hope was a lightning strike.

Please, God, he prayed. *Now! Let it be now!*

But though bolts crackled through the sky almost continuously, none of them hit the house. Groaning with fear and frustration, Jerry scrambled to his feet and sprinted after her. He had to stop her!

He caught her from behind and brought her down about two dozen feet from the house. She screamed and thrashed like an enraged animal, twisting and slashing at him again and again with the knife. She cut him along the ribs as he tried to pin her arms and was rearing back for a better angle on his chest when the night turned blue-white. He saw the rage on Steph's face turn to wide-eyed horror. Her body arched convulsively as she opened her mouth and let out a high-pitched shriek of agony that rose and cut off like a circuit being broken—

—only to be taken up by another voice from within the solarium. Jerry glanced up. Through the window he saw old lady Gati's body jittering in her chair like a hooked fish while blue fire played all about her. Her hoarse cry was swallowed and drowned as her body exploded in a roiling ball of flame. Fire was everywhere in the solarium. The very air seemed to burn.

He removed the knife from Steph's now limp hand and dragged her to a safer distance from the house. He shook her. "Steph?"

He could see her eyes rolling back and forth under the lids. Finally they opened and stared at him uncomprehendingly.

"Jerry?" She bolted up to a sitting position. "Jerry! What's going on?"

His grip on the knife tightened as he listened to her voice, searching carefully for the slightest hint of an accent, the slightest roll of an "r." There wasn't any he could detect, but there was only one test that could completely convince him.

"My name," he said. "What's my last name, Steph?"

"It's Pritchard, of course. But—" She must have seen the flames flickering in his eyes because she twisted around and cried out. "The house! It's on fire! Miss Gati—!"

She had said it perfectly. The real Steph was back! Jerry threw away the knife and lifted her to her feet. "She's gone," he told her. "Burnt up. I saw her."

"But how?"

He had to think fast—couldn't tell her the truth. Not yet.

"Lightning. It's my fault. I must have messed up the rods when I was up on the roof today."

"Oh, God, Jerry!" She clung to him and suddenly the storm seemed far away. "What'll we do?"

Over her shoulder, he watched the flames spreading throughout the first floor and lapping up at the second through the broken bay window. "Got to get out of here, Steph. They're gonna blame me for it, and God knows what'll happen."

"It was an accident! They can't blame you for that!"

"Oh, yes they will!" Jerry was thinking about the ground wire wrapped around the old lady's corpse. No way anyone would think that was an accident. "I hear she's got family in New York. They'll see me hang if they can, I just know it! I've got to get out of here." He pushed her to arm's length and stared at her. "Come with me?"

She shook her head. "I can't! How——?"

"We'll make a new life far from here. We'll head west and won't stop till we reach the ocean." He could see her wavering. "Please, Steph! I don't think I can make it without you!"

Finally, she nodded.

He took her hand and pulled her along behind him as he raced down the slope for the gatehouse. He glanced back at the old house and saw flames dancing in the second floor windows. Somebody down in town would see the light from the fire soon and then half the town would be up here to either fight it or watch it being fought. They had to be out of here before that.

It's gonna be okay, he told himself. They'd start a new life out in California. And someday, when he had the nerve and he thought she was ready for it, he'd tell her the truth. But for now, as long as Steph was at his side, he could handle anything. Everything was going to be all right.

Patrolman Grimes looked better now. He was back from the couple's apartment and stood in the hospital corridor with an open notebook, ready to recite.

"All right," Burke said. "What've we got?"

"We've got a twenty-three-year-old named Jerome Pritchard. Came out here from West Virginia nine months ago."

"I mean drugs—crack, angel dust, needles, fixings."

"No, sir. The apartment was clean. The neighbors are in absolute shock. Everybody loved the Pritchards and they all seem to think he was a pretty straight guy. A real churchgoer—carried his own Bible and never missed a Sunday, they said. Had an assembly-line job and talked about starting night courses at UCLA as soon as he made the residency requirement. He and his wife appeared to be real excited about the baby, going to Lamaze classes and all that sort of stuff."

"Crack, I tell you," Burke said. "Got to be."

"As far as we can trace his movements, sir, it seems that after the baby was delivered at 10:06 this morning, he ran out of here like a bat out of hell, came back about an hour later carrying his Bible and a big oblong package, waited until the baby was brought to the mother for feeding, then . . . well, you know."

"Yeah. I know." The new father had pulled a .10-gauge shotgun from that package and blown the mother and kid away, then put the barrel against his own throat and completed the job. "But why, dammit!"

"Well . . . the baby did have a birth defect."

"I know. I saw. But there are a helluva lot of birth defects a damn sight worse. Hell, I mean, her legs were only withered a little!"

Peacemaker

Charles Grant

In the darklight; a moment in late October between dusk and night, when the birds aren't quite sleeping and the wind has stopped blowing and the edges of the shadows don't blend with the black; when the houses are caves and the windows reflect nothing and the streetlamps are hazed by a mist without color; when perspective is missing and all roads lead to nothing, when the silence is complete and nothing breathes, nothing moves.

In the darklight, before midnight, the air touched with ice.

And he sat on the porch, in an old wooden rocker, his hands resting lightly on the flat of his thighs. The old sheepskin jacket granted protection from the chill, and on his head a western hat, its brim and crown time-worn to a shape that would have seemed ludicrous on another, rain-stained and snow-pocked and darker than its color; on his feet, western boots that a shine would only ruin.

Behind him, in the house, he could hear the furnace kicking on. The foyer clock chiming. A board creaking.

In the yard a nightbird chirped, a rustling, and nothing.

Immediately to his left, on the corner, the streetlamp dropped a stage of white on the pavement, and he watched it for signs of shadow, for signs of shape, and his left hand drummed his thigh while his right hand curled as if lightly gripping the air.

He knew what it was—it was excitement. The far-away-and-getting-closer kind that didn't prod action, only prodded the

senses. The sound of unseen horsemen, the chuff of a locomotive
slowing for a curve.

He puffed his cheeks, he blew a breath, he glanced at a dark
form beneath the yard's black oak branches.

One more time, he thought then, less a prayer than a command;
one more time before I get too old to count.

He shifted then. With a tightening of his lips to anticipate pain,
and cursing the twinge that stiffened his calves, he lifted his legs
until his boots were on the railing and he could see between his feet
across the street to Grandy's house. The downstairs lights were on,
and a spotlight hidden in the grass that aimed at the front door,
pinning a cob of dried maize to the white-curtained pane. On
either side of the steps were jack-o'-lanterns Grandy carved himself
every year, and in each of the windows were cardboard witches and
black cats and full orange moons with comic scowling faces.

The air drifted, wind coming.

Still watching the house, he allowed himself a brief smile for the
nights when Grandy would grumble about the kids, about their
vandalism, their lack of respect, their general cussed attitude for
things that ought not to be mocked. Yet every year, every holiday,
the window invitations were taped up and accepted.

But he never asked Rusty for the once-a-year favor.

Unlike the others, Grandy still had a hope.

Far down the street the brittle sound of voices—young voices
laughing and giggling and calling. A door slamming. A car starting.
And he glanced down at the floor to be sure the bag was still there,
let his left hand swing down to touch it, to be sure his eyes hadn't
lied.

Shadows then on the sidewalk, and low voices, one wondering
about the dark house, the other saying, "Hush!"

He shifted his attention to a hunched shape paused at the gate,
and to another running up the street, ghost-sheet flapping, a large
shopping bag slapping at its legs.

"Evening, Rusty," a man's voice said.

"Evening, Mr. Paretti. Having a good time?"

The man laughed and lifted one hand. "The kid's going to wear
me out if he keeps up like this."

Rusty nodded.

In a sudden rise of wind the man sighed loudly. "And would you believe that just yesterday I was going to ground him forever because he busted a cellar window? I don't know how he does it, Rusty. He always picks the days he knows I'm gonna be soft, you know what I mean?"

"I do."

"It's like he reads my mind or something."

Rusty said nothing. The moon lay silver patterns.

"Well," the man said with a half-hearted laugh, "I suppose I ought to catch up. I'm going to freeze before too long, I think."

"You keep moving, you keep warm."

"Right," the man said, and followed his ghost. "You moving tonight yourself?" the man called back, voice oddly high.

"Soon enough," he said softly, knowing he would be heard, and watched the man reach the corner and grab hold of the ghost, pull it close for a moment before shooing it onward, across the street to the next well-lit house.

The rocking chair creaked as he smiled and shook his head, creaked again when he brought one of his boots to the floor, then the other, before he put his hands on the railing and pulled himself up. A deep breath. A swallow. A slight tug at his hat.

He stepped away from the rocker, damning the cramp he felt in his left calf. He kicked out and it was gone, but he didn't feel much better. He was getting old. Every year a little older, every year a little slower. The fingers of his right hand brushed over his palm. Again. And again, harder. Until a faint burning warned him to stop and he slipped the hand into his pocket and moved to the top of the steps, leaned against the post, and watched the night.

Under the oak a perhaps plume of fog.

Not acknowledging the woman and four youngsters who hurried past the peeling white fence. Not breathing when one of them tugged at her coat and asked in a shrill voice why they didn't stop at Mr. Long's. She didn't answer. But he could see the fearful white of her cheek when she glanced in his direction before rushing on.

Not yet, he told her without moving his lips; not yet, ma'am, not yet. Maybe sometime we'll talk, but it's not your time yet.

The wind steadied as he waited, just enough to ruffle the fall of white over his collar, just enough to tease the weakest leaves off their branches, into the gutter.

An automobile, lights glaring, radio thumping, parked in front of a house three doors down. He couldn't count how many costumes piled out and raced up the walk, and he turned away from them when he saw they were only demons and comic book characters and one in a box painted silver—a robot.

He didn't know them.

He waited.

Someone would come, the evening wasn't done.

There was plenty of time. There had always been time, it seemed, and patience a damning virtue.

Too old

I'm getting too old, he thought, nearly bitter, and for the first time that night wondered why he bothered. Nobody cared but those he served, nobody thanked him, nobody gave him gifts or shook his hand. And sooner or later someone was going to take his place. He knew it. As sure as he knew the sun would rise in the morning and he'd have another year to wait and watch and listen and think, someone was going to come along and try to take his place.

Why the hell didn't he just take Grandy's advice? Just a few weeks ago Vell had said, "Tell you something, Rusty, this damned house is getting too damned big, and I'm getting too damned old for this stuff. I got half a mind to sell it and live in one of them condo things. They got guards there, you know, and elevators. The one I saw, I took a ride out the other day, it's got a swimming pool I could sit by and watch the ladies go around half-naked." He'd shaken his bald head and pulled out his pipe to stare unseeing at the bowl. "Trouble is, I leave it now and those kids'll tear it apart."

Rusty had said nothing, and Grandy Vell reached for the pouch that held his tobacco.

"Maybe," Vell said, "someday we'll talk."

"You know where I live."

Grandy only lit a match, and blinked when it blew out.

The wind a bit stronger, the sounds of children more fragile, and he took the steps down slowly, letting his heels crack, letting the spurs sound their warning. His arms were easy at his sides, his fingers slightly curled, and by the time he reached the gate the rhythm was set, senses alert, and it was a smooth and silent motion when he slapped at his leg and whirled, snapping up his hand to point a gun-finger at the porch.

"Bang," he said. And laughed. And made a slight sideways bow to the shape beneath the tree. "Don't lose many, do I?" he said, and laughed again and wondered if maybe he wasn't going crazy.

Someone giggled behind him.

He whirled again effortlessly and said, "Bang!" to Wendy Chambers, easily recognizable behind her burnt-cork hobo's face by the glasses she had to wear, and the braces on her teeth, and the stub of her nose that invited fingers to touch.

"You're funny," she said, holding onto a battered hat the wind tried to take.

"Just doing my job, little lady," he told her with a grin. "Gotta keep this street safe from the bad guys, y'know. Don't want 'em bothering good folks like you."

"Then shoot my brother," she said, a hateful look over her shoulder. "He won't let me walk with him. He says I'm too little."

Rusty pushed back his hat and leaned on the gate. "What about your Momma?"

"She yells a lot, but he still won't listen. She said I should talk to you. You gonna spank him, Mr. Long? My daddy used to before he died."

He rubbed his chin thoughtfully, finally nodded, and touched her shoulder. "He ever hit you, your big brother, I mean."

"Teddy always hits me," she grumbled, pushing her glasses back up her nose. "I don't like him."

He stared at her for a long time, watching the anger in her eyes, and the hurt, and the hope. Then he reached out and touched the tip of a finger to the tip of her nose.

She giggled again and shivered, but she didn't back away.

"All right," he said. "You tell him I say he has to watch for you tonight, okay? You tell him I said that, or there'll be trouble at the OK Corral."

Wendy frowned. "What's that?"

He almost laughed. "Never mind, little miss. You just tell him what I said."

She puckered her lips in determination, set her chin, and started off. And stopped and looked around. "What if he doesn't?"

"He will," Rusty promised, and watched her break into a run, shrieking her brother's name as she swept around the corner, dropped her bag, snatched it up, and disappeared. He watched the space she left behind for several long seconds, imagining himself as she had seen him—a cowboy having a shoot-out with his porch, with no gun, and no horse at the fence.

"Jesus," he whispered, and pulled up his collar when the wind found his neck, found the run of his spine and curled around him like a belt.

He decided then that he wasn't too old at all, he was just not old enough. Born too late to ride the range, be the hero, herd the cattle, play cards and drink whiskey and take the painted women upstairs for a slap and a tickle and a release for a dollar; too late to ride shotgun, to ride the Pony Express, to ride the Conestogas across the prairie to the mountains in the west.

Just an old man dreaming young man's notions of what it was like to be a god.

He looked up at the sky, at the moon, and wondered what the hell had gotten into him tonight.

His hand jumped on the gate.

Astonishment made him frown.

Afraid? Was he afraid? After all this time, was he scared?

He snorted in disgust, at himself and the idea, and turned back to the porch. Whatever the reason he was moody tonight, he would have to think about it later. And as he took the steps, cracking heels, sounding spurs, he felt a change in the autumn air—a vague dampness on the wind, a faint smell, a spectral touch on his cheek that made him stop with one hand on the post, one foot still on a step. A sideways look without turning his head, and he saw white shapes and dark shapes hurrying under the trees, veering like schools of startled fish into front yards, onto walks, up on porches where they gathered in ragged crescents, a demon choir.

They were here.

"Hey, anything for Halloween?"

In force at last, they were here.

"Trick or treat," it seemed, had died.

By the way they were moving, and stopping on the pavement to compare prizes and duds, he gave the first bunch fifteen minutes before they reached him. Unless they stopped at Grandy's first, where they'd be invited inside for apple cider or hot chocolate. Usually they went. No one in this town feared razors in candy and poison in gum; not anymore. And only those in the developments on the town's far side locked their doors at night and had alarms wired to the windows.

"You should talk to them," Bill Paretti had once suggested. "Maybe they don't know."

"They know," he had answered softly, and Paretti never spoke of it again.

He stood on the porch and heard the furnace that gave him no warmth, glancing up at the sky and closing his eyes before filling his lungs with air and letting it out slowly.

Too old.

You're going to die

At last reaching down to pick up the bag, resting it on the railing, dipping in a hand and pulling out a belt he strapped around his waist.

Old man. Stupid old man playing stupid children's games.

Reaching in again and pulling out the gun with the carved ivory grip and the long polished barrel.

He opened the chamber and filled each position, leaving one empty for the hammer to rest on when he closed it and spun it and dropped it into his holster.

Under the oak, something heavy moved.

Despite the watch of the moon, light snow began to fall, and the silence that followed was ringed by the keening wind. On Grandy's porch a devil saw him and told the others in a whisper; Paretti was on the corner, holding the ghost to his chest; and Wendy was at the fence, her brother behind her.

She was crying.

And they watched him as he stepped off the porch and took the walk, heels and spurs, opened the gate, patted her on the head, and stepped into the street.

The snow and the silence.

The moon, and the rising wind.

"Mr. Long?" Wendy said, sniffing. "He thinks you're a jerk."

He smiled without mirth and turned toward the sidewalk, watching, not staring, until the hobo moved away and the boy standing beside her straightened the bandanna at his throat.

"Old man," the kid said, with more a smirk than a smile.

"Not that old," said Rusty, as he drew and fired in a single motion, the gun back in its holster before the boy finished dying.

The devil on Grandy's porch cheered; Mr. Paretti clapped his hands.

Wendy looked at her brother lying on his back and shook her head. "He didn't listen," she said. "He never listened at all, you know what I mean?" Then she walked into the street and opened her bag of candy. "You want some gum or something?"

He winked at her. "No thanks, little miss."

Then he walked into the shadow of the oak by the gate, took hold of the reins and walked his black to the street. And once in the saddle, he looked around and nodded to the voices that sang his name.

"Mr. Long?"

He looked down.

It was Paretti.

"The window. You know, he never even said he was sorry?"

The black began walking, hooves with no echoes.

"Mr. Long?"

"Next year," Rusty told him. "Next year we'll talk."

Into the darklight, the color of blood.

Night They Missed
the Horror Show

Joe R. Lansdale

For Lew Shiner. A story that doesn't flinch.

If they'd gone to the drive-in like they'd planned, none of this
would have happened. But Leonard didn't like drive-ins when
he didn't have a date, and he'd heard about *Night of the Living
Dead*, and he knew a nigger starred in it. He didn't want to see no
movie with a nigger star. Niggers chopped cotton, fixed flats, and
pimped nigger girls, but he'd never heard of one that killed zom-
bies. And he'd heard too that there was a white girl in the movie
that let the nigger touch her, and that peeved him. Any white gal
that would let a nigger touch her must be the lowest trash in the
world. Probably from Hollywood, New York, or Waco, some
godforsaken place like that.

Now Steve McQueen would have been all right for zombie
killing and girl handling. He would have been the ticket. But a
nigger? No sir.

Boy, that Steve McQueen was one cool head. Way he said stuff
in them pictures was so good you couldn't help but think someone
had written it down for him. He could sure think fast on his feet to
come up with the things he said, and he had that real cool, mean
look.

Leonard wished he could be Steve McQueen, or Paul Newman
even. Someone like that always knew what to say, and he figured
they got plenty of bush too. Certainly they didn't get as bored as he
did. He was so bored he felt as if he were going to die from it
before the night was out. Bored, bored, bored. Just wasn't nothing
exciting about being in the Dairy Queen parking lot leaning on the

front of his '64 Impala looking out at the highway. He figured maybe old crazy Harry who janitored at the high school might be right about them flying saucers. Harry was always seeing something. Bigfoot, six-legged weasels, all manner of things. But maybe he was right about the saucers. He said he'd seen one a couple nights back hovering over Mud Creek and it was shooting down these rays that looked like wet peppermint sticks. Leonard figured if Harry really had seen the saucers and the rays, then those rays were boredom rays. It would be a way for space critters to get at Earth folks, boring them to death. Getting melted down by heat rays would have been better. That was at least quick, but being bored to death was sort of like being nibbled to death by ducks.

Leonard continued looking at the highway, trying to imagine flying saucers and boredom rays, but he couldn't keep his mind on it. He finally focused on something in the highway. A dead dog.

Not just a dead dog. But a DEAD DOG. The mutt had been hit by a semi at least, maybe several. It looked as if it had rained dog. There were pieces of that pooch all over the concrete and one leg was lying on the curbing on the opposite side, stuck up in such a way that it seemed to be waving hello. Doctor Frankenstein with a grant from Johns Hopkins and assistance from NASA couldn't have put that sucker together again.

Leonard leaned over to his faithful, drunk companion, Billy—known among the gang as Farto, because he was fart-lighting champion of Mud Creek—and said, "See that dog there?"

Farto looked where Leonard was pointing. He hadn't noticed the dog before, and he wasn't nearly as casual about it as Leonard. The puzzle-piece hound brought back memories. It reminded him of a dog he'd had when he was thirteen. A big, fine German shepherd that loved him better than his Mama.

Sonofabitch dog tangled its chain through and over a barbed wire fence somehow and hung itself. When Farto found the dog its tongue looked like a stuffed black sock and he could see where its claws had just been able to scrape the ground, but not quite enough to get a toehold. It looked as if the dog had been scratching out some sort of coded message in the dirt. When Farto told his old man about it later, crying as he did, his old man laughed and said, "Probably a goddamn suicide note."

Now, as he looked out at the highway, and his whisky-laced Coke collected warmly in his gut, he felt a tear form in his eyes. Last time he'd felt that sappy was when he'd won the fart-lighting championship with a four-inch burner that singed the hairs of his ass and the gang awarded him with a pair of colored boxer shorts. Brown and yellow ones so he could wear them without having to change them too often.

So there they were. Leonard and Farto, parked outside the DQ, leaning on the hood of Leonard's Impala, sipping Coke and whisky, feeling bored and blue and horny, looking at a dead dog and having nothing to do but go to a show with a nigger starring in it. Which, to be up front, wouldn't have been so bad if they'd had dates. Dates could make up for a lot of sins, or help make a few good ones, depending on one's outlook.

But the night was criminal. Dates they didn't have. Worse yet, wasn't a girl in the entire high school would date them. Not even Marylou Flowers, and she had some kind of disease.

All this nagged Leonard something awful. He could see what the problem was with Farto. He was ugly. Had the kind of face that attracted flies. And though being fart-lighting champion of Mud Creek had a certain prestige among the gang, it lacked a certain something when it came to charming the gals.

But for the life of him, Leonard couldn't figure his own problem. He was handsome, had some good clothes, and his car ran good when he didn't buy that old cheap gas. He even had a few bucks in his jeans from breaking into washaterias. Yet his right arm had damn near grown to the size of his thigh from all the whacking off he did. Last time he'd been out with a girl had been a month ago, and as he'd been out with her along with nine other guys, he wasn't rightly sure he could call that a date. He wondered about it so much, he'd asked Farto if he thought it qualified as a date. Farto, who had been fifth in line, said he didn't think so, but if Leonard wanted to call it one, wasn't no skin off his dick.

But Leonard didn't want to call it a date. It just didn't have the feel of one, lacked that something special. There was no romance to it.

True, Big Red had called him Honey when he put the mule in the barn, but she called everyone Honey—except Stoney. Stoney was Possum Sweets, and he was the one who talked her into wearing the grocery bag with the mouth and eye holes. Stoney was like that. He could sweet talk the camel out from under a sand nigger. When he got through chatting Big Red down, she was plumb proud to wear that bag.

When finally it came his turn to do Big Red, Leonard had let her take the bag off as a gesture of goodwill. That was a mistake. He just hadn't known a good thing when he had it. Stoney had had the right idea. The bag coming off spoiled everything. With it on, it was sort of like balling the Lone Hippo or some such thing, but with the bag off, you were absolutely certain what you were getting, and it wasn't pretty.

Even closing his eyes hadn't helped. He found that the ugliness of that face had branded itself on the back of his eyeballs. He couldn't even imagine the sack back over her head. All he could think about was that puffy, too-painted face with the sort of bad complexion that began at the bone.

He'd gotten so disappointed, he'd had to fake an orgasm and get off before his hooter shriveled up and his Trojan fell off and was lost in the vacuum.

Thinking back on it, Leonard sighed. It would certainly be nice for a change to go with a girl that didn't pull the train or had a hole between her legs that looked like a manhole cover ought to be on it. Sometimes he wished he could be like Farto, who was as happy as if he had good sense. Anything thrilled him. Give him a can of Wolf Brand Chili, a big Moon Pie, Coke and whisky and he could spend the rest of his life fucking Big Red and lighting the gas out of his asshole.

God, but this was no way to live. No women and no fun. Bored, bored, bored. Leonard found himself looking overhead for space-ships and peppermint-colored boredom rays, but he saw only a few moths fluttering drunkenly through the beams of the DQ's lights.

Lowering his eyes back to the highway and the dog, Leonard had a sudden flash. "Why don't we get the chain out of the back and hook it up to Rex there? Take him for a ride."

"You mean drag his dead ass around?" Farto asked.

Leonard nodded.

"Beats stepping on a tack," Farto said.

They drove the Impala into the middle of the highway at a safe moment and got out for a look. Up close the mutt was a lot worse. Its innards had been mashed out of its mouth and asshole and it stunk something awful. The dog was wearing a thick, metal-studded collar and they fastened one end of their fifteen-foot chain to that and the other to the rear bumper.

Bob, the Dairy Queen manager, noticed them through the window, came outside and yelled, "What are you fucking morons doing?"

"Taking this doggie to the vet," Leonard said. "We think this sumbitch looks a might peaked. He may have been hit by a car."

"That's so fucking funny I'm about to piss myself," Bob said.

"Old folks have that problem," Leonard said.

Leonard got behind the wheel and Farto climbed in on the passenger side. They maneuvered the car and dog around and out of the path of a tractor-trailer truck just in time. As they drove off, Bob screamed after them, "I hope you two no-dicks wrap that Chevy piece of shit around a goddamn pole."

As they roared along, parts of the dog, like crumbs from a flakey loaf of bread, came off. A tooth here. Some hair there. A string of guts. A dew claw. And some unidentifiable pink stuff. The metal-studded collar and chain threw up sparks now and then like fiery crickets. Finally they hit seventy-five and the dog was swinging wider and wider on the chain, like it was looking for an opportunity to pass.

Farto poured him and Leonard up Coke and whiskys as they drove along. He handed Leonard his paper cup and Leonard knocked it back, a lot happier now than he had been a moment ago. Maybe this night wasn't going to turn out so bad after all.

They drove by a crowd at the side of the road, a tan station wagon and a wreck of a Ford up on a jack. At a glance they could see that there was a nigger in the middle of the crowd and he wasn't witnessing to the white boys. He was hopping around like a pig with a hotshot up his ass, trying to find a break in the white boys so he could make a run for it. But there wasn't any break to be found and there were too many to fight. Nine white boys were knocking him around like he was a pinball and they were a malicious machine.

"Ain't that one of our niggers?" Farto asked. "And ain't that some of them White Tree football players that's trying to kill him?"

"Scott," Leonard said, and the name was dogshit in his mouth. It had been Scott who had outdone him for the position of quarterback on the team. That damn jig could put together a play more tangled than a can of fishing worms, but it damn near always worked. And he could run like a spotted-ass ape.

As they passed, Farto said, "We'll read about him tomorrow in the papers."

But Leonard drove only a short way before slamming on the brakes and whipping the Impala around. Rex swung way out and clipped off some tall, dried sunflowers at the edge of the road like a scythe.

"We gonna go back and watch?" Farto said. "I don't think them White Tree boys would bother us none if that's all we was gonna do, watch."

"He may be a nigger," Leonard said, not liking himself, "but he's our nigger and we can't let them do that. They kill him they'll beat us in football."

Farto saw the truth of this immediately. "Damn right. They can't do that to our nigger."

Leonard crossed the road again and went straight for the White Tree boys, hit down hard on the horn. The White Tree boys abandoned beating their prey and jumped in all directions. Bullfrogs couldn't have done any better.

Scott stood startled and weak where he was, his knees bent in and touching one another, his eyes big as pizza pans. He had never noticed how big grillwork was. It looked like teeth there in the night and the headlights looked like eyes. He felt like a stupid fish about to be eaten by a shark.

Leonard braked hard, but off the highway in the dirt it wasn't enough to keep from bumping Scott, sending him flying over the hood and against the glass where his face mashed to it then rolled away, his shirt snagging one of the windshield wipers and pulling it off.

Leonard opened the car door and called to Scott, who lay on the ground. "It's now or never."

A White Tree boy made for the car, and Leonard pulled the taped hammer handle out from beneath the seat and stepped out of the car and hit him with it. The White Tree boy went down to his knees and said something that sounded like French but wasn't. Leonard grabbed Scott by the back of the shirt and pulled him up and guided him around and threw him into the open door. Scott scrambled over the front seat and into the back. Leonard threw the hammer handle at one of the White Tree boys and stepped back, whirled into the car behind the wheel. He put the car in gear again and stepped on the gas. The Impala lurched forward, and with one hand on the door Leonard flipped it wider and clipped a White Tree boy with it as if he were flexing a wing. The car bumped back on the highway and the chain swung out and Rex clipped the feet out from under two White Tree boys as neatly as he had taken down the dried sunflowers.

Leonard looked in his rearview mirror and saw two White Tree boys carrying the one he had clubbed with the hammer handle to the station wagon. The others he and the dog had knocked down were getting up. One had kicked the jack out from under Scott's car and was using it to smash the headlights and windshield.

"Hope you got insurance on that thing," Leonard said.

"I borrowed it," Scott said, peeling the windshield wiper out of his T-shirt. "Here, you might want this." He dropped the wiper over the seat and between Leonard and Farto.

"That's a borrowed car?" Farto said. "That's worse."

"Nah," Scott said. "Owner don't know I borrowed it. I'd have had that flat changed if that sucker had had him a spare tire, but I got back there and wasn't nothing but the rim, man. Say, thanks for not letting me get killed, else we couldn't have run that ole pig together no more. Course, you almost run over me. My chest hurts."

Leonard checked the rearview again. The White Tree boys were coming fast. "You complaining?" Leonard said.

"Nah," Scott said, and turned to look through the back glass. He could see the dog swinging in short arcs and pieces of it going wide and far. "Hope you didn't go off and forget your dog tied to the bumper."

"Goddamn," said Farto, "and him registered too."

"This ain't so funny," Leonard said, "them White Tree boys are gaining."

"Well speed it up," Scott said.

Leonard gnashed his teeth. "I could always get rid of some excess baggage, you know."

"Throwing that windshield wiper out ain't gonna help," Scott said.

Leonard looked in his mirror and saw the grinning nigger in the backseat. Nothing worse than a comic coon. He didn't even look grateful. Leonard had a sudden horrid vision of being overtaken by the White Tree boys. What if he were killed with the nigger? Getting killed was bad enough, but what if tomorrow they found him in a ditch with Farto and the nigger. Or maybe them White Tree boys would make him do something awful with the nigger before they killed them. Like making him suck the nigger's dick or some such thing. Leonard held his foot all the way to the floor; as they passed the Dairy Queen he took a hard left and the car just made it and Rex swung out and slammed a light pole then popped back in line behind them.

The White Tree boys couldn't make the corner in the station wagon and they didn't even try. They screeched into a car lot down a piece, turned around and came back. By that time the taillights of the Impala were moving away from them rapidly, looking like two inflamed hemorrhoids in a dark asshole.

"Take the next right coming up," Scott said, "then you'll see a little road off to the left. Kill your lights and take that."

Leonard hated taking orders from Scott on the field, but this was worse. Insulting. Still, Scott called good plays on the field, and the habit of following instructions from the quarterback died hard. Leonard made the right and Rex made it with them after taking a dip in a water-filled bar ditch.

Leonard saw the little road and killed his lights and took it. It carried them down between several rows of large tin storage buildings, and Leonard pulled between two of them and drove down a little alley lined with more. He stopped the car and they waited and listened. After about five minutes, Farto said, "I think we skunked those father-rapers."

"Ain't we a team?" Scott said.

In spite of himself, Leonard felt good. It was like when the nigger called a play that worked and they were all patting each other on the ass and not minding what color the other was because they were just creatures in football suits.

"Let's have a drink," Leonard said.

Farto got a paper cup off the floorboard for Scott and poured him up some warm Coke and whisky. Last time they had gone to Longview, he had peed in that paper cup so they wouldn't have to stop, but that had long since been poured out, and besides, it was for a nigger. He poured Leonard and himself drinks in their same cups.

Scott took a sip and said, "Shit, man, that tastes kind of rank."

"Like piss," Farto said.

Leonard held up his cup. "To the Mud Creek Wildcats and fuck them White Tree boys."

"You fuck 'em," Scott said. They touched their cups, and at that moment the car filled with light.

Cups upraised, the Three Musketeers turned blinking toward it. The light was coming from an open storage building door and there was a fat man standing in the center of the glow like a bloated fly on a lemon wedge. Behind him was a big screen made of a sheet and there was some kind of movie playing on it. And though the light was bright and fading out the movie, Leonard, who was in the best position to see, got a look at it. What he could make out looked like a gal down on her knees sucking this fat guy's dick (the man was visible only from the belly down) and the guy had a short black revolver pressed to her forehead. She pulled her mouth off of

him for an instant and the man came in her face then fired the
revolver. The woman's head snapped out of frame and the sheet
seemed to drip blood, like dark condensation on a window pane.
Then Leonard couldn't see anymore because another man had appeared in the doorway, and like the first he was fat. Both looked
like huge bowling balls that had been set on top of shoes. More
men appeared behind these two, but one of the fat men turned and
held up his hand and the others moved out of sight. The two fat
guys stepped outside and one pulled the door almost shut, except
for a thin band of light that fell across the front seat of the Impala.

Fat Man Number One went over to the car and opened Farto's
door and said, "You fucks and the nigger get out." It was the voice
of doom. They had only thought the White Tree boys were dangerous. They realized now they had been kidding themselves. This
was the real article. The guy would have eaten the hammer handle
and shit a two-by-four.

They got out of the car and the fat man waved them around and
lined them up on Farto's side and looked at them. The boys still
had their drinks in their hands, and sparing that, they looked like
cons in a lineup.

Fat Man Number Two came over and looked at the trio and
smiled. It was obvious the fatties were twins. They had the same
bad features in the same fat faces. They wore Hawaiian shirts that
varied only in profiles and color of parrots and had on white socks
and too-short black slacks and black, shiny Italian shoes with toes
sharp enough to thread needles.

Fat Man Number One took the cup away from Scott and
sniffed it. "A nigger with liquor," he said. "That's like a cunt with
brains. It don't go together. Guess you was getting tanked up so
you could put the ole black snake to some chocolate pudding after
while. Or maybe you was wantin' some vanilla and these boys were
gonna set it up."

"I'm not wanting anything but to go home," Scott said.

Fat Man Number Two looked at Fat Man Number One and
said, "So he can fuck his mother."

The fatties looked at Scott to see what he'd say but he didn't say
anything. They could say he screwed dogs and that was all right

with him. Hell, bring one on and he'd fuck it now if they'd let him go afterwards.

Fat Man Number One said, "You boys running around with a jungle bunny makes me sick."

"He's just a nigger from school," Farto said. "We don't like him none. We just picked him up because some White Tree boys were beating on him and we didn't want him to get wrecked on account of he's our quarterback."

"Ah," Fat Man Number One said, "I see. Personally, me and Vinnie don't cotton to niggers in sports. They start taking showers with white boys the next thing they want is to take white girls to bed. It's just one step from one to the other."

"We don't have nothing to do with him playing," Leonard said. "We didn't integrate the schools."

"No," Fat Man Number One said, "that was ole Big Ears Johnson, but you're running around with him and drinking with him."

"His cup's been peed in," Farto said. "That was kind of a joke on him, you see. He ain't our friend, I swear it. He's just a nigger that plays football."

"Peed in his cup, huh?" said the one called Vinnie. "I like that, Pork, don't you? Peed in his fucking cup."

Pork dropped Scott's cup on the ground and smiled at him. "Come here, nigger. I got something to tell you."

Scott looked at Farto and Leonard. No help there. They had suddenly become interested in the toes of their shoes; they examined them as if they were true marvels of the world.

Scott moved toward Pork, and Pork, still smiling, put his arm around Scott's shoulders and walked him toward the big storage building. Scott said, "What are we doing?"

Pork turned Scott around so they were facing Leonard and Farto who still stood holding their drinks and contemplating their shoes. "I didn't want to get it on the new gravel drive," Pork said and pulled Scott's head in close to his own and with his free hand reached back and under his Hawaiian shirt and brought out a short black revolver and put it to Scott's temple and pulled the trigger. There was a snap like a bad knee going out and Scott's feet lifted in unison and went to the side and something dark squirted from his head and his feet swung back toward Pork and his shoes shuffled, snapped, and twisted on the concrete in front of the building.

"Ain't that somethin'," Pork said as Scott went limp and dangled from the thick crook of his arm, "the rhythm is the last thing to go."

Leonard couldn't make a sound. His guts were in his throat. He wanted to melt and run under the car. Scott was dead and the brains that had made plays twisted as fishing worms and commanded his feet on down the football field were scrambled like breakfast eggs.

Farto said, "Holy shit."

Pork let go of Scott and Scott's legs split and he sat down and his head went forward and clapped on the cement between his knees. A dark pool formed under his face.

"He's better off, boys," Vinnie said. "Nigger was begat by Cain and the ape and he ain't quite monkey and he ain't quite man. He's got no place in this world 'cept as a beast of burden. You start trying to train them to do things like drive cars and run with footballs it ain't nothing but grief to them and the whites too. Get any on your shirt, Pork?"

"Nary a drop."

Vinnie went inside the building and said something to the men there that could be heard but not understood, then he came back with some crumpled newspapers. He went over to Scott and wrapped them around the bloody head and let it drop back on the cement. "You try hosing down that shit when it's dried, Pork, and you wouldn't worry none about that gravel. The gravel ain't nothing."

Then Vinnie said to Farto, "Open the back door of that car." Farto nearly twisted an ankle doing it. Vinnie picked Scott up by the back of the neck and seat of his pants and threw him onto the floorboard of the Impala.

Pork used the short barrel of his revolver to scratch his nuts, then put the gun behind him, under his Hawaiian shirt. "You boys are gonna go to the river bottoms with us and help us get shed of this nigger."

"Yes sir," Farto said. "We'll toss his ass in the Sabine for you."

"How about you?" Pork asked Leonard. "You trying to go weak sister?"

"No," Leonard croaked. "I'm with you."

"That's good," Pork said. "Vinnie, you take the truck and lead the way."

Vinnie took a key from his pocket and unlocked the building door next to the one with the light, went inside, and backed out a sharp-looking gold Dodge pickup. He backed it in front of the Impala and sat there with the motor running.

"You boys keep your place," Pork said. He went inside the lighted building for a moment. They heard him say to the men inside, "Go on and watch the movies. And save some of them beers for us. We'll be back." Then the light went out and Pork came out, shutting the door. He looked at Leonard and Farto and said, "Drink up, boys."

Leonard and Farto tossed off their warm Coke and whiskys and dropped the cups on the ground.

"Now," Pork said, "you get in the back with the nigger, I'll ride with the driver."

Farto got in the back and put his feet on Scott's knees. He tried not to look at the head wrapped in newspaper, but he couldn't help it. When Pork opened the front door and the overhead light came on Farto saw there was a split in the paper and Scott's eye was visible behind it. Across the forehead the wrapping had turned dark. Down by the mouth and chin was an ad for a fish sale.

Leonard got behind the wheel and started the car. Pork reached over and honked the horn. Vinnie rolled the pickup forward and Leonard followed him to the river bottoms. No one spoke. Leonard found himself wishing with all his heart that he had gone to the outdoor picture show to see the movie with the nigger starring in it.

The river bottoms were steamy and hot from the closeness of the trees and the under and overgrowth. As Leonard wound the Impala down the narrow red clay roads amidst the dense foliage, he felt as if his car were a crab crawling about in a pubic thatch. He could feel from the way the steering wheel handled that the dog and the chain were catching brush and limbs here and there. He had forgotten all about the dog and now being reminded of it worried him. What if the dog got tangled and he had to stop? He didn't think Pork would take kindly to stopping, not with the dead burrhead in the floorboard and him wanting to get rid of the body.

Finally they came to where the woods cleared out a spell and they drove along the edge of the Sabine River. Leonard hated water and always had. In the moonlight the river looked like poisoned coffee flowing there. Leonard knew there were alligators and gars big as little alligators and water moccasins by the thousands swimming underneath the water, and just the thought of all those slick, darting bodies made him queasy.

They came to what was known as Broken Bridge. It was an old worn-out bridge that had fallen apart in the middle and it was connected to the land on this side only. People sometimes fished off of it. There was no one fishing tonight.

Vinnie stopped the pickup and Leonard pulled up beside him, the nose of the Chevy pointing at the mouth of the bridge. They all got out and Pork made Farto pull Scott out by the feet. Some of the newspaper came loose from Scott's head exposing an ear and part of the face. Farto patted the newspaper back into place.

"Fuck that," Vinnie said. "It don't hurt if he stains the fucking ground. You two idgits find some stuff to weigh this coon down so we can sink him."

Farto and Leonard started scurrying about like squirrels, looking for rocks or big, heavy logs. Suddenly they heard Vinnie cry out. "Godamighty, fucking A. Pork. Come look at this."

Leonard looked over and saw that Vinnie had discovered Rex. He was standing looking down with his hands on his hips. Pork went over to stand by him, then Pork turned around and looked at them. "Hey, you fucks, come here."

Leonard and Farto joined them in looking at the dog. There was mostly just a head now, with a little bit of meat and fur hanging off a spine and some broken ribs.

"That's the sickest fucking thing I've ever fucking seen," Pork said.

"Godamighty," Vinnie said.

"Doing a dog like that. Shit, don't you got no heart? A dog.

Man's best fucking goddamn friend and you two killed him like this."

"We didn't kill him," Farto said.

"You trying to fucking tell me he done this to himself? Had a bad fucking day and done this."

"Godamighty," Vinnie said.

"No sir," Leonard said. "We chained him on there after he was dead."

"I believe that," Vinnie said. "That's some rich shit. You guys murdered this dog. Godamighty."

"Just thinking about him trying to keep up and you fucks driving faster and faster makes me mad as a wasp," Pork said.

"No," Farto said. "It wasn't like that. He was dead and we were drunk and we didn't have anything to do, so we—"

"Shut the fuck up," Pork said sticking a finger hard against Farto's forehead. "You just shut the fuck up. We can see what the fuck you fucks did. You drug this here dog around until all his goddamn hide came off . . . What kind of mothers you boys got anyhow that they didn't tell you better about animals?"

"Godamighty," Vinnie said.

Everyone grew silent, stood looking at the dog. Finally Farto said, "You want us to go back to getting some stuff to hold the nigger down?"

Pork looked at Farto as if he had just grown up whole from the ground. "You fucks are worse than niggers, doing a dog like that. Get on back over to the car."

Leonard and Farto went over to the Impala and stood looking down at Scott's body in much the same way they had stared at the dog. There, in the dim moonlight shadowed by trees, the paper wrapped around Scott's head made him look like a giant papier-mâché doll. Pork came up and kicked Scott in the face with a swift motion that sent newspaper flying and sent a thonking sound across the water that made frogs jump.

"Forget the nigger," Pork said. "Give me your car keys, ball sweat." Leonard took out his keys and gave them to Pork and Pork went around to the trunk and opened it. "Drag the nigger over here."

Leonard took one of Scott's arms and Farto took the other and they pulled him over to the back of the car.

"Put him in the trunk," Pork said.

"What for?" Leonard asked.

"Cause I fucking said so," Pork said.

Leonard and Farto heaved Scott into the trunk. He looked pathetic lying there next to the spare tire, his face partially covered with newspaper. Leonard thought, if only the nigger had stolen a car with a spare he might not be here tonight. He could have gotten the flat changed and driven on before the White Tree boys even came along.

"All right, you get in there with him," Pork said, gesturing to Farto.

"Me?" Farto said.

"Nah, not fucking you, the fucking elephant on your fucking shoulder. Yeah, you, get in the trunk. I ain't got all night."

"Jesus, we didn't do anything to that dog, mister. We told you that. I swear. Me and Leonard hooked him up after he was dead . . . It was Leonard's idea."

Pork didn't say a word. He just stood there with one hand on the trunk lid looking at Farto. Farto looked at Pork, then the trunk, then back to Pork. Lastly he looked at Leonard, then climbed into the trunk, his back to Scott.

"Like spoons," Pork said, and closed the lid. "Now you, whatsit, Leonard? You come over here." But Pork didn't wait for Leonard to move. He scooped the back of Leonard's neck with a chubby hand and pushed him over to where Rex lay at the end of the chain with Vinnie still looking down at him.

"What you think, Vinnie?" Pork asked. "You got what I got in mind?"

Vinnie nodded. He bent down and took the collar off the dog. He fastened it on Leonard. Leonard could smell the odor of the dead dog in his nostrils. He bent his head and puked.

"There goes my shoeshine," Vinnie said, and he hit Leonard a short one in the stomach. Leonard went to his knees and puked some more of the hot Coke and whisky.

"You fucks are the lowest pieces of shit on this earth, doing a dog like that," Vinnie said. "A nigger ain't no lower."

Vinnie got some strong fishing line out of the back of the truck and they tied Leonard's hands behind his back. Leonard began to cry.

"Oh shut up," Pork said. "It ain't that bad. Ain't nothing that bad."

But Leonard couldn't shut up. He was caterwauling now and it was echoing through the trees. He closed his eyes and tried to pretend he had gone to the show with the nigger starring in it and had fallen asleep in his car and was having a bad dream, but he couldn't imagine that. He thought about Harry the janitor's flying saucers with the peppermint rays, and he knew if there were any saucers shooting rays down, they weren't boredom rays after all. He wasn't a bit bored.

Pork pulled off Leonard's shoes and pushed him back flat on the ground and pulled off the socks and stuck them in Leonard's mouth so tight he couldn't spit them out. It wasn't that Pork thought anyone was going to hear Leonard, he just didn't like the noise. It hurt his ears.

Leonard lay on the ground in the vomit next to the dog and cried silently. Pork and Vinnie went over to the Impala and opened the doors and stood so they could get a grip on the car to push. Vinnie reached in and moved the gear from park to neutral and he and Pork began to shove the car forward. It moved slowly at first, but as it made the slight incline that led down to the old bridge, it picked up speed. From inside the trunk, Farto hammered lightly at the lid as if he didn't really mean it. The chain took up slack and Leonard felt it jerk and pop his neck. He began to slide along the ground like a snake.

Vinnie and Pork jumped out of the way, and watched the car make the bridge and go over the edge and disappear into the water with amazing quietness. Leonard, tugged by the weight of the car, rustled past them. When he hit the bridge, splinters tugged at his clothes so hard they ripped his pants and underwear down almost to his knees.

The chain swung out once toward the edge of the bridge and the rotten railing, and Leonard tried to hook a leg around an upright board there, but that proved wasted. The weight of the car just pulled his knee out of joint and tugged the board out of place with a screech of nails and lumber.

Leonard picked up speed and the chain rattled over the edge of the bridge, into the water and out of sight, pulling its connection after it like a pull toy. The last sight of Leonard was the soles of his bare feet, white as the bellies of fish.

"It's deep there," Vinnie said. "I caught an old channel cat there once, remember? Big sucker. I bet it's over fifty feet deep down there."

They got in the truck and Vinnie cranked it.

"I think we did them boys a favor," Pork said. "Them running around with niggers and what they did to that dog and all. They weren't worth a thing."

"I know it," Vinnie said. "We should have filmed this, Pork, it would have been good. Where the car and that nigger-lover went off in the water was choice."

"Nah, there wasn't any women."

"Point," Vinnie said, and he backed around and drove onto the trail that wound its way out of the bottoms.

The Yard

William F. Nolan

It was near the edge of town, just beyond the abandoned freight tracks. I used to pass it on the way to school in the mirror-bright Missouri mornings and again in the long-shadowed afternoons coming home with my books held tight against my chest, not wanting to look at it.

The Yard.

It was always spooky to us kids, even by daylight. It was old, had been in Riverton for as long as anyone could remember. Took up a full city block. A sagging wood fence (had it *ever* been painted?) circled all the way around it. The boards were rotting, with big cracks between many of them where you could see all the smashed cars and trucks piled obscenely inside, body to body, in rusted embrace. There were burst-open engines with ruptured water hoses like spilled guts, and splayed truck beds, split and swollen by sun and rain, and daggered windshields filmed with dark-brown scum. ("It's from people's brains, where their heads hit the glass," said Billy-Joe Gibson, and no one doubted him.)

The wide black-metal gate at the front was closed and padlocked most always, but there were times at night, *always* at night, when it would creak open like a big iron mouth and old Mr. Latting would drive his battered exhaust-smoky tow truck inside, with its missing front fenders and dented hood, dragging the corpse of a car behind like a crushed metal insect.

We kids never knew exactly where he got the cars—but there were plenty of bad accidents on the Interstate, especially during the fall, when the fog would roll out from the Riverton woods and drape the highway in a breathing blanket of chalk white.

Out-of-towners who didn't know the area would come haul-assing along at eighty, then dive blind into that pocket of fog. You'd hear a squeal of brakes. Wheels locking. Then the explosion of rending metal and breaking glass as they hit the guardrail. Then a long silence. Later, sometimes a lot later, you'd hear the keening siren of Sheriff Joe Thompson's Chevy as he drove out to the accident. Anyway, we kids figured that some of those wrecked cars ended up in the Yard.

At night, when you passed the Yard, there was this sickly green glow shining over the piled up metal corpses inside. The glow came from the big arclamp that Mr. Latting always kept lit. Come dusk, that big light would pop on and wouldn't go off till dawn.

When a new kid came to school in Riverton we knew he'd eventually get around to asking about the Yard. "You been inside?" he'd ask, and we'd say heck yes, plenty of times. But that was a lie. No kid I knew had ever been inside the Yard.

And we had a good reason. Mr. Latting kept a big gray dog in there. Don't know the breed. Some kind of mastiff. Ugly as sin on Sunday, that dog. Only had one good eye; the other was covered by a kind of veined membrane. Clawed in a fight maybe. The good eye was black as a chunk of polished coal. Under the dog's lumpy, short-haired skull its shoulders were thick with muscle, and its matted gray coat was oil-streaked and spotted with patches of mange. Tail was stubbed, bitten away.

That dog never barked at us, never made a sound; but if any of us got too near the Yard it would show its fanged yellow teeth, lips sucked back in silent fury. And if one of us dared to touch the fence circling the Yard that dog would slam its bulk against the wood, teeth snapping at us through the crack in the boards.

Sometimes, in the fall, in the season of fog, just at sunset, we'd see the gray dog drift like a ghost out the gate of the Yard to enter the woods behind Sutter's store and disappear.

Once, on a dare, I followed him and saw him leave the trees at the far edge of the woods and pad up the slope leading to the

Interstate. I saw him sitting there, by the side of the highway, watching the cars whiz by. He seemed to enjoy it.

When he swung his big head around to glare at me I cut out fast, melting back into the woods. I was shook. I didn't want that gray devil to start after me. I remember I ran all the way home.

I once asked my father what he knew about Mr. Latting. Said he didn't know anything about the man. Just that he'd always owned the Yard. And the dog. And the tow truck. And that he always wore a long black coat with the frayed collar turned up, even in summer. And always a big ragged hat on his head, with a rat-eaten brim that fell over his thin, pocked face and glittery eyes.

Mr. Latting never spoke. Nobody had ever heard him talk. And since he didn't shop in town we couldn't figure out where he got his food. He never seemed to sell anything, either. I mean, nobody ever went to the Yard to buy spare parts for their cars or trucks. So Mr. Latting qualified as our town eccentric. Every town has one. Harmless, I guess.

But scary just the same.

So that's how it was when I grew up in Riverton. (Always thought Riverton was a funny name for a place that didn't have a river within a hundred miles of it.) I was eighteen when I went away to college and started a new life. Majored in engineering. Just like my Dad, but he never did anything with it. I was thirty, with my own business, when I finally came back. To bury my father.

Mom had divorced him ten years earlier. She'd re-married and was living in Cleveland. Refused to come back for the funeral. My only sister was in California, with no money for the trip, and I had no brothers. So it was up to me.

The burial that fall, at Oakwood Cemetery, was bleak and depressing. Attendance was sparse—just a few of Pop's old cronies, near death themselves, and a scattering of my high school pals, as nervous and uncomfortable as I was. On hand just to pay their respects. Nothing in common between any of us, nothing left.

After it was over I determined to drive back to Chicago that same night. Riverton held no nostalgic attraction for me. Get Pop buried, then get the hell out. That was my plan from the start.

Then, coming back from the cemetery, I passed the Yard.

I couldn't see anybody inside as I drove slowly past the pad-locked gate. No sign of life or movement.

Of course, twelve long years had passed. Old Latting was surely dead by now, his dog with him. Who owned the place these days? Lousy piece of real estate if you'd asked me!

A host of dark memories rushed back, crowding my mind. There'd always been something foul about the Yard—something wrong about it. And that hadn't changed. I shuddered, struck by a sudden chill in the air. Turned the car heater up another notch.

And headed for the Interstate.

Ten minutes later I saw the dog. Sitting at the wooded edge of the highway, on the gravel verge, at the same spot I'd followed it to so many years before. As my car approached it, the big gray animal raised its head and fixed its coal-chip eye on me as I passed.

The *same* dog. The same sightless, moon-fleshed eye on the right side of its lumped skull, the same mange-pocked matted fur, the same muscled shoulders and stubbed tail.

The same dog—or its ghost.

Suddenly I was into a swirl of opaque fog obscuring the high-way. Moving much too fast. The apparition at the edge of the woods had shattered my concentration. My foot stabbed at the brake pedal. The wheels locked, lost their grip on the fog-damp road. The car began sliding toward the guardrail. A milk-white band of unyielding steel *loomed* at me. Into it. Head on.

A smashing explosion of metal to metal. The windshield splintering. The steering wheel hard into my chest. A snapping of bone. Sundered flesh. Blood. Pain. Darkness.

Silence.

Then—an awakening. Consciousness again. I blinked, focusing. My face was numb; I couldn't move my arms or legs. Pain lived like raw fire in my body. I then realized that the car was upside down, with the top folded around me like a metal shroud.

A wave of panic rippled over me. I was trapped, jack-knifed inside the overturned wreck. I fought down the panic, telling myself that things could have been worse. Much worse. I could have gone through the windshield (which had splintered, but was still intact);

the car could have caught fire; I could have broken my neck. At least I'd survived the accident. Someone would find me. Someone.

Then I heard the sound of the tow truck. I saw it through the windshield, through the spider-webbing of cracked glass, coming toward me in the fog—the *same* tow truck I'd seen as a boy, its front fenders missing, hood dented, its front bumper wired together . . . The rumble of its ancient, laboring engine was horribly familiar.

It stopped. A door creaked open and the driver climbed from the cab. He walked over to my car, squatting down to peer in at me.

Mr. Latting.

And he spoke. For the first time I heard his voice—like rusted metal. Like something from a tomb. "Looks like you went an' had yerself a smash." And he displayed a row of rotting teeth as he smiled. His eyes glittered at me under the wide brim of his ragged hat.

Words were not easy for me. "I . . . I'm . . . badly hurt. Need to . . . get a doctor." I had blood in my mouth. I groaned; pain was in me like sharp blades. All through my body.

"No need to fret," he told me. "We'll take care'a you." A dry chuckle. "Just you rest easy. Leave things to us."

I was very dizzy. It took effort just to breathe. My eyes lost focus; I fought to remain conscious. Heard the sound of chains being attached, felt the car lifted, felt a sense of movement, the broken beat of an engine . . . Then a fresh wave of pain rolled me into darkness.

I woke up in the Yard.

Couldn't be, I told myself. Not *here*. He wouldn't take me *here*. I need medical care. A hospital. I could be dying.

Dying!

The word struck me with the force of a dropped hammer. I was dying and he didn't care. He'd done nothing to help me; I was still trapped in this twisted hulk of metal. Where were the police? Mechanics with torches to cut me free? The ambulance?

I squinted my eyes. The pale green glow from the tall arclamp in the middle of the Yard threw twisting shadows across the high-piled wreckage.

I heard the gate being slammed shut and padlocked. I heard Latting's heavy boots, crunching gravel as he came toward me. The car was still upside down.

I attempted to angle my body around, to reach the handle of the driver's door. Maybe I could force it open. But a lightning streak of pain told me that body movement was impossible.

Then Latting's skeletal face was at the windshield, looking in at me through the splintered glass. A grin pulled at the skin of his mouth like a scar. "You all right in there?"

"God, no!" I gasped. "Need . . . a doctor. For Christ's sake . . . call . . . an ambulance."

He shook his head. "Got no phone to call one with here at the Yard," he said, in his rasping voice. "Besides that, you don't need no doctors, son. You got *us.*"

"Us?"

"Sure. Me an' the dog." And the blunt, lumpy head of the foul gray animal appeared at the window next to Latting. His red tongue lolled wetly and his bright black unblinking eye was fixed on me.

"But . . . I'm bleeding!" I held up my right arm; it was pulsing with blood. "And I . . . I think I have . . . internal injuries."

"Oh, sure you got 'em," chuckled Latting. "You got *severe* internals." He leered at me. "Plus, your head's gashed. Looks like both yer legs is gone—an' your chest is all stove in. Lotta busted ribs in there." And he chuckled again.

"You crazy old fool!" I snapped. "I'll . . . I'll have the sheriff on you." I fought back the pain to rage at him. "You'll rot in jail for this!"

"Now don't go gettin' huffy," Latting said. "Sheriff ain't comin' in here. Nobody comes into the Yard. You oughta know that by now. Nobody, that is, but ones like you."

"What do you mean . . . like me?"

"Dyin' ones," the old man rasped. "Ones with mosta their bones broke and the heart's blood flowin' out of 'em. Ones from the Interstate."

"You . . . you've done this before?"

"Sure. Lotsa times. How do you think we've kept goin' all these years, me an' the dog? It's what's up there on the Interstate keeps us alive . . . what's inside all them mashed-up cars, all them rolled-over trucks. We *need* what's inside." He ruffled the mangy fur at the dog's neck. "Don't we, boy?"

In response, the big animal skinned back its slimed red lips and showed its teeth—keeping its obsidian eye fixed on me.

"This here dog is kinda unusual," said Latting. "I mean, he seems to just know *who* to pick out to cast the Evil Eye. Special ones. Ones like you that nobody's gonna miss or raise a fuss over. Can't have folks pokin' around the Yard, askin' questions. The ones he picks, they're just into the fog and gone. I tow 'em here an' that's that."

Numbly, through a red haze of pain, I remembered the fierce *intensity* of that single dark eye from the edge of the highway as I passed. Hypnotizing me, causing me to lose control and smash into the guardrail. The Evil Eye.

"Well, time to quit jawin' with ya and get this here job done," said Latting. He stood up. "C'mon, dog." And he led the animal away from the car.

I drew in a shuddering breath, desperately telling myself that someone must have heard the crash and reported it, that the Sheriff would arrive any moment now, that I'd be cut free, eased onto cool crisp linen sheets, my skin gently swabbed of blood, my wounds treated . . .

Hurry, damn you! I'm dying. Dying!

A sudden, shocking immediate smash of sound. Again and again and again. The cracked curve of safety glass in front of me was being battered inward by a series of stunning blows from Latting's sledge as he swung it repeatedly at the windshield.

"These things are gettin' tougher every year," he scowled, continuing his assault. "Ah, now . . . here she goes!"

And the whole windshield suddenly gave way, collapsing into fragments, with jagged pieces falling on my head and shoulders, cutting my flesh.

"There, that's better, ain't it?" asked the old man with his puck-ered-scar grin. "He can get at ya now with no bother."

Get at me?

The dog. Of course he meant the dog. That stinking horror of an animal. I blinked blood from my eyes, trying to push myself back, away from the raw opening. But it was useless. The pain was incredible. I slumped weakly against the twisted metal of the in-caved roof, refusing to believe what was happening to me.

The gray creature was coming, thrusting his wide shoulders through the opening.

The fetid breath of the hellbeast was in my nostrils; his gaping mouth fastened to my flesh, teeth gouging; his bristled fur was rank against my skin.

A hideous snuffling, sucking sound . . . as I felt him draining me! I was being . . . *emptied* . . . into him . . . into *his foul body* . . . all of me . . . *all* . . .

I felt the need to move. To leave the Yard. The air was cold, edged with the promise of frost. The sky was steel gray above me.

It was good to move again. To run. To leave the town and the woods behind me.

It was very quiet. I gloried in the strong scent of earth and concrete and metal which surrounded me. I was *alive.* And strong again. It was fine to be alive.

I waited. Occasionally a shape passed in front of me, moving rapidly. I ignored it. Another. And another. And then, finally, the *one.* Happiness rushed through me. Here was one who would pro-vide my life and strength, and the life and strength of my master.

I raised my head. He saw me then, the one in the truck. My eye fixed on his as he swept past me with a metallic rush of sound. And vanished into the fog.

I sat quietly, waiting for the crash.

In the Trees

Steve Rasnic Tem

It was a good climbing tree, a good climbing tree for a good boy. And Will's son was a good boy. A wild boy, sure, but a good boy, a beautiful boy. A boy like Will himself could have been, if only he hadn't had to grow up so quickly. The fact was, Will had never been very good at being a boy. He'd never had the knack. At his son's age he'd been cautious and forced, an old man in the soft skin of a boy.

"Go to sleep, son," he said softly, a whisper from the old man he'd always been. He stood in the doorway and gazed at his son's head, small face and soft dark hair barely out of the comforter, sunk to his red ears in the pillow. "You need your rest. You can't understand that now, but take it from me, you'll never have enough rest for what lies ahead."

Will could see past the bed, out the window to where the climbing tree stood, its leaves lighting up with the moonlight. Will took another pull off his beer and wished it were whiskey. The climbing tree was a beautiful thing, standing out from the surrounding trees that formed the edge of "the grove"—more like a forest—that spread out from this edge of town seven miles before farm land started breaking it up.

But few of the trees seemed fit for climbing, and none of the others were this close to the house.

"I'm a good boy, aren't I, Dad?" his son spoke sleepily from his bed. But even in the sleepy voice Will could hear the anxiety that had *no* reason to be there. "I try to be good, don't I?"

"Of course, son. You're a good boy, a *fabulous* boy."

"Then don't make me go to sleep. I *can't* sleep."

Will knew this couldn't be true. This was just the boy's natural excitement talking, his anxiety, all the life in him rising to the top that made it hard for him just to lie down and rest, to permit the night to pass without his presence in it. His son sounded sleepier the more he said. He wouldn't be surprised to hear his snores at any second. He had to go to sleep. Sleep was medicine. And he had to take his medicine. Had to grow up big and strong. And bury his old man someday if it came to that.

Will thought about what to say, tried to think about what his own father would have said, and drank slow and steady from the can, now lukewarm in his sweaty hand. "Tomorrow's another day," he finally managed, feebly. "You're young; you have a whole lifetime ahead. No sense rushing it; that was the mistake I made when I was a boy. I was always rushing things."

The wind picked up. The longest of the leafy branches thrashed the window. His son's dark head began to thrash, too, whipping back and forth across the pillow as if in fever.

"Stay still, son," Will implored, his hands shaking, full of pain. "That's no good. That's no good at all. You have to get your rest!"

"I can't sleep, Daddy! I just can't!"

Will moved to the side of the bed. It was a kid's bed, low and small; Will felt like a giant towering over it. "I'll help you sleep," he said, his own anxiety bubbling up at his throat. "I'll do anything I can."

Awkwardly Will dropped to his knees beside the bed. He put the can down on the rug, but it tipped over. Foam erupted from the opening and dribbled over the edge of the rug onto the wooden floor. But Will couldn't move his hands off his son's comforter. He reached over and stroked the good boy's hair, hair softer than anything in Will's experience. He felt the good boy's forehead for fever—not sure he would know a fever in a boy this small. He stroked the shallow rise of comforter that covered his chest and arms.

"I don't want to go to sleep, Daddy! I'm scared!"

"What are you afraid of?"

"I don't know," the good boy said, thrashing. "I never know." Will wasn't going to say there was nothing to be afraid of; he knew better.

Will looked around the room for something, anything, that might calm his son down and let him sleep. And let Will sleep as well, for he knew he couldn't leave the room until a night's rightful relief for his son was well on its way.

A stuffed tiger, a bear, a red truck, a pillow decorated with tiny golden bells. His son barely looked at the toys as Will piled them up around his tiny, soft, thrashing head. "Had your prayers yet?" Will asked the beautiful, anxious boy, as if it was still more medicine he was talking about, still more magic. Will rubbed his hands together, prayerful-like, now desperate for another drink.

"No! I'm not sleeping!" his beautiful son cried, his tiny head red as blood, the wave of black hair across his forehead suddenly so like the greasy wing of a dead bird. Will made his pained hands into fists, not knowing whether he was going to caress or strike the good boy.

Will put his shaking hands together and prayed for his son to go to sleep.

"I want to climb the tree!" the good son suddenly cried.

And Will, who had never before permitted it, said, "Tomorrow. I'll let you climb the tree tomorrow."

Will sat on the floor in his son's dark bedroom, drinking a beer. He watched the beautiful face—no longer bright red, or dark, now pale silver in the moonlight that had slipped through the open window—as his son slept, dreaming the dreams all good boys dreamed, but which Will, who had grown up all too quickly, had forgotten.

Behind and above the headboard of the bed was the open window, and the climbing tree beyond. The moonlight had planted silver flames in its branches. The boy's head was perfectly still. The boy's head no longer thrashed, but the climbing tree continued to thrash in the wind, making the silver flames break and spread, shoot higher up the limbs of the tree.

Will watched his beautiful son's face, relieved at its peace, but could see his nervous, living dreams torturing the bright flaming limbs of the climbing tree.

Again, the beer had grown warm in his hand, but he continued to drink. Tomorrow his wife and daughter would be back from their trip. Maybe *she* could get their son to sleep. Maybe *she* could talk him down out of the climbing tree. Will had been crazy to agree to the climb—it wasn't *safe*, it had never been safe. He'd never let his beautiful boy climb the tree before, no matter how much he'd begged. Now he didn't understand how he could have given in so easily. He'd change his mind and tell the boy, but Will had never been able to break a promise to his son before.

The curtains floated up on either side of his son's window, flapping severely as if tearing loose. Will hugged himself and imagined his small, good son hugging him, protecting him from the chill wind of adult pain.

It was a good tree, an outstanding tree. Will drank and watched his beautiful son play in the uppermost branches of the climbing tree.

His son was better at climbing trees than he had ever been. His son braved things that had terrified the young Will, left him motionless and dumb. And old, so old the other young boys were strangers to him, wild beasts scrapping in the trees. His son was a much better boy than Will had been. His son had all the right talents for being a boy.

He was a wild boy, but a good boy. The boy loved it when the branches almost broke, bent so far they threatened to drop him on his head. The boy *laughed* at terror; it thrilled him. Like other boys Will had known once upon a time, his sweet boy had no sense about danger.

The boy shook the upper branches and made as if to fly off with the tree, laughing. Will imagined the tree up-rooting, then turning somersaults in the darkening, early evening air.

Behind him, the wife said, "Will, it's getting late. It's time to get him in." Will's wife knew about a boy's safety.

But much to his surprise, Will discovered he didn't want his son to come down just yet. As the sky grew darker and the wind increased Will took pride in the way the boy held fast to the uppermost branches, shaking them like some small, fierce animal, dancing among them like some unnatural spirit. *That's it, son! That's it*, he thought, throwing his head back and permitting the flat beer to gush down his throat. *Don't leave the trees for a life down here on the ground. It happens soon enough—you'll understand that someday.*

A sudden wind caught Will full in the face: his hair stood up and his eyes were forced closed. Another gust knocked the empty can out of his hand. He could almost feel himself up in the tree with his son, just another boy to join that good, wild boy. Will staggered to his feet. The wind took away his lawn chair. He moved forward toward the base of the tree, trying to remember what his clever son had done to begin the climb.

"Daddy, I want to climb, too." Will knew the tug on his pants. He looked down at his little girl, who was using his leg to block the wind.

"You're too small!" Will shouted down. But the wind was dragging his words away.

"You let *him!*" She began to cry.

Will picked his little girl up in his arms. "Too dangerous," he spoke into her ear.

"Will!" His wife's scream beside him warmed his ear. The wind had grown cold; he could feel ice in the wrinkles of his clothes.

He turned. Her face was white, floating in the cold black air. "It's going to be okay!" Will cried against the wind. "He's a *good* boy! A *great* boy! Don't you see? A much better boy than I ever was!"

Will turned back toward the tree, where his son played and laughed, his son's face hot and glorious in the wind, the moon laying shiny streaks into his dark hair. Lightning played in the distant boughs of the forest, moving toward the house. Will started toward the climbing tree, his wife and daughter clinging to him. But he remembered he no longer knew how to climb, and stopped halfway between the house and the tree.

His beautiful son stopped laughing and stared down at Will. Will brought a nervous hand up to his lips, then realized he had no beer. He felt a sudden panic as he knew his son had seen what life was like back on the ground.

Lightning began to ripple the trees. Up in the highest part of the tree, his beautiful son laughed and started climbing higher.

It was a good climbing tree. A wonderful climbing tree. Will had taught his good son not to be afraid to do things. Will had taught him the lessons Will had never known. Will had taught him not to be afraid to live.

"No!" Will cried out to the trees. "Come back! It's not safe!"

But in the trees there were boys laughing and playing, unafraid and with no sense of danger. Dark hair flew as the boys climbed higher, pushing and wrestling in the weak, thin upper branches of the forest. Lightning bleached their hair. Wind and electricity gave them wings.

"Will! Get him *back!*" his wife screamed.

"He's a good boy, he's a wild boy, he's a beautiful boy!" Will shouted above the wind.

The climbing tree rose up and did a somersault, the kind Will had always been afraid of doing. The forest floated up out of its roots and shouted. And all the boys in the trees laughed so hard they cried, in love with themselves and in love with each other.

And Will's beautiful son was gone, climbing *so* high, climbing to where Will had always been afraid to go.

Dead Air

Gregory Nicoll

SCREAMIN' LORD SUTCH—Lord David Sutch was the Fifth Earl of Harrow, a full-blooded member of English nobility who also hacked out a reputation for himself as a hardworking rock 'n' roll revivalist during the 1960s. As Screamin' Lord Sutch and the Savages, Dave and his band were noted for spectacular and macabre shows which frequently started with Dave emerging from a coffin carried onstage by hooded monks. His recorded output is unfortunately rather spotty. Dave's best-known American release is *Hands of Jack the Ripper* (Cotillion Records, SD 9049, out of print), a live LP featuring members of The Who and the Jimi Hendrix Experience. A standout tune is the title track, over nine minutes' worth of delirious sonic mayhem which some listeners claim can . . .
—CARLTON AND WOOD, *Weird Heroes of Rock 'n' Roll, vol. 2 (DB Press, 1989)*

The broadcasting studio, long and narrow like a coffin, had soundproofed walls unbroken by windows. A torn and wrinkled poster for Mötley Crüe's *Shout at the Devil* was their only decoration.

This place is a tomb, Mary thought. *Feels like I'm buried alive.*

She struck a match and touched it to the end of a Marlboro, her fifth since she'd started her air shift. She was alone in the radio station, a squat building full of tiny, cramped offices and racks of old record albums in tattered covers.

Jimmy Page's fuzzy guitar screeched from enormous speakers overhead as Led Zeppelin's *Presence* rotated on the left-hand turntable at an even, digitally verified 33⅓ rpm. The room was damp and cold and smelled like cigarette smoke. It was almost a quarter to four in the morning, and Mary grimaced at the thought of staying there another three hours.

Maybe Neil will come in early and I can sweet-talk him into running the end of the shift for me . . .

She shivered, drawing the collar of her silver W-H-O-R satin jacket up around her neck. *Good ole Bert,* she thought sarcastically. *He spends a fucking fortune on these jackets for us, but won't shell out a nickel for some heat.*

As the Led Zep tune faded out, Mary quickly pulled on her headphones, potted up her mike, and set her hands on the knobs which controlled the right-hand turntable. The next song was Pink Floyd's "Another Brick in the Wall, Part 2," and fading it on cue was tricky enough when you did it as a straight segue—much more so when you had an ID and a back-sell to lead in with.

"That was the sizzling sound of Led Zeppelin," she announced as the song ended. "Comin' up we've got a lot more rock 'n' roll for you here on the Home of Rock—W-H-O-R, Atlanta, Georgia! A little later we'll be rollin' up to four A.M. with a Blue Oyster Cult superset, but right now let's each mix up a batch of mortar and pour ourselves a tall glass of Amontillado. It's time to help the Floyd put another brick . . . in the wall."

She punched the button, starting the right-hand turntable spinning, while at the same time she rotated the potentiometer all the way to maximum. The sound of the song rolled in precisely on cue.

And the two lights on the telephone began to flash like the eyes of a winking demon.

Here come the geeks, she thought, picking up her cigarette for one quick drag before she replaced the Led Zep LP in its sleeve. *Well, they can wait a minute.*

She took her time filing the album in the rack and had yet another hit on the Marlboro before she answered the first of the incoming calls.

"W-H-O-R! You're rockin' with Mary. It's your dime."

There was a snicker on the line. *"Yeah,"* said a deep male voice, blurry with alcohol.

"Somethin' I can do for you?" she asked, trying hard to feign enthusiasm. *God, does anyone listen to this station when they're sober?*

"Y-you're new there, ain't you?"

"Um-hmm. I started the night before last."

"I th-thought so." There was a long pause. "What do you look like?"

"What do you *think* I look like?"

"I bet you're one *fine*-lookin' lady. One *damn* fine-lookin' fox."

Mary shook her head. "You just might be right. Now, is there a song I can play for you?"

The drunk chuckled quietly. "What are you wearing right now?"

"My W-H-O-R jacket."

"And *nothing* else?"

She punched the button for the other extension, cutting off the first caller. "You're rockin' with Mary on W-H-O-R, the Home of Rock 'n' Roll. What can I do for you?"

"Uh, er . . ."

"Go ahead. Spit it out."

There was a moment's pause. Then a timid male voice, possibly belonging to a teenage boy, asked, "You takin' requests for that superset?"

"Sure," she said. "What d'you want to hear?"

"How about 'Smoke on the Water'?"

She rolled her eyes. " 'Fraid not. Like I said, the superset is by the Blue Oyster Cult. I'll play you something—but it's gotta be a BOC cut or nothin' at all."

"Oh."

Mary cued up "Don't Fear the Reaper" as she waited for the kid to make a choice.

"I know," he said at last. "How about 'Veteran of the Psychic Wars'?"

"That's a good one," she admitted, flipping through a nearby stack of Blue Oyster Cult albums to verify that she had a copy of *Fire of Unknown Origin*. "I'll be glad to play it for you. You're gonna be listenin', aren't you?"

"Damn straight," he answered, his tone firm with conviction. "Say, what's with your voice, Mary?"

"My voice?"

"It sounds real different tonight."

She smiled. "I'm new here. My name's Mary Clark. You must be thinking of Mary Kelly, the D.J. who used to have this shift."

"Ohhhhhh . . . Gee . . . Uh, what happened to her?"

Mary shrugged. "Beats me. The station owner didn't say."

"Well, I hope you stay around awhile. I like your voice."

"*Thanks*. And thanks for calling in. G'bye."

"G'bye."

The huge Favag dial clock overhead displayed the time as just shy of a quarter to four.

Mary sighed. *Another three hours, give or take a few minutes, depending on when Neil gets here. How the hell am I gonna make it?*

She massaged the back of her eyelids.

It had been a long night—and a rough one—starting at seven when Bert had picked her up at her apartment. His ancient Austin-Healey was probably a lot of fun in warm weather, she conceded, but in the autumn chill it had been intensely uncomfortable to ride in the ragtop. The wind sliced her cheeks, and the broken springs in the passenger seat impaled her fanny. Add to that a broken heater and you had the recipe for a ruined evening.

Of course, she thought, *Bert did his best to warm me up.*

She smirked. *Well, at least he tried . . . Poor guy. He probably couldn't get it up if he tied it to a toothbrush.*

Mary lifted the cigarette to her lips and drew deeply from it.

The first phone line lit up again.

"W-H-O-R, Rock 'n' Roll Radio. What's your pleasure?"

Silence came over the line.

"Hello? Anybody there?"

"I-I'll tell you wh-what my pleasure is," sniggered the same drunken voice that had called before. "I'm comin' over to that there radio station to see you in a minute, and I'm gonna bring a jar full of wet, squishy—"

She slammed down the handset.

The second line lit up.

Sure hope this is somebody else . . .

She balanced her Marlboro on the edge of the ashtray and lifted the handset to her ear again. "Hello. You're rockin' with Mary on W-H-O-R, the Home of—"

"*Mary?*"

Though it had said but a single word, the voice was instantly familiar. There was no mistaking that rich, deep English accent with its heavy suggestion of Big Ben, Buckingham Palace, the Tower of London, Prince Charles and Lady Diana, and all other veddy, veddy British things.

It was Bert.

"Oh," she said, her voice stopping cold in genuine surprise. "Ah, I didn't expect to hear from you so soon, Bert."

"Look, Mary," he said briskly, "about this evening. I'm frightfully embarrassed by what happened and I'd truly like to make it up to you—"

"Bert, there's really no call for that. I'm sorry for the way things worked out, and I want you to know that I'll never tell anyone wh—"

"Of course," he interrupted. "But I'd truly appreciate the opportunity to sit down with you and to explain why I couldn't—"

"Bert, I—"

"I don't want you to think it had anything to do with *you;* I mean with you *personally.*"

"Bert—"

"It's just that I—"

"Bert!"

He finally stopped talking.

"Bert," she said, *"please!* I feel bad enough about the whole thing already. Yes, we can talk about it sometime, but not *now*—I'm in the middle of my air shift, fer Chrissakes. Maybe tomorrow afternoon we could meet for breakfast or—"

"No, Mary, no. Not tomorrow. Tonight."

"Tonight? Oh, Bert," she protested. "There's just no way. I've been up for over fifteen hours straight now and I already feel like I've got rigor mortis. When my shift is over I'm going straight home and collapsing into bed. And let no man stand in my way!"

The line was silent for a few moments. Then Bert said one word. He said it quietly, but with an air of gentle persistence that she found irresistible. He said her name.

"Mary . . ."

She raised the cigarette back to her lips. "All right, Bert. You can come by here."

"Gracious thanks, Mary," he said. "You're sure it's all right?"

"Um-hmm." She rubbed her temples. "The question is, am *I* all right?"

"Whatever do you mean?"

She grimaced. "My head hurts like crazy. How many drinks did I have over at your place?"

"Only two, I'm afraid."

"Well, I'm sure feeling zonked. Maybe you oughta bring me some aspirin . . . and, uh, maybe a little hair o' the dog?"

"You've got it, Mary dear. I'll be there directly."

She hung up and swiveled back to face the console.

The speakers went dead. The song was over.

Damn, she thought, her eyes racing across the board in a panic, *I can't remember what I was going to do next!*

The station was broadcasting nothing but silence, the empty, lonely sound of dead air.

Tapping a button nearby, she activated her microphone. Using it without the headphones to monitor her own voice was difficult but it could be done. The trick was staying close to the mike and watching the needles on the VU meters to regulate her volume.

"Hope you en*joyed* the *Floyd*," she quipped, "and now, from that *rhyme*, we shift to the *time!*"

She glanced up at the Favag. It was almost four.

"Well, well, well, the clock here at H-O-R, the Home of Rock Radio, says it's time for the Blue Oyster Cult's superset . . . *after this!*"

She tapped the button which triggered the first audiocart deck. A waterbed store commercial—one of Neil's editing room wonders—squawked from the speakers.

Massaging her temples with one hand, Mary used the other to pluck a BOC album from the pile near her feet and slap it on the turntable. She cued it with the little monitor built into the console. When the waterbed spot ended a few seconds later, her headphones were on her head, her fingers poised on the controls of the turntable.

"Creeping up on four o'clock in the mornin' here at 1300 on your AM dial. You're rockin' with Mary Clark, and right now we're gonna kick off our salute to the Soft White Underbelly—*better known as the Blue Oyster Cult*—with their classic 'Don't Fear the Reaper'!"

She started the song, its haunting guitar lines chiming from the speakers at exactly the right instant.

The telephone extensions lit up again.

"Fuck you," she muttered. It was safe now—the mike was switched off. "Gimme a chance to pull my music."

She thumbed through the other BOC albums, selecting the ones she'd need. "Burnin' for You" would follow "Don't Fear the Reaper." That'd carry the set up to the station ID at the top of the hour. Then she'd come out of the ID with "Veteran of the Psychic Wars"—the trouble was that it was on *Fire of Unknown Origin*, the same album as "Burnin' For You," and they only had one copy of it.

"Well," she said, thinking aloud, "I guess I could always play it off the *Heavy Metal* soundtrack album . . . if we've got a copy of that around here."

She checked the card file. Sure enough, it was there—two of its songs, one by Don Felder and another by Sammy Hagar, were still in infrequent rotation on W-H-O-R's playlist.

Sliding back her chair to the record rack behind her, she located the *Heavy Metal* jacket and slipped the two discs out.

"Veteran of the Psychic Wars" was scratched. A deep gouge ran completely through all its grooves.

So much for that, she thought. *Unless . . . unless there's another copy back in the disc library . . .*

Glancing over at the turntables, she saw that "Don't Fear the Reaper" was less than a third of its way through. The flashing phone extensions, she decided, could wait—there was just enough time to go back to the stacks and hunt down another record with "Veteran of the Psychic Wars" on it. Mary stuck her cigarette back on the edge of the ashtray and got up, hastily making the circuit around the console to the door at the far end of the little room.

Her feet clicked on the slick floor of the hall outside. *Damnedest thing*, she thought. *Every other station I've worked at had carpeting at least a coupla inches thick. Guess Bert doesn't mind the background noises and echoes around here.*

Hell, who'd ever hear 'em? This is AM, after all. Ain't even stereo unless they've got one of those special receivers . . .

The record library was at the far end of the hall, two doors past Bert's office. Racks of albums ran from floor to ceiling, and piles of unsorted discs cluttered the tabletops around the room. A turntable set up in one corner bore a large sign, scrawled on a legal pad sheet, which warned, *"Do not use this record player. The needle is shot."*

Underneath, in a different handwriting, was scribbled, *"Then fix it, dammit!"*

Mary found a sealed copy of the *Heavy Metal* LP in the stacks. She tried to pick open the plastic, but her fingernails weren't up to the task.

Now, where the hell is that knife they keep around here?

It was on top of a carton containing twenty-five copies of the new Black Sabbath album. The knife had a slender eight-inch blade with a slight curve at its tip. It was mounted in a stout wooden handle.

Mary slipped it into the edge of the record jacket, and the plastic seal melted away. She tossed the knife back on the carton of records.

Something creaked in a faraway room.

"Hello?" she called. "Is that you, Bert?"

There was no response.

Instinctively she picked the knife back up. Then, feeling foolish, she replaced it on the box.

"Neil?"

There was a thump, as of a door closing.

The front door—I wonder if I forgot to lock it . . . Gee . . . I was pretty upset when I came in . . . I might've forgot all about it . . .

Another sound, fainter, indistinct—footsteps on the hall floor?

Christ! It might be that drunk asshole who called in! He said something about "comin' over" here . . .

Her heart beat faster.

"Hello?" she called. "Who is it?"

Still nothing.

Carefully placing the *Heavy Metal* album on a nearby table, she stepped out into the hall. She did her best to mute the clicks of her boots against the hall floor as she headed up to the reception area at the front door of the station. The mysterious sounds seemed to have come from there.

When she turned the corner, she discovered that the room was empty. The secretary's desk, a few chairs, and the huge pair of monitor speakers were the only things in the wood-paneled room, aside from the usual assortment of gold records and autographed photos hung on the walls.

Right now the speakers were kicking out the final bars of "Don't Fear the Reaper." The song was only seconds from its finale.

"Dammit!" Mary grunted, her professional training overcoming her personal terror. *I better get my ass back in the booth.*

She didn't make it.

For almost ten full seconds the station broadcasted nothing but dead air.

Fuckin' terrific. And with Bert probably on his way over here right now, no doubt listening to all this and wonderin' what the hell is goin' on.

Dammit dammit dammit.

He'll probably fire me the minute he walks in the door.

"Burnin' for You" was spinning on the right-hand turntable. To play "Veteran of the Psychic Wars" next, she'd have to go back to the record library and pick up that *Heavy Metal* LP she'd left there. For a few seconds she considered substituting another song.

No, she finally decided, *I promised that kid who called in that I'd play it next . . .*

Mary picked up her cigarette and discovered that it had burned out.

Jesus. This just ain't my night.

She went back into the hall and started toward the library.

Hey—what's that smell?

She stopped, turned around—and noticed a light under the closed door to Bert's office. There was a faint odor which seemed to be coming from that direction, the smell of something sour.

"Bert?"

She knocked tentatively on the door. "Bert, are you in there?"

Mary tried the handle. It turned, and the door swung open slowly to reveal—

Nothing. There's nobody here.

The sour smell was stronger inside the little room, but she couldn't see anything that might be causing it.

Bert probably left a milk carton in his wastebasket or something . . .

She reached over to the light switch on the far side of the desk, silently cursing whatever inconsiderate architect or electrician had positioned the switch so far from the door. To reach it she had to lean around the large bookcase which stood at a right angle to Bert's desk. In the process of bending her arm around the expanse of bookshelves she couldn't help but notice the long row of leather-bound volumes lining the space.

She chuckled.

Neil and some of the other W-H-O-R jocks had a running series of jokes about Bert's eclectic reading habits. Most of the staff, however, decided that Bert's book collection was just there for show—a form of wallpaper that must've cost nine dollars per square inch. The titles were certainly impressive enough—*Remembrance of Things Past, Best Plays of Shakespeare, Of Human Bondage, Gray's Anatomy, Beowulf, Discourses on Livy,* and *A Farewell to Arms*—although they kept strange bedfellows. On the shelf below were *The Book of Rock Lists, Up and Down with the Rolling Stones,* and *Elvis and Me.*

She flicked the light switch. It snapped down with a resounding *click.*

Mary shook her head as she shut the office door behind her. *Coulda sworn that light was already off the last time I passed by it . . .*

A minute later with the album in her hands, she was heading back up the hall when another sound stopped her short.

Water?

It sounded like a tap running—possibly the one in the rest room up near the reception area.

"Bert? Neil? *Anybody?*"

She walked to the other end of the hall but couldn't hear the sound any better there. *"Hello?"*

"Burnin' for You" was blasting from the reception room speakers. The song was into its final chorus.

Mary spun in place and ran back into the booth. She was in her seat, headphones in hand, when it ended.

Dead air again, dammit all!

She opened the mike. "It's just past four o'clock and time to rock—on the Home of Rock 'n' Roll Radio, W-H-O-R, Atlanta, 1300 AM!"

As she spoke, she slapped the *Heavy Metal* disc onto the left-hand turntable and lowered the tone arm to the appropriate groove. Then, holding her breath, she rotated the potentiometer up to full as the record began to spin.

Christ, I sure hope the needle fell in the right place!

The song began *in medias res*. Missing was a part of the opening instrumental, though not a significant portion.

Mary let her breath out slowly and switched off her mike. *Well,* she decided, *that coulda been a lot worse . . .*

She looked around at the stacks of records. What to play next? A superset was supposed to have at least four songs by the featured artist.

Noticing that the phone lines were both still flashing, she answered the first of the incoming calls.

"Home of Rock. What can I do you for?"

The voice was young, slightly nervous. "Uh, is this Mary?"

"You got me."

"Uh, can you, uh, can you play 'Godzilla' in this set?"

"Sure can."

"Er, *gee*, uh, you're really gonna play it?"

"Be happy to. It'll be right after 'Veteran of the Psychic Wars.' "

"Oh . . . okay. Great. Thanks!"

She switched over to the second call. "H-O-R, the Home of Rock 'n' Roll. What can I do you for?"

It was quiet on the line, although a faint hiss of presence indicated that someone was there.

"This is Mary. Hello? Is there somethin' I can play for you?"

"Yes," said a hesitant male voice. It sounded suspiciously like the drunk who'd called earlier, but she couldn't be sure. "I want you to play . . . 'Hands of Jack the Ripper.' "

Mary rolled her eyes. "Is that by the Blue Oyster Cult?"

There was no answer, only the vague sound of presence.

"I'm not familiar with 'Hands of Jack the Ripper.' Is that one of those import-only tracks, or is it something off the first live album?"

The caller *laughed*. It was a low, murky, horrible laugh. Then he whispered, "I'm coming for you now, Mary Clark."

The line went dead.

"Fuck you, too," she huffed, dropping the handset back on its cradle.

She lit another Marlboro and practiced blowing smoke rings at the microphone. Several of them successfully encircled its knoblike end before disappearing in the air.

The phone flashed again.

"Mary on the Rock. What's your pleasure?"

There was a twitter on the line. An *English* twitter.

"Bert?"

"Yes, yes. It's me." He chuckled. "*Really*, my dear, surely you knew before you answered."

"And how could I do *that?*" she asked, slightly annoyed.

"Oh, come on, then. Surely you were having me on! You don't always answer the phone like that, do you?"

"Not always, Bert, but I do try to be personable."

"Very well, then. I'll speak no more of it. I just rang over to tell you I'm on my way."

"Check. I'll see you when you get here. And by the way—hurry it up, okay? Some weirdo keeps calling me up, and he's starting to give me the heebie-jeebies. Maybe you could answer the phone for me for a while."

"I'd be delighted to, Mary. Fret not. I'll be there . . . And one more thing—a small favor, if you will."

"You're the boss."

"Play me a song for the drive over. 'Roll Over, Beethoven' would be nice."

"Sorry, chief. That one's scratched. I was gonna use it in the Beatles superset at two A.M. but there was an awful gash right through the grooves. By the way, there seems to be a lot of that going on around here. Some other song I could swap for it, maybe?"

"Well—we do have another version of it."

"That's news to me, Bert. Who's it by?"

"Screamin' Lord Sutch."

"Never heard of the dude. Is he one of those Brit rockers you've added to the playlist?"

"Well, actually I haven't added him yet, but the album's on my desk. You can't miss it. It's called *Hands of Jack the Ripper*. See you soon!"

She lowered the handset slowly to the cradle. *So that's what that asshole caller was asking for! Some obscure Limey wax which he must've heard Bert play on the oldies show . . .*

She took a drag on her cigarette and checked the turntable. "Veteran of the Psychic Wars" had about another two minutes to play. Plenty of time to zip down to Bert's office and pick up that LP he wanted her to use. She left the Marlboro in the ashtray and made a beeline down the hall.

The light in the office was on again.

What the fuck is going on?

She turned around and yelled up the hall, "Whoever's in here and running around playing games better cut it out *right now!* This shit isn't funny anymore!"

Probably Neil. If I hadn't had so much booze tonight, I'd probably think all this was funny as hell . . .

Bert's desk was cluttered with promo albums, wadded W-H-O-R T-shirts, Post-It notes of uncertain vintage, backstage passes from a half-dozen recent rock shows, and a McDonald's fish sandwich that looked at least three days old.

It was, without *any* further doubt, the source of the sour smell in the office.

"Phew!" Mary gasped. She felt an urge to puke and fought hard to suppress it. *The mayo on that thing must be blue-green by now.*

She groaned as she discovered that *Hands of Jack the Ripper* by Lord Sutch and His Heavy Friends lay beneath the sandwich.

"The things I do for rock 'n' roll," Mary muttered as she cautiously separated the LP from its noxious burden.

Back in the control room the Blue Oyster Cult was still singing as Mary resumed her seat. She relit her Marlboro and stuck it in her lips as she examined *Hands of Jack the Ripper*.

It was a gatefold album, its rather innocuous front cover opening to reveal a photo of a man dressed as Jack the Ripper stalking a woman in Victorian garb. There were also several photos of Lord Sutch and various musicians rehearsing in a small studio. Mary recognized Keith Moon of The Who in one shot and smiled at his goofy expression.

Then she remembered that Moon was dead.

Helluva loss, she thought. *The Who sure wasn't the same without him . . .*

Another picture showed Noel Redding, the bass guitarist of the Jimi Hendrix Experience.

Hunh . . . Hendrix is dead, too . . .

She squinted at the liner notes, a column of ultra-fine print on the right edge of the gatefold. Skimming them quickly, she spotted a reference to John Bonham of Led Zeppelin.

Another dead musician . . .

Shuddering, she flipped the record jacket over to its back cover where the song list was printed. "Roll Over, Beethoven" was the second song on side one. *Beethoven,* she noted with amusement, *still another dead man—although he's a lot colder than the others.*

The last song on side one was the title track, "Hands of Jack the Ripper." She raised an eyebrow as she noticed that it was 9¼ minutes long.

Must be a whole lotta rippin' goin' on in that one.

Beside the song list was a large photo of Lord Sutch. He was devastatingly handsome, his blond hair trimmed to a perfect Brian Jones pageboy, ruffled shirt hanging open to reveal a chest that would've made Tarzan proud.

He looked like he'd be a lot better in bed than Bert.

"Veteran of the Psychic Wars" neared its conclusion.

Mary dropped *Hands of Jack the Ripper* on the console and reached for the control board. It was too late. The record ended and her broadcast fell silent.

Dead air dead air dead air. All night long. Dead air dead air.

Tapping the controls, she set "Godzilla" spinning.

Dammit. This has been the worst shift of my life. What I need is some fresh air. Maybe during this song . . .

She was playing the long version of "Godzilla" off the live album. With a little fast work to get things in order, cueing up the next song and picking out a few more to follow it, she felt she could earn a brief fresh-air break. A stroll to her Mustang in the sandlot outside would be just what she needed. And if, while she was out that way, there happened to be any Jack Daniel's left in that bottle on the passenger seat . . .

Well, why not?

It'll be okay . . . I'll switch on the car's radio so I can keep tabs on the broadcast . . .

She cued up "Roll Over, Beethoven" from *Hands of Jack the Ripper* as the next song. With deep regret she eyed the running time of the title tune. "Beethoven" was only 2½ minutes long; the 9¼-minute "Hands of Jack the Ripper" would've made an even better cocktail song than "Godzilla."

But, she reminded herself, *I promised Bert I'd play "Roll Over, Beethoven" . . . and he is my boss.*

Unless he fires me over all that dead air that's been fouling up my shift.

Cigarette in hand, Mary walked out of the studio and around to the front door, which she propped open with a chair to expedite getting back inside when the time came.

I can just imagine fumbling for my key here in the dark while the record plays out on the turntable!

It was cold outside. She zipped her W-H-O-R jacket up as tightly as it would go.

Her Mustang was parked close to the door. She shook her head in disbelief when she saw the acute angle at which she had pulled it up to the edge of the lot.

Christ! Was I that blitzed when I got here tonight? How many gins did I drink over at Bert's?

She unlocked the door and flopped into the driver's seat. The car smelled of cigarettes and stale beer. The bottle of J.D. was right where she'd left it, and she was in luck—there was almost a pint left. She unscrewed the cap, letting its bracing aroma strike her nostrils with its delicious impact. The burning sweet scent easily cut through the car's odor. Mary raised the bottle to her lips and took a deep swallow.

It felt good going down. She could feel the warmth spreading through her chest.

She switched on the radio. "Godzilla" came blasting from the dashboard speakers. Mary turned it down so that it was just barely audible.

"Heavy metal," she muttered, "is *not* what my headache needs."

The radio station stood just a few hundred yards off North Druid Hills Road, and from the front seat of her car she could watch the occasional early morning vehicle pass by. At this hour the traffic was mostly newspaper carriers and dairy trucks. Even in a sprawling metropolis like Atlanta, people had to sleep *sometime*.

To the southwest she could see the city itself, skyscrapers and industrial centers interlaced with ribbons of expressway. A million tiny lights gave proof through the night that her listening audience was still there. Her *target* audience. It was still too early in her tenure at W-H-O-R to know if she was hitting it.

Of course, she thought wryly as she leaned back on the car seat, *any of 'em with even a lick of sense should be asleep right now.*

She looked up at the starlit sky.

Rising high into the air behind the station was the massive antenna tower. It loomed like a gallows against the starry night.

Smiling contentedly, she took another hit on the Marlboro, another hit on the bottle. "Godzilla" thundered along on the radio, showing no sign of concluding. Mary let out a peaceful sigh.

She turned east. North Druid Hills Road rose slightly as it rolled that way. Beyond the curving hill, past the lone telephone booth at its crest, the road stretched toward the outlying communities of Toco Hills and Decatur. Life was a lot different in that direction. Not two miles from the chic uptown boutiques of Lenox Square and Phipps Plaza, some people still lived in clapboard shacks and plowed their fields with mule teams.

She put them quickly out of her head.

After all, she thought, *certainly none of those people listen to my show.*

"Godzilla" ended.

Dead air!

She dropped the bottle of Jack Daniel's and tossed the cigarette aside, scrambling out of the Mustang and sprinting for the station door. Reaching the doorway, she tripped over the chair she'd used to prop it open and fell forward, hitting her head on the bare concrete floor.

Mary got up slowly. Her hands were shaking.

Dammit all . . .

It took a great deal of effort and willpower—and she was dangerously short of both—to crawl around to the studio and get back into her seat behind the console. Her head was spinning and her eyes found it hard to focus. Somehow the console—that standard radio station control board so familiar from fifteen years in the business—now looked as foreign as the dashboard of a 747.

She slipped on her headphones and stared idiotically at the buttons and dials and meters and switches in front of her.

Dead air dead air dead air. The story of my life!

She lit another cigarette, but with difficulty—her hands were still shaking. Mary inhaled. The tobacco restored her to her senses.

She opened her mike. "Here's a rare version of a rock 'n' roll classic for you on W-H-O-R, 1300 AM," she said. "This is 'Roll Over, Beethoven' as interpreted by Screamin' Lord Sutch!"

She tapped the button.

Nothing happened.

Dead air. Dammit. What the hell is——?

A voice shouted from the speakers. It was saying something about the next song.

Mary shook her head. The headphones fell off and clattered against the surface of the console, then plopped to the floor.

The voice coming from the speakers introduced the upcoming song as "Hands of Jack the Ripper."

What the hell?! Hey!!!

She swiveled in her chair and eyeballed the turntable. Reading a record's center paper as it rotates is a skill every D.J. has to master. A disc spinning at 45 rpm can be pretty tricky, but catching one at 33⅓ is not exceptionally difficult.

Sure enough, the needle was planted on the last track of side one, the title tune—"Hands of Jack the Ripper."

Satanic laughter and spookhouse horn effects boomed from the speakers.

Dammit. I know I cued up "Roll Over, Beethoven," not this song. That means . . . Well, I guess it means that . . .

That there's somebody else here in the station . . .

Its Halloween-show introduction over, the song began with a $3/4$-time rock 'n' roll beat. It was a standard chord progression, the classic "Woolly Bully" riff. The music proceeded for a few bars before a female chorus joined in, chanting every few seconds.

This is just too weird for me, Mary thought. She stood up and walked to the studio door. The hand that held her Marlboro was shaking so hard that she dropped the cigarette on the hall floor. She mashed it under her boot heel.

"Neil? *Bert?* Are you here, Bert?"

She stuck her head in his office and switched on the light. No— nothing there but his piles of junk, old records, and putrid fish sandwich.

Footsteps sounded in the distance—from the reception area?

"Bert?"

It had to be Bert. Neil certainly wouldn't be *this* early, even if he had a whole stack of audiocarts to dub for tomorrow.

She moved in the direction of the sound, trying hard not to stumble. Her head hurt even worse than before.

The footsteps continued. It sounded like someone was strolling all around the secretary's desk by the front door.

Who is it? And where the hell are they walking to?

She remembered the drunk who'd called and said he'd come over.

Christ! I sure as hell hope it isn't him . . .

She reached the source—the small room at the front of the building.

There was nobody there. Just the reception desk and monitor speakers. Two *silent* monitor speakers.

The footsteps proceeded around the room.

Mary's brow creased. *Is . . . is that sound on the record?*

A woman's voice, her accent a thick cockney, called out a greeting.

That's what it is, Mary decided. *It's a sound effect on the album . . . and those footsteps must've been in stereo, moving from speaker to speaker. I think . . .*

The woman with the cockney accent started gasping, "No! No!"

I wonder where the hell Bert is, Mary thought. *He should've been here by now . . .*

The woman on the record was screaming. The vocalist began to sing about a London physician who chased and butchered the local ladies of the night.

I better have another drink . . .

The song continued, Lord Sutch assuming the part of Jack the Ripper as he called out for the blood of his next victim, a woman named *Mary . . .*

Better not go out to the car again, though. Guess I'll just wait on Bert.

She walked back to the booth.

Maybe he hasn't left his apartment yet . . .

She found Bert's home phone number on the list posted beside the console and picked up the phone to dial it.

The line was dead.

What the——?

Mary tapped the plungers a few times, but the phone could not be resuscitated. She slammed down the handset angrily.

Goddamn Southern Bell piece a shit!

One of the extensions flashed. Somehow, some way, *a call was coming in.*

Mary lifted the receiver to her ear. "Hello?"

Nothing.

"This is W-H-O-R," she said firmly. "Is anybody there?"

There was a sound—a *laugh.* A laugh she'd heard before—low, murky, horrible.

Mary looked back at the base of the telephone. Her eyebrows rose as she saw that both of the lights for the two incoming extensions were unlit.

But there *was* a light—a tiny one at the opposite end of the phone's base.

The call was coming from *inside* the station.

She dropped the handset. *Oh. My. God.*

The doorknob at the far end of the broadcasting booth began to turn. It clicked softly as the bolt slid back, freeing the latch.

"Hands of Jack the Ripper" continued to boom from the booth's speakers. The gleeful, demented laughter of Screamin' Lord Sutch filled the air as the song rumbled along.

"Wh-who is it?" Mary shouted at the door.

It swung open—and Bert stepped in.

He was wearing an English-style overcoat and heavy boots. His expression was pleasant, though he seemed a bit puzzled.

"What's afoot here, Mary?" he asked. "The light was on down the hall."

"I went into your office to get that record," she said. Her heartbeat began to slow. "But I turned it off. I swear I did."

"Well, then, who—?"

She fumbled with the cigarette pack until she discovered that it was empty. She crumpled it and cast it aside.

"Bert, there's somebody *in* here. He called me on the internal line, and he's been playing tricks on me all night." She brushed her hair back and let out a long breath. "He even recued this record— I'd set it up to play 'Roll Over, Beethoven.' "

Bert glanced down at the spinning disc. "Looks like it's got a good five minutes to go. What say we look around together?"

She nodded. "Okay . . . Uh, did you bring me that drink?"

Bert smiled reassuringly. "I did indeed. But let's inspect the premises before we indulge."

"Okay. We can start with the record library."

There was nobody in the record library.

"Here," said Mary, picking up the knife the staff used to open new records. "You might need this."

He chuckled. *"O happy dagger . . ."*

She looked at him, her eyebrows knitted in confusion. "What?" "Um?"

"What's that you were saying?"

He held the knife up. *"O happy dagger . . ."* He smiled. "It's from Shakespeare. *Romeo and Juliet.*" There was a faraway look in Bert's eyes.

Mary smiled. "I keep forgetting that you're such a big reader."

Bert stepped closer to her. "Yes," he said, "From *Of Human Bondage* to human anatomy."

He raised the knife in front of her face.

"Put that down, Bert. You're scaring me—and my nerves are frazzled enough as it is."

He smiled again and moved the knife slowly downward, toward her chest.

"*Hey,*" she said, taking a step back. "Will you cut that out?"

"Precisely my intention—to cut something out, Mary Clark."

"What?"

Bert laughed. It was a horrible laugh—the laugh she'd heard on the phone.

All Mary could do was run.

She fled up the hall, her boot heels scraping the floor as she went. She ran through the reception area, the cries of Screamin' Lord Sutch from the speakers blending with the laughter of Bert right behind her.

At last reaching the door, she flung it open hard and stumbled awkwardly out toward her car, her right hand digging in her pocket for the ignition key.

But her pocket was gone. She was wearing a white dress.

Her car was gone, too.

And even North Druid Hills Road was gone. There was a fence or a wall or something where it should have been.

And the city lights of Atlanta were also missing, replaced by a solitary row of antique gaslights. They spread their amber glow across the cobblestones of the narrow street in which Mary stood.

Alone.

Bert's footsteps clattered on the cobblestones.

She turned to face him.

He was dressed in what looked like a Sherlock Holmes costume, complete with elegant cape and a deerstalker hat. There was a small black bag in his right hand.

And a knife in his left.

Eight inches of glistening steel, curving slightly at the tip.

She stumbled back against the fence. "No!" she screamed. *"No! No!"*

The blade entered her like a lover. Its thrusts were slow and careful at first, but they built to a climactic frenzy, plunging deeper and deeper . . .

On the left-hand turntable of the broadcast booth of W-H-O-R, "Hands of Jack the Ripper" rolled to its finale precisely 9¼ minutes after it had started. The record continued to spin, and with each rotation the tip of the diamond needle fell back into the closed groove at the edge of the center paper. To virtually everyone listening, the station seemed to be broadcasting nothing but dead air; but to a scattered few who, puzzled by the sudden silence, turned their stereos up louder, there was a faint but rhythmic scraping in the speakers.

Scritch . . .

Scritch . . .

Scritch . . .

Scritch . . .

Scritch . . .

The sound continued, straight on till morning.

The Third Dead Body

Nina Kiriki Hoffman

I didn't even know Richie. I surely didn't want to love him. After he killed me, though, I found him irresistible.

I opened my eyes and dirt fell into them. Having things fall into my eyes was one of my secret terrors, but now I blinked and shook my head and most of the dirt fell away and I felt all right. So I knew something major had happened to me.

With my eyes closed, I shoved dirt away from my face. While I was doing this I realized that the inside of my mouth felt different. I probed with my tongue, my trained and talented tongue, and soon discovered that where smooth teeth had been before there were only broken stumps. What puzzled me about this and about the dirt in my eyes was that these things didn't hurt. They bothered me, but not on a pain level.

I frowned and tried to figure out what I was feeling. Not a lot. Not scared or mad, not hot or cold. This was different too. I usually felt scared, standing on street corners waiting for strangers to pick me up, and cold, working evenings in skimpy clothes that showed off my best features. Right now, I felt nothing.

I sat up, dirt falling away from me, and bumped into branches that gridded my view of the sky. Some of them slid off me. The branches were loose and wilting, not attached to a bush or tree. I lifted my hands to push them out of the way and noticed that the tips of my fingers were blackened beyond my natural cocoa color. I looked at them, trying to remember what had happened before I fell asleep or whatever—had I dipped my fingers in ink? But no; the

skin was scorched. My fingerprints were gone. They would have
told police that my name was Tawanda Foote, which was my street
name.

My teeth would have led police to call me Mary Jefferson, a
name I hadn't used since two years before, when I moved out of my
parents' house at fifteen.

In my own mind, I was Sheila, a power name I had given myself;
no one could have discovered that from any evidence about me.

No teeth, no fingerprints; Richie really didn't want anybody to
know who I was, not that anybody ever had.

Richie.

With my scorched fingers I tried to take my pulse, though it was
hard to find a vein among the rope burns at my wrists. With my
eyes I watched my own naked chest. There were charred spots on
my breasts where Richie had touched me with a burning cigarette.
No pulse, but maybe that was because the nerves in my fingertips
were dead. No breathing. No easy answer to that, so I chose the
hard answer:

Dead.

I was dead.

After I pushed aside the branches so I could see trees and sky, I
sat in my own grave dirt and thought about this.

My grannie would call this dirt goofer dust; any soil that's been
piled on a corpse, whether the body's in a box or just loose like me,
turns into goofer dust. Dirt next to dead folk gets a power in it, she
used to say.

She used to tell me all kinds of things. She told me about the
walking dead; but mostly she said they were just big scary dummies
who obeyed orders. When I stayed up too late at night reading
library books under my covers with a flashlight, she would say,
"Maybe you know somebody who could give those nightwalkers
orders. Maybe she can order 'em to come in here and turn off your
light."

She had started to train me in recognizing herbs and collecting
conjo ingredients, but that was before I told the preacher what
really happened when I sat in Grand-père's lap, and Grand-père got
in trouble with the church and then with other people in the Parish.

I had a lot of cousins, and some of the others started talking up about Grand-père, but I was the first. After the police took Grand-père away, Grannie laid a curse on me: "May you love the thing that hurts you, even after it kills you." She underlined it with virgin blood, the wax of black candles, and the three of spades.

I thought maybe if I left Louisiana I could get the curse off, but nobody I knew could uncross me and the curse followed me to Seattle.

In the midst of what was now goofer dust, I was sitting next to something. I reached out and touched it. It was another dead body. "Wake up," I said to the woman in the shallow grave beside me. But she refused to move.

So: no fingerprints, no teeth. I was dead, next to someone even deader, and off in some woods. I checked in with my body, an act I saved for special times when I could come out of the numb state I spent most of my life in, and found I wasn't hungry or thirsty. All the parts of me that had been hurting just before Richie, my last trick, took a final twist around my neck with the nylon cord he was so fond of, all those parts were quiet, not bothering me at all; but there was a burning desire in my crotch, and a pinprick of fire behind my eyes that whispered to me, "Get up and move. We know where to go."

I looked around. At my back the slope led upward toward a place where sun broke through trees. At my feet it led down into darker woods. To either side, more woods and bushes, plants Grannie had never named for me, foreign as another language.

I moved my legs, bringing them up out of the goofer dust. All of me was naked; dirt caught in my curly hair below. I pulled myself to my feet and something fell out of my money pit, as my pimp, Blake, liked to call my pussy. I looked down at what had fallen from me. It was a rock flaked and shaped into a blade about the size of a flat hand, and it glistened in the dulled sunlight, wet and dark with what had come from inside me, and maybe with some of his juices too.

The fire in my belly flared up, but it wasn't a feeling like pain; it felt like desire.

I put my hands to my neck and felt the deep grooves the rope

had left there. Heat blossomed in my head and in my heart. I
wanted to find the hands that had tightened the rope around my
neck, wrists, and ankles. I wanted to find the eyes that had watched
my skin sizzle under the kiss of the burning cigarette. I wanted to
find the mind that had decided to plunge a crude blade into me
like that. The compulsion set in along my bones, jetted into my
muscles like adrenaline. I straightened, looked around. I had to find
Richie. I knew which direction to look: something in my head was
teasing me, nudging me—a fire behind my eyes, urging me back to
the city.

I fought the urge and lifted more branches off the place where I
had lain. If I was going to get to Seattle from here, wherever here
was, I needed some clothes. I couldn't imagine anybody stopping to
pick me up with me looking the way I did. I knew Richie had
worked hard to get rid of all clues to who I was, but I thought
maybe my companion in the grave might not be so naked of
identity, so I brushed dirt off her, and found she was not alone.
There were two bodies in the dirt, with no sign of afterlife in them
except maggots, and no trace of clothes. One was darker than me,
with fewer marks on her but same rope burns around her neck.
The other one was very light, maybe white. She was really falling
apart. They looked like they must smell pretty bad, but I couldn't
smell them. I couldn't smell anything. I could see and hear, and my
muscles did what I told them, but I didn't feel much except the
gathering fire inside me that cried for Richie.

I brushed dirt back over the other women and moved the
branches to cover their resting place again.

Downslope the trees waited, making their own low-level night.
Upslope, open sun: a road, probably. I scrambled up toward the
light.

The heat in my head and heart and belly burned hotter, and I
churned up the hillside and stepped into the sun.

A two-lane highway lay before me, its yellow dotted center stripe
bright in the sun. Its edges tailed into the gravel I stood on.
Crushed snack bags and Coke and beer cans lay scattered in the
bushes beside the road; cellophane glinted. I crossed the road and
looked at the wooded hill on its far side, then down in the ditch.

No clothes. Not even a plastic bag big enough to make into a bikini bottom.

The heat inside me was like some big fat drunk who will not shut up, yelling for a beer. I started walking, knowing which direction would take me toward town without knowing how I knew.

After a while a car came from behind me. Behind was probably my best side; my microbraids hung down to hide the marks on my neck, and Richie hadn't done any cigarette graffiti on my back that I could remember. A lot of tricks had told me I had a nice ass and good legs; even my pimp had said it, and he never said anything nice unless he thought it was true or it would get him what he wanted. And he had everything he wanted from me.

I could hear the car slowing, but I was afraid to look back. I knew my mouth must look funny because of the missing teeth, and I wasn't sure what the rest of my face looked like. Since I couldn't feel pain, anything could have happened. I bent my head so the sun wasn't shining in my face.

"Miss? Oh, miss?" Either a woman's deep voice came from the car behind me, or a man's high one; it sounded like an older person. The engine idled low as the car pulled up beside me. It was a red Volkswagen Rabbit.

I crossed my arms over my chest, hiding the burn marks and tucking my rope-mark bracelets into the crooks of my elbows.

"Miss?"

"Ya?" I said, trying to make my voice friendly, not sure I had a voice at all.

"Miss, are you in trouble?"

I nodded, my braids slapping my shoulders and veiling my face.

"May I help you, miss?"

I cleared my throat, drew in breath. "Ya-you goin' do down?" I managed to say.

"What?"

"Down," I said, pointing along the road. "Seaddle."

"Oh. Yes. Would you like a ride?"

"Mm-hmm," I said. "Cloze?" I glanced up this time, wondering if the car's driver was man or woman. A man might shed his shirt

for me, but a woman, unless she was carrying a suitcase or something, might not have anything to offer.

"Oh, you poor thing, what happened to you?" The car pulled up
onto the shoulder ahead of me and the driver got out. It was a big
beefy white woman in jeans and a plaid flannel shirt. She came
toward me with a no-nonsense stride. She had short dark hair. She
was wearing a man's khaki cloth hat with fishing flies stuck in the
band, all different feathery colors. "What ha—"

I put one hand over my face, covering my mouth with my palm.

"What happened—" she whispered, stopping while there was
still a lot of space between us.

"My boyfriend dreeded me preddy bad," I said behind my hand.
My tongue kept trying to touch the backs of teeth no longer there.
It frustrated me that my speech was so messy. I thought maybe I
could talk more normally if I touched my tongue to the roof of my
mouth. "My boyfriend," I said again, then, "treated me pretty bad."

"Poor thing, poor thing," she whispered, then turned back to the
car and rummaged in a back seat, coming up with a short-waisted
Levi's jacket and holding it out to me.

I ducked my head and took the jacket. She gasped when I
dropped my arms from my chest. I wrapped up in the jacket, which
was roomy, but not long enough to cover my crotch. Then again,
from the outside, my crotch didn't look so bad. I turned the collar
up to cover my neck and the lower part of my face. "Thank you,"
I said.

Her eyes were wide, her broad face pale under her tan. "You
need help," she said. "Hospital? Police?"

"Seattle," I said.

"Medical attention!"

"Won't help me now." I shrugged.

"You could get infections, die from septicemia or something. I
have a first aid kit in the car. At least let me—"

"What would help me," I said, "a mirror."

She sighed, her shoulders lowering. She walked around the car
and opened the passenger side door, and I followed her. I looked at
the seat. It was so clean, and I was still goofer dusted. "Gonna get it
dirty," I said.

"Lord, that's the last thing on my mind right now," she said. "Get in. Mirror's on the back of the visor."

I slid in and folded down the visor, sighed with relief when I saw my face. Nothing really wrong with it, except my chin was nearer to my nose than it should be, and my lips looked too dark and puffy. My eyes weren't blackened and my nose wasn't broken. I could pass. I gapped the collar just a little and winced at the angry dark rope marks around my neck, then clutched the collar closed.

The woman climbed into the driver's seat. "My name's Marti," she said, holding out a hand. Still keeping the coat closed with my left hand, I extended my right, and she shook it.

"Sheila," I said. It was the first time I'd ever said it out loud. She. La. Two words for woman put together. I smiled, then glanced quickly at the mirror, and saw a smile that was as bad as I'd thought. My mouth was a graveyard of broken teeth, brown with old blood. I hid my mouth with my hand again.

"Christ!" said Marti. "What's your boyfriend's name?"

"Don't worry about it," I said.

"If he did that to you, he could do it to others. My daughter lives in Renton. This has to be reported to the police. Who is he? Where does he live?"

"Near Sea-Tac. The airport."

She took a deep breath, let it out. "You understand, don't you, this is a matter for the authorities?"

I shook my head. The heat in my chest was scorching, urging me on. "I have to go to town now," I said, gripping the door handle.

"Put your seat belt on," she said, slammed her door, and started the car.

Once she got started, she was some ball-of-fire driver. Scared me—even though there wasn't anything I could think of that could hurt me.

"Where were we, anyway?" I asked after I got used to her tire-squealing cornering on curves.

"Well, I was coming down from Kanaskat. I'm on my way in to Renton to see my daughter. She's got a belly-dance recital tonight, and—" She stared at me, then shook her head and focused on the road.

The land was leveling a little. We hit a main road, Highway 169, and she turned north on it.

The burning in my chest raged up into my throat. "No," I said, reaching for her hand on the steering wheel.

"What?"

"No. That way." I pointed back to the other road we had been on. Actually the urge inside me was pulling from some direction between the two roads, but the smaller road aimed closer to where I had to go.

"Maple Valley's this way," she said, not turning, "and we can talk to the police there, and a doctor."

"No," I said.

She looked at me. "You're in no state to make rational decisions," she said.

I closed my hand around her wrist and squeezed. She cried out. She let go of the steering wheel and tried to shake off my grip. I stared at her and held on, remembering my grand-mère's tales of the strength of the dead.

"Stop," I said. I felt strange, totally strange, ordering a woman around the way a pimp would. I knew I was hurting her, too. I knew I could squeeze harder, break the bones in her arm, and I was ready to, but she pulled the car over to the shoulder and stamped on the brake.

"I got to go to Sea-Tac," I said. I released her arm and climbed out of the car. "Thanks for ride. You want the jacket back?" I fingered the denim.

"My Lord," she said, "you keep it, child." She was rubbing her hand over the wrist I had gripped. She heaved a huge sigh. "Get in. I'll take you where you want to go. I can't just leave you here."

"Your daughter's show?" I said.

"I'll phone. We're going someplace with phones, aren't we?"

I wasn't sure exactly where we would end up. I would know when we arrived. . . . I remembered the inside of Richie's apartment. But that was later. First he had pulled up next to where I was standing by the highway, rolled down the passenger window of his big gold four-door Buick, said he'd like to party and that he knew a good place. Standard lines, except I usually told johns the place, down one of the side streets and in the driveway behind an abandoned house. I had asked him how high he was willing to go. My pimp had been offering me coke off and on but I'd managed not to get hooked, so I was still a little picky about who I went with; but Richie looked clean-cut and just plain clean, and his car was a couple years old but expensive; I thought he might have money.

"I want it all," Richie had said. "I'll give you a hundred bucks." I climbed into his car.

He took me down off the ridge where the Sea-Tac Strip is to a place like the one where I usually took my tricks, behind one of the abandoned houses near the airport that are due to be razed someday. There's two or three neighborhoods of them handy. I asked him for money and he handed me a hundred, so I got in back with him, but then things went seriously wrong. That was the first time I saw and felt his rope, the first time I heard his voice cursing me, the first time I tasted one of his sweaty socks; not the worst thing I'd ever tasted, but close.

When he had me gagged and tied up and shoved down on the back seat floor, he drove somewhere else. I couldn't tell how long the drive was; it felt like two hours but was probably only fifteen or twenty minutes. I could tell when the car drove into a parking garage because the sounds changed. He put a shopping bag over my head and carried me into an elevator, again something I could tell by feel, and then along a hall to his apartment. That was where I learned more about him than I had ever wanted to know about anybody.

I didn't know his apartment's address, but I knew where Richie was. If he was at the apartment, I would direct Marti there even without a map. The fire inside me reached for Richie like a magnet lusting for a hammer.

Shaping words carefully, I told Marti, "Going to the Strip. Plenty of phones."

"Right," she said.

"On the other road." I pointed behind us.

She sighed. "Get in."

I climbed into the car, and she waited for an RV to pass, then pulled out and turned around.

As soon as we were heading the way I wanted to go, the fire inside me cooled a little. I sat back and relaxed.

"Why are we going to the—to the Strip?" she asked. "What are you going to do when we get there?"

"Don't know," I said. We were driving toward the sun, which was going down. Glare had bothered me before my death, but now it was like dirt in my eyes, a minor annoyance. I blinked and considered this, then shrugged it off.

"Can't you even tell me your boyfriend's name?" she asked.

"Richie."

"Richie what?"

"Don't know."

"Are you going back to him?"

Fire rose in my throat like vomit. I felt like I could breathe it out and it would feel good. It felt good inside my belly already. I was drunk with it. "Oh, yes," I said.

"How can you?" she cried. She shook her head. "I can't take you back to someone who hurt you so much." But she didn't stop driving.

"I have to go back," I said.

"You don't. You can choose something else. There are shelters for battered women. The government should offer you some protection. The police. . . ."

"You don't understand," I said.

"I do," she said. Her voice got quieter. "I know what it's like to live with someone who doesn't respect you. I know how hard it is to get away. But you *are* away, Sheila. You can start over."

"No," I said, "I can't."

"You can. I'll help you. You can live in Kanaskat with me and he'll never find you. Or if you just want a bus ticket someplace—back home, wherever that is—I can do that for you, too."

"You don't understand," I said.

She was quiet for a long stretch of road. Then she said, "Help me understand."

I shook my braids back and opened the collar of the jacket, pulled down the lapels to bare my neck. I stared at her until she looked back.

She screamed and drove across the center lane. Fortunately there was no other traffic. Still screaming, she fought with the steering wheel until she straightened out the car. Then she pulled over to the shoulder and jumped out of the car, running away.

I shut off the car's engine, then climbed out. "Marti," I yelled. "Okay, I'm walking away now. The car's all yours. I'm leaving. It's safe. Thanks for the jacket. Bye." I buttoned up the jacket, put the collar up, buried my hands in the pockets, and started walking along the road toward Richie.

I had gone about a quarter mile when she caught up with me again. The sun had set and twilight was deepening into night. Six cars had passed going my way, but I didn't hold out my thumb, and though some kid had yelled out a window at me, and somebody else had honked and swerved, nobody stopped.

It had been so easy to hitch before I met Richie. Somehow now I just couldn't do it.

I heard the Rabbit's sputter behind me and kept walking, not turning to look at her. But she slowed and kept pace with me. "Sheila?" she said in a hoarse voice. "Sheila?"

I stopped and looked toward her. I knew she was scared of me. I felt strong and strange, hearing her call me by a name I had given myself, as if I might once have had a chance to make up who I was instead of being shaped by what had happened to me. I couldn't see it being possible now, though, when I was only alive to do what the fire in me wanted.

Marti blinked, turned away, then turned back and faced me. "Get in," she said.

"You don't have to take me," I said. "I'll get there sooner or later. Doesn't matter when."

"Get in."

I got back into her car.

For half an hour we drove in silence. She crossed Interstate 5, paused when we hit 99, the Strip. "Which way?"

I pointed right. The fire was so hot in me now I felt like my fingertips might start smoking any second.

She turned the car and we cruised north toward the Sea-Tac Airport, my old stomping grounds. We passed expensive hotels and cheap motels, convenience stores, and fancy restaurants. Lighted buildings alternated with dark gaps. The roar of planes taking off and landing, lights rising and descending in the sky ahead of us, turned rapidly into background. We drove past the Goldilocks Motel, where Blake and I had a room we rented by the week, and I didn't feel anything. But as we passed the intersection where the Red Lion sprawls on the corner of 188th Street and the Pacific Highway, fire flared under my skin. "Slowly," I said to Marti. She stared at me and slowed the car. A mile further, past the airport, one of the little roads led down off the ridge to the left. I pointed.

Marti got in the left-turn lane and made the turn, then pulled into a gas station on the corner and parked by the rest rooms. "Now, wait," she said. "What are we doing, here?"

"Richie," I whispered. I could feel his presence in the near distance; all my wounds were resonating with his nearness now, all the places he had pressed himself into me with his rope and his cigarette and his sock and his flaked stone knife and his penis, imprinting me as his possession. Surely as a knife slicing into a tree's bark, he had branded me with his heart.

"Yes," said Marti. "Richie. You have any plans for what you're going to do once you find him?"

I held my hands out, open, palms up. The heat was so strong I felt like anything I touched would burst into flame.

"What are you going to do, strangle him? Have you got something to do it with?" She sounded sarcastic.

I was having a hard time listening to her. All my attention was focused down the road. I knew Richie's car was there, and Richie in it. It was the place he had taken me to tie me up. He might be driving this way any second, and I didn't want to wait any longer for our reunion, though I knew there was no place he could hide where I couldn't find him. My love for him was what animated me now.

"Strangle," I said, and shook my head. I climbed out of the car.

"Sheila!" said Marti.

I let the sound of my self-given name fill me with what power it could, and stood still for a moment, fighting the fire inside. Then I walked into the street, stood in the center so a car coming up out of the dark would have to stop. I strode down into darkness, away from the lights and noise of the Strip. My feet felt like match-heads, as if a scrape could strike fire from them.

Presently the asphalt gave way to potholes and gravel; I could tell by the sound of pebbles sliding under my feet. I walked past the first three dark houses to the right and left, looming shapes in a darkness pierced by the flight lights of airplanes, but without stars. I turned left at the fourth house, dark like the others, but with a glow behind it I couldn't see with my eyes but could feel in my bones. Heat pulsed and danced inside me.

I pushed past an overgrown lilac bush at the side of the house and stepped into the broad drive in back. The car was there, as I had known it would be. Dark and quiet. Its doors were closed.

I heard a brief cry, and then the dome light went on in the car. Richie was sitting up in back, facing away from me.

Richie.

I walked across the crunching gravel, looking at his dark head. He wore a white shirt. He was staring down, focused, his arms moving. As I neared the car, I could see he was sitting on a woman. She still had her clothes on. (Richie hadn't taken my clothes off until he got me in his apartment.) Tape was across her mouth, and her head thrashed from side to side, her upper arms jerking as Richie bound his thin nylon rope around her wrists, her legs kicking. I stood a moment looking in the window. She saw me and her eyes widened. She made a gurgling swallowed sound behind the sock, the tape.

I thought: he doesn't need her. He has me.

I remembered the way my mind had struggled while my body struggled, screaming silently: no, oh no, Blake, where are you? No one will help me, the way no one has ever helped me, and I can't help myself. That hurts, that hurts. Maybe he'll play with me and let me go if I'm very, very good. Oh, God! What do you want? Just tell me, I can do it. You don't have to hurt me! Okay, rip me off, it's not like you're the first, but you don't have to hurt me!

Hurt me.

I love you. I love you so much.

I stared at him through the glass. The woman beneath him had stilled, and she was staring at me. Richie finally noticed, and whirled.

For a moment we stared at each other. Then I smiled, showing him the stumps of my teeth, and his blue eyes widened.

I reached for the door handle, opened it before he could lock it. "Richie," I said.

"Don't!" he said. He shook his head, hard, as though he were a dog with wet fur. Slowly, he lifted one hand and rubbed his eye. He had a big bread knife in the other hand, had used it to cut the rope, then flicked it across the woman's cheek, leaving a streak of darkness. He looked at me again. His jaw worked.

"Richie."

"Don't! Don't . . . interrupt."

I held out my arms, my fingertips scorched black as if dyed or tattooed, made special, the wrists dark beyond the ends of my sleeves. "Richie," I said tenderly, the fire in me rising up like a firework, a burst of stars. "I'm yours."

"No," he said.

"You made me yours." I looked at him. He had made Tawanda his, and then he had erased her. He had made Mary his, and then erased her. Even though he had erased Tawanda and Mary, these feelings inside me were Tawanda's: *whoever hurts me controls me;* and Mary's: *I spoke up once and I got a curse on me I can't get rid of. If I'm quiet maybe I'll be okay.*

But Sheila? Richie hadn't erased Sheila; he had never even met her.

It was Tawanda who was talking. "You killed me and you made me yours," she said. My fingers went to the jacket, unbuttoned it, dropped it behind me. "What I am I owe to you."

"I—" he said, and coughed. "No," he said.

I heard the purr of car engines in the near distance, not the constant traffic of the Strip, but something closer.

I reached into the car and gripped Richie's arm. I pulled him out, even though he grabbed at the door handle with his free hand. I could feel the bone in his upper arm as my fingers pressed his muscles. "Richie," I whispered, and put my arms around him and laid my head on his shoulder.

For a while he was stiff, tense in my embrace. Then a shudder went through him and he loosened up. His arms came around me. "You're mine?" he said.

"Yours," said Tawanda.

"Does that mean you'll do what I say?" His voice sounded like a little boy's.

"Whatever you say," she said.

"Put your arms down," he said.

I lowered my arms.

"Stand real still." He backed away from me, then stood and studied me. He walked around, looking at me from all sides. "Wait a sec, I gotta get my flashlight." He went around to the trunk and opened it, pulled out a flashlight as long as his forearm, turned it on. He trained the beam on my breasts, my neck. "I did you," he said, nodding. "I did you. You were good. Almost as good as the first one. Show me your hands again."

I held them out and he stared at my blackened fingers. Slowly he smiled, then looked up and met my eyes.

"I was going to visit you," he said. "When I finished with this one. I was coming back to see you."

"I couldn't wait," said Tawanda.

"Don't talk," Richie said gently.

Don't talk! Tawanda and Mary accepted that without a problem, but I, Sheila, was tired of people telling me not to talk. What did I have to lose?

On the other hand, what did I have to say? I didn't even know what I wanted. Tawanda's love for Richie was hard to fight. It was the burning inside me, the sizzling under my skin, all I had left of life.

"Will you scream if I say so?" said Richie in his little boy's voice.

"Yes," said Tawanda; but suddenly lights went on around us, and bullhorn voices came out of the dark.

"Hold it right there, buddy! Put your hands up!"

Blinking in the sudden flood of light, Richie slowly lifted his hand, the knife glinting in the left one, the flashlight in the other.

"Step away from him, miss," said someone else. I looked around too, not blinking; glare didn't bother me. I couldn't see through it, though. I didn't know who was talking. "Miss, move away from him," said another voice from outside the light.

"Come here," Richie whispered, and I went to him. Releasing the flashlight, he dropped his arms around me, holding the knife to my neck, and yelled, "Stay back!"

"Sheila!" It was Marti's voice this time, not amplified.

I looked toward her.

"Sheila, get away from him!" Marti yelled. "Do you want him to escape?"

Tawanda did. Mary did. They, after all, had found the place where they belonged. In the circle of his arms, my body glowed, the fire banked but burning steady.

He put the blade closer to my twisted throat. I could almost feel it. I laid my head back on his shoulder, looking at his profile out of the corner of my eye. The light glare brought out the blue in his eye. His mouth was slightly open, the inside of his lower lip glistening. He turned to look down into my face, and a slight smile curved the corner of his mouth. "Okay," he whispered, "we're going to get into the car now." He raised his voice. "Do what I say and don't struggle." Keeping me between him and the lights, he kicked the back door closed and edged us around the car to the driver's side. Moving in tandem, with his arm still around my neck, we slid in behind the wheel, me going first. "Keep close," he said to me. "Slide down a little so I can use my arm to shift with, but keep close."

"Sheila!" screamed Marti. The driver's side window was open.

Richie started the car.

"Sheila! There's a live woman in the back of that car!"

Tawanda didn't care, and Mary didn't care, and I wasn't even sure I cared. Richie shifted from park into first and eased his foot off the brake and onto the gas pedal; I could feel his legs moving against my left shoulder. From the back seat I heard a muffled groan. I looked up at Richie's face. He was smiling.

Just as he gunned the engine, I reached up and grappled the steering-wheel-mounted gear shift into park. Then I broke the shift handle off.

"You said you'd obey me," he said, staring down into my face.

He looked betrayed, his eyes wide, his brow furrowed, his mouth soft. The car's engine continued to snarl without effect.

Fire blossomed inside me, hurting me this time because I'd hurt him. Pain came alive. I coughed, choking on my own tongue, my throat swollen and burning, my wrists and ankles burning, my breasts burning, between my legs a column of flame raging up inside me. I tried to apologize, but I no longer had a voice.

"You promised," said Richie in his little boy's voice, looking down at me.

I coughed. I could feel the power leaving me; my arms and legs were stiffening the way a body is supposed to do after death. I lifted my crippling hands as high as I could, palms up, pleading, but by that point only my elbows could bend. It was Tawanda's last gesture.

"Don't make a move," said a voice. "Keep your hands on the wheel."

We looked. A man stood just outside the car, aiming a gun at Richie through the open window.

Richie edged a hand down the wheel toward me.

"Make a move for her and I'll shoot," said the man. Someone else came up beside him, and he moved back, keeping his gun aimed at Richie's head, while the other man leaned in and put handcuffs on Richie.

"That's it," said the first man, and he and the second man heaved huge sighs.

I lay curled on the seat, my arms bent at the elbows, my legs bent at the knees. When they pulled Richie out of the car I slipped off his lap and lay stiff, my neck bent at an angle so my head stuck up sideways. "This woman needs medical attention," someone yelled. I listened to them freeing the woman in the back seat, and thought about the death of Tawanda and Mary.

Tawanda had lifted me out of my grave and carried me for miles. Mary had probably mostly died when Grannie cursed me and drove me out of the house. But Sheila? In a way, I had been pregnant with Sheila for years, and she was born in the grave. She was still looking out of my eyes and listening with my ears even though the rest of me was dead. Even as the pain of death faded, leaving me with clear memories of how Richie had treated me before he took that final twist around my neck, the Sheila in me was awake and feeling things.

"She's in an advanced state of rigor," someone said. I felt a dim pressure around one of my arms. My body slid along the seat toward the door.

"Wait," said someone else. "I got to take pictures."

"What are you talking about?" said another. "Ten minutes ago she was walking and talking."

Lights flashed, but I didn't blink.

"Are you crazy?" said the first person. "Even rapid-onset rigor doesn't come on this fast."

"Ask anybody, Tony. We all saw her."

"You try feeling for a pulse. Are you sure he wasn't just propping her up and moving her around like a puppet? But that wouldn't explain . . ."

"You done with the pictures yet, Crane?" said one of the cops. Then, to me, in a light voice, "Honey, come on out of there. Don't just lie there and let him photograph you like a corpse. You don't know what he does with the pictures."

"Wait till the civilians are out of here before you start making jokes," said someone else. "Maybe she's just in shock."

"Sheila?" said Marti from the passenger side.

"Marti," I whispered.

Gasps.

"Sheila, you did it. You did it."

Did what? Let him kill me, then kill me again? Suddenly I was so angry I couldn't rest. Anger was like the fire that had filled me before, only a lower, slower heat. I shuddered and sat up.

Another gasp from one of the men at the driver's side door. "See?" said the one with the shock theory. One of them had a flashlight and shone it on me. I lifted my chin and stared at him, my microbraids brushing my shoulders.

"Kee-rist!"

"Oh, God!"

They fell back a step.

I sucked breath in past the swelling in my throat and said, "I need a ride. And feeling for a pulse? I think you'll be happier if you don't."

Marti gave me back her jacket. I rode in her Rabbit; the cop cars and the van from the medical examiner's office tailed us. Marti had a better idea of where she had found me than I did.

"What's your full name?" she said when we were driving. "Is there anybody I can get in touch with for you?"

"No. I've been dead to them for a couple years already."

"Are you sure? Did you ever call to check with them?"

I waited for a while, then said, "If your daughter was a hooker and dead, would you want to know?"

"Yes," she said immediately. "Real information is much better than not knowing."

I kept silent for another while, then told her my parents' names and phone number. Ultimately, I didn't care if the information upset them or not.

She handed me a little notebook and asked me to write it down, turning on the dome light so I could see what I was doing. The pain of scorching had left my fingers again. Holding the pen was awkward, but I managed to write out what Marti wanted. When I finished, I slipped the notebook back into her purse and turned off the light.

"It was somewhere along here," she said half an hour later. "You have any feeling for it?"

"No." I didn't have a sense of my grave the way I had had a feeling for Richie. Marti's headlights flashed on three Coke cans lying together by the road, though, and I remembered seeing a cluster like that soon after I had climbed up the slope. "Here," I said.

She pulled over, and so did the three cars following us. Someone gave me a flashlight and I went to the edge of the slope and walked along, looking for my own footprints or anything else familiar. A broken bramble, a crushed fern, a tree with a hooked branch—I remembered them all from the afternoon. "Here," I said, pointing down the mountainside.

"Okay. Don't disturb anything," said the cop named Joe. One of the others started stringing up yellow tape along the road in both directions.

"But—" I was having a feeling now, a feeling that Sheila had lived as long as she wanted to. All I needed was my blanket of goofer dust, and I could go back to sleep. When Joe went back to his car to get something, I slipped over the edge and headed home.

I pushed the branches off the other two women and lay down beside their bodies, thinking about my brief life. I had helped somebody and I had hurt somebody, which I figured was as much as I'd done in my first two lives.

I pulled dirt up over me, even over my face, not blinking when it fell into my eyes; but then I thought, Marti's going to see me sooner or later, and she'd probably like it better if my eyes were closed. So I closed my eyes.

The Troll

Ray Bradbury

Once upon a time, when wishing *wasn't* having, there was an old man who lived under a bridge. He lived there for as long as people remembered.

"I'm a troll," he said.

When people passed on the bridge above he cried out, "Who goes there?"

When they told him, he would demand, "Where going?"

And when they had outlined their destination, he would say, "Are you a good, kind person?"

And when they said, "Oh, yes," he would let them pass.

He got to be quite a character with the people up in the village who said, "Go visit the troll. Don't be afraid. His bark is worse than his bite. He's much fun when you get to know him."

On summer days the children would hang over the stone rim of the bridge and call down into the cool spaces, "Troll, troll, troll." And the echoes would blow up cool and clear, "Troll, troll, troll. . . ." And then they saw his reflection in the slow running water, a wry, old face with a twisty green beard woven of moss and fresh reeds, it seemed, with green moss eyebrows and pointed wax-white ears. His fingers were horny and clawed and his naked body was clothed with reeds and green grass and verdigris, wet and gleaming.

And his reflection in the water would call back up to them. "What do you want?"

"Some crayfish, troll."

"Some snails, troll."

"Some tadpoles, troll."

"Some bright stones, troll."

And if they went away a while and didn't look, when they came back they would find some delicate, scuttling crayfish placed upon the bridge rail, along with some slow snails, a few wriggling tadpoles, and some bright pink and blue-white stones from the deepest part of the creek.

"Oh, thank you, troll."

"Thank you, thank you, thank you, troll," the child voices would call into the green coolness, into the water shadows.

Drip, drip went the water. No answer. The water slid under the bridge in the summertime, and the children went on their way.

But one summer day, as the troll was basking at his ease beneath the bridge, listening to the water purl between his soaking hooves, his eyes shut and at rest, he heard a great horning and tooting and something banged over the bridge above.

"One of those idiots with his new car," murmured the troll. "Damn fool, when he could be down here, in the water shadows all summer, watching the light on the stream, feeling it slide by with your hand or your hoof. Such rushing fools up there in that hot world!"

Not a minute later he heard two people pass on the bridge. By the tread of their shoes he knew it to be two men, and one of them was saying, "Did you see that red Jaguar? Boy, was he traveling!"

"Know who that was? Our fruitcake psychiatrist! You see his new office, most modern building downtown? He's come to get us nuts off the tree, cure our neuroses, put us back on the tree, or so he said on TV last night."

"Well, well," said the other. "He sure advertises! That car's a fire engine!"

"Believes in expression, no frustrations, so he said, loud and clear."

The voices passed.

The troll, listening idly, eyes shut, was only faintly stirred by the conversation. There was a nice long summer ahead, here in this midwestern town, and then when winter froze the stream to milk-glass, he would float south leisurely, like a clump of moss and reed, easing down toward the sea, to spend a few months in a creek under a bridge in the spring. It was not a bad life at all, one had one's perambulating stations, people respected you, and on occasion (here he licked his lips) you met up with a scoundrel, a thief, some perpetual criminal, and the world thanked you for services offered and services rendered. He thought of himself as a sieve hunkered here to strain the light and dark civilizations that passed above. He could guess the pace of murdering thieves forty paces away. None of them would last through an idling and suddenly violent summer.

This train of thought sat him up, musing. "Why," he wondered, "hasn't there been a really bad one through all June or July? Here it's getting almost August and I've had to make do on mini-frogs and crayfish. A frugal lunch, no dinner at all. Where, oh where is the dark flesh and rancid blood of a true, far-traveling villain?"

Hardly had he finished this half-prayer then he heard a sound of voices far off, and quick footsteps, a very defiant series of footsteps, hurrying down the road.

"I wouldn't go near there, if I were you," warned a woman's voice.

"Bosh!" a man said. "I'll find this so-called troll myself. I don't need your help."

"So-called troll?" The troll stiffened. He waited.

A moment later, a head popped over the rim of the bridge. A pair of beady black licorice eyes stared wildly down.

"Troll!" yelled the strange man. "You *there!?*"

Troll almost plunged into the water. He lurched back into the cool shadows.

"Is *that* what they call you, the damn-fool villagers here?" the stranger above wondered. "Or did you make the name up so you could blackmail pedestrians and grab their cash?"

Troll was so stunned, his mouth froze.

"Come on, speak up, come out, the game's up, cut the comedy!" shouted the stranger.

At last, Troll inched over and glared up at the loud man suspended in the noon glare.

"And who," muttered Troll, "are you?"

"I'm Dr. Crowley. Psychiatrist. Eminent. That's who," snapped the loud man, his face crimson from hanging upside down. "And since this is a very undignified posture, why don't you come up in the sunlight? Let's talk man to man."

"I have nothing to discuss with you, Dr. Crowley." The troll subsided against the bank below.

"Then, at least," barked the psychiatrist, "give me your name!"

"Troll."

The doctor snapped his fingers. "Come, come! Don't be ridiculous! Your *real* name!"

"Well, *Summer Bridge* Troll . . . or Green Moss Summer Bridge Troll, should you want the whole thing."

"When did this first come over you?" asked the irritable doctor.

"What?"

"To sit under *bridges*. When you were a child?"

"I've *always* sat under bridges."

"I see." The face vanished. Above, a pen scratched. A voice murmured, "*Always* sat under bridges. So." The face reappeared, perspiring. "Did you run away from home often, away from siblings?"

"Siblings!?" cried the troll, confused, "what in hell's that? I never *had* a home."

"Ah." The face vanished again. The voice murmured, the pen scraped. "Orphan. Psychologically dispossessed." Like a stringless puppet the doctor thrust himself down. "What would you say attracted you *most* about bridges. The shadows, the secrecy, eh? The stashed-away element, yes? Right?"

"No," said the troll, irritably, "I simply like it here."

"Like!" cried the psychiatrist. "There's no such thing as 'like.' Every thing has *roots!* You are probably suffering from a back-to-the-womb complex. Societal withdrawal. Paranoia. Leader complex. Yes, that's *it!* You hide down here and holler up at anyone who passes. Oh, I know about you. That's one reason why I came. I traveled a long way to investigate you and the people of this village with their superstitions. But especially *you!*"

"Me?"

"Yes, the word spread there was a troll in residence who asks each fool crossing, 'are you passing good or loping evil?' "

"What's wrong with that?" demanded Troll.

"My dear fellow, everyone knows there is no dichotomy of bad and good. It's all relative."

"Sorry," said Troll, "I don't see it that way."

"Did you ever consider environment as a factor when you asked people if they were good or evil?"

Troll snorted peevishly.

"Or heredity. Do you research the genetics of the people you supposedly eat? You *do* eat people?"

"I do."

"Tut! You only *think* you do. That's an extension of your preoccupation with curing people of their so-called sins. You imagine that by snacking on them you can digest their crimes. What you do, however, is convince yourself that each time a local thief vanishes, you have dined off his bones."

"*Haven't* I?"

"No comment. Now, how long have you lurked down there?"

"One hundred years."

"Poppycock. You're seventy at most. When were you born?"

"I was never born. I just grew. Some reeds, some crayfish, snails, grass, lots of moss, fermented, coagulated, here in the rock's shade a century back, and here I was."

"Highly fanciful but hardly of any help to me," the psychiatrist declared.

"Who asked you to come here?"

"Well, truthfully, I came on my own. You lured me as a neurotic manifestation within a culture."

"You mean to hang up there and tell me I haven't done a good job, doc?!" Troll shouted so the echoes roared. "You came to make me doubt my work, make me unhappy, yes?!"

"No, no, I came simply to help you to arise and flourish, so you can live in this world and be happy."

"I *am* happy! I *am* content. Go!"

"You only think you are. I'll come to interview you each day until we solve your problem."

"The problem is yours." Troll quivered. His hooves flinted the rocks. "A year ago, doctor, a very bad man, a man who shot and robbed people, crossed the bridge. I said, are you good or evil, and thinking I wouldn't guess he told the truth, he laughingly said, evil. An instant later the bridge was empty as I sat down to dine. Now, do you mean to tell me I erred in flaying and deboning that man?"

"What, without researching his life, to scan his love-starved youth, his starved ego, his need for love, for comfort and help?"

"I loved him immensely. I helped myself to *him*. What if I told you I've breakfasted on ten hundred such men in my lifetime, doctor?" asked the troll.

"I'd say you were an obsessional liar."

"What if I proved it?"

"Then? You'd be a murderer."

"Good or evil?"

"What?"

"A good or an evil murderer, Dr. Crowley?"

The doctor's face dripped sweat. "It's awfully hot up here in the sun."

"Your cheeks *are* red. How old are you, Crowley? Look like a heart case. Better not hang there too long with your scratch-pad. Answer my question. Am I a good or evil killer?"

"Neither! Yours was a lonely childhood. Obviously, you re-treated here years ago, to set yourself up as the town's moral ty-rant."

"Did the town complain?"

Silence.

"*Did* it?"

"No."

"They're satisfied to have me here, yes?"

"That's not the question."

"*They're* satisfied. They didn't send for you."

"You need me," said Dr. Crowley.

"Yes, I guess I do," said the troll at last.

"You *admit* it?"

"I do."

"You'll take my treatments?"

"Yes." The troll lay back in the shadows.

The doctor's face perspired in excess as his face blushed. "Glorious! Oh, but, god, it's hot!"

His spectacles blazed with sunlight.

"Fool," whispered the troll. "Why do you think I stay here? It's icehouse cool on the hottest day. Come down."

The psychiatrist hesitated.

"I believe I will," he said, finally. "Just for a moment."

His feet slid over the edge of the bridge.

In the late afternoon, three children passed above.

"Troll, troll," they called.

"Troll, troll," they sang.

"Troll, troll, troll."

"Give us a stone, give us a shell, give us a frog. Troll, troll, give us a gift, give us a nice gift, troll."

They walked off and then turned back.

And there, dripping in the little pool of cool water on the stone rim of the bridge, lay a shell, a tadpole, a fountain pen, a pad, and a pair of bright silver-rimmed spectacles.

The stream went under the bridge silently. And as they bent to call "Troll, troll!" they saw something that resembled a lazy, cool mass of green reed and green grass and green moss float slowly and slowly south and south in the tide, even as the skies clouded and birds circled and the first smell of autumn touched the air.

Brazo de Dios

Elizabeth Massie

The walls were dry, and the floor wet. There was a drain hole in the middle of the small room. Puddles of water stood in low places on the concrete. The concrete was coarse, laced with chunks of oyster and clam shells. Sand in the concrete sparkled in the dull light of the string of bulbs above Catherine's head. It had taken her more than an hour to find out this much about the cell. It had taken her that long to loosen her bruised arms from about her face to look around.

The welt on the side of her head rocked a terrible rhythm, driven on by the screams in the cells beyond her own. The blood on her wound had dried. She could smell her own sharp sweat. Her stomach cramped, bloated with fear.

This is a washing room, she thought. *A washing cell. They wash away signs of their crimes.*

Catherine put her fist to her mouth. A wave of anguish and pain took her and spun her violently. Tears cut her eyes.

God, help me.

She drew up against a dry wall. Her body shook.

A spider on the ceiling found a burned-out bulb between the bright ones, and began its determined web-making. Ceiling to floor, floor to ceiling, touching the wet concrete surface just barely before climbing up again.

Be rational, she forced herself to think. *Take it rationally. You're alive. You still have your clothes. Appeal to the law. You know the law.*

She had been taken in a jeep, in the very early morning. Quietly hanging out the mission linens alone, Catherine had watched the orange spot of the sun as it pushed itself into the sky. Dogs had growled at the groan of the engine but Catherine had thought nothing of it. When it stopped beside the mission garden, she had turned, too late. There were dark men with rifles. In their swift movement, she could not register faces, only shadows. Then a rifle came down on the side of her head and shattered the morning.

The law requires me to see a judge, she thought. *I've not been charged.* She looked at the spider, intent on its instinctive task. She remembered the grinning face of the captain of the fuerza as he had watched her in the village and near the mission. An ugly old man, he had winked at her and licked his lips. A sob caught Catherine's throat. "No," she whispered. "There is law to be followed here."

But they disdain the law. Remember dear Pablo. Holy Christ, remember Maria. The captain had taken notice of Maria as well.

Catherine dropped her aching head into her knees and gave her prayers and her consciousness to God. The peasants saw blessed visions, and heard miracles of holy voices. Catherine prayed for one. Nothing came but sleep. It was filled with fever.

Someone awakened her with a gentle shaking of the shoulder. She blinked, then shuddered. She pressed the heel of her hand to her temple to catch the pain, and looked up. The man above her wore black, similar to the garb of the mission's priest. She did not know this man. He nodded to her.

"You are all right?" he asked.

Catherine looked beyond him. The spider had made quite a web. To be a spider now. To be mindless and overlooked by men. This man in black would take her to the captain. God help her.

There was no saliva in her mouth. Her words were strained through cactus thorns. "What time is it, señor?" she asked. She squinted; the throbbing of her eyes made it difficult to focus.

"It is morning, sister."

"What time is it?"

"I do not wear a watch. I do not know."

Screams from nearby cells made the backs of Catherine's arms go cold. "I hear the others," she said. "Campesinos, aren't they? The Fuerza de Seguridad Publica has taken me."

"The security force has brought you here, yes," said the man. "No harm intended to you, sister. They let me come to talk with you, to help you not be afraid. The campesinos, the peasants you hear, are criminals. You need not worry for them."

"The captain has asked for my arrest?"

"The captain? I don't know what you mean."

A woman, not far away, separated only by the walls, cried, "Jesus!" Her voice spiraled upward, an animal shriek.

"What crime is that woman guilty of?" Catherine whispered.

"Campesinos want what is not theirs. You work with them, you know they are often greedy beyond their station." The man smiled and patted Catherine's arm. His hand was soft and the nails of his fingers trimmed and clean. Padre Felipe, back at the mission, had broken nails and dark grooves in the skin of his hands. Padre Felipe's hands were beautiful and worn.

Catherine swallowed but the motion was worthless. Thirst made her cough. "Señor," she said. "I know the laws of this country. I'm an American but I've chosen this place in which to serve my God and brothers. I learned a lot before I came, and have learned a lot since being here."

The man smiled, nodding his head. His teeth were fine and even.

"The law says I must be brought before a judge before twenty-four hours are up."

"I understand what you say," said the man. "I, too, know the law. We are good people, with good laws. Do not be afraid. Trust me. The policía have their job. It is a difficult one, you can imagine."

"Have I been here twenty-four hours?"

The man stood, still smiling, and opened the door. "I tell you I do not wear a watch. But what is time to the faithful? Rest, sister. I will come visit again."

Catherine tried to count her breaths to steady them. It did not work. "The captain . . ." she murmured.

"I do not know what you mean," said the man.

He went outside. The door closed behind him.

Catherine rose onto her knees and prayed the prayer of her mission.

"Father, still the hand of the tormentor. Open the hearts of the oppressor. Bring understanding and peace to those in danger."

A child from another cell, a boy or girl, she could not tell, cried out in exquisite pain. "Yatagan, no, no!" Catherine spun about on her knees and threw her face against the door. "God stop them, don't let the torturing go on." Her teeth ground against each other. "Please," she said. "Don't let them torture me."

It was a number of hours before anyone came again to her cell. The activity beyond her room quieted, and although the bulbs above her head burned in unflickering yellowed constancy, and the shadows were the same as when she had arrived, not one traveling across from corner to corner as would happen in a windowed room, Catherine guessed it to be a meal time. Even the fuerza would stop to eat.

The door rattled and unlocked, and the man in black entered, carrying a scratched aluminum tray with food. He set the tray before Catherine on the floor. His eyebrows jumped as if in apology for the lack of a proper table.

"You are feeling better?" he asked as he took a paper napkin from the top of a bowl of rice and corn. A small loaf of bread lay beside the bowl along with a mug of coffee.

Catherine's head pounded, but she did not say so.

"May we talk, then?"

Catherine looked at the bread and wished the man would leave her alone so she could perform the Lord's supper. "This is my body, broken for you . . ."

"May we talk?"

Catherine said, "Yes." She took the coffee and sipped tentatively.

"You come from America. What state is that?"

"Kentucky."

"What is Kentucky like?"

"Hills. Mountains. Trees."

"Like our country in some ways?"

"In some ways."

"You have problems in your state in America?"

"Of course."

"Campesinos, wanting land that does not belong to them? Building huts where they should not be, ignoring the capataz who tells them to leave?"

"No, not like that. Every place has problems. We have poverty, yes. But our problems are different in other ways. Ours are not the same as the ones here."

"Why do you not stay in Kentucky and stop the problems there? Why do you feel you need to come here?"

Catherine hesitated. Her bowels were full and she shifted uncomfortably. She wiped at the salty grit in the corner of her eyes. She put the cup of coffee back onto the tray. She knew the answer. How would it sound, out on the air of this cell of terror? "The church sent me."

"But why? Why does the church send you? It seems presumptuous to me. Can you see why?"

"Missions take us beyond our own backyard. We are to take the Word into the world."

"Most of our people are Christians. They have the Word."

"They're suffering," said Catherine. She winced at the pain in her head, and at what she had said. People the world over suffered. People in her own Kentucky suffered. There was no right answer here. It was a labyrinth. What would Padre Felipe do? Would he remain silent?

"Hmmmmm," said the man. "And you would do what you could to reduce suffering?"

Catherine said, "Yes."

"Anything you could?"

Catherine looked the man in the eyes. They were black eyes, possibly kind eyes, possibly cruel eyes. She could not tell. He was here, he knew the security force and believed them to be right, therefore the eyes must disguise cruelty. But he had not abused her, he had not been the one who had arrested her, he had not beaten her or raped her. So the eyes might be kind. They might be the eyes of a friend in an insane world. Perhaps the eyes of the Savior would be found here, a miraculous vision of hope. "I pray so, yes," she said.

"You are a Christian," said the man. "God must love you very much. Enjoy your meal. Forgive its simplicity." He rose and left the cell.

Catherine uttered a trembling grace, then tasted the corn and rice. The flavor was bland, without hot spices. She ate a small bit. Minutes later, the screaming began again, and she threw up the meal over the wet drain hole.

Catherine slept then awoke. Her neck throbbed from the angle her head had rested at as she lay on the floor. Surely it had been twenty-four hours. She knew the chances of being brought before a judge for an official charge were slim. The fuerza rarely followed the laws of its country. This was one reason she had come to this place. Innocent, illiterate people were losing their land and their property to military leaders who forged legal documents and drove the campesinos away with threats, arrests, and murders. Those arrested were usually tortured, sometimes to death. Many others joined the ranks of the "disappeared." Surely Christ wept over the inhumanity of His children. And therefore, those who served Him should not look away, should not count the dangers.

Her clothes, simple jeans and work shirt, were now not only dirty from her work on the school repairs, but stinking from her hours in the prison. She needed to use a restroom, but was afraid to bang on the door to ask for help. Maybe it would be better to be alone and, perhaps, forgotten. Cautiously, and with humiliation, she emptied her bladder and bowels over the drain hole in the center of the cell.

Kentucky, your problems should have been mine, she thought with shame. *The screams of your starving, your ignorant, your cruel, I didn't hear. I didn't follow.*

She paced around the cell walls. She looked at the spider's web, praying to see a divine message, but there was nothing, only the mass of white, tangled threads.

The memories of girlhood ebbed and flowed through her mind, filling her with touches of warmth, making her seasick. She could have become a teacher. She could have had a little house and an azalea garden. She could have become a wife. Scott, her high school love, who had first aroused in her sweet dreams of passion, might at this moment have been making tender love to her. Instead, a crazed captain would soon rape her for his own horrendous pleasure.

The wetness on the floor had begun to dry. Who had been in the cell before her? Whose anguish had been rinsed away by casual buckets of water? A beautiful olive-skinned child, nails torn out while his mother must listen in the next room, then confessed and still died?

Had Pablo, the old farmer, been repeatedly subjected to the capucha, the rubber suffocation hood, nearly to the point of death, as reported by campesinos who knew of the atrocities of the security force?

Or had Sister Maria been raped here? Had the policía used the electric prods on her and in her, anointing her with water so the shocks rode directly to her core?

Sweet Jesus, to see the hills of her home again, to walk the valley and smell the magnolia and lilac. To be content to bloom where she had been planted, to serve those with whom she had lived.

To be Scott's wife. To raise children.

That would have been as good.

Would that have been as good?

Who would have come then, to this dangerous country?

Who, then, has stayed behind to help those of my own mountains?

She could not think. She could not know. God did not answer. Perhaps the man was wrong. She was too confused to call herself a Christian. She was too frightened. Her head pounded. Her muscles were cramped with fear.

She sat and waited. She looked for Jesus' face in the patterns of her hands and saw nothing.

Some time later, the man returned. He wore the same clothes; Catherine could not guess if he had gone home, wherever that might be, or if he had stayed at the detention center. She wondered if he had family. Did he have a wife who loved him? Was he the father of little children? Did they know of the place where he worked, and of what went on there? The man brought a pitcher of water and a glass. Catherine sat on the floor and turned away. She was surprised he did not gag at the stench in the room.

"Sister," said the man.

"How long has it been?" she asked. "Twenty-four hours?"

"These things take time," said the man. He put the pitcher and glass on the floor beside Catherine. She was thirsty but did not reach for them.

"What things? What things take time? Why am I here?"

"I am not of the fuerza. I do not know the specifics."

"I'm to be questioned?"

"I do not know. I do not believe so. Have some water."

Catherine shook her head.

"You have great faith," said the man.

Catherine said nothing.

"Your love is great. What does your faith say to you?"

Catherine did not want to talk. She said, "That Christ gave His life for us. We should love as He loved."

"You believe life is sacred?"

"Yes."

"But Christ gave up His life? He did not see His life as sacred?"

Catherine closed her eyes, then opened them. The smell of the cell made them burn. "Life is sacred. Love is more sacred. Sacrifice for others is the ultimate love. You aren't a Christian?"

"I have interest in Christianity." The man sat down beside Catherine. He folded his hands. "You would do whatever you could to stop suffering and death, sister?"

Catherine felt sweat between her breasts and under her arms. Of course she would, she was a sister, a Christian. Christ could expect no less of her.

"You would do whatever you could?" the man repeated.

"I would do whatever I could," said Catherine. There was glass in her words. Her throat felt gouged and bloody with the commitment.

"Life is sacred," said the man. "Christ said so."

"Yes."

"The screams of the campesinos bother you."

Catherine nodded. "Dear God, yes."

"You would like to save a life, sister?"

Catherine's heart flipped. Now, oh God, she would know why she was here.

The man took Catherine's hand in his own. He said, "The name of your mission, the name of Padre Felipe's mission, is 'Brazo de Dios,' is it not?"

Catherine stared at him. Slowly, she said, "Yes." It was all she could do to not jerk her hand away from the smooth clasp of the man in black. "The Arm of God. We are part of the body of Christ. The arm of God reaches out to the poor and needy."

"You have a lovely arm," said the man. And he lowered his smooth, smiling lips to Catherine's arm and kissed the flesh. Catherine flinched. "God should be proud of His creation."

"Please," said Catherine. *Think of God,* she thought. *Pray for a sign. Think of the love of Christ. Christ help me.* "I know a little nursing. I help children at the mission when they're hurt. I would do what I could to help stop pain. Shall I minister to those the fuerza interrogate? Is that why you brought me here?"

"Sister," said the man. He let go of Catherine's arm, and she immediately drew it up about herself. "It would not be right for you to see what goes on behind the hidden walls. It is very ugly."

Catherine picked up the glass and tried the pitcher, but it shook too much to pour. The man took it from her and filled the glass. Catherine sipped, choked, and sipped again. In her ears her heart thundered.

"Come, my sister," said the man. "Our time is here." He stood and reached out his hand for Catherine. The glass fell from her fingers and shattered on the concrete floor by her knee. She took the man's hand and stood.

"The captain," she said.

"Shhh, now," said the man.

Pray for us now and in the hour of our death, amen.

A blindfold was tied across Catherine's eyes, but the man did not use handcuffs as had the policía when she had been brought here. He was not rough, but decidedly gentle. *Yes,* she thought anxiously. *Maybe he is a good man, in a place of bad men. His kiss might not have been lecherous, but fatherly. He would not take her to the captain, he would let her free.*

The cell door was opened; Catherine could feel cooler air against the skin of her face. She walked carefully, following the man's steady lead.

Human shrieks were clearer now. Low growling voices of the policía, inhuman laughter at the plight of their captives.

Mama, take me home. Sweet Jesus, Mary, Mama, Daddy, I want to go home. Tears leaked through the cloth of the blindfold. Catherine swayed, horror stealing her balance.

They walked the corridor. The man squeezed Catherine's hand as if they were lovers on a first date, pressing his shoulder to her so she would not fall.

"I'm with you, sister," said the man. "Do you trust me?"

Catherine began to sob.

"Do you trust me?"

Catherine said, "I want to."

"Trust me," the man said.

They stopped, and a door was opened. There were no screams in this room, and through the blindfold Catherine was aware of bright lights. At the man's urging, she stepped carefully over the high threshold.

The blindfold was removed. They stood in a room that resembled a clinic. It was clean and white. There was a little window, and through the window Catherine could see the shadowed shape of branches and leaves outside. A white-sheeted bed sat in the middle, surrounded by floor lights and a wheeled table. A second man in white, a doctor, she thought, washed his hands at a steel sink.

"Christ sacrificed his life," said the man in black. "We do not ask that of you."

Catherine's legs gave. She dropped to the floor. Her head bobbed as though her neck was broken. "No," she said. "I'll tell you anything. What are you going to do? Please, no."

"Sister."

"Don't let the captain have me. Please let me go!"

"Sister," the man said again. "There is no captain here." He put his arms beneath hers and took her to the table. "We do not ask your life. We do not ask that you tell us anything, for we know everything you might know. Do you not trust me? I have not lied to you at any time. I merely ask to see your faith."

Catherine watched the doctor put on gloves. The disinfected smell was that of lilacs and magnolias. The doctor's face swam, shimmering, becoming that of her father and of Padre Felipe and of Pablo. On his face was the demonic grin of the captain, and she could hear the shrieks of Maria as he had abused her body.

"I am interested in Christianity."

Catherine looked away from the doctor to the man in black. He nodded, and gestured to the table. Catherine shook her head. The man smiled patiently, and with a swift movement, lifted Catherine onto the table and lay her on her back. Catherine tried to hit him away but he held her hands down. "Now, now," he said.

"Twenty-four hours," Catherine managed. "Listen to me, please. Wait, listen." *God, a miracle now, a message, a vision, now or never, amen!* "How long have I been here? I'm to have a judge. You said you knew the law. Please listen to me."

"This is not a matter of law," said the man. "It is a matter of faith."

The doctor moved to the table's side. He removed Catherine's shoes and put them on the floor. The sensation of bare feet cut Catherine with a surge of mortification and helplessness. Her breaths convulsed her entire body. The light above the table seared her skin as if it were the fire of hell.

"Twenty-four hours. My mother, I mean Padre Felipe won't know what's happened. I've got to go home."

Home, the mountains, Kentucky, the mission, God, where is home?

"Your mother did not worry when you came to our country, she knows you did it with faith." The man in black stroked Catherine's shoulder while the doctor unbuttoned her blouse and lifted her slightly to slide it off. "Now," the man said. "You told me you would do what you could to save a life. You have heard the screams of many dying here. Worthless lives, I believe, but you said you would save one. Did you not?"

Catherine closed her eyes to the light and the men. She tried to think of Kentucky and of the familiar roads and farms and forests. No visage of God appeared on her lids.

"Your church sent you here. You believe its teachings. Can you follow your words?"

"The Lord is my shepherd," prayed Catherine. There was a wonderful Wednesday night mass in her hometown. Father Altman would sing with his guitar and there would be a covered dish dinner afterwards. Scott would be there. He and Catherine held hands under the long folding table. Catherine would make fried chicken. Her mother had taught her to fix chicken the good way. Crunchy and with lots of pepper. "I shall not want."

"I will give you the chance to save a life."

Fried chicken and lilacs. Simple pleasures. Given of God. Given of God and taken away.

"Will you give your arm to save a life?"

"My arm?" gasped Catherine. Her eyes remained closed.

The man in black slapped Catherine's face. Her eyes sprang open. "The chance to save a life," he said. "Will you give your arm to save a life?"

"My arm?"

"Brazo de Dios. Arm of God. Given for His children. Are you willing to do what He would do?"

Catherine looked at her hands, her arms. They would take her arm away to save a life. They would take an arm away to test her faith and to save a life. A sudden, violent tremor twisted Catherine, and she screamed, "Not my arm! Don't cut off my arm!"

There was silence for a moment, and the man in black said, "Not even for a life, sister?"

Campesinos, Catherine thought wildly. *They expect violence, they live it, they are used to it. They won't know what I've done here. I can't lose my arm.* Catherine bent her head to her chest. *They'd never know my sacrifice.*

"Not even for a life?"

Catherine thought, *Without my arm I couldn't make fried chicken. I couldn't hold the bowl and stir the coating.* Her lungs felt crushed. She struggled for air.

"My arm," she hissed. "Oh God, no."

"Very well, then," said the man in black. "We shall let you go back to the mission. I see what Christianity is now."

"Yes," said Catherine then, and her soul wailed at what fate her voice had sealed. "Take the arm, oh dear God, take the arm from me." Acid tears drew savage lines on her face. "What arm will you take, you bastard?"

The doctor turned and pulled a syringe from the wheeled table.

He forced fluid through the tip, then pinched the skin beneath Catherine's right forearm.

The man in black kissed Catherine's cheek. "I am not a bastard. There is no pain. We will make you feel nothing. I could be a Christian, could I not?"

There was a sting, and the needle was moved in and out of Catherine's upper arm, numbing it instantly in several places. A moment later, the entire arm was deadened. The doctor silently patted the skin, and frowned with duty. He tied a rubber tourniquet about the arm, just beneath Catherine's armpit.

"You toy with me," Catherine said. "You filthy bastard."

The doctor brought out a small knife and a surgical saw.

"I am a good man," said the man in black. "The policía would have raped you many times and beat you for their pleasure. The capucha on a woman fills them with lust, and they would use you until your death. I am not a bad man." He rubbed his mouth, nodding, seeming to consider his words. Then he said, "Turn away, now. This will be ugly."

Catherine turned away. *I'm saving a life,* she thought. *Remember this, Lord.* Her eyes found the window and the shimmering trees beyond. Leaves caught sunlight, reflecting it like chips of liquid emerald. Catherine tried to watch it, to become part of it. Part of the beauty that was God's natural world. Harmony, sweetness, peace, gentleness.

And she would no longer be natural. Her body was being destroyed on a whim. And she was enduring it, for the sake of faith. She had no promise a life would be spared for this obscene test.

Certainly God did not want this. This was evil's desire. No. God would not want this.

No.

"No!" cried Catherine. "Don't take my arm!"

She looked back at the doctor.

He was holding her arm. It was no longer attached to her shoulder. Blood poured in a hot stream as he held it, looking confused at Catherine's sudden cry.

Catherine looked at the short stump, at the deep scarlet pool and the flap of skin the doctor would stitch up to cover the raw end.

She screamed, a supreme and mortal sound. She thought she saw the man in black mouth, "Trust me." She fell into unconsciousness.

Her sleep was as empty as the hole of hell.

There was the sound of rumbling and the sensation of rough waters. There was heat and a taste of brine.

Catherine opened her eyes. She was in a jeep, and it was traveling the pocked roads of the night countryside. She was alone except for the driver beside her. She could not see who it was. His clothes were as black as the sky. She tried to think of who he might be, or why she might be with him, but something in her veins made thinking difficult. Her heart pumped betrayal to her limbs and her mind. She felt bile rise and, with effort, she swallowed it back.

"Where?" she asked.

The driver did not look at her but when he spoke she remembered him.

"We are going back to Brazo de Dios," said the man in black.

The jeep hit a pit and Catherine fell against the low door. Her arm, however, did not come in contact with the frame. There was no specific pain, just a sickening sensation of nothingness. She looked over to see why she was leaning on her side.

Her right arm was gone. The stump was bandaged and pinned neatly. Catherine moaned. Nausea came and went.

"And you'll kill me now, won't you?" she said then. "I'll become one of the disappeared."

"We are going back to Brazo de Dios," the man repeated. "You will listen to me, because I tell the truth. I am not a liar nor a bad man."

Catherine looked up and could not see the moon. Stars hid themselves behind the dark clouds of a coming storm. God did not show Himself.

"Sister, I know the captain of whom you spoke. That is the only lie I have told you today. The captain of the fuerza is a strange man. A brutal man. He has no respect for religion or things of God. But he did not send for you today. I had you taken by the force."

Catherine touched her face with the fingers of her left hand. Her lips were cracked. She fought to keep her eyes open. She fought to listen to the man.

"The captain has plans tomorrow morning to come to your mission. All of the people who work there will die."

Catherine felt the drugs tug her stomach. She leaned forward and spit on the floor. Her shoes were spattered. "What do you mean?" she said slowly.

"What I say I mean," said the man. "The captain has plans to find all the sisters and brothers and even your Padre Felipe and take them to the field. There they will be gunned down. You, having caught his attention, would have been molested before your death. You would have been passed around to any of the men in his favor. And then you would join the others of the mission, in a ditch in the field. You see, church is trouble to the captain. He does not tolerate trouble."

Catherine shook her head. "He can't do that. I love those people." Then she said, "You took my arm from me."

The man drove in silence. Catherine could see the familiar rise of a knoll and knew they were, indeed, driving toward the mission.

"The captain," said the man in black, "does have a love, or a sympathy. I do not know the difference. The captain's sister is a cripple. His sister, not a sister of the church, but his true sister, do you understand?"

Catherine understood, but could not nod.

"The captain's sister was wounded as a child when he was but a boy himself. He was playing with his father's gun and there was an accident. The gun went off and shot his sister in the arm. It tore the arm up badly, and poor treatment made amputation necessary."

"Why are you telling me this? You are taking me to the mission. We are all going to be killed!"

"He loves his sister. He has sympathy, maybe guilt. He will not harm cripples."

The jeep reached the top of the knoll. Dim lights spotted various windows in the mission's dormitory. A dog, belonging to some campesinos living nearby, barked at the approaching vehicle.

The man in black drove to the gateway and stopped the jeep. He looked at Catherine. "He will not harm cripples. He will see you, and he will let you live. He will kill the others. There is nothing anyone can do. Nothing I can do. Nothing you can do. But he will leave you alone, he will let you live because of your affliction."

Catherine pressed her left hand to her mouth. She thought she felt the phantom right hand pressing her heart.

"Go, then," said the man. Catherine dragged herself out, holding to the door so she would not drop to the dirt. "Say your prayers, sister. The Lord has been with you."

The jeep made a sharp turn and then rattled off into the darkness.

Catherine watched as it vanished down the knoll. And in the specter of its image she saw the face of Christ.

Her Wild Wild Eyes

Brad Strickland

Raymond Kingsley met her the night of the slashing.

He had left the studio after the deed was done, had gone out into the hot dark streets to walk and brood and curse his fate. It was not a neighborhood for nightwalking: even at 2:00 A.M., trios and quartets of young men congregated on the street corners, smoking, jiving, scattering hoots of laughter, casting furtive eyes his way. Kingsley was in the wrong place, at the wrong time, to be secure.

Early on, a man from one of the streetlamp groups actually broke away and approached him, speaking in a voice sweet and soft as molasses: "I gotcha, man. Got what you need, right here—"

Without speaking, Kingsley waved him off. The man stopped, his dark eyes going round. "Hey, O.K., man, shit—" He backed away, shaking his head and muttering, "It's cool, it's O.K." He went back to the others, and they watched Kingsley silently as he strode away. A few blocks farther along, Kingsley noticed the stickiness on the base of his thumb, and under a streetlight, he saw the crimson palm he had showed the pusher. He had been caught red-handed, as it were. In this part of town, that color could mean only one thing.

No wonder the kid backed off, he thought, carelessly scrubbing his hand against his jeans, feeling the half-dried acrylic paint peel away, smelling the plastic scent of it, cloying on the humid night air.

His walk had taken him past closed Korean groceries and open, dimly lighted bodegas, past doorways spilling the aroma of whiskey or the sound of salsa, to a place where the street ended in a narrow alley between two buildings, an asphalted bluff overlooking the riverfront. Kingsley stood in a patch of dry weeds at the end of the street where a chest-high barrier kept traffic from spilling over into the stream. Looking out across the black water, he saw the lighted towers and spires of the city.

Once upon a time, someone like Raymond Kingsley, an aspiring artist, would have lived in that great city, even if it were in a garret, and he would have enjoyed the bohemian company of other starving servants of the muse. No more. Rents were too high, space too dear, and the world had turned on.

There's a picture, Kingsley thought, staring at the night city, smelling the garbage reek of alleyways, the dead-fish stench of the stale water below, hearing the faraway electronic shrieks of sirens, mad laughter leaking from an asylum of eight million. He flexed his right hand, feeling the remnants of the crimson paint, sticky and warm.

He bent his elbows and rested them on the guardrail, hearing the summer-withered weeds crackle underfoot. His eyes caught the thousand shimmering colors shining in the lights of the high concrete towers, dancing in the leftover heat of the August day. It was almost a painting complete in itself, needing no artist's touch to make it art. *Almost.*

"God damn," he said sincerely, directing the thought at himself. "You could paint it."

For a vertiginous moment, Kingsley thought the voice was in his head, conjured by imagination: feminine, soft, breathy. Then he turned and peered through the darkness and saw her.

The streetlight down the block defined her, shone from behind her to halo her cascading blonde hair, to make her bare shoulders gleam, to lose itself in her black dress. Looking at her, Kingsley had the odd impression that she was the center of the night, that darkness flowed in toward her, black water spiraling down an endless drain: everything else seemed obscured by her presence. *She draws the light into herself,* he thought.

But that was not wholly true, for her golden hair had captured the light, and the highlight on her neck was a graceful long *S*, and her face—

Her face was almost self-luminous, like a pale moon shining through a layer of cloud.

"You could paint it," she said again. She stood perhaps twenty feet away from Kingsley, her arms at her sides, her left leg straight, her right just a little bent. He felt himself pulled toward her, drawn on the tide of night.

"That's the trouble," he said. "I can't." His attempted laugh was miserable, a cough of despair. He took a few steps toward her.

She was shorter than he had thought; as he came closer, she tilted her chin to look up at him. "You're an artist."

"I've been known to call myself that." He shivered, though the night was still heavy with summer heat. "I don't remember seeing you in the neighborhood—?"

She ignored the invitation to name herself. "I know you, though. You are capable of great things . . . Ray."

There was something about her voice. Despite her knowing his name, she did not sound familiar; no, the quality of her speech was not familiarity, but rather, strangeness. Kingsley realized that her voice carried no accent, no geographical quality. And yet it was soothing, musical, lilting almost.

Striving to recognize her, he stared intently into her face, the features just visible in the lightscatter from the city. She had high cheekbones and a mouth well defined, probably red, but looking black in the shadows. Her eyes were wide and very dark, though he could not tell their color. He laughed again, no more successfully this time than the first.

"Did I say something funny?" she asked without a trace of the smile.

"One funny word. Capable. I used to think that I was. Tomorrow, though—no, forget it."

She tilted her head. "Forget what?"

He shrugged. "Tomorrow I've got to take the subway into town and see the art director at Helios Press and tell him I can't do the cover for *Mother Kali*. So I don't get the check I was counting on. So I'll be evicted sometime next month. Not much."

"*Mother Kali?*"

He looked away. The fairy city burned on the other side of the river, and its reflection jeweled the dark water. "Science fiction novel," he said. "You've heard of Penelope Lowell?" When the woman did not respond, Kingsley continued: "Well, anyway, she started as a science fiction writer, then hit big as a mainstream novelist. Stories in *The New Yorker, The Atlantic.* You know the book *Female Trouble?* Best-seller last year? That was hers. This new book, *Mother Kali,* is her return to the field, and the Helios limited edition will be her first science fiction novel in ten years. I lucked into the assignment. Now I'm losing it." He paused. "I don't know why I'm babbling."

He felt her hands on his arm, soft pressure, a childlike tug. "You're not babbling. I'm interested. Take me to see."

He shook his head. "I wouldn't want you to look at them. Or anybody else, for that matter."

"What's wrong?"

"The work's no good. I don't have it."

"What?" Somehow she was close to him, her breath right in his face, warm and sweetly scented, a honey-and-ginger sort of fragrance. "What don't you have?"

"Damned if I know. Whatever artists have to have," he said, his voice going ragged. A car came toward them, and he pulled her from the street onto the sidewalk. In the glare of the headlights, he saw her eyes were deep blue, the color of midnight, and her lips as red as blood. "What I'm lacking is talent. Inspiration. Whatever the hell it takes. I've lied to myself for five years, but the truth is, I'm no artist."

She did not reply. He swept his hand toward the city. "You said I could paint that. I can't. I can *see* the painting in it; I can even sense what it should feel like—but if I put it on canvas, it would be dead. Perfectly composed, but dead—like a funeral-parlor corpse. Like the dead paintings hanging in my studio now."

She pulled his arm again, gently insisting. "Come. Take me." He caught himself hearing an entirely different invitation in her words, one he could not dismiss.

Because she made him less alone, because he could not make

himself believe that she meant only what the surface of her words said, he did take her to the studio. She expressed no surprise at the building, which a hundred years ago had been a modest warehouse for tobacco shipped north from Virginia, and now was all but derelict. She had nothing at all to say about his top-story living quarters (three brick-walled rooms, all still smelling faintly of tobacco: bathroom, kitchen/sleeping area, and a long, high-ceilinged room with a northern tier of windows running its entire length). She showed no dismay at its untidiness or its fusty smell of ripe garbage, oils, and acrylics. She did cry out, very softly, when she saw the remnants of his slashed paintings.

"They were no good," he said, leaning against the windows. "Nothing I've done in the past five years is any damn good." He nodded at a set of panels on the floor against the south wall. "Some of the early stuff, the student works, had a glimmer. But nothing since I came to the city."

"You were married?"

He shook his head, smiling. "Never. Well, once, sort of; it lasted nearly a year, but we didn't have a ceremony or anything. And she's living abroad now."

"Long ago?"

"Seems like it. I last saw her, let's see, three years ago in October. She threw a party for my twenty-fifth birthday and told me the next morning that she had to leave, sorry, we all have to grow, blah, blah, blah. You don't want to hear this."

She raised a mischievous eyebrow. "You think not?" She wandered the length of the studio, fingering ripped canvas, her neat, small feet in their black pumps crunching broken composition-board panels. Standing before the arched doorway, she turned to give him a dark, level look. Her eyes were extraordinary, a rich midnight blue, the darkest blue eyes he had ever seen. "Are you coming?"

"Where?"

She went into the bedroom, already reaching to unfasten the black dress. Kingsley swallowed. He pushed away from the window, followed her into the bedroom. The dress lay on the floor. She had pulled the covers off the bed and lay there in the dimness, her whole body now seeming to glow with that faint luminescence, that bashful-moon lambency. He saw her in shadow, but he saw enough to make his throat ache.

He reached for the buttons of his shirt. "We're crazy for doing this," he said. "We don't even know each other's—"

"My name is Lisbet." The voice throaty, purring almost, sensual. "And yours is Ray." She drew in her breath, sighed, and raised her arms toward him. He went to her. He kissed her, not once but many times, and at last he kissed her eyes, felt the soft flesh of her eyelids trembling at the touch of his lips. After a while he had no more thoughts of strangeness, but only of her and of the release she gave him.

Daylight woke him. He had painted the windows in the bedroom black. The bedroom/kitchen and bathroom had once been the office and rest room of the warehouse, and they shared the row of windows that ran the whole length of this side of the building. The windows were all right for a warehouse, and wonderful out in the old hallway that now was his studio, but he had felt exposed sleeping with the city looking in.

But sunshine spilled in from the studio through the open archway. He felt in bed for Lisbet, failed to find her, and sat up quickly. Black spots blossomed in his vision and swam to the hum of tinnitus. Kingsley closed his eyes until the dizziness passed, and in the warm darkness behind his eyelids, he heard a lingering melody, a fairy song, that faded into the humming of his ears.

After a moment that, too, faded, and he opened his eyes, feeling steadier. He eased out of bed, stood, and padded barefoot to the bathroom, his head as light as if he were a little drunk. She was not there; her dress was no longer on the bedroom floor. The wreck of the paintings still littered the studio.

Kingsley felt detached, as if he had dreamed the whole thing and was now dreaming himself. He took a shower, his legs rubbery, his breath coming shallow. Toweling himself dry, he had another moment of vertigo and had to sit on the toilet for a moment to collect himself. Recovered, he dressed slowly, looking at his watch as he strapped it on: 11:44.

His appointment at Helios was for 1:30. The painting was due there then. Kingsley groaned, got his shoes on, and wandered through the three rooms again, half-convinced that Lisbet was hiding somewhere, and half-believing that she was only a dream, no more real than the half-remembered melody of his sleep.

Real or dreamed, she was not in the apartment, and walking through it only made him aware of his strange weakness, his unaccustomed lethargy. Kingsley's stomach fluttered at the thought of breakfast, but he did brew and swallow a half pot of bitter black coffee.

On the way to the subway, and then during the ride into town, he felt curiously empty, as if there were the smallest gap between the world and his perception of it, as if he were an actor in the declining weeks of a play's long run. *Scared,* he thought. *Scared to face Jake. That's what's wrong with me. Unless I caught twenty-four-hour AIDS.* The bleak joke pleased him and made him laugh aloud. A woman in a babushka did not look at him, but edged frantically away.

Helios was not a large outfit, though it had a growing reputation as a publisher of collector's editions. Its offices were small, noisy, and crowded with stacks of manuscripts, boxes of books, furniture that might have been new the year before the Japanese bombers appeared over Pearl Harbor.

Jacob Rubin was the art director at Helios, and his cubbyhole of an office, a corner location with a narrow window looking out onto a busy street six floors below, was a haven of quiet, where the constant sound of telephones muted itself to background noise. Rubin stood five feet four, but he was so thin that he gave the impression of lankiness. With his bulbous bald head and long wrists, he reminded Kingsley of the little articulated wooden mannequin that used to pose for him in art school.

"I don't see a canvas," Rubin said as soon as Kingsley walked in. His waspish voice took on a rasping edge: "Let me guess. I'm not getting the picture. I'm getting an excuse."

Kingsley sank into a worn armchair. "Not even that, Jake. I'm sorry. It's beyond me."

Rubin let his breath out in a long hiss that managed to sound exasperated but resigned. "God damn it, Ray."

"I know what this means—"

The art director grunted, took off his round glasses, polished them with a handkerchief. "No, Ray, you don't know what it means. If you did, you wouldn't screw me like this. I can do it, you said. I need a chance, you said. And I put it all on the line for you, Ray. They told me, Frank and the others, they said you'd fuck up. Did I listen? Go with your gut feeling, I told myself. How long will it take?"

Kingsley shook his head. "You won't get a painting. Not from me. You've got to assign the project to some other artist. I know it's short notice—"

Rubin flapped his hand as if shooing flies. "Like hell. It's late, Ray, very late. Lowell's a name now, kid. There'll be a trade edition from her regular house in December; and if we don't beat it to press, if ours isn't a real first, we lose our shirts. What, should I send it out with a white cover and just the words? Get another artist, he says." He sighed. "This headache I didn't need. Look, I can give you to the beginning of September, but that is absolutely—"

Kingsley stood. "Jake, understand me. I can't do it. I tried. It won't—I don't know; it won't live for me. I—"

Pushing back from the desk, Rubin tilted his head to stare up at Kingsley. "You look like hell, you know. You're not doing something you should tell me about, are you?"

For a second Kingsley stared at him, uncomprehending. Then he grinned. "Drugs? Jake, I've got barely enough money to buy paint. I can't support two habits."

"You look sick as hell. Look, show me what you have. I—"

Kingsley shook his head. "I have nothing. The preliminary sketch you approved is all there is. I ripped the painting apart last night."

Rubin's glasses were opaque with reflected light, making his gaze blank-eyed, pitiless. "That was a damn fool thing to do." He opened a desk drawer, took out a sheaf of photocopies, shuffled through them. "Here. Take these and get out. I've got to find an artist."

Kingsley frowned down at the top sketch Rubin tossed onto the desk. It was bad, not as bad as his botched painting had been, but not good, not half the vision he had in his head. It was a woman's face, seen in three-quarter profile, dark-skinned, black-haired, sloe-eyed: the concept was not the horrific Kali of Hindu legend, not the blood-smeared dancer, but a woman subtly terrible in her beauty. Only—"It's not what it ought to be," Kingsley said.

"You're telling me? It should've been a painting by now, damn it."

Kingsley reached for a pencil—a coffee mug full of them perched on the corner of Rubin's desk—and turned the photocopy over, its blank side upward. "No, it's just wrong, badly thought out. But see it like this."

For a moment he had the same odd sensation that he had felt last night, when he first saw Lisbet in the street: the world darkened, and the darkness flowed toward a point, but this time the point was the end of the pencil, pressed against the paper on the desk before him. His head swam. He felt his hand moving, heard the scratch of graphite on paper, but he saw nothing of what he was doing—"

"Yeah," Rubin said, and the spell broke.

Kingsley blinked. The page bore a sketch now, a sketch so unlike his usual stiff, overworked style that part of his mind rejected it as his own work. But the pencil was in his hand, and the paper was in front of him.

There was the cityscape he had imagined the night before, suggested in verticals and starbursts; a hasty shading indicated night sky. And there was Kali.

The destroying goddess, she balanced on her left leg, caught in the dance of death. Her right leg, lifted and partly extended, balanced the gracefully outspread arms. Framed by billowing, ink-black hair, her face, even in a hasty pencil sketch, seemed illuminated, had the quality of the moon shining through cloud—

Kingsley's heart thumped. No, the face was not Lisbet's, but there was a sisterhood there, in the calm features, the full mouth, the wide eyes—

He saw the stars of midnight shining through those wide eyes.

"This is it," Rubin said, his voice trembling. "By God, this is it. How soon, Ray?"

"Huh?"

Rubin picked up the sketch. "God damn, man. Why didn't you tell me you were changing the concept? Not that I disagree—this is great—but when can we have it? Has to be by the first."

"Three weeks," Kingsley heard himself say.

"Acrylic?"

He nodded.

"Today's the tenth. Ray, listen to me. I can give you till the thirty-first. That is absolutely, my hand to God, the last possible day. If you miss that, you've screwed us. And if you screw us—"

"I'll never work in this town again," Kingsley finished. Rubin did not smile.

"So what the hell are you waiting in my office for? You got painting to do."

He had painting to do.

Kingsley cut a cold-press panel to twenty-four by thirty-seven inches, considerably larger than his first attempt, the oil-on-canvas, had been. The jacket art would be reduced to six by nine-and-a-quarter inches, and much of the detail he saw in his mind would undoubtedly be lost. Still, he knew, he felt, that nothing smaller would allow him to do justice to the vision.

He applied three coats of progressively thinner gesso, smoothing each coat with ultrafine sandpaper. The sweet smell of the gluelike paste nearly maddened him, urged him to hurry so that the actual painting could begin. When the last coat of gesso had dried, and he had sanded it to glassy smoothness, he assembled his materials.

Normally Kingsley dragooned one of his few friends to pose for figure paintings: the aspiring actress who waited on tables at the deli down the street, her roommate (a trim secretary who did not mind shedding her clothes for nude studies), the affable homosexual bodybuilder who took Kingsley's rejection of his advances easily and still remained the artist's friend—these and his other acquaintances had posed for him in the past for the price of conversation and a shared bottle of cheap wine. This time, though, he worked without a model, seeing everything, down to the last nuance of light and shadow, in his mind.

His timidity seemed to have vanished, his insecurity to have fled. Where normally he would have worked details with a tiny #000 brush, he now used a comparatively massive #1, its bristles flattened to give him the fine point he needed. The first three days of work saw the background and figure blocked in, the relative values established. From then on, Kingsley worked feverishly at overpainting, at layering hues and shades to produce a delicate, compelling translucence.

He worked as long as he could hold a brush. When his fingers grew too tired for that, he grabbed something to eat—something cheap, for his resources were dwindling—and fell exhausted into bed for four or six hours of sleep. He developed a blister on his right middle finger from holding the brush, but he ignored it until it thickened into a callus.

By the end of the second week, he could see his success. Kali danced for him, goddess of time and destruction, called from his imagination by paint and talent. Her skin was pale, glowing almost, her features not cruel, but terribly, inhumanly dispassionate. The face was classic in its awful serenity, the billows of jet-black hair a net that trapped and enslaved the fairy cityscape in the background. And the eyes . . .

The eyes were hers, Lisbet's.

Wide they were, and deep midnight in color; and after you looked at the painting for a while, you came to realize that the eyes were the eyes of a mask, hollow, and the lights you saw in their depths were the lights of distant stars that neither saw nor cared for you.

Kingsley stopped once, breathing hard, and wept at what he had done. Before him was the magnificence he had dreamed.

He worked on into the third week, texturing the sky, adding the highlights of the twinkling fairy city, impatiently drying the layers with forced air from a hair dryer set on "cool." Finally one morning he woke up, rolled out of bed, and went barefoot and naked into the studio, not caring if anyone could see him from the taller buildings across the way.

He stood staring at it for a long time, barely daring to breathe
lest the illusion be broken. But it was no illusion: there was Kali, in
all her terror and beauty, and the painting was more than an illustration. It was art.

He had been crossing days off a calendar since starting the
painting. The last X was through August 30. The painting was due
today. Still naked, Kingsley rummaged for a can of Clear Coat that
still had some pressure in it, found one, and sprayed the panel. The
clear aerosol burned his eyes, brought a sweetish alcohol taste to his
tongue as he breathed the fumes.

Kingsley showered, found some clothes that did not reek, and
carefully packed the panel. He caught the subway just after rush
hour, rode it to the island, and then walked four blocks to the
Helios offices. Jake Rubin met him in the reception room. "Let's
see," he said as soon as they were in his cubbyhole.

Kingsley passed the package over. Rubin shook his head. "This
is it, kid. I like you. My bosses tell me I'm crazy, but I like you.
And I liked that sketch. Let's see—" He tore open the package,
lifted the panel out by its edges, and stood with his head bowed
over it.

Kingsley licked his lips. "Well?"

"My God," Rubin said, his tone reverent. When he looked up,
Kingsley saw with surprise that his eyes glistened. "Damn, Ray, this
is too good for a book cover. You must know that."

Kingsley felt himself go weak, as if invisible strings supporting
him had suddenly broken. He fell more than sat in the disreputable
armchair. "I'm glad," he said, his voice hoarse. "I kept thinking it
was just me, that I'd lost my mind."

"This—kid, we're not paying you enough." Rubin shook his
head, and he almost whispered, "We can't pay you enough."

Kingsley gave him a weak smile. "About that. Uh, Jake—"

Rubin looked at him, and his blue eyes grew sharp. "The hell,
Ray? When did you eat last?"

Kingsley shook his head. "Day or two ago. It's all right; I was
working—"

"Stay here." Rubin left, taking the painting with him. Left alone,
Kingsley covered his eyes and felt himself trembling.

A hand shook him awake a moment later. "Ray. Here. Take it."

Blinking, Kingsley accepted the check. "This is early, Jake. It can't have gone through your Accounts Payable—"

"Take it, take it; you have to know where every dime comes from?"

Kingsley's throat was tight, his voice shaky: "Thanks, Jake. This is—thank you."

"No," Rubin said softly. "Thank you. Now get out of here, you bum, and get some food under your belt. Take care of yourself; I think we're going to be doing business again soon."

The check let Kingsley pay his rent, pay his overdue bills at the art-supply house, buy food; but food was not what he needed.

He needed her, Lisbet.

No one had seen her; no one knew of her: not the Chuns who ran the corner grocery, not the waitresses at the deli, or the kids who played stickball down the block, no one.

The lack of her ate at Kingsley. The fact that she did not know what power she had given his art—for he associated his success with *Mother Kali* completely with the night she had spent with him—pained him like a hollow and aching tooth.

The pain was worse when he tried to work.

The new pieces were all right, at least as good as the best he had done before meeting Lisbet, but they were far inferior to the painting he had done for Helios. They did not satisfy him.

In the three weeks after he turned *Mother Kali* in to Helios, he worked at his easel in a desultory way during the days, and at night he went out looking for her, without success. It was late September when he received a letter bearing the Helios logo and a scrawled "Rubin" as a return address. He opened it and read, "Get a telephone, you cheap bastard. Call me earliest. Jake." When he made the call from the pay phone in the deli, Rubin said, "Penny Lowell wants to meet you."

For a second, Kingsley did not place the name. Then he got it: "The writer? Why?"

"Wants to make you an offer on your painting." Rubin's voice dropped to a soft murmur: "Five thousand, kid. Stick her for that much at least. She's got it, and God knows we couldn't pay you what the cover's worth."

Kingsley's lips were numb. Part of him did not want to give up the painting, the sight of those deep eyes, but part of him never wanted to see them again. Rubin set up the meeting; and a few days later, during the first week of October, Kingsley and Penny Lowell had lunch together. Before it was over, she passed him a personal check, for considerably more than five thousand.

"There, that's done," she said, sipping her coffee. She looked forty, Kingsley thought, though he knew she was closer to sixty. Trim, tennis-muscled, fair-haired, she radiated authority. Her mouth was a brilliant scarlet, the same color as Lisbet's had been— but Lisbet's lip color had not come off, as Penny Lowell's did on the rim of her coffee cup. "Would you like another job?" she asked, pinning Kingsley with a direct stare.

Her eyes were ice gray, he noticed. He smiled. "Not another book cover, not yet. I—"

The author shook her head. "A commissioned portrait," she said. "Not me. A friend of mine." She reached across the round table and tapped the pinkish orange check with a pointed red nail. "That again as fee. But I want the same life in it as I saw in *Mother Kali*. That's a condition."

Kingsley sipped his own coffee, a frothy cappuccino, and thought. After all, this was something like what he had dreamed of. "Let me consider it," he said.

Penny Lowell sniffed and tossed her head. It was a girlish gesture, though she looked anything but girlish in a forest-green suit over a pale beige silk blouse. "I need your answer now," she said.

Kingsley sighed. "Let me make a sketch or two. If you think they're what you would want, fine. If not—"

"Fine. Is tomorrow acceptable?"

Thinking of the cleanup he'd have to do, Kingsley shrank inwardly. But he said, "That ought to do."

"Good," she said, nodding like a woman who always got her way. She opened her checkbook again and uncapped a pen, a real fountain pen with a gold nib, and began to write. "Ten percent as a deposit. No more until you've got the work underway."

"All right."

She tore the second check free and held it out, her eyes almost hostile. "You know, you're a pretty good artist, for a man."

The friend was named Isabel, a nineteen-year-old slip of a woman, pale, dark-haired, brown-eyed, thin: neurasthenic, they used to call her type. A Poe illustration, Kingsley thought to himself; or a Dickinson one. She spoke very little, held Penny's hand as much as she could, and posed in uneasy alertness, like a bird disturbed by a nearby footfall and ready for flight.

"Just relax," Kingsley urged her as he set up his camera.

Isabel's eyes jittered, as if she were terrified. She reached out blindly, and Penny Lowell was there, taking her hand. "Just relax, dear," the writer purred. "And before you know it, I'll have something to remember you by forever." Isabel did become a little more at ease, though not much, and she posed satisfactorily as the afternoon went on. Kingsley took several reference photographs, then did some pencil impressions of the woman, trying to see beyond her tenseness to her natural state of repose. When the sitting was over, Penny kissed the girl on the mouth.

Kingsley made an appointment to show some preliminary sketches to the writer in a week's time. When the two women left, he stared critically at the roughs. They were not what he wanted them to be.

He had the photographs developed and printed, and on the third day, he tried to work the reference sketches and pictures into something approximating the portrait Penny Lowell wanted.

Nothing happened.

He walked again that night, walked to the alley overlooking the river, walked back alone, climbed the fire escape to the roof of the warehouse, stood gazing out toward the distant city, hazed by distance and mist. "Where are you?" he asked aloud.

"Here," Lisbet's voice said behind him.

He turned, and there she was, dressed just as he recalled her: and again the night seemed to flow into her, as if the night were coalescing, becoming her. They were in each other arms in a moment; and in a few moments more, they were downstairs and in his bed.

He whispered to her during intervals between lovemaking, spilled the whole story in her ear, marveled at the burning touch of her flesh on his, caressed her and held her tight. "I know," she murmured. "I know it all."

This time he fought sleep for her sake; this time, when she slipped naked from the bed, he rose on his elbow. "Tell me about you," he said then.

She stood with her back to him as the black dress rustled down over her nakedness. "There is nothing to tell."

"Not true." He was sitting up in bed now, fully awake. "What's your name, your whole name?"

She bent to kiss him. "You know."

He held to her hand. "I know only Lisbet," he said. "That's not enough."

Her smile was unreadable in the gray light of a foggy dawn. "It will have to be."

"I want you to stay—"

She touched his face. "You look so tired, Ray. Rest now." She hummed, a curious, plaintive melody, the same alien tune he had dreamed before.

And somehow he was dreaming again, dreaming of Lisbet's mouth and her eyes and of the cold, distant stars.

When Kingsley woke, it was late afternoon, and he rose feeling shaky and wretched, as if recovering from a bout of flu. But when he glanced at the sketches, he saw exactly what was wrong, saw how the final painting would have to look—

Trembling with exhaustion, he started work.

This time there was hardly a pause, a moment to go to the bathroom, five minutes to eat something while standing looking at the panel on the easel, and then back to work again. He felt charged, felt energy flowing through him like electricity through the filament of a bulb; and like the filament, he felt himself being used up in the process. As soon as an area of paint was dry enough to be overpainted, he was working at it, the strokes of the brush firm and knowing; while that section was setting, he moved to another part, putting the painting together as a man sentenced to life imprisonment might assemble a billion-piece jigsaw puzzle, with infinite patience.

She came a day ahead of schedule. He had just touched up the painting—God, it had gone fast!—when he heard the knock at the door. He opened it and saw Penny Lowell there, alone. She blinked, and her nostrils twitched.

Kingsley realized that he stank. He had not bathed in—how long had it been? "I'm sorry," he said. "I didn't expect you until Wednesday."

She frowned at him. "This is Wednesday. Did you—oh." Her gray eyes were looking past him, at the panel. "Oh my God." She pushed past Kingsley, went to stand six feet from the panel. "That's it," she said. "Oh my God, I can see her breathe."

Kingsley came to look over her shoulder. Isabel was there, a book in her lap, her head side-tilted as if she had been disturbed in her reading and had looked up to see—whom? Friend, lover? Death, the gentleman caller? Her expression was unreadable; the eyes, the dark eyes, held mystery beyond mystery.

"It looks ready to go. Is it? When will it be finished?" Penny asked, not looking around.

The word spun in Kingsley's brain: *finished, finished, finished.* He put out a hand to steady himself—

"Ray? Can you hear me?"

He opened his eyes. The face was familiar, the round glasses, the balding dome. "Jake?" he asked, surprised at how thin his own voice sounded. "What are—"

"Don't excite yourself," Rubin said.

Only then did Kingsley realize that he was no longer at the studio. He smelled disinfectant, hospital odors. "What happened?" His right hand itched abominably; reaching to scratch it, he found an IV connection. He lifted his head from the pillow and looked to his left: an aged man lay in a fetal position there on a hospital bed, his eyes vacant of everything but misery. "Jake?"

Rubin put a hand on his shoulder. "Easy, don't raise up. You passed out, kid. Scared the piss out of Penny. She called the EMTs, they got you here, and then she called me. How're you feeling?"

Kingsley closed his eyes; they felt as if the insides of the lids were coated with grit. "Dead. Overdue for burial. What day is it?"

Rubin's laugh was a hiss of air. "Wednesday afternoon, kid. You been here a couple of hours. What have you been doing to yourself? You look like hell, must've lost fifteen pounds."

Kingsley rasped his left hand over his jaw. A bristly growth of beard prickled him. "Working too hard, that's all."

"Dehydrated, the doctor says. So they're dripping glucose in you to plump you out some."

The old man in the other bed groaned softly and, with infinite labor, turned over onto his back, then onto his side. Kingsley glanced at him, was horrified to see the mummylike body revealed by the slit hospital gown, the ribs like a washboard, the buttocks flat, the hipbones gaunt beneath the skin.

Jake was saying something. Kingsley rolled his head and brought the art director's face back into focus. "What?"

"I asked you a question," Rubin said with what seemed forced patience. "You been eating at all?"

"Sure."

"You don't look like it."

The living skeleton in the other bed groaned again. Kingsley resisted the temptation to look. "Jake, tell me something. When can I get out?"

Rubin shook his head, evidently misunderstanding. "Don't worry about the cost—Frank's letting Helios pick it up, and it's only a semi-private room. Least the cheap bastard can do after paying you what he did for *Mother Kali*—"

"Jake. When?"

Behind the round glasses, Rubin's eyes grew worried. "There's no law to keep you here. Anytime, kid, I guess. But maybe you should have some tests run, or—"

"No tests," Kingsley said. "I know what's wrong with me."

The man in the next bed took in a long breath and held it forever.

He got back to the studio near midnight. Penny Lowell had had the presence of mind to find his keys and lock up for him. He had reclaimed the keys from the hospital desk, and he was relieved to see the studio intact; nothing was missing, except for the portrait. Pushpinned to the easel in its place was a salmon-colored check. She had occupied herself by making it out while she waited for the ambulance.

His knees shaking, Kingsley climbed the fire escape again, up to the roof. The night air was cool, Halloween coming on in a few weeks, then winter. He smelled it all, the burning leaves of fall, the nose-stinging coldness of snow, in one deep, quivering breath. The roof was empty, the fire escape the only way up. Holding on to its iron railing, Kingsley cleared his throat. "Where are you?" he asked.

"Here." She came softly behind him. He felt her palm, cool, smooth, on the back of his neck. "I'm here."

He reached for her hand, but she pulled it away.

"No, Ray. It's too soon. You need rest."

Kingsley could not bring himself to look at her. "It's you," he said, squinting at the distant blur of the city lights. "After you—we make love, then I have it, I have the gift, just for a short time. And then it goes away again, until you come back and—"

"Yes," she said.

He swallowed, his throat stringy and tight with phlegm. "But you take something from me. Every time there's less left for me."

"Yes."

He dared to look at her then. The lights of the distant city were no longer necessary to show her to him: she would be visible in the deepest night, in the blackest pit, for she burned with an unmistakable inner lambency now, a vitality that had come, he knew, from him.

"Why?" he asked.

Her voice was soft, but it held no regret: "It's what I am."

"Some kind of goddamn vampire?"

She sighed, a rustle like a dry leaf being swept by the wind. "People have called us that, but we are not blood drinkers. We do not feed as you do; we must take life from others."

"How?"

"In our own way. I can't tell you; you couldn't understand. But in exchange for what we take, we give our own gifts, such as we may."

The lights shimmered as tears came to his eyes. "That's crazy. Maybe I'm crazy."

"We live in your darknesses, and we live long lives. I could tell you stories—but you wouldn't believe them."

Kingsley started to speak, and could find his voice for only one rusty word: "Try."

The autumnal sigh again. "There was a poet in England, nearly two hundred years ago by your people's counting. He wrote a poem, 'La Belle Dame sans Merci—' "

"Keats, wasn't it?"

"Yes."

Kingsley drew in a deep, shuddering breath. "I remember a little of the poem. 'And then I shut her wild wild eyes with kisses four.' But Keats died of tuberculosis, I think."

"Of consumption, yes. He thought so, too."

Kingsley shook his head. "Maybe I'm not insane, after all. Maybe it's just you. Are you telling me he died from—because of your kind?"

"No. Because of me." Her palm again, so cool and soft on his neck. "He was my first."

"Crazy," Kingsley said again, and now he was weeping in earnest. "Crazy." He gathered himself and turned on her. "Why didn't you tell me?"

She smiled at him, but no mirth lived in that miserable smile. "Telling is forbidden."

"But now—?"

She was quiet for a long moment. "I don't want you to misunderstand me. We do not feel love, not as your people do. But I do feel—something—for you."

He snorted. "I'm a better lay than Keats, is it? Or a better meal?"

She shook her head. "I knew you wouldn't believe or understand."

"I understand that you said you'd kill me." His heart was thudding very fast now, so hard that it seemed to him that he trembled with every beat.

"No," she said. "It's not that way. Not for you. I will give you a choice." She was close, so close that he could feel her breath on his face, could smell its honey-and-spice sharpness. "You may have your years back, if you will; such years as you would have left, anyway."

"Have them back?"

"Yes. I can go away now, tonight. I can find someone else, someone who needs me and whom I need."

"Prey."

She did not flinch. "Prey. All right. That's your word. But notice how your people prey on each other before you judge me: the writer Lowell draws life from that wretch of a woman. The men who pay for your work care only for the work, not for the anguish you put into it. How many husbands, how many wives, build their lives on the other's ruins? There are many different kinds of predators, Ray; one for every possible type of prey, I'd think."

He swallowed. "If you don't leave me, what then?"

She kissed him. Her lips were hot, pliant; they carried no flavor of lipstick, but left his mouth and tongue burning, as if he had tasted some exotic sweet spice. She pushed away, stood with her palms against his chest. Her face was placid, soft, luminous. "I take what I must. I give what I may. You must choose. Now. You may have me, and your art, and your life, for a year or perhaps two; or you may have almost as many years as you would have lived if you had never met me."

The world revolved very slowly around the rooftop. His voice shaking, Kingsley muttered, "What if I want to make it on my own? I can do it. You've showed me that I can do it. It may take me years to get even half as good as I was with the Kali painting, but by God, it would be *me*, myself, and not some damned inhuman—" His words broke off in a sob.

"Choose." Was there a hint of sadness in her voice? If so, it sounded to Kingsley like no human sadness. "You must choose."

His heart beat against his ribs, a panicked scarlet bird battering
itself against the bars of its cage. Already knowing the decision that
he had not yet consciously made, Kingsley stared at Lisbet's pale,
beautiful face. Her unpainted lips were the shade of fresh blood,
her unblinking eyes the color of midnight unending.

The Snatchers

Jane Yolen

You could say it all began in 1827 (though my part of it didn't start until 1963) because that was the year Tsar Nicholas I decided to draft Jews into the army. Before that, of course, only Russian peasants and undesirables had to face the awful twenty-five-year service.

But it was more than just service to the state the Jewish boys were called to do. For them, being in the army meant either starvation—for they would not eat non-kosher food—or conversion. No wonder their parents said *kaddish* for them when they were taken.

After Tsar Nicholas' edict, the army drafted sons of tax evaders and sons of Jews without passports. They picked up runaways and dissidents and cleaned the jails of Jews. Worst of all, they forced the *kahal*, the Jewish Community Council, to fill a quota of thirty boys for every one thousand Jews on the rolls—and those rolls contained the names of a lot of dead Jews as well as living. The Russian census takers were not very careful with their figures. It was the slaughter of the innocents all over again, and no messiah in sight.

The richest members of the community and the *kahal* got their own sons off, of course. Bribes were rampant, as were forgeries. Boys were reported on the census as much younger than they were; or they were given up for adoption to Jewish families without sons of their own, since single sons were never taken. And once in a while, a truly desperate mother would encourage her sons to mutilate themselves, for the army—like kosher butchers—did not accept damaged stock.

In my grandfather's village was a family known popularly as Eight-toes because that is how many each of the five sons had. They'd cut off their little toes to escape the draft.

So many boys were trying in so many ways to avoid conscription that a new and awful profession arose amongst the Jews—the *khaper*. He was a kidnapper, a bounty hunter, a Jew against Jews.

My Aunt Vera used to sing an old song, but I didn't know what it meant until almost too late:

> *I had already washed and said the blessing*
> *When the snatcher walked right in.*
> *"Where are you going?" he asks me.*
> *"To buy wheat, to buy corn."*
> *"Oh no," he says, "you are on your way*
> *Trying to escape. . . ."*

One of my uncles remarked once that the family had come over to escape the *khapers* in the 1850s, and I thought he said "The coppers." For years I was sure the Yolens were but one step ahead of the police. Given my Uncle Louis' reputation as a bootlegger, why should anyone have wondered at my mistake? But I learned about the *khaper*—the real one—the year I was sixteen. And I understood, for the first time, why my family had left Ykaterinislav without bothering to pack or say goodbye.

I was sixteen in the early sixties, living with my parents and two younger brothers in Westport, Connecticut. My father, a member of a lower-class family, had married rather late in life to a young and lovely Southern Jewish intellectual. He had become—by dint of hard work and much charm—part of the New York advertising fraternity. He had also rather successfully shaken off his Jewish identity: of all the Yolens of his generation, he was the only one without a hint of an accent. If he knew Yiddish, he had suppressed or forgotten it. My mother's family were active leftists, more interested in radicalism than religion. I was reminded we were Jews only when we went—infrequently—to a cousin's wedding or bar mitzvah.

I was undersized, over-bright, and prone to causes. My glasses hid the fact that I was more myopic about people than things. Recently I had fallen under the spell of a local pacifist guru who was protesting American involvement in Vietnam even before Americans were aware we *were* involved. While my friends were playing football and discussing baseball stats, I was standing in protest lines or standing silently in vigils in the middle of the bridge over the Saugatuck River. I even took to writing poems, full of angst and schoolboy passion. One ended:

> *Death you do not frighten me,*
> *Only the unknown is frightening.*

which the guru's group published in their mimeoed newsletter. It was my first by-line, which my father, a staunch Republican, refused to read.

It was while I was standing next to Bert Koop, the pacifist guru, basking in his praise of my poetry and wishing—not for the first time—that *he* was my father, that I noticed the man in black. We were used to onlookers, who usually shouted something at us, then walked away. But he was different. Wearing a long, ankle-length black coat and high boots with the pants pushed into the tops, he stood in the shadow of the town library's front door. He had an odd cap pulled down to his eyebrows which effectively hid his face, though I could tell he was staring at us. He didn't move for long minutes, and I thought he was watching the entire line of us. It was only much later that I understood he had been staring at me.

"FBI?" I whispered to Bert.

"CIA," he told me. "But remember—we have rights." He turned his face toward the man in black, as if defying him.

I did the same. And then, as bravado took over—sixteen is the high point of bravado even today—I slammed my fist against my chest, shouting across the noise of the traffic: "Doug Yolen. American. I have my rights."

At that the man in black nodded at me, or at least he tucked his chin down, which totally obscured his face. I turned to gauge Bert's reaction. He was smiling proudly at me. When I looked back, the man in the doorway was gone.

The next time I saw him, I was at a basketball game, having been persuaded by Mary Lou Renzetti to go with her. I had had a crush on Mary Lou since second grade, so it didn't take much persuading. She thought of me as her little brother, though we were the same age, give or take a couple of months.

The man was on the other side of the gym, where the Southport crowd sat in dead quiet because their team was losing, and badly. I didn't see him until the second half. He was wearing the same black coat and cap, even though it must have been 100° in the gym. This time, though, it was clear he was staring at me, which gave me the shivers, bravado notwithstanding. So I turned away to look at Mary Lou's profile, with its snub nose and freckles. Her mother was Irish and she took after that side.

Jack Patterson made an incredible basket then and we all leaped up to scream our approval. When I sat down again, I glanced at the Southport benches. The man in black was gone.

It went on like that for days. I would see him for a minute and then look away. When I looked back he wasn't there. Sometimes it was clear where he had gone, for a nearby door would just be closing. Other times there was nowhere for him to have disappeared.

At first I found it uncomfortable, spooky. Then when nothing at all happened, I tried to make a joke of it.

"So—you see that guy over there, Mary Lou?" I said. "The one with the black cap?" We were standing outside in the parking lot after school. I gestured over my shoulder at the running track, now covered with new-fallen snow. "He's been following me."

She put her hand on my arm, so I enlarged on the story, hoping she'd continue to hold on. "He's probably heard my dad is rich or something and wants to kidnap me. You think my dad will give him anything? I mean after the report card I brought home? He'll probably have to send my dad one of my fingers or something to prove he means . . ."

"Douggie, there's no one there."

I felt her hand on my arm, the fingers tight. I liked how they felt, and grinned at her. Slowly I turned my head, careful not to jiggle her hand loose. He wasn't there, of course. The snow on the running track was unbroken.

I thought about saying something to my father then. Or to my mother. But the more I rehearsed what I could say, the sillier it sounded. And though I had made a joke of it with Mary Lou, the truth is that the report I'd brought home the week before hadn't really put me in my parents' good graces. It was "Douggie—you're too bright for this!" from my father. And a searching, soulful look from Mom. To make matters worse, the twins brought home all A's. But then so had I at age thirteen.

So I shrugged the whole thing off as nerves. Or glands. Or needing new glasses. Or someone playing a bizarre joke. Or a hallucination. Only I had never joined the drinking crowd at school. Wine gave me headaches and I hated the taste of beer, especially when it repeated up my nose. Drugs had yet to hit high school—or at least to hit our crowd. They filtered in slowly over the next few years so that by the time the twins were seniors, Todd had experimented with everything in sight, and Tim joined an anti-drug crusade. But that's another story entirely.

Finally I spoke with Bert Koop about it and he was, predictably, sympathetic. And—as it turns out—totally wrong.

"Definitely CIA," he said. "They've been bugging my phone, too. Probably going to try and get to me through you."

"Well, if they think going to war is brave," I said. "I'll show them what *real* courage is. I won't say a word."

"Death . . ." Bert quoted, "you do not frighten me."

"Right," I said, and really meant it. After all, I had never actually seen anyone dead. Jews don't believe in open caskets. So death *didn't* frighten me. But the man in black was beginning to.

It was about a week after I first saw him that the man in black turned up at our house. Not *in* the house, but *at* it, walking slowly down the road. Grounded on weekdays till my grades improved, I had been working on my homework curled up on the sofa in the living room. I was pretty involved in writing a term paper on *War and Peace*. Tolstoy had been a pacifist, too, and I was writing about the difference between a war in fiction and a war in real life, especially Vietnam. I don't know what made me look up at that moment, but I did. And through the picture window I saw him walking along Newtown Turnpike toward the Weston line.

I leaped off the sofa, scattering my notes and the AFSC pamphlets about war resistance all over the floor. Sticking my feet quickly into boots and, without lacing them, I ran out the door after him. By the time I got down the driveway and to the main road, I was shivering uncontrollably. It was late November and we'd already had two snowfalls; I hadn't taken a coat. But I walked way past the Hartleys' house, at least a quarter mile on up the road, right to the Weston line.

There was no sign of him.

That night I came down with a raging fever; missed a whole week of school, an interfaith peace vigil I had helped put together, the start of the big basketball tournament, and the due date for my Tolstoy paper. Evidently I had also spent one whole day—twenty-four solid hours—ranting and raving about the man in black. Enough so that both my mother *and* my father were worried. They had called the town cops, who questioned my friends, including Mary Lou. A police car made special rounds the entire week by our house. It seems my father really *did* have a lot of money, and there had been a kidnapping just six weeks earlier of an ad man's kid in Darien. No one was dismissing it as a prank.

But then they found the gang that had kidnapped the Darien kid, she identified them all, and the special patrols stopped. And once I was well again, I swore it had all been some kind of wild nightmare, a dream. After all, I had a healthy distrust of the police because of my association with Bert Koop. I think everyone was relieved.

Except—and this was the really funny thing—except my father. He made these long, secret phone calls to his brothers and sisters, and even to his Uncle Louis, who scarcely had an aggie left, much less the rest of his marbles. My father rarely spoke to his family;

they were the embarrassing past he'd left behind. But since my night of raving, he insisted on calling them every night, talking to them in Yiddish. *Yiddish!* After that, he started going to work late and driving the twins and me to school before getting on the train to the city. Further, he established a check-in system for all of us. I was sixteen and embarrassed; sixteen is the high-water level of being embarrassed by one's parents.

It was two weeks before I saw the man in black again. By that time, with my grounding rescinded—not because my grades had gone up but because we all had other things to think about—and Mary Lou starting to pay a different kind of attention to me, I had all but forgotten the man in black. Or at least I had forgotten he scared me. I had walked the long block to Mary Lou's for a study date. Study on her part, date on mine, but I still got to hold her hand for about a quarter of an hour without her finding an excuse to remove it. Her parents kicked me out at ten.

The moon was that yellow-white of old bone. It made odd shadows on the snow. As I walked my breath spun out before me like sugar candy; except for the noise of my exhalations, there wasn't a sound at all.

I was thinking about Mary Lou and the feel of her hand, warm and a bit moist in mine, and letting my feet get me home. Since I had gone around that block practically every day since second grade—the school bus stop was in front of Mary Lou's driveway—I didn't need to concentrate where I was going. And suddenly, right at the bend of the road, where Newtown Turnpike meets Mary Lou's road, a large shadow detached itself from one of the trees. He had made no sound but somehow I had heard something. I looked up and there he was. Something long and sharp glittered in his hand. He was humming a snatch of song and it came to me across the still air, tantalizingly familiar. I couldn't quite place it, though a line ran through my mind: "You are on your way trying to escape . . ."

I turned and ran. How I ran! Back past Mary Lou's, past the Pattersons', past the new row of houses that just barely met the two acre standards. I turned left and right and left again. It was dark—the moon having been hidden behind clouds—then light once

more and still I ran. I had no breath and I ran; I had a stitch in my
side and I ran; I stood for a moment by the side of the road
vomiting and vomiting up something and then nothing and I ran.

I got home at three a.m. My mother lay fast asleep on the sofa, a
box of Kleenex by her side, her eyes red with crying. She didn't
rouse when I slipped in the door. I thought of waking her, of
hugging her with gratitude that I was home and safe. But I was so
exhausted, I went right to bed.

I took off my shoes and, still in my clothes, lay down. A shadow
detached itself from my closet. Something long and sharp glittered
in its hand. I tried to scream and couldn't, then saw it was my
father and relaxed.

"Dad . . ." I began.

"This . . ." he said as he always did when he was going to
punish me, "is going to hurt me more than it does you."

He was wrong of course. On cold nights, especially winter
nights, that missing toe aches more than anything.

But I have never seen the man in black again.

All Flesh Is Clay

John J. Ordover

Again there is a knock on my workshop door, a dry white sound that scrapes along the wood. The empty figure stands there as always, grinning as always. It moves slowly in; its thinning tendons pull at its yellowed bones.

I have a reputation among the dead. My name is whispered in the graveyards and given to the dying as a sign of hope. I gesture, and moved by love or hate or desperation the skeleton seats itself in my special chair.

I have no sympathy for them; if I were freed of life I would never return. To me there could be no reason strong enough; no lover, no child, no need for vengeance powerful enough to pull me back.

I examine the body carefully, measure the sleeve and inseam, use tiny instruments to check the shape and pattern of the cheekbones and chin. A woman, I see by the pelvis, Caucasian by the arms, Irish by the eye sockets. I speak to her.

"I can do it," I say, "can you pay the fee?" Her jaw opens and her hand comes up. From behind silver-filled teeth she takes a photograph and a money card authorized to the estate of Joan McFarrel. She'd prepared well. Few anticipate the need.

I slide the chair down flat and begin. The remnants of her tendons are useless and I cut them away, paralyzing her. Then I turn to the head.

The textbooks I studied to be licensed for my craft require a layered approach; start with the organs, they say, lash the plastic replicas in place within the ribs; put in the simulated blood tubing, then set the contracting fiber muscles; connect the metal tendons and give motion to the body; then progress to the dermal coverings and finally the head. They condemn any other practice as grotesque and unlikely to be successful.

I disagree.

I bring out a bowl of dull red putty and roll it into long thin snakes. I place them on her skull and circle her empty sockets with them, then flatten them out, spread them, knead them flat. There are still no eyes, and her cheekbones are white and rough. Her teeth still grin at me.

I lay the muscles and tendons into the red mask on her blank face, then cover them with a second layer, then a third, the cosmetic layer that looks like human skin. From a box on my desk I take round white balls, styrofoam, with black buttons glued on. Sculpting carefully, I match them to the sockets, then lay them to one side.

I build the eyelids out of cardboard backed with clay, then anchor them above the empty sockets. I place two saline-soaked pads inside the skull, then reach for the puppet eyes. The first stage is complete and I wait for the soul to merge.

There are many reasons, apparently, to leave your coffin and go walking through the night. Most are better done without flesh: flesh that can hurt; flesh that can die again. Often the reason becomes unimportant when the pain of living returns.

That is why I start with the eyes. The books tell you to finish the limbs and torso first, to work your way backward through the anatomy text. Many of those operations are successful, but the patients, reminded now of life, remain dead of their own choosing.

The full process is lucrative, and the estate pays win or lose. Many of my colleagues consider the fee and follow the book precisely, wasting time.

Her eyes come to life, blinking and staring, salt tears from the pads running down and back into her empty brain-case. The styrofoam softens and the black eye-buttons turn light blue. I check the photograph and find blue eyes.

I will continue.

The face is the simplest part, and the part that gets the most praise. I am not a visual artist, but any craftsman can follow a design. I do it quickly, matching her to the picture she brought. Soon her face is staring at me from below a bare bone headcap.

The tone of the flesh, the general appearance—that requires no true talent or genius. But will the skin feel like skin, the muscles feel like muscles, not from the outside, but from the inside, to the wearer?

I run my fingers along soft but muscular arms that hours ago were nothing but bone. The hands require much precision, and I work on them closely under bright lights. Her eyes follow me as I work, sometimes closing in fear, sometimes spreading wide as I trip over a too-soon-functioning nerve; they have dampened further, the no-longer-button pupils contract and dilate in the light.

Her hands are shaped and finished, and her arms and legs and feet, but her ribs are still bone and lie empty, her pelvis fleshless and stark white. I stop for lunch before I move on.

I watch her face as I eat. Without lungs the newly-made mouth cannot speak, but somehow with nothing in her skull she can still think, still have emotions that come in waves of silent laughter or lips set in grim, determined lines. The constant use is changing the face quickly, the clay fading into true skin, the eyes already filling with their own tears.

As always, I wonder what reason she has that is worth the pain I inflict. I have heard many explanations, some trivial or misconceived; many tragic: one man, shot dead by a woman he could not make love him, thought this act of suffering would win his murderess's heart; one rich young woman strangled by a husband who she did not know would kill her daughter next; when I told her she had no child left behind she slumped back to clay before my eyes. People return to wives and lovers; to hate and pain; to uncompleted follies: swept away by what they think they feel.

After lunch I place the major organs. They are pre-packaged yet complex, both boring and difficult. I tear the cellophane wrapping from her lungs and tie them carefully inside her ribs. With air from a tube I inflate them, and check them for leaks or punctures. They work well, and I attach the trachea to the back of her throat. The sound of the air rushing through her mouth is a scream muffled by clay walls.

I put a respirator in her, then watch the inflating lungs change color and become at least somewhat alive. I unblock her throat and speak to her.

"Hello," I say pleasantly. "Things are going well." She tries to speak, then tries again. I think I understand her. "Yes, quite well," I say, then turn back to my work while she breathes deeply and tries to talk. Despite the distraction I secure the heart and stomach and liver, then discover the gallbladder is too wide and trim it back.

Her lungs are working better now. She is crying with the pain, yelling it out, the sound sinking into my padded walls. Her volume lifts and falls, going up whenever I touch her, softening when I step away.

Her pain comes from her own choice. I can see in her eyes that she knows this, that she does not regret the ordeal. How foolish.

I finish inside her, her heart beating slowly, intestines and uterus in place. The law requires that my creations be sterile, but I refuse to be less than thorough and connect her ovaries. She must be complete.

Her arms and legs have motion now, and I cuff them down to keep myself and her new body safe. There is still no skin between her neck and thighs, and there are many nerves to place. An unrestrained reflex could destroy her.

Her screams increase in number as I lay the skin in and the new connections start to grow. If I placed her brain now, it would be far worse. This way the impulses are implied, not sensed, and some of the pain is lost. At least that's what the souls tell us.

The first and second layers done, I start on her breasts. She is clothed in the photo she gave me, but I can guess at the shape her body had and I improve it slightly. I make the men just a trifle longer, too. No one complains.

I build her vulva and vagina carefully, using the standard pattern for her genetic type. I plant the area with scattered hair, slightly darker than the bright red I will use on her head. I feel inside her for a moment, getting the texture perfect and the small glands placed correctly. I stroke her gently until I feel her contract once on my fingers, then I withdraw them and step back.

She looks perfect, and when I run my hands along her she feels perfect, still more like clay than flesh but evolving quickly. I walk around her and put my hands on her head.

Her brain-case is still empty. Gently I remove the package from the cool, dark place it is stored, then peel back its wet covering. The grey rubber mass is slippery and must be connected exactly right.

The brain sealed in place, I secure her red hair and sit waiting, coffee in hand, for the true scream.

It comes an hour later, an average time, and she shakes the house with her voice, shouting her pain outward like a baby. She does it twice, then pants heavily. I walk over to her.

I examine her again for texture, ask a few questions about how this or that feels to her. She pants as she answers, her tone reflecting relief and memory of pain. I help her up and go to fetch clothes for her, all part of the service.

When I get back she dresses and asks for coffee. I use it to test her senses; taste, smell, heat, touch, and the numerous small reflexes of drinking and swallowing. She works perfectly, nature and determination again making up for lack of precision, smoothing over any errors in duplication.

She does not now look or feel like clay.

"Was it worth it?" I ask her. No one ever says no; they would look idiotic.

She turns her eyes on me, surprised. "Of course," she says.

"Was being dead so bad?" I ask, watching her face carefully.

She thinks about it while sipping at her coffee. "It was a great opportunity," she begins, "you know, a chance to be forgiven and begin again. But you can't finish what you'd already started."

"And you have something to finish?" I say, a patronizing tone in my voice. "A marriage, a love affair, a child you think needs you?"

"A painting," she answers flatly. "It's sitting on my easel, only half-finished. I tried to forget about it. . . ." she sips again at her coffee, then looks helpless and shrugs, ". . . so I came back."

"A painting?" I ask. For some reason the thought upsets me.

She shrugs again. "So sue me, I don't like to stop in the middle of something." She stands up. "My will said to leave my studio alone. Can you call me a cab?"

I do so, and when she leaves I think about my next client, and my next. I work a lot, and there is always the chance that something will happen, that between the lungs and liver my heart will fail, or I will fall, and there will be a canvas on my table that I will never finish, never make whole. The image chases me and I shake; I think of the pain of merging and I shake again. For most of the night I balance the fears.

In the morning I call my lawyer, then arrange for nude photos to be taken, from many angles. I will be ready, I tell myself, if I become a canvas for someone else. If I become the one strapped empty to a table, desperate for life, I am prepared.

I love my work.

The Boy Who
Came Back from the Dead

Alan Rodgers

Walt Fulton came back from the grave Sunday evening, after supper but before his mom had cleared the table. He was filthy, covered from head to toe with graveyard dirt, but all the things the car had crushed and broken when it hit him (things the mortician hadn't quite been able to make look right) were fixed.

"Mom," Walt called, throwing open the kitchen door, "I'm home!" His mother screamed, but she didn't drop and break the porcelain casserole dish she was holding.

There's something in an eight-year-old boy that lets him understand his mother, though he could never know that he had it or put words to what it told him. Walt couldn't have told anyone how when his mother saw him she first wanted not to believe that it was him—the boy was dead and buried, by God, and let the dead rest—but because she was his mother and mothers *know*, she knew that it was him returned from the grave.

Then Walt saw the shock setting in, saw her begin to paralyze. But she was stronger than that; she set her teeth, shook off the numbness. She was a strong woman. His return brought her joy beyond words, for she loved him. But she wanted him to go away and never come back, because seeing him again meant remembering the moment at the highway rest stop when she'd looked up to see him running out into traffic after his ball—and then suddenly splattered like a fly across the front bumper of a late model Buick. And she couldn't bear to have that dream again.

Walt didn't resent any of it, not even knowing that she felt that way about him. The same thing that let him know what she was thinking (despite the fact that it was impossible) made sure that he would always love her.

After a minute and a half she composed herself. "Walt," she said, "you're late for dinner and you're filthy. Wash your hands and face and sit down at the table." His father and sister smiled; Dad had tears in his eyes, but he didn't say anything. Mom got up and set him a place at the table.

And Walt was home.

The morning after he came back Walt sat at the kitchen table for hours, coloring in coloring books, while his mother fussed about the house. There was a certain moodiness and elegance in his crayon-work; he wondered at the strangeness that grew on the pages as he colored.

"Walt," his mother said, peeking over his shoulder and humming in surprise, "you can't imagine how much trouble it's going to be to get you back in school." She walked into the kitchen and bent down to look into the cabinet underneath the sink. "They're all certain that you're dead. People don't come back from the dead. No one's going to believe that it's you. They'll think we're both crazy."

Walt nodded. She was right, of course. It was going to be a lot of trouble. He looked down at the floor and scuffed his feet against the finish.

"I ought to tell someone," he said.

"What's that, Walt?" His mother's head was buried deep inside the cabinet under the sink, among the cleansers and the steel wool and the old rusty cans.

"About being dead," he told her. "I remember it."

Walt knew his mother wasn't listening. "That's nice. You all ready for school this afternoon? We have an appointment with the principal for one o'clock, right after lunch."

"Yeah," he said, "school's okay." He scratched his cheek. "I know people need to know what it's like, about being dead, I mean. It's one of those things that everybody has needed to know forever."

Walt's mother pulled her head out of the cabinet slowly. She turned to stare at him, her mouth agape.

"*Walt!* You'll do nothing of the sort. I won't have that." Her voice was frantic.

"But *why?* They need to know."

But she only clamped her lips and turned beet red. She wouldn't talk to him again until after lunch.

The principal, Mr. Hodges, was a man with dry red skin and grey-black hair who wore a navy blue suit and a red silk cloth in his breast pocket. Walt didn't like him and he never had. He never acted friendly, and Walt thought the man would do him harm if he only could.

"He's Walt all right," Mom told the man. "Never mind what I *know*; Sam and I went out to check the grave this morning as soon as the sun was up. All the dirt is broken, and you can see where he crawled up out of it."

"But it can't be done. We don't even have the files anymore. They've been sent away to the fireproof vault downtown." He stopped for a moment to catch his breath. "Look, I know it's horrible to lose a child. Even worse to see him die while you're watching. Walt's not the first kid I've had die in an accident. But you can't delude yourself like this. Walt's dead and buried. I don't know who this young man is, much less why he's preying on this weakness of yours. . . ."

Walt's mother looked outraged, so angry that she couldn't speak. He wanted to settle things, to quiet them: "What kind of proof do you want?" he asked the man. "What would make you certain that I'm me?"

Neither his mother nor the principal could respond to that at first. After a moment Mr. Hodges excused himself and left the room.

For twenty minutes Walt sat staring out the window of the principal's office, watching the other kids at recess. His mother never got out of the seat by the principal's desk. She stared at the wall with her eyes unfocused while her fingers twisted scraps of paper into tiny, hard-packed balls.

Finally, Mr. Hodges opened the door and came back into the room. He looked tired, now, and even shell-shocked, but he didn't look mean any more. He set two thick file folders onto his desk.

"Any proof I'd want could be manufactured, Walt. But it isn't right for me to try to stop you this way. If nothing else, you've got a right to call yourself anything you want." He opened one of the files. "I can't connect you to these files without moving heaven and earth. But I don't think you need them. There's nothing here that would make us treat you any differently than we'd treat a new student." He began to read. "You're in the third grade. The class you were in has gone on now, but your teacher, Miss Allison, still works for us. You haven't been gone quite a year; you've already been through this part of the third grade, but I don't think the review will do you any harm."

Later, before Walt and his mother finished filling out the forms, the principal called Miss Allison in to see them. Walt looked up when she opened the door to Mr. Hodges's office, and he felt her recognize him when she saw him.

Miss Allison screamed, and her legs went limp underneath her. She didn't faint—she was never unconscious—but when she fell to the floor it looked as though she had.

She screamed again when he went over to help her up.

"*Wal—ter!*" long and eerie, just like something out of an old horror movie.

"It's all right," Walt said. "I'm not a ghost."

"What are you?" Her voice was still shrill with terror.

"I'm just . . . just Walt. I'm Walt."

Miss Allison glared at him impatiently.

"Really. I'm Walt. Besides, Mom said I couldn't tell."

Walt heard his mother snap the pencil she was chewing on. "Tell her," she said. Her voice was furious. "Tell me."

Walt shrugged. "It was the aliens. They were walking all around the graveyard, looking into people's dirt."

"What aliens?"

"A whole bunch of them, all different kinds. They landed in a spaceship over in the woods. A couple of them looked kind of like fish—or snakes, maybe—one of them kind of like a bear, a couple looked like mole crickets when you see them in a magnifying glass. Others, too.

"But the one I paid attention to—it was the one telling all the rest what to do—that one was really gross. It had this big lumpy head—shaped like the head on that retarded kid Mrs. Anderson had—"

"Walt! Billy Anderson is a mongoloid. You mustn't speak ill of those less fortunate than you."

Walt nodded. "Sorry. Anyway, the thing had this big, lumpy, spongy head, and this face that looked kind of like an ant's—with those big pincer things instead of a mouth—and kind of looked like something you dropped on the floor in the kitchen. It drooled all over the place—"

"Walt!"

"—and it kept making this gross sound like someone hawking up a great big clam.

"But it wasn't what it looked like that bothered me so much. What scared me was when it first got to my grave, and it looked down like it could see me right through the dirt. And its pincers clacked and rubbed against each other just exactly the way a cat licks its lips when it sees a mouse, and its elbows flexed backward like it wanted to pounce. It made this whining sound, like a dog when it begs, and I thought it was going to reach right through the dirt and eat my putrid body. And even though I knew I was dead and I couldn't get any deader, it scared me. It was bad enough being something trees couldn't tell from mulch, without being dinner for a ghoul. But then the thing turned away and went back to looking at other people's dirt. After it looked at everyone, it came back to me and broke up my dirt and shined its ray down on me. It didn't hurt—but nothing does when you're dead. After five minutes I was alive again, and I felt things but I couldn't just know them anymore, and I pushed my way out of the dirt.

"But when I got up to the ground the aliens had already gone. So I went home."

It was Miss Allison who finally said it.

"Walt, that can't be. How could you know all that when you're dead, buried in the ground? Even if your eyes were open, how could you see through all the dirt?"

Walt shrugged. "That's what I need to tell them. About what it's like to be dead. They've all been needing to know forever, because they're all afraid. It's like the feeling of your fingernails on a dusty chalkboard, like being awake so long you get dizzy and start hearing things. And you can't feel anything, and you know everything that's going on around you, and some things far away. It's bad, and it's scary, but not so terrible that you can't get used to it."

Neither Miss Allison nor his mother spoke to Walt again that afternoon.

No one saw any sense in disrupting things by bringing him into class in the middle of the day. Tomorrow morning was soon enough. (Maybe too soon, the look on Miss Allison's face said, but everyone did his best to ignore that.) When they got home Anne, his sister, had a hug for him, and they played cards until supper time. After dinner Dad and Walt and Anne roughhoused and threw pillows at each other in the playroom.

It was fun.

Before bed Walt wanted Dad to tell him a story—he'd missed Dad's ghost stories—but Dad wouldn't. After a while, Walt stopped asking. He wasn't dumb; he knew why it scared his father.

But what could he do? He sure didn't want to go away, go back to being dead. He liked being alive. He liked having people see him, hear him, know he was there. The dead make poor companions. Almost all of them are quiet and tired, waiting for the resurrection, not so much world weary as exhausted by its absence.

Tuesday and Wednesday were quiet days in school. Almost no one in his new class had known Walt before the accident. Those few who did took a while to reason out that Walt was something they'd only seen on Saturday afternoon horror movies.

But by Thursday word had got around, and the boldest of the boys from his class the year before—four of them—looked for him and found him in an empty corner of the school yard during recess.

"Hey Zombie," Frankie Munsen called at him from behind, throwing a dirt clod that caught Walt in the soft part of his shoulder, just below his neck.

"Count Dracula, I presume. . . ?" Donny James taunted him, stepping out from behind a tree on Walt's left. He draped his blue Windbreaker over his forearm and shielded his chin with it, the way vampires do with their chins in the movies. "You got bats in your belfry, Walt? What's it like to be *un*dead?"

Walt flinched when a dirt clod hit him in the belly from the right. He looked over to see John Taylor and Rick Mitchell standing in a knot of pine trees throwing dirt clods. As he saw them a clod hit him on the forehead and the dust splattered in his eyes.

When he could finally open them again he saw four boys standing over him, surrounding him.

"What's the matter, Zom-boy? Smoke get in your eyes?" Donny jeered, shoving Walt by the shoulders so that he fell on his back. Donny straddled Walt's chest and pinned him by digging his knees into the muscles of his upper arms. "Ain'tcha gonna fight back, Zom-boy?" He snickered. "Too late now, sucker."

Walt's voice wasn't frightened, wasn't scared at all, just a little angry: "What's the matter with you? I haven't done anything to you."

"Don't like to see dead people walking around our school, Zom-boy." Donny drooled spit into Walt's eyes. "Want you to leave, sucker."

Walt rolled over, surprising Donny, throwing him off. As he stood up he wiped the spit from his eyes with one arm and grabbed Donny's collar with the other. Walt hauled the older boy to his feet.

"I'm not dead," he said. His voice was furious now, trembling. He threw Donny against a tree where his head made a liquid cracking sound.

None of the other boys said or did anything. They didn't run yet, either. Donny sat up, drooling bloody spit into the dirt.

"I bit my tongue," he said. He swayed back and forth unevenly.

Walt turned away. "Don't do anything like this again," he said. And he went home.

Someone should have done something about that—called his house, sent someone after him, marked him truant at least. But no one did. It was not as though no one noticed him gone. And certainly no one missed seeing what he'd done to Donny James. But Miss Allison couldn't bring herself to report him, and no one would challenge her.

When his mom got home, he was sitting by the TV with a coloring book spread out over the coffee table. He had the sound turned almost all the way down.

"You're home early, dear. Why's that?" she asked. Walt mumbled without using any real words, just low enough that she'd think his answer got lost in the sound of her walking.

"Sorry, dear, I didn't hear you. Why was it?"

Walt's hand pressed too hard, and his crayon left a dark, flaky wax mark on the paper. It looked like a scar to Walt.

"I got into a fight," he said. "I think I hurt Donny James pretty bad. He looked like he was going to have to go see a doctor. I didn't want to have to talk to them any more. So I went home."

"You just left school? Just like that?"

"Mom, they think I'm a monster. They think I'm some sort of a vampire or something." Walt wanted to cry, mostly from frustration, but he didn't. He set his head down onto his arms so that his nose rubbed against the coloring book.

Mom sat down beside him and lifted him up so that she could put her arms around him. In front of them, on the television with the sound turned down, the characters in a soap opera worried at each other silently, the way a dog worries a bone.

"You aren't a monster, Walt," she said as she held him, hugging him tighter to her. "Don't let them tell you that." But her voice was so uncertain that even though he wanted to more than anything else in the world, Walt couldn't make himself believe her.

Walt went out an hour before dinner time, looking for something to do. He walked a long way, blocks and blocks into the neighborhood, trying to find someone he knew, or a sandlot game to watch or even play in, or *something*, but all he found were some floating waterbugs (the ones his mom told him never to bring home because they were really *roaches*) in the creek down on Dumas Street. It wasn't much fun. Walking home, the stars were gloriously bright, even though it wasn't very dark out yet. Walt tried to find Betelgeuse—he loved the star's name, so he got his father to show him how to find it—but the star was nowhere Walt could see. Three stars turned to meteors as he watched. At first he just stared, marveling at the pencil-marks of light that the shooting stars left behind them—but then they all began to spiral down and each in turn to head toward him. Three blocks away there was a big woods, fifteen or twenty square blocks' worth of land where no one had ever got around to putting in streets or building houses. Walt ran there, as hard and fast as he could. He ran deeper into the woods than he'd ever been before, until he couldn't see any houses or landmarks that he knew, and he wasn't sure where he was. When he heard the sound of people running toward him he climbed into the biggest, tallest, leafiest tree he could find. He hid there.

The aliens should have found him. Walt knew that.

There were seven of them, each one strange and different from every other. The only one he really saw was the one who held the gadget that looked like a Geiger counter, the one with the giant ant pincers for a mouth—it was a maw, really, not a mouth. (Walt knew that. He'd gone to the library on Tuesday and spent hours reading about bugs.)

That was the same one that'd stared at him right through the graveyard dirt when he was still dead. The thing came right up to the tree Walt had hidden in, where the widget in its hands beeped and whirred maniacally. Walt stared at the thing from above, chewing on his lower lip. So close, it was even uglier than when it'd looked into his grave. The things at the ends of its arms weren't hands at all, really. It didn't have palms or fingers, just muscley, wormy flaps of skin dangling and fluttering at the ends of its wrists. Its skin was just exactly the color a roach is when you squish it. It smelled kind of like rotten eggs and kind of like the mouse that nested in the TV one summer and chewed on the wrong wire and got itself electrocuted. Its arms looked ordinary at first (or something in Walt's eyes wanted to make them look ordinary) but then the thing reached out to lean on the tree trunk, and its arm bent *back* double-jointed, and then the thing leaned even harder and the arm wasn't just bent double, it was *bending* in an arc under the weight. The legs were like that, too, and they bent ass-backward in a half-crouch when it walked. It had a tunic on, so Walt mostly couldn't see its torso, but then it bent sideways and the cloth (or was it some stretchy, rubbery plastic?) stretched thin enough to see through, and Walt could see that it was twisted off like a sausage in the middle, two big, bulbous pieces connected only by a touch.

Its eyes were the worst things, though. They were big, bigger than the saucers in Mom's good china, and they were sort of like what they say a spider's eyes look like when you see them up close. But not quite. More like a bowl full of eggs, broken and ready to scramble, but still intact. Around each eye's half dozen yellow pupils, through the clear matter, Walt could see veins and nerve endings pulse against the eye socket. Phlegm dripped down steadily from the eyes, into the maw. That was why the thing kept making that sound like somebody hawking up a big wad of snot.

The thing spent a long time prowling around the base of Walt's tree, sifting through every log and bush and leaf pile, while the other aliens combed through the rest of the woods. But it never looked up. None of the aliens, not one of them, ever looked up.

They searched for him carefully, methodically, sticking electronic probes deep into the ground, turning every stone and rotted log, sifting every drift of mulch.

But not once did any of them check the branches of a tree.

Stupid aliens, Walt thought. Later, reflecting on it, he decided he was right.

After they'd prowled around him for three-quarters of an hour they gave up and left. Walt stayed in the tree twenty minutes longer, against the possibility that they were hiding, waiting for him. He'd meant to wait longer but he couldn't make himself be still.

That was just as well. No one came to get him when he climbed out of the tree.

The aliens are more impatient than me, Walt thought. The idea of jittery aliens made him want to laugh, but he didn't.

It was night, now, and Walt didn't know this part of the woods at all. The moon at least was already up and nearly full, so there was light enough to see by, to see the trail (not a very well used one at all; thick clumps of grass grew out of it in places) that led, in both directions, in ways he didn't recognize.

He wasn't worried so much for himself—after all, he was lost not far from home, almost a silly thing to be—but he knew that his mother would be concerned. By the time he got home she'd be angry at him. He hurried as best he could.

After about fifteen paces the trail opened up into Walt's cemetery.

The one he'd spent eleven months and seven days buried in. The tree he stood by was the tree whose roots would almost tickle him on sunny mornings. In front of him was his headstone, desecrated with graffiti.

Even by the dim moonlight he could see it; bold strokes of spray paint crowding out the letters carved in the granite.

It had to be new. He'd looked back to see the stone the night he'd crawled out of the grave, and it was clean then.

And someone had packed the dirt back into his grave and tucked the sod grass back in above it.

Walt stood on the grave, kicking the toe of his shoe into the roots of the grass, staring at the gravestone, reading it over and over again. He tried to read the graffiti, too, but it wasn't made up of words or even letters, but of strange squiggles like the graffiti that covered the subways Walt had seen when Dad took him to New York. (Dad said the graffiti in the city was that way because the kids who painted it could never learn to read or write, that they were too dumb to ever even learn the alphabet. That seemed too incredible to believe, but Walt couldn't imagine any other reason why they didn't know how to use letters.) He thought maybe the aliens had left the graffiti, but then he thought, *Why would the aliens use bright red spray paint?* and he knew it couldn't be them.

Looking at the grave made him feel sleepy and comfortable. It was getting late, and he knew he should go home. But he couldn't stop himself, not really. He lay down on his grave, rested his head on the headstone (the paint was still fresh enough that Walt could smell it), and for an hour he stared into the sky, watching the stars.

Not to search for alien starships, but because nothing in the world could be more comfortable.

His mom wasn't in when Walt got home. Just Dad and Anne, watching TV in the den.

"Hiya, Walt," Dad called when he walked in. "Late night with the Cub Scouts?"

Walt chuckled. "Yeah," he said. It wasn't *really* a lie; Dad was just being facetious. Walt sat down at the card table behind Dad's recliner. Anne, sitting in the love seat against the wall, didn't turn away from the TV until the commercial was on.

"Cards?" she asked him.

"No, I'm going to bed early, I think."

"There's dinner left over for you in the refrigerator, Walt," Dad said. "Stuffed pork chops and green beans."

Walt nodded. "Thanks." He got up and started toward the kitchen.

"Oh, and Walt," Dad said, "I forgot. The man from that newspaper called. *The Interlocutor.* He wants to come by and talk to you tomorrow morning. Before school."

"Huh." Walt wasn't certain what he thought.

"Yeah," Dad said. "It should be interesting. I wonder how they found out so soon."

Walt shrugged, then realized his father couldn't see that. "I don't know. Someone at school, I guess."

"Yes." His father nodded at the television set. "I guess that would have to be it."

In the kitchen he took the plate from the refrigerator and tried to eat what his mom had left him. Walt loved stuffed pork chops. Even cold. But he couldn't find the appetite to eat them or the green beans, and after twenty minutes he left the plate virtually untouched on the kitchen table, and went to bed.

His mom came in through the back door while he was on the stairs up to his room. He turned to say good night to her, and she was already on the stairway just below him, charging up to God knew what, not seeing him at all in the dark.

"Mom," Walt said, trying to get her attention before she collided into him.

"*Oh my God!*" His mother screamed. In the darkness she swung her arm out and her fist hit Walt hard just below the right eye. That knocked him down; he would have rolled down the stairs if his left ankle hadn't jammed against her feet.

For five minutes, trembling and breathing deeply, she leaned into the banister that was screwed into the wall. Walt didn't move—it didn't seem safe to—he just lay on the stairs at her feet. In a moment his father and sister got to the foot of the stair, and they could see. They stood there, watching. They didn't say anything.

"Walt," his mother finally said (her voice was colder and more inhuman than it would ever seem to any stranger). "A hundred times I've told you to turn the lights on when you use the stairs and hallways."

"Sorry," he said, afraid she'd get angrier if he said anything else.

"*Don't* do it again."

He nodded. "I was going to bed. I meant to say good night."

"Good night," she said, her voice colder and lonelier than his grave had ever been.

In bed, drifting off to sleep, he realized that he'd hardly eaten all week, and that he hadn't been hungry since he came back from the dead.

Dad woke him up real early in the morning, shaking him by the shoulder with his big soft hand. Walt took a shower and got dressed before he'd really woke up; later he discovered that he'd put his shirt on backward.

When he got to the kitchen his mom was already cooking breakfast—scrambled eggs and bacon—and the man from *The Interlocutor* was sitting at the kitchen table. He stared at Walt the way Walt remembered staring at the lizards in the House of Reptiles at the zoo when he was six. But the lizard couldn't see him, or it acted like it couldn't.

"Hi, Walt." The man held out his hand to shake, but he still stared. "I'm Harvey Adler from *The National Interlocutor*. I'm here to take your story." He smiled, but it reminded Walt of the lizards' smiles: more a fault in their anatomy than a true expression.

"Are you going to eat with us?" Walt asked. He wasn't sure why he did.

"Ahh—" Adler began uncomfortably, but then Walt's mom set a plate in front of him and another in front of Walt. "Well. It looks like I am." Walt felt somehow betrayed.

"Coffee, Mr. Adler?" Walt's mom asked. That was even worse; Walt didn't know why.

"No thank you, Mrs. Fulton. I've already had two this morning." He turned back to Walt. "Did you really die, Walt? And come back from the dead? What was it like to die?"

Walt picked at his food with his fork. "I started to run across the highway, and I forgot to look. There was a screaming sound. I guess it was the car trying to stop. But I didn't see. I never even turned my head. It happened too fast. Then everything was black for a while."

Adler had his tape recorder on, and he scribbled notes furiously. "Then what, Walt?"

Walt shrugged. "Then I was dead. I could see and hear everything around me. Just like the other dead people. But I couldn't move."

"You were like that for a year? It must have been pretty lonely."

"Well. You know. You don't care that much when you're dead. And the dead people can hear you. And can talk to you. But they don't much. They just don't ever want to."

They went on like that for an hour. He told the man everything—about the aliens, about climbing out of his grave, about his friends and school and all. Finally, Walt was late for school. It probably wasn't a good day for that; when he finally got to class Miss Allison still wasn't talking to him from the day before.

At morning recess, Donny James (black and blue but not really hurt) found Walt and asked him to come to the Risk game they always had on Friday afternoons. He acted like nothing had happened, maybe even a little bit embarrassed. Walt could never understand that, and though later in life he knew that people could do such things, he could never expect or believe it.

It came to trouble with Miss Allison about an hour after recess. She asked the class a question ("Where is the Malagasy Republic?") that she meant no one to answer. But Walt raised his hand and answered it quite thoroughly ("The Malagasy Republic *is* the island of Madagascar off the southeast coast of Africa. The people are black, but they speak a language related to Polynesian."), which made her look awfully silly, and the class giggled. Walt didn't mean to do it. But as soon as he opened his mouth he knew that he'd made her look silly. Answering questions was a compulsion for him, and he knew the answer because the old man in the grave next to his had been a sailor in the Indian Ocean for thirty years, and when he did talk (which was almost never) it was always about Africa or India or the Maldives or some such.

Miss Allison didn't take it well at all. She hadn't taken anything well since Walt got back. And it didn't help any when Walt (feeling bold since he'd explained everything to the man from *The Interlocutor* at breakfast) tried to explain how it was he knew such an odd fact and why, after all, it really wasn't so important. For the third time this week Miss Allison's expression grew violent, and she pulled her hand back to strike him, and for the third time Walt glared at her as though if she did it might be the last thing she ever did. (Not that he meant it or even was able to carry out the threat. It was a bluff. But he knew her well enough to know that it would make her stop.) Miss Allison didn't go back to her desk, shaking, the way she did the times before, though. She ran out of the classroom and slammed the door behind her. She didn't come back for twenty minutes, and when she finally did Mr. Hodges, the principal, was with her.

He took Walt away from Miss Allison's class and moved him ahead a year—into the class he'd shared with Donny James, Rick Mitchell, and all the rest.

He liked it better there. Even if the fourth-grade teacher was a battle-axe, at least she wasn't hysterical.

In the afternoon he walked home with Donny and helped him set up the Risk game. Six boys showed up all together—Walt, Donny, Rick, Frankie, John, and Donny's little brother Jessie—and the game went well enough. Walt didn't win, but he didn't lose either. Nobody lost, really. It got to be dinner time before anyone got around to conquering the world, so they left it at that.

When he got to the house, his father and sister weren't home yet. His mom was sitting at the kitchen table drinking coffee with the aliens.

He knew the things were there before he even banged into the kitchen; when he opened the front door he could smell electrocuted flesh and sulfury-rotten eggs, and he knew they were there for him. His first thought was that they'd taken his mother hostage, kidnapped her to make him go with them. He rushed into the kitchen (where the smell came from) on the tide of one of those brave reflexes a boy can have when there isn't time to think.

But there was no need for him to save her.

As soon as he opened the kitchen door he knew that he should turn around and run right then, but he didn't. Shock paralyzed him. He backed up against the wall by the door he'd just come through, and stared at them with his eyes open wide and his mouth agape.

His mom sat at the kitchen table drinking coffee with the aliens. The ugly one, the one with skin the color of roach guts and eyes like a spider's corpse, sat right there at the table with her. Behind them, in the hall that led from the garage, the rest of the aliens crowded together at the doorway to stare at him.

"Walt," his mom said, "this is Mr. Krant. He's going to take you with him."

Walt wanted to scream, but his throat cramped, jammed, and he couldn't make any sound. Something in his knees wanted to spring loose and let him fall to the ground, so he leaned his body into the wall enough for it to take his weight.

"That's why they woke you up, dear. They wanted you. They're here for you. They're here to help you."

Walt didn't believe a word of it, not for a minute. His mother's tone was saccharine and *too*-sincere; she'd lied to him just like that just after he had died.

"*No!*" he shouted. His voice was shrill. He still wanted to scream, but now he wanted to cry, too. *God*, why his mom? Why did *she* have to be with them?

"It's okay, Walt." She was still lying. "You don't have to go with them, if *you* don't want. But listen. Talk to them. Hear them out."

Right away he knew that was the last thing he should do. The alien reached into the purse it carried and took out a gadget that Walt got dizzy looking at.

A hypnotizer, Walt thought, and he turned his head away as fast as he could.

"Relax, Walter." The thing's voice sounded like the air that bubbles up in a toilet when the pipes are doing funny things. Walt could hear it tinkering with the gadget. "You can call me Captain Krant. We've come a long way to find you. From galaxies and galaxies away." Walt couldn't help himself; he turned to see it talking. The pincers didn't move much, but the maw jumped and squirmed crazily. That made booger-clotted mucous drool down the thing's chinless jaw. Walt watched it ooze down the cloth of the alien's tunic and feed into the stain-ring below the neck—

—and he had to puke, even though he hadn't eaten in days, and his legs propelled him through the aliens toward the bathroom—

—and he realized he could move again, could run—

—so where the hall split he went straight, through the garage and out the side door, to run and run and run without looking back at his mother's house.

Which, maybe, he should have done, because he never saw it again.

He didn't pay much attention to where he ran, so it didn't surprise him much when he found himself, moments later, panting and crying and leaning over his own headstone. The grave was his home, probably the best one he'd ever had—though there was an element of bias, of bitterness, in that thought. Walt didn't mind it. There was nothing wrong with bitterness when your mom turned against you like she was a rabid dog—maybe there was even something right about it. Mothers were supposed to be the ones who *protected* you, not the ones who sold you into slavery (worse: gave you away) when the aliens came for you.

"Walt?" and a hand on his shoulder. He jumped and nearly screamed, but stopped himself. He hadn't heard it coming. Not at all.

"Walt, are you okay?" His sister. No one else. No one with her. His heart stomped up and down like a lunatic inside his chest.

"Yeah." He took a deep breath, let it out real slow. "Okay. I ought to say good-bye, though. Got to run away."

"Huh? Why's that?"

"Mom—" He stopped. "You wouldn't believe me."

Anne shook her head.

"It's hard to believe you're alive. What could be worse?"

Walt tried to think about that for a moment, then decided he didn't want to. He shrugged. "The aliens, the ones who made me alive again. They came back for me. Mom wants me to go with them."

She shrugged. "Maybe she's right. Something is wrong. Hasn't been right since you came back."

"*God!* Not you, too. If you saw them, if *you* had to go with them. . . ! They're *scary!*" Walt was trying not to cry, but it wasn't doing much good. "I don't want to go. I don't want Mom to try to get rid of me."

Anne stood there, empty-faced, not saying anything. Walt didn't really know why or how, but he knew there was no way she could respond to what he'd said.

And there was nothing left for him to say. "Yeah," he said finally, because he needed to fill the space with something—he didn't really mean anything when he said it. "Well. I guess good-bye, then."

She nodded, and she hugged him and she wished him luck. She turned around and before she'd gone five paces he was in the woods, quietly skulking his way into the darkest place he could find. He didn't see her again for a long time.

He sat in the woods for hours, trying to figure out what he was supposed to do next.

He still didn't know at midnight, when he heard his dad's footsteps. Dad didn't have to say anything for Walt to know who it was; he knew his walk by the sound of it.

"Son," Dad called, almost as though he could hear him breathing. "Walt. . . ? Are you still out there, son?"

Walt tucked himself deeper into the niche between the two big rocks where he was resting.

"It's okay, son," Dad called. In the sound of his voice Walt heard everything he wanted to believe: that his dad loved him, wanted him, needed him. That his mom was just having a bad time, and that soon she'd be loving him just like she always had. Real soon—next week, maybe the week after at the latest.

"It's all right, Walt," Dad called again. "Nobody's going to make you do anything you don't want to do. Really, son. Your mom's a little upset, sure, but it'll work out okay. Maybe you and me and Anne can take a week or two and rent a cabin up by the lake." Lake Hortonia in Vermont, where they went every year for vacation since Walt was three. "And let your mom have a little time to herself, time to get used to things."

Dad was real close now, but Walt wasn't really trying to hide any more. He wasn't getting up and letting his dad know where he was, either, though. He'd gotten cautious. Reflex wouldn't let him just stand up. Then his leg twitched and made some dirt clods fall.

That gave him away.

"Walt?" His dad's voice was tense now, sharper. The flashlight spun around, and there he was, trapped in it.

Walt wanted to scream in terror, in frustration at being caught. But what happened was a lot more like crying even though he tried as hard as he could for it not to be, and then he was running to his dad with his arms stretched out, and calling "Daddy," and hugging his dad with his arms around his waist and his face buried in Dad's big soft belly. And crying into his soft flannel shirt, and smelling clean laundry because his dad never sweated.

"Daddy," Walt said again, and he hugged him harder.

"Oh God, Walt, oh God, Walt, I love you son, you know that."

And Walt nodded into his dad's stomach even though it wasn't really a question.

"And I hope to God that some day you'll forgive me what I'm

doing. God, your mother *made* me, she *made* me. . . !" And then his father's hands wrapped around his wrists, tight and hard as iron neck bands, and he shouted back in the direction of the cemetery, "I've got him," and. . . .

Something down inside Walt busted and without his even thinking, without his even knowing what he did, a scream bubbled up from some black, fireless pit at the base of him.

A scream so horrible and true that it shook the woods and, for weeks, the dreams of everyone who heard it.

His father's hands fell loose from Walt's hands.

And Walt *ran.*

Walt ran all night. He wasn't going anywhere. Not yet. He hadn't thought that far yet.

So he kept moving, because he knew they were looking for him. More than once he heard their walking just behind him—his mother's, his father's, the weird rhythms of the aliens. Others, later.

It was after moonset but before even the beginning of dawn when he heard the shrill, grating stage whisper of a hiss.

"Hssit. Walt."

He thought at first it came from Donny James's house—he was in the woods behind it—but then he realized it came from Mr. Hodges's next door.

Walt couldn't imagine why the school's principal would call him. He went to the back window—it was open but it had a screen—to find out.

"What's happened, Walt? Your parents have been here, and then the police, looking for you. They must've gone to every house in the neighborhood. What did you do?"

Walt shrugged. "I ran away, I guess. The aliens that made me alive again came back for me. Mom wants to give me to them."

Mr. Hodges didn't believe a word of it. "Even if that is what happened—I suppose it's no more preposterous than anything else about you these days—why would your mother call the police? They'd just complicate matters for her later."

Walt shrugged again. "Mom's tricky."

Mr. Hodges shook his head. "I don't know what you are, Walt, but you're strange." He looked out into the woods, back and forth. "You want to come in for cocoa?"

Walt knew he shouldn't trust the man; he knew from experience that he shouldn't trust anyone tonight. But he was tired of being scared and bored of running, so he nodded and said, "Yes."

"Come around to the side door," Mr. Hodges told him, and he did.

Inside, it was still dark. They sat at the kitchen table while the principal made cocoa (he brewed coffee for himself) with only the light that came in through the windows from the street lamp out front.

"Best to leave the lights out," he said, "the way they're searching out there, they're sure to see you if we turn them on."

"Yeah." Walt nodded.

There was nothing, really, for them to talk about. Walt had already said more about himself and about the aliens than he ever meant to say to anyone. Besides, he didn't know much, really. There was school, but Walt felt uneasy telling the principal anything interesting; he might get someone in trouble.

"Miss Allison is in the hospital," Mr. Hodges said. "She had a breakdown yesterday afternoon. Right in her own classroom. The janitor came in at four o'clock to sweep and mop, and there she was, looking off into the distance just like she was waiting for something. And nothing anyone did would even make her blink— though if you watched long enough you might see her do that on her own."

Walt nodded and stirred his cocoa with his finger. "She was acting strange this morning."

Mr. Hodges lit his pipe, sucking in fire from a butane lighter three times with a hissing-sucking sound. Smoke billowed up to freeze in the street light. The smell was rich, but bitter and powdery.

Walt knew the sun would rise soon. He felt himself slipping away just like a fade out on a television set; felt his muscles let go bit by bit, felt his head sinking down to the cushion of his arm on the table beside the cocoa. He tried to make himself be taut, awake, but it didn't do any good.

"Walt? Are you going to be okay?"

Mr. Hodges's asking woke him up. He shook his head. "Sorry. I'm all right."

"Do you want to camp out on the couch here? Do you need to sleep?"

"Could I?" Walt was tired, but he was scared, too. He pictured his mother finding him while he slept, and giving him to the aliens without even waking him to let him know. He could see himself waking on a spaceship, already light-years from home, in the arms of some *thing* that looked and felt like tripe and smelled like rotten eggs. He tried not to shudder, but it didn't do any good.

"Walt? Should I get you a pillow and a blanket? Don't fall asleep there; you might fall off the chair and break your neck."

"Please." He stumbled into the living room, to the couch. He was almost asleep before Mr. Hodges got back.

The clean muslin of the pillowcase felt comfortable and wonderful but somehow alien to Walt. He'd got used to the satin of his coffin, even though he couldn't feel it when he was dead. Muslin seemed too coarse, too absorbent. He lay awake a lot longer than he wanted to, getting used to it.

Walt woke in the early evening; Mr. Hodges wasn't home yet, and he hadn't left a note. Walt went to the bathroom to wash up as best he could without a change of clothes. He didn't know what he would do next; it seemed to him that there was no place to go, no life left for him to gather up the pieces of. He even thought for a moment that he would rather be dead, but he knew that wasn't so.

For the moment, at least, the doorbell decided for him. Walt put down the towel he'd used to dry his face and looked around the corner where the hallway ended, into the living room.

Through the window in the alcove he could see three policemen, their hands clasped in front of them just like busboys at some fancy restaurant. His mother stood behind them.

Walt dropped the washcloth that he had in his hand. He had to go or they'd get him. He ran to the bedroom in the back, popped the screen out of the window frame, climbed out, and began to run.

"Walt!"

His heart lurched and tried to jump out his throat. He thought they had him, but then he turned and recognized the voice at the same time: Donny James, sitting on a lawn chair in his backyard; the Jameses' house was right next door to Mr. Hodges's.

"Quiet!" Walt stage-whispered. He tried to be quiet, but it didn't work. "They're looking for me. Don't shout."

"Huh. . . ?" Donny was running to catch up to him. Over on the far side of the woods, where the storm drain passed under the interstate highway, there was a big concrete sewer pipe, big enough for a boy to walk through, but too small for an adult. He could hide there, and even if they found him they couldn't get in to catch him. Or even trap him. He could be long gone before they could get around the nearest highway overpass and surround him at the far end of the pipe.

"Where're you going, Walt?" Donny asked. Walt didn't answer.

"Just come on," he said.

There still wasn't any sign of his mom or the policemen when they reached the pipe. Walt walked in first—duck-walked, half-squatting, really. In the middle of the pipe he sat down and leaned his back against the curved wall. It was cool and dry and dark. There weren't any bugs around, at least not that Walt could see.

"The police came to school today, looking for you," Donny said. "When they didn't find you they asked everybody questions."

Walt nodded. He'd kind of expected that.

"What happened to you? Why were you running? Why were they looking for you?"

Walt didn't know what to say; he kicked his leg against the far side of the pipe, trying to think.

"The aliens that made me alive again came back for me." He kept expecting people not to believe that, and they kept believing it. Strange. "I didn't want to go 'cause they're real gross. But Mom wanted to make me. So I ran away."

Donny flicked a pebble at the entrance they'd come in through. "Where're you going to go now?"

Walt *still* hadn't thought about that. Not really. He shrugged. "I don't know, I guess."

Donny and Walt sat thinking about that, not talking, for a good five minutes.

"Well," Donny said, "you can't go back home, you know. She'll just pack you away with the aliens. But you got to have some place to stay."

"Yeah." Walt nodded. He hadn't thought that far before. He'd been avoiding it, he guessed.

"And wherever you go, it better be pretty far away. Or your mom'll find you."

"Yeah." It was true. It was why he'd been trying not to think about what he'd do. He didn't *want* to run away. He wanted to go home and stay there and grow up just like any other boy.

But there was just no way in hell. He felt like he needed to cry— more out of frustration than anything else—but he didn't want to do that where anybody could see it. Especially Donny.

"I guess I better go," Walt said.

Donny nodded. "Where're you going to go?"

"I don't know. I'll be back sooner or later, though. I'll see you again."

But he never did. By the time Walt got back to town Donny had been gone a long time.

In the window of the 7-Eleven by the on ramp to the interstate, Walt saw himself on the cover of the *National Interlocutor.*

BOY CRAWLS OUT OF GRAVE

Walter Fulton, age 8, dug his way out of his grave last week, after being buried for more than a year. Walt died last year when a car hit him as he crossed a street.

"Dying wasn't so bad," says Walt. "Two angels took my arms, lifted me from the car wreck, and brought me up to heaven.

"Heaven's a great place, and everybody's happy there," Walt continues, "but it's no place for an 8-year-old boy. There isn't any mud, no baseball bats, and nobody ever gets hurt in the football games."

Dr. Ralph Richards of the Institute for Psychical Research in Tuskegee, Alabama, speculated that Walt's experience may not have been mystical in nature at all. "It's possible that young Fulton wasn't dead at all when he was buried, but suffering from a Thanatesque condition, from which he later recovered."

(continued on page 9)

Walt marveled at the newspaper, reading it again and again, staring at the photos. There were two of them: one a photo of the cemetery, focused on his tombstone. There was no graffiti on it yet, and the ground before it was still crumbled and spilling out from Walt's crawling out. Policemen—fifteen or twenty of them— milled about the cemetery. Walt had never seen the photo, but he knew it must have been taken not long after the caretaker found Walt's grave abandoned. That would be the Monday after his resurrection. The other photo was a head shot of Walt. He recognized it; it had to have been cut from his first-grade class picture, the group photo where the whole class had stood in three parallel lines and posed for the camera together.

Walt went into the 7-Eleven and bought a copy of the paper with some of the lunch money he'd hoarded this week. He hadn't been hungry at all at lunch.

The paper amazed him; it was as though they'd written the article before they'd sent the man to talk to him. He took the paper off the counter, paid the woman, walked out of the store, and wandered out to the street, still reading the article over and over again. He felt awed; the paper had the aura of The Mysteries— even things mystical—about it.

Out on the street, Walt set his teeth and pointed himself at the ramp to the interstate highway. He walked for thirty minutes, thumb out, hitchhiking along the grassy strip to the right of the southbound lane.

It was almost dark when the station wagon stopped for him.

"Where're you going?" the guy in the front passenger seat asked him. There were four people in the car already. The smell of burning marijuana drifted out from the window. Walt could see beer cans littering the floor, and at least one of the four men was drinking.

"South," Walt said. "A long way."

"You want to ride on the back shelf?"

It was mostly empty.

"Sure."

"Open the door and let him in, huh, Jack?"

Jack opened the door and leaned away from it enough for Walt to climb over him; Walt settled in among the duffel bags and piles of etcetera. He rode for hours lying on his back with his head on a pillow made of what felt like clothes. He stared up into the sky as he lay there, watching the stars.

Meteors whizzed back and forth over the highway in the sky above them. And three times police cars screamed by them, lights flashing, sirens wailing.

Once Jack asked him if he wanted a hit off a joint, but he didn't. Jack and everybody else in the car laughed uproariously.

At four in the morning they stopped at a rest area to use the men's room. When they stopped moving the odor in the car became unbearable.

"We're going to get off the highway at the next exit," Jack told him. He got back before the others did. "If you're still going south, this is probably a better place to get a ride than that is."

Walt nodded. "Yeah," he said. He started to climb out, relieved at the chance to get away from the stink. As he got up, he saw what it came from: the pile he'd been using for a pillow. Dirty socks and underwear. His stomach turned, he retched a little, but nothing came out. It'd been too long since he'd eaten, and thank God for that.

"Take it easy, kid," Jack said. He was awfully close when Walt's body was trying to puke. "You okay? You going to be all right?"

Walt got out of the car. He stood bent over with his hands on his knees. "I'll be all right," he said. The smell was horrible, and it was in his hair and clothes, and he was so *tired.* "Thanks for the ride."

He went to the water fountain by the picnic tables, and he drank water for ten minutes, hardly even pausing to breathe. When he looked up, the station wagon was gone.

Home was miles and miles away, and he was tired and he stank.

He went into the men's room and tried to clean himself, but it didn't help. The smell had ground its way into his pores.

He needed someplace to sleep. He was sure his mom or someone would find him if he fell asleep on one of the benches in the little roadside park. If nothing else he'd be so conspicuous that some highway patrolman who had nothing to do with any of this would find him. But he couldn't stand the thought of trying to get another ride. He looked past the fence that wrapped itself around the rest stop and thought about the great thick woods that surrounded the highway. It was deep and dark and big; silent and endless. It extended as far as he could see.

The fence was three strands of barbed wire strung through rough wood posts. This far from any city there was no need for anything more elaborate. Walt pressed down the lowest wire and slipped between it and the wire above. His shirt snagged and tore on one of the barbs; another barb gave him a long bloody scratch on his upper arm. But he didn't care. He was too tired. He just wanted to find a dry, soft, comfortable bed of pine needles and sleep for a million years.

But he went much deeper into the forest than he meant to. He needed the hike, he guessed; at the same time he wanted to collapse, something like a nervous tick in his legs kept pushing him deeper and deeper into the woods. Maybe it was his body trying to bleed off excess adrenaline, or maybe it was a need to get as far away from the highway as he could, just to be safe.

Not long before dawn, his right foot caught on a gnarled, twisty root he hadn't seen, and he came down chest-first into an enormous heap of soft, wet, acid-smelling dung. It splattered all over the front of his shirt, onto his upper arms (even into the fresh cut), and under his chin. He started sobbing then; it wasn't so bad to cry since no one was looking. He took his shirt off and used the back of it to wipe off his arms and neck. It didn't do any good. It took some of the clumps off him, but the shitty edges smeared him where he was clean. He threw the shirt onto a pile of rocks and crawled away from the bear shit, over to the base of a pine tree.

He sat there with his back to the tree until the sun came up, paralyzed with frustration and hopelessness. He thought about dying again, but he didn't think that would do any good either.

Late in the morning he fell asleep, still filthy, his skin beginning to burn and itch where the shit was. He hadn't moved since he'd crawled over to the tree. He barely noticed the transition between wakefulness and sleep.

The touch of something cool and clean and wet woke him. Before he opened his eyes, while he was still waking up, he thought it was rain.

But it wasn't.

When his eyes finally focused he saw it was the alien, wiping Walt's body clean with a white cloth that smelled like lemons or something citrus. Its hand brushed him, and it felt just exactly like tripe in the refrigerator case in the grocery. Behind the citrus was the alien's smell of sulfur and . . . preserved meat. Walt's first impulse was to scream in stark raving bloody terror—was it cleaning him the way you clean an animal before you slaughter it?—but all the heart for screaming had worn out of him. If this was the end, then that was that: whether he'd meant to or not he'd already come to terms with it. He stared calmly and coolly into its drooling eyes.

"You are hurt?" the alien asked him, its voice bubbles in a fish tank, its breath rotten eggs. Walt turned his face away from it.

"No," Walt said. He sighed. "I'm okay."

The alien nodded its head back and forth slowly like a rocking chair. It finished wiping off Walt's right shoulder and reached over to clean the left. Walt could feel that under his chin was already clean. "Stop that," he said.

The alien looked startled, but it pulled its hand back. "It burns your skin," the thing said.

"Just don't."

The alien sat there staring at him for a long minute. "You can't go back home," it told him. "Your mother would be unhappy with you. She would hurt you."

"I know," Walt said. He'd known it for a while now.

"Where will you go? Where will you have a life?"

Walt shrugged.

"You were unhappy being dead. That's strange for your people; almost all of them rest content. We needed an assistant, so we woke you." The alien looked down into the dirt. "You don't have to come."

Walt could feel the bear shit deep in his pores, even where the creature had cleaned him. He could feel the filth matted into his hair in the station wagon. His clothes were filthy, kind of greasy; he'd been wearing them for three days now. And the alien—hands like tripe, smelling like something dead and something rotten— didn't seem gross or disgusting at all. Not in comparison.

He went with the aliens. Whether that was the right choice or not, he never regretted it.

And he had fun.

And when he grew up, he lived a great and full life out among the galaxies, a life full of stars and adventures and wonders. When he was forty he came home to the world to make his peace.

His father and he and his sister and her family spent a week of reunion and celebration. It was a good week, as joyful as thirty Christmastimes at once.

But his mother was already dead when he came back. She hadn't lived a long life; she died not long after Walt left. He went to her grave to say good-bye to her.

She didn't answer. She did her best to ignore him.

The Dark Country

Dennis Etchison

Martin sat by the pool, the wind drying his hair.

A fleshy, airborne spider appeared on the edge of the book which he had been reading there. From this angle it cast a long, pointed needle across the yellowing page. The sun was hot and clean; it went straight for his nose. Overweight American children practiced their volleyball on the bird-of-paradise plants. Weathered rattan furniture gathered dust beyond the peeling diving board.

Traffic passed on the road. Trucks, campers, bikes.

The pool that would not be scraped till summer. The wooden chairs that had been ordered up from the States. Banana leaves. Olive trees. A tennis court that might be done next year. A single color TV antenna above the palms. By the slanted cement patio heliotrope daisies, speckled climbing vines. The morning a net of light on the water. Boats fishing in Todos Santos Bay.

A smell like shrimps Veracruz blowing off the silvered waves.

And a strangely familiar island, like a hazy floating giant, where the humpback whales play. Yesterday in Ensenada, the car horns talking and a crab taco in his hand, he had wanted to buy a pair of huaraches and a Mexican shirt. The best tequila in the world for three-and-a-half a liter. Noche Buena beer, foil labels that always peel before you can read them. Delicados con Filtros cigarettes.

Bottles of agua mineral. Tehuacan con gas. *No retornable.*

He smiled as he thought of churros at the Blow Hole, the maid who even washed his dishes, the Tivoli Night Club with Reno cocktail napkins, mescal flavored with worm, eggs fresh from the nest, chorizo grease in the pan, bar girls with rhinestone-studded Aztec headbands, psychoactive liqueurs, seagulls like the tops of valentines, grilled corvina with lemon, the endless plumes of surf. . . .

It was time for a beer run to the bottling factory in town.

"¡Buenos días!"

Martin looked up, startled. He was blinded by the light. He fumbled his dark glasses down and moved his head. A man and a woman stood over his chair. The sun was at their backs.

"¿Americano?"

"Yes," said Martin. He shielded his forehead and tried to see their faces. Their features were blacked in by the glare that spilled around their heads.

"I told you he was an American," said the woman. "Are you studying?"

"What?"

Martin closed the book self-consciously. It was a paperback edition of *The Penal Colony*, the only book he had been able to borrow from any of the neighboring cabins. Possibly it was the only book in Quintas Papagayo. For some reason the thought depressed him profoundly, but he had brought it poolside anyway. It seemed the right thing to do. He could not escape the feeling that he ought to be doing something more than nursing a tan. And the magazines from town were all in Spanish.

He slipped his sketchbook on top of Kafka and opened it awkwardly.

"I'm supposed to be working," he said. "On my drawings. You know how it is." They didn't, probably, but he went on. "It's difficult to get anything done down here."

"He's an artist!" said the woman.

"My wife thought you were an American student on vacation," said the man.

"Our son is a student, you see," said the woman. Martin didn't, but nodded sympathetically. She stepped aside to sit on the arm of another deck chair under the corrugated green fiberglass siding. She was wearing a sleeveless blouse and thigh-length shorts. "He was

studying for his Master's degree in Political Science at UCLA, but
now he's decided not to finish. I tried to tell him he should at least
get his teaching credential, but—"

"Our name's Winslow," said the man, extending a muscular
hand. "Mr. and Mrs. Winslow."

"Jack Martin."

"It was the books," said Mr. Winslow. "Our boy always has
books with him, even on visits." He chuckled and shook his head.

Martin nodded.

"You should see his apartment," said Mrs. Winslow. "So many."
She gestured with her hands as if describing the symptoms of a
hopeless affliction.

There was an embarrassing lull. Martin looked to his feet. He
flexed his toes. The right ones were stiff. For something further to
do, he uncapped a Pilot Fineliner pen and touched it idly to the
paper. Without realizing it, he smiled. This trip must be doing me
more good than I'd hoped, he thought. I haven't been near a college
classroom in fifteen years.

A wave rushed toward the rocks at the other side of the cabins.

"Staying long?" asked the man, glancing around nervously. He
was wearing Bermuda shorts over legs so white they were almost
phosphorescent.

"I'm not sure," said Martin.

"May I take a peek at your artwork?" asked the woman.

He shrugged and smiled.

She lifted the sketchbook from his lap with infinite delicacy, as
the man began talking again.

He explained that they owned their own motor home, which was
now parked on the Point, at the end of the rock beach, above the
breakwater. Weekend auto insurance cost them $13.70 in Tijuana.
They came down whenever they got the chance. They were both
retired, but there were other things to consider—just what, he did
not say. But it was not the same as it used to be. He frowned at the
moss growing in the bottom of the pool, at the baby weeds poking
up through the sand in the canister ash trays, at the separating
layers of the sawed-off diving board.

Martin could see more questions about to surface behind the

man's tired eyes. He cleared his throat and squirmed in his chair, feeling the sweat from his arms soaking into the unsealed wood. Mr. Winslow was right, of course. Things were not now as they once were. But he did not relish being reminded of it, not now, not here.

A small figure in white darted into his field of vision, near the edge of the first cabin. It was walking quickly, perhaps in this direction.

"There's my maid," he said, leaning forward. "She must be finished now." He unstuck his legs from the chaise longue.

"She has keys?" said the man.

"I suppose so. Yes, I'm sure she does. Well—"

"Does she always remember to lock up?"

He studied the man's face, but a lifetime of apprehensions were recorded there, too many for Martin to isolate one and read it accurately.

"I'll remind her," he said, rising.

He picked up his shirt, took a step toward Mrs. Winslow and stood shifting his weight.

Out of the corner of his eye, he saw the maid put a hand to the side of her face.

Mrs. Winslow closed the pad, smoothed the cover and handed it back. "Thank you," she said oddly.

Martin took it and offered his hand. He realized at once that his skin had become uncomfortably moist, but Mr. Winslow gripped it firmly and held it. He confronted Martin soberly, as if about to impart a bit of fatherly advice.

"They say he comes down out of the hills," said Winslow, his eyes unblinking. Martin half-turned to the low, tan range that lay beyond the other side of the highway. When he turned back, the man's eyes were waiting. "He's been doing it for years. It's something of a legend around here. They can't seem to catch him. We never took it seriously, until now."

"Is that right?"

"Why, last night, while we were asleep, he stole an envelope of traveler's checks and a whole carton of cigarettes from behind our heads. Can you beat that? Right inside the camper! Of course we never bothered to lock up. Why should we? Everyone's very decent around here. We've never had any trouble ourselves. Until this trip. It's hard to believe."

"Yes, it is." Martin attempted to pull back as a tingling began in his stomach. But the man continued to pump his hand, almost desperately, Martin thought.

"The best advice I can give you, young man, is to lock your doors at night. From now on. You never know."

"Thanks, I will."

"He comes out after the sun goes down." He would not let go of Martin's hand. "I figure he must hit the beach three, four in the morning, when all the lights are out. Slips right in. No one notices. And then it's too late."

Martin pretended to struggle with the books so that he could drop his hand. "Well, I hope you're able to enjoy the rest of your vacation." He eyed the maid. "Now I'd better—"

"We're warning everybody along the beach," said Winslow.

"Maybe you should report it."

"That don't do no good. They listen to your story, but there's nothing they can do."

"Good luck to you, then," said Martin.

"Thank you again," said the woman peculiarly. "And don't forget. You lock your door tonight!"

"I will," said Martin, hurrying away. I won't, that is. Will, won't, what did it matter? He side-stepped the dazzling flowers of an ice plant and ascended the cracked steps of the pool enclosure. He crossed the paved drive and slowed.

The maid had passed the last of the beachfront houses and was about to intersect his path. He waited for her to greet him as she always did. I should at least pretend to talk to her, he thought, in case the Winslows are still watching. He felt their eyes, or someone's, close at his back.

"*Buenos días,*" he said cheerfully.

She did not return the greeting. She did not look up. She wagged her head and trotted past, clutching her uniform at the neck.

He paused and stared after her. He wondered in passing about

her downcast eyes, and about the silent doorways of the other
cabins, though it was already past ten o'clock. And then he noticed
the scent of ozone that now laced the air, though no thunderhead
was visible yet on the horizon, only a gathering fog far down the
coastline, wisps of it beginning to striate the wide, pale sky above
the sagging telephone poles. And he wondered about the unsteadi-
ness in Mrs. Winslow's voice as she had handed back the sketchbook. It was not until he was back at the beach that he
remembered: the pages he had shown her were blank. There were
no sketches at all yet in the pad, only the tiny flowing blot he had
made with his pen on the first sheet while they talked, like a
miniature misshapen head or something else, something else, stark
and unreadable on the crisp white sulfite paper.

He was relieved to see that the private beach had finally come alive
with its usual quota of sunbathers. Many of them had probably
arisen early, shortly after he'd left for the quiet of the pool, and
immediately swarmed to the surf with no thought of TV or the
morning paper, habits they had left checked at the border sixty
miles from here. A scattered few lagged back, propped out on their
patios, sipping coffee and keeping an eye on the children who were
bounding through the spume. The cries of the children and of the
gulls cut sharply through the waves which, disappointingly, were
beginning to sound to Martin like nothing so much as an enormous screenful of ball bearings.

There was the retired rent-a-cop on holiday with his girlfriend,
stretched out on a towel and intent on his leg exercises. There was
the middle-aged divorcee from two doors down, bent over the
tidepools, hunting for moonstones among jealous clusters of aqua-
marine anemones. And there was Will, making time with the
blonde in the blue tank top. He seemed to be explaining to her
some sort of diagram in the slicked sand between the polished
stones. Martin toed into his worn rubber sandals and went down
to join them.

"Want to go to a party?" Will said to him as he came up.

"When?"

"Whenever," said the blonde in the blue top. She tried to locate

Martin's face, gave up and gazed back in the general direction of the southern bungalows.

There a party was still in progress, as it had been since last Wednesday, when Will and Martin had arrived. The other party, the one on the north side, had apparently been suspended for a few hours, though just now as Martin watched a penny rocket streaked into the sky from the bathroom window, leaving an almost invisible trail of powder-blue smoke in the air above the water. The sky-rocket exploded with a faint report like a distant rifle and began spiraling back to earth. Martin heard hoarse laughter and the sudden cranking-up of stereo speakers inside the sliding doors. So the party there was also nearly in full swing again, or had never let up. Perhaps it was all one big party, with his cabin sandwiched like a Christian Science reading room between two pirate radio stations. He remembered the occasional half-dressed teenager staggering around the firepit and across his porch last night, grunting about more beer and did he know where those nurses were staying? Martin had sat outside till he fell asleep, seeing them piss their kidneys out on the steaming stones by the footpath.

"Bummer," said the girl seriously. Martin noticed that she was lugging around an empty twelve-ounce bottle. She upended it and a few slippery drops hit the rocks. "You guys wouldn't know where the Dos Equis's stashed, wouldjou?"

"*No es problema,* my dear," said Will, steering her toward the patio.

Martin followed. Halfway there the girl wobbled around and hurled the bottle as high as she could away from the shoreline. Unfortunately, her aim was not very good. Martin had to duck. He heard it whistle end-over-end over his head and shatter on the flat rocks. Will caught her under the arms and staggered her inside. Next door, a Paul Simon song was playing on the tape deck.

By the time Martin got there she was on her way out, cradling a bottle of Bohemia. Again she tried to find his eyes, gave up and began picking her way across the rocks.

"Take it slow," yelled Will. "Hey, sure you don't want to lie down for a while?"

Martin grinned at him and walked past into the high-beamed

living room. The fireplace was not lighted, nor was the wall heater, but a faint but unmistakable odor of gas lingered in the corners.

"We better stock up on Dos Equis from now on," said Will.

"Is that her favorite?"

"She doesn't care. But we shelled out a deposit on the case of Bohemia. Dos Equis is no return."

Martin stood staring out at the island in the bay. The fishing boats were moving closer to shore. Now he could barely make out the details of the nearest one. He squinted. It wasn't a fishing boat at all, he realized. It was much larger than he had imagined, some kind of oil tanker, perhaps. "Guess what, Will? We're going to have to start locking the doors."

"Why? Afraid the *putas* are gonna OD on Spanish fly and jump our bones in the middle of the night?"

"You wish," said Martin. He sniffed around the heater, then followed the scent to the kitchen and the stove. "The gas pilots," he said. "It's the draft. You—we're—always going in and out. The big door's open all the time."

"Got a match, man?" Will took out a bent cigarette, straightened it and crumpled the pack. The table was littered with empty packs of cheap Mexican cigarettes, Negritos and Faros mostly. Martin wondered how his friend could smoke such garbage. He took out his Zippo. Will struck it with an exaggerated shaking of his hands, but it was out of fluid. He stooped over the gas stove and winked at Martin. He turned the knob. The burner lit. He inhaled, coughed and reached for the tequila. He poured himself a tall one mixed with grapefruit juice. "Mmm. Good for the throat, but it still burns a little."

"Your system runs on alcohol, Willy. You know that, don't you?"

"Don't all machines?"

"Myself, I could go for some eggs right now. How about you? What've we got left?" Martin went to the sink. It was full of floating dishes. "Hey, what the hell is it with the maid? We did remember to leave her a tip yesterday. Didn't we?"

"One of us must have."

That was it, then. That was why she had skipped them, and then snubbed him this morning. That had to be it. Didn't it?

The tape deck next door was now blaring a golden oldie by Steely Dan. Martin slid the glass door closed. Then he snagged his trousers from the back of a chair and put them on over his trunks. Started to put them on. They did not feel right. He patted his back pocket.

Will slid the door back open halfway. "You're serious, aren't you? Look at it this way. Leave it like this and the gas'll just blow on outside. Relax, man. That's what you came down here for, isn't it? After what happened, you need . . ."

Martin checked the chair. On the table were a deck of playing cards from a Mission Bay savings and loan, the backs of which were imprinted with instructions about conserving energy, a Mexican wrestling magazine with a cover picture of the masked hero, El Santo, in the ring against a hooded character in red jumpsuit and horns, and an old mineral water bottle full of cigarette butts. On the floor, lying deflated between the table legs, was his wallet.

"There's another reason, I'm afraid." Martin twisted open the empty wallet and showed it to his friend.

"Who in the hell. . . ?"

"Well, it certainly wasn't the maid. Look at this place." Outside, a small local boy came trudging through the patios. He was carrying a leather case half as big as he was. He hesitated at the cabin on the south side, as three teen-aged American boys, their hair layered identically and parted in the middle, called their girls out into the sun. "It must have happened during the night."

"Christ!" said Will. He slapped the tabletop. He reached for his own wallet. It was intact. "There. I was over there partying all night, remember? They must've passed by every place where anybody was still up."

The small boy opened his case and the American girls began poring excitedly over a display of Indian jewelry, rings and belt buckles and necklaces of bright tooled silver and turquoise. From a distance, an old man watched the boy and waited, nodding encouragement.

"You should have gone with me," said Will. "I told you. Well, don't you worry, Jack. I've got plenty here for both of us."

"No, man. I can wire my agent or—"

"Look," said Will, "I can even kite a check if I have to, to cover the rental till we get back. They'll go for it. I've been coming here since I was a kid."

I've got to get away from here, thought Martin. No, that isn't right. Where else is there to go? I've come this far already just to get away. It's hopeless. It always was. You can run, he told himself, but you can't hide. Why didn't I realize that?

"Here," said Will. "Here's twenty for now."

"Are you sure?"

"Don't worry about it. I'd better go see if the nurses got hit, too. Saw a bunch of people in a huddle down the beach a while ago." He drained his glass. "Then I'll make another beer run. The hell with it. We're gonna party tonight, God damn it! You going by the office, Jack?"

"Sure."

"Then you might as well report it to the old lady. I think she's got a son or a nephew in the federales. Maybe they can do something about it."

"Maybe," said Martin, cracking open a beer. He could have told Will that it wouldn't do any good. He stopped in at the office anyway. It didn't.

He wandered on up the highway to Enrique's Cafe. On the way he passed a squashed black cat, the empty skin of it in among the plants, the blood-red flowers and spotted adder's-tongues and succulents by the roadside. The huevos rancheros were runny but good. When he got back, Will's four-wheel-drive was still parked under the carport. He took the keys and made the beer run into town himself, police cars honking him out of the way to make left turns from right-hand lanes, zigzagging across the busy intersections of the city to avoid potholes. He bought a case of Dos Equis and, for forty cents more, a liter of soft, hot tortillas. As the afternoon wore on he found himself munching them, rolled with butter and later plain, even though he wasn't really hungry.

That evening he sat alone on a bench by the rocks, hearing but not listening to a Beatles song ("Treat Me Like You Did the Night Before"), the smoke from his Delicado wafting on the breeze, blending with wood smoke from the chimneys and rising slowly to leave a smear like the Milky Way across the Pleiades. It's time for me to leave this place, he thought. Not to run away, no, not this time; but to go back. And face the rest of it, my life, no matter how terrible things may have turned back home since I left.

Not Will, though; he should stay awhile longer if he likes. True, it was my idea; he only took the time off at my suggestion, setting it all up to make me comfortable; he knew I couldn't take any more last week, the way things were up there. He's my friend. Still, he was probably waiting for just such an excuse in order to get away himself.

So I'll call or wire the agency for a plane ticket, give them a cock-and-bull story about losing everything—the truth, in other words. It was the truth, wasn't it? I'll say the trip was part of the assignment. I had to come down here to work on some new sketches for the book, to follow a lead about headstone rubbings in, let's see, Guanajuato. Only I never made it that far. I stopped off for some local color. Charge it against my royalty statement. . . . I'll talk to them tomorrow. Yes, tomorrow.

Meanwhile, there's still tonight. . . .

But I should tell Will first.

He resumed walking. There was a fire on the breakwater by the Point. He went toward it. Will would be in one of the cabins, partying with a vengeance. Martin glanced in one window. A slide show was in progress, with shots that looked like the pockmarked surface of another planet taken from space. He pressed closer and saw that these pictures were really close-ups of the faces of newborn seals or sea lions. Not that one, he thought, and moved on.

One of the parties he came to was in the big cabin two doors north of his own. That one was being rented, he remembered, by the producer of a show in the late seventies called STARSHIP DISCO. Martin had never seen it.

An Elvis Costello tape shook the walls. A young card hustler held forth around the living room table. A warm beer was pushed into Martin's hand by a girl. He popped the beer open and raised

it, feeling his body stir as he considered her. Why not? But she
could be my daughter, technically, he thought, couldn't she? Then:
what a disgusting point of view. Then: what am I doing to myself?
Then it was too late; she was gone.

Will was not in the back rooms. The shelf in the hallway held
three toppling books. Well, well, he thought, there are readers
down here, after all. Then he examined them—*By Love Possessed* by
Cozzens. *Invitation to Tea* by Monica Lang (The People's Book Club,
Chicago, 1952), *The Foundling* by Francis Cardinal Spellman. They
were covered with years of dust.

He ducked into the bathroom and shut the door, seeing the
mirror and razor blade lying next to the sink, the roll of randomly-
perforated crepe paper toilet tissue. There was a knock on the
door. He excused himself and went out, and found Will in the
kitchen.

"*¡Dos cervezas,* Juan!" Will was shouting. "Whoa. I feel more like I
do now than when I got here!" With some prodding, he grabbed
two cold ones and followed Martin outside, rubbing his eyes.

He seemed relieved to sit down.

"So," began Martin. "What did you find out? Did anyone else
get popped last night?"

"Plenty! One, the nurses. Two, the bitch from San Diego. Three,
the—where is it now? Ojai. Those people. The . . ." He ran out
of fingers. "Let's see. Anyway, there's plenty, let me tell you."

The ships were now even nearer the shore. Martin saw their
black hulls closing in over the waves.

"I was thinking," he said. "Maybe it's time to go. What would
you say to that, man?"

"Nobody's running scared. That's not the way to play it. You
should hear 'em talk. They'll get his ass next time, whoever he is.
Believe it. The kids, they didn't get hit. But three of those other
guys are rangers. Plus there's the cop. See the one in there with the
hat? He says he's gonna lay a trap, cut the lights about three
o'clock, everybody gets quiet, then bam! You better believe it.
They're mad as hell."

"But why—"

"It's the dock strike. It happens every year when there's a layoff.

The locals get hungry. They swoop down out of the hills like bats."

Just then a flaming object shot straight through the open front door and fizzled out over the water. There was a hearty "All r-r-ight!" from a shadow on the porch, and then the patio was filled with pogoing bodies and clapping hands. The night blossomed with matches and fireworks, 1000-foot skyrockets, bottle rockets and volleys of Mexican cherry bombs, as the party moved outside and chose up sides for a firecracker war. Soon Martin could no longer hear himself think. He waited it out. Will was laughing.

Martin scanned the beach beneath the screaming lights. And noticed something nearby that did not belong. It was probably a weird configuration of kelp, but . . . he got up and investigated.

It was only this: a child's broken doll, wedged half-under the stones. What had he supposed it was? It had been washed in on the tide, or deliberately dismembered and its parts strewn at the water-line, he could not tell which. In the flickering explosions, its rusty eye sockets appeared to be streaked with tears.

A minute after it had begun, the firecracker war was over. They sat apart from the cheering and the breaking bottles, watching the last shot of a Roman candle sizzle below the surface of the water like a green torpedo. There was scattered applause, and then a cry went up from another party house down the beach as a new round of fireworks was launched there. Feet slapped the sand, dodging rocks.

"Do you really believe that?"

"What?"

"About someone coming down from the hills," said Martin. *Like bats.* He shuddered.

"Watch this," said Will. He took his bottle and threw it into the air, snapping it so it flew directly at a palm tree thirty feet away. It smashed into the trunk at the ragged trim line.

Instantly the treetop began to tremble. There was a high rustling and a shaking and a scurrying. And a rattling of tiny claws. A jagged frond dropped spearlike to the beach.

"See that? It's rats. The trees around here are full of 'em. You see how bushy it is on top? It never gets trimmed up there. Those rats are born, live and die in the trees. They never touch down."

"But how? I mean, what do they eat if—?"

"Dates. Those are palm trees, remember? And each other, probably. You've never seen a dead one on the ground, have you?"

Martin admitted he hadn't.

"Not that way with the bats, though. They have to come out at night. Maybe they even hit the rats. I never saw that. But they have mouths to feed, don't they? There's nothing much to eat up in the hills. It must be the same with the peasants. They have families. Wouldn't you?"

"I hate to say this. But. You did lock up, didn't you?"

Will laughed dryly. "Come on, I've got something for you. I think it's time you met the nurses."

Martin made a quick side trip to check the doors at their place, and they went on. They covered the length of the beach before Will found the porch he was looking for. Martin reached out to steady his friend, and almost fell himself. He was getting high. It was easy.

As they let themselves in, the beach glimmered at their backs with crushed abalone shells and scuttling hermit crabs. Beyond the oil tankers, the uncertain outline of the island loomed in the bay. It was called Dead Man's Island, Will told him.

He woke with the sensation that his head was cracking open. Music or something like it in the other room, throbbing through the thin walls like the pounding of surf. Voices. An argument of some kind. He brushed at the cobwebs. He had been lost in a nightmare of domination and forced acquiescence before people who meant to do him harm. It returned to him in fragments. What did it mean? He shook it off and rolled out of bed.

There was the floor he had pressed with his hand last night to stop the room from spinning. There was the nurse, tangled in the sheets next to him. He guessed she was the nurse. He couldn't see her face.

He went into the bathroom. He took a long draught of water from the faucet before he came out. He raised his head and the room spun again. The light from the window hurt his eyes—actual physical pain. He couldn't find his sock. He tottered into the other room.

A young man with blown-dry hair was playing the tape deck too loudly. The sound vibrated the bright air, which seemed thin and brittle, hammering it like beaten silver. There was the girl in the blue tank top, still seated next to the smoldering fireplace. An empty bottle of Damiana Liqueur was balanced against her thigh. Her eyes were closed and her face was stony. He wondered if she had slept that way, propped upright all night. On the table were several Parker Brothers-type games from stateside: *Gambler, Creature Features, The Game of Life.* A deck of Gaiety Brand nudie cards, with a picture on the box of a puppy pulling a bikini top out of a purse. Someone had been playing solitaire. Martin couldn't remember.

There was a commotion outside.

"What's that?" he said, shielding his eyes.

"Talking Heads," said the young man. He showed Martin the tape box. "They're pretty good. That lead guitar line is hard to play. It's so repetitious."

"No, I mean . . ."

Martin scratched and went into the kitchen. It was unoccupied, except for a cricket chirping somewhere behind the refrigerator. Breakfast was in process; eggs were being scrambled in a blender the nurses had brought with them from home. Martin protected his eyes again and looked outside.

There was Will. And there were three or four tan beach boys from the other party. And the cop. He wasn't doing his leg exercises this morning. They were having an argument.

Martin stumbled out.

"But you can't do that," one of them was saying.

"Stay cool, okay, motherfuck? You want the whole beach to know?"

"You think they don't already?"

"The hell they do! We drug him over out of the way. No one'll—"

"No one but the maids!"

"That's what I'm *saying.* You guys are a bunch of jack-offs. Jesus

Christ! I'm about *this* close to kicking your ass right now, do you know that?"

"All right, all right!" said Will. "That kind of talk's just digging us in deeper. Now let's run through the facts. One—"

Martin came up. They shot looks at each other that both startled him and made him unreasonably afraid for their safety as well as his own. They stopped talking, their eyes wild, as if they had gobbled a jar of Mexican amphetamines.

Will took him aside.

"We've got to do something!" said the one with the souvenir hat. "What're you—?"

"Hold on," said Will. "We're all in this together, like it or—"

"I'm not the one who—"

"—Like it or not. Now just try to keep a tight asshole another minute, will you, while I talk to my friend Jack? It's his neck, too."

They started back up the beach. Will propelled him ahead of the others, as to a rendezvous of great urgency.

"They got him," said Will.

"Who?"

"The thief, whoever he was. Poor bastard. Two guys from next door cornered him outside our place. Sometime around dawn, the way I get it. Apparently he fell on the rocks. He's dead. They found me here a little while ago. Now—"

"*What?*"

"—Now there's no use shitting bricks. It's done. What we have to do is think of a way to put ourselves in the clear—fast. We're the strangers here."

"We can make it look like an accident," said the one in the hat. "Those rocks are—"

"Accident, hell," said the security cop. "It was self-defense, breaking and entering. We caught him and blew him away. No court in—"

"This isn't the USA, you dumb shit. You know what greaser jails are like? They hate our guts. All they want's our money. This buddy of mine, he got . . ."

And so it went till they reached the porch, the surrounding beach littered with the casings of burnt-out rockets, vomit drying on the rocks, broken clam shells bleaching between the rocks, the rocks like skulls. And here blood, vivid beyond belief even on the bricks of the patio, great splotches and gouts of it, like gold coins burnished in the sun, a trail that led them in the unforgiving light of day to the barbecue pit and the pile of kindling stacked in the charcoal shade.

Martin knelt and tore at the logs.

And there.

The body was hidden inside a burlap sack. It was the body of the boy who had come by yesterday, the boy who had wanted to sell his jewelry.

He felt his stomach convulse. The small face was scraped raw, the long eyelashes caked and flaking, the dark skin driven from two of the ribs to show white muscle and bone. A great fear overtook Martin, like wings settling upon him, blocking out the sun. He folded under them momentarily and dry-heaved in the ashes.

Will was pacing the narrow patio like a prisoner in a cell, legs pumping out and back over the cracking cement, pivoting faster and faster at the edges until he was practically spinning, generating a hopeless rage that would not be denied but could not be released. His hands were shaking violently, and his arms and shoulders and body. He looked around with slitted eyes, chin out, lips drawn in, jaws grinding stone. Far down the beach by the Point an elderly man came walking, hesitating at each house and searching each lot. He was carrying a leather case.

Will said, "You kicked him to death, didn't you? You stomped this child until he was dead." Then, his voice a hiss, he began to curse them between his teeth with an unspeakable power and vileness. The one in the hat tried to break in. He started shouting.

"It was dark! He could've been anyone! What was he doing creepin' around here? He could've been——"

But Will was upon him, his arms corded, his fingers going for the throat. The others closed in. People on the beach were turning to stare. Martin saw it all as if in slow motion: himself rising at last to his full height, leaping into it a split-second before the others could grab hold, as he fell on their arms to stop the thumbs from Will's eyes, to break Will's hands from the other's throat. Every-

thing stopped. Martin stepped between them as the young one fell
back to the flagstone wall. Martin raised his right hand, flattened
and angled it like a knife. With his left he cupped the back of the
young man's neck, holding it almost tenderly. The young man's
eyes were almost kind. They were eyes Martin had seen all his life,
outside recruiting offices and Greyhound bus depots the years over,
and they were a law unto themselves. He brought his right hand
down sharp and hard across the face, again, again, three times, like
pistol shots. The tan went white, then red where he had slapped it.
For a moment nobody said anything. The old man kept coming.

They passed motorcycle cops, overheated VWs, Jeeps, Chevy Luvs,
Ford Couriers with camper shells, off-road vehicles with heavy-duty
shocks and, a mile outside of town, a half-acre of pastel gravestones
by the main road. Martin fit as best he could among the plastic
water jugs, sleeping bags and Instamatic cameras in the back seat.
The boys from next door were piled in with him, the one in the hat
in front and Will at the controls of the four-wheel drive.

The twenty-mile access road behind Ensenada wound them
higher and higher, pummeling them continuously until they were
certain that the tie rods or the A-frame or their bodies would shake
loose and break apart at the very next turn. The lane shrank to a
mere dirt strip, then to a crumbling shale-and-sandstone ledge cut
impossibly around the backs of the hills, a tortuous serpentine
above abandoned farmland and the unchecked acreage between
the mountains and the sea. Twice at least one of the wheels left the
road entirely; they had to pile out and lay wild branches under the
tires to get across fissures that had no bottom. Martin felt his
kidneys begin to ache under the endless pounding. One of the boys
threw up and continued to retch over the side until Will decided
they had gone far enough, but no one opened his mouth to complain. After more than an hour, they set the hand brake at the start
of a primitive downslope, blocked the wheels with granite chips
and stumbled the rest of the way, numb and reeling.

The silence was overpowering. Nothing moved, except for the
random scrabbling of lizards and the falling of individual leaves and
blades of grass. As they dragged the sack down to the meadows,

Martin concentrated on the ribbon of dirt they had driven, watching for the first sign of another car, however unlikely that was. A small, puddled heat mirage shimmered on the dust, coiled and waiting to be splashed. A squirrel darted across the road, silhouetted as it paused in stop-motion, twitched its pointed head and then ran on, disappearing like an escaped shooting gallery target. Great powdered monarch butterflies aimlessly swam the convection currents; like back home, he thought. Yes, of course: I should have known. Only too much like home.

"Dig here," said Will.

The old wound in Martin's foot was hurting him again. He had thought it would be healed by now, but it wasn't. He rocked back wearily on one heel. A withered vine caught at his ankle. It snapped easily with a dull, fleshy sound as he shook free. He took another step, and something moist and solid broke underfoot. He looked down.

He kicked at the grass. It was only a tiny melon, one of dozens scattered nearby and dying on the vine. He rolled it over, revealing its soft underbelly. Too much rain this season, he thought absently; too much or too little, nourishing them excessively or not enough. What was the answer? He picked it up and lobbed it over their heads. It splattered on the road in a burst of pink. Watermelons, he thought, while fully-formed seeds pale as unborn larvae slithered off his shoe and into the damp grass. Who planted them here? And who will return for the harvest, only to find them already gone to seed? He stooped and wiped his hand. There was a faint but unmistakable throb and murmur in the ground, as though through a railroad track, announcing an unseen approach from miles away.

"What are you going to do, Jackie?"

Martin stared back at Will. He hadn't expected the question, not now.

"It's like this," said Will, taking him to one side. "Michael, for one, wants to get back to his own van and head on deeper into Baja, maybe San Quintin, lay low for a few days. He wasn't registered, so there's no connection. Some of the others sound like they're up for the same, or for going north right away, tonight. Kevin's due to check out today, anyway."

"And you?"

"Don't know yet. I haven't decided. I'll probably stay on for appearances, but you do what you want. I wouldn't worry about the maid or anyone coming by to check up. Anyway, we hosed off the patio. Nobody else saw a thing, I'm sure. The girls don't know anything about it."

There was a grunt. The sack, being lowered, had split open at the seams. Hands hurried to reclose it.

"What's that?"

Will grabbed a wrist. A silver bracelet inlaid with polished turquoise glittered against a bronze tan in the afternoon light.

"I—I bought it."

"Sure you did," said Will.

"I brought it with me on the trip. Ask my girl. She—"

Will stripped it off the arm and flung it into the shallow grave. "You want to get out of this alive, kiddo? That kind of work can be traced. Or didn't you think of that? You didn't think, did you? What else did you steal from him while you were at it yesterday? Is that why he came back last night? Is it?"

"Lookit, man, where do you get off—"

"We all hang together," said Will, "or we all hang together. Get it?"

He got to his knees to close the sack. As an afterthought, he reached deep and rifled the dead child's pockets for anything that might tie in with Quintas Papagayo.

His hand stopped. He withdrew a wad of paper money which fell open, a flower on his palm. A roll of American dollars, traveler's checks, credit cards.

"Hey, that's—"

"I had eighty bucks on me when—"

Martin joined him in examining the roll. The checks were signed NORMAN WINSLOW. Two of the cards, embossed on the front and signed on the back, read JACK MARTIN.

"Knew I was right!" said the one in the felt hat. "Fuck if I wasn't! Lookit that! The little son of a bitch. . . ."

* * *

Martin straight-armed the wheel, running in darkness.

He reminded himself of the five-dollar bill clipped to the back of his license. Then he remembered that his wallet was flat, except for the credit cards. Motorcycle cops passed him like fugitive Hell's Angels. He kicked on the lights of his rented car and thought of the last news tape of the great Karl Wallenda. He had been running, too, though in wind, not fog, toward or away from something.

Did he look back, I wonder? Was that why it happened?

. . . Heading for the end, his last that day was weak. Or maybe he looked ahead that once, saw it was the same, and just gave up the ghost. No, not Wallenda. For him the game was running while pretending not to—or the other way around. Was that his private joke? Even in Puerto Rico, for him the walk was all. *Keep your head clear*, he wanted to tell Wallenda. For that was how it finished, stopping to consider. But Wallenda must have known; he had been walking for years. Still he should have remembered. . . . Martin put on his brights, gripped the steering wheel and made for the border.

He turned on the radio, found an American station.

It was playing a song by a group called The Tubes. He remembered the Tivoli Night Club, the elevated band playing "Around the World" and "A Kiss to Build a Dream On." He remembered Hussong's Cantina, the knife fight that happened, his trip to the Blow Hole, policía with short hair and semiautomatic rifles. The housetrailers parked on the Point, the Point obscured by mist. The military guns with silencers . . .

The doll whose parts had been severed, its eyes opening in moonlight.

Shaking, he turned his mind to what lay ahead. He wanted to see someone; he tried to think of her face. Her eyes would find his there under the beam ceiling, the spider plants in the corners growing into the carpet, the waves on Malibu beach, the Pleiades as bright, shining on what was below: the roots between the rocks, the harbor lights like eyes, the anemones closed inward, gourds and giant mushrooms, the endless pull of riptide, the seagulls white as death's-heads, the police with trimmed moustaches, the dark ships at anchor. . . .

He came to a bridge on the tollway. Ahead lay the border.

To his right a sign, a turnoff that would take him back into Baja. He sat with the motor running, trying to pick a direction.

Nobody's Perfect

Thomas F. Monteleone

L ydia thought she might be able to like this guy. He seemed
different from all the others. There was something mysterious about him, something exotic, and her intuition told her
to expect an interesting evening.

Salazar noticed her . . . *aberration* as he sat in her living room
watching her. She stood in the kitchen struggling to open the twist-
off cap of a Michelob bottle.

He smiled just slightly. Odd he had not observed the deficiency
previously . . .

Not that it mattered much, if at all. If anything, it somewhat
intrigued him. He would still dispose of Lydia like all the others,
and he was confident that her meat would steam with exquisite
flavor.

Salazar allowed himself a small anticipatory smile. He was not
certain what excited him the most, what provided him with the
most pleasure—the initial search for suitable prey, the stalking-time
when one had been selected, or the final act of consummation.
There was a grandness about it all which *inspired* him, drove him
with a fervor that religious zealots would envy.

The ritual was so wonderful, and the meat always so utterly
tasty . . .

. . . It had been a Saturday two weeks earlier when Salazar fixed
upon *The City Paper*'s classified ad for volunteers. He had been

scanning the "Personals," which had proved to be a good place to find prey—although he had been careful not to establish any patterns which the police might notice—when his eye drifted down to the "Help Wanteds" and read:

VOLUNTEERS needed to read and record literature.
Books For The Blind. For details call 555-1010.

For some reason, he re-read the listing, and a familiar wave of heat rippled his body, exciting him in an almost sexual way. In that single instant he knew the Fates were reaching out to him, directing him to his next mission.

This would be perfect, he thought with a thoughtful nod of the head. Visions of young, single women—most of them probably unattached and bookish—burned in him. Young women with time on their hands. Soulful and naive do-gooders. Yes. This set-up would be perfect.

He called the number and was given an address downtown near the bohemian section of the city. It was a waterfront neighborhood which had recently enjoyed a renaissance in the form of countless new bars with catchy off-beat names, art galleries, little theatres, antique shops, and several alfresco restaurants. Yes, Books For The Blind was open on Saturdays, and yes, they would be glad to have him come down for an audition.

It was not unusual for Lydia to spend her Saturday doing volunteer work. She found it a pleasant change of pace from her weekday position as a systems analyst for Westinghouse, and since she liked to read anyway, the Books For The Blind seemed ideal. The day had turned out to be bright and crisp, suggesting better weather still ahead.

As Lydia walked through the quaint neighborhood of Fells Point, she did not, as she often did, let herself dwell upon all the pain in the world, all the discomfort and sadness, the injustice and the plainly cruel. Sometimes, when she reflected upon the daily horror in the world, it affected her physically as well as mentally— tiny needles of pain would tingle up the right side of her body, as if a precursor to a special kind of heart failure. Throughout her young life, she had probably absorbed more than her share of the world's pain, but it had left her undaunted, making her even stronger and more positive in the long run.

"You'll do just fine," said Mr. Hawthorne, a reed-thin, nobly balding gentleman, who looked to be in his late fifties. He sat opposite a folding table, wearing headphones which were connected to an ancient, boxy reel-to-reel recorder.

"That is wonderful," said Salazar. "When do I start?"

Hawthorne looked at his watch. "If you can wait until four or so this afternoon, we're going to have an orientation class for all the volunteers we've selected today."

"That would be fine."

"Very good. You'll be getting a schedule for when you can come in at night and read into one of our recorders. We want to make sure everyone knows how to operate them properly." Mr. Hawthorne smiled primly. "Plus, you'll need to know a few basics about how to handle mistakes—so that when the tapes are edited, they will sound as smooth as possible."

"So it will not be necessary to take the machines home with us?" said Salazar.

"No, they're a bit too bulky to be very portable, I'm afraid. If we could get a larger budget, we would like to buy some new equipment, but . . ."

"I see." Salazar did not want his evenings tied up with such obligations. The thought touched him that perhaps this had been a bad idea after all.

"Is there something wrong?" asked Hawthorne. "Didn't I tell you the hours?"

"No."

"Sorry about that. Does your work schedule conflict? Do you work in the evenings?"

"No, not really," said Salazar. "It is just that I am often very busy at night."

"Well, perhaps you'd like to try it for a while and see how it's working out." Hawthorne smiled a weak, thin-lipped smile. "If it sounds like I'm cajoling you, I am. You see, we don't get that many men to volunteer for this kind of work."

"Really?" His waning interest in the project sparked and crackled.

"That's right," said Hawthorne with a smile that tried to be sly. "Lots of young women, though."

Lots of young women.

"It will be no problem. I will return at four."

Passing the audition proved easy for Lydia. She'd always enjoyed theatre, and had also done a little singing. Everyone told her she had a pleasant voice, a good voice. She entered the orientation room and took a seat in front of one of the old tape recorders which had been carefully arranged on long tables. Other volunteers were already seated and others slowly drifted in. There was nothing to do but wait for things to get started.

He passed some time by walking around the neighborhood, in and out of some of the art and photography galleries, which he loathed. To see the garbage which passed for true art these days ignited within him a burning anger of righteousness. He wallowed in the ferocity of his outrage, drawing strength and resolve from it. The decadence of art was only one of the many signs pointing to the coming Apocalypse. Such signs, and he saw them *everywhere*, beautifully reinforced his own special preparations for survival.

For March, the weather was surprisingly mild and many people herded along the sidewalks, pretending to be enjoying themselves. He looked closely at many of the couples, immediately despising the males and thinking his usual thoughts about the females.

Despite the intoxicating surges of rage which powered him as he walked the streets, he did not actually prefer being out among the mortals for long periods of time. He felt far more comfortable, more secure in the relative solitude of the post office, where he operated his mail sorting machines with mind-numbing efficiency, where he need not speak to anyone other than himself, where he could concentrate on his special thoughts without distraction or interruption. And of course, nothing matched the solitude of his fortress-like row-house in one of the city's forgotten neighborhoods. Like a great womb, the old house encapsulated and protected him. It was the place where he'd been born, had lived his entire life, even after his mother died. It was the place where he believed he would achieve his immortality.

Growing tired of the sidewalks and galleries, and still having almost an hour to kill, he drifted into one of the trendy bars where they served sushi and many foreign ales and beers. The dark interior was more suitable to his mood, even though he found it somewhat crowded as he straddled a stool. He did not like crowded places.

Sipping upon a seltzer and lime, he glanced around the bar to see several young women, and some who were not so young, studying him as well. This did not surprise or excite him, however. His Mediterranean face was softly featured, naturally handsome. His liquid, puppy-dog eyes and warm, resonant voice attracted women. His delicate manner of speaking, the way he carefully pronounced all his words without contractions, charmed most females.

But Salazar ignored them because he knew better than to be seen associating with any of them in public. It was too easy to be seen, to be witnessed and thereby connected.

No. He had his own methods. Methods proved successful over many years.

He arrived at the volunteer center a few minutes late and the receptionist ushered him into a large room filled with long tables and many people sitting at them. Mr. Hawthorne was already droning on about how to operate the recorders as Salazar moved quickly to the closest open chair. Taking a seat in the second row, he looked with great disinterest at the old Webeor which squatted in front of him.

A growing excitement smoldered in him like early bursts of heat from a pile of oily rags. He loved the overall somatic control he conjured up at such times. All his senses operated at the brink of overload; he never felt so incredibly alive as when he plunged into a new hunt. Salazar absorbed the scent of the woman to his right—a faint blend of Halston perfume and perspiration. It was a natural pheromone to him. His peripheral vision recorded a splash of blonde hair, small movements of her left arm. Stealing a quick glance to his right, he was rewarded with a stunning vision.

Instantly he knew that it was not mere chance which had placed him next to a very special prey. Truly the Fates did conspire to help him, a belief he often pondered. The young woman to his right possessed not the glitz of a Cosmo covergirl or the sexual artifice of a Playmate . . . just a natural grace, an innocence which seemed to radiate from her soul like a beacon. In an instant, he had mentally photographed her.

Sea-green eyes, long lashes. High cheekbones, and sculpted facial planes. Pert nose and streamlined lips with just the hint of fullness. Strawberry blonde hair, long and full. It was rare indeed that he found one so perfect.

She wore a loose, baggy lavender sweater with macrame laces up the front. It was not something designed to be sexy or revealing. But the way she leaned forward over the table, enabling her to inspect some facet of the recorder's controls, gave him a perfect view of her breasts.

More perfection. Full and upthrusting, but not actually large or pendulous. Delightfully pink aureoles, fully defined, as though swollen, protruded from the rest of the breast. The nipples themselves, while semi-erect, were not thick or obtrusive.

Hawthorne's voice had deteriorated to something less than the idiot-hum between radio stations. Salazar flirted with the state of total rapture.

"Hi!"

The utter cheeriness of the soft voice was like a slap in his face. Stunned, Salazar looked up to the beautiful woman smiling at him. Her age could have been anywhere between eighteen and thirty.

"Hello . . ." he said, trying to keep his voice from cracking. He was not accustomed to be caught staring. "I just wanted to see if we all had the same kinds of machines . . ."

"I think so," she whispered.

Salazar noticed that Hawthorne had stopped talking and everyone was fiddling with their tape machines, obviously testing out some procedure.

"I'm . . . Tony . . . Tony Vespa," he said in a half-whisper.

He used the phony name he'd given Hawthorne. "Nice to meet you."

"Lydia McCarthy," she said, still smiling. "Likewise."

"Which category did you sign up for?" He didn't really care, but a desperate urge burned within to preserve their contact. Even though he had not availed himself of any of the other prey available, he *knew* she was the one.

"Oh, I picked the Classics . . ." said Lydia, a seasoning of regret in her voice.

He smiled at her. Most women found his smile disarming and ingenuous. She reciprocated, and his pulse jumped. Salazar was certain she had no idea how she affected men. No teasing. No flirting. Everything was very natural with her. She would be perfect.

"What're you going to be reading?"

"What?"

"The tapes," she said. "What category did you pick?"

"Oh . . . I'm doing some spy thrillers and some mysteries." He could care less about the goddamned blind . . .

"All right, now, I think you've all got the basics," said Hawthorne, his voice intrusive and alien. "Don't forget—it's okay to make mistakes . . ."

Lydia's attention returned to the front of the room. Salazar stared at her, invaded the front of her sweater with his hungry gaze. She would be so sweet . . .

"I'm going to call you out by the category you selected," said Hawthorne. "When you hear your group called, please come up and get your assignments and schedules. If you have any conflicts, you can work them out with our receptionist. Are we ready? All right . . . let's take the Classics first."

"That's me," said Lydia, gathering up her purse and down jacket. "It was nice meeting you . . ."

Salazar was stunned by her sudden movement. His gaze left the front of her sweater and searched out her green-flecked eyes. But before he could say anything, she had turned away, slipped into the stream of other readers moving quickly past Hawthorne's table. A surge of panic choked through him. He should change his category! He should follow her.

But he could do no such thing. He could not draw attention to himself, or worse, connect himself with her in any way. Occupied with precautionary thoughts, he was barely aware of her receiving her book-assignment and exiting the room.

Hawthorne, meanwhile, had moved down his list, calling on Biography, General Non-Fiction, Contemporary Fiction, Romance—Gothics, and Science Fiction, before finally hitting Spy & Mystery. Salazar played out the charade, accepted his schedule with feigned interest, then exited as quickly as possible without appearing to be in a hurry.

The hallway was empty and so was the lobby, other than the receptionist's desk. Lydia McCarthy was gone and if her phone number was unlisted it was possible he'd lost her forever. But he didn't give up that easily, retreating back down the hall to Mr. Hawthorne's vacant office. Moving quickly, Salazar rifled through a folder full of applications on the pristine blotter.

More quickly than he expected, he found Lydia's form, instantly committing her phone number to memory. Right away, the familiar, explosive sensation of great warmth suffused him. Intimate. Comforting. He felt full of power and confidence as he strode triumphantly out into the hall, through the lobby, and out into the cold, late afternoon.

It had been so easy after all. The digits of her phone number blazed in the center of his skull.

The temptation to rush home to call was seductive, almost overpowering, but he told himself he would wait until Tuesday.

Tony Vespa.

At first the caller's name meant nothing to her, but he ignored her initial confusion and re-introduced himself. The handsome, dark-eyed guy at the volunteer center—she suddenly connected the name and the face. He had seemed so very nice. So polite and charming. And as he spoke, he continued to reinforce that first impression.

She was pleased that he'd called, and she was not really all that surprised that, after some small talk, he asked her out—some drinks and maybe some dancing at Edgar's. Saturday night, around eight?

"Yeah, that would be great," she heard herself say, perhaps a little too enthusiastically. "I've never been there, but people at work say it's real nice."

He confirmed her address, then prepared to end the conversation.

"Gee, do you have to go so quick?" asked Lydia, hoping she didn't sound too forward.

"What do you mean?"

"I thought maybe we could talk for a while. Maybe get to know each other a little better . . ."

He chuckled softly. A seductive sound, even through the receiver. "Plenty of time for that, Lydia. Good night."

Saturday night, eight o'clock. She had opened her apartment door to him wearing a dark blue jacket-and-pants ensemble over an ivory satin blouse. The silky material conformed to her flesh in such a way it was obvious she was braless.

And then she'd asked him if he wanted a beer while he waited for her to finish getting ready . . .

. . . and Salazar now watched her working hard to twist off the cap with her left hand while she held the Michelob bottle awkwardly in the crook of her flipper-like right arm.

How had he not noticed it?

He could not keep his gaze from the deformity. Foreshortened, stick-thin, slightly twisted. Just beyond the permanently half-bent elbow protruded three stiff, semi-formed and useless fingers. A withered arm.

The thought lit up his mind like a cheap neon sign. He looked away from the kitchen, trying to seem interested in the contemporary decor of her living room. A withered arm.

So taken had Salazar been with the perfection of the rest of her, he had somehow failed to notice. He had not actually seen her . . . *all* of her. He wondered if this sudden knowledge would make any real difference, and his first inclination was probably not. His image of perfection was of course destroyed, but he could still feel his hot blood pounding in his head. No, it would be all right.

"Here we go," said Lydia brightly as she exited the kitchen and extended the bottle to him with her left hand.

Looking up, he tried to smile, tried to keep his gaze from drifting down to that hideous thing sticking out of her sleeve.

"Thanks . . ." He accepted the bottle and took a careful sip. It was not a good thing to drink alcohol, but the charade must be played out. He knew that one bottle would not foul his plans.

"I'm almost ready," she said, turning down the hall towards her bedroom. "Just a few minutes, really."

"We have all the time in the world," he said.

A single, unsettling thought that something was not quite right touched her mind as soon as she climbed into his beat-up Chevrolet. The interior was rimed with a furry patina of grime and dust, the windows so fogged with dirt she could barely see the streetlights in the distance. An aroma of Lysol spray, trying to mask a deeper, more hideous odor, assailed her as he closed the door. There was something familiar about the smell—a slightly rancid, yet somehow metallic redolence, but she couldn't place it. She had never been in such a filthy car.

In addition, he never spoke to her after slipping into his seat and keying the ignition. Watching him, Lydia noticed how he gripped the wheel with both hands, knuckles taut, arms rigid. He stared straight ahead, eyes not even blinking. There was something chilling about him, *a sudden coldness that was reptilian.* She could almost *see* it lurking beneath the surface of his handsomeness like the creature in the black lagoon. How could she have not noticed it before?

The Chevrolet accelerated quickly under his unflinching control, changing lanes in the heavy city traffic like a checker zigzagging across its board. Landmarks blinked past her window and she realized they weren't headed for the hotel district where Edgar's was located. With a shudder, Lydia knew she wanted out of the car—as soon as possible.

She tried to make a few jokes, to get him talking, but he ignored her completely. His coldness radiated outward, touched her, and the inside of the car felt like the bottom of a well.

"Where are we going?" she asked sternly.

He turned a corner roughly, leaving a wide thoroughfare for a narrow neighborhood street. Poorly lit, the street assumed a mantle of foreboding shadows.

"I said, where are we going? Why won't you answer me?"

This time, he turned and smiled at her.

"We're almost home," he said in a reverent whisper. He sounded stagy, but also frightening.

She knew she didn't want to be anywhere near this creep's home. As the car slowed for a red traffic light, she whirled awkwardly in her seat so her left arm could reach the door handle.

Yanking it upward, she gasped when nothing happened. Almost without effort, he lashed out with the back of his hand. The force of impact almost unhinged her jaw. Stinging flashes of pain lit up the inside of her skull; nausea and dizziness welled up like a black geyser behind her eyes. She collapsed into the corner of the seat and the door, fighting the urge to pass out, to give in to him.

No. She would never do that. She kept repeating the thought as though it would give her strength.

Her mind raced with half-panicky thoughts. How could she have let this happen? He'd seemed so normal, so nice . . . and she had so few dates, so few chances to get out and be like everybody else.

But even her earliest memories confirmed she'd never been treated like everybody else. Just because her pregnant mother had been prescribed a drug called thalidomide. Lydia had survived as an outsider. She learned as a small child how to live with the special pain of rejection, of words like *freak* and *monster*. She knew intimately the simple cruelties, and countless, unseen injuries. Like a grey, mottled tumor, her pain clung to the depths of her soul. But rather than allowing it to become a malignant destroyer, she had used her pain as a source of power, of soul-energy. She had learned to accept the pain, break it down into its molecular parts, and rebuild it into a driving engine of confidence and inner strength.

Lydia had always faced the torment with a special dignity, always growing more formidable in the process.

But now, she faced something far darker . . .

Salazar was feeling very strong since slapping her across the face. The contact with her flesh exhilarated him. Electricity danced upon the tips of his fingers, singing to him in a chorus of power. Whipping the steering wheel to the left, he jockeyed the car down another side street, then left again into the alley behind his house. As he braked to a halt, his passenger lunged for the door latch. He smacked her again—this time hard enough to break the skin across her cheekbone and to stun her into semi-consciousness. Moving quickly, he grabbed a roll of duct tape from the glove compartment, tearing off a strip to seal her mouth. Then before she regained her senses, he pulled her from the car and fireman-carried her towards the house. Draped limply over his shoulder, she felt almost weightless to him. His entire body *hummed* with infinite vitality: the sensation was intoxicating, sensuous, almost divine. He moved with stealth and silence even though the high fences shielded him from the eyes of any curious neighbors. The light of a half moon cut a pale blue path through his trash-littered backyard. Salazar followed it to the outside cellar steps and descended with his prey into the familiar darkness.

Tiny flames flickered in the distance. With a great effort, Lydia lifted her head to stare at the candles casting orange light and long shadows across the cellar. She forced herself to sharper awareness. Something was restricting her good arm, holding it almost straight up, and she gradually realized he'd manacled her against a damp, chilly wall of stone. A second bracelet and chain hung past her right shoulder, rendered useless by her withered arm. But the cold metal looped both ankles; short chains tethered her spread-legged to the wall.

The bastard. . . !

Her anger threatened to banish the numbing chill of the cellar. The first tendrils of rage were reaching into the core of her being, seeking the energy which seethed there. She would—

The tape was ripped savagely from her mouth, twisting her neck to the side. Stinging pain ate into her face as she detected movement in the shadows. He appeared out of the darkness, his eyes wide with pleasure. He appraised her with a grin and chuckled to himself. The taut muscles of his chest and arms strained against a plain white T-shirt, over which he wore a thick leather apron. Slowly he raised a barber's straight razor until it was level with her eyes. The blade looked insanely sharp.

Lydia recoiled from the shining weapon, thrashed against the chains, but no sound could escape her throat.

"It's okay if you want to scream," he said in a whisper. "Nobody can hear you down here. They never heard any of the others."

Behind him, next to a workbench full of tools, an old gas stove heated two large stewing pots. Adjacent to the stove at the end of a large, darkly stained wooden table sat an electric rotisserie. Its interior glowed a deep orange from the glow of its heating elements.

An alarm was going off in her head. It was the Klaxon of sheer panic. Naked fear capered like a demon across her mind. She was going to *die*. She was going to be sliced and gutted like a sacrificial pig. For an instant the alarm screeched so loud, so insistently, she felt she was plummeting into the abyss of madness.

"Going to cut you up," said the monster in the leather apron. His face moved to within inches of her own. His breath smelled of decay, his eyes as flat and dead as a shark's. "And then, I'm going to eat you . . ."

No.

The single word went to substance in the very core of her being. It rose up in her, gathering the stuff of anguish and suffering, and plating itself with it like newly forged armor. A vortex of anger whirled into life, kicking out sparks of defiance. A silent cry of pure, sweet outrage streaked out of her like an explosion of radio waves from a star going nova.

In that single instant, she hated him. Completely. With a cosmic finality.

Her anger and her hate fused into something new, becoming a tapline which drove down into the deepest core of her soul.

"Here we go," said the monster as he slipped the razor's edge into her blouse, bringing it down with slow precision. The blade separated her clothing effortlessly, slicing it away like rice paper. He continued down until he had opened her garments as if they'd been zippered. With a technique smoothed by years of practice, he began removing the tatters of her clothes. As the last of her blouse fell off her right shoulder, revealing her deformity, he paused as if to study the withered appendage. His gaze seemed to traverse the short length of her slightly twisted humerus. Twig-thin, punctuated by the suggestion of an elbow and a stump of misshapen flesh, it looked unfinished. Three proto-fingers jutted stiffly from the stump.

He reached out and touched her right arm, slowly running his fingers down the useless travesty of a hand. She wanted to recoil from his touch—for most of her life she had avoided touching her right arm as much as possible—but she refused to give him even the slightest satisfaction that he had offended her. The limb had always been numb, essentially dead, but as his fingers played along its length, she felt a slight warmth beneath the shriveled skin.

"Never seen anything like this," he said as though to himself. "Maybe I'll save it as a souvenir."

He looked up from her twisted arm, smiled widely.

"Why don't you scream?" he asked softly. "It's okay if you want to scream."

More expert snicks of the blade, and everything fell away except her panties. Her pale skin goose-fleshed from the chilly dampness, then flushed as a wave of humiliation passed over her.

But she would not let the indignity deter her from the climax of her rage. The maelstrom of hate for him continued to expand inside her, faster and more deadly than a metastasizing growth. Like a hungry cancer it fed upon the storehouse of her pain and humiliation—a lifetime's worth. In a frenzy of building pressure, her loathing sought an outlet . . .

"This will be nice," he said, slipping the edge of the razor inside the elastic band of her panties. Slowly he moved it down, paring away the last boundary of her nakedness. Lydia stared straight ahead into the distant shadowed corners of the room as her underpants fell away in ribbons. He placed the cold steel of the blade flat against her lower abdomen, moved the blade downward over her mons, scything her blonde pubic hair like wheat, until he reached the beginning of her labia. Slowly he rotated the blade so that its cutting edge faced upward and perpendicular to her body.

"This seems like a good place to start," he said in a half-whisper.

No!

The rage from the core of her being, engorged from the surfeit of her pain, sought form. She blinked her eyes, flinching away from the blade, and sensed that things were somehow slowing down. The warmth in her withered arm surged, bursting forth with white heat in all the places where he'd touched her.

All the years of suffering, the humiliation and exquisitely distilled anguish of her were taking substance now. Time almost stopped for her. The catalytic moment had arrived. Something shifted in the cosmos, and the great wheel of being sought a new balance-point. When he touched her dead flesh, he'd unwittingly switched on the radiant energy of her soul.

He moved the blade upward; the cold edge of steel touched her. It was only an instant, but she could feel the heat expanding, suffusing her arm with a life it had never known. Time slowed, spiraling down into a dark well. A total spectator, Lydia watched as her withered arm moved—moved for the first time in her life. Its pale flesh almost incandescent with vengeful energy, her limb lengthened, swung forward.

Things were happening so fast, and yet she could see it all unfolding with exacting detail. Time fugued around her like a storm.

He looked up as her arm moved, for the moment forgetting his intended upward thrust of the razor. His eyes widened as the stump of flesh flattened out and the stick-like projections swelled and grew into taloned, grasping fingers. Like a spade-claw, it raked his face, and she could hear him scream slowly through the underwater-like murk of distended time.

The sound of his own pained voice, his scream of pain and terror, stunned him as much as the transformation he was witnessing. As his own blood warmed his ruined cheek, he found himself marvelling at the exquisite tang of his own coppery fear, his own pain-fire burning. So different . . . so ironically reversed . . . fascinating as much as horrific. The girl's face had become twisted into an unrecognizable mask. The gaze of her sunken eyes stared through him, past him, and into a timeless place. Her transformation was a gift from the gods, he realized in the final moment. It was a miracle, and only he had been chosen to witness the event. Salazar smiled through his pain and his fear, and awaited her special anointing . . .

In an instant the hand reached *into* his face, index and middle fingers puncturing his eyes, the newly-formed thumb hooking the roof of his mouth. Gristle and bone collapsed from the unrelenting pressure; the razor fell away from his hand. Then the arm shot out, straightening, as the hand held his head like a ten-pin bowling ball. For a moment, he hung there, suspended, a grim marionette, legs and arms flailing through a final choreography of nerve-shock and death.

Then, like a crane jettisoning its cargo, the hand released his stilled body; and powered by the last sparks of her rage and her pain, it yanked free the manacles from her wrist and ankles. Lydia blinked her eyes in the candlelight as her time-sense telescoped back to normal. The right side of her body seemed aflame and her heart raged in her chest as if it might explode. The monster lay at her feet and she'd killed him. Her stomach lurched, sending a hot column of bile halfway up her throat.

The horror of knowing she'd actually killed someone was tempered by her realization of how it had been done. Looking down at her new right arm, her new hand, it seemed impossible that it could really be there.

She kept waiting for it to fade away, to shrink back into the desiccated parody she'd always known.

But it never did.

Blind

Joyce Carol Oates

Sometime during the night, which is a terrible dark here in the country on moonless nights, the electricity went off.

I was wakened by it, I think. I was asleep, and suddenly wakened. A low rumbling sound like the sound of collapse. Amid a harsh pelting rain drumming on the roof over my head which is a low ceiling and a low roof of rotting shingles close over my head. And blown slantwise against the windows so I sat up terrified hearing the **hiss! hiss!** of the rain seeking entry.

I did not speak to *him*, nor even wake *him*.

Let the old fool slumber, let them all sleep. Snoring and snuffling and a rattle in their throats. At that age, what can you expect?

I am not a tearful woman; in truth I am a strong and practical-minded woman with the experience of years. Overseeing the household in our other house, and here—in our retirement. (*His* retirement: how is it mine?) Thus I am not fearful of storms except in a practical way; you must use your common sense in a household, one member of the household at least. Hearing the rain like that streaming down the window as it was streaming down the walls of the house vertical and plunging because the eaves' gutters had not yet been cleaned, and were overflowing; thus the water runs down the house to the old stone foundation and into the cellar, oh God. That was my fear. That, and not the storm itself. Because of course *he* had not gotten around to cleaning the gutters, no matter how I reminded him.

One day soon, now it was April at last in this cold windy place, I

would drag the aluminum step-ladder out of the barn myself, to rid
the eaves of rotted leaves and other debris to shame him. That old
man. But I had neglected to do so, yet—and now, too late. And
now the **hiss! hiss!** of the rain seeking entry.

It was then that I attempted to switch on the bedside light but
the power was off. The room so utterly dark I could not see my
hand in front of my face. Groping for the lamp, and almost knocking it over blundering against the shade, muttering to myself but to
no avail the power was off. (Did *he* hear my distress?—snoring and
snuffling the ratchety noise of phlegm in his throat? Never!) Several
times during the winter the power had gone off, once it was off for
eighteen hours, and when I telephoned to complain the girl said in
a smirky little voice, The company is doing all it can, ma'am, power
will be restored as soon as possible. And each time I called, the
girl said in a smirky little voice, The company is doing all it can,
ma'am, power will be restored as soon as possible. Until at last I
shouted into the phone, You're a liar! You are all liars! I pay for our
electricity and we want better service! And there was silence, I
believed I had gained the little snip's respect at last, but then said
the smirky little voice, I could all but see the red lipstick pursing in
mockery of decent respect for one's elders, Ma'am, I have told
you—the company is doing all it can.

So in fury I slammed the receiver down. So hard, it clattered to
the floor. Hairline cracks in the cheap plastic.

I tried then to see the time. Peering into the dark where the
clock should be. But even the green-luminescent numerals were
gone, it was so dark. But I judged (by the pressure on my bladder: I
am wakened regularly each night by this discomfort) that it was
between 3:00 A.M. and 3:30 A.M. The very middle of the night so
you would know the electric company would be slow to get a repair
crew out, and use that as an excuse.

I was breathing hard now, in exasperation and worry, and had to
use the bathroom, and in this pitch dark!—swinging my legs
(which are slightly swollen, the ankles especially) off the bed and
rising unsteady on bare feet. Where were my slippers?—I groped
for them, but could not find them.

I sighed and may have murmured to myself, as I acknowledge it is my habit to do, where once I addressed the cat and in other years the canary, *he* being deaf when it suited him, murmuring aloud, God have mercy! though from my tone you would judge God is no friend of mine any longer. Not for many years you may be sure. But *he* did not hear, slumbering on, no doubt lying on his back, his jaw drooping and a strand of spittle leaking across his cheek I did not doubt.

I am not a heavy woman, still less fat. I have grown a bit stout, which puts pressure on the legs and back. Sometimes I grow short of breath, as with natural impatience.

In my place, I tell my daughters, when rarely they call, you would be no different. Oh don't you tell *me!*

Slowly then, painstakingly I groped my way to the bathroom, for my bladder *was* pinched, and I was in near-distress. Had I shut my eyes I alight have been unerring, for the room, the entire house, is memorized in my mind, but I tried to see which is in such circumstances a mistake. Thus stubbing my toe, thus bumping against the bureau, groping for the door which did not seem to be where I knew it must be, but a few feet to one side. Panting, muttering to myself, for at my age you come to expect more respect from the world of objects if not from the world of humankind, but of course *he* did not hear, lost in selfish slumber.

Fortunately the bathroom is in the hall right outside the bedroom. So I had not far to go.

Inside, forgetting the lights were off, I fumbled for the wall switch, so strong is the force of habit.

I was able to use the toilet with little trouble, though. Noting that the bathroom was, I thought, darker somehow than the bedroom and the hall; though there is a window behind the toilet overlooking a steep-sloped roof and an old overgrown pasture. (Bathed in moonlight many times these past twelve years since moving to this place I had stood at the window, looking out. To see what? In expectation of what?) But now the window too was lost in darkness. Utter blackness. You would not have believed a window was there at all, except for the pelting rain, the noise and damp.

I flushed the toilet once, twice, a third time before the mechanism took hold. Cursing the plumbing as many times in the past, for something was always breaking down in this old house and who then would call the plumber?—and who make out the check, to pay the bill? And my daughters saying, Why do you nag Daddy, why don't you let Daddy alone you know his nerves poor Daddy they say, or used to say. As if the little fools knew—

Well it was my fault I suppose. Agreeing so readily in fact so vehemently to sell our old house, to move *here*. Leaving our house in the college town where we'd lived for forty-three years, to move *here*. This farmland and monotony of trees that held a memory for *him* (because when he was a boy, his family had taken him to visit some relatives here in the summer—happiest memories of his life he said) but not for *me*. Leaving my three women friends without saying goodbye because they'd slighted me, took me for granted and I would not tolerate it, so moving away was my revenge and I took it. And too late to regret it now.

I groped my way back to bed in the terrible black, hearing the rain louder than before, that **hiss!** against the windowpanes and drumming on the roof. *He* wasn't snoring so loud now, or the wind was loud enough to drown him out; he'd never stirred when I got out of bed. I could have had an attack or fit or fallen down the stairs in the pitch black and would he take notice?—don't make me laugh. Lowering myself into bed, and the box springs creaked. Still, *he* never stirred.

So I tried not to think about the rain, and the cellar. The overflowing eaves. I tried to calm my mind seeing waves of black water move toward me, shallow waves, where I might rise, and float, as I'd learned to float at the pool, on my back; what a surprise I could float so easy and feel no fear when the younger women had trouble, the skinny ones had the worst time of all. When it's so easy. You just give yourself up to it. And float.

But my mind wouldn't rest. It was like knitting—the steely needles clicking and flashing.

All the years *he* locked himself away in his study not to be disturbed typing over his lecture notes, always the same lecture notes, working on his scholarly articles, his single book—the source of some ancient Greek tragedy no one ever read who hadn't been assigned to. Well we were proud of him I suppose, his wife and daughters I suppose, there is natural pride in us all thus we must be proud of something I suppose! And of course his salary as a professor of classics supported us, I grant that. Poor fool sucking on that pipe of his not knowing what it was, he sucked. None of them do. And when he was forbidden actual smoke he sucked on the unlit pipe like a baby with a rubber nipple, now that *is* pathetic. They held the retirement party in the classics common room, just sweet red wine and cheese cubes on toothpicks, a few toasts, the chairman praising and *him* rising to thank, tears gleaming in his eyes while the younger professors exchanged smirks and even the senior professors, next to go, swallowed yawns like swallowing pits almost too big to go down. Now that was funny to observe!

All toasts to Professor Emeritus, and *him* raising his wine glass so solemnly. Never knowing. Poor vain fool never guessing what it was the first thing to come into *my* mind, about that occasion.

Yet, then, in a weakness of my own, seeking revenge on my only friends, I let him talk me into moving out here.

His retirement: how is it mine?

I tried to sleep but the rain continued hard as before, and the thunder began to come nearer like something huge rolling across the countryside aimed for this very house so my eyes flew open in terror as the thing, it was a gigantic round object, *rolled over the house and away across the fields to disappear. But no lightning! Not before, or after. The night was dark as any night I had ever seen.*

Now I tried to wake *him*. Seized his shoulder, shook *him.*

Wake up! help us! Something terrible has happened!

My voice climbed high as a mad soprano's yet had no effect on *him.* In this pitch black I could not see *him*, not so much as a blur.

Yet I was certain it must be *him*, my husband of fifty-one years lying beside me slack and heavy as a bag of fertilizer, the mattress sagging beneath him. I groped feeling his whiskery jaws, his thin hair and the bony skull beneath. I groped feeling his eyes, which were wide open like my own.

Myron! What is it! What has happened to you!

Yet he lay there unmoving. And now a dank sickish odor arose from the bedclothes pinching my nostrils hard.

I realized I had not heard his breathing for some minutes. That snoring-snuffling, that rattle in his throat.

Anger rose in me in clots like phlegm. Sucking that pipe of his not knowing what he sucked, hadn't the doctor warned him!—and I, and his doting daughters, warned him!

But, no: Professor's mind was off in the ancient world, or poking about in the stars (for the Universe was one of his "interests").

Wake up! Wake up! Wake up! How dare you leave me, at such a time!—and I struck his shoulder hard, with my fist.

Did *he* groan, or was it my imagination?—drowned out in any case by a sudden swelling of thunder again, rolling over the countryside and the house so I whimpered for mercy like a child. And still there was no lightning, not the briefest of flashes!

Which was not natural, I knew. For thunder must be preceded by lightning, for thunder is precipitated by lightning splitting the sky in pieces, that fact I knew.

Unless the sound was not of thunder at all but something else?

Suddenly I was in the grip of a panic seizing me from the outside as from the dark, I pushed *him from me as of no further use, for had he* known who I was, or so much as looked at me these many years?—the thought coming to me, *No one can help anyone now, this is the dark of the very beginning, and the end.*

That would have been about 4 A.M., by my subsequent calculations. At the time, in my panicked state, in the first knowledge that *he* was dead, and that I should get help, I was not able to absorb the significance of such wisdom. Knowing only that I was alone, oh and so terrified! my heart beating like a wild creature's so terrified! That *he* had abandoned me at the very start of this siege, this terror abroad in the world beyond my knowledge.

I climbed out of our common bed desperate to be gone as from a grave.

The ceiling was leaking?—the bedclothes were damp, something sticky on the coverlet. That foul sickish-sweet odor in the air despite the fresh smell of the rain. Oh I blamed *him!* I blamed *him!* Fumbling for the telephone in the dark, overturning a lamp, and I shrieked, oh I screamed, and began sobbing like a young bride having lost *him*, whose face I had not truly seen for a long time, though not so long a time as *he* had not seen mine.

Once, my elder daughter had discovered me, in the kitchen of our old house in University Heights, and said, shocked, Why Mother, why are you crying?—and I hid my face from her young eyes murmuring in anger and shame, Because your father and I are no longer husband and wife, we have not loved each other in twenty years, and my daughter drew in her breath sharply as if she had heard an obscenity from this middle-aged woman, her mother's lips; and said, Oh Mother!—I don't believe that!—turning away from me in distaste for she meant instead, as they all mean, the children who spring from our bodies and stride away quick and brisk as they can, I don't want to hear such a thing from *you*.

And now *he* was dead, and I must get help, except, on my hands and knees groping for the fallen telephone, I understood that, if he was dead, it was for the same reason that the power was out; if the power was out, it was for the same reason that he was dead—thus beyond all human help.

And did I want strangers coming into this room, even should they be able to find this house, this room, in the pitch-black night?

My fingers scrambled against the coarse material of the carpet but I could not locate the plastic telephone, nor hear its dial tone which meant, I realized, that the telephone lines too were down; all communication with the outside world had ceased.

That foul sickish odor. *His. Him.* Suddenly it was unbearable, cooped up in here with *him*. A wildness came over me, that I had to escape.

I crawled on hands and knees in the direction of the door, whispering to myself yes! yes! like this! have courage! There was a kerosene lamp on the bureau, and matches, for just such emergencies; but I seemed to know that I would not be able to find it, still less light the wick with my trembling fingers.

So it was, on hands and knees trailing my nightgown stinking of the grave, I escaped.

*　*　*

Slowly, painstakingly, panting with strain, I descended the steep stairs into the dark.

So many steps!—I had never counted them before, and, descending them now, lost count at twenty.

I grasped the banister (which was not very steady) with my left hand and groped along the wall with my right hand. My eyes were dry of tears now and wide open staring seeing nothing below me except the dark, blunt and depthless as a smear of black paint. I understood that there was something mysterious about this dark which was like no other dark of my life.

I must see, I must have light to see.

I was desperate to get downstairs, to get the flashlight out of the cupboard; to light candles. In my haste I had forgotten my bathrobe, my slippers. I could not have said which year it was, nor where I was, which house this was of the houses I had lived in. Oh, a woman of my age, coarse gray hair trailing down between her shoulder blades, heavy flaccid breasts, hips, thighs, belly flaccid too, panting like a dog, and sweating, even on these drafty stairs sweating, barefoot and ungainly, how my former friends would stare in pity, how my daughters would sneer! Never do you dream as a young woman that, one day, this will be *you.*

The rain and the thunder continued, but still there was no lightning. Except for the pull of gravity I did not seem to be going *down* until suddenly, lowering a foot to the next step I discovered there was no next step, I had come to the end of the stairs.

I was trembling badly, crouched as if to ward off an attack. But the darkness was empty.

And here the foul odor of that upper room was dissipated. I could still smell it—it clung to my flannel nightgown, my hair—but less strongly. A sharp smell of rain and earth prevailed, a smell I associated with spring. The rains of spring, and the thaw after the long winter. Each year the thaw seems to come later in the season, thus it is more welcome. On gusty days, when the Sun shines, such smells can make you feel as if you are *alive.*

I was clutching at the newel post trying to get my bearings. To my right was the parlor, to my left the kitchen. It was the kitchen I sought.

Like stepping off into black water then I groped in the direction of the kitchen yet colliding at once with a chair (but who had left a chair in such a place?) and knocking the side of my head against the sharp edge of something (a shelf?—*there?*), finally entering the kitchen knowing it was that room by the odor of cooking and grease and the cold linoleum beneath my feet.

Here too I fumbled for the light switch on the wall—so strong is the force of habit.

But no light of course. The darkness remained steady and depthless.

It crossed my mind here to attempt the telephone another time, for there was need to get help, a terrible need wasn't there?— though memory was blurred, as to exactly why. But the telephone, on the wall beside the sink, was on the far side of the expanse of floor black and fearful as deep water, and my bowels clenched at the risk. And *what if I was not alone? What if something waited for me to make a false move?* All unexpectedly I found myself at the refrigerator, the door open, cold wafting out, ravenous with hunger; suddenly I reached blindly yet unerringly for a piece of frosted cinnamon coffee cake I had wrapped in cellophane yesterday morning, a quart container of milk, able to see in my mind's eye as I could not see in the dark. And shameless and trembling with animal appetite I stood there, the door open wastefully, devouring cake until the last crumb was gone and drinking milk so greedily some dribbled on my nightgown. Then, appetite sated, I felt the disgust of my behavior, and the folly, quickly shutting the door to conserve the precious cold.

The electricity being off, and who knows when it might be restored, perishables in the refrigerator and the freezer were in danger of spoilage. Of course a freezer will keep certain foods (for instance meat) for hours before defrosting begins but once the process starts it cannot be reversed, under threat of food poisoning.

I was in dread of being without food if the storm continued, if the roads were out and I dared not leave the house for days. For the telephone was of no use, for even should my call go through, I would be greeted by mockery and derision. I would be provoked into screaming curses, and then they would know my name.

I had to have light, now in a panic ravenous for light as for food I groped my way to the cupboard where the flashlight was kept, amid the canisters and aerosol spray cans; but where was the flashlight?—had *he* misplaced it?—in my haste knocking an object to the floor where it shattered, a cup perhaps, shattering at my feet and now the added danger of stepping in broken glass with my poor bare feet, O God have mercy! So distraught now whimpering aloud *Why? why? help me!* seeking the lost flashlight I wondered if unknowingly in my past I had committed some terrible sin for which I must now be punished, some meanness or hardness of the heart committed not willfully perhaps but in the absence of will or conscious intention as in our blind lives we perform so many actions only half thinking, half *seeing* the effects of our behavior. And if so, may You forgive me!

(Yet I could not believe I had truly committed any such sin, for I remembered nothing. As if the electrical failure here had erased all memory too. As if, in absolute dark, there need be no time save absolute Now.)

And then in my desperation trying an adjacent cupboard, where the flashlight had never once been, I discovered it!—snatched it up at once and pushed the little switch with my thumb; but, though it clicked on at once, *there came no light.*

How was it possible? Was the battery dead? And yet, I had used the flashlight only recently, down in the cellar—in the dark alcove where my canned fruits are kept.

And yet: *there came no light.*

Sobbing aloud now in frustration and despair I took a step unwisely and my foot came down on a splinter of glass. Fortunately I had not put my full weight upon the foot, yet the cut stung, and was surely bleeding.

Carefully then as I could, trying to control my sobbing (for I am as I have said a practical-minded woman, the capable wife of this and previous households for beyond a half-century), I groped my way to the far side of the kitchen, located the counter beside the sink, the drawer beneath, where loose candles and matches were kept for such emergencies, and moving my lips in prayer to You for mercy (I, who had cast off in disdain my belief in You so many years ago!) struck matches, holding them with trembling fingers against a candle's invisible wick, and how vexing! how much trickier a task than lighting a candle you can see! finally after numerous clumsy attempts, I succeeded, I swear, for one of the matches *did* catch fire, and I smelled sulphur—but I saw *no flame.*

Then it was clear and irrefutable to me, what I had only suspected previously—that there was something mysterious about this dark, this night; something that made it unlike any other dark or any other night. For it was not the mere absence of light (which is of course derived from our Sun) but the *presence of dark itself thick and opaque as any matter.*

Thus I realized it could have no visible effect whether a match was "lighted"—whether a candle wick "burned." What would have been light under normal circumstances was immediately sucked away, vanished, as if it had no existence. For indeed it had no existence.

If I could bear this, till dawn—!

With dawn, surely all would be well? (The storm seemed to be abating. Yet even if the rain continued, and the sky remained overcast, there *would* be light—for what evil force could withstand the strength of our Sun?)

I did not believe in God, but I believed in our Sun. Though never listening with much attention when *he* would prattle on reading to me out of one of his science magazines, the billion-billion-billion age of the Sun, or size of the Universe, or whether Time might be collapsed into something small enough to fit in my thimble!—as if, sighing with my housewifely tasks, I had the patience for such.

How exhausted I was suddenly, my search for light so futile, and my dignity rent, I turned in haste to grope my way back out into the hall thinking in my confusion that I would climb the stairs and return to bed—not remembering in my confusion what it was that had usurped my bed, thus my sleep, how I abhorred it, what wickedness it sought to inflict upon me, and another time I stepped upon glass this time cutting my foot more severely. Fool! fool! fool! I cried feeling the blood slippery against the linoleum floor; yet, spared of seeing it, unexpectedly I seemed hardly to care.

I groped, stumbled, blundered my way into the hall, and into the parlor, sobbing aloud in anger, and if anything or anyone awaited me, in that dark smelling of mildew and dust (had I not cleaned in that room, vacuumed and polished, only last week?) I did not care in the slightest—I did not. So exhausted now that my legs were as water beneath me, I groped for the sofa, a handsome old leather sofa of *his* purchase as I recalled it, smooth to the touch but fine-cracked in places with age, and cold. But by now I did not care what sort of thing it was I lay down on. I wanted only to shut my eyes, and sleep.

And did I sleep, indeed?—was it sleep I slipped into, or a greater, bottomless dark, whimpering and moaning to myself, unable to find a position on the sofa that did not pinch my neck, distend my spine?—release formless terrors to my brain?

I did not dream. I "saw" nothing. Until waking at last to the Sun, I "saw" myself waking eager and smiling to the new day, a pale but unmistakable sunlight leaking through the lacy curtains of the parlor window—At last! at last!

Except, cruelly, this *was* a dream—and when I sat up blinking and dazed, I found myself staring into the dark, as before; the unchanged, hideous dark. For long minutes I simply could not grasp what had happened, where I was, for I was *not* in my bed, nor in any bed I knew; calling out, so great was my confusion, Myron! Myron! Where are you! What has happened to us!

And then, as if a black tide swept upon me, and swept me away with it, I remembered. I knew.

Should you track me to my hiding place supposing me, a woman of my age, alone, thus vulnerable, you would be mistaken. For the darkness in this place is so complete, none of you will ever penetrate it.

And I have driven in three-inch spikes, to seal the door from within.

I am in no danger of running out of provisions. I have stocked all I could of fresh and canned goods from the kitchen; I have here, in the cellar, dozens of jars of preserves—pears, cherries, tomatoes, rhubarb, even pickles; and there is an apple bin, and a sack of Idaho potatoes. Devoured raw, some foods are more delicious than cooked.

(The preserves I had prepared out of a need to keep busy, here in the country where I knew no one, and cared to know no one. Even as *he* went about shaking hands, smiling in *his* hope, poor fool, of being accepted as one of you. And which of us now stands vindicated?)

I am no longer fearful of the dark. For here, in this place, it is *my* dark.

When it was exactly, how many days (days? nights? now there is no distinction, the very words sound foolish) I understand what had happened and how, with no more delay, I must hide, I cannot recall—it may have been the equivalent of a month, it may have been only a few hours ago. In perpetual night, Time does not apply.

I do remember though long months through the preceding winter when the sky was overcast and the Sun, burning through, had a look of tarnished pewter; the many evenings the lights in the house would dim and flicker. My complaints to the power company fell on deaf ears—of course.

Then came the storm: the actual attack.

And when I woke to dawn it was to night though hearing certain but unmistakable sounds—the cries of birds close about the house—understanding that it *was* dawn; yet without the Sun.

And the rain had ceased. And the thunder. Groping to a window in what was the parlor I pressed both hands against the pane feeling, yes, the warmth of the Sun, it *was* the Sun, though invisible. As, earlier, there had been the struck flame of a match and a candle's burning wick. But the change was upon the world, *there could be no light.*

I had no time then to comprehend what had happened, what disaster of nature, knowing only that I must act quickly! Homeowners like myself would have to protect themselves against looting, burning, rape, and pillage of every kind—for the world would now divide itself into those *with* shelter and provisions and those *without.*

Those *with* a secure hiding place, and those *without.*

So I have barricaded myself here. In the cellar, in the dark, I require no eyes.

I have memorized all this space by touch. Never can I be enticed to leave. Thus do not appeal to me, do not threaten me, do not even approach. I know nothing of *before* the catastrophe, and have no interest. Should any of you claim to be kin of mine, even to be my daughters, be advised: I am not the woman you once knew, *nor any woman at all.*

In *his* prattle *he* once marveled at certain dangers to the Earth from outer space, a warning, or was it a prophecy, that one day a malevolent celestial body (comet? asteroid?) would strike Earth with an impact equivalent to the release of numberless nuclear explosions, thus rocking Earth off its natural course, raising pulverized rock and dust to block all sunlight henceforth casting sinful mankind into perpetual night. If this is Your wish, so it is Your wish. It is the end of the old world yet not the end to those of us who were prepared.

Even now I hear sirens in the distance. I am sure that that foul, acrid smell is a smell of smoke.

But I have no curiosity; I have made my own peace.

As I've said I have provisions to last for many months—for the remainder of my life. I have food, and water; not water out of the well but water fresh enough for me, dank, earthy-smelling but plenteous here in the cellar darkness where it lies in some areas to a depth of four or five inches; and, when rain returns, it will trickle freely down the rock walls where I can lap it delightedly with my tongue.

Gingerbread

S. P. Somtow

When we went to live in Hollywood, we saw many wonderful things. We saw many cruel things. Some people touched our hearts and some people touched our bodies. We grew up much too fast, and when we were all grown we found we'd been trapped in our childhood forever.

This is me, Greta Blackburn, writing all this down so my brother Johnny will one day remember if he chooses to. I can write real good now because there are a lot of books here and they let me take as many as I want into my room and I can keep them there without signing for them or anything.

On Sundays, a screenwriter comes to the institution and tells us stories. His name is Bob, and he is unemployed. But I've never seen him panhandling for money, and he wears expensive clothes. He is nice, kind of, and he never lays a hand on us. He is a volunteer. The Writers Guild has this program where they send writers to talk to people like us. It's supposed to keep us anchored to the real world.

Bob encourages me to write and he makes me keep a diary. Every week he reads what I've written and corrects most of the grammar. He doesn't correct all of it because sometimes he thinks it's charming the way it is.

I know I am too old to listen to stories, but I go because of my brother. He doesn't talk much anymore, but I think he is taking it all in. The time Bob told us the story of Hansel and Gretel, I could see that Johnny was paying attention, because he fixed on Bob with those clear blue eyes. That made me listen too. That's how I finally figured out what Titania Midnight was. I hadn't been able to put my finger on it, not until I heard Bob read us that fairy tale, but the moment I realized it, it was obvious.

Titania Midnight was a witch.

We didn't meet her until the second time. The first time our parents tried to dump us, they didn't succeed. That's because Johnny had snuck down to the kitchen for a Snickers bar, and he overheard them in their prayer meeting. He woke me up by banging on the ladder that goes up to the top bunk. "Greta," he said, "they're gonna take us away and . . . and they're gonna *ditch* us."

I was groggy and I thought he'd wet the bed again, but he just kept shaking me, and finally I crept out of bed, just so he'd calm down, and I went downstairs with him.

They were in the living room. There was a drape we used to hide behind whenever we listened to them arguing. It was a nice living room with big vinyl sofas, a mahogany piano and a painting of Jesus, with big kind eyes, over the fireplace. I couldn't see Daddy but I knew he was standing right in front of that painting and drawing his authority from the Lord. "It's all settled, Martha," he was saying, "no ifs, ands or buts about it. I've prayed on it, and I've begged the Lord to take this cup from us, but he said, 'I've made up my mind, Jed, and there ain't nothing more to say about it.' And you'd best obey me, because you're my wife, and the apostle Paul says—"

"Maybe it wasn't the Lord talking to you. I mean, to abandon your own kids . . . maybe it was . . . someone else . . . you know . . . *mimicking* the Lord."

"You calling me a Satanist, Martha?"

"Told you," Johnny whispered, and he gulped down his second candy bar.

"But how can we know they'll be all right?" Mom said.

"We have to trust in the Lord. They'll be provided for, long as they don't stray from the paths of righteousness."

I hugged my brother and said, "We have to make a plan."

Later, when we were settled in again, Daddy came into our

bedroom. He checked to make sure Johnny was snoring. Then he sat down on the bottom bunk next to me and slowly peeled down the sheet. I half opened my eyes. In the blue glow of the Smurfs nightlight my father's face looked like the face of a demon. As usual, I pretended to be fast asleep, and I waited for it to end. But this time he didn't start right away. Instead, he began to talk, in a sweet voice full of hurting, a voice I'd never heard him use before.

Daddy said, "Forgive me, I'm not a bad man, there's just something that comes over me and I can't help myself . . ." and then, "if only you knew how much I love you baby but I can't talk about those things I'm just a sinner and your mother don't understand . . ." and then he called me tender nicknames he would never use when I was awake. But after a while his voice grew harsh, and he said, "God damn them to hell, them ayrabs and them chinks that take away a decent Christian's job, and them usury-practicing kikes that caused this damn recession and take bread out of our mouths . . . the krauts should've never let them crawl out of them ovens, damn them, damn damn damn," and he called me *bitch* and *whore* and I just squeezed my eyes tight shut and made myself very small and very far away until he was all done with me.

The next morning, after breakfast, they made sure we brushed our teeth, then we got into the station wagon and set off. Daddy had to go to a job interview first, and we waited in the car. He came out looking dour.

"God damn all them Goldbergs and Goldsteins and Goldfarbs and Gold-shitass-Satan-worshiping, baby-sacrificing jewboys," he said. "A decent Christian can't get enough to feed his family, and they own half the damn country."

"Jed, please don't curse," said our mother, "not in front of the children."

They left us at some shopping mall, told us they'd pick us up in an hour, and went away. But we were prepared for that, and we had memorized every turn and every street name, and by sunset we managed to walk all the way home.

Daddy prayed on it all night. He didn't even come into our bedroom. Johnny peed the bed, but I overslept and didn't strip the sheets. They didn't notice, just fed us breakfast and told us to wait in the garage.

The second time, they locked us in the trunk and they drove and drove, and Johnny was carsick and we could hardly breathe. Johnny cried all the way. Partly it was the sugar that made him hard to deal with. I guess that's why they wanted to ditch us. Still, I was the one who took care of him most of the time. I'm a good girl.

When we woke up, we were in a blind alley, and it was night. There was a dumpster leaning against the wall, so I knew that we wouldn't go hungry. But it was cold and I didn't know how late it was or how long we had been there. Johnny was whimpering because he hadn't had a candy bar in a long time. From beyond the wall we could hear a buzzy kind of music and there were neon lights flashing in rhythm to it. There were people chattering, too, and the sound of spiked heels on concrete, and, now and then, a police siren. But inside the alley it was all quiet and dark.

"It hurts all over," Johnny said.

"Maybe we should go back to sleep for a while," I said, because I knew that when you're asleep there is no pain. We curled up together but the pavement was damp and cold, and finally we climbed up on the dumpster and found comfy places among the trash, which was not bad; back home, Daddy sometimes made us sleep in the garbage to teach us a lesson. He'd say, "You're poor, and you're white, so you might as well be trash too." I got a better deal because Johnny had a lot of fat on him and his butt made a pretty good cushion after I wedged it tight against the metal casing with a beer bottle.

The next time I woke up, it was still night, and I was looking into Titania Midnight's eyes. She was shining a flashlight in my face, and she was all in shadow, except for her eyes. They were sunken into a mess of wrinkles, but they were young eyes, and kind, like the painting of Jesus in our living room. "By Isis and Hecate," she said, "I've struck gold tonight."

That was when Johnny woke up and he started carrying on like he always does. "Double gold," said Titania Midnight, "even though the second nugget is a little . . . dare I say it . . . *larded.*"

"That ain't nice," I said. "Johnny can't help being, um, *ample*. It's his glands."

"Oh, I daresay, I daresay. But within the chrysalis, something beautiful, no? You'll come with me, of course; you'll want food."

"I had pizza earlier. It was still warm even, two slices, pepperoni. But Johnny has to have his sugar fix or he'll get crazy."

"I've just the thing." She rummaged in a tote bag and gave something to Johnny. "Baked it meself. Gingerbread is best. I think it blends a lot better than brownie mix."

"Blends with what?" I said.

"Oh, oh, you innocent, wide-eyed creature. Fundamentalist parents, I'll bet. Raped you too, I wouldn't wonder. Maybe not the boy, he's so *gelatinous*. No wonder you bolted."

I didn't understand what she was talking about, but she seemed kind, like in the parable of the Good Samaritan. Johnny gobbled the gingerbread cookie greedily and asked for another one.

"Oh, nonsense," she said, "you'll be stoned out of your everloving mind."

She asked us our names and she told us hers. I thought it was a fishy-sounding name, but I didn't want to be impolite. I'm a good girl.

"Well," she said. "Come along now. You'll be wanting to freshen up. Get a decent night's sleep and all that. No time to stand around chit-chatting. Hollywood's like the Forest of Arden. Anything can happen. Sorcery. Gender confusion. Love potions that make you see a donkey as a sex object. Whew! But it's a magic place. You'll see. Wonder piled on wonder."

I helped Johnny out of the trash and dusted him off a little bit. We followed Titania out of the alley and that's when the lights and the music hit us full blast. God, it was wild. Posters tall as buildings with painted ladies on them and musclemen in just their underwear, and a big Chinese dragon that lit up and wall-to-wall cars and hip-hop making the pavement quake and skateboarders with long hair on one side and bald on the other and people snapping pictures everywhere and stars on the sidewalks and a dinosaur climbing up the side of one building . . . oh, it was Disneyland. I held Johnny's hand tight because he gets frightened easily. But actually he didn't seem to mind even though he had never been among so many people in his life. His eyes just seemed to go all glassy. The gingerbread must have been real good.

Everyone seemed to know who Titania was. People would come up to her and she would smile at them or wave. The colors of the lights kept changing and sometimes she seemed young and sometimes she seemed old. She had a nose like a parrot's beak and her lips were red as cherries and her eyelids were all covered with gold paint. A man in a white suit came up to her and pointed at us, but she said, "Don't you touch any of my babies, you hear? They're too good for the likes of you."

And I whispered in Johnny's ear. "She's nice. She'll protect us. Maybe she's our guardian angel."

"Yeah," Johnny said, and then he giggled for no reason at all.

We turned down a side street and then another one. This was a narrow street and all dark, except for one neon sign, blinking, and it read

PSYCHIC READER AND ADVISOR
DONUTS

and I knew that there had never been any place like *that* where we came from. From the street it seemed like just a regular doughnut place and there were a couple of customers inside, including a policeman. Next to the entrance was a narrow unpaved alley with high walls and there was a side door. Titania used three keys to let us in, and then she punched in a code on the security pad inside the doorway.

Inside there was a dingy living room. A black girl was lying on the rug watching *Murphy Brown*. The clock on the wall said three A.M., so it must have been a videotape. She looked up at us. "Hey," she said, "I thought you said no more kids."

"No jealous fits, now, Laverne," said Titania, "you really must learn to share."

"Where they gone sleep?" Laverne said. "And what about *lardass* there? You could strip him and sell him for parts, maybe, but in one piece, he wouldn't even make it round the block." She frowned and flicked the remote to MTV. I knew it was MTV, even though we didn't have cable back home, because it showed Satanic stuff.

"Oh, you cruel heartless beast," Titania said, but there was no malice in the way she said it. "Put on the light; let's have a look at this one. Ai, ai, ai . . . what are we to do with him?"

Laverne got up and switched on a naked light bulb that swung from the ceiling. All of a sudden everything was harshly lit. One side of the room was all drapes; they were a tad open and I could see through to a big kitchen, maybe where they made the doughnuts. The walls were covered with signed photographs of famous actors. The shag carpeting was spotty . . . one or two places looked like puke stains. Titania and the black girl were leading Johnny by the hand until he was right under the light, and they were studying him, like dissecting a frog in school.

"You know," Titania said, "Laverne, you are too ready to flush people down the toilet bowl of existence. This one has possibilities. Notice the eyes, how big they are. They are the eyes of an angel. And the flesh, well, the flesh . . . even though we are not Michelangelo, can we not see David in this block of marble? Can we not whittle? Hone? Hollow the pudginess so the cheekbones stand proud, even arrogant? And look at his sullenness. The lips can be worked into a willful pout. Strip him for parts indeed!" They were all poking him and looking at his teeth and looking down his shorts and Johnny started to cry. And Titania let go of him and made Laverne step back, and she said, "That's it. The finishing touch. Listen to that weeping. It's like the cry of the sea gulls over some solitary isle in the bitter cold North Sea."

"I think I know what you're getting at," Laverne said slowly.

"What *is* she getting at?" I said, and I could feel my stomach curl up.

"He will be our fortune!" Titania cried, and kissed Johnny wetly on the lips, which caused him to make one of his goofy faces. They laughed. "He'll have the beautification room," Titania said. "As for . . . Greta, was it? . . ."

"I ain't sharing my room with no honky greenhorn," Laverne said.

"Oh, you were always selfish."

"You can tell she's not right for us!" Laverne said. "She gots a strong firm body like a ho', but she don't have a ho's eyes. She be needing one of your magic potions every time she goes to work."

Suddenly, for the first time, I panicked. "You can't split us up!" I said. "We've never been apart, not for one minute! And I'm the only one who can tell when his sugar's off."

That set both of them to laughing, and Johnny to carrying on still more, and I could feel a few tears brimming up in my eyes too, until it dawned on me that there would be no visit from Daddy tonight. I realized I had died and gone to heaven.

The beautification room was about the size of a large closet but it had a TV and a VCR. It could only be locked from the outside. The door had a little glass pane where you could look in. There was no toilet but Titania gave him a potty that she made me empty once a day. She fed him on nothing but water and little blue pills. I told her he needed sugar but she said, "It's okay, hon, this is just for a little while; the dexies will get him thinned down, bring out those dimpled cheekbones."

Titania was the only one who had the key, but you could talk to Johnny by sticking your ear right on the pane to listen, and putting your lips up to the glass and talking soft enough so the sound wouldn't carry beyond the corridor. But I couldn't touch Johnny and I knew that upset him. Still, I didn't want to complain too much to my host. I was a good girl, and I had been through a lot worse times than this.

It wasn't much fun sleeping with Laverne at first, though. She used to hog the thing you folded out to sleep on (she called it a "foo-ton") and she would talk about me as though I wasn't there, and even when she talked directly *to* me, she made it sound like I was stupid. But a lot of the time she was gone all night, and I could sleep by myself, which was great because it was a tiny room, the size of a large bathroom maybe, with no windows.

When Laverne got home—it didn't matter how late it was—she kicked me out of the futon so I was at least halfway on the floor. She would turn on the television and smoke cigarettes.

She was addicted to the Jeffrey Dahmer case, which was on the

late, late news every day. "I *love* Jeff," she would say. "I think he's
beautiful. He eats people alive. He's the grim reaper."

I didn't know if that was a satanic thing to say or not. I shut up
about it mostly. But no matter how late she came in, she would
always go flick, flick, flick with the cable controller until she found
some piece of news about him. It was scary how obsessed she was.
The third night, even though I was afraid she'd bully me and tell
me to shut up, I just came out and asked her why she didn't watch
something more pleasant. She only said, "Sometimes I wish he'd
carve *me* up."

"But why would you say that?" I said. "Aren't you happy here?"

"Sure," she said, "sure, Laverne happy."

In the dark room all I could see were her eyes, large and round
and full of disappointment. I thought she was just contrary. Things
were good for us girls. We had a lot to eat. And even though
Titania didn't let Johnny eat anything at all, it was true that Johnny
was shedding his rolls of fat. By the third day, looking at him
through the pane in the door, I could see what Titania meant.
Johnny was beautiful, and I cussed myself out because I, his own
sister, hadn't seen fit to notice a plain fact like that, right under my
very own nose. His eyes were getting more and more like the eyes of
the Jesus that hung in our living room over the fireplace.

"Titania," I said over dinner, "you must know magic or something."

"I do," she said. "Finish your corn muffins and take Johnny his
pills. And empty his chamberpot and weigh him and get dolled up,
because we're going into Beverly Hills."

I used to watch *Beverly Hills, 90210* every week, of course, so
naturally this was the most exciting moment for me since we arrived in Hollywood. Titania made me borrow some of Laverne's
clothes. They were tight and skimpy but Titania kept telling me I
looked beautiful. Then she made me put on makeup so I looked
like a painted whore of Babylon. I guess I did anyway, because
though I had never been to Babylon I'd heard Daddy talking about
them often enough, and I knew they weren't good girls like me. But
I was afraid not to do what Titania said because she had been so
good to me. And then again I thought of Johnny, locked up in the

beautification room, with the ugliness melting away from him with the pills and the starvation, and I knew that what Titania was doing was a dark mystery . . . like the changing of water into wine. If Titania could really work miracles, she had to be connected to the Holy Spirit somehow, because Daddy told me that Satan can't *really* do miracles, he can only deal in illusion.

And when I looked in the little hand mirror Titania gave me, I really was beautiful. It wasn't an illusion. I looked like, I don't know, Julia Roberts. It sure made me happy to know I could be beautiful even though I had never been in a movie.

Titania came out of her room and she was wearing a long black gown, studded with rhinestones. She wore so much makeup she seemed to have no wrinkles at all. In the harsh light of the living room her face seemed to be made of porcelain. Laverne came in for a moment and when she saw me dressed that way she turned her nose up at me.

"Bitch," she said.

"Now don't you carry on," Titania said. "You can be *so* immature sometimes, Laverne."

But I was sorry because I figured Laverne was a little envious because she wasn't coming with us, and I said, "Why can't we bring her along?"

Laverne said, "She taking you 'cause you white."

"Now you know very well that that simply isn't true," said Titania. "Each of us has his appointed place in the cosmos. You have yours, and Greta will have hers . . . and a splendid place it will be," she added, handing me a gingerbread cookie out of her clutch. I nibbled it as she went on, "Come on, now, Greta. It's time you learned the ropes. And really, dear, we must do a little better than *Greta.* So *plain,* so, I don't know, *Teutonic!* What about Anastasia? Or Renée? Carina? Perhaps some advice, Laverne? You people always have such unusual names."

"I hate you," Laverne said. "Gimme one of them cookies."

"In time," said Titania, and it seemed that her porcelain face grew taut and brittle, "but now, get your black ass back out on the street and don't come back until you've made your quota for the night." She didn't sound like the same woman at all; she had a scary voice, like those women who sometimes get possessed and have to have the devil cast out of them in church. Then Titania turned on the charm again and said to me, "Honey, we're off."

A limo picked us up and we went onto the freeway. Actually we went way past Beverly Hills—I got a chance to look at all the posh houses—and then down a winding road that hugged the ocean. I watched television and Titania fussed with my hair. I flick-flick-flicked until I saw the image of Jeffrey Dahmer on the television. He was being tried and his face filled the whole screen. I didn't think he was beautiful at all, and I sure didn't want to get cut into pieces and eaten. I wondered what it could be that made Laverne think that way. After all, life is a precious gift.

The limo drove past solitary beach houses. There was a house shaped like a monster's face, peering from the side of a cliff. There was a house that seemed to be made of vines, and another all glass, and another all chrome. It was gloomy and you could hear the ocean sighing even through the closed windows of the limo. Titania was putting on more makeup. For the first time since I'd known her, she seemed nervous, tapping the armrest with her tapered fingernails, smudging and redoing her lipstick over and over. When she thought she was all done, she said to me, "Now, Anastasia, I'm going to introduce you to a *very important* person. He can really change your life if you're good to him. I want you to do what he says, even if it seems a tad peculiar to you . . . do you under-stand?"

I nodded as I watched on television that they weren't going to send Dahmer to the electric chair after all, since they don't do that kind of thing in Milwaukee. That was strange to me, that you could kill all those people and not be killed yourself. It went against the Bible. But I had been thinking less and less about the Bible the last few days.

Where the party was there was a long wooden deck that ran on stilts beside the sea. The house was wooden and all white. There were maids in black uniforms and all the guests wore black even though it wasn't a funeral. Inside the house there were big splotchy paintings and sculptures made of wire and the guests sat in small groups, drinking and sniffing some kind of Nutrasweet into their noses. I was scared and stood in a shadowed corner, but Titania just plowed right into the crowd, screaming out endearments like "darling" and "honey" to people even though I could tell she didn't care about them at all.

"Titania Midnight!" said a woman who was wearing enough jewelry to sink a ship. "You have just *got* to do a reading for me."

"Well," said Titania, "the moon is full and the night is bright." She blinked her gold-lidded eyes and her lashes *rippled*. I don't know how to describe it except once, in school, before my parents took us out because they'd been teaching about evolution, I saw a paramecium-thingy in a microscope, and it had those little legs, *cilia* they call them, and they were just like Titania's eyelashes. "Come, Anastasia," she said, and it took me a minute to remember it was me, and we went out to the deck, to a private place that was surrounded by potted plants.

Titania sat on the redwood planks, in front of one of those electric waterfalls where the water comes down all in beads, and she pulled a deck of cards out of her clutch, and she handed them to me. The woman squatted across from us and I realized I had seen her before, in *All My Children* maybe. Titania shuffled and the television star woman shuffled and then they handed me the deck and whenever Titania held out her hand I was to give her one of the cards, face down. And Titania would turn it up and lay it down on the deck in a cross kind of pattern, which reminded me of the Lord's crucifixion. Then she closed her eyes and mumbled to herself . . . I guess she was praying in tongues . . . and she said things like, "Oh no, oh no. You won't want to hear this, honey, but . . . the other one . . . he is darker, isn't he? I think, a swarthy man, hairy also, and . . . wearing a gold chain—thick."

"Oh, my God," said the television person, "I can't wait until I totally tell all my friends . . . this is, oh God, *uncanny*. Well, it's a platinum chain actually. Herbie's, you know, *allergic* to gold and all. Can you relate?" she added, turning to me, but I don't think I was supposed to answer.

Then I looked up and saw the blond beautiful man with long hair. He was wearing a black suit and he had an earring in the shape of a scythe dangling all the way down to his shoulder. He wore mirror shades. Maybe Laverne was in love with Jeff Dahmer, but she'd probably think again if she saw *this* man. He had a little stubble, like Jeff did in the courtroom.

"You old witch," he said to Titania. "What have you conjured up today?"

Titania saw that I was staring at him with my mouth wide open. She said to me, "Anastasia," and she nudged the base of my skull so I'd look more demure, with downcast eyes, "this is your host and mine, Dana Harrington. I think you had better call him Mr. Harrington."

"But what about the dark hairy man with the platinum chain?" said the television star woman. "Do we get to, you know, like, *do* it?"

"Hold your horses, hon," said Titania, taking the next card and flipping it through the air, "you have the Death card. I think you should wait until after the divorce. Or else . . ." She made a throat-slitting gesture.

"*Shit,*" said the television person, "the fucking trust fund. The palimony. I'd better lay in a supply of Seconals."

"Go with Mr. Harrington," Titania said to me.

I followed Mr. Harrington through the party crowd, which parted for him like the sea. We reached a bedroom that was all white and didn't even have a television in it. There were toys on the white carpet . . . boy's toys, but the kind that are a few years out of date, I mean, Transformers, Teenage Mutant Ninja Turtles action figures, and stuff. Above the bed there was a huge painting in a gold frame, and it was a picture of a boy. He was a thin boy with big eyes, but in a strange kind of way he reminded me of Johnny. I couldn't help thinking of Johnny at that moment, wondering what he was doing and whether he had wet himself yet. There was a tray of chocolates next to the bed and the man offered them to me. I had one. There was a weird liquid in the middle, which tasted the way Daddy's breath used to smell some nights. It made me feel a bit woozy, but part of that was from the gingerbread I'd had earlier. I had a few more chocolates.

"How old are you, Anastasia?" said the blond beautiful man.

"Fourteen. And my name's really Greta."

I said I was older than I really was. Later I found out you can get more money if you say you're younger.

"Do you like the chocolate liqueurs? Have some more." He smiled. He was nice. I wondered if he would start calling me names, like Daddy. But he just made me sit next to him on the bed and he toyed with my hair. I was scared my hair would get messed up and Titania would be mad at me so I just sat there, all stiff, eating the chocolates.

"I want you to know that I'm not a bad man," said Mr. Harrington. "I do have . . . *weaknesses* . . . but I'm in therapy now. You really needn't worry about me hurting you or anything like that. I'm the last person in the world who would do that."

"I know you're a good man, Mr. Harrington," I said.

"I'm an important man," said Mr. Harrington. "Maybe I could do something for you one day."

"I got everything I need," I said. "You don't have to worry about me, Mr. Harrington." But he had already slipped a hundred dollar bill into my hand. "You sure got a lot of art here."

"I'm a collector. I only have the most beautiful things in the world here. Like you. I have an insatiable appetite for beauty. I eat it up. I consume it and afterward I'm still hungry. You know, the Chinese food syndrome."

I wasn't sure what was so great about some of those splotchy paintings, but I was too good a girl to point that out to him. Mr. Harrington took off his shades. He had the clearest eyes; I couldn't decide if they were more like Jeff Dahmer's or more like Jesus's.

"Who's that?" I said. I pointed to the portrait that reminded me so much of Johnny . . . not fat little Johnny but the Johnny that Titania was squeezing out of Johnny's flesh . . . the ideal Johnny, Johnny Angel.

"It's my son," he said.

"He looks nice."

"He's dead."

"I wish I'd of known him."

"You would have liked him. Everyone did. He was everybody's favorite Hollywood kid. He was precocious but not obnoxious. He

was bright enough to be witty but not enough to be an egghead."
Mr. Harrington looked away from me, remembering.

"How did he . . . I mean . . ." I knew I shouldn't have said
that. Because Mr. Harrington turned to me and he was so full of
rage I was afraid he was going to slap my face.

"Don't!" I said, and I shrank back, and that left him kind of
dazed, staring at his hand.

"Violently," he said at last. "He died violently." I saw a tear in
the corner of one eye form slowly, like a drop of condensation on a
glass of soda, and slide down his cheek. I wondered whether, right
now, Daddy was crying over me. Probably not, I thought. Mr.
Harrington was a very special kind of man, blond, beautiful, and
caring. He wiped his eye on a sleeve, and he smiled a little, and put
his mirror shades back on again so I couldn't see his eyes anymore.

Then he fucked me.

Titania Midnight allowed me to keep ten dollars out of the hundred, and things got better for me after that night. I did parties and
dates every night except Sunday, when I helped out in the doughnut shop, stirring the big vat of batter and putting the croissants
into the monster oven in batches, a hundred at a time. Sometimes I
made as much as a hundred dollars a week. I became good at
makeup. I became more beautiful. And so did Johnny. But when I
went into his little room to take him his pills and empty his potty,
I tried not to look at him too much. He would mumble things I
didn't understand. I think it was because of all the videotapes he
watched. He didn't have anything to do but look at television. It
was lucky there were a lot of tapes: musical comedies, slasher movies, pornos, and even some that weren't in English.

Johnny's skin had a shine to it now, like a polished vase. It
glowed as though there were a candle burning inside him, and I
could see what Titania meant about his cheekbones. But I'd clear
out of the room as quickly as I could every morning. I felt guilty, I
suppose. I knew that somehow I had betrayed him. Once in a while
I'd slip him a piece of gingerbread.

Titania had taught me how to make it, from sautéing the dried
marijuana in butter beforehand to kill the taste, to rolling the

dough and fashioning it into flat little men with raisin eyes, noses, and mouths. "Creating life in the laboratory," Titania called it, sipping her coffee and wolfing down three or four powdered doughnuts, her favorite. It sure seemed to give Johnny life because he'd just wolf that thing down. He was always sad and that was part of what made him beautiful.

Titania even showed me the larder where she kept all the fixings for her special treats. There was a jar full of white powder, a mortar and pestle, and dried toadstools, and a big brown envelope full of marijuana. There was a corrugated brown box marked *Valium*. And a whole lot of other stuff that you could use in baking to get unusual results.

The best times of all were when it was real late at night, and Titania would let me sit in on her readings. They were in a big room way in back, and it was hung with black velvet drapes and there would always be music playing there, the kind of music where you can't quite catch the melodies even though they are almost the same thing, over and over, twisting around one or two notes. I would sit in shadow and hand her the cards. Sometimes she told them I was a mute, or retarded, because they were afraid I would betray their secrets. They would look at me and say, "Poor thing," and stuff, and I had to pretend I couldn't understand.

After the last customer left, Titania would show me how it all worked. Every card, she said, is a window into another world. There's what you see and there's what you don't see. Look at this one: what are the wolves howling at that's just beyond the edge of the picture, the thing that we can't see? Is that a lobster or is it a scorpion in the water? When you open yourself up, she told me, you can hear what the wolves are saying. And more. You can hear the voices that speak from all over that hidden world. You can hear the weeping of the moon. Listen. Listen. Turn over another card.

Tonight the card was Death.

The first time I'd flipped up Death had been at Mr. Harrington's party. Death was a bent old skeleton-man with a scythe, grinning. Mr. Harrington had a scythe hanging from his left ear. The ground beneath Death was strewn with severed heads. Jeffrey Dahmer had heads in his refrigerator, apartment 213, the same number as our area code in Hollywood. Looking at the card this time made me all shivery and I wanted to cover it with another card.

Laverne poked her head in the doorway. "Eww," she said, "someone gone die tonight."

Titania took both my hands in hers and said, "Dear, dear, dear! The first lesson for the good clairvoyant is this: *Thou shalt not kill the goose that layeth the golden eggs!* Imagine, honey, the horror of telling some Hollywood fashion plate, 'Eww, someone gone die!' You'd never survive a fortnight in the biz."

"But what if I get the feeling that someone *is* going to die?" I said. "I have to tell the truth, don't I? Ain't that what the gift of prophecy is all about?"

"Laverne, go check on the chocolate dips, there's a dear." Laverne threw a roll of twenties on the floor, slammed the door, stalked off down the hall. The money crossed the Death card and all you could see was the tip of the scythe. Titania flicked the money out of the way and whispered, "Now, my dear dear dear disciple, now we come to the greatest mystery of them all. Death is not death. Death is transformation."

"Oh, I get it. Like the death and resurrection of the Lord."

"Bingo! Aren't you the clever one."

"So if I draw the Death card, I have to tell the questioner that . . ."

"There will be a transformation. No, no, there is no death. Chrysalis and butterfly, corpse and maggot, life rolls over into life, death is a tango through eternal night. Look at your little brother . . . how he has shed his fleshy self . . . how he is translated into the ethereal! Ai, ai, ai, Johnny Angel indeed!"

I stared and stared at that card, but I couldn't figure it out.

In the morning, Johnny moaned and carried on, and he was mumbling and muttering and he had a fever. His skin was all translucent, and you could see the veins. I mopped up his sweat with a dish towel. He tossed and turned in my arms, but I couldn't understand anything he was saying, until, looking straight past me, he said, "The man with the big curvy sword."

The room became all cold. I thought I felt someone breathing on my neck. Johnny seemed to see someone, standing behind me, swallowing both of us in his shadow. Maybe it was the fever, or maybe he really could see something; he's gifted that way. In church, he always used to know when someone was possessed.

After the blast of icy breath died away, I couldn't feel anything anymore. But Johnny could still see whatever it was he saw. I knew it was terrifying him because he started to piss himself, which he normally only does in his sleep.

I fed him gingerbread men until he dozed off. Then Titania came in with a Polaroid camera, and she made me lay him down, very carefully, like a dead body on a bier, and she took three or four snapshots of him all lying there, asleep with his eyes wide open.

I have a lot of men inside me now. I've sucked little pieces of them into myself. One day the little pieces will dissolve and I'll be able to piss them away and become all clean again inside.

They liked it when I called them Daddy. Maybe they didn't have daughters of their own. Sometimes when she sent me out to work, Titania brewed me what Laverne used to call her magic potion. The potion made me crazy. I learned how to buck and heave and make those little panting noises. But oftentimes they liked it better when I played dead, closed my eyes, pretended to be asleep. That was the easiest to do, because I learned it from home. It was different from home though. Because sometimes they told me jokes, bought me little gifts, tried to treat me like a real person. They didn't call me names. And they gave me money, so that I wasn't worthless anymore.

I hardly ever watch television or go to the movies these days. You never know when one of them's going to appear. And then I'll feel all queasy inside and I have to excuse myself to go to the bathroom.

After a while, maybe because she wasn't Titania's favorite any-more, Laverne kind of drifted away from us, and sometimes she'd stay out all night. One day they were yelling at each other and Titania screamed, "Go away, get what you want, I dare you," and sent Laverne sulking into the neon night, and Laverne never came back.

I saw one evening on *A Current Affair* how Jeff Dahmer had his own groupies who used to hang around the courtroom waiting for a glimpse of him. You'd think they would all be a bunch of fat wannabes but no, some of them were good-looking, not the kind of people who needed to get a life. I had this idea that Laverne had maybe taken the bus out to Milwaukee to become one of the groupies. Since the verdict, Jeff had not come on television as often anymore, so that was probably why I had not seen Laverne on TV. Maybe in a year or two, if they ever had one of those "What ever happened to——?" type shows, I could see Laverne, hovering outside the walls of a bleak gray prison, and she'd still be calling out to him. "Come and get me too, because I love you."

I did see Laverne on television, but it wasn't how I imagined it. They were pulling her body out of a dumpster. I think it was the same one Johnny and I had slept in, that first night in Hollywood.

Later Titania and I went down to the morgue to identify the body, because we were all the kin Laverne had. She was in pieces, but it was her all right. Her hands had been cut off and strung around her neck with a length of her own intestine, and one of her feet was poking up out of her, you know, down there. Her skin was just like Johnny's, translucent. She had never been that black but now she was almost yellow. Her eyes stared past me the way Johnny's stared that time, seeing someone I could not see. It still seemed to me that she was sneering at me, even now that she had been shuffled and redealt.

In the pocket of her jeans, they had found a Jeffrey Dahmer trading card. I knew then that this death had been the death she'd prayed for. It was hard to believe that a man in a prison far away could have reached out, heard her wishes, and granted them, maybe by sending down some divine ambassador to wield the scythe that had sliced her into thirteen pieces. After all, Daddy had always told me that only God can do things like that. But he also said God can be anyone, anywhere, anytime.

Maybe even inside a serial killer.

It made me sick, and later I asked Titania how she could still say to me, "There is no death."

But all she would say was, "You have to look past those things." And she took a sip of the hospital cafeteria coffee.

Sure, she'd said, *sure, Laverne happy.*

Now I couldn't get any of them out of my head: the bone man swinging the scythe and Dahmer and the head in the refrigerator and Mr. Harrington and the dead boy who'd died violently, *violently,* and my brother transforming into an angel inside that beautification room. "God, why'd you have to bring me here?" I screamed at her. "Did you make this happen when you told her she would get what she'd always wanted? Is this another one of your magic spells?"

"Temper, temper," she said. "I have to open all the doors in the dark castle, dear; you have to gaze at the searing face of the deity; yes! Oh, Anastasia, oh, Renée, you have looked the demon in the eye and know him to be yourself!"

It was then that I knew Titania Midnight was crazy. Only Johnny could know if she was sick in the head or whether some devil had taken possession of her body. I was half crazy myself, because I loved the old woman, because she was what I had to cling to in the madness that whirled around me. The city of night had given me a thousand fathers, but only one mother. I cried then, and I hugged her and told her it would all come out all right in the end.

After all, she still had me, and I could do double the work to keep us all afloat. And I did.

There was another party at the Harrington place. It was another Harrington place, actually, not the one in Malibu, but the one actually *in* Beverly Hills. The house was different but the room was the same. It was uncanny. The room was a kind of shrine, I guess. There was probably one like it in every house the beautiful blond man owned.

The bed, the portrait of Mr. Harrington's son, even the outdated toys that were scattered on the rug were in exactly the same places. Mr. Harrington gave me two hundred dollars this time because by now he had found out my real age, plus now I was real good at behaving just the way he wanted. Right after it was over, I fell into a deep sleep because it was the best way to stop feeling the pain.

When I woke up, Titania Midnight was in the room, and so was Mr. Harrington, fully dressed now in his tuxedo, ready to go to some premiere. They were sitting on the edge of the bed.

"Can we talk? She won't wake up, will she?" said Mr. Harrington.

"Not if she drained that Valium cocktail to the last drop."

Mr. Harrington said, "You've been very good to me, Titania. In accommodating . . . well, my tastes. But there was something else you were going to look for . . . I don't know how much progress you've made."

"A lot. I want you to see some Polaroids," Titania said. I kept my eyes closed because I didn't want them to know I could hear them. I could hear Titania rummaging in her purse, could hear papers rustling, and then I heard Mr. Harrington sigh. "The eyes. The sadness. The crisp hard curl of a lower lip that can't quite twist into a smile. He's so beautiful you could eat him up," Titania said.

"No poetry, Titania," said Mr. Harrington. And he sighed again.

"No poetry? But how can you say that when you see these pictures? But it gets better. No papers. No dental records. No milk cartons. No television appeals. He does not exist. Not until you spring him, fully formed, into the world. Come for him tomorrow midnight."

"I'll have the cash."

They didn't talk for a long time. It took time for the weight of what they were saying to settle in. I pretended to sleep until they left the room. Then I got up and prowled around. I didn't go back down to the party because then they might know I'd overheard them. I tiptoed across the toy-strewn rug. Titania had left her purse on the dresser. I was sure she'd been showing Mr. Harrington the Polaroids of Johnny, and I was right. That's what they were. I held one of them up to the lava lamp, then I glanced up at the portrait of Mr. Harrington's son. Titania had caught the look exactly.

Somehow, she had turned Johnny into this dead boy. It was like Johnny's body was an empty glass and you could pour in any soul you wanted. Maybe the pills did more than melt away his fat. And Mr. Harrington was a collector, he'd told me. Was he planning to collect Johnny? I became real frightened, and I guess my hand was trembling because I knocked the purse onto the floor.

A lot of stuff fell out: a key ring, a pack of Dunhills, a driver's license. I knelt down and tried to put everything back in. I looked at the license too. It showed Titania's picture, but the name on it was Amelia Goldberg. Hadn't Daddy said something about Goldsteins and Goldfarbs . . . sacrificing babies and taking away his job? It didn't seem possible that Titania Midnight could be one of those people. She didn't even know who my father was, so how could she take his job? And it wasn't *her* who had killed Laverne.

Or was it?

I didn't want to think such terrible things about the woman who had taken me in, given me a job with decent wages, and tried to share so much of her wisdom with me. But it sure made me think. There was more to all this than I had ever dreamed. It really scared me.

Especially when I finally put my clothes back on and I went back down to the party, and I saw Mr. Harrington gliding through the thick of the crowd, smiling a little, in a world of his own, and the scythe in his ear catching the light from the crystal chandelier. He moved among the chatter, and the clinking of cocktail glasses, but he himself seemed to be inside his own private silence.

That night I dreamed about the beautiful blond man, and the scythe swinging and people screaming and their heads flying through the air like bloody soccer balls. When I woke up I wished Laverne would be lying on the futon next to me, even if she would kick me half onto the floor. It was real late and I knew that even Titania would be asleep by now, either in her bedroom or in the reading room, slumped over a deck of tarot cards, or in the easy chair in the big kitchen among the unbaked doughnuts.

I had a feeling I had to see Johnny. It was Johnny who had spied on Daddy's prayer meeting and who had had the presence of mind to come and warn me. It was only fair I should tell him about things I overheard. So I pulled on a long *Beverly Hills, 90210* T-shirt, and I crept down the corridor to the beautification room.

I looked in at my brother. He was leaning against the wall, staring at the television. He didn't seem to see me. I put my lips to the pane and whispered his name a couple of times, but he didn't look up. Then I tried the door. It was unlatched. I wondered how many times it had been unlatched in the past, how many times we could have escaped. Except where would we have escaped to? Titania had fed us . . . me, anyway . . . loved us, for all I could tell. I slipped into the room and I was almost touching him before he seemed to notice me. "Johnny," I said, "Johnny, I think they want to do something to you, I don't know what."

Johnny said, "I don't like the pornos that much. I seen all that stuff before, at home. Westerns are cool. The horror movies are the best. I love Freddy Krueger's fingernails."

"Johnny, can't you hear me?"

"When I close my eyes, the movie still goes on. The man with the curvy sword is dancing in the street. Under the neon lights. The flashing sign makes a dragon on his face because his face is like a mirror."

God, I thought, thinking of Mr. Harrington's shades as he moved up and down, up and down, seeing my face get big and small, big and small. "Johnny," I said, "are there mirrors over his eyes? Is the curvy sword dangling from his ear? Is he a beautiful blond man dressed in black?"

Johnny giggled. But that was because of something on the television. "You have to tell me," I said, "it's real important."

But Johnny began to babble in tongues. He was always a lot closer to the Lord than I could ever be. He carried on for a while, waving his arms and making his eyes roll up in their sockets, but without the gift of interpretation I couldn't understand what he meant. But finally he switched back to English and he said, "The skull." And pointed straight at the television screen. But all I could see was a Madonna video.

"Come on, Johnny. Let's run away. I don't think this place is safe anymore. I think they're gonna do something really bad to you.

Look, I got a couple hundred bucks saved up, tips and stuff. I know we don't remember how we got here, but maybe we can find a better daddy and mommy. I met a hundred new daddies here, and most of them were pretty nice to me. You could have all the candy bars you wanted. You wouldn't have to be this way."

Johnny turned to me at last. The room was dark except for the pool of gray light in front of the television. He sat up. He was wearing only a pair of yellowing BVDs and his whole body was shiny, like the TV screen, and his eyes were haunted and deep. His hair was as pale as the hair of the blond beautiful man, and his fingers tapped at the empty air. "We can't go," he said softly. "You can't run away from the man with the curvy sword."

I hugged Johnny and said, "I got a plan, Johnny. We'll be okay." I didn't know what the plan would be yet, but my mind was racing. We'd use my money to buy a bus ticket to Disneyland. We'd find a mommy and a daddy and a tract house in a green green suburb. We'd overdose on gingerbread and fly into the sky.

I tugged at Johnny. He started to budge, then I heard the key turn in the latch of the prison door. I looked up sharply and saw Titania's face in the television's ghostly light. She must have just come back from a Beverly Hills reading, because her face was powdered to a chalky whiteness, and her lips painted the crimson of fresh blood, and there were charcoal circles around her eyes. She sniffed like a hungry she-wolf, and her lips twisted into a sharp-toothed smile. Then she faded into shadow.

Titania Midnight was more than mad. She was evil.

I held Johnny in my arms the whole night long, and didn't sleep until dawn.

The blond beautiful man with long hair was coming at midnight. I knew that from overhearing that conversation. I didn't have that long to do what I had to do. I went to Titania's secret larder and pulled out about forty Valium; I ground them up with the mortar and pestle, and I folded and sifted them with a half cup of powdered sugar. I poured the mixture into an envelope, tucked it in my jeans, and went out to work.

Work was not too bad that day. All my dates were regulars, and

I already knew how they all liked it. So I didn't really have to concentrate very hard. I just let myself drift, and I swallowed just enough gingerbread to loosen up my soul, and not enough to cut the kite string that held me to the real world. Everyone was pleased with me and I got a lot of extra money, which was good because maybe me and Johnny would need it later.

I stayed out as late as I dared. When I came home it was only an hour before midnight. I found Titania in the kitchen of the dough-nut shop. She had turned off the neon and pulled down all the shades and hung up a sign on the door that read ON VACATION—CLOSED. She had a whole pot of coffee out and, even though she wasn't going out anywhere, was dressed to the teeth. She had on a long black robe embroidered with suns and moons and stars. Her eyelids were painted in rainbow glitter, and her lips were midnight blue. When she saw me, she became all agitated and she started to cackle.

"Tonight's the night, my baby Anastasia," she said. "No more slaving over a hot kitchen for you! No more blowjobs in BMWs. You're going to be a princess now, and Titania's going to be queen of the wood. Be a dear and do me up some powdered doughnuts. Mama Titania'll be back in a few minutes."

I fetched the doughnuts and dipped them in the Valium powder. She was gone for a long time, and I became more and more nervous. I took the croissants out of the oven and stacked them up. I wondered why she was still baking if we were supposed to be on vacation . . . and rich besides.

When Titania came back, she had Johnny with her. He was wearing a brand new blue suit with crisp, sharply creased short pants. Titania had moussed his hair and brushed it. It was hard for Johnny to stand in the light. He kept blinking and he seemed not to know where he was.

Titania said, "Things will be different now, Johnny. You'll be able to eat anything you want. Would you like some candy? Would you care for a doughnut?" She snatched one from the plate I had so carefully arranged and handed it to him. Then she stuffed one into her own mouth. While she was busy chewing, I pried the doughnut

loose from Johnny's fist and gave him something else, a chocolate
éclair. He sucked on it, savoring the cream.

"My two little darlings," said Titania Midnight, "tonight Mr.
Harrington is going to come for you. Well, the deal is only for
Johnny, but I think we can manage to get Anastasia thrown into the
package . . . oh, my angels, how I slaved to make you ready for
this moment! But tomorrow it's curtains for Titania Midnight,
reader, advisor, pimp, and doughnut manufacturer extraordi-
naire . . . and now . . . for my next transformation . . . enter
Amelia Goldberg . . . rich bitch from Encino . . . estate bro-
ker . . . millionairess . . . queen of the gliterati . . . oh, it'll
be splendid, splendid, splendid, my honey babies!"

I said, "There's a picture on Mr. Harrington's wall. He says it's
his son. He says his son died violently."

"I know," said Titania. "So sad, isn't it? Torn to pieces by a mad
slasher. Time, indeed, for a new son."

"You're lying!" I said. "You made Johnny into an angel so Mr.
Harrington could kill him! He's the man with the big curvy sword,
the grim reaper, the Jeffrey Dahmer man!" How could I have been
so stupid before? Daddy always told me that people like her liked
to sacrifice babies. He said they shouldn't have let them crawl out
of the ovens. Titania had sent Laverne out to die with a single
sentence. She had said that death and transformation were the same
thing, and now she was telling us to get ready for transformation.
Right. For death.

He's so beautiful you could eat him up.

Wasn't that why the oven was still on?

"We ain't going where you tell us anymore," I said. "We ain't
going to die for you. It's too much to ask."

Her face started to transform then. There really was a demon
inside. I could tell by the way her eyes burned and her fingernails
raked the air.

"Whore!" she screamed. "I take you in . . . you *nothings* . . . I
make something of you, I see the chance to pull all of us out of the
gutter . . . and you dare defy me . . ." She lunged at me, but
that was when the Valium kicked in and she sort of folded up, and
then I pushed her with all my might. Right into the oven. She slid

in easy. I slammed the door but that didn't keep out the stench. And then fumes began pouring into the kitchen. There was a smell like burning plastic, maybe from her clothes, and another smell, like barbecuing lamb, that made my mouth water in spite of what I knew it was.

I started coughing. The smoke detector went off and the alarm screeched and I could hear clanging and buzzing and a siren in the distance. I stood there for a long time, too numbed to move, until I realized that the fire was going to eat all of us up unless I took Johnny by the hand and steered him out of the doughnut shop.

There was smoke all over the street. The whole place was burning up. There was a Rolls Royce parked in the alley and the blond beautiful man was standing there, all dressed in black, with the scythe dangling from his ear.

"Get away from him," I said to Johnny. "He'll cut you in pieces."

But Johnny just stared at him, and he kind of smiled. And he began walking toward him. I ran after him, trying to pull him back, crying out, "No, Johnny, no!" but he wouldn't listen.

Mr. Harrington took off his mirror shades. He was just staring at Johnny as though he were looking at a man from Mars. Then he started to weep.

"He does look just like him," he said softly. "Titania was right." He started to reach forward to touch Johnny, and that was when I lost control.

"I killed Titania! Now you can get out of our lives too!" I screamed. And I pummeled his black silk jacket with my fists. But he was hard and strong and hollow.

"She's dead?"

"I shoved her in the oven," I said. "God damned baby-sacrificing kike."

"Oh, my God," said Mr. Harrington. "Where did you learn to say such hateful things?"

"From Daddy," I said.

"You killed her." He started to back away from us. "She wasn't an evil woman. In her way she did try to help you. It's true that she trafficked in young flesh . . . but . . . no one is so evil they deserve to be . . ." The odor of burning meat wafted across the alley. "Poor Titania."

"Poor Titania? She was gonna give Johnny to you . . . so you'd kill him and cut him in pieces and eat him . . . like Jeffrey Dahmer."

"She didn't tell you? I was going to adopt him. Both of you, probably. You could have lived in Beverly Hills with me and had everything you ever wanted. For years I've wanted a new son . . . and Titania knew the dark country where you live, the forgotten, the abandoned children. I promised to pay her well to find me a kid who looked so much like . . . like. . . ."

"Don't give me that bullshit. You fucked me."

He winced. "I wish you wouldn't use that language."

The smoke blended right into the smog of night. I just glared at Mr. Harrington. I think he saw my anger for the first time. Maybe I shouldn't have lain there, leaving my body behind while my mind drifted far away. Maybe I should have looked him straight in the eye and shown him all my rage, all my frustration at being so weak and powerless. Then maybe he wouldn't have done it to me. But it was too late now. I could see now that the powerful emotion that had shaken him when he first saw us might have been the beginning of love. But it was fading now.

"I'm not a bad man," he said. "I'm . . . a weak man. I would have been good to you."

Johnny said softly, "I'm gonna pee my pants."

"But of course I can't adopt either of you now. My reputation . . . the scandal . . . you know how it is. I'd better go." Now I could see that he thought of us as slimy things . . . cockroaches . . . vermin. "I'll call 911 from the car."

He kissed Johnny on the forehead and touched my hair. Then he got back in his Rolls Royce and drove away, and we stood in front of the burning doughnut shop, waiting for the fire department.

Sometimes I see the blond beautiful man on television. But I change the channel. In a few months the court will send us to a foster home, if they can find one. But it might be hard since I'm a murderer.

After Bob read the last entry in my diary, the one where I talked about the fire at the doughnut shop, he told me that it made him cry. I don't know why. *I* never cry. I don't have time because I have to look after Johnny.

After he read *Hansel and Gretel* to us, I told Bob my witch theory, and he shook his head slowly and said, "Greta, there's only one kind of magic in the world. You made magic when you wrote the words that made me cry. Words can be black magic and they can be white magic, but they are the only things that can transform us. Even a movie starts with just words on a page, a screenplay."

That's why I go on writing it all down. If I write enough words down, maybe we can still have the things we long for . . . the tract house, the mommy and daddy, the green green suburb far away. But so far nothing has come true.

I guess I'm not that good at witchcraft.

Graves

Joe Haldeman

I have this persistent sleep disorder that makes life difficult for me, but still I want to keep it. Boy, do I want to keep it. It goes back twenty years, to Vietnam. To Graves.

Dead bodies turn from bad to worse real fast in the jungle. You've got a few hours before rigor mortis makes them hard to handle, hard to stuff in a bag. By that time they start to turn greenish, if they started out white or yellow, where you can see the skin. It's mostly bugs by then, usually ants. Then they go to black and start to smell.

They swell up and burst.

You'd think the ants and roaches and beetles and millipedes would make short work of them after that, but they don't. Just when they get to looking and smelling the worst, the bugs sort of lose interest, get fastidious, send out for pizza. Except for the flies. Laying eggs.

The funny thing is, unless some big animal got to it and tore it up, even after a week or so, you've still got something more than a skeleton, even a sort of a face. No eyes, though. Every now and then we'd get one like that. Not too often, since soldiers don't usually die alone and sit there for that long, but sometimes. We called them "dry ones." Still damp underneath, of course, and inside, but kind of like a sunburned mummy otherwise.

You tell people what you do at Graves Registration, "Graves," and it sounds like about the worst job the army has to offer. It isn't. You just stand there all day and open body bags, figure out which parts might belong to which dog tag, not that it's usually that important, sew them up more or less with a big needle, account for all the wallets and jewelry, steal the dope out of their pockets, box them up, seal the casket, do the paperwork. When you have enough boxes, you truck them out to the airfield. The first week maybe is pretty bad. But after a hundred or so, after you get used to the smell and the god-awful feel of them, you get to thinking that opening a body bag is a lot better than winding up inside one. They put Graves in safe places.

Since I'd had a couple years of college, pre-med, I got some of the more interesting jobs. Captain French, who was the pathologist actually in charge of the outfit, always took me with him out into the field when he had to examine a corpse in situ, which only happened maybe once a month. I got to wear a .45 in a shoulder holster, tough guy. Never fired it, never got shot at, except the one time.

That was a hell of a time. It's funny what gets to you, stays with you.

Usually when we had an in situ it was a forensic matter, like an officer they suspected had been fragged or otherwise terminated by his own men. We'd take pictures and interview some people and then Frenchy would bring the stiff back for autopsy, see whether the bullets were American or Vietnamese. (Not that that would be conclusive either way. The Viet Cong stole our weapons and our guys used the North Vietnamese AK-47s, when we could get our hands on them. More reliable than the M-16 and a better cartridge for killing. Both sides proved that over and over.) Usually Frenchy would send a report up to Division and that would be it. Once he had to testify at a court-martial. The kid was guilty but just got life. The officer was a real prick.

Anyhow we got the call to come look at this in situ corpse about five in the afternoon. Frenchy tried to put it off until the next day, since if it got dark we'd have to spend the night. The guy he was talking to was a major, though, and obviously proud of it, so it was no use arguing. I threw some C's and beer and a couple canteens into two rucksacks that already had blankets and air mattresses tied on the bottom. Box of .45 ammo and a couple hand grenades.

Went and got a Jeep while Frenchy got his stuff together and made sure Doc Carter was sober enough to count the stiffs as they came in. (Doc Carter was supposed to be the one in charge, but he didn't much care for the work.)

Drove us out to the pad and, lo and behold, there was a chopper waiting, blades idling. Should of started to smell a rat then. We don't get real high priority, and it's not easy to get a chopper to go anywhere so close to sundown. They even helped us stow our gear. Up, up, and away.

I never flew in helicopters enough to make it routine. Kontum looked almost pretty in the low, golden red sun. I had to sit between two flamethrowers, though, which didn't make me feel too secure. The door gunner was smoking. The flamethrower tanks were stenciled NO SMOKING.

We went fast and low out toward the mountains to the west. I was hoping we'd wind up at one of the big fire bases up there, figuring I'd sleep better with a few hundred men around. But no such luck. When the chopper started to slow down, the whir of the blades deepening to a whuck-whuck-whuck, there was no clearing as far as the eye could see. Thick jungle canopy everywhere. Then a wisp of purple smoke showed us a helicopter-sized hole in the leaves. The pilot brought us down an inch at a time, nicking twigs. I was very much aware of the flamethrowers. If he clipped a large branch we'd be so much pot roast.

When we touched down, four guys in a big hurry unloaded our gear and the flamethrowers and a couple cases of ammo. They put two wounded guys and one client on board and shooed the helicopter away. Yeah, it would sort of broadcast your position. One of them told us to wait, he'd go get the major.

"I don't like this at all," Frenchy said.

"Me neither," I said. "Let's go home."

"Any outfit that's got a major and two flamethrowers is planning to fight a real war." He pulled his .45 out and looked at it as if he'd never seen one before. "Which end of this do you think the bullets come out of?"

"Shit," I said, and rummaged through the rucksack for a beer. I gave Frenchy one and he put it in his side pocket.

A machine gun opened up off to our right. Frenchy and I grabbed the dirt. Three grenade blasts. Somebody yelled for them to cut that out. Guy yelled back he thought he saw something. Machine gun started up again. We tried to get a little lower.

Up walks this old guy, thirties, looking annoyed. The major.

"You men get up. What's wrong with you?" He was playin' games.

Frenchy got up, dusting himself off. We had the only clean fatigues in twenty miles. "Captain French, Graves Registration."

"Oh," he said, not visibly impressed. "Secure your gear and follow me." He drifted off like a mighty ship of the jungle. Frenchy rolled his eyes and we hoisted our rucksacks and followed him. I wasn't sure whether "secure your gear" meant bring your stuff or leave it behind, but Budweiser could get to be a real collectors' item in the boonies, and there were a lot of collectors out here.

We walked too far. I mean a couple hundred yards. That meant we were really spread out thin. I didn't look forward to spending the night. The God-damned machine gun started up again. The major looked annoyed and shouted "Sergeant, will you please control your men?" and the sergeant told the machine-gunner to shut the fuck up and the machine-gunner told the sergeant there was a fuckin' gook out there, and then somebody popped a big one, like a Claymore, and then everybody was shooting every which way. Frenchy and I got real horizontal. I heard a bullet whip by over my head. The major was leaning against a tree looking bored, shouting "Cease firing, cease firing!" The shooting dwindled down like popcorn getting done. The major looked over at us and said "Come on. While there's still light." He led us into a small clearing, elephant grass pretty well trampled down. I guess everybody had had his turn to look at the corpse.

It wasn't a real gruesome body, as bodies go, but it was odd-looking, even for a dry one. Moldy, like someone had dusted flour over it. Naked and probably male, though incomplete: all the soft parts were gone. Tall; one of our Montagnard allies rather than an ethnic Vietnamese. Emaciated, dry skin taut over ribs. Probably old, though it doesn't take long for these people to get old. Lying on its back, mouth wide open, a familiar posture. Empty eye sockets staring skyward. Arms flung out in supplication, loosely, long past rigor mortis.

Teeth chipped and filed to points, probably some Montagnard tribal custom. I'd never seen it before, but we didn't "do" many natives.

Frenchy knelt down and reached for it, then stopped. "Checked for booby traps?"

"No," the major said. "Figure that's your job." Frenchy looked at me with an expression that said it was my job.

Both officers stood at a respectful distance while I felt under the corpse. Sometimes they pull the pin on a hand grenade and slip it under the body so that the body's weight keeps the arming lever in place. You turn it over and—Tomato Surprise!

I always worry less about a hand grenade than about the various weird serpents and bugs that might enjoy living underneath a decomposing corpse. Vietnam has its share of snakes and scorpions and megapedes.

I was lucky this time; nothing but maggots. I flicked them off my hand and watched the major turn a little green. People are funny. What does he think is going to happen to him when he dies? Everything has to eat. And he was sure as hell going to die if he didn't start keeping his head down. I remember that thought, but didn't think of it then as a prophesy.

They came over. "What do you make of it, Doctor?"

"I don't think we can cure him." Frenchy was getting annoyed at this cherry bomb. "What else do you want to know?"

"Isn't it a little . . . odd to find something like this in the middle of nowhere?"

"Naw. Country's full of corpses." He kneeled down and studied the face, wiggling the head by its chin. "We keep it up, you'll be able to walk from the Mekong to the DMZ without stepping on anything but corpses."

"But he's been castrated!"

"Birds." He toed the body over, busy white crawlers running from the light. "Just some old geezer who walked out into the woods naked and fell over dead. Could happen back in the World. Old people do funny things."

"I thought maybe he'd been tortured by the VC or something."

"God knows. It could happen." The body eased back into its original position with a creepy creaking sound, like leather. Its mouth had closed halfway. "If you want to put 'evidence of VC torture' in your report, your body count, I'll initial it."

"What do you mean by that, Captain?"

"Exactly what I said." He kept staring at the major while he flipped a cigarette into his mouth and fired it up. Nonfilter Camels; you'd think a guy who worked with corpses all day long would be less anxious to turn into one. "I'm just trying to get along."

"You believe I want you to falsify—"

Now "falsify" is a strange word for a last word. The enemy had set up a heavy machine gun on the other side of the clearing, and we were the closest targets. A round struck the major in the small of his back, we found on later examination. At the time, it was just an explosion of blood and guts and he went down with his legs flopping every which way, barfing, then loud death rattle. Frenchy was on the ground in a ball holding his left hand, going "Shit shit shit." He'd lost the last joint of his little finger. Painful but not serious enough, as it turned out, to get him back to the World.

I myself was horizontal and aspiring to be subterranean. I managed to get my pistol out and cocked, but realized I didn't want to do anything that might draw attention to us. The machine gun was spraying back and forth over us at about knee height. Maybe they couldn't see us; maybe they thought we were dead. I was scared shitless.

"Frenchy," I stage-whispered, "we've got to get outa here." He was trying to wrap his finger up in a standard first-aid-pack gauze bandage, much too large. "Get back to the trees."

"After you, asshole. We wouldn't get halfway." He worked his pistol out of the holster but couldn't cock it, his left hand clamping the bandage and slippery with blood. I armed it for him and handed it back. "These are going to do a hell of a lot of good. How are you with grenades?"

"Shit. How do you think I wound up in Graves?" In basic training they'd put me on KP whenever they went out for live grenade practice. In school I was always the last person when they chose up sides for baseball, for the same reason, though to my knowledge a baseball wouldn't kill you if you couldn't throw it far enough. "I couldn't get one halfway there." The treeline was about sixty yards away.

"Neither could I, with this hand." He was a lefty.

Behind us came the "poink" sound of a sixty-millimeter mortar, and in a couple of seconds there was a gray-smoke explosion between us and the treeline. The machine gun stopped and somebody behind us yelled "Add twenty!"

At the treeline we could hear some shouting in Vietnamese and a clanking of metal. "They're gonna bug out," Frenchy said. "Let's di-di."

We got up and ran and somebody did fire a couple of bursts at us, probably an AK-47, but he missed, and then there was a series of poinks and a series of explosions pretty close to where the gun had been.

We rushed back to the LZ and found the command group, about the time the firing started up again. There was a first lieutenant in charge, and when things slowed down enough for us to tell him what had happened to the major, he expressed neither surprise nor grief. The man had been an observer from the Battalion and had assumed command when their captain was killed that morning. He'd take our word for it that the guy was dead—that was one thing we were trained in—and not send a squad out for him until the fighting had died down and it was light again.

We inherited the major's hole, which was nice and deep, and in his rucksack we found a dozen cans and jars of real food and a flask of Scotch. So as the battle raged through the night, we munched on Ritz crackers, pickled herring in sour cream sauce, little Polish sausages on party rye with real French mustard. We drank all the Scotch and saved the beer for breakfast.

For hours the lieutenant called in for artillery and air support, but to no avail. Later we found out that the enemy had launched coordinated attacks on all the local airfields and Special Forces camps, and every camp that held POWs. We were much lower priority.

Then about three in the morning, Snoopy came over. Snoopy

was a big C-130 cargo plane that carried nothing but ammunition and Gatling guns; they said it could fly over a football field and put a round into every square inch. Anyhow, it saturated the perimeter with fire and the enemy stopped shooting. Frenchy and I went to sleep.

At first light we went out to help round up the KIAs. There were only four dead, counting the major, but the major was an astounding sight, at least in context.

He looked sort of like a cadaver left over from a teaching autopsy. His shirt had been opened and his pants pulled down to his thighs, and the entire thoracic and abdominal cavities had been ripped open and emptied of everything soft, everything from esophagus to testicles, rib cage like blood-streaked fingers sticking rigidly out of sagging skin, and there wasn't a sign of any of the guts anywhere, just a lot of dried blood.

Nobody had heard anything. There was a machine gun position not twenty yards away, and they'd been straining their ears all night. All they'd heard was flies.

Maybe an animal feeding very quietly. The body hadn't been opened with a scalpel or a knife; the skin was torn by teeth or claws—but seemingly systematically, throat to balls.

And the dry one was gone. Him with the pointed teeth.

There is a rational explanation. Modern warfare is partly mindfuck, and we aren't the only ones who do it, dropping unlucky cards, invoking magic and superstition. The Vietnamese knew how squeamish Americans were, and would mutilate bodies in clever ways. They could also move very quietly. The dry one? They might have spirited him away just to fuck with us. Show what they could do under our noses.

And as for the dry one's odd mummified appearance, the mold, there might be an explanation. I found out that the Montagnards in that area don't bury their dead; they put them in coffins made from hollowed-out logs and leave them aboveground. So maybe he was just the victim of a grave robber. I thought the nearest village was miles away, like twenty miles, but I could have been wrong. Or the body could have been carried that distance for some obscure purpose—maybe the VC set it out on the trail to trap the Americans and make it easier to ambush them.

That's probably it. But for twenty years now, several nights a week, I wake up sweating with a terrible image in my mind. I've gone out with a flashlight and there it is, the dry one, scooping steaming entrails from the major's body, tearing them with its sharp teeth, staring into my light with black empty sockets, unconcerned. I reach for my pistol and it's never there. The creature stands up, shiny with blood, and takes a step toward me—for a year or so that was it; I would wake up. Then it was two steps, and then three. After twenty years it has covered half the distance, its dripping hands raising from its sides.

The doctor gives me tranquilizers. I don't take them. They might help me stay asleep.

The Old School

Ramsey Campbell

The house was locked. Dean strolled around the outside for a quarter of an hour, gazing through the tall windows at displays of roped-off rooms, and then he climbed the wide steps to the balcony. A lawn broader than his eyesight offered shrubberies and formal gardens and tree-lined walks. At the edge of the lawn, almost half a mile away, woods blotted out every vestige of the further world.

He'd known for years that the house was less than an hour's drive from home. Even better, it was only half an hour from the new town and the school. He could drive here after teaching, when he needed to relax and be taken out of himself. He was gazing at a distant shrubbery, where either mossy statues were hidden in the foliage or the topiary itself was shaped into faces, when the August sun found a gap in the flock of fat white clouds. Sunlight wakened all the drops of rain that still lingered from the afternoon, seeds of rainbows everywhere he looked, and the sight washed away his thoughts.

As he leaned on the parapet, no longer aware of the cold stone through the leather that patched the elbows of his jacket, he heard a sound he would have hoped to have left behind in the new town. Someone was kicking a tin can. He sighed and straightened up, automatically brushing his hair back over as much of his scalp as it would cover these days. Perhaps the tinny footballer was a gardener, and would desist when he saw the place had a visitor.

Dean heard a more determined kick, and the can landed deep in a bush. Three children appeared around the side of the house, two boys and a girl who wore high heels and lipstick so crimson Dean could see it even at that distance. The boy with a black eye poked at the bush with a stick while the other boy, whose pate looked dusty with stubble, danced hyperactively around him. Branches snapped, the can sprang into the air, and the boys jostled after it towards the steps.

The game ended when the hyperactive boy leapt on the can and trod it flat. His friend made a gesture of generalised menace with the stick and chopped twigs off bushes as he went back to demand a share of the girl's cigarette. The children were about eleven years old, Dean saw. He ought to interfere, though he felt as if there were nowhere his job would leave him alone this side of the grave. When he saw the children whisper and glance warily about, not noticing him, before converging on the nearest window, he went down the steps.

The children veered away at once. The girl blinked over her shoulder at him and nudged her companions, who glanced back, whistling tunelessly. The boy with the stick turned first, raising his shoulders like a boxer, and Dean saw that the bruise around his right eye was a birthmark. "Hello, sir," the boy said like a challenge.

They were from the school where Dean taught. He'd seen the boy in the junior schoolyard, thumping children for calling him Spot the Dog. Surely Dean needn't play this scene like a schoolmaster. "Enjoying your holidays?" he said in his best end-of-term voice.

They stared at him as if he'd made an insultingly feeble joke. "They're all right," the girl mumbled, treading on her cigarette.

"So long as you don't enjoy them at other people's expense. Spoiling them for others might mean you'll spoil them for yourselves."

The hyperactive boy jiggled his head as if to a beat only he could hear, the boy with the black eye swung his stick like a rod divining violence, the girl dug her hands into the pockets of her short faded secondhand dress and stared morosely at her budding breasts. "So have you something to do?" Dean said.

"Like what?" said the boy with the stick.

"Surely you know a few games."

"We've nothing to play with," the girl complained.

"Can't you play with yourselves?" Dean said, and had to laugh at his choice of words. At least that prompted the children to laugh out loud too. "If I were you," he said, "I'd be using this place to play hide and seek."

"Why don't you, then?"

"He won't play with us," the boy with the birthmark said with what sounded like bitterness.

If he were in Dean's class Dean wouldn't treat him with undue sympathy, would insist he join in activities like everyone else. "Of course I'll play if you want me to," Dean blurted, and added when they smirked incredulously: "I'm off school too, you know."

"Suppose so," the girl said as if she were humouring him. "You know how to play Blocko, don't you?"

"Remind me."

"Whoever's It has to count fifty and then try and find us, and run back here and shout 'Blocko Tina one two three' if they've seen me, or Burt if it's him, or Jacko if it's him. Watch out with that stick, Jacko, or you'll hit someone."

She had already been addressing the teacher in the same maternal tone. She began to point at each of them in turn as she chanted:

> *"Girls and boys come out to play,*
> *The moon does shine as bright as day.*
> *Eeny meeny miney mo,*
> *Bone in the wind and it points at you."*

"It's sir," Burt shouted, eager to be running. Jacko struck his own thigh several times with the stick while Tina removed her shoes so as to be quicker. Dean covered his eyes and turning to the steps, began to count. "You have to count so we can hear you," Tina told him.

"One!" Dean pronounced in a voice capable of travelling the length of both schoolyards. "Two! Three! . . ." He heard the children scatter, and then only his voice. ". . . Forty-nine! Fifty! Here I come!" he shouted, and swung around to find a couple in their sixties staring warily at him from beside a corner of the house. "I beg your pardon?" the woman said in a voice that refused to admit where she came from.

"Blocko," Dean explained with a conspiratorial grimace.

The man's face grew alarmingly like empurpled blancmange, and he pointed at Dean with his knuckly cane. "What did you say to my wife?"

"Blocko. The children's game, you know. You'll see the children any minute."

The woman grabbed her husband's arm. "What's that about children? Is he raving?"

"Everything's under control, madam. I'm a teacher."

"He says he's their teacher," the man communicated even more loudly.

"Not *their* teacher," Dean said, and gave up. He crept towards the shrubberies while the couple watched him suspiciously. They distracted him, and so did noticing that there weren't any statues or anything like faces where he thought he'd seen some. He was out of sight of the steps when Tina announced her return there and the boys joined her, shouting.

The suspicious couple had stayed near the steps. As Dean jogged back the woman announced "He said he wasn't their teacher."

"Then he's up to no good."

Tina brandished her shoes at them. "You leave him alone. He's from our school."

Burt commenced swinging his stick in defence of her or of Dean, and the teacher said hastily "Time for another game. Off you all go."

This game wasn't too successful. When he pounced on a movement which he glimpsed beyond a shrubbery, he came face to face with the elderly couple, though he'd thought he had heard them retreating around one corner of the house. They glared at him as if he'd invaded their bedroom, and he could only jog away as if he hadn't noticed them, trying not to swing his arms too vigorously and yet concerned that he might appear sloppy otherwise, feeling as if he were trapped into miming enjoyment while pretending that he had no audience. When he turned tail and ran back to the steps they followed him, though he was running because he'd seen Tina lurch into view beyond a hedge behind them. "Blocko Tina one two three," he declared.

Tina put on her shoes and stamped. "That wasn't fair. Burt or Jacko scared me, whispering behind me."

The boys appeared around opposite corners of the house, and Dean counted them out. "It couldn't have been the boys, Tina. They were nowhere near you."

"Thank God something frightens her," the woman told nobody in particular. "Children respect nothing these days."

"We aren't frightened of *you*," Burt said, punching the air.

"You wouldn't dare say that to anyone if you were from the boarding school," the man rumbled, jabbing his cane in the direction of the woods. "That's what teaching should be. You'd be terrified to open your mouth until you were told."

"You're right, Tina, it isn't fair. I'll be It again," Dean said. He began counting very slowly, staring at the couple until they moved away. As the children ran off between the shrubberies, arguing in low voices about something, he closed his eyes.

Now that he'd started counting so slowly he found that he couldn't speed up. In the pauses between numbers he heard the wind in the leaves, the footsteps of the couple marching regally away along the gravel drive, stealthy movements that must be the children tiptoeing around him at some distance, though once he thought he heard a whisper unexpectedly close to him. "Fifty!" he shouted at last, and looked.

The lawn was deserted. He'd already deduced from the movements he'd heard that the children had crept around the house. He was cupping each ear in turn towards the ends of the facade when he caught sight of a child among the trees at the edge of the lawn.

It was a boy—he wasn't sure which one. Dean might have called out, but that wouldn't be fair until he could say the name. In any case, the child wouldn't be able to reach the steps before Dean. He paced towards the trees, keeping his gaze on the boy's face.

At first he thought the child was staying still and hoping that Dean hadn't seen him, and then he realised that the small face was withdrawing through the tall undergrowth at exactly the speed of Dean's approach. The sight made Dean's eyes feel shaky, the child's face seeming to appear and vanish as the shadows of foliage camouflaged it, made it shift and turned it greener. He sprinted towards the woods so as to be able to put a name to it, and at once he couldn't see it at all. Presumably the other children were also in the woods, or they would have been able to saunter to the steps by now. He peered between the trees as he ran to the edge of the lawn.

He could see no obvious path into the woods. Here and there the undergrowth had been trampled, but not for any great distance. Dean headed straight for the place where he had last seen the boy, who must have reached it by another route, since the undergrowth between it and the lawn was undisturbed. Stepping over ferns and spiky grass, raindrops speckling his trousers and darkening his shoes, Dean stole into the woods. As soon as he was out of the direct sunlight, he saw a child's face blurred by shadows, watching him from the undergrowth between the trees ahead.

The sound of children's voices made him glance towards the house. Three children were walking away along the drive: Tina and the two boys. If they'd tired of the game, whom was Dean tracking? He swung round and glimpsed the boy's face in the instant before it disappeared, leaving a patch of ferns and grass swaying. The boy was several years younger than Tina and her friends. The idea of such a young child roaming the woods, especially so close to nightfall, dismayed Dean. "Hold on," he called. "I wasn't chasing you. Don't run away."

The trees had begun to vibrate with his scrutiny when he saw the face again, five or six trees further off. He held up one hand and was opening his mouth when the face was swallowed by shadows again and reappeared deeper into the woods. "Don't be frightened," Dean shouted. "I'm a teacher."

The child's face quivered and disappeared. The movement was so violent that it must have been mostly of the low foliage through which the child had been watching. Dean was wondering if he should pretend indifference—if that would coax the boy into the open—when he realised that the child had fled because he'd identified himself as a teacher. He had to assume that the boy was from the boarding school beyond the woods.

Sometimes Dean found it necessary to play the ogre with his classes, but he didn't enjoy it much. The idea of relishing children's fears, as the elderly couple had, disgusted him. When he managed to locate the boy's face again, in the midst of a cluster of leaves, he went forward. He wanted to see the child safe, but also to judge whether the school was as terrible as the couple would like to believe, though he didn't know what he would do if he found that it was.

The woods proved to be even more extensive than they had appeared from the balcony. He must have walked in as straight a line as the trees and patches of marshy ground would allow for nearly half an hour. Before long he saw that there was more than one child. As soon as he glimpsed any of the faces in the foliage or undergrowth, they retreated into the leafy shadows. They were letting him see them, he realised: they were continuing the game he'd started with Tina and the boys. He wished he could enjoy it more. Once when he was sick in bed with a childhood fever, he'd seen the wallpaper piled high with faces like skulls in a catacomb, and since then the kind of picture puzzle where you had to discover faces hidden in foliage had made him feel feverish too. But now he was nervous also because the boys—five or six of them, he thought there were—seemed to be fleeing from him as much as playing.

By the time he came close enough to the far edge of the woods to be able to distinguish a building through the trees, he was having to pick his way over roots. In the growing dimness the faces of the children were barely visible through a bush at the edge of the woods. He wasn't even sure that he was seeing them, for when a breeze rustled through the foliage, the greenish faces appeared to separate into fragments that recombined grotesquely. Increasingly nervous, he stumbled out of the woods.

The sight of the school made him catch his breath. For a moment he thought that the long Victorian building, all gloomy red brick and high pinched windows, looked decaying only because the twilight was filling the windows with darkness, and then he saw that it was derelict. The windows were empty of glass, the grounds were rubbly and overgrown; the school must have been abandoned years ago. All the same, he knew instinctively that it had been almost as grim and daunting when it was in use.

A movement at one of the windows overlooking the woods drew his attention. A face was watching him from inside the school—the face of the boy he had followed into the woods. "Stay right where you are, son," Dean shouted. "Don't run off in there, it could be dangerous."

He gritted his teeth as the face vanished. The boy must have stepped back into the dimness. In the poor light the face had seemed to collapse into itself. "What's the matter with you?" Dean said through his teeth, and ran towards the school, across lumps of stone that had been a harsh schoolyard.

The entrance door nearest to the woods was ajar. Presumably that was how the boy, and whoever else was inside, had got in, since the windows were too high for even Dean to reach. He squeezed past the door, which appeared to be wedged open, and halted in the corridor.

He was standing still in order to listen for movements that would help him locate the children, but more than that had halted him. Something was wrong with the place, with the long bleak stone-floored corridor that led past a series of classroom doors, their upper panels gaping. He hadn't time to stand there, he had to take the children somewhere safer before night fell. He strode along the corridor, pushing the doors open.

He could see nothing of significance in any of the rooms. In the corner of one a legless desk crouched, its distorted lid grinning beneath the single blotchy socket of the inkwell; in another classroom a few chalk marks glimmered on a blackboard like bones hovering in darkness. Despite the emptiness, something was waiting for him beyond the doors, accumulating like the twilight as he went from room to room, as he stared at the desertion where ranks of desks trapping children had stood, no doubt silent as the emptiness was now, except for a single voice and a timid response: it was fear.

It wasn't his, he told himself, except insofar as the place reminded him of the worst of his own schooldays. How afraid must the children have been for their fear to have lingered almost palpably in the air? They wouldn't have been able to see the outside world from their desks, and the outside world wouldn't have been able to see in, not that it would have bothered to look. The children must have felt they were in prison without visitors, at the absolute mercy of the staff.

Dean tried to think he was exaggerating, but that would mean some of the fear was his. Certainly the rooms were beginning to make him nervous, because he'd realised what was wrong with them: they were too empty, and so was the corridor. Where were the dust and cobwebs and dead leaves that the building should have accumulated? He was also wondering how the child had managed to look out at him from such a high window when there was nothing to stand on in the classrooms; the broken desk wouldn't have served. He could only think the boy had balanced on someone else's shoulders.

He'd peered into at least a dozen rooms, which seemed more and more to him like huge pitiless cells, when he came to the assembly hall that divided the corridor from its twin. The hall would have held several hundred children, and he felt as if it had retained their fear, imprisoned or awakened by the growing dark. He mustn't let the place or his imagination get to him. He was heading for the opposite corridor when he noticed a door under the stage at the far end of the hall.

It was half open. In the dark beyond it he thought he saw the glint of an eye, watching him. He crossed the hall quickly, his footsteps echoing through the school as though to demonstrate the extent of the darkness. Fumbling a book of matches out of his pocket, he ducked under the stage. His fingertip counted the matches: one, two, three, only four. He tore one out and struck it, and the gleam leapt at him.

He hadn't seen an eye after all, but the smashed glass on a school photograph. Photographs were stacked as high as the underside of the stage, and a few leaned against the stack. Apart from the photographs, the space was as bare as the rest of the school so far. The picture in front of him was older than the wars, he saw from the date on the frame. Tiny faces brown with age stared at him through the broken glass as the match burned down, and just as it singed his fingers he thought he recognised some of the faces. He shook it out and struck another, and shuffled forward on his knees to pull the photograph towards him. Among the unsmiling teenagers in the tallest rank of schoolboys lined up in front of the building, there were older versions of the faces of all the boys he'd followed through the woods.

The boys in the photograph must have grown up to be their grandparents, he thought, but what possessed the parents to let their children play here so late? He let go of the photograph, intending to back out from under the stage. The photograph fell flat, taking several with it and revealing the one closest to the stack. Pressed beneath the glass of that photograph were faces more familiar than those he'd just seen.

Dean hobbled forward, bruising his knees, holding the match high, hoping to be proved wrong—but there was no mistake. At the front of the photograph, where the youngest boys sat cross-legged, were all the children whose faces he'd seen in the woods. He lowered the match shakily to the frame, and read the date. The photograph was ten years older than the other he'd examined. The match went out, burying him in darkness.

The photograph was too old for the boys to be still alive, let alone looking like children. His mind flinched from that and from an even more dismaying thought: why would they have come back here, when there could have been nowhere they were more afraid of? He was staring into the dark, no longer searching but trying to hide, when he heard movement behind him.

He scrabbled round on all fours, afraid to see, more afraid not to. The fear around him was almost suffocating, and he felt as if it had changed the texture of the floor beneath him. Just beyond the doorway under the stage, dim shapes that looked thin and mal-formed were crowding, blocking his way. Though his hands were trembling so badly that he almost dropped the matchbook, he managed to light the third match.

The figures—far more numerous than in the woods—were mostly faces and spidery limbs. The nearest face was the one he'd first seen. This close he was able to see that it and its companions had no eyes to speak of, though they appeared to have done their best not to look incomplete. The substance of the faces and of their token bodies was shifting, not only because the match was quivering. All at once the wind that he could hear blundering about the school flung the figures at him.

As Dean shrank back, they collapsed like discarded puppets. The nearest face fell inward, as it had when he'd seen it at the window, and the materials of which the figures had been composed fluttered across the boards at him: dust, dead leaves and other vegetation, cobwebs loaded with husks of insects. The wind that was driving all this blew out the match, and he was crouching in the dark when he heard the wind slam the entrance door with a click of the lock that resounded through the school.

Dean pressed his hands and his scalp against the underside of the stage, as if that could give him strength or at least stop his shivering, but the wood felt softened by fear. Only his brain seemed capable of action, his thoughts chattering desperately as though an explanation could somehow end what was happening. Suppose, he thought, the experience of finding yourself suddenly dead and bodiless was so terrifying that you would use anything you could grasp to persuade yourself that you still had substance, however temporarily? Suppose finding yourself dead was so reminiscent of the greatest terror of your life that you were snatched back to it? Suppose you felt so vulnerable that your mind could only take refuge in the familiarity of remembered terror and imprison you there? None of these ideas helped him deal with the movements he could just see between him and the doorway, shapes wavering up from the floor, remaking themselves. He was struggling not to retreat further under the stage, away from any possibility of escape, when he heard the remains of a voice, hardly a whisper, more like a thought that wasn't his. "He's a teacher," it said.

The shapes leaned towards him, jerrybuilt heads wavering on rickety necks. "Not like the teachers who were here," Dean pleaded in a voice whose smallness shocked him. "I wouldn't have treated you like that."

There was a rustle of dead things as they crowded around him. "Chase us," said part of the rustling.

They wanted to be frightened, Dean thought in dismay: it was all they knew now. He needn't be frightened, his mind babbled; they were nothing but cobwebs and litter. He wouldn't play, they couldn't make him play. He brandished the unlit match at them as if the threat would keep them off. Perhaps when they saw he wasn't playing they would leave him alone, give him the chance to escape without having to touch them, and if not, he had only to stay still. "I won't ever come back here," he was muttering over and over, like a promise to them or to himself. "I mustn't come back here." He need only stay still until he could see his way out, until dawn.

At first he managed not to run, even when they started touching him to make him chase them. Eventually the touch of spindly disintegrating fingers proved unbearable. He crawled sobbing from under the stage and began to run back and forth through the lightless building, up and down the corridors, in and out of the rooms, leaping at the inaccessible windows, turning tail whenever he ran into something hiding in the dark. Soon he didn't know if he was giggling with fear or if they were, or whether he was chasing or being chased. He only knew that he was willing to play. Indeed, it seemed he might never stop.

The Ghost Village

Peter Straub

1

In Vietnam I knew a man who went quietly and purposefully crazy because his wife wrote him that his son had been sexually abused—"messed with"—by the leader of their church choir. This man was a black six-foot-six grunt named Leonard Hamnet, from a small town in Tennessee named Archibald. Before writing, his wife had waited until she had endured the entire business of going to the police, talking to other parents, returning to the police with another accusation, and finally succeeding in having the man charged. He was up for trial in two months. Leonard Hamnet was no happier about that than he was about the original injury.

"I got to murder him, you know, but I'm seriously thinking on murdering her too," he said. He still held the letter in his hands, and he was speaking to Spanky Burrage, Michael Poole, Conor Linklater, SP4 Cotton, Calvin Hill, Tina Pumo, the magnificent M. O. Dengler, and myself. "All this is going on, my boy needs help, this here Mr. Brewster needs to be dismantled, needs to be *racked* and *stacked*, and she don't tell me! Makes me want to put her *down*, man. Take her damn head off and put it up on a stake in the yard, man. With a sign saying: *Here is one stupid woman.*"

We were in the unofficial part of Camp Crandall known as No Man's Land, located between the wire perimeter and a shack, also unofficial, where a cunning little weasel named Wilson Manly sold contraband beer and liquor. No Man's Land, so called because the C.O. pretended it did not exist, contained a mound of old tires, a piss tube, and a lot of dusty red ground. Leonard Hamnet gave the letter in his hand a dispirited look, folded it into the pocket of his fatigues, and began to roam around the heap of tires, aiming kicks at the ones that stuck out furthest. "One stupid woman," he repeated. Dust exploded up from a burst, worn-down wheel of rubber.

I wanted to make sure Hamnet knew he was angry with Mr. Brewster, not his wife, and said, "She was trying—"

Hamnet's great glistening bull's head turned toward me.

"Look at what the woman did. She nailed that bastard. She got other people to admit that he messed with their kids too. That must be almost impossible. And she had the guy arrested. He's going to be put away for a long time."

"I'll put that bitch away, too," Hamnet said, and kicked an old gray tire hard enough to push it nearly a foot back into the heap. All the other tires shuddered and moved. For a second it seemed that the entire mound might collapse.

"This is my *boy* I'm talking about here," Hamnet said. "This shit has gone far enough."

"The important thing," Dengler said, "is to take care of your boy. You have to see he gets help."

"How'm I gonna do that from here?" Hamnet shouted.

"Write him a letter," Dengler said. "Tell him you love him. Tell him he did right to go to his mother. Tell him you think about him all the time."

Hamnet took the letter from his pocket and stared at it. It was already stained and wrinkled. I did not think it could survive many more of Hamnet's readings. His face seemed to get heavier, no easy trick with a face like Hamnet's. "I got to get home," he said. "I got to get back home and take *care* of these people."

Hamnet began putting in requests for compassionate leave relentlessly—one request a day. When we were out on patrol, sometimes I saw him unfold the tattered sheet of notepaper from his shirt pocket and read it two or three times, concentrating intensely. When the letter began to shred along the folds, Hamnet taped it together.

We were going out on four- and five-day patrols during that period, taking a lot of casualties. Hamnet performed well in the field, but he had retreated so far within himself that he spoke in monosyllables. He wore a dull, glazed look, and moved like a man who had just eaten a heavy dinner. I thought he looked like a man who had given up, and when people gave up they did not last long—they were already very close to death, and other people avoided them.

We were camped in a stand of trees at the edge of a paddy. That day we had lost two men so new that I had already forgotten their names. We had to eat cold C rations because heating them with C-4 would have been like putting up billboards and arc lights. We couldn't smoke, and we were not supposed to talk. Hamnet's C rations consisted of an old can of Spam that dated from an earlier war and a can of peaches. He saw Spanky staring at the peaches and tossed him the can. Then he dropped the Spam between his legs. Death was almost visible around him. He fingered the note out of his pocket and tried to read it in the damp gray twilight.

At that moment someone started shooting at us, and the Lieutenant yelled *"Shit!"*, and we dropped our food and returned fire at the invisible people trying to kill us. When they kept shooting back, we had to go through the paddy.

The warm water came up to our chests. At the dikes, we scrambled over and splashed down into the muck on the other side. A boy from Santa Cruz, California, named Thomas Blevins got a round in the back of his neck and dropped dead into the water just short of the first dike, and another boy named Tyrell Budd coughed and dropped down right beside him. The F. O. called in an artillery strike. We leaned against the backs of the last two dikes when the big shells came thudding in. The ground shook and the water rippled, and the edge of the forest went up in a series of fireballs. We could hear the monkeys screaming.

One by one we crawled over the last dike onto the damp but solid ground on the other side of the paddy. Here the trees were much sparser, and a little group of thatched huts was visible through them.

Then two things I did not understand happened, one after the other. Someone off in the forest fired a mortar round at us—just one. One mortar, one round. That was the first thing. I fell down and shoved my face in the muck, and everybody around me did the same. I considered that this might be my last second on earth, and greedily inhaled whatever life might be left to me. Whoever fired the mortar should have had an excellent idea of our location, and I experienced that endless moment of pure, terrifying helplessness— a moment in which the soul simultaneously clings to the body and readies itself to let go of it—until the shell landed on top of the last dike and blew it to bits. Dirt, mud, and water slopped down around us, and shell fragments whizzed through the air. One of the fragments sailed over us, sliced a hamburger-size wad of bark and wood from a tree, and clanged into Spanky Burrage's helmet with a sound like a brick hitting a garbage can. The fragment fell to the ground, and a little smoke drifted up from it.

We picked ourselves up. Spanky looked dead, except that he was breathing. Hamnet shouldered his pack and picked up Spanky and slung him over his shoulder. He saw me looking at him.

"I gotta take *care* of these people," he said.

The other thing I did not understand—apart from why there had been only one mortar round—came when we entered the village.

Lieutenant Harry Beevers had yet to join us, and we were nearly a year away from the events at Ia Thuc, when everything, the world and ourselves within the world, went crazy. I have to explain what happened. Lieutenant Harry Beevers killed thirty children in a cave at Ia Thuc and their bodies disappeared, but Michael Poole and I went into that cave and knew that something obscene had happened in there. We smelled evil, we touched its wings with our hands. A pitiful character named Victor Spitalny ran into the cave when he heard gunfire, and came pinwheeling out right away, screaming, covered with welts or hives that vanished almost as soon as he came out into the air. Poor Spitalny had touched it too. Because I was twenty and already writing books in my head, I thought that the cave was the place where the other *Tom Sawyer* ended, where Injun Joe raped Becky Thatcher and slit Tom's throat.

When we walked into the little village in the woods on the other side of the rice paddy, I experienced a kind of foretaste of Ia Thuc. If I can say this without setting off all the Gothic bells, the place seemed intrinsically, inherently wrong—it was too quiet, too still, completely without noise or movement. There were no chickens, dogs, or pigs; no old women came out to look us over, no old men offered conciliatory smiles. The little huts, still inhabitable, were empty—something I had never seen before in Vietnam, and never saw again. It was a ghost village, in a country where people thought the earth was sanctified by their ancestors' bodies.

Poole's map said that the place was named Bong To.

Hamnet lowered Spanky into the long grass as soon as we reached the center of the empty village. I bawled out a few words in my poor Vietnamese.

Spanky groaned. He gently touched the sides of his helmet. "I caught a head wound," he said.

"You wouldn't have a head at all, you was only wearing your liner," Hamnet said.

Spanky bit his lips and pushed the helmet up off his head. He groaned. A finger of blood ran down beside his ear. Finally the helmet passed over a lump the size of an apple that rose up from under his hair. Wincing, Spanky fingered this enormous knot. "I see double," he said. "I'll never get that helmet back on."

The medic said, "Take it easy, we'll get you out of here."

"Out of *here?*" Spanky brightened up.

"Back to Crandall," the medic said.

Spitalny sidled up, and Spanky frowned at him. "There ain't nobody here," Spitalny said. "What the fuck is going on?" He took the emptiness of the village as a personal affront.

Leonard Hamnet turned his back and spat.

"Spitalny, Tiano," the Lieutenant said. "Go into the paddy and get Tyrell and Blevins. Now."

Tattoo Tiano, who was due to die six and a half months later and was Spitalny's only friend, said, "You do it this time, Lieutenant."

Hamnet turned around and began moving toward Tiano and Spitalny. He looked as if he had grown two sizes larger, as if his hands could pick up boulders. I had forgotten how big he was. His head was lowered, and a rim of clear white showed above the irises.

I wouldn't have been surprised if he had blown smoke from his nostrils.

"Hey, I'm gone, I'm already there," Tiano said. He and Spitalny began moving quickly through the sparse trees. Whoever had fired the mortar had packed up and gone. By now it was nearly dark, and the mosquitoes had found us.

"So?" Poole said.

Hamnet sat down heavily enough for me to feel the shock in my boots. He said, "I have to go home, Lieutenant. I don't mean no disrespect, but I cannot take this shit much longer."

The Lieutenant said he was working on it.

Poole, Hamnet, and I looked around at the village.

Spanky Burrage said, "Good quiet place for Ham to catch up on his reading."

"Maybe I better take a look," the Lieutenant said. He flicked the lighter a couple of times and walked off toward the nearest hut. The rest of us stood around like fools, listening to the mosquitoes and the sounds of Tiano and Spitalny pulling the dead men up over the dikes. Every now and then Spanky groaned and shook his head. Too much time passed.

The Lieutenant said something almost inaudible from inside the hut. He came back outside in a hurry, looking disturbed and puzzled even in the darkness.

"Underhill, Poole," he said, "I want you to see this."

Poole and I glanced at each other. I wondered if I looked as bad as he did. Poole seemed to be a couple of psychic inches from either taking a poke at the Lieutenant or exploding altogether. In his muddy face his eyes were the size of hen's eggs. He was wound up like a cheap watch. I thought that I probably looked pretty much the same.

"What is it, Lieutenant?" he asked.

The Lieutenant gestured for us to come to the hut, then turned around and went back inside. There was no reason for us not to follow him. The Lieutenant was a jerk, but Harry Beevers, our next lieutenant, was a baron, an earl among jerks, and we nearly always did whatever dumb thing he told us to do. Poole was so ragged and edgy that he looked as if he felt like shooting the Lieutenant in the back. *I* felt like shooting the Lieutenant in the back, I realized a second later. I didn't have an idea in the world what was going on in Poole's mind. I grumbled something and moved toward the hut. Poole followed.

The Lieutenant was standing in the doorway, looking over his shoulder and fingering his sidearm. He frowned at us to let us know we had been slow to obey him, then flicked on the lighter. The sudden hollows and shadows in his face made him resemble one of the corpses I had opened up when I was in graves registration at Camp White Star.

"You want to know what it is, Poole? Okay, you tell me what it is."

He held the lighter before him like a torch and marched into the hut. I imagined the entire dry, flimsy structure bursting into heat and flame. This Lieutenant was not destined to get home walking and breathing, and I pitied and hated him about equally, but I did not want to turn into toast because he had found an American body inside a hut and didn't know what to do about it. I'd heard of platoons finding the mutilated corpses of American prisoners, and hoped that this was not our turn.

And then, in the instant before I smelled blood and saw the Lieutenant stoop to lift a panel on the floor, I thought that what had spooked him was not the body of an American POW but of a child who had been murdered and left behind in this empty place. The Lieutenant had probably not seen any dead children yet. Some part of the Lieutenant was still worrying about what a girl named Becky Roddenburger was getting up to back at Idaho State, and a dead child would be too much reality for him.

He pulled up the wooden panel in the floor, and I caught the smell of blood. The Zippo died, and darkness closed down on us. The Lieutenant yanked the panel back on its hinges. The smell of blood floated up from whatever was beneath the floor. The Lieutenant flicked the Zippo, and his face jumped out of the darkness. "Now. Tell me what this is."

"It's where they hide the kids when people like us show up," I said. "Smells like something went wrong. Did you take a look?"

I saw in his tight cheeks and almost lipless mouth that he had not. He wasn't about to go down there and get killed by the Minotaur while his platoon stood around outside.

"Taking a look is your job, Underhill," he said.

For a second we both looked at the ladder, made of peeled branches leashed together with rags, that led down into the pit.

"Give me the lighter," Poole said, and grabbed it away from the Lieutenant. He sat on the edge of the hole and leaned over, bringing the flame beneath the level of the floor. He grunted at whatever he saw, and surprised both the Lieutenant and myself by pushing himself off the ledge into the opening. The light went out. The Lieutenant and I looked down into the dark open rectangle in the floor.

The lighter flared again. I could see Poole's extended arm, the jittering little fire, a packed-earth floor. The top of the concealed room was less than an inch above the top of Poole's head. He moved away from the opening.

"What is it? Are there any—" The Lieutenant's voice made a creaky sound. "Any bodies?"

"Come down here, Tim," Poole called up.

I sat on the floor and swung my legs into the pit. Then I jumped down.

Beneath the floor, the smell of blood was almost sickeningly strong.

"What do you see?" the Lieutenant shouted. He was trying to sound like a leader, and his voice squeaked on the last word.

I saw an empty room shaped like a giant grave. The walls were covered by some kind of thick paper held in place by wooden struts sunk into the earth. Both the thick brown paper and two of the struts showed old bloodstains.

"Hot," Poole said, and closed the lighter.

"Come on, damn it," came the Lieutenant's voice. "Get out of there."

"Yes, sir," Poole said. He flicked the lighter back on. Many layers of thick paper formed an absorbent pad between the earth and the room, and the topmost, thinnest layer had been covered with vertical lines of Vietnamese writing. The writing looked like poetry, like the left-hand pages of Kenneth Rexroth's translations of Tu Fu and Li Po.

"Well, well," Poole said, and I turned to see him pointing at what first looked like intricately woven strands of rope fixed to the bloodstained wooden uprights. Poole stepped forward and the weave jumped into sharp relief. About four feet off the ground, iron chains had been screwed to the uprights. The thick pad between the two lengths of chain had been soaked with blood. The three feet of ground between the posts looked rusty. Poole moved the lighter closer to the chains, and we saw dried blood on the metal links.

"I want you guys out of there, and I mean *now*," whined the Lieutenant.

Poole snapped the lighter shut.

"I just changed my mind," I said softly. "I'm putting twenty bucks into the Elijah fund. For two weeks from today. That's what, June twentieth?"

"Tell it to Spanky," he said. Spanky Burrage had invented the pool we called the Elijah fund, and he held the money. Michael had not put any money into the pool. He thought that a new lieutenant might be even worse than the one we had. Of course he was right. Harry Beevers was our next lieutenant. Elijah Joys, Lieutenant Elijah Joys of New Utrecht, Idaho, a graduate of the University of Idaho and basic training at Fort Benning, Georgia, was an inept, weak lieutenant, not a disastrous one. If Spanky could have seen what was coming, he would have given back the money and prayed for the safety of Lieutenant Joys.

Poole and I moved back toward the opening. I felt as if I had seen a shrine to an obscene deity. The Lieutenant leaned over and stuck out his hand—uselessly, because he did not bend down far enough for us to reach him. We levered ourselves up out of the hole stiff-armed, as if we were leaving a swimming pool. The Lieutenant stepped back. He had a thin face and thick, fleshy nose, and his Adam's apple danced around in his neck like a jumping bean. He might not have been Harry Beevers, but he was no prize. "Well, how many?"

"How many what?" I asked.

"How many are there?" He wanted to go back to Camp Crandall with a good body count.

"There weren't exactly any bodies, Lieutenant," said Poole, trying to let him down easily. He described what we had seen.

"Well, what's that good for?" He meant, *How is that going to help me?*

"Interrogations, probably," Poole said. "If you questioned someone down there, no one outside the hut would hear anything. At night, you could just drag the body into the woods."

Lieutenant Joys nodded. "Field Interrogation Post," he said, trying out the phrase. "Torture, Use of, Highly Indicated." He nodded again. "Right?"

"Highly," Poole said.

"Shows you what kind of enemy we're dealing with in this conflict."

I could no longer stand being in the same three square feet of space with Elijah Joys, and I took a step toward the door of the hut. I did not know what Poole and I had seen, but I knew it was not a Field Interrogation Post, Torture, Use of, Highly Indicated, unless the Vietnamese had begun to interrogate monkeys. It occurred to me that the writing on the wall might have been names instead of poetry—I thought that we had stumbled into a mystery that had nothing to do with the war, a Vietnamese mystery.

For a second music from my old life, music too beautiful to be endurable, started playing in my head. Finally I recognized it: "The Walk to the Paradise Garden," from *A Village Romeo and Juliet* by Frederick Delius. Back in Berkeley, I had listened to it hundreds of times.

If nothing else had happened, I think I could have replayed the whole piece in my head. Tears filled my eyes, and I stepped toward the door of the hut. Then I froze. A ragged Vietnamese boy of seven or eight was regarding me with great seriousness from the far corner of the hut. I knew he was not there—I knew he was a spirit. I had no belief in spirits, but that's what he was. Some part of my mind as detached as a crime reporter reminded me that "The Walk to the Paradise Garden" was about two children who were about to die, and that in a sense the music *was* their death. I wiped my eyes with my hand, and when I lowered my arm, the boy was still there. He was beautiful, beautiful in the ordinary way, as Vietnamese children nearly always seemed beautiful to me. Then he vanished all at once, like the flickering light of the Zippo. I nearly groaned aloud. That child had been murdered in the hut: he had not just died, he had been murdered.

I said something to the other two men and went through the door into the growing darkness. I was very dimly aware of the Lieutenant asking Poole to repeat his description of the uprights and the bloody chain. Hamnet and Burrage and Calvin Hill were sitting down and leaning against a tree. Victor Spitalny was wiping his hands on his filthy shirt. White smoke curled up from Hill's cigarette, and Tina Pumo exhaled a long white stream of vapor. The unhinged thought came to me with an absolute conviction that *this* was the Paradise Garden. The men lounging in the darkness; the pattern of the cigarette smoke, and the patterns they made, sitting or standing; the in-drawing darkness, as physical as a blanket; the frame of the trees and the flat gray-green background of the paddy.

My soul had come back to life.

Then I became aware that there was something wrong about the men arranged before me, and again it took a moment for my intelligence to catch up to my intuition. Every member of a combat unit makes unconscious adjustments as members of the unit go down in the field; survival sometimes depends on the number of people you know are with you, and you keep count without being quite aware of doing it. I had registered that two men too many were in front of me. Instead of seven, there were nine, and the two men that made up the nine of us left were still behind me in the hut. M. O. Dengler was looking at me with growing curiosity, and I thought he knew exactly what I was thinking. A sick chill went through me. I saw Tom Blevins and Tyrell Budd standing together at the far right of the platoon, a little muddier than the others but otherwise different from the rest only in that, like Dengler, they were looking directly at me.

Hill tossed his cigarette away in an arc of light. Poole and Lieutenant Joys came out of the hut behind me. Leonard Hamnet patted his pocket to reassure himself that he still had his letter. I looked back at the right of the group, and the two dead men were gone.

"Let's saddle up," the Lieutenant said. "We aren't doing any good around here."

"Tim?" Dengler asked. He had not taken his eyes off me since I had come out of the hut. I shook my head.

"Well, what was it?" asked Tina Pumo. "Was it juicy?"

Spanky and Calvin Hill laughed and slapped hands.

"Aren't we gonna torch this place?" asked Spitalny.

The Lieutenant ignored him. "Juicy enough, Pumo. Interrogation Post. Field Interrogation Post."

"No shit," said Pumo.

"These people are into torture, Pumo. It's just another indication."

"Gotcha." Pumo glanced at me and his eyes grew curious. Dengler moved closer.

"I was just remembering something," I said. "Something from the world."

"You better forget about the world while you're over here, Underhill," the Lieutenant told me. "I'm trying to keep you alive, in case you hadn't noticed, but you have to cooperate with me." His Adam's apple jumped like a begging puppy.

As soon as he went ahead to lead us out of the village, I gave twenty dollars to Spanky and said, "Two weeks from today."

"My man," Spanky said.

The rest of the patrol was uneventful.

The next night we had showers, real food, alcohol, cots to sleep in. Sheets and pillows. Two new guys replaced Tyrell Budd and Thomas Blevins, whose names were never mentioned again, at least by me, until long after the war was over and Poole, Linklater, Pumo, and I looked them up, along with the rest of our dead, on the Wall in Washington. I wanted to forget the patrol, especially what I had seen and experienced inside the hut. I wanted the oblivion which came in powdered form.

I remember that it was raining. I remember the steam lifting off the ground, and the condensation dripping down the metal poles in the tents. Moisture shone on the faces around me. I was sitting in the brothers' tent, listening to the music Spanky Burrage played on the big reel-to-reel recorder he had bought on R&R in Taipei. Spanky Burrage never played Delius, but what he played was paradisal: great jazz from Armstrong to Coltrane, on reels recorded for him by his friends back in Little Rock and which he knew so well he could find individual tracks and performances without bothering to look at the counter. Spanky liked to play disc jockey during these long sessions, changing reels and speeding past thousands of feet of tape to play the same songs by different musicians, even the same song hiding under different names—"Cherokee" and "KoKo," "Indiana" and "Donna Lee"—or long series of songs connected by titles that used the same words—"I Thought About You" (Art Tatum), "You and the Night and the Music" (Sonny Rollins), "I Love You" (Bill Evans), "If I Could Be with You" (Ike Quebec), "You Leave Me Breathless" (Milt Jackson), even, for the sake of the joke, "Thou Swell," by Glenroy Breakstone. In his single-artist mode on this day, Spanky was ranging through the work of a great trumpet player named Clifford Brown.

On this sweltering, rainy day, Clifford Brown's music sounded regal and unearthly. Clifford Brown was walking to the Paradise Garden. Listening to him was like watching a smiling man shouldering open an enormous door to let in great dazzling rays of light. We were out of the war. The world we were in transcended pain and loss, and imagination had banished fear. Even SP4 Cotton and Calvin Hill, who preferred James Brown to Clifford Brown, lay on their bunks listening as Spanky followed his instincts from one track to another.

After he had played disc jockey for something like two hours, Spanky rewound the long tape and said, "Enough." The end of the tape slapped against the reel. I looked at Dengler, who seemed dazed, as if awakening from a long sleep. The memory of the music was still all around us: light still poured in through the crack in the great door.

"I'm gonna have a smoke *and* a drink," Hill announced, and pushed himself up off his cot. He walked to the door of the tent and pulled the flap aside to expose the green wet drizzle. That dazzling light, the light from another world, began to fade. Hill sighed, plopped a wide-brimmed hat on his head, and slipped outside. Before the stiff flap fell shut, I saw him jumping through the puddles on the way to Wilson Manly's shack. I felt as though I had returned from a long journey.

Spanky finished putting the Clifford Brown reel back into its cardboard box. Someone in the rear of the tent switched on Armed Forces Radio. Spanky looked at me and shrugged. Leonard Hamnet took his letter out of his pocket, unfolded it, and read it through very slowly.

"Leonard," I said, and he swung his big buffalo's head toward me. "You still putting in for compassionate leave?"

He nodded. "You know what I gotta do."

"Yes," Dengler said, in a slow quiet voice.

"They gonna let me take care of my people. They gonna send me back."

He spoke with a complete absence of nuance, like a man who had learned to get what he wanted by parroting words without knowing what they meant.

Dengler looked at me and smiled. For a second he seemed as alien as Hamnet. "What do you think is going to happen? To us, I mean. Do you think it'll just go on like this day after day until some of us get killed and the rest of us go home, or do you think it's going to get stranger and stranger?" He did not wait for me to answer. "I think it'll always sort of look the same, but it won't be— I think the edges are starting to melt. I think that's what happens when you're out here long enough. The edges melt."

"Your edges melted a long time ago, Dengler," Spanky said, and applauded his own joke.

Dengler was still staring at me. He always resembled a serious, dark-haired child, and never looked as though he belonged in uniform. "Here's what I mean, kind of," he said. "When we were listening to that trumpet player—"

"*Brownie,* Clifford *Brown,*" Spanky whispered.

"—I could see the notes in the air. Like they were written out on a long scroll. And after he played them, they stayed in the air for a long time."

"Sweetie-*pie*," Spanky said softly. "You pretty hip, for a little ofay square."

"When we were back in that village, last week," Dengler said. "Tell me about that."

I said that he had been there too.

"But something happened to you. Something special."

"I put twenty bucks in the Elijah fund," I said.

"Only twenty?" Cotton asked.

"What was in that hut?" Dengler asked.

I shook my head.

"All right," Dengler said. "But it's happening, isn't it? Things are changing."

I could not speak. I could not tell Dengler in front of Cotton and Spanky Burrage that I had imagined seeing the ghosts of Blevins, Budd, and a murdered child. I smiled and shook my head.

"Fine," Dengler said.

"What the fuck you sayin' is *fine?*" Cotton said. "I don't mind listening to that music, but I do draw the line at this bullshit." He flipped himself off his bunk and pointed a finger at me. "What date you give Spanky?"

"Fifteenth."

"He last longer than that." Cotton tilted his head as the song on the radio ended. Armed Forces Radio began playing a song by Moby Grape. Disgusted, he turned back to me. "Check it out. End of August. He be so tired, he be *sleepwalkin'*. Be halfway through his tour. The fool will go to pieces, and that's when he'll get it."

Cotton had put thirty dollars on August thirty-first, exactly the midpoint of Lieutenant Joys' tour of duty. He had a long time to adjust to the loss of the money, because he himself stayed alive until a sniper killed him at the beginning of February. Then he became a member of the ghost platoon that followed us wherever we went. I think this ghost platoon, filled with men I had loved and detested, whose names I could or could not remember, disbanded only when I went to the Wall in Washington, D.C., and by then I felt that I was a member of it myself.

2

I left the tent with a vague notion of getting outside and enjoying the slight coolness that followed the rain. The packet of Si Van Vo's white powder rested at the bottom of my right front pocket, which was so deep that my fingers just brushed its top. I decided that what I needed was a beer.

Wilson Manly's shack was all the way on the other side of camp. I never liked going to the enlisted men's club, where they were rumored to serve cheap Vietnamese beer in American bottles. Certainly the bottles had often been stripped of their labels, and to a suspicious eye the caps looked dented; also, the beer there never quite tasted like the stuff Manly sold.

One other place remained, farther away than the enlisted men's club but closer than Manly's shack and somewhere between them in official status. About twenty minutes' walk from where I stood, just at the curve in the steeply descending road to the airfield and the motor pool, stood an isolated wooden structure called Billy's. Billy himself, supposedly a Green Beret Captain who had installed a handful of bar girls in an old French command post, had gone home long ago, but his club had endured. There were no more girls, if there ever had been, and the brand-name liquor was about as reliable as the enlisted men's club's beer. When it was open, a succession of slender Montagnard boys who slept in the nearly empty upstairs rooms served drinks. I visited these rooms two or three times, but I never learned where the boys went when Billy's was closed. They spoke almost no English. Billy's did not look anything like a French command post, even one that had been transformed into a bordello: it looked like a roadhouse.

A long time ago, the building had been painted brown. The wood was soft with rot. Someone had once boarded up the two front windows on the lower floor, and someone else had torn off a narrow band of boards across each of the windows, so that light entered in two flat white bands that traveled across the floor during the day. Around six thirty the light bounced off the long foxed mirror that stood behind the row of bottles. After five minutes of blinding light, the sun disappeared beneath the pine boards, and for ten or fifteen minutes a shadowy pink glow filled the barroom. There was no electricity and no ice. Fingerprints covered the glasses. When you needed a toilet, you went to a cubicle with inverted metal boot prints on either side of a hole in the floor.

The building stood in a little grove of trees in the curve of the descending road, and as I walked toward it in the diffuse reddish light of the sunset, a mud-spattered jeep painted in the colors of camouflage gradually came into view to the right of the bar, emerging from invisibility like an optical illusion. The jeep seemed to have floated out of the trees behind it, to be a part of them.

I heard low male voices, which stopped when I stepped onto the soft boards of the front porch. I glanced at the jeep, looking for insignia or identification, but the mud covered the door panels. Something white gleamed dully from the back seat. When I looked more closely, I saw in a coil of rope an oval of bone that it took me a moment to recognize as the top of a painstakingly cleaned and bleached human skull.

Before I could reach the handle, the door opened. A boy named Mike stood before me, in loose khaki shorts and a dirty white shirt much too large for him. Then he saw who I was. "Oh," he said. "Yes. Tim. Okay. You can come in." His real name was not Mike, but Mike was what it sounded like. He carried himself with an odd defensive alertness, and he shot me a tight, uncomfortable smile. "Far table, right side."

"It's okay?" I asked, because everything about him told me that it wasn't.

"*Yesss.*" He stepped back to let me in.

I smelled cordite before I saw the other men. The bar looked empty, and the band of light coming in through the opening over the windows had already reached the long mirror, creating a bright dazzle, a white fire. I took a couple of steps inside, and Mike moved around me to return to his post.

"Oh, hell," someone said from off to my left. "We have to put up with *this?*"

I turned my head to look into the murk of that side of the bar, and saw three men sitting against the wall at a round table. None of the kerosene lamps had been lighted yet, and the dazzle from the mirror made the far reaches of the bar even less distinct.

"Is okay, is okay," said Mike. "Old customer. Old friend."

"I bet he is," the voice said. "Just don't let any women in here."

"No women," Mike said. "No problem."

I went through the tables to the furthest one on the right.

"You want whiskey, Tim?" Mike asked.

"Tim?" the man said. "*Tim?*"

"Beer," I said, and sat down.

A nearly empty bottle of Johnny Walker Black, three glasses, and about a dozen cans of beer covered the table before them. The soldier with his back against the wall shoved aside some of the beer cans so that I could see the .45 next to the Johnny Walker bottle. He leaned forward with a drunk's guarded coordination. The sleeves had been ripped off his shirt, and dirt darkened his skin as if he had not bathed in years. His hair had been cut with a knife, and had once been blond.

"I just want to make sure about this," he said. "You're not a woman, right? You swear to that?"

"Anything you say," I said.

"No woman walks into this place." He put his hand on the gun. "No nurse. No wife. No *anything*. You got that?"

"Got it," I said. Mike hurried around the bar with my beer.

"Tim. Funny name. Tom, now—that's a name. Tim sounds like a little guy—like him." He pointed at Mike with his left hand, the whole hand and not merely the index finger, while his right still rested on the .45. "Little fucker ought to be wearing a dress. Hell, he practically *is* wearing a dress."

"Don't you like women?" I asked. Mike put a can of Budweiser on my table and shook his head rapidly, twice. He had wanted me in the club because he was afraid the drunken soldier was going to shoot him, and now I was just making things worse.

I looked at the two men with the drunken officer. They were dirty and exhausted—whatever had happened to the drunk had also happened to them. The difference was that they were not drunk yet.

"That is a complicated question," the drunk said. "There are questions of responsibility. You can be responsible for yourself. You can be responsible for your children and your tribe. You are responsible for anyone you want to protect. But can you be responsible for women? If so, how responsible?"

Mike quietly moved behind the bar and sat on a stool with his arms out of sight. I knew he had a shotgun under there.

"You don't have any idea what I'm talking about, do you, Tim, you rear-echelon dipshit?"

"You're afraid you'll shoot any women who come in here, so you told the bartender to keep them out."

"This wise-ass sergeant is personally interfering with my state of mind," the drunk said to the burly man on his right. "Tell him to get out of here, or a certain degree of unpleasantness will ensue."

"Leave him alone," the other man said. Stripes of dried mud lay across his lean, haggard face.

The drunken officer startled me by leaning toward the other man and speaking in a clear, carrying Vietnamese. It was an old-fashioned, almost literary Vietnamese, and he must have thought and dreamed in it to speak it so well. He assumed that neither I nor the Montagnard boy would understand him.

This is serious, he said, and I am serious. If you wish to see how serious, just sit in your chair and do nothing. Do you not know of what I am capable by now? Have you learned nothing? You know what I know. I know what you know. A great heaviness is between us. Of all the people in the world at this moment, the only ones I do not despise are already dead, or should be. At this moment, murder is weightless.

There was more, and I cannot swear that this was exactly what he said, but it's pretty close. He may have said that murder was *empty.*

Then he said, in that same flowing Vietnamese that even to my ears sounded as stilted as the language of a third-rate Victorian novel: *Recall what is in our vehicle (carriage); you should remember what we have brought with us, because I shall never forget it. Is it so easy for you to forget?*

It takes a long time and a lot of patience to clean and bleach bone. A skull would be more difficult than most of a skeleton.

Your leader requires more of this nectar, he said, and rolled back in his chair, looking at me with his hand on his gun.

"Whiskey," said the burly soldier. Mike was already pulling the bottle off the shelf. He understood that the officer was trying to knock himself out before he would find it necessary to shoot someone.

For a moment I thought that the burly soldier to his right looked familiar. His head had been shaved so close he looked bald, and his eyes were enormous above the streaks of dirt. A stainless-steel watch hung from a slot in his collar. He extended a muscular arm for the bottle Mike passed him while keeping as far from the table as he could. The soldier twisted off the cap and poured into all three glasses. The man in the center immediately drank all the whiskey in his glass and banged the glass down on the table for a refill.

The haggard soldier who had been silent until now said, "Something is gonna happen here." He looked straight at me. "Pal?"

"That man is nobody's pal," the drunk said. Before anyone could stop him, he snatched up the gun, pointed it across the room, and fired. There was a flash of fire, a huge explosion, and the reek of cordite. The bullet went straight through the soft wooden wall, about eight feet to my left. A stray bit of light slanted through the hole it made.

For a moment I was deaf. I swallowed the last of my beer and stood up. My head was ringing.

"Is it clear that I hate the necessity for this kind of shit?" said the drunk. "Is that much understood?"

The soldier who had called me pal laughed, and the burly soldier poured more whiskey into the drunk's glass. Then he stood up and started coming toward me. Beneath the exhaustion and the stripes of dirt, his face was taut with anxiety. He put himself between me and the man with the gun.

"I am not a rear-echelon dipshit," I said. "I don't want any trouble, but people like him do not own this war."

"Will you maybe let me save your ass, Sergeant?" he whispered. "Major Bachelor hasn't been anywhere near white men in three years, and he's having a little trouble readjusting. Compared to him, we're all rear-echelon dipshits."

I looked at his tattered shirt. "Are you his babysitter, Captain?"

He gave me an exasperated look and glanced over his shoulder at the Major. "Major, put down your damn weapon. The Sergeant is a combat soldier. He is on his way back to camp."

I don't care what he is, the Major said in Vietnamese.

The Captain began pulling me toward the door, keeping his body between me and the other table. I motioned for Mike to come out with me.

"Don't worry, the Major won't shoot him, Major Bachelor loves the Yards," the Captain said. He gave me an impatient glance because I had refused to move at his pace. Then I saw him notice my pupils. "God damn," he said, and then he stopped moving altogether and said "God damn" again, but in a different tone of voice.

I started laughing.

"Oh, this is—" He shook his head. "This is really—"

"Where have you *been?*" I asked him.

John Ransom turned to the table. "Hey, I know this guy. He's an old football friend of mine."

Major Bachelor shrugged and put the .45 back on the table. His eyelids had nearly closed. "I don't care about football," he said, but he kept his hand off the weapon.

"Buy the sergeant a drink," said the haggard officer.

"Buy the fucking sergeant a drink," the Major chimed in.

John Ransom quickly moved to the bar and reached for a glass, which the confused Mike put into his hand. Ransom went through the tables, filled his glass and mine, and carried both back to join me.

We watched the Major's head slip down by notches toward his chest. When his chin finally reached the unbuttoned top of his ruined shirt, Ransom said, "All right, Bob," and the other man slid the .45 out from under the Major's hand. He pushed it beneath his belt.

"The man is out," Bob said.

Ransom turned back to me. "He was up three days straight with us, God knows how long before that." Ransom did not have to specify who *he* was. "Bob and I got some sleep, trading off, but he just kept on talking." He fell into one of the chairs at my table and tilted his glass to his mouth. I sat down beside him.

For a moment no one in the bar spoke. The line of light from the open space across the windows had already left the mirror, and was now approaching the place on the wall that meant it would soon disappear. Mike lifted the cover from one of the lamps and began trimming the wick.

"How come you're always fucked up when I see you?"

"You have to ask?"

He smiled. He looked very different from when I had seen him preparing to give a sales pitch to Senator Burrman at Camp White Star. His body had thickened and hardened, and his eyes had re-treated far back into his head. He seemed to me to have moved a long step nearer the goal I had always seen in him than when he had given me the zealot's word about stopping the spread of Communism. This man had taken in more of the war, and that much more of the war was inside him now.

"I got you off graves registration at White Star, didn't I?"

I agreed that he had.

"What did you call it, the body squad? It wasn't even a real graves registration unit, was it?" He smiled and shook his head. "I took care of your Captain McCue, too—he was using it as a kind of dumping ground. I don't know how he got away with it as long as he did. The only one with any training was that sergeant, what's his name. Italian."

"DeMaestro."

Ransom nodded. "The whole operation was going off the rails." Mike lit a big kitchen match and touched it to the wick of the kerosene lamp. "I heard some things——" He slumped against the wall and swallowed whiskey. I wondered if he had heard about Captain Havens. He closed his eyes. "Some crazy stuff went on back there."

I asked if he was still stationed in the highlands up around the Laotian border. He almost sighed when he shook his head.

"You're not with the tribesmen anymore? What were they, Khatu?"

He opened his eyes. "You have a good memory. No, I'm not there anymore." He considered saying more, but decided not to. He had failed himself. "I'm kind of on hold until they send me up around Khe Sahn. It'll be better up there—the Bru are tremendous. But right now, all I want to do is take a bath and get into bed. Any bed. Actually, I'd settle for a dry level place on the ground."

"Where did you come from now?"

"Incountry." His face creased and he showed his teeth. The effect was so unsettling that I did not immediately realize that he was smiling. "Way incountry. We had to get the Major out."

"Looks more like you had to pull him out, like a tooth."

My ignorance made him sit up straight. "You mean you never heard of him? Franklin Bachelor?"

And then I thought I had, that someone had mentioned him to me a long time ago.

"In the bush for years. Bachelor did stuff that ordinary people don't even *dream* of—he's a legend."

A legend, I thought. Like the Green Berets Ransom had mentioned a lifetime ago at White Star.

"Ran what amounted to a private army, did a lot of good work in Darlac Province. He was out there on his own. The man was a hero. That's straight. Bachelor got to places we couldn't even get close to—he got *inside* an NVA encampment, you hear me, *inside* the encampment and *silently* killed about an entire division."

Of all the people in the world at this minute, I remembered, the only ones he did not detest were already dead. I thought I must have heard it wrong.

"He was absorbed right into Rhade life," Ransom said. I could hear the awe in his voice. "The man even got married. Rhade ceremony. His wife went with him on missions. I hear she was beautiful."

Then I knew where I had heard of Franklin Bachelor before. He had been a captain when Ratman and his platoon had run into him after a private named Bobby Swett had been blown to pieces on a trail in Darlac Province. Ratman had thought his wife was a black-haired angel.

And then I knew whose skull lay wound in rope in the back seat of the jeep.

"I did hear of him," I said. "I knew someone who met him. The Rhade woman, too."

"His *wife*," Ransom said.

I asked him where they were taking Bachelor.

"We're stopping overnight at Crandall for some rest. Then we hop to Tan Son Nhut and bring him back to the States—Langley. I thought we might have to strap him down, but I guess we'll just keep pouring whiskey into him."

"He's going to want his gun back."

"Maybe I'll give it to him." His look told me what he thought Major Bachelor would do with his .45, if he was left alone with it long enough. "He's in for a rough time at Langley. There'll be some heat."

"Why Langley?"

"Don't ask. But don't be naïve, either. Don't you think they're . . ." He would not finish that sentence. "Why do you think we had to bring him out in the first place?"

"Because something went wrong."

"Oh, everything went wrong. Bachelor went totally out of control. He had his own war. Ran a lot of sidelines, some of which were supposed to be under shall we say tighter controls?"

He had lost me.

"Ventures into Laos. Business trips to Cambodia. Sometimes he wound up in control of airfields Air America was using, and that meant he was in control of the cargo."

When I shook my head, he said, "Don't you have a little something in your pocket? A little package?"

A secret world—inside this world, another, secret world.

"You understand, I don't care what he did any more than I care about what *you* do. I think Langley can go fuck itself. Bachelor wrote the book. In spite of his sidelines. In spite of whatever *trouble* he got into. The man was effective. He stepped over a boundary, maybe a lot of boundaries—but tell me that you can do what we're supposed to do without stepping over boundaries."

I wondered why he seemed to be defending himself, and asked if he would have to testify at Langley.

"It's not a trial."

"A debriefing."

"Sure, a debriefing. They can ask me anything they want. All I can tell them is what I saw. That's *my* evidence, right? What I saw? They don't have any evidence, except maybe this, uh, these human remains the Major insisted on bringing out."

For a second, I wished that I could see the sober shadowy gentlemen of Langley, Virginia, the gentlemen with slicked-back hair and pinstriped suits, question Major Bachelor. They thought *they* were serious men.

"It was like Bong To, in a funny way." Ransom waited for me to ask. When I did not, he said, "A ghost town, I mean. I don't suppose you've ever heard of Bong To."

"My unit was just there." His head jerked up. "A mortar round scared us into the village."

"You saw the place?"

I nodded.

"Funny story." Now he was sorry he had ever mentioned it. "Well, think about Bachelor, now. I think he must have been in Cambodia or someplace, doing what he does, when his village was overrun. He comes back and finds everybody dead, his wife included. I mean, I don't think *Bachelor* killed those people—they weren't just dead, they'd been made to beg for it. So Bachelor wasn't there, and his assistant, a Captain Bennington, must have just run off—we never did find him. Officially, Bennington's MIA. It's simple. You can't find the main guy, so you make sure he can see how mad you are when he gets back. You do a little grievous bodily harm on his people. They were not nice to his wife, Tim, to her they were especially not nice. What does he do? He buries all the bodies in the village graveyard, because that's a sacred responsibility. Don't ask me what else he does, because you don't have to know this, okay? But the bodies are buried. Generally speaking. Captain Bennington never does show up. We arrive and take Bachelor away. But sooner or later, some of the people who escaped are going to come back to that village. They're going to go on living there. The worst thing in the world happened to them in that place, but they won't leave. Eventually, other people in their family will join them, if they're still alive, and the terrible thing will be a part of their lives. Because it is not thinkable to leave your dead."

"But they did in Bong To," I said.

"In Bong To, they did."

I saw the look of regret on his face again, and said that I wasn't asking him to tell me any secrets.

"It's not a secret. It's not even military."

"It's just a ghost town."

Ransom was still uncomfortable. He turned his glass around and around in his hands before he drank. "I have to get the Major into camp."

"It's a real ghost town," I said. "Complete with ghosts."

"I honestly wouldn't be surprised." He drank what was left in his glass and stood up. He had decided not to say any more about it. "Let's take care of Major Bachelor, Bob," he said.

"Right."

Ransom carried our bottle to the bar and paid Mike. I stepped toward him to do the same, and Ransom said, "Taken care of."

There was that phrase again—it seemed I had been hearing it all day, and that its meaning would not stay still.

Ransom and Bob picked up the Major between them. They were strong enough to lift him easily. Bachelor's greasy head rolled forward. Bob put the .45 into his pocket, and Ransom put the bottle into his own pocket. Together they carried the Major to the door.

I followed them outside. Artillery pounded hills a long way off. It was dark now, and light from the lanterns spilled out through the gaps in the windows.

All of us went down the rotting steps, the Major bobbing between the other two.

Ransom opened the jeep, and they took a while to maneuver the Major into the back seat. Bob squeezed in beside him and pulled him upright.

John Ransom got in behind the wheel and sighed. He had no taste for the next part of his job.

"I'll give you a ride back to camp," he said. "We don't want an MP to get a close look at you."

I took the seat beside him. Ransom started the engine and turned on the lights. He jerked the gearshift into reverse and rolled backwards. "You know why that mortar round came in, don't you?" he asked me. He grinned at me, and we bounced onto the road back to the main part of camp. "He was trying to chase you away from Bong To, and your fool of a lieutenant went straight for the place instead." He was still grinning. "It must have steamed him, seeing a bunch of round-eyes going in there."

"He didn't send in any more fire."

"No. He didn't want to damage the place. It's supposed to stay the way it is. I don't think they'd use the word, but that village is supposed to be like a kind of monument." He glanced at me again. "To shame."

For some reason, all I could think of was the drunken Major in the seat behind me, who had said that you were responsible for the people you wanted to protect. Ransom said, "Did you go into any of the huts? Did you see anything unusual there?"

"I went into a hut. I saw something unusual."

"A list of names?"

"I thought that's what they were."

"Okay," Ransom said. "You know a little Vietnamese?"

"A little."

"You notice anything about those names?"

I could not remember. My Vietnamese had been picked up in bars and markets, and was almost completely oral.

"Four of them were from a family named Trang. Trang was the village chief, like his father before him, and his grandfather before him. Trang had four daughters. As each one got to the age of six or seven, he took them down into that underground room and chained them to the posts and raped them. A lot of those huts have hidden storage areas, but Trang must have modified his after his first daughter was born. The funny thing is, I think everybody in the village knew what he was doing. I'm not saying they thought it was okay, but they let it happen. They could pretend they didn't know: the girls never complained, and nobody ever heard any screams. I guess Trang was a good-enough chief. When the daughters got to sixteen, they left for the cities. Sent back money, too. So maybe they thought it was okay, but I don't think they did, myself, do you?"

"How would I know? But there's a man in my platoon, a guy from—"

"I think there's a difference between private and public shame. Between what's acknowledged and what is not acknowledged. That's what Bachelor has to cope with, when he gets to Langley. Some things are acceptable, as long as you don't talk about them." He looked sideways at me as we began to approach the northern end of the camp proper. He wiped his face, and flakes of dried mud fell off his cheek. The exposed skin looked red, and so did his eyes. "Because the way I see it, this is a whole general issue. The issue is: what is *expressible?* This goes way beyond the tendency of people to tolerate thoughts, actions, or behavior they would otherwise find unacceptable."

I had never heard a soldier speak this way before. It was a little bit like being back in Berkeley.

"I'm talking about the difference between what is expressed and what is described," Ransom said. "A lot of experience is unacknowledged. Religion lets us handle some of the unacknowledged stuff in an acceptable way. But suppose—just suppose—that you were forced to confront extreme experience directly, without any mediation?"

"I have," I said. "You have, too."

"More extreme than combat, more extreme than terror. Something like that happened to the Major: he *encountered* God. Demands were made upon him. He had to move out of the ordinary, even as *he* defined it."

Ransom was telling me how Major Bachelor had wound up being brought to Camp Crandall with his wife's skull, but none of it was clear to me.

"I've been learning things," Ransom told me. He was almost whispering. "Think about what would make all the people of a village pick up and leave, when sacred obligation ties them to that village."

"I don't know the answer," I said.

"An even more sacred obligation, created by a really spectacular sense of shame. When a crime is too great to live with, the memory of it becomes sacred. Becomes the crime itself—"

I remembered thinking that the arrangement in the hut's basement had been a shrine to an obscene deity.

"Here we have this village and its chief. The village knows but does not know what the chief has been doing. They are used to consulting and obeying him. Then—one day, a little boy disappears."

My heart gave a thud.

"A little boy. Say: three. Old enough to talk and get into trouble, but too young to take care of himself. He's just gone—*poof.* Well, this is Vietnam, right? You turn your back, your kid wanders away, some animal gets him. He could get lost in the jungle and wander into a claymore. Someone like you might even shoot him. He could fall into a booby trap and never be seen again. It could happen.

"A couple of months later, it happens again. Mom turns her back, where the hell did Junior go? This time they really look, not just Mom and Grandma, all their friends. They scour the village. The *villagers* scour the village, every square foot of that place, and then they do the same to the rice paddy, and then they look through the forest.

"And guess what happens next. This is the interesting part. An old woman goes out one morning to fetch water from the well, and she sees a ghost. This old lady is part of the extended family of the first lost kid, but the ghost she sees isn't the kid's—it's the ghost of a disreputable old man from another village, a drunkard, in fact. A local no-good, in fact. He's just standing near the well with his hands together, he's hungry—that's what these people know about ghosts. The skinny old bastard wants *more.* He wants to be *fed.* The old lady gives a squawk and passes out. When she comes to again, the ghost is gone.

"Well, the old lady tells everybody what she saw, and the whole village gets in a panic. Evil forces have been set loose. Next thing you know, two thirteen-year-old girls are working in the paddy, they look up and see an old woman who died when they were ten—she's about six feet away from them. Her hair is stringy and gray and her fingernails are about a foot long. She used to be a friendly old lady, but she doesn't look too friendly now. She's hungry too, like all ghosts. They start screaming and crying, but no one else can see her, and she comes closer and closer, and they try to get away but one of them falls down, and the old woman is on her like a cat. And do you know what she does? She rubs her filthy hands over the screaming girl's face, and licks the tears and slobber off her fingers.

"The next night, another little boy disappears. Two men go looking around the village latrine behind the houses, and they see two ghosts down in the pit, shoving excrement into their mouths. They rush back into the village, and then they both see half a dozen ghosts around the chief's hut. Among them are a sister who died during the war with the French and a twenty-year-old first wife who died of dengue fever. They want to eat. One of the men screeches, because not only did he see his dead wife, who looks something like what we could call a vampire, he saw her pass into the chief's hut without the benefit of the door.

"These people believe in ghosts, Underhill, they know ghosts exist, but it is extremely rare for them to see these ghosts. And these people are like psychoanalysts, because they do not believe in accidents. Every event contains meaning.

"The dead twenty-year-old wife comes back out through the wall of the chief's hut. Her hands are empty but dripping with red, and she is licking them like a starving cat.

"The former husband stands there pointing and jabbering, and the mothers and grandmothers of the missing boys come out of their huts. They are as afraid of what they're thinking as they are of all the ghosts moving around them. The ghosts are part of what they know they know, even though most of them have never seen one until now. What is going through their minds is something new: new because it was hidden.

"The mothers and grandmothers go to the chief's door and begin howling like dogs. When the chief comes out, they push past him and they take the hut apart. And you know what they find. They found the end of Bong To."

Ransom had parked the jeep near my battalion headquarters five minutes before, and now he smiled as if he had explained everything.

"But what *happened?*" I asked. "How did you hear about it?"

He shrugged. "We learned all this in interrogation. When the women found the underground room, they knew the chief had forced the boys into sex, and then killed them. They didn't know what he had done with the bodies, but they knew he had killed the boys. The next time the VC paid one of their courtesy calls, they told the cadre leader what they knew. The VC did the rest. They were disgusted—Trang had betrayed *them*, too—betrayed everything he was supposed to represent. One of the VC we captured took the chief downstairs into his underground room and chained the man to the posts, wrote the names of the dead boys and Trang's daughters on the padding that covered the walls, and then . . . then they did what they did to him. They probably carried out the pieces and threw them into the excrement pit. And over months, bit by bit, not all at once but slowly, everybody in the village moved out. By that time, they were seeing ghosts all the time. They had crossed a kind of border."

"Do you think they really saw ghosts?" I asked him. "I mean, do you think they were real ghosts?"

"If you want an expert opinion, you'd have to ask Major Bachelor. He has a lot to say about ghosts." He hesitated for a moment, and then leaned over to open my door. "But if you ask me, sure they did."

I got out of the jeep and closed the door.

Ransom peered at me through the jeep's window. "Take better care of yourself."

"Good luck with your Bru."

"The Bru are fantastic." He slammed the jeep into gear and shot away, cranking the wheel to turn the jeep around in a giant circle in front of the battalion headquarters before he jammed it into second and took off to wherever he was going.

Two weeks later Leonard Hamnet managed to get the Lutheran

chaplain at Crandall to write a letter to the Tin Man for him, and two days after that he was in a clean uniform, packing up his kit for an overnight flight to an Air Force base in California. From there he was connecting to a Memphis flight, and from there the Army had booked him onto a six-passenger puddle jumper to Lookout Mountain.

When I came into Hamnet's tent he was zipping his bag shut in a zone of quiet afforded him by the other men. He did not want to talk about where he was going or the reason he was going there, and instead of answering my questions about his flights, he unzipped a pocket on the side of his bag and handed me a thick folder of airline tickets.

I looked through them and gave them back. "Hard travel," I said.

"From now on, everything is easy," Hamnet said. He seemed rigid and constrained as he zipped the precious tickets back into the bag. By this time his wife's letter was a rag held together with Scotch tape. I could picture him reading and rereading it, for the thousandth or two thousandth time, on the long flight over the Pacific.

"They need your help," I said. "I'm glad they're going to get it."

"That's right." Hamnet waited for me to leave him alone.

Because his bag seemed heavy, I asked about the length of his leave. He wanted to get the tickets back out of the bag rather than answer me directly, but he forced himself to speak. "They gave me seven days. Plus travel time."

"Good," I said, meaninglessly, and then there was nothing left to say, and we both knew it. Hamnet hoisted his bag off his bunk and turned to the door without any of the usual farewells and embraces. Some of the other men called to him, but he seemed to hear nothing but his own thoughts. I followed him outside and stood beside him in the heat. Hamnet was wearing a tie and his boots had a high polish. He was already sweating through his stiff khaki shirt. He would not meet my eyes. In a minute a jeep pulled up before us. The Lutheran chaplain had surpassed himself.

"Goodbye, Leonard," I said, and Hamnet tossed his bag in back and got into the jeep. He sat up straight as a statue. The private driving the jeep said something to him as they drove off, but Hamnet did not reply. I bet he did not say a word to the stewardesses, either, or to the cabdrivers or baggage handlers or anyone else who witnessed his long journey home.

3

On the day after Leonard Hamnet was scheduled to return, Lieutenant Joys called Michael Poole and myself into his quarters to tell us what had happened back in Tennessee. He held a sheaf of papers in his hand, and he seemed both angry and embarrassed. Hamnet would not be returning to the platoon. It was a little funny. Well, of course it wasn't funny at all. The whole thing was terrible—that was what it was. Someone was to blame, too. Irresponsible decisions had been made, and we'd all be lucky if there wasn't an investigation. We were closest to the man, hadn't we seen what was likely to happen? If not, what the hell was our excuse?

Didn't we have any inkling of what the man was planning to do?

Well, yes, at the beginning, Poole and I said. But he seemed to have adjusted.

We have stupidity and incompetence all the way down the line here, said Lieutenant Elijah Joys. Here is a man who manages to carry a semiautomatic weapon through security at three different airports, bring it into a courthouse, and carry out threats he made months before, without anybody stopping him.

I remembered the bag Hamnet had tossed into the back of the jeep; I remembered the reluctance with which he had zipped it open to show me his tickets. Hamnet had not carried his weapon through airport security. He had just shipped it home in his bag and walked straight through customs in his clean uniform and shiny boots.

As soon as the foreman had announced the guilty verdict, Leonard Hamnet had gotten to his feet, pulled the semiautomatic pistol from inside his jacket, and executed Mr. Brewster where he was sitting at the defense table. While people shouted and screamed and dove for cover, while the courthouse officer tried to unsnap his gun, Hamnet killed his wife and his son. By the time he raised the pistol to his own head, the security officer had shot him twice in the chest. He died on the operating table at Lookout Mountain Lutheran Hospital, and his mother had requested that his remains receive burial at Arlington National Cemetery.

His mother. Arlington. I ask you.

That was what the Lieutenant said. *His mother. Arlington. I ask you.*

A private from Indianapolis named E. W. Burroughs won the six hundred and twenty dollars in the Elijah Fund when Lieutenant Joys was killed by a fragmentation bomb thirty-two days before the end of his tour. After that we were delivered unsuspecting into the hands of Harry Beevers, the Lost Boss, the worst lieutenant in the world. Private Burroughs died a week later, down in Dragon Valley along with Tiano and Calvin Hill and lots of others, when Lieutenant Beevers walked us into a mined field where we spent forty-eight hours under fire between two companies of NVA. I suppose Burroughs's mother back in Indianapolis got the six hundred and twenty dollars.

The Great Lover

Dan Simmons

Editor's Prologue by Richard Edward Harrison III:

The following secret wartime journal of the poet James Edwin Rooke was "discovered" in the Imperial War Museum in London in September of 1988. In fact, the journal had been correctly logged and catalogued as one of several thousand Great War diaries found or donated to the Museum almost seventy years earlier, but the small notebook had been misfiled with bureaucratic detritus of little interest to scholars through all or most of the intervening decades. Once "discovered," however, the ensuing reaction it has created in scholars might be described as nothing less than sensational.

That it is the actual writing of James Edwin Rooke has now been verified beyond question. The handwriting has been confirmed. The poems, most of them in their earliest work state, have been identified as holistic versions of several of the more famous verses in Trench Poems *by James Edwin Rooke, copyright 1921 by Faber and Faber Ltd., London. Indeed, although the diary was not signed and was one of hundreds of nearly identical cheap journals recovered at aid stations, burial centres, or on the battlefield itself, many of the passages in this journal were "signed" by Rooke's hasty symbol ☺, which was to become so famous on the cover of the 1936 Faber edition of* Trench Poems.

But even when there was no further doubt as to the authenticity of this diary, there remained a shocked disbelief. The reasons are varied and profound.

*First, James Edwin Rooke's Somme diary from the Great War had already been found and published (*One Infantry Officer's Memoirs: James Edwin Rooke's Somme Diary, *copyright 1924 by George Falkner & Sons) and while it contained some disturbing imagery of trench warfare, the tone* was of the more temperate and often wryly humorous variety which so typified officers' diaries of that time. In point of truth, most of Rooke's published Somme Diary comments were terse operational notes with few personal asides of interest to any but the most dedicated literary scholar or military historian.

Certainly there was nothing of the sort of shocking material present in this more recently discovered journal.

Secondly, there were the legal rights of the Rooke estate to be considered and the surviving members of the Rooke family to be consulted. The editor wishes to thank Mrs. Eleanor Marsh of Tunbridge Wells for her kind permission to reprint the following pages.

Finally, there was the factor of the contents themselves. The reputation of James Edwin Rooke, as both poet and man, has seemed secure for most of this century. While the demands of honest scholarship require full disclosure, drastically altering the reputation of an historical figure so central to British pride and British literary tradition is no light undertaking. Thus it is that this, the first publication of James Edwin Rooke's secret Somme diary, was delayed for several years due as much to this editor's concern about the effect it would have on the image and literary legacy of the famous "trench poet" as to the serious and extended effort required to verify all aspects of the journal's authenticity.

But having verified the diary's authenticity and carefully weighed the effect such revelations will have on the memory of one of this century's premiere poets, the burden of honest scholarship compels this editor to publish the journal without amendation or expurgation.

The journal itself has suffered waterstain, some damage from the terrible war environment it describes, and the inevitable decomposition from seven decades in storage under less than optimum conditions at the Imperial War Museum. More than that, several pages are missing and may have been torn out by the author. Many passages have been scrawled over or marked out. Some of these have been retrieved through various X-ray techniques; others appear to have been lost forever.

Because of the many years and cultural differences that now separate us from those terrible months along the Somme in 1916, I have inserted a few editorial comments for purposes of clarification. Where the text is illegible or ambivalent, I have noted my own best guess reconstruction of a word or phrase. I have footnoted the bits of verse in the journals.

Other than these few editorial intrusions, the words and impressions are totally *those of the twenty-eight-year-old Lieutenant James Edwin Rooke, late of C Company, No. 4237, 13th (S) Battalion, The Rifle Brigade.*

—REH
Cambridge
December, 1992

Saturday, 8 July, 8.15 A.M.—

Because I had been here as observer the week before during the Big Push and "knew the way" through the endless maze of trenches, I was appointed last night to lead the entire Rifle Brigade from the reserve trenches on the Tara-Usna Ridge into our section of the Front at la Boisselle. I accepted with good enough grace, despite the fact that the lines had changed dramatically along this section of the Front in the intervening week. Since la Boisselle itself had fallen, it now lies behind the front line, while the section of enemy trench we had undermined and blown heavenward with such a ferocious bang on the morning of 1 July now exists merely as a gigantic crater to the right of our new forward line. (As I write this, the crater is in the process of becoming a mass grave for our comrades in the 34th Division whom I watched go over the top so bravely and so futilely only seven days ago. Their bodies have been out in the No Man's Land since the morning of the attack, and only the successful advance this morning during which la Boisselle finally fell has allowed our troops to reach the wire where most of the bodies have lain since the previous Saturday.)

We arrived after 10 P.M. last night, in the pouring rain, and, without sleep or a proper meal, were put to the task of burying the dead before the sun rose. The Colonel explained to the officers that burial teams had been sniped at during daylight hours so that we were to begin our business at night. The other officers and I called together the NCOs in our respective companies and passed on the explanation. The NCOs explained nothing to the men, but roused them out of their muddy nooks and crannies, out from under their dripping oilsheets, and away from their midnight brew-ups to get on with the grisly business.

The trenches here are a nightmare to navigate, even in the day-time, a confusing rat's maze even before the hasty advance and the

addition of new trenches in the past two days, and last night, in the
rain, the maze was almost beyond human mastery. Nonetheless, I
led burial parties to places along the row of old German trenches,
hoping all the while not to leave our section altogether and blunder
into active Boche lines. There was little to do except to direct the
men in the pulling of corpses dressed in khaki off the rolls of still-
standing wire. There were more bodies in the innumerable shell
craters, of course, but I decided to leave those alone in the dark and
rain. A living man can drown in one of those craters. The dead are
in no hurry to leave them.

This entire front stinks of death and decay and the smell has
already permeated my new uniform. It never leaves one and one
does not seem to grow completely used to it according to my
chums in the 34th who have been here since replacing the French.
It was worse, of course, out among the corpse-filled craters and
body-strewn wire of what only yesterday had been No Man's Land.

Our burial parties moved forward warily under the sputtering
light of Very flares and the incessant heat-lightning flash of artillery. Neither the German guns nor our own had let up their duel-
ing from the day's battle (we lost thirteen men merely moving the
mile from the Tara-Usna Ridge to the forward communications
trenches behind the Front) and whatever advantage we held over
snipers in the dark certainly seemed negated by the effect of the
heavier nighttime shelling.

There were hundreds of bodies on the wire just in our small
section of line and I had the NCOs tell the men to concentrate on
these, ignoring, as I said, those in the shellholes and former German trenches. Naturally there were hundreds of German bodies
there as well as the British dead, and the other two lieutenants and I
decided that it would be easier to sort these out in the daylight.

The procedure was rather straightforward. Each detail consisted
of men to pull our comrades' bodies from the wire, often leaving
chunks of the corpse behind, other men to gather identity disks,
stretcher bearers to carry each corpse to the crater, and a final
group of men to gather up rifles and other recoverable equipment.
At the crater, the bodies were merely tipped over without memorial
service or farewell. In the red light of flares, I watched as several of

these dead men—some of whom I may well have met or known during my week of liaison with the 34th Division—went rolling gently, almost comically, down the muddy slope in the rain and dark. No effort was made to identify individuals at this point. Their identity disks will be perused later and the appropriate letters written and posted.

The bodies roll very slowly, usually burying themselves in the chalk and sucking mud before reaching the noxious green lake of gas and decay at the bottom of the crater. Once, as I watched, a shell struck the lip of the crater where a work party of six men were lifting corpses off stretchers and bits of the recently quick and the recently dead all went spiraling out over the hungry maw of the pit. Two wounded men were helped back toward the aid station—I do not know if their helpers ever *found* the aid station—while the rest of the mutilated burial detail (or at least as much as could be found) were merely shoved down into the crater along with the bodies they had been handling only moments before.

We are ordered to occupy the forward trenches, but these are also mass graves.

> *And clink of shovels deepening the shallow trench.*
> *The place was rotten with dead; green clumsy legs*
> *High-booted, sprawled and grovelled along the saps*
> *And trunks, face downward, in the sucking mud,*
> *Wallowed like trodden sandbags loosely filled;*
> *And naked sodden buttocks, mats of hair,*
> *Bulged, clotted heads slept in the plastering slime*[1]

But I must write of what has caused me to start this new and private diary.

I know that I will die here at the Somme. I am certain of it.

And I know now that I am a coward.

During the past few months of training at Auxi-le-Château, or the billet time before that at Hannescamps, I had suspected that my nervous tendencies and poetic inclinations indicated a lack of nerve. But I had told myself that I was merely green, that it was merely a case of the usual jitters, of the new subaltern getting the wind up during his first exposure to the Front.

But now I know better.

I am a coward. I want to live and nothing—not King, not Country, not even saving home and family and Western Civilization from the slavering Hun—seems worth dying for.

It was getting on toward dawn and I had sent back the last burial party—Sergeant Jowett, Corporal Newey, Bobby Wood, Frank Bell, and several of the other boys who had worked at W. H. Smith's in Nottingham and who had joined together—when I tried to find my way back to Battalion H.Q. via a series of low communications trenches. Any trip through these interlocking lines of zigzagging wounds in the wet earth can take an absurd amount of time—last week I became lost trying to find 34th Divisional Headquarters and spent almost an hour traversing a few hundred yards—but this morning I was completely, totally, irrevocably, irretrievably lost. And alone. Finally, when I realized that the trench system which I was traversing was deeper than any British trench I had ever seen, that the junction signs—too dim to decipher in Very light without igniting a flame on my trench lighter, which I was not about to do —were nonetheless visibly written in *Fraktur*, and that the corpses against which I had been brushing were wearing higher boots and sharper tin hats than the honest British dead, I decided that I had blundered into a section of German trench which was—I sincerely hoped—only recently captured and not yet manned against counterattacks.

I sat down to wait for daylight.

It was several minutes before I realized that someone was sitting directly opposite me in the rain, his pale face appearing to study me quite intensely.

I admit that I started rather violently and reached for my pistol before I realized that it was only another corpse. It was helmetless, and I could not make out the color of the uniform fabric—all uniforms seem composed of mud at any rate—but the protruding legs seemed booted more in the Boche manner than in Blighty leather. {*Ed. note—British Tommies along the Somme at this time often referred to England and things English as Blighty.*}

As I sat there waiting for dawn to reach forth her rosy fingertips, or at least for the black rain to turn to grey drizzle, I studied the man—what had been a man only days or hours before—in the red light of flares and the orange and magnesium-white pulse of exploding shells. I think the rain had let up a bit, or I had become used to it. I had left my valise {*Ed. note—some officers carried their sleeping gear in a sort of portmanteau*} and oilsheet where the Brigade had come onto the line, so I merely huddled miserably against the front of the trench since my friend seemed comfortable leaning against the parados {*Ed. note—the backside of the trench, the front being the parapet*} and satisfied myself in letting the rain drip from my tin hat onto my drenched lap.

Rats had been busy with my friend. This was no surprise, since most of the corpses we had witnessed this long day and longer night had a dead rat or two as quiet company. Sergeant Jowett, who has spent more time in the forward trenches than any of the rest of us, explained that a certain number of the giant vermin literally gorge themselves to death on the flesh of our comrades. During the first days on the line, he explained, the men tend to take it personally and to use bayonets to stab the slower-moving overstuffed creatures and toss them out into No Man's Land. But soon enough, he says, one learns to ignore the living rats, much less the dead.

There were no dead rats here tonight. At least none that I could see in the rain and mud. I began to make deductions about my friend's fate. He appeared to be almost one with the trench wall, as if he had been slammed back into it by a great force of exploding shell or a tossed Mills bomb. But his clothing and limbs were visibly intact, so that presumption seemed less than probable. It was more likely that he had been shot, had slumped against this trench wall, and one or more days of rain had brought the mud packing down around him in a sort of vertical burial. His hands were visible and very white. His clothes seemed to fit him wonderfully well, better than any quartermaster had ever clothed any living German infantry soldier—or British one either for that matter—but this sartorial precision was the result of gasses bloating the body so that expanding wet wool and leather almost creaked in protest.

I had seen this before, this deceptive rotundity of the dead.

My friend's fatal wound seemed quite visible and—to me—
most terrible.

The rats and carrion birds had taken his eyes, of course, but the
eyelids seemed intact right down to the lashes and he seemed to
gaze at me with these black oval pits. And there was a third eye
precisely in the center of his pale forehead. Sometimes, when the
Very flares sputtered near the end of their descending lifetime, one
or more of these three eyes seemed to wink and blink at me in
some sort of necromantical conspiracy, as if saying—*You too will
soon know this stillness.*

A Lee Enfield such as those the men in my rifle brigade carry
and which almost certainly inflicted the visible wound in my friend,
does not leave a dramatic entrance hole. Usually the German shooting victims we had passed on the roads coming up had little more
than a neat, bluish, bloodless, eye-sized or smaller aperture in the
side that had been facing our marksmen. Of course, they—like my
friend here—might have an exit hole large enough to put one's fist
in, large enough to spill the entire contents of his cranium out in a
widening fan of brain and blood, but these details were mercifully
hidden by the trench wall of which he seemed intent on becoming a
part.

I confess here that this single, simple wound caused terror in me
because I have always had an abnormal fear of being struck in the
face. When other boys had faced off with fists at school, I had
backed away from confrontation. Not, I told myself, because I
feared pain—I feel that I deal with pain as well as the next boy or
man—but precisely because the thought of a closed fist *coming
toward my eyes and face* made me sick with revulsion and terror.

And now this. A bullet from one of our rifles, or—more rele-
vantly, from its counterpart German Mauser—travels at almost
half a mile per second, arriving twice as quickly as the sound of the
shot itself.

*Directly toward one's face. At one's eyes. Sharp metal flying directly at the
eyes—the "darling of one's senses."* The thought is insupportable.

I watched my friend and eventually I tore my gaze away from his
unblinking tripartite stare.

I believe he had been young. Younger than my twenty-eight years certainly. Through the mud, there was the hint of short blond hair. The rats had left the flesh of his face surprisingly alone, suiting themselves to only a few long strips torn away around the cheek-bones and jaw. These looked like mere finger scratches in the flarelight as water dripped from his nose and brow and strong chin.

What fascinated me were his teeth. The lips themselves may once have been full, even sensuous, but a day or more in the July sun had withered these and pulled them away from the teeth and gums so that even in the dim light I could see the bulging expanse of white and pink. The teeth were too perfect and protruded as if my friend were trying to spit out some final discharge, even if only an epithet at the injustice of his own banal death here.

As I sat staring, accustomizing myself to his presence there and my own presence *here*—here in the theatre of almost certain death where pieces of sharp metal come flying at one's eyes faster than one can perceive or dodge—I realized that those teeth, that jaw, were moving.

At first I thought it a trick of the flickering light, for although the shelling had subsided somewhat, more flares were drifting down as both the Boche and British lines anticipated the pre-dawn patrols through No Man's Land.

It was not the light. I leaned forward, thrusting my own face within a yard of my friend's.

The jaw was moving. I could hear it as dried and withered tendons stretched and popped.

The great white teeth—dentures, I realized now, for although the face was young, the teeth were certainly artificial—began to part. The entire face began to squirm, as if my friend were attempting to separate himself from the muddy trench wall and lean forward to join me in an open-mouthed kiss at the center of the pit.

I could not move. I could not breathe, even as the white teeth opened further and a great hiss of escaping gas billowed out and over me, bringing a stench of internal corruption worse than mustard gas or phosgene. The jaws worked. The throat writhed as if my dead friend were struggling against all the bonds of Hades to make one final utterance, perhaps to impart one final warning.

Then the dentures fell out, tumbling and chattering across the sunken, muddy chest, the throat and jaw writhed a final time, the mouth opened wide into a purely black, hissing oval, then stretched further into some obscene simulacrum of birth . . . and then an oily black rat—huge, its sleek body as long as a weasel's, its eyes black and arrogant—forced its way out between withered lips and rotting gums.

I did not move as the rat scuttled over me in its slow escape. It was well fed and in no hurry.

I did not move for some time after the rat had gone, but sat staring at my friend's chest and belly and wondering if I perceived other movement there.

I—my kind, my comrades and I—had brought about this young man's terrible pregnancy.

Who, I wondered, *will bring this gift to me?*

I did not move until the sun was well and truly up and three men from B Company, 13th Platoon, found me while foraging for souvenirs. This trench was not a true connecting trench at all, only a fortified extension of a sunken road the Germans had defended. It was beyond our lines, but well back from the new German position and somewhat shielded by a low ridge. The boys from B Company led me back.

I returned to the Battalion H.Q., made sure that the men of my company had been billeted in their rough dugouts, and then absently joined two men from my brigade, a certain Rifleman Monckton and Corporal Hoyles, as they brewed their morning tea.

A few minutes ago, just as I finished the first part of this entry, the Colonel came along with an officer from Staff. The Staff Captain climbed onto the firestep, peered oh-so-cautiously above the parapet toward the old No Man's Land where my men had been retrieving bodies from the wire all night, spied the hundreds of sun-blackened British corpses still lying about, and said to Colonel Pretor-Pinney, "Good God, I didn't know we were using Colonial troops!"

The Colonel said nothing. Eventually they left. "Dear God," Monckton muttered to the Corporal near him, "hasn't that bastard ever seen a dead man before?"

I moved away from the enlisted men before duty required me to officially overhear and reprimand them. I began laughing then. I was able to stop only seconds ago. My tears of laughter have smudged some of the lines on this page.

It is just 9 A.M. So begins our first day on the line.

Sunday, 9 July—

Have not slept since Thursday. The Captain says that the Rifle Brigade has been chosen to lead the way when we go over the top —probably tomorrow.

The Colonel came up to ask me about the Big Push of July the first. He had sent me up to visit my friend Siegfried {*Ed. note— Siegfried Sassoon*} in A Company and to watch the attack so that I could later describe it to him, the Colonel, but I wasn't able to locate Siegfried or Robert {*Ed. note—Graves perhaps? James Edwin Rooke had known both of these poets before the war*}. I *did* run across another friend, Edmund Dadd, and he allowed me to watch with the other officers from their position in reserve. Dadd and his fellows in the Royal Welch Fusiliers had a brilliant view of the 21st Division advance and the Manchester Pals attack.

Colonel Pretor-Pinney came by today in the early afternoon, peered up at the mirror above our parapet—vibrating now as the enemy was dropping 5.9s near us—and said, "Well Jimmy. What did you see last week?"

In the past week I had grown confident that the Old Man would never ask. Now, with our own Big Push less than twenty hours away, I could see that he needed to know. "Where do you want me to start, Sir?" I asked.

The Colonel offered me a cigarette from a gold case, tamped his against the case, lighted both of ours with his trench lighter, and said, "The barrage. Start with the barrage. I mean, we heard it in Albert, of course . . ." He trailed off. Our bombardment of German lines had gone on for seven days. It was said in the trenches that they had heard the guns in Blighty. Everyone from Sir Douglas {*Ed. note—Sir Douglas Haig, Commander-in-Chief of British forces*} on down had said that after such a bombardment, the Big Push would be a walkover. Most of the lads I'd known in the 34th had been worried that they wouldn't get to the German trenches in time to find the best souvenirs.

"It was a sight to watch, Sir," I said.

"Yes, yes, but the *effect*," said the Colonel. His voice was still soft—I had rarely heard the Colonel raise his voice—but there was more emotion there than I had heard before. I watched him pick a shred of tobacco from his tongue while he composed himself. "What was the effect on the wire, Jimmy?"

"Negligible, Sir. The wire was uncut in most places. The Manchesters had to bunch up in the few places where there were holes in the German wire. Most of them fell then."

The Colonel was nodding. He had heard the casualty reports during the past week. Forty thousand of our finest men had fallen before breakfast that day. "So the shelling had little effect on their wire?"

"Almost none, Sir."

"How soon did the German snipers and machine guns open up?"

"Immediately, Sir. Men were hit as soon as they lifted their heads above the parapet of the New Trench."

The Colonel continued nodding but I could see that the movement was automatic. He was thinking of something else. "And the men, Jimmy? How did the Manchesters comport themselves?"

"Brilliantly," I said. It was both the absolute truth and the greatest lie I had ever told. The Manchesters had shown profound courage—walking upright into the machine-gun fire as if they were on dress parade. As if they were walking to the theatre. But is it brilliance when one advances like a lamb to slaughter? Our Battalion had buried thousands of these brilliant lads in the past twenty-four hours.

"Good," said Colonel Pretor-Pinney, absently tapping my shoulder. "Good. I know our chaps will be equally splendid in the morning."

It was the first confirmation I had heard that the Push was definitely set for tomorrow morning. I have always disliked Mondays.

After the Colonel had left, squelching down the line of trench, chatting up the lads along the firesteps as he went, I glanced down at my hand holding the burning cigarette. It was shaking as if palsied.

Monday, 10 July, 4.45 A.M.—

No sleep again tonight. I was tapped for a night patrol. Absolute waste of our time, three hours of crawling around in No Man's Land with ten of my men. All as terrified as I, only they were allowed to show it. No intelligence garnered. No prisoners gathered. But no casualties either. We were lucky to find our way back through the desolation.

The Night Patrol

[Ed. note—Several lines were crossed out here.]

> . . . *and everywhere the dead.*
> *Only the dead were always present—present*
> *As a vile sickly smell of rottenness;*
> *The rustling stubble and the early grass,*
> *The slimy pools—the dead men stank through all,*
> *Pungent and sharp; as bodies loomed before,*
> *And as we passed they stank: then dulled away*
> *To that vague foetor, all encompassing*
> *Infecting earth and air.*[2]

[Ed. note—A page has been roughly torn out here with only two words remaining on the serrated stub—"pure terror . . ." The verse on the next page appears to be a separate poem.]

> *We had no light to see by, save the flares.*
> *On such a trail, so lit, for ninety yards*
> *We crawled on belly and elbows, till we saw,*
> *Instead of the lumpish dead before our eyes,*
> *The stakes and crosslines of the German wire.*
> *We lay in shelter of the last dead man,*
> *Ourselves as dead, and heard their shovels ring*
> *Turning the earth, then talk and cough at times.*
> *A sentry fired and a machine gun spat;*
> *They shot a flare above us, when it fell*

414 · Dan Simmons

> *And spluttered out in the pools of No Man's Land,*
> *We turned and crawled past the remembered dead:*
> *Past him and him, and them and him . . .*
> *And through the wire and home, and got our rum.*[3]

Monday, 10 July, 8.05 A.M.—

A beautiful morning. I know I am to die and it seems a cruel irony to die on such a perfect day.

In the night, during the patrol, all was mud and slime and slither. Then a summer sunrise. A vapor is rising from the trenches and shell holes as the fierce summer sun strikes the pools of foetid water. Here in the forward trench, German corpses remain and I can see vapor streaming skyward from the sodden wool uniforms on several of the bodies. Like souls fleeing heavenward from . . .

. . . from Hell? It seems so banal to write that. It does not sound like Hell. I can hear a lark from the direction of la Boisselle.

Colonel Pretor-Pinney and Captain Smith from D Company came by seconds ago and the Colonel said softly, "We go over at 8.45. Set your watches."

I did so, removing my father's silver watch and carefully setting it to match the Colonel's and the Captain's. It is 8.22. My father's watch had read 8.18 when I had to reset it to 8.21. I lost three minutes of life merely by setting a watch.

A strange calmness has descended upon me.

Oddly, there has been no bombardment for the past hour or so. The silence is deafening. I had overheard Colonel Pretor-Pinney tell Major Sir Foster Cunliffe that the bombardment had ended ten minutes early on July the first because of a mistaken communication to the artillery blokes. I wonder if a similar mistake has been made this morning.

From my position near the periscope—actually just a mirror set on a pole above the parapet—I can see a small wood a few hundred yards ahead of the trenches. To the right of the wood—largely splintered trunks, but a few whole trees remaining—lies another copse of shattered trunks and the remnants of the village of Contalmaison. Our chaps in the 23rd Division chased Jerry out of that village yesterday evening and now our Battalion is set to chase them out of their trenches. I wish we had learned more from the patrol last night.

The nearest Germans are only a 150 yards or so ahead of us. One could kick a football there. (My friend from the 2nd Welch Fusiliers, Eddie Dadd, told me that some of the chaps *did* kick a football ahead of them on the morning of the Big Push. It was a Pals Battalion of footballers and South African ruggers who'd joined up together. Eddie said that out of one 40-man platoon, only one man returned . . .)

8.30. Sergeants Laney on my left and Cross on my right are going up and down the lines, warning the men not to bunch up. "If you bunch up, they'll pick you off like rabbits," Sergeant Laney is saying. The words are oddly calming.

Of course they will pick us off like rabbits. I remember, as a child of about six, watching my father skin a rabbit. One incision and a tug and the fur slipped off like a guest shedding a coat, with only sticky strands of thin, gummy stuff connecting it to the pale blue flesh.

8.32. What is a poet doing here? What are any of us doing here? I would say something inspiring to the men, but my mouth is so dry that I doubt if I could speak.

8.38. Hundreds of bayonets. They gleam in the bright sunlight. Sergeant Cross is snapping at the men to keep their bayonets below the line of the parapet. As if the Germans do not know we are coming. Where the goddamn hell is the bombardment the Colonel said they promised us?

8.40. I know what might save me. A litany of life. The things I love in ways that only a living person may love and a poet can articulate—

—white cups, clean-gleaming

—wet roofs beneath the lamp-light

—the strong crust of friendly bread and many-tasting food

—the comfortable smell of friendly fingers

—live hair that is shining and free

—the unpassioned beauty of a great machine

8.42. Jesus Christ, oh Jesus. I do not love God but I love life.

The cool kindliness of sheets. Radiant raindrops crouching in cool flowers. The rough kiss of clean blankets.[4] Christ, to lose all this?

8.43. Women. I do love women. The clean-smell powder-and-talc scent of women. Their pale skin and pale pink nipples in candlelight. Their gentleness and firmness and the muskscent terrible wetness . . .

8.44. I will think of women. I will close my eyes and think of a litany of femaleness, scent and touch of life womanness. All things alive and vital in {*Ed. note—This line unfinished.*}

8.45. Whistles blowing down the line. I will try to blow mine. Sergeants pushing the men up and out. Other NCOs leading. Will follow in . . . {*Ed. note—illegible*} . . . not fair.

A litany of feminine life force. Muse protects.

Good-bye.

{*Ed. note—It is well known that J.E.R.'s other trench diary ends here. Or, rather, with the following terse note.*}

10-7–16, 8.15 A.M.—The Colonel passes among us a final time and I prepare my men to go over the top. Our big guns remain silent. Perhaps the Staff do not want to spoil the surprise we have in store for the Germans. I joked with Sergeant Cross that I hoped Jerry was cooking breakfast as I was ravished with hunger. Gave the chaps a good laugh.

{*Ed. note—It might be noted that the poems seen here in rough form have often been misdated. "The Night Patrol" is often quoted as being the result of J.E.R.'s observation of a night patrol returning on 30 June while he was observing with the 2nd Welch Fusiliers. The bit of verse beginning "And clink of shovels . . ." is usually attributed to the previous Christmas when the 13th Rifle Brigade was comfortably billeted at Hannescamps and Lieutenant Rooke was assigned to his first burial detail. What has been described elsewhere as ". . . a brilliant young poet's active imagination turned toward the perceived horrors of the Front" turns out to be simple reportage rather than poetic imagination.*

Finally, the segment dealing with the actual experience of a night patrol—"We had no light to see by, save the flares."—is not to be found in any edition of Trench Poems. *It is obvious, to this bibliographer at least, that J.E.R. was working toward a longer, more definitive version of* The Night Patrol *and would have realized it had not circumstances intervened.*}

Friday, 14 July—

The Lady is not with me tonight. She was here earlier, but the doctors made noise and she has not returned. I smell her scent.

Brickers, next to me, the one with half a face who has managed to moan every hour I have been conscious, died a few minutes ago. The gargle and rattle were unmistakable.

The Lady was here then. She is not here now. I pray for her return.

Saturday, 15 July, 9.30 A.M.—

I am more cognizant of my whereabouts today. I recognize the pounding of guns. Sister Paul Marie, the nicer of the two nuns who nurse us, tells me that there is another Big Push underway. The thought makes my skin crawl.

I believe my Lady was here in the night—I remember her touch—but everything else from the past few days is a strange, pain-riddled blur. When I first became aware of myself and my surroundings yesterday, on my bedside table there were two items which I had brought back from No Man's Land: my father's watch, stopped now at 10.08, and the secret diary in which I had been scribbling just before we went Over the Top. It seems that I carried these two things in my hands during the attack. When I finally reached the dressing station some two days later, the watch was still firmly gripped in my left hand and the journal had somehow been transferred to the pocket of my blouse—almost the only bit of clothing on me that had not been shredded.

Let me describe my surroundings. I am in an RAMC forward hospital {*Ed. note—Royal Army Medical Corps*} just outside of Albert. Because this village is only two miles from the Front, this place is a kind of way stop between the crude dressing stations and field surgical hospitals closer to the Front and the true Base Hospitals much further back. (Many in England herself.) This "hospital" consists of three whitewashed rooms in what may have been part of the convent here. From my window I can see the Golden Virgin. {*Ed. note—In the center of the village of Albert was a large church and on its spire was a gilded statue of the Virgin Mary holding the infant Jesus above her head. The statue was struck by a German shell in 1915 and had been leaning at right angles to the spire ever since. The journals of Sassoon, Graves, Masefield and a hundred lesser names mention marching to the Front under this bizarre landmark. A legend had grown up on both sides of the Front that if the Virgin fell, the war would end. German troops added the coda that if the statue did indeed fall, Germany would be the victor. French engineers then quickly secured the hanging Madonna and Infant with steel hawsers. It remained in that position until Germans reoccupied Albert in 1918 and began using the steeple as an observation post, at which time British gunfire brought down both steeple and Virgin. }*

Albert is all but abandoned by civilians but somehow manages to continue to exist here so close to the fighting. Some of our artillery is *behind* the village. Troops move through in both directions by day and night and sleep is almost impossible due to the noise of their tramping, the clomp of horses' hooves, and the cursing of men tugging large guns through the mud. My hospital mates here are all officers and I understand from Sister Paul Marie's comments that this place is only for those too seriously injured to travel toward Amiens and home, or for those injured so slightly that they will soon return to the Front. I count myself unlucky to be listed in the latter category.

There are about a dozen men in my ward, several of them officers from the Rifle Brigade. Most are dying. One chap, a captain, has had both legs blown off and the stench of gangrene fills the ward at all times. Another fellow, a lieutenant such as myself, was shot through the brain and talks incessantly, wooing the poor nun as if she were his lover. An older man, a major, returns to the surgical tent every day to have a bit more of his leg sawed off. He also has the smell of gangrene and death around him, but he never complains, but merely lies on his bed and stares fixedly at the ceiling.

Sister Paul Marie tells me that Colonel Pretor-Pinney is receiving special care in the field hospital next door, still too badly wounded to be sent down the rail line to hospital. She said that his left arm had been shredded by machine-gun bullets. I knew that. I saw it happen.

Almost all of the officers in our Battalion have been killed, including all four company commanders. I also saw them die. Most of the other platoon commanders were also killed. I understand that Lieutenant Fitzgibbon was a fellow survivor, but he was so badly wounded that he was sent immediately home to Blighty. Most of our sergeants were cut down—including Cross and Monckton—but there is hope that some survived. There is much confusion after a battle.

I seem to be the only "slightly wounded" in the ward, suffering as I am from what is described as "concussion paralysis" and a case of pneumonia from the two nights lying in the shell hole. The pneumonia is bothersome, especially as they come in to drain my lungs every day with a needle literally the size of a bicycle pump— they hold me in place while they insert the needle through my back—but much worse than that is the terrible pain of feeling finally returning to my numbed legs. It is as if they have been asleep for four or five days, and the pins-and-needles sensation of their awakening may well drive me mad.

The young officer with no legs has just died. First they put a screen around his bed, then men come in with a stretcher to remove his body. Covered as he is, the form under the blanket looks much too small to have ever been a man.

The lieutenant who is shot through the skull continues to call for his nurse/nun/lover in a voice that grows increasingly wild. I suspect that he will not last the night.

I think of this place as the vestibule of Hell. Obviously some other literate soul has had similar thoughts, for written in charcoal on the wall near the window through which I can see the Golden Virgin are the words "PER ME SI VA NE LA CITTA DOLENTE, PER ME SI VA NE L'ETTERNO DOLORE, PER ME SI VA TRA LA PERDUTA GENTE." Sister Paul Marie tells me that the nuns leave it there because the officer who scribbled it told them that it was a poem attesting to the gentleness of care at this place. Obviously none of the nuns know neither Italian nor their Dante.

The quote is from the Inferno, of course, and reads—"THROUGH ME THE WAY INTO THE SUFFERING CITY, THROUGH ME THE WAY TO THE ETERNAL PAIN, THROUGH ME THE WAY THAT RUNS AMONG THE LOST."

The doctors are coming with their accursed needle. I will write later.

Saturday, 15 July, almost midnight—
The guns are very loud. I can see the Virgin and Child backlighted by the gunflashes as light from the incessant bombardment falls across the whitewashed floorboards like the flickering from some unseen fireplace.

The only other person in the ward who seems to be awake is the victim of phosgene gas who lies across the aisle from me. The noise he makes is a terrible thing. I try not to look at him, but every few seconds I steal a glance.

> . . . the white eyes writhing in his face,
> His hanging face, like a devil's sick of sin;
> If you could hear, at every holt, the blood
> Come gargling from the froth-corrupted lungs,
> Obscene as cancer, bitter as the cud
> Of vile, incurable sores on innocent tongues . . .[5]

Each breath the poor devil takes extorts a terrible price in pain and effort. I can not imagine he can live until morning, or even through ten more of such terrible breaths . . . but I have counted ten even while I waited to write this. Perhaps he will be doomed to live until morning and even beyond, although why such pain is inflicted on any living thing is quite beyond me. It makes Christ's so-called agony on the cross a petty thing.

I have not been able to sleep because I wait for the Lady's visit. Traces of her violet perfume remain on my own wrist and pajama sleeve and I raise these to my face when the stench from the gangrene becomes too bad.

I was sure that she would return tonight.

I think that I will write about the attack while I wait. Perhaps if I write about it, I will not dream about it again.

We went up and over at 8.45. I knew that at places in front of us, the Jerries' line was a third of a mile or so away, but our objective was a bit of enemy trench only a couple of hundred yards in front of us. I convinced myself that this was a definite advantage for our chaps, and then I clambered up the side of the trench and was out.

My first impression upon leaving the trench was a sort of light-headedness at being able to walk above ground. Then I thought giddily, *There are bees up here.* The air was absolutely filled with a *zzzp-zzzp* sound, precisely like the time when I was a boy and had disturbed a large hive of bees in Mr. Alknut's garden. When I saw the tufts of dirt leaping up ahead of and to the side of me, I realized that the noise was nothing less than bullets. I almost stopped then, so terrible was my fear of a steel-jacketed bullet striking me square in the face, but I squinted until my eyes were almost closed, leaned forward a bit, and forced myself to move forward with the lads.

All up and down the line, our men were moving forward into this murderous fire—first the officers and NCOs, then the riflemen with bayonets fixed, and then the Lewis gunners and their ammunition carriers struggling under loads. I noticed then that everyone out there—myself included—walked into the enemy fire in a sort of a diagonal crouch, as if we were all leaning into a strong wind or rain. Sergeants continued shouting at members of their platoons to keep apart and not to bunch up. Men began to fall as I watched through squinted eyes.

It was strange, actually. Men just fell over, almost casually, as if they were children playing at war. I thought at first that some of this was pure funk . . . but there was no more cover where they fell, and even as I watched more bullets struck their bodies, causing them to jerk only slightly. The sound of bullets striking flesh was almost exactly like the *pat-thud* of bullets striking the sandbags which we had all heard from the trenches. And everywhere the air continued to be filled with the *zzzp-zzzp*.

My fear was so terrible at this point that it was everything I could do to stay upright and balanced as I advanced, stepping carefully over shell holes and rotting corpses. The earth leaped up in front of me and behind. Somehow, my mind stayed quite detached.

I had begun the walk with a dozen or more of the lads from my platoon, but one by one they had fallen away. I stopped by one lying prone and asked, "Are you hurt?"

"What the fuck do you think I'm doing down here, you bleeding toff bastard?" the rude fellow shouted at me. "Picking fucking daisies?" Then a machine-gun bullet struck the precise center of the man's helmet, he vomited brains, and I moved on.

Finally only a man whom I vaguely recognized as Corporal Woodlock from No. 11 Platoon, and I, were left. We were less than fifty yards from the enemy wire when Corporal Woodlock began laughing. "Jesus Christ, Sir!" he shouted, as giddy as a schoolboy. "Jesus Christ, Sir, I think we're the only ones who're going to get through this bloody lot!" He giggled. "Jesus Christ, Sir . . ." he began again just as several bullets tore the khaki above his chest into maroon shreds. He fell sideways into a shallow crater and I put my notebook into my blouse pocket, checked my watch, and ambled forward.

There was only a single gap in the wire in front of us and No. 8 Platoon, which had preceded us, made for it. I thought then that they looked a bit like lambs filling up a chute to the slaughter. The German machine guns opened up from fifty feet away and every member of that platoon went down in a bloody heap.

My eyes almost closed, I thought of women I had known and seduced. I visualized their skin, their lips, the color of their eyes, and their sweet smell. I imagined their touch.

Shells started falling. Bits of Corporal Woodlock erupted from his shell hole, mixed with the fragments of corpses which had been there since the Big Push of July first. The Corporal's head, helmet still firmly affixed and chin strap tightened, landed at my feet and rolled.

The hole in the wire ahead of me was clogged three high with the bodies of the men of No. 8 Platoon, so I turned left and began making for a stretch of No Man's Land where I could see men of the Rifle Brigade still standing, still advancing. I knew from the maps that somewhere ahead of me was the so-called "chalk pit," a small quarry which the enemy had fortified.

At this point I glanced to my right to see the 25th Division which was supposed to have been supporting us on that flank. No one was there. I looked far to the left to see the 23rd Division who were supposed to be attacking on our left. The field was empty. I turned around, hearing the *zzzzp-zzzzp* past my ears, to see if the 13th Fusiliers had come out in the second wave as planned. There was no second wave.

"Get down, man!" It was Colonel Pretor-Pinney crouching in a shell hole. I stepped down into it with him.

"Jimmy," he gasped. "I don't believe we can . . ." A runner stumbled into the hole and thrust a message into the Colonel's hands.

"Attack canceled, Sir," panted the boy.

The Colonel stared unbelievingly at the message. "That explains the lack of bombardment. The reason the 23rd and 25th did not come out." He crumpled the message. "It was canceled before we shoved off, Jimmy. This just did not get to us in time." He leveraged himself up over the front edge of the hole. More 5.9s and whizz-bangs were falling near us now.

"Jimmy," he said, "the chaps from Thirteen Platoon have already made it into the Boche trenches. Someone will have to go forward and tell them . . ."

"I will, Sir!" said the young runner.

Colonel Pretor-Pinney nodded and the boy leapt out of the shell hole with the speed and courage of the very young who know that they are immortal. The machine guns caught him less than ten yards out and almost tore him in half.

The Colonel looked at me. "Well, there's nothing for it then, Jimmy." We clambered out of the trench and moved forward together, leaning into the noise as if breasting a strong wind.

Some men were still alive in shell holes. Most had rid themselves of pack and rifles, clutching themselves into small spheres of fear. I saw the Colonel look left, and there in one hole were all four of our company commanders and several of their aides, crouching and pointing in different directions.

"Break that up, you bloody fools!" shouted Colonel Pretor-Pinney and then an explosion absolutely filled the crater with dust and shrapnel. When the smoke cleared, only bits of men remained.

We had almost reached the bit of fortified road near the chalk

pit when the Colonel spun and went down heavily. I crouched next
to him for a moment. The twin bones of his forearm were clearly
visible through the mangled flesh. His lips formed words but I was
quite deaf to them. I knew that this was my only opportunity to
live; to pick up the Colonel and carry him back to the trenches. I
might even receive a medal.

Squinting even more fiercely, I turned away and walked toward
the enemy trenches.

I do not remember reaching the German lines, nor dropping
into their trenches, but I clearly remember the German sergeant
who came around the corner of a zigzag and shouted something at
me. I am not sure which of us was more startled. I remember
thinking *The man is wearing his wool greatcoat . . . in July! He must be
mad.* And then the heavyset sergeant stopped shouting and began
fumbling for the rifle that was—inexplicably in such a context—
slung over his shoulder.

One of our lads had fallen here, his face in the mud, his Lee
Enfield lying just beyond the reach of his outflung hand. Without
thinking, I lifted the heavy rifle and marched forward at double
time, letting my father's watch dangle from the chain I had
wrapped twice around my wrist somewhere between the crater
where the Colonel had fallen and here.

The German had just got his own weapon to port arms when I
drove the bayonet under his guard and into his chest just below his
sternum. The bayonet was twenty-one inches long. It slid into the
thick wool of the man's greatcoat and out of sight so easily that it
seemed as if he and I were conspiring together in some amateur
magic act. I felt the sharpened-steel tip strike the mud of the trench
behind the sergeant.

The man looked at me quizzically, lifted his own rifle a bit so
that he could see the point of entry where my bayonet disappeared
into the wet wool over his belly, and then he sighed softly and
leaned back against the trench wall. I could feel a vibration coming
from the point where my steel had severed his spine. The sergeant
opened his mouth as if he were about to say something, but smiled
instead. When he fell more heavily against the trench wall, I
dropped my rifle as if it had grown suddenly hot to my touch. The

butt of it wedged in the mud and held the corpse almost upright, the rifle and his two splayed legs making a sort of tripod, his dead hands still clutching the rifle. The man's greatcoat hung in folds like a shroud.

I turned and walked back down the trench to find 13 Platoon to tell them that the attack had been canceled.

It was while coming back that the bad thing happened.

I had found the remnants of the Rifle Brigade fighting in captured trenches, unaware that the attack had been canceled or that it had been a mistake in the first place. The Germans had reinforced both the sunken road and their lines near the chalk pit so that the place was a viper's nest of concrete emplacements, machine-gun revetments, dugouts as deep as thirty feet, and a maze of duckboards and tunnels. Our lads had cleaned them out of a long stretch of this line and were holding their own against disorganized counterattacks.

Trench fighting is terrible in the best of circumstances, and in this warren, with the Battalion depleted and low on ammunition, it was worse than terrible. By early afternoon the Rifle Brigade had used up their Mills grenades and were perilously low on rounds for rifles and their two remaining Lewis guns. All of the telephone lines brought across No Man's Land at such a cost of life had been cut almost immediately by shellfire and attempts to communicate with our trenches via semaphore flasher or flags brought fire down on the signaler without fail.

I conferred with the one officer I could find, Captain Revere, and we decided to try to make our way back as soon as it was dusk.

True twilight did not deepen in this part of France until almost ten o'clock, and as soon as we thought it was dark enough to start back without drawing the attention of the Boche, Captain Revere ordered the men out of the trenches they had spilled so much blood to capture and defend through the long, hot day. They left in groups of three or four, fading away into the shadows of No Man's Land. The German machine-gunners seemed to take pity on us. Or perhaps they were as exhausted as we were.

I had shaken hands with Captain Revere and was finding my

own way across when the barrage opened up. I knew immediately from the sound that they were eighteen-inchers and that they were our own guns firing on us.

The fierce and terrible bombardment which had been promised us for the attack that morning had never arrived . . . until now. The entire field of No Man's Land that separated us from our own forward lines—about a thousand yards at this point—suddenly erupted in a solid sheet of flame and shrapnel. Once again I was squinting and leaning forward as the very atmosphere filled with metal. This time the fragments screamed by with a noise like *wwhh-hiiit* . . . the final consonant added when the shrapnel embedded itself in something. Many of the blasts were airbursts, which we all feared most deeply since the head was usually struck first and anything short of a dugout with a solid roof offered no cover whatsoever.

Behind us, the German machine guns opened up. The Boche had obviously already counterattacked and retaken the trenches we had just abandoned. There was no going forward. There was no going back. I felt like giggling as Corporal Woodlock had in his final seconds.

From what I have heard yesterday and today, I think that the 13th Rifle Brigade ceased to exist as a fighting unit about this time. Thinking that it was the Germans counterattacking from Con-talmaison, our own artillery tore us to shreds.

As for me, I found myself running aimlessly from shell hole to shell hole, ducking when the larger explosions came near, running through dirt and smoke when they seemed to be landing further away. I realized that my father's watch was still gripped tightly in my left hand, the chain still wound around my wrist.

This insanity could not continue forever and it did not. One minute I was running toward what I thought were friendly lines still some hundreds of yards away, and the next instant I felt a great blast behind me and I was literally flying, looking down on the battlefield as if from a great height. I thought at that second that I had been killed and that my soul had fled my body.

Then I landed and tumbled into a deep shell crater, my legs splashing into a pool of foetid green water in the bottom. I was unconscious for a while and when I awoke it was full dark and the bombardment was continuing. I had no doubt that another shell would find me at any moment, but I was beyond caring for the time being.

The blast had shredded my trousers until I was essentially naked from the waist down and I could not feel my legs where they disappeared into the brackish water. My upper tunic was also in rags, although my blouse had survived in front. My helmet was gone. I felt little pain above the great numbness that spread from my back down to my legs, but I was sure that I had to have been hit by some mortal piece of metal that even at that second lay deep in my numbed flesh. My hands were smudged as black as the rest of me, but they seemed intact and—after some moments of drifting in and out of consciousness—I used them to try to drag myself up and out of the water.

This was not a good idea. The top of my head was only inches below the edge of the steep shell crater, and as soon as I rose above this ad-hoc parapet, bullets and shrapnel whizzed by. I gave up struggling against the mud and slipped back down so that my legs disappeared again up to the thighs beneath dark water.

There were one or two others sharing my hole. I say one or two because to this day I do not know if it was one body or two lying across the six-foot pool from me. The bottom half of a torso lay on the mud, toes almost touching the lip of the crater. The bit of spinal cord visible glowed white each time a flare drifted down or an explosion lit the scene. The puttees and boots were decidedly British and I would have thought it was the lower half of my own body lying there if I had not already glimpsed my naked legs.

The top half of some chap's head protruded from the water, visage toward me. He had managed to keep his helmet on and the chinstrap seemed firmly attached. His eyes were open and staring at me very intensely indeed. I would have guessed that this was a clever fellow lying doggo, waiting for the bombardment to ease before lurching up for another try, except for the fact that both the man's mouth and nostrils were under water. There were no bubbles. He did not blink as minutes faded into hours.

With my legs useless, my wounds unable to be assessed while the general numbness persisted, and the bombardment continuing, I lay back in the shell-hole mud and waited to die as the barrage continued. When it ended, if I survived it, the Germans would send out patrols to finish the last of us with bayonets.

I admit that I lay there and tried to think philosophical thoughts, but the best I could do was remember the faces and names of all the girls I had bedded. It was not an unpleasant way to pass the time.

And then the pain in my back and chest began in earnest. I had prepared for this eventuality by bringing the regulation four morphia tablets allowed to each officer. Now I reached for them in my trouser pocket.

I had no trousers. Only rags and lacerations there.

I patted my blouse pocket, hoping against hope that I had put the morphia there in a fit of absent-mindedness, but all I found were this journal, a stub of pencil, and my silver whistle.

The pain rolled in like poison gas. I would have *welcomed* poison gas at this point, if only to put an end to the pain. I am, as I have admitted in these pages, not brave.

It was sometime after midnight and before dawn, as I writhed in the mud on the pinpoint of my dead comrade's unblinking stare, that *she* came.

The Lady. The one for whom I wait this night.

But perhaps the scratch of my pen or my upright posture keeps her from visiting. I will set the journal aside until another time and wait in the darkness between the flashes of the big guns.

Post Script: the gas victim across the aisle no longer breathes.

Sunday, 15 July, 9.00 A.M.—

The Lady did not come. Or at least I do not remember her being here. I cannot express the depth of my disappointment.

The nun—the brusque one, not Sister Paul Marie—explains the frenzied sound of our big guns by saying that there is a terrible battle being waged for High Wood. Most of the casualties streaming in, she says, are from the 33rd Division, especially the Church Lads' Brigade. She says that the wounds are more terrible than anything she has seen to date.

I have come to realize that this practice of filling Kitchener's quota by recruiting Pals Battalions will reap a terrible whirlwind of grief and that while it was almost certainly a grand idea from the recruitment point of view, it is leading to empty villages, churches, fire brigades, and entire professions where the cream of our generation there will have been wiped out in a single afternoon. {*Ed. note—Even now, few can have missed or forgotten the image of Lord Kitchener pointing from his poster stating unequivocally "Your Country Needs You." What modern readers may have forgotten, however, is that Kitchener did not bring in conscription to fill the ranks until January of 1916. Thus James Edwin Rooke and some two and a half million other men in khaki were volunteers. Rooke's opinion of the "Pals Battalions," where friends and acquaintances could join en masse, turned out to be entirely correct. Much of the impact of the carnage of WWI on Great Britain has been not just the numbers of dead, but the terrible focus of such loss on specific locales brought about by destruction of "Pals." Pals Battalions suffering more than 500 casualties (out of a battalion consisting of 1,000 men) at the Somme included the Accrington Pals, Leeds Pals, The Cambridge Battalion, Public Schools Battalion, 1st Bradford Pals, Glasgow Boys' Brigade Battalion, and the Co. Down Volunteers. And this was on the single day of 1 July.*}

The doctors and nurses came through a while ago to push the needle through my back and into my lungs. The noise it makes extracting fluid is beyond description, but rather reminds me of a circus elephant I once watched sucking up the last of a bucket of water. The circus was passing through Weald of Kent that leafy summer, and I wish to God I were there now.

The doctor left some papers he had wearily set down and I pilfered one of the forms to read. It is an autopsy report. I have been awake since before seven—the bells in the damaged steeple under the leaning Golden Virgin work very well indeed and are somehow more intrusive than the constant rumble and roar of guns—and I have been struggling with the poem I began last night about the gas victim whose breathing I still seem to hear despite his most definite absence.

The autopsy report seems more effective as poetry than my poor scribblings. I will reproduce it verbatim:

Case four: Aged 39
Years.
Gassed 4 July 1916.
Admitted to casualty clearing station
The same day.
Died about ten days later.
Brownish pigmentation present over large surfaces
Of the body. A white ring
Of skin
Where the wrist watch was.
Marked superficial burning of the face and
Scrotum.
The larynx much congested. The whole of the trachea
Was covered by a yellow membrane. The bronchi
Contained abundant gas. The lungs fairly
Voluminous.
The right lung showed extensive collapse at the base.
Liver congested
And fatty.
Stomach showed numerous
Submucous haemorrhages. The brain substance was
Unduly wet
And very congested.[6]

Merde. Poetry does not serve as poetry in this new age. And nonpoetry cannot masquerade as serviceable verse. Perhaps poetry is dead. Perhaps it deserved to die. Perhaps the poets do also.

The bells have stopped. Perhaps the half dozen faithful civilians still living in Albert have been driven in to Mass. The guns do not hesitate for a second. I pity The Church Lads' Brigade. For what they are about to receive, may those of us who are not there by truly thankful.

It is almost time to write about the Lady. I have hesitated to do so because anyone finding and reading my journal would think me mad.

I am not mad.

And this journal will be destroyed . . . *must* be destroyed. It is a poet's place to lay bare thoughts that others must deny even having, but poetry is dead and I soon will be and I refuse to leave these thoughts where prying eyes will find them.

And yet I must write about it all or go mad.

We had attacked on the 10th, watched our Rifle Brigade be destroyed by ten P.M., on the 10th, and all that night of the 10th I lay in the shell hole, half-delirious with the pain from legs that would not work for me, half out of my mind with thirst and fear. I admit that I drank from the green slime of that corpse-littered crater. I would have drunk my own urine by that second night. I almost certainly did.

I cannot forget the sound. It started that first night and had not died away completely by the time I crawled out of that hell on the evening of the 12th.

The sound was constant, yet it rose and fell almost like the precisely composed vagaries of a wind-tossed surf or the rustling of a million leaves on an autumn evening in Kent. Only there was nothing lulling or meditative about this sound: it was the noise of a thousand teeth scraping on a hundred slabs of slate; it was the noise of broken fingernails scrabbling; it was the hiss and gurgle and blood-rasp gaspings of gas victims fighting vainly for another mucous-filled breath.

It was the sound of the hundreds of our wounded lads in No Man's Land.

I confess that I added to that chorus. My own moans and inarticulate cries seemed to come from somewhere outside of me and at times I listened to them joining the common call of pain with a feeling more of embarrassment than horror.

Occasionally, above the dull explosions and rumble of guns and hammer of machine guns, there would be audible the flintlike clarity of a single rifle shot. And then one voice in the chorus of pain would be silenced. But the rest of us sang on.

All that second day—Tuesday the 11th—I lay between the shards of wire and bone. At one point I managed to drag myself up and sideways so that my nerveless legs were out of the water; I told

myself that I was afraid they would rot, but my real fear was that
something would grab me from beneath the surface of green scum.
The dead soldier continued to stare at me, with only the dark pits
and egg-whites of his eyes visible above the waterline and beneath
the helmet shadow. Those eyes receded visibly as I watched, sinking
into theskull as if retreating from the sight of me. The night before,
even in the unsteady light of flares and explosions, the dark of his
irises and pupils had been visible, but this second day the eyes were
white with the bubbled mass of fly eggs.

The bluebottle flies were so thick that sometimes I thought they
were a cloud of Valkyries that had descended on us. But they were
only flies. Their buzzing reminded me of the bullets; the buzzing
of bullets above me reminded me of the flies. I gave up trying to
brush the flies from my face and stirred only when they crawled
from my lips into my open mouth.

The steady background of moaning had slackened toward dusk
that second evening, but when it grew dark the volume rose again,
as if the dead had joined the dying in our song. I tried pulling
myself up when it was truly dark, my hands grabbing stones, my
elbows digging into mud, but as soon as my head came above the
lip of the shell hole, machine guns opened up. As many tracer
rounds came from the British line as from the German. Our lads
were obviously nervous and frightened of a counterattack.

One of these bullets took a warning nick out of my left ear.
Another cut through the tattered cloth of my blouse between my
left ribs and inner arm. I gave up the thought of crawling two
hundred yards through this and slid back into my brackish tomb.
The soldier seemed to welcome me back with a white wink. Rats
were tugging at the bottom half of the torso in the dark so that the
legs seemed to be attempting a feeble dance.

My hands had gained enough feeling so that I pitched stones at
the vermin. They ignored me. I preferred that to being the focus of
their attention.

I dozed in a half-conscious state where the growling of the big
guns wove the texture of my dreams. Suddenly, sometime before
dawn, I awoke. The Lady had come.

It seems insane now to admit that I felt little surprise. There had been talk of nurses coming as far as the Front lines, but this was only barracks' fantasy. At any rate, I knew this was no nurse. She did not stumble and slide down the steep crater wall; one minute she was simply *there*. I awoke to the touch of her hand on my cheek.

To describe her, even now after several of her visits, seems somehow sacrilegious. But perhaps if I do so with even a small fraction of the reverence I feel toward her, it will not harm the chances of her future coming.

She is fair. Not merely English fair as in an absence of sun, but fair with the radiance of a fine piece of white Carrara marble. There is a light about her features, which are classical but not refined to the point of what we now think of as ideal feminine beauty. Her nose is long and straight, her chin strong, her eyes set wide apart and quite dark. Her hair is not done in the current style; when I was in Paris and London last, the ladies were wearing their hair cut shorter, dressed low on the forehead and pulled back, covering only part of their ears and often ending in a coil or bun in the back. The Lady's hair is clasped somehow with combs on the side, but it still hangs loose, rather like that of a lady of my mother's generation when preparing for bed.

When she touched my cheek, I tried to speak, to warn her of the terrible danger out here in No Man's Land, but the Lady only touched my cracked lips with a finger and shook her head as if to silence me.

I noticed dully that she was wearing a gown quite unsuitable for a nurse or our environment; she wore a material which looked soft and silky such as crêpe de chine set in a style somewhere between a chemise and nightdress. But this was no undergarment or nightdress. The Lady's outfit was perfectly suited to her strong face and full figure. I felt as if Penelope had come for me to take me home from my wanderings.

I closed my eyes then, and in my half-dream I was still with her. We were no longer on the battlefield, but on the terrace of a fine home in the moonlight. The trees and summer night scent were familiar; I thought it might be Kent. The Lady was waiting for me at a wrought-iron table under an arbor. I approached and took my seat across from her, noticing that she was no longer wearing the soft gown but a more normal outfit, two pieces of peach-colored cotton, a basqued jacket shirred at the waist, broad sleeves ending in flounced cuffs, and an ankle-length skirt. Her auburn hair—I could see the color clearly now in the moonlight—was tied up in a more conventional manner and partially covered by a straw hat with a furred plume and a softly curving brim.

There was a tea set on a silver tray between us. When she tried to pour my tea, I reached to touch her. She pulled away, but was smiling.

"This is an hallucination," I said.

"Do you really think so?" she said softly. Her voice excited me as much as did her eyes.

"Yes," I said. "I'm dying in some . . ." I paused before saying "bloody shell hole." I may have been hallucinating upon the point of death, but that was no reason to lose my manners in front of a lady. ". . . in some banal shell hole in France," I continued. "And all this . . ." I waved toward the arbor, the gardens from which the July scent of hibiscus wafted, and the estate dimly visible in the moonlight. "All this is the delusion of my dying brain."

"Do you really think so?" she said again. And took my hand in hers. Her fingers were ungloved.

The word "galvanized" is too inactive to describe my reaction at her touch. It is as if I had never contacted a woman's skin until that instant. It is as if I was a stammering boy again rather than the seasoned ladies' man I had allowed myself to become since my days at Clare College, Cambridge.

I tried to speak then, to say that I was certain that none of this was real, but clouds moved from in front of the moon and touched the soft curve of flesh visible above her *décolletage*, and the words stayed stuck in my throat.

"I think this is quite real," she whispered. Her fingertip traced an oval on my upturned palm. "But you will have to return to your friends before we can meet again."

"Friends?" I whispered, embarrassed that my lips were so dried and cracked. At that moment I could remember neither the names nor faces of any friends. All my comrades in the war were dust. Less than dust. Only the Lady held the firmness of my attention.

She smiled at me. It was not the simpering smile of so many of the London ladies I had known, nor the coquettish smile of so many of the French lasses, and certainly not the cruel smile of certain widows and well-off wives I had included in my acquaintance. It was a pleasant enough smile, but weighted with irony and some challenge.

"Do you wish to see me again?" she asked. The moonlight made her lashes gleam.

"Oh, yes," I said, not thinking how naïve it sounded. And not caring.

She patted my hand a final time. "We will talk again when you have returned to where you must go."

"Where must I go?" I asked. My legs were in the brackish sludge again. My hands were twitching in nervous spasms. My father's watch, its chain wrapped around my blackened wrist, gleamed in the moonlight.

"Back," she whispered. She was wearing the chemise-robe now. I worried about it. There were so many pleats. Lice bred on us everywhere here at the Front, especially along the seams of our uniforms and in the pleats of the Scots' kilts. My uniform was new—had been new—purchased at a special officers' store in Amiens only weeks before, but already I was lousy.

No, the thought of the Lady with lice was absurd. I realized that she was touching me. Her fingers were on my bare leg, rising up my bare thigh. The soldier in the water watched with his white eyes stirring in the moonlight.

"Go back," she whispered, leaning closer. Her scent was violets and a hint of jasmine. Her fingernails raked the inside of my thigh gently, more as if in testing than in teasing. "Then we will meet again."

I started to speak then, but the Lady glanced to her left as if she had been called and then rose above the edge of the crater somehow more gently than if merely walking. Then I was alone again with the staring face, the lower torso, the tugging rats, and the cloud of flies.

I crawled out of the shell hole just before dawn, was fired at as soon as the sun came up, lay doggo another long July day, and began pulling myself toward British lines as it grew dusky on Wednesday the 12th. It was almost dawn again before someone challenged me. I heard the bolt of the rifle slamming home.

I was challenged out of the darkness to advance and be recognized or to give the code word. I could do none of these things, lying as I was exhausted and bleeding within the coils of my own wires. I *felt* the muzzle of the rifle aiming at me in the dark and could feel the unseen sentry's concentration as he prepared to fire at the sound of my croaking.

With my last strength then I could have rasped out my name and unit, perhaps a stirring "God Save the King," but none of these, I think, would have been understandable through my cracked lips and parched throat. So, inexplicably, absurdly, I began singing. The tune somewhat resembled "Here We Go Round the Mulberry Bush":

> *We don't want a girl from Givenchy-le-Noble,*
> *From Givenchy-le-Noble,*
> *From Givenchy-le-Noble,*
> *If you go for a walk she will get into trouble.*
> *So we don't want a girl from Givenchy-le-Noble.*
> *We don't want a girl who comes from les Comptes,*
> *Who comes from les Comptes,*
> *Who comes from les Comptes,*
> *For they all eat onions, and their breath rather haunts,*
> *So we don't want a girl who comes from les Comptes.*[7]

I lowered my face to the mud and waited.

"Sweet baby Jesus," came the sentry's voice. "It's someone from The Rifle Brigade. Pull him out of there, lads."

They covered my semi-nakedness with a blanket, carried me back through communication trenches, and left me at what they thought was a dressing station behind the lines.

The bells have started up again, either to celebrate the end of the last mass or to drag people in to the next. Either way, I cannot concentrate. Some mule driver is cursing at his team just outside the window as they try to pull a cart out of the mud while an entire brigade waits.

I cannot concentrate. I hurt. I will write more later.

Monday, 17 July, 2.00 P.M.—

I awoke to the Lady's scent last night, but the ward was empty except for the doomed, the dying, and me. I feel certain that she had been there only seconds before.

The long needle extracted only thimbleful of fluid this morning, I was able to stagger to the latrine with the aid of two canes, and Sister Paul Marie tells me that I will be pronounced cured within a day or two to make way for more seriously injured chaps. Several of my previous wardmates have died—the Major was found this morning, staring as fixedly at the ceiling in death as he had in his last days of life—and the new fellows seem to be from the 33rd Division. As I imagined when I heard of the fighting over the weekend, the Church Lads' Brigade seems to have met the same fate as our Brigade.

Sister tells me that Colonel Pretor-Pinney was finally shipped back to Base Hospital. There is hope that he will live. Sergeant Rowlands stopped by to see me yesterday afternoon. Rowlands had been a good man, but had been ordered back here to Albert just before our 10 July attack so that he could serve Headquarters Detail as orderly sergeant. He is bitter about missing the show, but the reassignment almost certainly saved his life.

Rowlands told me that when they took roll-call of the Brigade on the 12th, more than three hundred names carried an "M." {*Ed. note—"M" stood for "Missing."*} Of course no one at Headquarters knew if these men were dead, dead and buried, dead and still unburied, dead and blown to atoms, captured, wounded, wounded and evacuated, wounded and lying out in No Man's Land, at dressing stations, or already sent back to hospital. According to Rowlands, no one at Headquarters was very interested in finding out. So the Sergeant himself has used most of the past week in bicycling around every field hospital and dressing station asking after our Rifle Brigade chaps. On Friday he brought his own list to the Colonel here at the big dressing station and Pretor-Pinney wept

openly, which is almost unimaginable. According to Rowlands, all
the Colonel could say, again and again, was, "What a mess they've
made of my Battalion. What a *mess* they've made of my Battalion."

Rowlands would not have found me at a dressing station had he
sought me out last Wednesday. The lads who found me at the
Front had commandeered a motorcycle with sidecar and brought
me back almost to Albert, dropping me off at what they were sure
was a dressing station. There was a huge tent filled with casualties
on stretchers, a few workers moving around under lights on the far
side, and rows of overflow stretchers and blanketed wounded on the
yard outside the tent. It was a warm night; the stars were clear. The
sentry and his chum lifted me out of the sidecar, found me an
empty stretcher, tucked a blanket to my chin, wished me luck, and
returned to their duties on the line.

Fading in and out of consciousness as I was, so giddy at being
alive and out of No Man's Land, it was an hour or two before I
noticed that no one was checking on me. Not a doctor. Not a
nurse. Not even an enlisted man taking temperatures or carrying
out *triage*.

I also noticed the silence. For the first time in three days, the
chorus of wounded men did not grate on my nerves and sanity.
This group made no noise at all.

It was, of course, a burial station, not a dressing station, and it
seemed that the enlisted men in charge of the detail had knocked
off for the night just as my friends from the Front had left me to
their tender mercies. I lay outside, alone, with the noble dead. My
legs did not work, but I was able to sit up and look around. Many
of the bodies had not been covered with blankets. Starlight gleamed
from exposed bone and still-open eyes. I actually recognized a few
of the lads from 13th Platoon.

Shouting did no good, as my lungs were already so congested
that I could only cough hollowly. I lay back, sure that someone
would come along. From time to time horses or motorcars came
along the road no more than ten meters away, but a small rise
separated the rows of dead from the thoroughfare, and my gasping
coughs would not have been heard at any rate.

I considered crawling for help, but now, three and a half days after my last meal—and I had eaten little breakfast the morning of the attack, not only out of nervousness but due to the soldier's fear of a stomach or intestinal wound after eating—I had no strength left in my upper body. I was quite sure that I would die of thirst or my wounds before morning.

It rained sometime before dawn. The soft mist awakened me and I pitched my head back, opened my mouth, and swallowed what I could. It was not enough. I tried cupping my hands to catch the blessed moisture, but my hands were shaking too fiercely to serve me. Knowing that the soft rain would end soon, I peered around madly in the darkness trying to find some vessel with which to capture the water and save my life—a tossed-aside canteen, a jerry can, a helmet, anything. There was nothing. Then I noticed the water pooling in the folds and wrinkles of uniforms on the uncovered corpses nearby. I admit that I crawled where I could, lapping up these minuscule pools of water before they soaked in or evaporated. I remember using my tongue like a cat at a saucer of cream as I drank water pooled in the cold hollow of a young man's throat. I had no shame then and I feel none now. The gods had abandoned me and I defied them to do their worst. I would survive to spite the Fates.

She came then.

She walked between the rows of silent forms, treading lightly. I do not know if she was barefoot or in soft slippers. Her gown was the same as the previous night's—gauzy but not diaphanous, draped in Pre-Raphaelite folds which rearranged themselves in the starlight. I lay back on my stretcher then, pulling the rough blanket up around me, my thirst forgotten. I was afraid that she was searching for me in the darkness and more afraid that she was not.

I do not pretend that I did not know who she might be, must be. It did not matter. Her hair, when she bent over me, unfolded itself around us like a curtain. The scent of her neck was the hint of violets, a trace of jasmine, and all woman's warmth.

I wanted to say no, that my lips were cracked and caked, that my breath must be rank, but she touched my mouth with her cool finger to silence me. A second later she placed her lips where her finger had been. Her kiss was both firm and soft, endless and too brief. The stars seemed to circle in my vertigo. When she pulled back, I could sense the soft form of her left breast through the material.

"Wait," I rasped, but she was already stepping away, lifting the hem of her gown so that it did not touch the curled fingers or raised faces of the others lying there in the damp.

"Wait," I whispered again, but already sleep was coming. Shivering, knowing that I would have followed her at that moment if strength and the proper time had been mine, I managed to pull the sodden blanket higher as I slipped off into a sleep as dreamless as that of the dead around me.

Tuesday, 18 July, 3.30 P.M.—

A dreadful day. They make ready to discharge me but a bad night of fever and coughing kept me in bed one last day. My legs feel as if they are attached by sutures and not my own to control, but I can stand on them now with the aid of only one cane.

Fit to serve in Kitchener's Army again.

News so bad today that I can only laugh at whatever god of irony rules the universe. With The Rifle Brigade down to half strength and less, I knew that it is finished as a fighting unit. At least for some while. That meant that when I returned to the Battalion it would be to some "cushy" duty in a quiet section of the Front . . . or more probably in reserve behind the Front. Sergeant Rowlands had said yesterday that he had seen orders sending the Battalion to Bresle today, and then on to relatively comfortable duty near Calonne. He says that the billets are in houses there and that it is away from the fighting and the Somme.

I was beginning to think that I might live to see Christmas. Today my transfer papers arrived.

I had put in for a transfer *last* Christmas when the Brigade was in Hannescamps and I was feeling left out and rather low. I've never got along with the common sort well, and the other officers in the Brigade did not seem like gentlemen. I'd approached the Colonel and filled out forms for a transfer to 34th Division, rather hoping that I might end up with Dickie, John, Siegfried {*Ed. note—Siegfried Sassoon*}, or some of the other chaps I'd known at Cambridge. The

Colonel had told me how unlikely it was that any such transfer would be approved, but I sent the papers through, heard nothing, and had forgotten about it. Today I find that I *have* been transferred—to the 1st Battalion of the 1st Rifle Brigade of the 14th Division.

Wonderful. Fucking bloody wonderful. I've been in three Divisions during my short time in this fucking army: The Rifle Brigade was trained as part of the 37th, we were told that we had been moved to the 34th when we joined the line less than two weeks ago (less than two weeks?), and now I am to pack up and join the bloody fucking 14th. I know no one in the 14th. Worse than that, Sergeant Rowlands tells me that the 14th is moving *into* position on the line even while my old Brigade is leaving it.

If I had not lost my pistol in No Man's Land, I would put it in my mouth and pull the bloody fucking trigger.

Wednesday, 19 July, 7.00 P.M.—

Earlier I went outside to watch The Rifle Brigade march out of Albert. A beautiful evening. The air was actually cool and crisp, as if autumn were approaching despite the fact that it is high summer. There was only a hint of dust and cordite and the smell of decaying bodies in the air. The Golden Virgin and her child caught the light as the Battalion marched away under her.

I did not recognize many of the faces. Hundreds of new men have been incorporated into the ranks here in Albert so that the Battalion *looks* a bit like a battalion. Those faces I did recognize looked years older than when I last saw them nine days ago. An eternity ago. I stood on the hill outside the old convent here and waved, but many of the chaps I'd known from the old Brigade stared straight ahead, seeing nothing. Many wept. After they marched out of sight I came inside, expecting to sleep or perhaps write a letter to my sister, but there was a delegation if important ladies from Blighty here and we had to all be on our best behaviour. The nuns had put screens around the lads in worst condition—the new gas case, the Church Lad who's lost both legs, his right arm, and at least one eye, two or three others—so that our visitors would not be offended. I was simply not up to speaking to them, so I feigned sleep. One of them commented to another what a handsome lad I was. The brusque sister said that I was all well and would soon be returning to the Front. The Blighty lady, some old crone with her hair done up in a Gibson Girl bun—I peeked through lowered lids—said how wonderful it was that I was going back to give it another go.

I would like to give her another go.

THE GLORY OF WOMEN

You love us when we're heroes, home on leave,
Or wounded in a mentionable place.
You worship decorations; you believe
That chivalry redeems the war's disgrace.
You make us shells. You listen with delight,
By tales of dirt and danger fondly thrilled.
You crown our distant ardours while we fight,
And mourn our laurelled memories when we're killed.
You can't believe that British troops "retire"
When hell's last horror breaks them, and they run,
Trampling the terrible corpses—blind with blood.
    O German mother dreaming by the fire,
    While you are knitting socks to send your son
    His face is trodden deeper in the mud.[8]

I do not think that *she* will come tonight. I wish to God that she would.

Still, I do not think that she has abandoned me. We will meet again soon enough.

To sleep now. My last night in hospital. Perhaps my last night ever between clean sheets.

Saturday, 22 July—

I was wrong about the clean sheets. I have slept between sheets—although not quite so clean as in hospital—each night since coming back to Amiens to join up with my new Rifle Brigade in the 14th Division.

Shells were raining down on Albert as I left on Thursday. German 5.9s were rearranging the rubble of the town centre and falling perilously close to the large field hospital and the convent hospital where I had recovered. I suspect that I look rather romantic with my limp, my cane, and my haggard expression contrasting with my new uniform; certainly the salutes I have been receiving from new troops heading toward the Front have been snappier and more respectful than I was used to. I also have begun growing a mustache. I notice grey hairs that were not there two weeks ago.

Amiens is some fifteen miles behind the lines, but it might as well be fifteen hundred. There is a real world here: a bookshop run by a certain Madame Carpentier whose daughter flirts with officers, restaurants with names such as Rue du Corps Nu sans Tête, la Cathédrale, Josephine's Oyster Bar, the wonderful Godebert, and one merely called "Officers Dining Room" where a veritable covey of subalterns hang out, not to mention such other Amiens wonders such as the barbershop in Rue des Trois Cailloux where one can, after a haircut, shave, and session with hot towels, receive a *friction d'eau de quinine* which makes one's scalp tingle for hours afterward.

It is a cruel respite. The 14th moves up to the line on Monday and this reminder of what human life is like will make the Front all the more unbearable.

I had the Devil's own time of trying to find the 14th—Amiens is full of billeted troops arriving and departing and the outskirts of town looks as if a thousand circuses were setting up tents—but I finally reported to an arrogant colonel whom I did not care for at all, and then to a certain Captain Brown who seemed a pleasant enough chap. Brown introduced me to my platoon sergeants and explained that the 1st Brigade was being built back up to strength because of all the "loans" they had made to more active units. I am beginning to see this entire war as one giant game of musical chairs, where the loser dies due to being in the wrong place at the wrong time when the music stops.

I think of the Lady every night, but I know that she will not visit me here. The thought of seeing her once more is the only thing attractive about moving northeast to the Front once again.

Sunday, 23 July, noon—

Word is that Australian and New Zealand troops attacked against Pozieres sometime after midnight. Captain Brown says that despite the usual rosy reports from Headquarters and the patriotic babble from the journalists, the result will probably turn out to be much the same as with the 34th on July 1st and my own Rifle Brigade on the 10th: i.e. thousands dead in the mud for nothing.

We will be heading up to Albert tomorrow, then into the Line.

The other big news today concerns the death of Major-General Ingouville-Williams, commander of the 34th Division. I remember Dickie and Siegfried telling me that the men called him "Inky Bill." It seems that he was killed yesterday by an exploding shell while hunting for souvenirs in Mametz Wood. The officers are all sombre about the loss, but I heard Corporal Cooper say to another enlisted man that "it serves him bloody right for leaving his cushy bloody dugout to go pokin' around for souvenirs where the rest of us have to fight a bloody war." At any rate, there was quite a commotion behind the lines to find a set of four matching black horses to pull the caisson carrying his body back down the line. Captain Brown says that a suitable team was found at C Battery of the 152nd Brigade.

I suppose these things are important.

> *On, marching men, on*
> *To the gates of death with a song.*
> *Sow your gladness for earth's reaping.*
> *So you may be glad, though sleeping.*
> *Strew your gladness on earth's bed,*
> *So be merry, so be dead.*[9]

The four thousand men of our brigade march toward the Front tomorrow. I suspect that there will be no black horses to carry home the thousands who do not march back this way again.

Tuesday, 25 July, 10.00 P.M.—

The Golden Virgin and her child hung over the road as we marched back through Albert yesterday and the cloud of dust our

Brigade had raised set a sort of orange halo around the Madonna and Child. Our way to the Front was not quite the same as when I visited the 34th for the Big Push on the 1st or where The Rifle Brigade went into line to die as a Brigade on the 10th. Our Brigade marched through Fricourt, but instead of taking either the road toward Pozieres or Contalmaison, we went by way of Sausage Valley to the right of la Boisselle and reached the new line in front of Pozieres without exposing the men to much in the way of enemy fire. The Germans know that huge numbers of men are using Sausage Valley, but they have no direct fire so we had hoped that our only worry was the occasional 5.9 dropping in blindly to welcome us.

They used gas. I suppose if I were Jerry, I would have chosen gas as well. It makes things difficult for us with very little effort on Jerry's part. Yesterday it was just tear gas, but in sufficient quantities that we all had to don goggles or gas masks. The sight was quite absurd—literally thousands of lorries, buses, messengers on bicycles and motorbikes, long lines of ambulances, artillery caissons, horse-drawn wagons, even a detachment of cavalry—all mixed in with thousands of marching men in a cloud of white dust that rose a thousand feet in the air and mixed with tear gas so thick that the valley was absolutely drenched in it. Some of the lorry and wagon drivers had no masks—evidently they were not considered combatants and had been issued none—and the image of them trying to drive their vehicles or teams of horses with tears streaming down their faces, mucus literally dripping from their chins, was beyond absurdity.

The number of dead horses lining the roads up Sausage Valley is absolutely staggering. It is as if someone had decided to pave the roadsides with rotting horseflesh. It is not uncommon to see the remains of two or three horses mingled so that one cannot tell which spill of intestines belongs to which carcass. And everywhere the occluded, staring eyes, so much more reproachful, I think, than the gaze of our human dead. The flies are everywhere, of course, as well as the stink. Many of us who have been this way before brought perfume purchased in Amiens so as to hide the stink of decay that sets into our skin and uniforms, but that is a losing proposition. Better to ignore it. Meanwhile, the snarl of traffic, shouts of drivers, the sobbing and slobbering of men and horses caught without masks, the muffled curses of sergeants—all viewed and heard distantly through our clumsy masks.

One old lorry driver I talked to while the Brigade was waiting an hour for the snarl ahead to lessen told me not to trust the awkward mass of mica and canvas with its clumsy nosepiece tube with which the army has issued us. Through that abomination, I asked him what he was using. It looked like an old rag but appeared to be doing the trick.

"Piss on one of me socks," he said. He held it up to show me that he was not jesting. "Works better than that bloody froggy headpiece you're peering out of. Want to give it a try?"

I restrained my eagerness.

The Anzacs {*Ed. note—Australian and New Zealand troops*} made up the bulk of the traffic both toward and away from the Front yesterday. Evidently their attack that began sometime after 1 A.M. on Sunday morning is still going on in bloody stages. At least the idiots at Headquarters have learned not to send men over the top in daylight. Little good the darkness seems to have done the Scots and Anzacs who have been fighting for Pozieres and the little copses of woods around it: the ambulances are full and there are dozens of burial centres working overtime just back of the trenches.

It seems my lot always to come to war in the command of burial parties. While the 14th is to stay in reserve behind the Australians, our first order of business is to put our lads to work burying Australians. It is dirty work, but at least the bodies have not been out on the wire for a week or more.

The shelling is very fierce. I was pleased to find that our reserve trenches were on the Front just a few days ago, so the dugouts are deep and the facilities well prepared. I am sharing a dugout that must be twenty feet below ground level with two other lieutenants named Malcolm and Sudbridge. Captain Brown is just down the trench a bit and his dugout is even deeper than ours.

We have bunks in ours, shelves, a rotty strip of burlap to keep the light in and the gas out, and even a table at which to sit and play cards. The whole place is lit by two hurricane lamps and the effect is rather cozy. It is much cooler than the cauldron of mid-summer dust and heat above.

An hour or two ago Lieutenant Malcolm suggested that we level the ground under the table, which seemed a good idea since the platform was a bit wobbly. Young Malcolm and Sudbridge had set to with a will, digging out clay to make a nice flat area under each leg, when suddenly Malcolm scraped away the last layer of lime above some rotting blue cloth. "It looks like some Frog soldier lost his tunic," Malcolm said naïvely, still digging.

The smell filled the dugout a second before the remnants of the hand and arm were exposed.

I went for a walk to smoke my pipe and confer with Captain Brown. When I returned sometime later, the dirt had been filled back in and the boys were playing cards on the wobbly table.

I had chosen an upper bunk on the silly assumption that it would be more difficult for the rats to reach me up here—I hate the thought of those huge, sleek buggers crawling across my face in the dark—but a few minutes ago I noticed that the reinforcing timber above me seemed to be shimmering slightly, as if the surface of the wood were moving. I raised a lantern to the timber and found that it was literally crawling with lice. For half an hour after I turned out the light, I could feel the things falling on my chest and cheeks. Unable to sleep, I came out here to the firestep to write this by the light of the bombardment.

The Lady has not come. I would say that this place is not worthy of her, but I know that is not the reason. I have faith that I will see her again though.

Though we are in the reserve trenches, we are still within direct view and rifle shot of the German lines outside of Pozieres. Bullets strike the sandbags above my head with a familiar sound.

I can feel the lice seeking the warm folds and pleats of my almost-new uniform. I know from experience that I will try to find and crush them for several days, then give it up and live with the constant crawling on my flesh.

It is time now to go back in to my bunk to sleep. I have my first inspection tour of the platoon in the trenches in three hours.

Friday, 28 July, 8.00 A.M.—

The Colonel called me back to his elaborate dugout yesterday and demanded to know why I had requested transfer to the 14th Division. I admitted that I had not—that I had wanted to join the 34th to be with some of my school chums. The Colonel, a dyspeptic, pale little man, slammed down some flimsies and muttered an oath. It seems that Headquarters had got wind of a screw-up—my papers *should* have specified the 34th after all—and now everyone had their bowels in an uproar over some clerk's error.

"Well, what the hell do you propose we do about this, O'Rourke?" growled the Colonel, despite the fact that my name was quite plainly printed on the various forms in front of him.

I was at a loss. It seemed inconceivable to me that in the midst of all this carnage—my men had been burying Australians, Scots, and New Zealanders all week—anyone would give a tinker's damn about one junior lieutenant posted to the wrong division.

"We can't send you to the 34th," grumbled the Colonel. "They don't have any paperwork on you and are busy rebuilding. And we bloody well can't keep you here if Headquarters keeps sending up rockets."

I nodded and wished that the whole thing would just be dropped. I had begun to get to know the other subalterns—Malcolm and Sudbridge particularly—and had struck up an actual friendship with Captain Brown and several of the sergeants.

"Here, sign this," said the Colonel, sliding papers toward me across a battered table.

I looked at the forms. "A request to transfer back to The Rifle Brigade, Sir?" I said. It already seemed like an age since I had seen the few survivors of my old Brigade march out of Albert.

The Colonel had turned back to more important papers. "Yes, yes," he said, waving at me over his shoulder to sign. "You'll stay here until we can get a replacement, but that shouldn't be more than a week or two. Let's just send you back to where you belong, eh, O'Rourke?"

"Lieutenant *Rooke,* Sir," I said, but the brown-toothed little homunculus was paying no attention to me. I signed the papers and left.

It is only now, some hours later, that I think about what this might mean. Yesterday I heard from Sergeant Rowlands, and he mentioned in his note that the reserve trenches near Calonne were quite as cushy as the survivors of the Brigade had hoped. They had every wish to sit out the rest of the war there. If my transfer comes through . . .

This way lies madness. I have too much faith in the God of Irony to believe that anything as simple as another transfer will save me.

9.00 P.M., the same day—

A hot, sticky night. The sky over No Man's Land is the color of boiled lemons. Everyone here is moving slowly, desultory with the heat, almost wishing back the heavy rains that have plagued us all summer here along the Somme. Even the dugouts are too stuffy so men take their sleep shifts fully clothed, lying full length on duck-boards, a sandbag for a pillow. Luckily for us, it seems that even the German snipers are too enervated to ply their trade with much enthusiasm.

Word is that the Australians tried once again to take the windmill that has been such a sticking point near Pozieres. All we see are the hundreds and hundreds of wounded men trying to get back to dressing stations. Some are on stretchers. Some are being helped along by their friends. Others stagger along by themselves until someone gives them a hand or they simply collapse in one of the trenches or supply roads.

This afternoon I was coming back with Sergeant Ackroyd and two privates from a detail down in Sausage Valley when I happened to glance aside at a line of British bodies lying alongside the trail. What caught my eye was that all seven of the men were wearing kilts. This was no surprise since the Royal Scots Brigade of the 51st Division had been taking heavy losses for two weeks. These bodies had been covered with tarps and each foot was tagged with the yellow card which meant that the burial detail would return later, but I noticed that one of the tarps had been pushed aside. The man lying under it had red hair and looked to be an officer. A large cat was lying on the man's tartan chest and was quite happily eating his face.

I stopped and shouted. The cat ignored me. One of the privates threw a rock. It struck the body but the cat did not look up. I nodded to Sergeant Ackroyd who ordered the two men to chase the cat away.

The result was quite surprising. The cat did not deign to lift its face from its meal until the two men were quite close. Then, as they shouted and waved their arms, the overfed beast leaped at them, spitting and clawing. The Irish Private—O'Branagan I think his name is—had bent down to shoo the cat away and lurched back with bloody clawmarks across his face.

The cat ran into the basement of a cottage tumbled by shell fire, and the Private hesitated. He had unslung his rifle and was holding it in the proper attitude for defense against bayonet attack.

"Oh bloody hell," muttered the Sergeant and he and I went forward and descended into the basement. It was obvious that unless we did something about the cat, it would return to its meal as soon as we had departed.

The basement was a mass of tumbled stones, charred beams, and shadowy recesses. We had to advance through the catacombs in a sort of half-crouch. What little light that made its way through the rafters, beams, and charred floorboards above was weak indeed. The Sergeant had borrowed the frightened Private's rifle; I considered taking my pistol out of its holster, but contented myself with holding my cane a bit higher. The whole thing had become laughable.

A shifting of loose rocks in the deepest regions of the sloping basement caused the Sergeant and me to turn. There was a sort of root cellar beneath the cellar. I would have given a quid at that moment to have been carrying a hand torch. I am afraid that I hesitated a second too long at the sepulchral opening to that lower circle of darkness, for the Sergeant said in a hearty voice, "Here, Sir, let me go first. I've always had crackerjack vision in the dark."

I let the burly NCO squeeze past and crouched to see what I could see. I had the distinct image of him bayoneting that ghoulish monster and something about the thought of the blade sliding into soft fur brought back the memory of wet wool and made me a bit queasy.

Suddenly I heard the Sergeant whisper "Mother of Christ," and he stopped on the middle of six stone steps leading into the deeper cellar. I did take my pistol out then, and stepped down to stand next to him.

It took a minute for my eyes to adapt to the very dim light. There were three human bodies in there, perhaps four. They had been there long enough and the cellar was cool enough that the stench was not much greater than the constant background scent of decay this close to the Front. I could see now from the bits of rotting cloth and remaining blonde hair that it looked like a mother had brought her two toddlers and a very small baby down to escape the shelling. But the shelling had found them. That or poison gas.

But it was not the human remains that had brought the Sergeant up short and which now caused me to grip my cane and pistol with renewed strength. The five kittens—although they were too large, too fat, to be called kittens—raised their faces from their nibbling. They were *inside* the mother and the larger of the children. Nothing was left of the baby except yellowed lace and white bones.

The Sergeant let out a cry then and rushed forward with his bayoneted rifle. The kittens scattered—the backs of the corpses were as obviously hollow as the front—and before he could reach any of them, the animals were in the tumble of blackened timbers where we could not follow.

I happened to look up then at the tangle of beams above us and a larger set of yellow eyes was watching us with what I perceived as demonic interest. At that moment the cat and kittens began to yowl—or so I tell myself now—and the sound rose in volume until the Sergeant and I could only stand with our heads swiveling, not believing the intensity of the noise.

I had heard this chorus before. In No Man's Land. And I had been part of it.

"Come on," I said to the Sergeant. We returned to the surface and stood guard over the ruins until O'Branagan returned with two canvas bags of heavy Mills grenades, three wine bottles, and the jerry can of petrol I had ordered him to scrounge or steal.

The grenades threw up a huge pall of dust and rock chips. The
Sergeant and I made sure that we had lobbed at least one bomb
into every recess we could find there. O'Branagan had filled the
bottles, we used bits of an old shirt from the other Private's pack
for fuses, and then I lit each wick with my trench lighter. The
explosions were impressive enough, but the fire was even more so. I
noticed that the Sergeant had kept the Private's rifle and watched
carefully while the ruins burned and the already-blackened timbers
fell into the smoldering pit.

Nothing emerged either before or after the fire.

A platoon of the 6th Victoria Brigade were plodding toward the
Front as we finished our work, and I noticed the strange looks they
gave us.

Just minutes ago I was riding my bicycle back that way in the
dusk to carry a message to Headquarters when I glanced up to see
the smoke still rising. The tarp was intact across the Scot's body,
just as it had been when we set it back in place. But it seemed that
the canvas over the face was rucked too high, and moving slightly.

I told myself that it was a trick of the failing light-and pedaled
on.

Tuesday, 1 August, 2.30 A.M.—

Writing this on the firestep outside Captain Brown's dugout.
The bombardment is heavy enough that I can see the page to move
my pencil.

I have come to understand that Death is a jealous suitor.

I think of the women waiting at home—mothers, sisters, lovers,
wives—and of the proprietary way they speak of us—of the dead
and doomed to die. It is an arrogant conceit on their part to think
that they can hold the memory of us like ashes and bones in an
urn.

Even our memory is being devoured here.

> *When you see the millions of the mouthless dead*
> *Across your dreams in pale battalions go . . .*
> *Then, scanning all the o'ercrowded mass, should you*
> *Perceive one face that you loved heretofore.*

It is a spook. None wears the face you knew.
Great death has made all his for evermore.[10]
{*Ed. note—In the last line here, Rooke has crossed out "hers" and substituted the "his" we know from his published poem.*}

God Almighty, I love life. Even this vile place, where the trees are shattered stubs and where nothing grows but craters, even the sights, scents, sounds, and stirrings of this place are preferable to the unchanging nothingness of the Great Darkness.

As much as I love nature, music, exercise, riding to hounds, spring mornings, autumn evenings . . . as much as I love these things and bring them to mind when I think *life* . . . I love women more.

I was just fifteen when I took my fifteen-year-old second-cousin on a walk down in the Weald to the hop-farm there with its unusual line of white-cowled hop-kilns. Twenty tall hop-kilns, rising above the barns like the imagined Alps above equally imagined alpine chalets, the tops of the kilns tipped white like the apex of the icing-cone Mr. Leeds used at the bakery to put writing on the celebration cakes.

Her name was Evelyn, my second-cousin, and we walked into the edge of the forest near the hop-farm quite innocently. The trail there was little used, but a quicker return to our house above the Weald. I remember the heat of that day, much like the recent hot days here on the Somme but nothing at all like them as well. The air was still that day, but leaf-dappled and alive to the hop of insects in the tall grass, birds in the upper tiers of the forest, and the scrabble of squirrels and unseen wild things behind and within the hedges.

Evelyn had brought two sweet cakes and we sat to eat them in a sheltered place near the stream that was almost lost in undergrowth. The last time I had seen my cousin she had been dressed in a hand-embroidered kimono frock that was such the rage for children then; today she was dressed in a girlish version of a Gibson Girl outfit: long skirt, a shirt with pale blue stripes and long cuffs the same color as the stripes, a lemon-colored cravat, and a straw boater. Her hair was clasped near the base of her neck, her lashes were long, her blouse was gathered at her thin waist, her cheeks were rather pink—all and all she looked very grown up.

How things started between us that day, I do not recall precisely. A game. How things proceeded after they started, however, I recall absolutely. Her blouse had fewer buttons than most ladies' things, but far too many for my patience or fumbling fingers. And then it simply flowed away. She wore thin petticoats which made no sound when they moved. Her chemise was loose except where strings gathered it under the soft curve of her still-budding breasts. The sunlight and shadow seemed part of the texture of her skin there.

I remember how gently we kissed at first, how briefly, and then how urgently. Her drawers reached her thighs but once beyond the initial elastic there, they were loose and offered no resistance to my exploring hand. And somehow, inexplicably, miraculously, neither did Evelyn.

This mystery—so warm, slightly moist, and moistening more as exploration continued, the shocking humanness of the downy hair, this incredible, heart-stopping *absence*—this mystery is part of what I thought of as I crossed No Man's Land last month, squinting against the bullets.

The Lady came to me tonight while I slept. While Lieutenants Malcolm and Sudbridge slept not three feet away from me, their snores filling the dugout.

I felt her breasts pressing against me even before I fully awakened, and I admit that I started rather violently, thinking *rat.* Then I smelled her scent and felt her cheek so close to mine. I opened my eyes and made no sound.

She was standing next to the bunk, leaning forward so that part of her upper body brushed against my arm. Her face was warm against my neck. It was raining hard outside and cool in our dugout, but I could feel her warmth wherever she touched me.

She was no phantom. I could see the faint light from the flickering beyond the half-open burlap curtain playing on her lashes. I could feel the weight of her right breast against my bare forearm. Her breath was sweet.

She kissed me. Her left hand slid between the open buttons of my undershirt. I remembered Evelyn and all the girls since her.

Always, except for the few times where professionals were involved, I had been the seducer. It had been I who first slipped fingers between cotton or muslin or wool.

Not this night. I saw her smile as her long, thin fingers slid down my rough undershirt and touched the drawcords of my pyjamas. She must have felt my excitement. She seemed to smile again and she lowered her face to my throat and kissed my pulse.

When she backed away I followed, sliding down off the bunk as quietly as possible. For some reason I slid my hand across my bunk, found this journal where I had tucked it, and brought it with me. It was as if this little notebook held proof of the bond between the Lady and me.

Malcolm snored on in the lower bunk. His face had been scant inches from the Lady's translucent gown when she had roused me. I was surprised that her scent had not awakened him. Sudbridge slept in the smaller bunk across the dugout, his face turned to the sweating wall. He did not stir.

My Lady parted the burlap and went up the plank steps. She was no ghost. The burlap moved to the touch of her fingers, just as I had. The orange heat lightning of the counterbombardment cast her shadow on the planks. I followed her up and out.

She was a shadow out here in the trench; then less than a shadow. I was busy pulling on my boots, and when I looked up she had blended with the other shadows near where the trench zigs to the right so that a shell there would not send shrapnel here.

"Wait!" I said aloud. At that moment I heard the distant pop of a *grenatenwerfer* being launched and I threw myself down as several "pineapples" exploded just above the trenches, showering red hot shrapnel up and down the line. A man shouted somewhere as I began moving toward the shadows where the Lady had just passed. I must have looked an absurd sight in my rough cotton pyjama bottoms, undershirt, and boots, my diary clutched to my chest like a talisman. I had forgotten my cane and I limped a bit.

Just then I heard a sound a thousand times more terrifying than a *grenatenwerfer* pop—the sound of some of our own 18-pounders falling short and dropping shells on our line with that whistle and rush that tells one that the huge piece of metal and explosive is coming *here*. Once again I threw myself face down in the mud, and this time not a second too soon. The noise deafened me. The ground seemed to reach up and smack my chest so that for a second I thought the Boche had also tunneled under us and detonated a huge mine. With that amazing alacrity of visual image in a moment of crisis, I could imagine the entire section of trench along this part of the line bubbling up a hundred meters into the air the way the explosion did opposite our line on the morning of the 1st.

Mud and timbers dropped all around. Men cursed. I dug myself out and started back to the dugout.

The 9-inch shell from the 18-pounder had been a direct hit on our dugout. Sergeant Mack and several of the others had already rushed to begin digging, but one look at the terrible concaveness of the crater told me everything that I needed to know. The Sergeant and his men continued to dig, however, until they came across the splinters of our bunks and table and a few bits and pieces of Malcolm and Sudbridge. They stopped then, merely shoveling some of the mud back in the pit. It was not a burial, but it would do until morning came.

Captain Brown was very good; he gave me a stiff tot of his own whiskey, loaned me kit, blouse, and trousers until I can get refitted, and insisted that I sleep in his batman's bed in his own dugout. I was grateful, but I prefer to sit out here until the sun rises.

The air smells slightly of violets.

Friday, 4 August, 11.00 A.M.—
The shelling has become almost intolerable. There is a continued battle for the outskirts of Guillemont—a battle in which our 14th Division has not yet been asked to take part, thank whatever god deserves to be thanked—but the artillery exchange involves us all. It has gone on day and night for four days now, and everyone's nerves are stretched to the breaking point as we huddle in our dugouts when off duty, clutching the chalky soil and sandbags of the trenches when on duty.

It is interesting how the ear becomes educated to the precise signature of approaching death. Even above the constant cacophony, one can hear the individual German guns fire. Their small field guns have a *crack* not unlike a golf ball being struck smartly. Their shells arrive with a banshee shriek. The medium guns sound like someone tearing *The Times* lengthwise while the arrival of their shells sounds rather like heavily loaded farmcarts rumbling downhill, brakes screeching. The firing of their heavy guns can be felt in one's eardrums and sinuses, it is as if someone has come up from behind and cuffed you on the side of the head, while the shell's arrival is a slow whistling across the sky, rather like a train heard distantly, until the locomotive rush and rumble of it comes roaring directly into one's living room.

The trench mortar is child's play compared to their heavier calibre guns, but I believe we all fear it most. There are so many of the damned things and they fire so quickly. One mortar can lob twenty-two shells a minute at us, eight in the air at any given time, and the explosions—although minor compared to the concussive terror of their 5.9s or larger guns—are so frequent and so well-aimed that they make us feel that a malevolent intelligence is stalking us, unlike the more disinterested malevolence of the heavy artillery.

Yesterday a German mortar shell came whistling down on our position as I sat chatting with three men at an observation post. We all ducked and cowered, knowing from the noise that this was meant for us and that there was no escape. The damned thing makes a *woof-woof* sound as it falls, and this one sounded like a rabid dog rushing at us from out of the sky.

It *was* meant for us. The shell struck not five yards from where we crouched, collapsed a sizable section of the parados, and came rolling almost to our feet. The shell was the size of a two-gallon oil drum and was dribbling yellow paste that smelled like marzipan. It was a dud. If it had burst upon impact the way it had been designed to, the concussive force would have been felt a mile away and there would have been nothing left of the three of us except bits of tatters and shoe leather in a smoking crater the size of my mother's living room in Kent.

The last four days they have been laying down mortar shells every three yards on our position at ten-minute intervals. We can hear their gunnery chief blow his whistle before each shot. And this is in addition to the howitzers that have been blasting swimming pool-sized craters up and down our lines all day and all night. It can grow to be tiresome.

We all retreat into ourselves in some way. I tend to sit and stare at whatever book I am holding in white-clenched fingers: Today it was a new book of verse by the chap Siegfried and I were so excited about—Eliot. I read not a word, turned not a page. Some of the men curse constantly, adding their frightened litany to the incredible onslaught of noise. Others shake, some just noticeably, others almost uncontrollably. No one thinks less of them for it.

Dust and atomized chalk and cordite coat everything during a bombardment like this. When we do move around, it is with white eyes staring from grimy faces. We officers stand around the table stabbing at soiled maps with filthy fingers and dirt-rimmed nails. I am amazed that our lice continue to call us home, as foul as we all are.

I heard a Cockney singing a bit of doggerel as he stood on the firestep last night about dusk during a minute's lull in explosions. It was rather fine.

> The world wasn't made in a day,
> And Eve didn't ride in a bus,
> But most of the world's in a sandbag,
> And the rest of it's plastered on us.[11]

I wait each night for the Lady but I haven't seen her since the night Malcolm and Sudbridge were blown to bits. Captain Brown has been quite nice about sharing his dugout, but tomorrow night I will be moving into less exalted quarters with two new subalterns who have just come up. They look like children.

No word about my transfer to the 13th Battalion. I am beginning to know the men of this Rifle Brigade and to think that my destiny should lie here. However limited or common these chaps may be as individuals, their common effort and good nature under these conditions makes one feel something akin to love toward them. Each death is an affront. I think that they may soon be called upon to go over the top and the wastage appalls me in a most personal way.

For some reason Marvell comes to mind as I watch the lads from my platoon eat their ration of bully beef while the bombardment rages:

> *My love is of a birth as rare*
> *As 'tis for object strange and high:*
> *It was begotten by Despair*
> *Upon Impossibility.*[12]

Tuesday, 8 August, 4.00 P.M.—

The 55th Division has gone over the top on yet another attempt to capture Guillemont. The word is that the French attacked simultaneously on their right. It is nice to know that the French are still in the war.

Captain Brown came back from Headquarters a while ago with the word that the French were stopped cold by enfilade fire and our lads in the 55th were cut to ribbons by the German counterbombardment. He says that a few of our chaps made it to the enemy trenches, seized a stretch of them, and then were annihilated to a man by machine-gun bullets directed from Waterlot Farm, Guillemont Station, and the trenches in front of the village. All afternoon the shattered remnants of the 55th and supporting groups such as the 5th King's Liverpools have been straggling through our reserve trenches, trying to find their officers or reach dressing stations. We help when we can.

A heavy mist has been hanging over the hills and fields all day, mixing with the smoke and dust from the terrible bombardment. Brown says that two of our own Battalions ended up slaughtering each other in the mist and confusion this afternoon.

All of us in the 1st Rifle Brigade expected to be thrown into this meat grinder tomorrow, but word now is that the Reserve Battalions have been chosen as sacrifice. It is terrible to feel relief because another man will die.

Wednesday, 9 August, midnight—

She came tonight.

This afternoon I had done foot inspection—our M.O. {*Ed. note—Medical Officer*} was killed yesterday by a sniper—and the act of going down the line inspecting scores of men's bare and stinking feet had put me in a somewhat Christlike mood. Since the bombardment had let up a bit, I stayed in the advanced trenches after the 9 P.M. tour of the platoon's posts. It is a clear, cool night for a change, and the stars above the trench are very bright. I must have fallen asleep on the duckboard where I was smoking a pipe and meditating in one of the shelter niches in the sandbags.

I awoke to the scent of violets and the touch of her hand. We were on the same patio where she had taken me before for tea. It was all purple twilight. The manor house was candlelit behind us, there were candles in hurricane lamps set around the flagstone terrace, and I could hear hounds baying softly from the kennels beyond the barn. The Lady was wearing a pale evening dress with a frilly, flesh-colored chemisette covering a low *décolletage*, with matching sleeves reaching just to her elbows. Her skirt was tight to the hips and high-waisted, belted with a subtle jeweled corselet. Her head was bare except for small, jeweled combs holding her hair at the back. Her long neck caught the lamplight.

She led the way into a dining room where a table had been set for two. The china and silver reminded me a bit of my aunt's, but the napkins were a stylish pale blue. The table was set for only two. The main course had already been set out—Cornish hens under glass with a watercress salad. A fire burned in the marble fireplace, but this seemed appropriate since there had been an autumn tang to the air outside.

We joined arms and I escorted her to her seat. Her skirt rustled softly as I set her chair in place. When I sat down, I pinched the loose skin on the top of my hand under the table. I felt the pain of it, but the verisimilitude only made me smile.

"You believe that you are dreaming?" asked the Lady with a slight smile. Her voice was as low as I had imagined, but I could not have imagined the effect it had on me. It was as if her fingertips were on my skin again.

"I forgot you speak," I said stupidly.

Her smile became more pronounced. "Of course I speak. Would you have me dumb?"

"Not at all," I stammered. "It is just . . ."

"Just that you are not sure of the rules," she said softly, filling our glasses with wine from a bottle that had been set near her place.

"There are rules?" I said.

"No. Only possibilities." Her voice was just above a whisper. The fire crackled and I could hear a wind coming up in the trees outside. "Are you hungry?" she asked.

I looked at the hen, the candlelight on fine silver, the wine in sparkling crystal, and the perfectly fresh green salad. I had not had a meal such as this in months. "No, I am not hungry," I said truthfully.

"Good," she said, the playfulness apparent in her voice now. The Lady stood, I took her cool fingers, and she led me from the dining room through an ornate drawing room, from the drawing room to the hall, up a wide flight of stairs, down a landing lined with dark portraits, and into a room which I knew at once was her bedroom. A fire had been set here as well, and the flickering light fell on the parted lace of the curtained bed. Broad doors opened to a balcony and the stars were visible above the trees.

She turned to me and raised her face. "Please kiss me."

Feeling that I should have a script, that there should be footlights rather than firelight, I stepped forward and kissed her. Immediately all thoughts of the theatre disappeared. Her lips were warm and moist, and when they opened slightly under the pressure of mine, I felt a pleasant vertigo, as if the floor were no longer so solid. I could feel her arm and hand move until her perfect fingertips touched the back of my neck just above the collar.

When the kiss finally ended, I could only stand there, caught in a surge of passion such as none I had ever known. At some time during our embrace, my arms had encircled her. I could feel the warmth of her bare back through the lace of her blouse. She lifted her fingers from my neck, put her hand behind her, and loosened her hair.

"Come," she whispered and stepped toward the high-canopied bed. Both her small hands surrounded my single large one.

My hesitation was only for the briefest second, but she turned, my hand still in hers. One eyebrow lifted ever so slightly in query.

"Even if you are Death," I said, my voice husky, "it may well be worth it."

Her smile was just perceptible in the soft light and shadows. "You think me Death? Why not your Muse? Why not Memnosyne?"

"You could be Death," I said, "and still be my Muse."

There was a moment of silence broken only by the crackling of burning logs and the renewed rustle of wind in treetops. She lifted her finger and traced a complicated pattern on the broad back of my hand. "Does it matter?" she said.

I did not reply. When she stepped toward the bed again, I followed. She had stopped to lift her face to mine again when the wind in the trees became a train whistle, the train whistle grew to a locomotive rush, and then I was falling from the duckboard, covering my face with hands as the trench mortar shell exploded not ten yards from where I had been sleeping. The five men I had visited there not twenty minutes earlier were blown to fragments. Hot shrapnel rattled on my helmet and bits of red meat decorated the sandbags of my niche like scraps set out for the kennel dogs.

Saturday, 12 August, 6.30 P.M.—

I was cycling back on the sunken road between Pozieres and Albert this noon, carrying a message from the Colonel to Headquarters, when I stopped to watch what promised to be a bit of comedy.

One of our observation balloons was hanging like the fat sausage it was when an enemy monoplane came buzzing across the lines. I considered finding a convenient shell hole to cower in, but the insect-droning machine seemed uninterested in finding a target to bomb; it made a beeline for the balloon. Usually it is funny to watch our chaps up there when an enemy machine appears. They do not wait for the attack but immediately parachute to safety. I cannot say I blame them—the balloons explode so ferociously that

I doubt that I would choose to wait around to see the flicker of enemy machine guns.

Both observers jumped just as the German plane turned toward them and I nodded in satisfaction to see their parachutes open at once. The plane made a single pass, its guns hammered for less than three seconds, and the balloon did what all such hydrogen targets do when punctured by hot lead—it exploded into a giant mass of flaming gas and rubberized shreds. The wicker basket beneath it ignited like tinder.

Unfortunately, there was almost no wind, so rather than drift toward Albert or our rear lines, the observers descended almost directly under the balloon, their parachutes settling down in slow spirals like seeds from a shaken dandelion. The flaming mass caught the first man still two hundred feet above the ground. I distinctly heard him scream as first his parachute ignited and then his clothes.

The second man jerked desperately at the lines connecting him to his silk umbrella, and for a moment I was sure that he had avoided the fate of his friend. The tumbling mass of wicker, steel cable, flaming rubber, and burning gas missed him by five yards— enough to singe him but not enough to ignite his parachute or pull him down. Then I saw the Medusa-like mass of ropes and cables trailing behind the central mass. These whipped about like the *flagella* of some dying creature, and it was only bad luck that one of these steel cables lashed around the lines of the parachute, tugged it and the man sideways in a terrible jerk, and pulled him down.

The umbrella did not quite fold up and the observer might have survived if the cable had not pulled him into the burning mass of debris on the ground. As it was, I and several other passing messengers ran to the edge of the great pyre, but there was no chance of running in to help the poor chap. The flame must have covered a diameter of thirty yards. He was able to stand, run a few yards, fall into the flames, stand, run again, and fall again. This happened four or five times before he did not rise. I rather thought that the boys back in the trenches could hear his screams three miles away.

I delivered the message to Headquarters, ran into a chap there

whom I had known in college, and accepted his offer of a whiskey
and soda before cycling back toward the Front.

Monday, 14 August, 7.45 P.M.—
   Every sort of evil omen today.
   After two weeks of sunny, hot August weather, the skies opened
up today. It poured. As if in response to the counterbarrage of
thunder and lightning, the big guns on both sides retreated into
relative silence with only an occasional salvo to keep us or the
Germans honest. This is not rain, it is deluge.
   After an hour the duckboards were all under water. After three
hours, the sandbags began to slip in places as entire trench walls
became the consistency of very moist coffee grounds. Shell holes
have become lakes with their deadly green scum of solidified poison
gas running off in rivulets into streams and tributaries. Everywhere
bodies are washing up and washing out, and a walk in any direction
shows green hands and plastered clumps of hair rising from the
mud as if the trumpet for the Second Coming had sounded.
   Captain Brown and Sergeant Ackroyd tell me that the River
Ancre has flooded its banks and is filling the valley behind us.
Ahead of us, the village of Thiepval is awash, as are the German
trenches. We can tell that because the lads coming back from the
fighting in Thiepval Wood say that the water the Germans pump
out of their cushy trenches runs downhill to our lads' precarious
positions among the shattered tree trunks. Word is that the Australians have captured the windmill that has eluded them for so
long, but the Anzacs are so exhausted that all the living can do is lie
in the mud with their dead and dying and suffer the deluge.
   The second evil omen is that early this morning we were ordered
to rear billets "for rest and refitting." By noon we had marched
back to the temporary camp between Pozieres and Albert and were
drying off in tents rather than our leaking dugouts. This would
seem to be good news, but as we have not been directly involved in
any of the fighting so far, the "rest and refitting" has to fall under
the category of preparation for our own go at the objectives that
have eluded so many of our dead and rotting predecessors.

The final evil omen was at the 4 o'clock meal when the men received hot stew, fresh-baked bread, hot rather than tepid tea, and oranges and chestnuts. It was the oranges and chestnuts that tied it all up in a ribbon. They only serve us these delicacies when they are fattening us up for the slaughter. I would have taken the daily trenchfare of bully beef and beans, even with its usual cloud of flies, rather than this final meal.

She has not come again since I wrote last. I think she will tonight, although I share this tent with young Lieutenants Julian and Raddison, whom the others call Raddy. The rain is pounding the canvas with fists. Everything leaks. The only course of action is to eat our fine meal, smoke our new cigarettes, and crawl into our new, lice-free blankets.

Tuesday, 15 August, 1.20 P.M.—

She did not visit last night, nor this morning when I was alone. It may seem insane to wish for her, but I do. And I know why I do.

It is official. Captain Brown returned from Headquarters this morning, his face slack. We go over the top on Friday, the 18th.

Brown tried to put the best face on it, explaining to all the subalterns that it will be the 33rd Division with the yeoman's task ahead of it—securing ground between Delville Wood and High Wood while simultaneously securing High Wood itself. All our Brigade has to do, says Brown, is attack on the right flank of the 33rd and to the left of Delville Wood and secure an area of enemy front known as Orchard Trench. Our effort will be part of a general attack stretching from Guillemont to Thiepval Ridge, and Captain Brown says that the boffins in Headquarters cannot see how we can fail to take High Wood and Delville Wood this time.

This Friday, 18 August, will be the fiftieth day of this battle.

A while ago, alone in my tent, I took out my revolver, made sure it was loaded, and seriously considered shooting myself. It would have to be a fatal shot, since any attempt at a self-inflicted wound is punishable by execution.

The irony makes me laugh.

Wednesday, 16 August, 2.30 P.M.—

Late this morning, Brigadier-General Shute himself—the commander of our entire Brigade—showed up with the pompous Colonel and several red-tabbed Staff adjutants in tow. The men were
assembled in the rain, three companies on a side of an open square.
The order went out to stand at ease and there we were, several
thousand men in dripping waterproofs and sodden khaki caps (we
put away our tin hats this far behind the lines), with all eyes on
General Shute astride his tall black horse in the centre of our
square. The horse was nervous and had to be reined in, which the
General did without apparent thought.

"Well, I think that . . . yes . . . ahem, it seems to be incum-
bent upon me . . . that is to say, all you chaps should know that
action with the enemy is . . . well, imminent, shall we say?" The
General cleared his throat, reined in the nervous black horse, and
sat higher. "I have no doubt that each and every man jack of you
will comport himself with, you know, courage. And uphold the
honour of this Division, which has covered itself with, well, glory
since the Battle of Mons."

At this point the horse wheeled around as if leaving and we
thought the lecture was over, but the General reined in the recalci-
trant animal, almost stood in his stirrups, and got to the crux of
his address. "And one more thing, lads," he said, voice rising. "I
visited your reserve trenches two days ago and I was, well, *appalled.*
Simply *appalled.* Sanitary arrangements were far from satisfactory.
Hygiene was as lax as the discipline. Why, I saw *human excrement*
lying about in places. You all know the regulations about burying
one's waste. I need to tell you that I won't have it—*I simply won't
have it!* Do you hear? I know that you have been under some artillery
harassment recently, but that is no reason to behave like animals.
Do you hear me? After this attack, if I find anyone not keeping
their section of trench clean and disinfected according to precise
regulations, I shall have that man or those men *up on charges!* And I
include officers as well as the lower ranks in this charge."

As we all stood stunned in the increasingly heavy rain, General
Shute wheeled his black horse a final time and almost galloped to

the rear, his covey of adjutants and aides-de-camp racing to their motorcars to catch up.

We were not finished. We were called to attention and made to stand there for another forty minutes as first the Colonel ticked us off with spittle flying, echoing his commander's sentiments about human waste found lying around, and then—when the Colonel had left—the Sergeant-Major gave a stern lecture about how the severest military penalties would apply to any slacker who held back during the attack. Then the Sergeant-Major read an endless list of names—names of men executed for such offenses, complete with the date of their cowardice, their rank and unit, and finally the date and hour of their execution. It was profoundly depressing, and when we returned to our leaking tents our thoughts were more on floating shit and firing squads than on covering ourselves with glory for Blighty or King.

Same day, 9.00 P.M.—

I may have found a way out of this war more clever, or at least more certain, than shooting myself.

After I penned that last entry, I sat in my tent and wrote a poem. Because I wrote it on foolscap rather than in this journal, Lieutenant Raddison—Raddy—evidently came across it later and showed it to some of the chaps. I was furious, of course, but it was too late. The poem has made the rounds of the camp by now and I have heard laughter from a hundred sources. Even the stern old NCOs are reported to be delighted by it, and many of the lower ranks have begun singing it as a marching ditty.

As of now, only a few of the other officers know that I was the wit behind this broadside, but if it is discovered by the Colonel or anyone of higher rank, I have no doubt that my name will be on the list the next time the men must hear of executions. Captain Brown knows, but he merely gave me an exasperated look and said nothing. I suspect that he secretly enjoyed the poem.

Here it is.

> *The General inspecting the trenches*
> *Exclaimed with a horrified shout,*

> "I refuse to command a Division
> Which leaves its excreta about."
>
> But nobody took any notice
> No one was prepared to refute,
> That the presence of shit was congenial
> Compared with the presence of Shute.
>
> And certain responsible critics
> Made haste to reply to his words
> Observing that his Staff advisers
> Consisted entirely of turds.
>
> For shit may be shot at odd corners
> And paper supplied there to suit,
> But a shit would be shot without mourners
> If somebody shot that shit Shute.[13]

Thursday, 17 August, 4.00 P.M.—

Marched the Brigade back to the reserve trenches by noon, then forward to the advanced trenches held by the devastated 55th until this morning. All the way back here in the rain I kept hearing snatches of the Brigade's new "marching song." But the singing died as we reoccupied our old trenches and then moved forward to the advanced line opposite Orchard Trench.

I would like to write now that I feel fatalistic about all this, that I have been through it all before and that nothing can frighten me after what I have seen, but the truth is that I am more terrified than ever before. The thought of dying is like a great void opening within me. Marching here, I look at a field mouse scurrying away from the road in the valley and I think, *Will that mouse be alive in forty-eight hours when I am dead?* The idea—no, the probability—that I will be condemned to an eternity of non-sight, non-sound, non-touch while other things continue to live and sense the universe is almost unsupportable.

For the past hour I have been trying to read *The Return of the Native.* I do not want to die before I finish this book.

The men are pooling their cash to be divided amongst the survivors after the attack. Their feeling is admirable—*If I should die, better this money goes to some chum or fellow sufferer than rot in the mud of No Man's Land or be looted by some souvenir-hunting Hun.* If the attrition is as bad as it was with my 13th Battalion, or the 34th, or the Church Lads' Brigade of the 33rd, or the 51st or 55th who still lie in silent rows, their faces to the rain, in the fields behind us . . . well, there will be some wealthy chaps this time tomorrow evening.

The religious fellows in the platoon attended a communion service not an hour ago. The altar was two stretchers on which the blood of the wounded was visible on the stained canvas beneath the chalice holding the Blood of Our Savior. I envy the men who found comfort there.

This advance trench is only seven feet deep, barely deep enough to keep our tin hats out of sight. An hour ago a Lance-Corporal from D Company peeked his head up for the briefest second and a bullet caught him square in the ear and took his face quite off. We are all aware that to show any part of ourselves, for even the briefest time, would bring a bullet.

And tomorrow we will stand up there on those sandbags and walk out toward the enemy? It hardly seems sane.

Captain Brown was talking about the barrage, and how the artillery chaps will try a different approach this time—walking a "curtain" across No Man's Land in front of us. God knows they have tried everything else. For the Australians, our officers commanding the 17-pounders followed the old recipe of twenty-four hours of barrage, then the crescendo . . . and then waited ten minutes for the Germans to come flocking out of their dugouts and reinforced bunkers . . . and then resumed it again, trying to catch them in the open.

We do not know how effective this clever plan was—the Australians who went out by the thousands to capture those trenches did not, by and large, return.

Captain Brown is quite sanguine about our Brigade reaching and taking its objective. At times I want to shout at him that the objective is not worth the floating shit that General Shute found so offensive. What use is another hundred yards of bombed-out trench if it costs a hundred thousand lives . . . or three hundred thousand . . . or a million? It is common knowledge that General Sir Douglas Haig calls the deaths of thousands of us "the usual wastage" and has said that half a million casualties before this battle is over would be "quite acceptable."

Acceptable to whom, I wonder? Not to me. My life is all I have. I thought that at the advanced age of twenty-eight, I would be less worried about losing my life. Instead, I hold every second of experience to this point as sacred and detest those who would take away my chance to see another sunrise or eat another meal or finish *The Return of the Native*.

My hand is shaking so that I can hardly read this writing. What will the men think come morning if their Lieutenant cannot muster the courage to lead them over the top? Who cares what the men would think if my funk would gain me even a minute more of life and breath.

I would care. For whatever bizarre reason, I care. Perhaps it is just fear of having one's comrades think poorly of one that sends us each over the top.

It is time for high tea. Bully beef and a bulb of onion for the men tonight. The days of oranges and chestnuts are past. It is the flies' favorite meal for us tonight—and tomorrow? Many of us will be meals for flies.

Friday, 18 August, 3.15 A.M.——

She was here tonight. I am writing this by the light of Very flares. The entire Brigade are packed into these trenches and it is very crowded. Men are sleeping with their backs to the sandbags, their feet on the duckboard or in the ten inches of water beneath. Men are crouching on the firesteps, trying to sleep, or pretending to sleep. I was one of the latter until the Lady came.

The periscope above the trench here is a slanted piece of mirror on a broomstick. I had been looking up at it idly—one can sometimes see the flash of their big guns before the sound reaches us—when suddenly the surface of the mirror reflected only her face and flowing gown. I stood then, my helmet almost showing above the parapet, and would have reached for the mirror—and almost certainly would have been shot by the snipers who already tonight had culled two of the curious from our platoon—if she had not reached for me instead.

And then we were within the shelter of her curtained bed.

She was wearing only the softly translucent gown I had first seen her in. My own clothes had been removed and were lying, neatly folded, on the chair just outside the curtains. They were no longer mud-caked or lousy. Nor was I. My hair was still slightly damp, as if from the bath.

She lifted the covers slightly so that I could slide within that inviting envelope. The autumn air had turned cooler and now it ruffled the bed curtains with a sensuous languor. The light from the fireplace and a single candle filtered through the lace and fell on damask and silk with a buttery touch. We lay on the pillows, she and I, studying each other's faces in the masked light.

When she touched my cheek, I took her wrist and held it firmly.

"You are afraid," she asked, or said, for although her dark eyes were questioning, I did not hear a rising inflection.

I did not answer.

After a moment she said, "But you know me."

I held the silence another moment. "Yes," I said at last, "I know you."

In my mother's drawing room there was a mirror in which I had, in silent, narcissistic intensity, contemplated my own face a thousand times or more. And I remember the other details of my mother's drawing room: the beeswaxed parquet floor, the cat's half-empty bowl of milk under the gate-legged table, the urn of fresh flowers which the servants replaced daily . . . or nightly, I should say, so that when I was a small child I had thought that the invisible appearance of these blooms in season was magical, rather like the coming of Father Christmas only much more prompt and reliable.

I remember the Herndon photograph of the painting by G. F. Watts—*Love and Death*—with the attractive spectre of feminine Death, the folds of her robe elaborated in all their Pre-Raphaelite glory, her face lowered and turned away so that when I was very young I thought that she either possessed no head or had darkness for a skull . . . beautiful Death with her right arm raised above a cherubic boy-child whose partially concealed right arm was also raised, as if touching Her face, or perhaps attempting, futilely, to hold Her at bay. The photograph of the painting hung directly opposite the mirror which I found so endlessly fascinating, so that each time I studied my young poet's features—for I was sure even when I was seven or eight that I must be a poet—this image of Love and Death was visible above my right shoulder, Death's posture reversed from leaning right to leaning left above young Eros, so that it seemed that the form in the image had moved of Her own accord.

"Yes," I said again to the beautiful woman in whose bed I now lay, "I know you."

She smiled once more and this time there seemed less mockery and more pleasure there. I released her wrist, but rather than stroke my cheek, the Lady slid her pale hand under the bedclothes. I started ever so slightly when her fingers touched my side and she held them still there, just above the ridge of my hip, as someone does when trying not to startle an animal which might or might not allow itself to be petted.

Her eyes, I noticed, were not all black but merely very brown, the iris actually surrounded by an infinitely thin band of green that somehow added to the lustre there.

She slid her hand slowly across the bone of my hip and down my thigh, bending her fingers back slightly so that the pads of her fingers rather than her long nails would touch my skin. I admit that the tender flesh along my thigh rippled like the pelt of some forest animal as her fingers slid lower. Never had a woman been so bold with me, behaving as if my body were hers with which to play. When her fingers curved around my rigid sex, I closed my eyes.

Friday, 18 August, 5.45 A.M.—

Dawn ends this seemingly endless night. Routine takes over. Before breakfast, each company dumps its tent packs and stacks blankets into bundles of twelve.

There is reassurance here. Each man is thinking that there is safety in routine, that Death must wait if we are called on to complete the Army's tasks.

The cooks have made an effort to brew fresh coffee and tea, although the water is often bad. Sometimes they have to lower their cans into the shell holes for water. They say that boiling it kills the germs that the foetid corpses breed, but if the cooks have miscalculated and captured the green scum on the surface left from the residues of poison gas, boiling the water merely releases and reactivates the bubbles of deadly gas. Normally we would worry about this in the advance trenches, but now with only hours until we go over the top, such a bellyache would be welcomed as an excuse to go back to hospital.

There is also an attempt at a good British breakfast—sausages, baked beans, even stewed tomatoes and eggs for some of the officers—but few of us take advantage of it. The thought of a ruptured stomach or intestines, of metal and filthy cloth driven through a gut full of such food, still drives away appetite from most of us. Fear stops the rest from eating.

We know that the order to go over the top today will come later than usual—Captain Brown thought mid-afternoon—and this makes the waiting more miserable than last time for me. At least we were up and murdered and all but finished with it by 9 A.M. during the last go.

10.10 A.M.—

I have not mentioned the barrage this morning, but it is insane. Our own position here is slightly higher than that of the Germans only a few hundred yards in front of us, and this topography dictates that our guns have to lower their aim so severely that the air above is filled with shells flying literally inches above our parapets. Half an hour ago the inevitable occurred and a chap in C Company had his head blown quite off. The effect on those crowded into that section of trench was rather terrible, since blood and brain matter drenched dozens of them and two men were carried rearward with shrapnel wounds from splinters of flying skull.

The Sergeants are going around now with a bottle of rum,

doling out spoonsful to the chaps and taking frequent swigs themselves. I notice that Sergeant Ackroyd's red face has grown noticeably redder.

12.30 P.M.—

For the past fifteen minutes there has been a strange diversion.

First the guns fell silent on both sides, as if our and the German artillery chaps had all gone out for dinner. At first the men became more tense rather than less, believing that the lull in the barrage meant that our attack was imminent, but Captain Brown sent the subalterns down the length of the trench, telling the men that the attack had been set for 3 P.M. We all relaxed. Some of the chaps had a brew up while others surrendered to hunger and heated up some of their bully beef.

To add to the sense of relief from both barrage and anxiety over the uncertainty of when we were to go over the top, the rain that has plagued us for the past four days finally relented. While the sun did not actually emerge, the clouds *did* lift from their low-lying sullenness to a solid but much brighter ceiling some three or four thousand feet above the trenches.

And that is when the aeroplanes appeared.

At first they were a mere droning sound in the unaccustomed silence, then two specks broke free of the clouds some miles to the west, and soon we could make out the machines themselves, although with my nearsightedness there was no question of my actually telling friend from foe. The men did, though, and when what I perceived as the smaller of the two droning crosses quickly circled into a position behind the larger, the troops along our entire section of trench sent up a cheer.

For the next ten minutes or so it was as if we were spectators to some aerial Punch and Judy show as the two machines whirled and circled and dipped and climbed into and out of the cloud ceiling. All sniping and harassing machine-gun fire stopped as both sides of No Man's Land became engrossed in the spectacle. For the first time in weeks, the Front became so silent that one could hear bird song from the river behind us or the cough of men many yards away. And then came the tiny hammering sound of the machine guns in the aeroplanes themselves—just occasionally when one had the advantage on the other—and then so briefly as to make all of us on the ground—*under* the ground—feel like wantons for our constant and endless expenditure of ammunition.

And then, just as the aerial display threatened to become repetitious and boring, one of the machines—the larger—burst into flame and went spiraling down in tighter and tighter circles until it disappeared behind the German trenches in the direction of Guillemont. A moment later a great column of black smoke rose into the sky and our lads gave a triple hurrah followed by so many whistles and shouts that I thought that I was sitting in the working class seats at a football match.

The celebration was premature. A moment later the circling smaller machine—British or French, I assumed, although I could not make out the markings—suddenly emitted a burst of smoke.

"Coo, 'e's on fire. See the bloody flames?" said a Lance Corporal near me.

I could see no flames, but I *could* hear the sputter of the aeroplane's engine as the last of the cheering in our line died away. Evidently the machine was too high to return safely to earth before the flames consumed the pilot—or perhaps there was simply no place for it to come down in our thousand square miles of cratered earth here along the Front—for rather than descend, the aeroplane appeared to climb and try several awkward sideslipping motions, as if the frenzied pilot were attempting to keep the flames away from his body. It must not have worked; a moment later even I could see the flames and thin line of smoke trailing behind the sputtering cruciform shape.

The men along the line of trench shouted and moaned for several seconds before I could make out the reason for their lamentation. Then I saw what they had already perceived: the pilot had jumped from the machine just below the ceiling of clouds. Even someone as ignorant of the details of aerial machinery and warfare as I knew that pilots did not carry parachutes up with them as our balloon observers do, although whether this abstemiousness is from lack of room in the flying machine or a function of their code of airborne chivalry, I do not know. At any rate, even while knowing that the plummeting figure was doomed by his lack of a few yards of silk, one hoped during the entire plummeting descent that this chap might be an exception and that the circle of white would pop open at the last moment, bearing the warrior gently down to the waiting arms of his comrades.

It did not. He fell into No Man's Land a few hundred yards to the east of our position, close enough that we could see his arms and legs thrashing as if seeking purchase in the air; close enough that even I could see a white scarf trailing like the tail of an aberrant kite. There was a long silence along the trenches when he struck. I glanced up once, expecting to see the burning aeroplane descending as rapidly as its driver had, but the machine—now blossoming in full flame like Apollo's chariot—continued to fly along until it passed into the clouds, became an eerie glow through the white ceiling, and then disappeared completely, never to reappear.

A moment later the German machine guns opened up as if the schoolmaster had blown his whistle, ending our little recess. A moment after that the barrage began again.

It is after 1 P.M. We go up and over at 3.00.

2.10 P.M.—

I did not go to sleep. I did not close my eyes.

But one moment I was here, in the slimy trenches under an atmosphere of screaming metal, and the next moment I was *there*— next to my Lady between clean sheets with the cool air ruffling balcony drapes and bed curtains.

She touched me still. And I responded still.

Brusquely, I moved her hand away from my sex, thrust aside the bedclothes, and sat in the cooling air with my back to her.

I could feel rather than see her moving toward me, feel the featherbed indent as she rested on one elbow behind me. "You do not desire me?" Her voice was the softest of whispers.

I forced an ironic smile. My clean uniform still lay folded neatly over the Empire chair, but I could see no bulge of cigarette case in the pocket of my blouse. It would have helped at that moment to have had a cigarette. "All men must desire you," I said, my own voice rough and ragged, nowhere near a whisper.

"I am not interested in all men," she said. I could feel the warmth of her breath on my bare back. "I am interested only in you."

That statement should have made me shudder, but instead it increased my arousal. I *did* want her . . . more than I had wanted any woman or any thing. I said nothing.

She laid her hand flat against my back. I could feel the outline of her palm and each slender finger as a locus of warmth. Outside, the wind blew as if leading in a storm.

"At least lie next to me," she said, rising so that her lips were next to my neck. "Lie next to me and keep me warm."

I managed an ironic chuckle. "Keep you warm so that I may be cold forevermore? Or will you keep me warm by pulling a blanket of earth over us?"

She pulled back. "You are unfair," she said.

I turned to look at her then, knowing even as I did so that such a glance might seal my fate . . . although I would be Eurydice to her Orpheus.

Neither of us vanished. She was beautiful in the candlelight. Her hair lay loose, her chemise had pulled aside so that I could see the creamy skin above one elegant shoulder, and her left breast was outlined through the thin fabric by the glow behind her. Although my breath caught in my throat, I said, "How can one be unfair to a metaphor?"

She smiled then. "You think me a metaphor?" Her right hand touched my cheek.

"I think you a seductress," I said through a tightening throat.

Her laugh was soft, pleasant, and it held no scorn. "Then you would be wrong. I am no seductress." Her fingers slid along my lips. "It is you who seeks to seduce me; it is you who has courted me since birth. It is always thus." Her face came closer and we kissed before I could speak.

Outside, the storm arrived suddenly with a gust of cold air, a blast of the terrace doors being blown open, and an endless roll of thunder.

"Good Christ," gasped the Lance Corporal huddled next to me on the firestep, "that fuckin' barrage is too fuckin' close for me fuckin' peace of mind."

2.35 P.M.—

The Sergeant and I moved along the trenches a moment ago, checking a final time that the men's kit was in battle order. Normally the chaps wear their haversacks on the left side, but in preparation for the attack they move it to the back below the shoulder blade. Beneath their haversack, their groundsheet must be rolled tightly. Our objective is to seize and *occupy* Orchard Trench and we pack as if there is no doubt that this objective will be achieved. A partial list of the men's kit includes—

> *Entrenching tool*
> *Pull-through*
> *Rifle with fixed bayonet*
> *Bootlaces*
> *Spine protector*
> *Gas mask*
> *Tin of grease*
> *Waterproof sheet*
> *Latherbrush*
> *Razor and case*
> *Holdall*
> *Housewife*
> *Towel*
> *Water bottle*
> *Bottle of oil*
> *150 rounds of rifle ammunition*
> *Paybook*
> *Toothbrush*
> *Cardigan*
> *Cap comforter*
> *Knife, fork, spoon*
> *Comb*
> *Soap*

Socks (3 pairs)
Shirt
Mess tin

In addition, each man now carries an extra 180 rounds of rifle ammunition in a spare bandolier over his right shoulder and a 5-pound Mills grenade in each tunic pocket. Many of the men carry extra canisters for the Lewis gun. Other extra burdens include Very flares, wirecutters for every tenth man, periscopes, signal lamps, wire for the telephone lines, and extra water because of the heat. The Sergeant always demands that the men show him their filled water bottles carried on the right side and the white linen bag containing an extra iron ration. My grim job is to remind the men of their field dressing sewn into the lower right flap of their tunics, and to show them how to use the iodine on the wound before wrapping it with the temporary dressing. The lads look at me—at my chalky, wasted face and cane—and they listen, believing me to be a man of more experience than I actually have.

It is no wonder, with these tons of superfluous detritus, that after each battle No Man's Land looks like a gigantic garbage heap of bandages, torn papers, toilet paper, abandoned weapons, spent cartridges, and bits of the men who carried all this there.

Earlier today the men had their teaspoon of rum to give them courage during the long wait; now the Sergeant has gone around with the attack-ration of rum: one sixty-fourth of a gallon per man, carefully doled out in a small tin cup. The easy joking of this morning's ration is not matched by horseplay now—the men accept their dole in silence, as if receiving Communion.

2.48—

The barrage intensifies, if such a thing is possible. Captain Brown just came by and reminded us that the officers will be leading the attack for each company. Previously, some stayed behind until all men were out of the trenches, but this time the military police will make sure that there are no laggards. The same police will follow the attack, using their bayonets on shirkers if need be.

Captain Brown patted me on the shoulder and said, "We'll knock back a pint after all this settles, Jimmy. See you in Orchard Trench." And then he was off to reassure the men with jokes and pats on the back.

2.56—

Numbness. I am so frightened that I am as numb as when I was shellshocked during the last attack. I only pray that my legs will carry me up the side of the trench and into the killing ground.

I will bring my cane.

2.58—

I cannot hear the barrage for the pounding of my heart. I see men's mouths moving in shouts but hear nothing—perhaps I have gone death. {sic}

For some reason I recall a snatch of Byron—

> The winds were wither'd in the stagnant air,
> And the clouds perish'd; Darkness had no need
> Of aid from them—She was the Universe.[14]

My father's watch says it is only 2.59 but the barrage has moved away and whistles are blowing up and down the

{Ed. note—The next several pages of James Edwin Rooke's diary are missing and appear to have been torn out. A fragment of one page exists and has the following verse scribbled in pencil:}

> Who are these? Why sit they here in twilight?
> Wherefore rock they, purgatorial shadows?
> Drooping tongues from jaws that slob their relish,
> Baring teeth that leer like skulls' teeth wicked? Stroke
>   on stroke of
> pain—but what slow panic,
> Gouged these chasms round their fretted sockets?
> And from their hair and through their hands' palms

Misery swelters. Surely we have perished
Sleeping, and walk in hell; but who these hellish?[15]

{*Ed. note—the journal resumes several pages later in mid-sentence with no date or time of entry*}

none of this makes any sense, so will try again . . . thusly . . .

Whistles blow. I thrust my journal in my pocket, grasp my cane like a sword, and climb the ladder. The ladder. Up. For weeks, showing the smallest part of one's head above the parapet means a sniper bullet through the brain. Death, instant, inevitable. Now they order us to climb up there. Above.

I climb. The men throng like terrified cattle thrust too many to a chute above which the slaughterhouse executioner waits. Bayonets from below make retreat down the ladder impossible once the ascent has begun. Mud on the soles of the boots of the man ahead of me—Captain Brown. He is shouting. The barrage has not ended, but is moving across No Man's Land like a curtain.

Standing on the lip of our own trench, up in sunlight and still alive—miraculous! Energy flows through me like an electric current. Up here and alive!—I wave the men up and out with my cane. Then I turn to lead the advance . . .

. . . turn to lead the advance . . .

and am hit quite squarely between the eyes.

My feet fly out from under me, I feel blood fly from my shattered brow, a great weight seems to descend out of the sky to fall upon me, and I sense my body tumbling backwards, over the edge of the trench, and then down, flying blindly into my own grave with a great splintering of duckboard and splash of muck.

Blackness for minutes or seconds. Then I open my eyes expecting to see the Lady, but instead see snatches of greying sky through a film of red. Wiping blood from my eyes, I sit up. Some great heifer of a man with a red face—Sergeant McKay from B Company—is helping me up, pulling me out from under a dead weight which seems to cling to me. I see sprawling white hands, blood-soaked khaki, and for an instant I think that the Sergeant is pulling my soul from my shattered body as if he were God's midwife.

"Just bloody bad luck for him," the red-faced NCO is saying. "Are ye all right though, Sir? I think it be just a scratch on yer noggin, Sir."

I shake my head and try to focus on what the Sergeant is saying. Men are rushing by, climbing ladders. I have been unconscious for mere seconds, if at all.

". . . another go, Sir?" McKay is saying, half-holding me upright as we shuffle toward the ladder through the throng of frightened men. "Careful, Sir," he says, pulling me to one side, "best not to step on the gentleman's face."

I look down. Almost under my boot lies Captain Brown. The machine-gun bullets have stitched a bloody row from his groin to his forehead, shattering his teeth and Adam's apple along their route. I realize numbly that it is the brim of Captain Brown's helmet that had caught me between the eyes seconds before; the weight of his near-eviscerated body driven into mine that had tumbled me back into the trench.

"Upsy-daisy, Sir," says the Sergeant, speaking to me in a tone one would use with a child as he helps me up the ladder.

No, I scream in my mind, *there is some mistake. I have already climbed up there. No one should have to do it twice.*

"Thank you, Sergeant," I say, my voice shaky. I wipe blood from my eyes again.

Incredibly, the Sergeant finds my cane where it had fallen near the wire and hands it to me. Bullets whine past our ears. The barrage is now some hundreds of yards ahead, but enemy 5.9s are falling all around us. I see my company—Company C—some mere 20 yards ahead, advancing with rifles at port arms, heads lowered as if advancing into a strong rain. Company B, McKay's chaps, are rising out of the trenches now two platoons abreast every 200 yards, a man every two yards, all of their pacing straight from the Infantry Manual.

"Thank you, Sergeant," I say again, dusting myself off although the khaki is soaked more with mud and water than dust. I take a step, wobble, steady myself with my cane, and start toward the enemy lines.

No Man's Land is as repugnant as I remember it. Some shell

holes still smoke and stink of cordite, while others resemble ancient lunar craters with their stagnant ponds and scum of poison gas. Bodies and bits of bodies lie everywhere here between the wire. The filthy litter is everywhere; I notice a clean, well-oiled rifle lying untended and consider sweeping it up before I notice the clutched hand and severed forearm still attached.

I turn to shout to Sergeant McKay but a series of explosions hides him and the rest of his platoon from sight. Ahead of me, C Company have taken shelter in a slight dip in the terrain and are lying in almost perfect battle order. Beyond them, D Company continue on toward enemy wire. I stagger the thirty paces or so to the muddy fold in the ground and collapse next to a Lance Corporal who is keeping his head down. A machine gun stitches its way across the soil inches from my head. For the first time I notice that I have lost my helmet in the tumble back into the trench.

After a few moments of sheer gratitude at being alive, I see that while our barrage continues to move forward toward the enemy lines, the German counterbarrage is now churning up the debris between the muddy depression in which we lie, and our own wire. And it is moving closer. Not wanting to appear the insufferable officer-wallah, but also not wanting C Company either to die where they have taken shelter or to fall too far behind D Company's attack, I stand up amidst the bee-hum of bullets and pace back and forth on the far side of the depression, urging the chaps to their feet with gestures of my cane since no one can hear my voice.

None of the men move a muscle. I admit that I feel a momentary surge of uncharacteristic anger at this general funk, but it passes when I realize that if I hadn't earned these damned subaltern pips due to my college and social standing, I would be lying there with the other chaps hoping that the goddamned lieutenant would either shut up or lie down or get shot.

I drop down into the low ravine next to the Lance Corporal and begin pulling him to his feet, hoping that our example will shame the other men into movement. The Corporal almost comes apart in my arms.

He is dead, of course. They are all dead, lying there in their proper battle lines, faces against the stocks of their rifles, arms thrown across their faces as if frozen in the act of flinching. I check two other men—a private named Dunham and a bantam-sized little pipefitter named Bennett—and see from the wounds that shrapnel has dropped them like leaves from a tree. It may have been our own barrage, or perhaps the first lucky counterstrokes of the German counterfire, but a hailstorm of shrapnel has cut these men down in their tracks.

Limping, using the cane now for support rather than inspiration, I hobble forward ahead of the enemy barrage.

Just before reaching the enemy wire, I drop into a smoking shell hole where Sergeant Ackroyd is arguing with Raddy—my bunk-mate, young Lieutenant Raddison. Their voices are inaudible but I can see the spittle flying from the open mouths in their white faces. It takes me a moment to understand the source of their disagreement, but then I comprehend. Both men have had their guts opened as if by a butcher's knife and they kneel there in the bile-colored mud, their intestines spilled out in a common, smoking heap. Each man is attempting to tuck himself back in, as if they were schoolboys embarrassed at having been caught with their shirts outside their trousers, and each is arguing with failing strength about which strand of grey-white gut belongs to whom.

The argument ends as I watch with wide eyes; first Raddy quits shouting and heels slowly to his left, eyes showing only whites, finally tumbling into his own viscera, and then Sergeant Ackroyd leans forward with almost ballet-like grace, the scooping movement of his arms and hands slowing, slowing, until all motion halts like the last, tired movements of a worn machine. I begin pawing my way backwards, up and over the crater lip, back into the cleanliness of the machine-gun fire, but not before I see Sergeant Ackroyd stir, his bloodless face turning toward me, his bloodless lips forming words I mercifully cannot hear.

A pitiful remnant of D Company has breached the enemy wire and seized a fifty-yard section of forward trench. Twice more I am knocked down by shellfire, once blown into the wire, which is painful, but eventually I extricate myself and drop down the muddy parapet into German trenches for the second time in my life.

A beefy sergeant and a wire-thin private whirl toward me and crouch as if ready to bayonet me.

"At ease, men," I manage. My voice sounds alien to me and I cannot imagine they can hear any of it. Both the enemy and friendly barrages have joined now into a maelstrom of metal and flame falling along this mile of trench line.

But the Sergeant lowers the Private's Lee Enfield, averts his own bayonet, and leans close. "Good Christ Almighty, Sir. You're wounded bad. Lie down, Sir."

For a moment I am sure that he is right and that I am dying, perhaps already dead, but then I glance down at myself and have to rub muddy knuckles against my lips to keep from laughing or sobbing. The front of my tunic is absolutely soaked with Captain Brown's blood. My shoulders are caked with drying brain matter. And blood continues to flow from the deep scratch on my forehead from where the captain's helmet struck me. My face is caked with dried blood. I realize that I must look like a combination of a Red Indian and a demon from hell to these exhausted and shell-shocked men. Realizing that there is no time for irony, I lean forward and say, "Situation please, Sergeant."

The old NCO sags upward almost to attention. I read his lips more than hear his voice. Even above the cordite and trench stink, I can smell the rum on his breath. "We've secured this bit o' trench, Sir," he reports. "Me an' about ten o' the lads from Lieutenant Hall's platoon. Jerry keeps counterattackin', Sir, but 'e don't do much but throw them stick bombs what're easy to throw back, Sir."

As if to demonstrate this piece of acumen, a German grenade on its throwing stick comes sizzling and bouncing into the trench not three yards from us. The wire-thin private calmly sets down his rifle, lifts the bomb, and tosses it back over the sandbagged revetment. The explosion follows in less than a second.

"They're set for a bloody eight seconds, Sir," reports the Sergeant with disdain in his voice. "Fritz don't like to hold 'em for no more than two seconds or so. Oodles of time, Sir."

I nod and glance around. This is not Orchard Trench. We are some distance from our objective, perhaps as much as a hundred yards. We have captured some form of forward observation trench

from the looks of the hastily sandbagged emplacement, but because
it is connected to Jerry's main line, he obviously wants it back. As if
to demonstrate the veracity of my assumption, there is shouting
around the corner and the surviving half-dozen men of D Company fall back to this small section of trench, firing and throwing
Mills bombs as they go. I press against the parados as stick grenades bounce in and are thrown back. Enemy 5.9s explode in No
Man's Land a few yards behind us; "friendly" 18-pounders throw
up soil and bits of corpses a dozen yards to our front. The Sergeant and I bury our faces in the muddy sandbags and wait for the
clods and shrapnel to settle.

When I lift my face, it is to shout at the Sergeant, "Where is
Lieutenant Hall?"

The rum fumes wash over me. "He went down way back there,
Sir. Near where C Company is hidin'. Why the fuck don't they
come up to support us the way they was told to? Sir?"

I wave away his question. "We'll hold this section of trench until
relieved or ordered to fall back," I shout. All five of the men are
gathered around me now. Two have fallen just seconds ago when a
stick grenade had a shorter fuse than the private and his chum had
thought.

I look at their faces. They understand that my order is a death
sentence. They show no anger. Two go off to the corner where the
trench zigzags on our right and begin firing down it. Two others
move to the corner on our left. The Sergeant begins pulling bando-
liers off the dead private and the other man who has just been
killed. "Ammunition won't last 'til it gets dark," he says.

I want to say something inspiring now—"We'll hold," perhaps,
or "It will last until A Company arrive"—but I merely nod and
move along the trench, swinging my cane and throwing back the
occasional stick bomb. Instead of letting up, the barrage increases
in severity as both sides focus on this section of shallow trench.
When I raise my head to look back, one of the two men guarding
our left flank is writhing on the ground and holding the bloody
mass that was his groin just seconds ago. His mate stares in horror.
To our right, I hear shouts in German . . . *German!* . . . and the
Lance Corporal at the corner there fires seven rounds in rapid

succession. He seems to be praying, but as I come closer I can hear his dry-lipped litany—"I'd give me fockin' left bollock for a fockin' Lewis gun now . . . I'd give me fockin' left bollock for a fockin' Lewis gun now . . ." He squeezes off three more rounds and reloads.

I clap him on the shoulder and walk back toward the left flank, half expecting men in grey to come flying over the parados or around the corner and bayonet me before I reach the Sergeant. I am swinging my cane and whistling softly. I am very happy.

The marble bannister under my hand was cool. I was wearing only a silk robe that rustled softly against my skin. The wind continued to rise, shimmering the treetops in the darkness like a squall moving across brittle water.

"Come to bed," she said softly from the room behind me.

I glanced over my shoulder at the wind-stirred bed curtains and the glimmering firelight. "In a moment," I said, still wishing for a cigarette.

She did not wait. I heard the rustle of her long gown and she stood next to me against the railing. Starlight sketched the curve of her cheek and set soft highlights in her tumbled hair. Her eyes looked soft and moist. She set her hand on mine and I could feel the warmth of her hand above, alternating with the chill of the marble under my palm.

"It is not fair," I said at last.

"What, my love?"

I did not turn to look at her. "It is not fair that you use the act of love to steal men from life."

I thought that I could almost hear the mockery in her silence, but when I finally turned to look at her, there was no mockery in her downcast face. Her fingers trembled against the back of my hand. She asked, "How can one steal by giving?"

Pulling my hand away, I looked toward the dark woods. "Sophistry," I mutter.

"What else can one expect from a . . . metaphor?" Her whisper was just audible above distant thunder.

I turned quickly and seized her by the throat. Her neck was so slim that it fitted nicely into my one hand. Applying pressure, I could feel her breath stop suddenly. Fragile structures lay just beneath the webbing between my straining thumb and forefinger. Her eyes widened inches from my own.

"Would you like to taste death?" I whispered in her face.

The Lady did not struggle although I could sense her weakening as no breath or blood flowed above my firm grip. Her hands stayed at her sides. I think that if she had raised one to scratch or strike me, I would have snapped her neck then like a spent match. Her gaze never left me.

"Can Death die?" I breathed into her small ear and then pulled back to watch her face. Starlight and lack of blood made it pale as porcelain. Her dark eyes seemed to answer my question with a question.

"Damn," I cursed myself and dropped my hand away. She did not raise her small hands to her throat, but I could hear her labored breathing and see the red marks my fingers had left there. Beyond us, the wind died as suddenly as it had come up.

"Damn," I said again and kissed her.

Her lips were moist and open and I could feel a sense of mutual surrender flowing through and from our contact. It was exhilarating, like the instant when one has launched oneself into space before gravity's unsubtle intervention. Her fingers did rise then, finally, and migrated, hesitant and softly fluttering, to the back of my neck. Her body pressed against mine so that I could feel her thighs and the soft cusp of her belly against me through the thin layers of silk which were all that separated us.

Our kiss ended just as I grew dizzy. She pulled her head back as if also gasping for breath or equilibrium. I gave her time for neither. Sweeping her up in my arms, her gown so low on her left breast that I could see the pale nipple above the laced border there, I carried her from the balcony into the bedroom.

The gas shells make a different sound from High Explosive, a sort of double cough, a bit like a crass tradesman loudly clearing his throat to be noticed.

"Gas!" screams the Sergeant and we scramble through our canvas kits for the masks. I pull mine on and fumble with the clumsy straps. The thing is awkward and imperfect, a thrown-together contraption of army shirt material, thick mica eyepieces, and a nosepiece tube holding sodium thiosulphate. It will not tighten properly and I frenziedly pull at straps to cinch the gaps. Someday they will invent a true gas mask, but in the meantime my life depends upon this absurdity.

The Sergeant and I peer around, attempting to see if the gas is visible. The Germans have been using copious quantities of tear gas recently, but it is a nuisance gas and one can spot the white clouds before they disperse. In the last year or so, there has been much more use of the killing gases chlorine and phosgene. In hospital, I had seen the results of German battlefield experiments with a mixture of ethylene in a solution of sodium chloride—the so-called mustard gas. In recent weeks they have loaded these various gases in shells rather than release them from canisters.

The effect, at least on the half-dozen of us still alive in the forward trench, might be described as comic. The Sergeant and I are peering around like frightened frogs. The other four chaps have set down their rifles and have been digging through kit for their masks. If the Germans want the trench now, all they have to do is waltz in to take it.

I see no visible gas. Phosgene. Almost certainly phosgene.

Chlorine is bad enough—a thousand parts per million in the air means death. The gas destroys the small bronchial tubes and alveoli of the lungs so that one cannot absorb oxygen; a man then literally drowns in the water his own lungs create. Our Brigade buried a few victims of chlorine, and the skin of these men was invariably a bright blue, their stiffened arms were thrown wide with terror, and their staring eyes told all.

Phosgene is worse. Twenty times more lethal than chlorine, invisible, and much more difficult to detect. One can smell chlorine long before the dose is lethal, but phosgene, even in deadly amounts, smells only faintly of moldy hay. It does its job, though. When I was in hospital, one poor chap who had tried only a whiff of phosgene vomited four pints of a thick, yellow fluid from his lungs *each hour* for the forty-eight hours or so until he mercifully drowned in his own excretions.

I do not know much about this new mustard gas, but Captain Brown said that it blisters and burns the flesh, blinds the eyes, rots mucus membranes, seeks out and attacks the genitals, and scours right through to the bone. He said that our chaps who are developing it were delighted that the symptoms do not appear until hours after exposure. Soldiers will not know whether they are doomed or not. I remember the autopsy report I tried to set to verse. Evidently the Germans have perfected it before us. Fritz was always clever at chemistry.

The Sergeant is shouting something now, but even leaning so that my canvas mask touches his, I cannot understand him. But I look to where he is pointing.

One of our chaps cannot find his mask. His maskless face becomes a contorted mask itself. I can clearly hear *his* screams.

"I smell it! I bloody smell it!" He throws down his kit, abandons his rifle, and scrambles up over the parapet toward No Man's Land.

I am screaming at him, urging him to piss on his sock. The Sergeant is trying to grab him. Another private attempts to grip his friend's puttees while tightening the straps on his own mask. More shells are coughing near us. It is all a comic farce.

The fleeing private gets only ten yards or so before a German machine gun slams him aside like a struck ten-pin. He had forgotten that there are more common ways to die here.

The other four men in the trench lift their weapons and prepare to fight off another counterattack. I pick up the dead private's rifle, slide the bolt back to make sure that there is a cartridge in the chamber, and join the other chaps on the firestep we have erected from sandbags at the rear of the trench. I am sweating so heavily in this clumsy canvas bag of a mask that the thick mica eyepieces, barely serviceable at the best of times, are fogged up on the inside. A clip in the gas mask keeps me from breathing through my nose so only by gasping in the bit of air that makes it through canvas and filter can I get barely enough oxygen to survive. I imagine that I can smell moldy hay. I am essentially blind.

"There!" comes the Sergeant's scream through filter and mask. "They're comin'!"

Something moves, vague shapes are visible through the opaque eyepieces. Bayonets, perhaps. German bayonets. Stick bombs come bouncing and hissing into our trench but we are all too busy to deal with them. I pant through my mouth and squeeze off several shots at the attacking shadows.

The great attraction and the great danger of passion is that it is something outside of oneself, a strong wind from nowhere in the face of which the forest of everyday thought and behaviour cannot stand.

She was beautiful, my Lady. I carried her from the balcony to the bedroom, across the firelit parquet floor, feeling rather than seeing the soft nap of Persian carpet under my bare feet in the second before parting the bed curtains and setting this woman, *my* woman, gently on the high mattress there. Her hair flowed back over my forearm where it remained, still cradling her. The pale-pink circles of her nipples were visible through thin fabric.

The time for subtlety was past. I cast off my silk robe, grasped her thin garment by its lacy collar, and tore it down the front. She raised her arms above her head on the pillow and the reflected firelight painted the lower curves of her breasts with warm tones. Her legs were long and smooth, her belly slightly curved, the triangle of darkness below meeting its apex at the juncture of her shadowed thighs.

She opened her arms to me as I stretched myself out against the length of her. She must have felt my rigid sex against her thigh, for a kind of gentle shivering went through her and she closed her eyes. To quiet her, I set my fingers in her hair, kissed her eyelids, and laid myself atop her like a blanket. When we kissed, she opened her legs to me and slid her nails lower on my back. I could feel the opening warmth of her against the head of my sex, and I paused a second to savor that briefest of moments where the two of us were on the verge of becoming one.

Our kiss seemed to continue on past consciousness, she opened

her mouth to me, our tongues met in urgent strife, and I slid
forward into my Lady.

The Sergeant dies just before darkness comes.

We have held off two attacks, fighting in our crude gas masks,
the air swirling with invisible phosgene and then—before the second assault—with vaporous clouds of tear gas. The Germans are
vague shapes through the fog outside and the fog inside our thick
mica lenses. We fire at the shapes and some go down. I glance at a
twitching corpse just around the bend of our trench and see that
the German masks are not much more refined than ours. This man
has been shot through the eyepiece and blood runs from the
tapered snout of the mask's tube. It is as if I have killed a demon.

There were five of us counting the wounded private, the Sergeant, and myself. And then, after several stick bombs go off on the
first attack, there is only the Sergeant and myself. We gather the last
of the ammunition from our dead comrades, patting their pockets
for more Mills bombs or cartridges. Setting our masks together so
that we can be heard, the Sergeant and I decide that we cannot hold
the entire section of trench with just the two of us to guard the
approaches. We retreat to the right where the trench zigzags back
toward the main German lines. There are grey-clad bodies stacked
in the mud for the length of the next section of trench. The rats are
already busy feeding.

The Sergeant rests his rifle on a niche in the trench wall to cover
this approach while I stack other sandbags to create a crude revetment. Anyone coming around the far corner will have to pass down
the full length of our abandoned trench under my sights.

Then tear gas and smoke billow around us. My eyes are running
with tears, I cannot breathe, but this has been the case for the past
half hour in my mask so I do not know if there is a leak. I peer
down the sights of my Lee Enfield waiting for the first of them to
come around the corner. His back to mine, the Sergeant stares
down his section of trench.

They come over the top, leaping down from the parados with
guttural cries. From the distant place I have gone, I calmly notice

how much longer the upper sections of their boots are than those issued to our chaps.

I shoot two of them. Another throws a stick bomb at us and flees. The Sergeant kicks the hissing bomb around the corner of the trench and I shoot the running German in the back. He continues to crawl. I shoot him again and feel nothing.

Two more men leap into our trench from almost directly overhead. I shoot one in the face and my rifle jams; the bolt will not eject the cartridge. The surviving German shouts something through his gas mask and drops into the stance for bayonet attack. With no time to turn and fire, the Sergeant shifts his rifle into a defensive diagonal and steps between the German and me.

The German lunges, the Sergeant clumsily deflects the blade, and lunges back. Both men have scored. The German's thin bayonet has entered the Sergeant's throat just under where the gas mask is tightened. Four inches of the Sergeant's blade is embedded in the German's abdomen. The two men sag to their knees, still attached by steel. Each pulls the bayonet from the other as if in a single, choreographed motion. As I watch, panting, almost fainting from lack of oxygen, the two forms thrust their bayoneted rifles at each other again even while they are on their knees. Neither has the strength to penetrate the other much more than skin deep. They drop their rifles and fall together at the same second.

Ignoring the threat of other Germans coming over the top, I drop my rifle and roll the Sergeant to his side, tugging off the mask. His mouth is wide and almost filled with blood, as round as a shell crater. His eyes are wide. I never learned his name.

The German is still alive, writhing in pain. I prop him up against the front wall of the trench, pull off his mask and study his face.

He is just a man: dark stubble, brown eyes, sweat-matted hair, and a shaving nick on his throat. He gasps for water—I know the German word for that at least—and I lift my water bottle to his lips. He swallows, starts to speak, suddenly convulses, and dies without uttering another word.

Leaving my own rifle in the mud, I lift the Sergeant's, wipe the blood from the stock as best I can, check to make sure that there is a full magazine loaded, and sag against my tumbled sandbags. Whistles are blowing in the German trenches and I guess that they are readying another attack.

Then the shells begin to fall with deadly aim, tumbling the trench walls in, exploding parts of bodies into the air, and filling the length of the trench with screaming shrapnel. I know the sound of these guns. They are British 18-pounders. There will be no relief. Headquarters has decided that no British troops have made it this far. The barrage has begun again.

Our motion is liquid, oiled with passion and sweat. Her warmth surrounds and consumes me.

Death did not claim me when I first touched her, I am able to think through the rising surge of sensation. *Nor when I kissed her. Nor when I entered her.*

We roll among the bedclothes, never allowing ourselves to lose that most intimate of contact with the other, her legs around me, thighs gripping me. When she is above me, her breasts hang like fruit I must gather, the nipples visible like rising seeds between my fingers. Her hair is a curtain around us.

It must be when I reach the ultimate ecstasy. The so-called "little death" will not be so little this time. I do not care. I roll with her until we tumble off the bed and I lie atop her on the Persian carpet amidst the tangle and drape of bedclothes, the fireplace light showing me her face contorted with the same passion I feel.

We—I—move more rapidly now, beyond thought, past stopping, beyond return, past anything except the consummation of the passion that increases our rhythm to this sliding crescendo.

Wednesday, 23 August, sometime in the afternoon—

Ten minutes ago they jammed the needle through my back and drained a pint of fluid from my lungs. They are still not sure whether it is the probably fatal pneumonia caused by the gas I inhaled, or merely a return of the pneumonia I suffered earlier.

At least the liquid is not increasing. If I am drowning, I am drowning slowly.

The wound on my right leg worries me more. They have cut

away flesh all around the wound, but the smell of gangrene fills the ward and I constantly sniff at my own bandages to see if I am contributing to the stench.

"It's your own damned fault," said the curt Dr. Babington while on his rounds after the needle extracted fluid today, "for fighting in such fertile fields."

I have not spoken since entering this place, but the doctor took my silence as query. "It's the French fields," he continued, "best fertilized in the world, don't you know. Yes, tons and tons of manure. Human waste as well, don't you know. You chaps have it saturated in your uniforms. Then a piece of metal like this passes through flesh and drives all that *merde*-soaked fabric in with it. The wound itself is nothing . . . nothing." He snapped his fingers. "But the sepsis . . . ah, well . . . we will know in a few days." And he passed on down the ward.

There are no windows in this canvas field hospital, but I asked one of the overworked nurses and she said, yes, the Madonna and Child still lean over the street in Albert in the valley below us here. The small hospital I was in last time is gone, destroyed by shelling. I find myself worrying about the kind nun who had helped me there.

Thursday, 24 August, 9.00 A.M.——
Wakened early this morning, but instead of being served the gruel we receive for breakfast, I was painfully set onto a sort of wheeled cart and pushed out into a courtyard between the tents. It was raining, but they left us there—myself and two other officers I recognized from the 1st Battalion Rifle Brigade. These two men were wounded more seriously than I. One had his face tightly wrapped in gauze, but I could tell that most or all of his lower jaw was missing. The other showed no visible wounds, but was unable to sit up in the wicker wheelchair. His head lolled as if unattached to his pale neck.

We had been left there in the rain for ten or fifteen minutes when a Colonel and several aides came out of the adjoining mess tent. It was the Colonel who had spoken to the Brigade with General Shute.

Oh, no, I thought. *I do not want a medal. Just wheel me in out of the rain, please.*

The Colonel spoke for only a minute. There were no medals.

"I expect you all to know," he began with his Harrow drawl so similar to General Shute's, "that I'm damned disappointed in you chaps. Damned disappointed." He slapped his crisply trousered thigh with a riding crop. "It is important for you chaps to . . . ah . . . understand . . . that you've let down the side. That's what you've done. Just let down the side." He wheeled as if he were going to leave but then turned back, surprising his aides who had also wheeled away as if disgusted with the three of us on our carts and wheelchairs.

"One more thing," said the Colonel. "You should know that your Battalion was the only one of the Brigade to have failed . . . the only one! And I do not want to hear any complaining about the fact that the 33rd Division did not push forward on your right . . . do you hear? I shan't have that bandied about as an excuse. The 33rd's failure is the 33rd's shame. The 1st Battalion's failure is our shame. And you chaps are responsible. And I'm . . . well . . . I'm damned disappointed."

And he and the pilot fish in his wake disappeared back into the mess tent. I could smell some sort of cake or confectionery from the baking ovens. The three of us sat or lay out in the rain for another ten minutes or so, not speaking, until someone remembered to fetch us back to the ward.

Afterwards, she lies in the protective harbor of my arm while we watch the firelight fade to embers.

"Would you like to hear a passage of His Nibs's private diary?" she whispers.

I am brought back from pleasant reverie. "What? Whose?"

"General Sir Douglas Haig," she says and smiles. "You are not the only one who keeps a private journal."

I play with a strand of her hair. "How do you know what the General writes in his private diary?"

She ignores me, closes her eyes, and recites as if from memory. " 'Saturday, 19 August—The operation carried out yesterday was most successful. It was on a front of over eleven miles. We now hold the ridge south-east of and overlooking Thiepval. Nearly five hundred prisoners were taken here while the battalion which carried out the attack only lost forty men! During their advance our men kept close to the artillery barrage.' "

I look at her in the fading light. "Why do you tell me this?"

She shifts sideways so that her bare shoulder becomes a faintly lit crescent leading to her shadowed face. "I thought that you might like to know that you were part of a success."

"My battalion was destroyed," I whisper, feeling very strange at bringing the War into our bed. "More than forty men died in C Company alone."

She nods slightly against the pillow. I cannot see her eyes for the shadows. "But the leading battalion lost only forty. And gained several hundred yards of mud. General Sir Douglas Haig is pleased."

"Fuck General Sir Douglas Haig," I say.

I expect some sound of shock from my Lady, but she sets her hand playfully on my bare chest and if there is a sound, it is a soft laugh.

Saturday, 26 August, 7.00 P.M.—

It is getting dark earlier. This is the one week anniversary of my waking up in the casualty clearing station.

I remember nothing of leaving the trench or making my way back across No Man's Land. I remember no help in finding the station. I remember nothing of taking my mask off and choking on the remnants of gas, nor of receiving the shrapnel wound that has turned my right leg into a throbbing mass of suppurating pain.

I do remember awakening. After the first attack, when I thought I was waking in hospital, I found myself among the dead. After this attack, when I was sure that I would lie unwaking among the dead, I awoke to the flare of acetylene torches with a surgeon bending over me. If he is God or the Devil, I thought, then God or the Devil dresses in army-issue white smock liberally spattered with blood. His archangels on high looked to be a sister in nurse whites,

an orderly with pince-nez glasses, and a tired anaesthetist with a
smock as gored as the surgeon's.

And then I remember very little except arriving here on the 21st,
not even being aware of time as I scribbled in my journal, trying to
make sense of all those fragmented images.

And fuck General Sir Douglas Haig, and the Colonel, and
Shute, and whoever else is intent upon killing me. I defy them. I
defy the gods. I defy God Himself.

Sunday, 27 August, 5.00 A.M.—

Awoke coughing, retching yellow fluid, and drowning at 3.22
A.M. Had to shout for a nurse, who came slowly, obviously irritated
at being wakened.

Could not breathe. Thought *All right, then . . . so this is the way of
it. It was worth it. She was worth it.* And then all such rational thoughts
fled as I gasped for air and flailed about like the drowning man I
was. Every time I inhaled I vomited yellow bile. My throat was full,
my nose was full. Black spots danced all around my vision, but
blessed oblivion did not condescend to arrive as I thrashed and
retched and pounded the stained mattress as if it were the ocean.

I remember my last coherent thought was *Dying is not so easy as they
make it out . . . Tolstoy, this is how peasants die!* and then a bored
orderly sauntered in with one of the bicycle-pump needles, they
slapped it through my shoulder blade into my right lung, and a few
minutes later they had extracted enough of the thick fluid that I
could breathe . . . after a fashion . . . although the terrible
sucking, mucusy sound must have kept many of the other chaps
here awake. They said nothing.

Same day, 11.15 A.M.—

A priest came through to give Communion to the Catholic lads.
I watched and listened to his gentleness for almost an hour, seeing
how truly moved he was by the plight of the more seriously
wounded. When he passed my bed, glanced at my chart, and saw
"NONE" typed in above the line that says "RELIGION," he nonetheless
stopped and asked if there was anything he could do for me. Still
unable to talk, I could only shake my head and try to hide my tears.

An hour later the doctor in charge of the ward sat tiredly on the edge of my bed. "Listen, Lieutenant," he said, his voice more tired than stern, "it seems as if the gangrene may be getting better. And the orderlies assure me that the lung problem is minor." He polished his glasses and then leaned forward. "If you think these . . . minor accidents of war . . . are going to assure you of a cushy rest period back in the arms of England, well . . . the War goes on, Lieutenant. And I expect you to be back in it as soon as we can get you out of here to free up this bed for a truly wounded man. Do you understand me?"

I started to nod, but then I spoke for the first time in the week I have been here. "Yes, Sir," I said through the phlegm and fluid that filled my throat. "I expect to go back to the Front. I *want* to go back to the Front."

He cleaned his glasses and frowned at me, as if I were having some sport with him, but in the end he only shook his head and moved on.

I was not having sport with him. I was telling the truth. What I could not tell him is what the Lady told me this morning.

It is morning, a beautiful autumn morning, and we are having a light breakfast of tea and croissants on her patio. She is wearing a dark skirt and a light-blue blouse, gathered at the cuffs and midriff, fastened at the throat by an emerald brooch. Her dark hair is tied up in an intricate manner. Her eyes are smiling as she pours my tea.

"We will not meet again for a while," she says, setting the silver teapot aside. She adds the single lump of sugar I prefer.

I am stunned into silence for only a minute. "But I want . . . I mean, we must . . ." I break off, appalled at my own incoherence. I want to tell her that I used to be a poet who understood language.

She sets her hand on mine. "And we will," she says. "We will see each other again. It will be a short while for me. A bit longer for you."

I frown at my lack of understanding. "You realize that I understand nothing," I say honestly. "I had thought that our love would . . . had to . . ."

She smiles. Her hand does not leave mine. "Do you remember the photograph of the painting in your mother's drawing room?"

I nod, my face reddening. Discussing this is somehow more intimate than our night of total intimacy. "G. F. Watts," I say. "*Love and Death.* The woman figure of Death . . ." I pause, unable to say "you," ". . . the robed figure standing above the child . . . Eros, I presume. Love."

Her fingernails trace small patterns on the back of my hand. "You used to think it had a secret meaning," she says, very quietly.

"Yes." I can think of nothing intelligent to say. The secret meaning had eluded me then. It eludes me now.

She smiles again, but again there is no mockery there. I remember her face in the firelight. "Perhaps," she says, "just perhaps, instead of the female Thanatos looming over the threatened Eros, it is your feminine . . . metaphor . . ." She smiles more broadly now. ". . . of Love who is stopping the capricious young prankster Death from playing his tricks."

I blink, struck stupid.

My Lady laughs softly and pours herself tea, lifting the cup and saucer. The absence of her hand on mine is like a harbinger of winters to come.

"But love . . . of whom?" I say at last. "Of what? What great passion would forestall death?"

Her graceful eyebrow arches. "You do not know? You, a poet?"

I do not know. I say as much.

She leans forward so that I can hear the rustle of her starched cotton blouse and the silk beneath. Our faces are so close that I can feel the warmth from her skin. "Then you need more time to learn," she whispers, her voice as filled with emotion as when she cried out last night.

I set my own hand, shaking, on the small iron table. "And how much time will we have . . . now . . . together . . . until we part?" I ask.

She does not laugh at my redundancies. Her eyes are warm. "Time enough for tea," she says, and raises her cup to her lips.

Thursday, 31 August, 1.00 P.M.—

Discharged from the field hospital near Albert today. Can barely walk, but found a ride in an empty ambulance going back to Carnoy Valley where General Shute has pulled the brigade to rest before another offensive.

One of the other surgeons, over Dr. Babington's terse report that my wound and pneumonia were healed sufficiently to return to duty, recommended strongly that I be shipped back to Blighty for at least a month of recuperation. I thanked the other surgeon, but said that Dr. Babington's suggestion suited me.

I know very few of the chaps here in the valley camp. I did run into Sergeant McKay, the gentleman who had helped me up out of the trenches after I had been knocked backwards by poor Captain Brown, and we were so delighted to see that the other had survived the attack that I think we barely restrained from hugging one another. Most of the other faces in C and D Companies are fresh and strange.

Sergeant McKay asked me if I had heard the storm the night before. I admitted that I had slept through it.

"One 'ell of a show, Sir," he said, his red face beaming. "Soaked us all good, it did. The lightnin' was worse than the barrage on the day we went over. At the 'eight of it, Sir, it struck two of our observation balloons and blowed them right up, Sir. Quite a show. Beggin' your pardon, Sir, but I can't see how no one could sleep through such a show. No disrespect meant, Sir."

I grinned at him. "No disrespect inferred, Sergeant." I hesitated only a second. "It sounds like quite a storm, but it was just . . . ah . . . well, last night was my last night in Albert, and I . . . well, I was not alone, Sergeant."

The NCO's smile grew broader, his face screwed up in a wink worthy of the stage, and he saluted me. "Yes, Sir," he said. "Well, glad you're back, Sir. And wishin' you good health while you're here, Sir."

Now I sit on my bunk and try to rest. My chest aches, my leg aches, but I try to ignore these distractions. Word is that there will be a general attack on Delville Wood within forty-eight hours and that General Shute wants his lads—us—in the forefront of it.

But forty-eight hours is a goodly amount of time. I have books to read—*The Return of the Native* here in my locker, as is the new Eliot which I have not yet finished—and after reading a bit, I may take a stroll around the camp. The storm seems to be over. The air is clear. It is a lovely evening.

Editor's Afterword—

Here ends the newly discovered war diary of Lieutenant James Edwin Rooke.

There was an attack on Delville Wood on the 2nd of September, 1916, although Rooke's Battalion did not bear the brunt of it. The Gloucestershire Regiment, 5th Division—the so-called "Bristol City Battalion"—had the honor of leading the way. The Battalion was all but destroyed in thirty hours of fierce fighting.

Rooke did participate in the larger offensive of 15 September. This battle marked the first time tanks were used on a battlefield, although there were too few and they were poorly used. Rooke was not injured during this final attack on Delville Wood, although 40% of his platoon were reported missing, wounded, or dead after the action.

The poet did not see Thiepval finally captured on 27 September. A forgotten transfer had come through shortly after the 15 September offensive, and Rooke returned to his old unit, the 13th Battalion Rifle Brigade. There are only two letters extant from this quiet period in the "cushy" trenches near Calonne, but in both letters to his sister, Rooke appears to have been simultaneously contemplative and quietly joyful. He wrote no poetry.

The 13th Rifle Brigade returned to the Somme on 11 November, 1916, when winter was setting in and trench conditions were particularly dreadful. James Edwin Rooke participated in the terrible fighting during the attack on Serre on November 13–15. The objective was not attained. Rooke was in the field hospital near Pozieres, dealing with a third and more serious bout of pneumonia, when word came that the Battle of the Somme was "over" on 19 November, 1916.

Actually, there was no formal end to the battle. It had merely petered out amidst the mud, snow, and freezing temperatures of that particularly early and harsh winter.

More than 1,200,000 men died during the five months of fighting along the Somme in 1916. No major breakthroughs were achieved.

James Edwin Rooke returned to his unit and stayed along the Front at the Somme—where casualties still ran at about 30,000 men a month for the

British—until he was wounded again at the battle called Third Ypres, or Pass-chendaele, in August of 1917. Rooke was hit by two machine-gun bullets while leading an attack on a German pillbox with the strange name of Springfield Farm.

Survivors of Passchendaele later remembered and spoke mostly of the mud there; General Sir Douglas Haig himself wrote:

". . . the low-lying clayey soil, torn by shells and sodden with rain, turned into a succession of vast muddy pools, the valleys of the choked and overflowing streams were speedily transformed into long stretches of bog, impassable except by a few well-defined tracks, which became marks for the enemy artillery. To leave those tracks was to risk death by drowning."

Indeed, in one of his few letters to his sister in which he mentions details of the war itself, Lieutenant James Edwin Rooke—then convalescing in Sussex—described how a friend of his, a certain Sergeant McKay, did drown in the mud of a shell hole while the wounded lieutenant lay nearby and could do nothing to help.

Of James Edwin Rooke's life after the Great War, much has been written. Of his decision to write no poetry for publication from that time on, many have lamented. When Rooke decided to join the Roman Catholic Church in 1919, his family and friends reacted with shock. When he actually became a priest in 1921, family and friends essentially disowned him. Only his younger sister, Eleanor, continued to correspond with him during the years that followed.

While Rooke's Trench Poems took on a fame and life of their own, the man himself retreated from the literary scene. Few of the poets of the 1930s and 40s who patterned their verse after his knew that the poet himself was still alive, although in relative seclusion, in various monasteries in France. Indeed, Rooke's literary production in those decades, while well picked-over by scholars, consists almost entirely of correspondence with his sister and the intermittent (but lively) letters he exchanged with his friend, Teilhard de Chardin. The one book he did print, privately, was the now legendary Songs from Silence (John Murray Publishers, Ltd., 1938), a series of prose poems describing the contemplative life he had led in the Benedictine Abbey of St. Wandrille and the long visits he had made—some lasting years—to the Cistercian Monastery of La Grande Trappe, the Abbey of Solesmes, and the Rock Monasteries of Cappadocia.

Scholars have shown that within the Church itself, Father Rooke seemed any-thing but monastic. Always expressing a love for life that sometimes bordered on the apostate, Father Rooke became as famous within his small theological circles for his theory of "life ascendent" as his friend Teilhard did for his theories of moral

and spiritual evolution. These two continued their lively and impassioned corre-
spondence until Teilhard's death in 1955.

In 1957, Rooke's sister Eleanor wrote him a letter in which she asked the aging
priest why he had forsaken the comforts of wife and family for all of the years since
the War. Father Rooke responded in a letter which has become famous but which,
until now, has not been totally clear. I present that letter now in its entirety:

15 September, 1957
The Abbey of St. Wandrille

My dearest Eleanor,

I read your letter while strolling on the Rouen-Yvetot road
this evening and it delighted me, as your letters always do,
with your keen intelligence and gentle wit. But it also sad-
dened me that you feel hesitant to ask me a question . . .
"have waited these forty years," you wrote, "and know that I
should wait forty more."

There is no need to wait forty more, my dear, nor even
another day. The question is asked, and I take no offense.

Tonight, when the Abbot tapped his mallet and the reader
ceased his reading and intoned *"Tu autem Domine miserere nobis,"*
and we all rose and bowed as we chanted our thanksgiving, I
was—as I have every morn and noon and evening for almost
forty years—thanking not a personal or impersonal God, but
merely the fact of Life itself for its gift of life.

As to my celibacy—or as you so quaintly put it—"my
long denial of life's physicality," well, Eleanor, have you ever
known a more physical person than your brother? Even this
afternoon, as I labored to finish weeding the last patch of
peas in the garden between the Abbey and the forest, can you
not imagine me taking sheer physical pleasure in the sweat
that ran into my eyes and trickled under my rough robes?

But I know you speak of marriage, or more precisely, of
physical love.

Do you not remember that I wrote many years ago that I
was married? Not *felt* married or *acted as if I were married*, but
married. I should wear a wedding ring like the nuns in Rouen
who show they are wed to Christ.

Only I am not wed to Christ. I respect him and grow more interested in his teachings as each year passes—especially the idea that God is, indeed, quite literally, Love—but I am not wed to the Galilean.

Yes, my dear, I know that this is heresy, even to such a casual C of E sometime-believer as yourself. Imagine if the Abbot or dear Brother Theophylaktos or serious Father Gabriel heard me utter these words! Thank heavens for vows of silence.

I am wed, not to Christ, nor to any conventional image of God, but to Life herself. I celebrate Her daily and look forward to seeing Her even as life seems to abandon me. I find Her in the smallest things each day—the sunlight on the rough plaster of my cell, the touch of rough wool, the savor of those fresh beans I defended with my hoe for so many hot months.

Eleanor, do not think that I have abandoned God in my love of Life. It is merely that I understand—have been made to understand—that God is found in *this* Life and that to wait for another is folly.

Of course you must ask how I can shut myself away if I believe in embracing Life. The answer is difficult even for me to understand.

First, I do not consider my life in these abbeys as a retreat from life. It is—as I hope I showed in the simple little book I sent you fifteen or sixteen years ago (my God, time moves on, does it not, my baby sister?)—my way of savoring life. As imperfect as those writings were, they were my attempt to share the exquisite simplicity of such a life. It is as if I were a connoisseur of fine food, and rather than discourage my appetite through gluttony, I indulge it by ingesting only small portions of the finest cuisine.

I love Life, Eleanor. It is that simple. Had I the choice, I would live forever, accepting pain and loss as my due and learning—across time—even to appreciate the sharp seasoning of this sadness. The alternative is the Child Who Devours.

I know this makes no sense, my dear. Perhaps this poem I shall enclose, written some time ago, might cast some light on the murky cloud of verbiage I have stirred up. Poets rarely get to the point.

Please write again soon. I wish to hear about your dear husband's health (improving, I hope and will pray) and the continued fortunes of Charles and Linda in the big city. (I would not recognize London were some miracle to transport me there. The last time I saw it was during the Blitz, and while morale was very high amongst the populace, the old city itself had seen better days. Tell me, are the barrage balloons still there? Just kidding—the pub (I still call it that) near the station in the nearby village boasts a television and I caught a glance of a film set in London just last month on my way to a conference in Rouen. And there were no barrage balloons.)

Do write, Eleanor, and forgive your brother's continued obtuseness and perversity. Someday I shall grow up.

I remain—

> Your loving brother,
> James

{*Ed. note—The following poem was enclosed.*}

THE GREAT LOVER

I have been so great a lover: filled my days
So proudly with the splendour of Love's praise,
The pain, the calm, and the astonishment,
Desire illimitable, and still content,
And all dear names men use, to cheat despair,
For the perplexed and viewless streams that bear
Our hearts at random down the dark of life.
Now, ere the unthinking silence on that strife
Steals down, I would cheat drowsy Death so far,
My night shall be remembered for a star
That outshone all the suns of all men's days.
Shall I not crown them with immortal praise
Whom I have loved, who have given me, dared with me

High secrets, and in darkness knelt to see
The inenarrable godhead of delight?
Love is a flame;—we have beaconed the world's night.
A city:—and we have built it, these and I.
An emperor:—we have taught the world to die.
So, for their sakes I loved, ere I go hence,
And the high cause of Love's magnificence,
And to keep loyalties young, I'll write those names
Golden for ever, eagles, crying flames,
And set them as a banner, that men may know,
To dare the generations, burn, and blow
Out on the wind of time, shining and streaming . . .

These I have loved:
          White plates and cups, clean-gleaming,
Ringed with blue lines; and feathery, faery dust;
Wet roofs, beneath the lamp-light; the strong crust
Of friendly bread; and many-tasting food;
Rainbows; and the blue bitter smoke of wood;
And radiant raindrops couching in cool flowers;
And flowers themselves, that sway through sunny hours,
Dreaming of moths that drink them under the moon;
Then, the cool kindliness of sheets, that soon
Smooth away trouble; and the rough male kiss
Of blankets; grainy wood; live hair that is
Shining and free; blue-massing clouds; the keen
Unpassioned beauty of a great machine;
The benison of hot water; furs to touch;
The good smell of old clothes; and other such—
The comfortable smell of friendly fingers,
Hair's fragrance, and the musty reek that lingers
About dead leaves and last year's ferns . . . Dear names,
And thousand others throng to me! Royal flames;
Sweet water's dimpling laugh from tap or spring;
Holes in the ground; and voices that do sing:
Voices in laughter, too; and body's pain,

Soon turned to peace; and the deep-panting train;
Firm sands; the little dulling edge of foam
That browns and dwindles as the wave goes home;
And washen stones, gay for an hour; the cold
Graveness of iron; moist black earthen mould;
Sleep; and high places; footprints in the dew;
And oaks; and brown horse-chestnuts, glossy-new;
And new-peeled sticks; and shining pools on grass;——
All these have been my loves. And these shall pass.
Whatever passes not, in the great hour,
Nor all my passion, all my prayers, have power
To hold them with me through the gate of Death.
They'll play deserter, turn with traitor breath,
Break the high bond we made, and sell Love's trust
And sacramented covenant to the dust.

——Oh, never a doubt but, somewhere, I shall wake,
And give what's left of love again, and make
New friends, new strangers . . . But the best I've known,
Stays here, and changes, breaks, grows old, is blown
About the winds of the world, and fades from brains
Of living men, and dies. Nothing remains.

O dear my loves, O faithless, once again
This one last gift I give: that after men
Shall know, and later lovers, far-removed
Praise you, 'All these were lovely': say, 'He loved.'[16]

{*Ed. note——James Edwin Rooke died of cancer in July of 1971. He was 83 years old.*}

Notes to "The Great Lover"

About the real poets:

1. Siegfried Sassoon, "And clink of shovels . . ."

Born in 1886, educated at Marlborough and Clare College, Cambridge, Sassoon served with the Sussex Yeomanry and Welch Fusiliers. He was known as an incredibly brave officer and had been seriously wounded and awarded the Military Cross even before he saw action at the Battle of the Somme.

Sassoon was the first major poet to be critical of the lack of progress in the war, and his brutal, realistic verse became the archetype for an entire generation of wartime poets. His antiwar poetry and protests were at first diagnosed as shell shock, and he was committed to a sanatorium where he met Wilfred Owen, another brilliant young antiwar poet. Owen wrote of Sassoon—"I hold you as Keats + Christ + Elijah + my Colonel + my father confessor + Amenophis IV in profile."

Unlike most of the younger poets, Sassoon survived the war and became the literary editor for the *Daily Herald*. Throughout his writing career, Sassoon was obsessed with his wartime experiences and his fictional autobiography, *Memoirs of an Infantry Officer*, may be the best-known memoir of that war. Sassoon died in 1967.

2. A. G. West, "The Night Patrol"

3. A. G. West, "We had no light . . ."

4. Images adapted from "The Great Lover" by Rupert Brooke.

Rupert Brooke was the quintessential romantic war poet. Born in

1887, educated at Rugby and King's College, Cambridge, Brooke was given a commission in the Royal Naval Division by his admirer—the First Lord of the Admiralty, Winston Churchill—saw some action at Antwerp in 1914, wrote patriotic verse about his willingness (almost eagerness) to die for his country, and died of blood poisoning while being transported to Gallipoli in 1915. He was buried on the Greek island of Scyros and his life, verse, death, and burial instantly became the stuff of legend.

Rupert Brooke's brilliant but romanticized view of the war differs wildly from the bitter verse of his contemporaries who survived to see the horrors of later battles and the high-level stupidity of the long war of attrition.

5. Wilfred Owen, ". . . the white eyes writhing in his face"

Born in 1893, educated at Birkenhead Institute and University of London, Owen enlisted in the Artist's Rifles in 1915 and fought in France from January 1917 to June 1917, when he was invalided out. Suffering from nervous collapse, Owen was sent to the sanatorium where he met Siegfried Sassoon, who soon became his mentor. Sassoon introduced Owen to the poets Robert Graves and Robert Nichols, both of whom had been at the Somme.

Although bitter about the mishandling of the war and converted to pacifism, Owen returned to the Front and became a Company Commander dedicated to keeping his men alive. "My senses are charred," he wrote shortly before he died. "I don't take the cigarette out of my mouth when I write Deceased over their letters."

Wilfred Owen was awarded the Military Cross for exceptional bravery in October 1918, and was killed by machine-gun fire at the Sambre Canal on November 4, 1918. Many consider him the finest poet of the war.

6. From an Official Medical History of the War (HMSO).

7. Marching song of the 13th (S) Btn, The Rifle Brigade.

8. Siegfried Sassoon, "The Glory of Women"

9. Charles Sorley, "On, marching men, on . . ."

10. Charles Sorley, "When you see the millions of the mouthless dead . . ."

Born in 1895, educated at Marlborough, Sorley won a scholarship to University College, Oxford, but enlisted in the Suffolk Regiment in August 1914. Within a year he had obtained the rank of captain. He was killed in action at Loos on October 13, 1915. Although Sorley was only twenty at the time of his death, John Masefield and others considered him the most promising of the war poets. His *Marlborough and Other Poems* was published in 1916 and proved extremely popular. His "Song of the Ungirt Runners" is his most famous poem and has been recited by generations of schoolchildren.

In a letter home in which he had included some poetry, Sorley once wrote: "You will notice that most of what I have written is as hurried and angular as the handwriting: written out at different times and dirty with my pocket: but I have had no time for the final touch nor seem likely to have for some time."

11. Soldiers' doggerel, "The world wasn't made in a day."

12. Andrew Marvell, "The Definition of Love"

This was quoted by Guy Chapman in *A Passionate Prodigality*, published in 1933. This memoir is an excellent introduction to an officer's view of the war and the Battle of the Somme. Chapman dedicates the book to "certain soldiers who have now become a small quantity of Christian dust." Born in 1889, Guy Patterson Chapman served with the 13th Battalion and the Royal Fusiliers from 1914 to 1920. Chapman is one of the few writers who reenlisted after the war. Later becoming a barrister, writer, publisher, historian, and professor of Modern History at Leeds University, Chapman died in 1972.

The poet Andrew Marvell lived from 1621 to 1678.

13. A. P. Herbert, "The General inspecting his trenches . . ."

An officer in the Royal Naval Division, Alan (A. P.) Herbert was present when General Shute dressed down the 63rd Division for their filthy trenches. The division had just gone into the line formerly held by the Portuguese, and the men resented Shute's comments. Herbert's "poem" became a song sung to the tune of "Wrap Me Up in My

Tarpaulin Jacket" and soon spread throughout the division, and then through the entire army.

The irony of the situation was that although General Shute was renowned as a spit-and-polish man and a bit of a mariner, he was admired by many of his men for his tremendous courage and willingness to crawl into No Man's Land with scout patrols. Thanks to Herbert's limerick, what tends to be remembered now about Shute is "The General inspecting his trenches . . ."

14. Byron (George Gordon, Lord), "The Prisoner of Chillon and Other Poems of 1816."

15. Wilfred Owen, "Who are these? . . ."

16. Rupert Brooke, "The Great Lover."